THE WORLD OF DON CAMILLO

Giovanni Guareschi

THE WORLD OF DON CAMILLO

THE LITTLE WORLD OF DON CAMILLO

DON CAMILLO AND THE PRODIGAL SON

DON CAMILLO'S DILEMMA

DON CAMILLO AND THE DEVIL

COMRADE DON CAMILLO

LONDON   VICTOR GOLLANCZ LTD   1980

THE LITTLE WORLD OF DON CAMILLO Copyright 1950 by Giovanni Guareschi
English translation Copyright 1950 by Una Vincenzo Troubridge

DON CAMILLO AND THE PRODIGAL SON Copyright 1952 by Giovanni Guareschi
English translation Copyright 1952 by Frances Frenaye

DON CAMILLO'S DILEMMA Copyright 1954 by Giovanni Guareschi
English translation Copyright 1954 by Frances Frenaye

DON CAMILLO AND THE DEVIL Copyright 1957 by Giovanni Guareschi

COMRADE DON CAMILLO Copyright 1964 by Giovanni Guareschi
English translation Copyright 1964 by Frances Frenaye

ISBN 0 575 02933 1

Printed in the United States of America

CONTENTS

THE LITTLE WORLD OF DON CAMILLO

DON CAMILLO
AND THE
PRODIGAL SON

DON CAMILLO'S DILEMMA

DON CAMILLO
AND
THE DEVIL

COMRADE DON CAMILLO

INTRODUCTION

I AM perpetually irritated by the virtue of the punctilious penpushers who have penetrated the most unsuspected places and lie in ambush wherever I go. They favour me with a bored and pitying glance when I rush in at the last minute before the dead-line with my typewritten pages and India-ink drawings.

"Poor Guareschi! Just under the rope, as usual!" they are obviously thinking.

At such times I am full of coffee, nicotine, bicarbonate of soda and fatigue. My clothes are sticking to me because I haven't taken them off for three days; I have dirty hands and stubble on my chin. My mouth is furry and my head, stomach, heart and liver are all aching. A lock of unkempt hair is hanging down over my nose and black dots dance before my eyes.

"Why do you always wait until the very last minute?" they ask me. "Why don't you do your work little by little, while there is still plenty of time?"

But if I had paid attention to the punctilious penpushers, I wouldn't have got even as far as I am today.

I remember distinctly the day of December 23, 1946. Because of Christmas, the work had to be in "ahead of time," as the penpushers put it. At that time, beside editing the magazine *Candido*, I wrote stories for *Oggi*, another weekly put out by the same publisher. On December 23, then, I was up to my ears in trouble. When evening came I had done my piece for *Oggi* and it had been set up by the printer, but the last page of *Candido* was still unfinished.

"Closing up *Candido*!" shouted the copy boy.

What was I to do? I lifted the piece out of *Oggi*, had it reset in larger type and put it into my own paper.

"God's will be done!" I exclaimed.

And then, since there was another half hour before the dead-line of *Oggi*, I wrote a hasty story to fill the gap.

"God's will be done!" I said again.

And God must have willed exactly what proceeded to happen. For God is no punctilious penpusher. Because, if I had heeded all the good advice poured into my ear, Don Camillo, Peppone and all the other characters in this book would have perished on the day they were born, that December 23, 1946. For the very first story of the series was written for *Oggi*, and if it had appeared there, it would have gone the way of its predecessors, and no one would have heard of it again.

But after it came out in *Candido*, I received so many letters from my two dozen subscribers that I wrote a second story about the big priest and the big Red mayor of a village in the Po River valley.

And so I am not in the least bit sorry to have put off until the morrow that which I could perfectly well have done the day or the month before. At times it saddens me to look over the things I have written, but I don't suffer too awfully much because I can honestly say that I did my best not to write them. And I outdid myself in putting them off them from day to day.

There, my friends, is the story of how the priest and the mayor of a village in the Po River valley were born. Two hundred times I have pulled the strings and made them do the most extravagant things that anyone can imagine. So extravagant that often they are literally true. Over and over I complain: "Now that I've brought them into the world, what shall I do about them? Kill them off and call it a day?"

It is not that I claim to be their "creator"; all I did was put words into their mouths. The river country of *The Little World* created them; I crossed their path, linked their arms with mine and made them run through the alphabet, from one end to another. In the last weeks of 1951, when the mighty river overran its banks and flooded the fields of the happy valley, readers from other countries sent me blankets and parcels of clothing marked "For the people of Don Camillo and Peppone." Then, briefly, I imagined that instead of being an unimportant fool I was an important one.

G.G.

THE
LITTLE WORLD
OF
DON CAMILLO

THE LITTLE WORLD

THE LITTLE WORLD OF Don Camillo is to be found somewhere in the valley of the Po River. It is almost any village on that stretch of plain in Northern Italy. There, between the Po and the Apennines, the climate is always the same. The landscape never changes and, in country like this, you can stop along any road for a moment and look at a farmhouse sitting in the midst of maize and hemp—and immediately a story is born.

Why do I tell you this instead of getting on with my story? Because I want you to understand that, in the Little World between the river and the mountains, many things can happen that cannot happen anywhere else. Here, the deep, eternal breathing of the river freshens the air, for both the living and the dead, and even the dogs, have souls. If you keep this in mind, you will easily come to know the village priest, Don Camillo, and his adversary, Peppone, the Communist Mayor. You will not be surprised that Christ watches the goings-on from a big cross in the village church and not infrequently talks, and that one man beats the other over the head, but fairly—that is, without hatred—and that in the end the two enemies find they agree about essentials.

And one final word of explanation before I begin my story. If there is a priest anywhere who feels offended by my treatment of Don Camillo, he is welcome to break the biggest candle available over my head. And if there is a Communist who feels offended by Peppone, he is welcome to break a hammer and sickle on my back. But if there is anyone who is offended by the conversations of Christ, I can't help it; for the one who speaks in this story is not Christ, but my Christ—that is, the voice of my conscience.

A CONFESSION

DON CAMILLO HAD BEEN born with a constitutional preference for calling a spade a spade. Upon a certain occasion when there had been a local scandal involving landowners of ripe age and young girls of his parish, he had, in the course of his mass, embarked upon a seemly and suitably generalised address, when he had suddenly become aware of the fact that one of the chief offenders was present among the foremost ranks of his congregation. Flinging all restraint to the four winds and also flinging a hastily snatched cloth over the head of the Crucified Lord above the high altar in order that the divine ears might not be offended, he had set his arms firmly akimbo and had resumed his sermon. And so stentorian had been the voice that issued from the lips of the big man and so uncompromising had been his language that the very roof of the little church had seemed to tremble.

When the time of the elections drew near Don Camillo had naturally been explicit in his allusions to the local leftists. Thus there came a fine evening when, as he was going home at dusk, an individual muffled in a cloak sprang out of a hedge as he passed by and, taking advantage of the fact that Don Camillo was handicapped by his bicycle and by a large parcel containing seventy eggs attached to its handlebars, belaboured him with a heavy stick and promptly vanished as though the earth had swallowed him.

Don Camillo had kept his own counsel. Having arrived at the presbytery and deposited the eggs in safety, he had gone into the church to discuss the matter with the Lord, as was his invariable habit in moments of perplexity.

"What should I do?" Don Camillo had inquired.

"Anoint your back with a little oil beaten up in water and hold your tongue," the Lord had replied from above the altar. "We must forgive those who offend us. That is the rule."

"Very true, Lord," agreed Don Camillo, "but on this occasion we are discussing blows, not offences."

"And what do you mean by that? Surely you are not trying to tell me that injuries done to the body are more painful than those aimed at the spirit?"

"I see your point, Lord. But You should also bear in mind that in the beating of me, who am Your minister, an injury has been done to Yourself also. I am really more concerned on Your behalf than on my own."

"And was I not a greater minister of God than you are? And did I not forgive those who nailed me to the Cross?"

"There is never any use in arguing with You!" Don Camillo had exclaimed. "You are always in the right. Your will be done. We must forgive. All the same, don't forget that if these ruffians, encouraged by my silence, should crack my skull, the responsibility will lie with You. I could cite several passages from the Old Testament. . . ."

"Don Camillo, are you proposing to instruct me in the Old Testament? As for this business, I assume full responsibility. Moreover, strictly between Ourselves, the beating has done you no harm. It may teach you to let politics alone in my house."

Don Camillo had duly forgiven. But nevertheless one thing had stuck in his gullet like a fish bone: curiosity as to the identity of his assailant.

Time passed. Late one evening, while he sat in the confessional, Don Camillo discerned through the grille the countenance of the local leader of the extreme leftists, Peppone.

That Peppone should come to confession at all was a sensational event, and Don Camillo was proportionately gratified.

"God be with you, brother; with you who, more than any other man, have need of His holy blessing. It is a long time since you last went to confession?"

"Not since 1918," replied Peppone.

"You must have committed a great number of sins in the course of those twenty-eight years, with your head so crammed with crazy notions. . . ."

"A good few, undoubtedly," sighed Peppone.

"For example?"

"For example, two months ago I gave you a hiding."

"That was serious indeed," replied Don Camillo, "since in assaulting a minister of God, you have attacked God Himself."

"But I have repented," exclaimed Peppone. "And, moreover, it was not as God's minister that I beat you, but as my political adversary. In any case, I did it in a moment of weakness."

"Apart from this and from your membership of your accursed Party, have you any other grave sins on your conscience?"

Peppone spilled all the beans.

Taken as a whole, his offences were not very serious, and Don Camillo let him off with a score of Paters and Aves. Then, while Peppone was kneeling at the altar rails performing his penance, Don Camillo went and knelt before the crucifix.

"Lord," he said. "You must forgive me, but I am going to beat him up for You."

"You are going to do nothing of the kind," replied the Lord. "I have forgiven him and you must forgive him also. All things considered, he is not a bad soul."

"Lord, you can never trust a Red! They live by lies. Only look at him; Barabbas incarnate!"

"It's as good a face as most, Don Camillo; it is your heart that is venomous!"

"Lord, if I have ever served You well, grant me just one small grace: let me at least break this candle on his shoulders. Dear Lord, what, after all, is a candle?"

"No," replied the Lord. "Your hands were made for blessing, not for striking."

Don Camillo sighed heavily.

He genuflected and left the sanctuary. As he turned to make a final sign of the cross he found himself exactly behind Peppone who, on his knees, was apparently absorbed in prayer.

"Lord," groaned Don Camillo, clasping his hands and gazing at the crucifix. "My hands were made for blessing, but not my feet!"

"There is something in that," replied the Lord from above the altar, "but all the same, Don Camillo, bear it in mind: only one!"

The kick landed like a thunderbolt and Peppone received it without so much as blinking an eye. Then he got to his feet and sighed with relief.

"I've been waiting for that for the last ten minutes," he remarked. "I feel better now."

"So do I!" exclaimed Don Camillo, whose heart was now as light and serene as a May morning.

The Lord said nothing at all, but it was easy enough to see that He too was pleased.

A BAPTISM

ONE DAY THE CHURCH was unexpectedly invaded by a man and two women, one of whom was Peppone's wife.

Don Camillo, who from the top of a pair of steps was cleaning St. Joseph's halo with Brasso, turned round and inquired what they wanted.

"There is something here that needs to be baptised," replied the man, and one of the women held up a bundle containing a baby.

"Whose is it?" inquired Don Camillo, coming down from his steps.

"Mine," replied Peppone's wife.

"And your husband's?" persisted Don Camillo.

"Well, naturally! Who else do you suppose gave it to me?" retorted Peppone's wife indignantly.

"No need to be offended," observed Don Camillo on his way to the sacristy. "Haven't I been told often enough that your Party approves of free love?"

As he passed before the high altar Don Camillo knelt down and permitted himself a discreet wink in the direction of the Lord. "Did you hear that one?" he murmured with a joyful grin. "One in the eye for the Godless ones!"

"Don't talk rubbish, Don Camillo," replied the Lord irritably. "If they had no God, why should they come here to get their child baptised? If Peppone's wife had boxed your ears it would only have served you right."

"If Peppone's wife had boxed my ears I should have taken the three of them by the scruff of their necks and . . ."

"And what?" inquired the Lord severely.

"Oh, nothing; just a figure of speech," Don Camillo hastened to assure Him, rising to his feet.

"Don Camillo, watch your step," said the Lord sternly.

Duly vested, Don Camillo approached the font. "What do you wish to name this child?" he asked Peppone's wife.

"Lenin Libero Antonio," she replied.

"Then go and get him baptised in Russia," said Don Camillo calmly, replacing the cover on the font.

The priest's hands were as large as shovels and the three left the church without protest. But as Don Camillo was attempting to slip into the sacristy he was arrested by the voice of the Lord.

"Don Camillo, you have done a very wicked thing. Go at once and bring those people back and baptise their child."

"But Lord," protested Don Camillo, "You really must bear in mind that baptism is not a jest. Baptism is a very sacred matter. Baptism is . . ."

"Don Camillo," the Lord interrupted him. "Are you attempting to teach me the nature of baptism? Did I not invent it? I tell you that you have been guilty of gross presumption, because, suppose that child were to die at this moment, it would be your fault if it failed to attain Paradise!"

"Lord, do not let us be melodramatic," retorted Don Camillo. "Why in the name of Heaven should it die? It's as pink and white as a rose!"

"Which means exactly nothing!" the Lord admonished him. "What if a tile should fall on its head or it should suddenly have convulsions? It was your duty to baptise it."

Don Camillo raised protesting arms: "But Lord, just think it over. If it were certain that the child would go to Hell, we might stretch a point; but seeing that despite being the son of that nasty piece of work he might very easily manage to slip into Paradise, how can You ask me to risk anyone going there with such a name as Lenin? I'm thinking of the reputation of Paradise."

"The reputation of Paradise is my business,' shouted the Lord angrily. "What matters to me is that a man should be a decent fellow and I care less than nothing whether his name be Lenin or Button. At the very most, you should have pointed out to those people that saddling children with fantastic names may involve them in annoyances when they grow up."

"Very well," replied Don Camillo. "I am always in the wrong. I must see what I can do about it."

Just at that moment someone came into the church. It was Peppone, alone, with the baby in his arms. He closed the church door and bolted it.

"I do not leave this church," he said, "until my son has been baptised with the name that I have chosen."

"Look at that," whispered Don Camillo, smiling as he turned towards the Lord. "Now do You see what these people are? One is filled with the holiest intentions and this is how they treat you."

"Put yourself in his place," replied the Lord. "One may not approve his attitude, but one can understand it."

Don Camillo shook his head.

"I have already said that I do not leave this place unless you baptise my son as I demand!" repeated Peppone. Whereupon, laying the bundle containing the baby upon a bench, he took off his coat, rolled up his sleeves and advanced threateningly.

"Lord," implored Don Camillo. "I ask You! If You think it just that one of your priests should give way to the threats of a layman, then I must obey. But in that event, if to-morrow they should bring me a calf and compel me to baptise it You must not complain. You know very well how dangerous it is to create precedents."

"All right," replied the Lord, "but in this case you must try to make him understand. . . ."

"And if he hits me?"

"Then you must accept it. You must endure and suffer as I did."

Don Camillo turned to his visitor. "Very well, Peppone," he said. "The baby will leave the church baptised, but not by that accursed name."

"Don Camillo," stuttered Peppone, "don't forget that my stomach has never recovered from that bullet that I stopped in the mountains. If you hit low, I shall go for you with a bench."

"Don't worry, Peppone. I can deal with you entirely in the upper storeys," Don

Camillo assured him, landing him a neat one above the ear.

They were both burly men with muscles of steel, and their blows fairly whistled through the air. After twenty minutes of silent and furious combat, Don Camillo distinctly heard a voice behind him. "Now, Don Camillo! The point of the jaw!" It came from the Lord above the altar. Don Camillo struck hard and Peppone crashed to the ground.

He remained where he lay for some ten minutes; then he sat up, got to his feet, rubbed his jaw, shook himself, put on his jacket and re-knotted his red handkerchief. Then he picked up the baby. Fully vested, Don Camillo was waiting for him, steady as a rock, beside the font. Peppone approached him slowly.

"What am I to name him?" asked Don Camillo.

"Camillo Libero Antonio," muttered Peppone.

Don Camillo shook his head. "No; we will name him Libero Camillo Lenin," he said. "Yes, Lenin. When you have a Camillo around, such folk as he are quite helpless."

"Amen," muttered Peppone, gently prodding his jaw.

When all was done and Don Camillo passed before the altar the Lord smiled and remarked: "Don Camillo, I am bound to admit that in politics you are My master."

"And also in fisticuffs," replied Don Camillo with perfect gravity, carelessly fingering a large lump on his forehead.

ON THE TRAIL

DON CAMILLO HAD LET himself go a bit in the course of a little sermon with a local background, allowing himself some rather pointed allusions to "*certain people*" and it was thus that on the following evening, when he seized the ropes of the church bells—the bell-ringer having been called away on some pretext—all hell broke out. Some damned soul had tied crackers to the clappers of the bells. No harm done, of course, but there was a shattering din of explosions, enough to give the ringer heart failure.

Don Camillo had not said a word. He had celebrated the evening service in perfect composure, before a crowded congregation from which not one was absent, with Peppone in the front row and every countenance a picture of fervour. It was enough to infuriate a saint, but Don Camillo was no novice in self-control and his audience had gone home disappointed.

As soon as the big doors were closed, Don Camillo snatched up an overcoat and on his way out went to make a hasty genuflection before the altar.

"Don Camillo," said the Lord, "put it down."

"I don't understand," protested Don Camillo.

"Put it down!"

Don Camillo drew a heavy stick from beneath his coat and laid it in front of the altar.

"Not a pleasant sight, Don Camillo."

"But, Lord! It isn't even oak; it's only poplar, light and supple . . ." Don Camillo pleaded.

"Go to bed, Don Camillo, and forget about Peppone."

Don Camillo had raised his arms and had gone to bed with a temperature. And so when on the following evening Peppone's wife made her appearance at the presbytery, he leaped to his feet as though a cracker had gone off under his chair.

"Don Camillo," began the woman, who was visibly greatly agitated. But Don Camillo interrupted her. "Get out of my sight, sacrilegious creature!"

"Don Camillo, never mind about that foolishness. At Castellino there is that poor wretch who tried to do in Peppone! They have turned him out!"

Don Camillo lighted a cigar. "Well, what about it, comrade? I didn't make the amnesty. And in any case, why should you bother about it?"

The woman started to shout. "I'm bothering because they came to tell Peppone, and Peppone has gone rushing off to Castellino like a lunatic. And he has taken his tommy-gun with him!"

"I see; then you have got concealed arms, have you?"

"Don Camillo, never mind about politics! Can't you understand that Peppone is out to kill? Unless you help me, my man is done for!"

Don Camillo laughed unpleasantly. "Which will teach him to tie crackers to the clappers of my bells. I shall be pleased to watch him die in gaol! You get out of my house!"

Ten minutes later, Don Camillo, with his skirts tucked up almost to his neck, was pedalling like a lunatic along the road to Castellino astride a racing bicycle belonging to the son of his sacristan.

There was a splendid moon and when he was about four miles from Castellino Don Camillo saw by its light a man sitting on the low parapet of the little bridge that spans the Fossone. He slowed down, since it is always best to be prudent when one travels by night, and halted some ten yards from the bridge, holding in his hand a small object that he happened to have discovered in his pocket.

"My lad," he inquired, "have you seen a big man go by on a bicycle in the direction of Castellino?"

"No, Don Camillo," replied the other quietly.

Don Camillo drew nearer. "Have you already been to Castellino?" he asked.

"No. I thought it over. It wasn't worth while. Was it my fool of a wife who put you to this trouble?"

"Trouble? Nothing of the kind . . . a little constitutional!"

"Have you any idea what a priest looks like on a racing bicycle?" sniggered Peppone.

Don Camillo came and sat beside him on his wall. "My son, you must be prepared to see all kinds of things in this world."

Less than an hour later, Don Camillo was back at the presbytery and went to make his report to the Lord.

"All went well according to Your instructions."

"Well done, Don Camillo, but would you mind telling me who it was that instructed you to take him by the feet and tumble him into the ditch?"

Don Camillo raised his arms. "To tell you the truth, I really can't remember exactly. As a matter of fact, he appeared to dislike the sight of a priest on a racing bicycle, so it seemed only kind to prevent him from seeing it any longer."

"I understand. Has he got back yet?"

"He'll be here soon. Seeing him fall into the ditch, it struck me that as he would be coming home in a rather damp condition he might find the bicycle in his way, so I thought it best to bring it along with me."

"Very kind of you, I'm sure, Don Camillo," said the Lord with perfect gravity.

Peppone appeared just before dawn at the door of the presbytery. He was soaked to the skin, and Don Camillo asked if it was raining.

"Fog," replied Peppone with chattering teeth. "May I have my bicycle?"

"Why, of course. There it is."

"Are you sure there wasn't a tommy-gun tied to it?"

Don Camillo raised his arms with a smile. "A tommy-gun? And what may that be?"

"I," said Peppone as he turned from the door, "have made one mistake in my life. I tied crackers to the clappers of your bells. It should have been half a ton of dynamite."

"*Errare humanum est*," remarked Don Camillo.

EVENING SCHOOL

IN THE EMPTY CHURCH, by the faint light of the two altar candles, Don Camillo was chatting with the Lord about the outcome of the local elections.

"I wouldn't presume to criticize Your actions," he wound up, "but I should never have allowed Peppone to become mayor with a council in which only two people really know how to read and write properly."

"Culture is entirely without importance, Don Camillo," replied the Lord with a smile. "What counts is ideas. Eloquent speeches get nowhere unless there are practical ideas at the back of them. Before judging, suppose we put them to the test."

"Fair enough," conceded Don Camillo. "I really said what I did because, in the event of the lawyer's party coming out top, I had already been given assurances that the bell tower of the church would be repaired. In any case, should it fall down, the people will have compensation in watching the construction of a magnificent People's Palace with dancing, sale of alcoholic liquors, gambling and a theatre for variety entertainments."

"And a lock-up for such venomous reptiles as Don Camillo," added the Lord.

Don Camillo lowered his head. "Lord, You misjudge me," he said. "You know what a cigar means to me? Well, look: this is the only cigar I possess, and look what I am doing with it."

He pulled a cigar out of his pocket and crumbled it in his enormous hand.

'Well done," said the Lord. "Well done, Don Camillo. I accept your penance. Nevertheless, I should like to see you throw away the crumbs, because you would be quite capable of putting them in your pocket and smoking them later on in your pipe."

"But we are in church," protested Don Camillo.

"Never mind that, Don Camillo. Throw the tobacco into that corner." Don Camillo obeyed while the Lord looked on with approval, and just then a knocking was heard at the little door of the sacristy and Peppone came in.

"Good evening, Mr. Mayor," said Don Camillo deferentially.

"Listen," said Peppone. "If a Christian is in doubt about something that he has done and comes to tell you about it, and if you found that he had made some mistakes, would you point them out to him or would you simply leave him in ignorance?"

Don Camillo protested indignantly: "How can you dare to doubt the honesty of a priest? His primary duty is to point out clearly all the penitent's mistakes."

"Very well, then," exclaimed Peppone. "Are you quite ready to hear my confession?"

"I am ready."

Peppone pulled a large sheet of paper from his pocket and began to read: "Citizens, at the moment when we are hailing the victorious affirmation of our Party . . ."

Don Camillo interrupted him with a gesture and went to kneel before the altar. "Lord," he murmured, "I am no longer responsible for my actions."

"But I am," said the Lord promptly. "Peppone has outwitted you, and you must play fair and do your duty."

"But, Lord," persisted Don Camillo. "You realize, don't You, that You are making me work on behalf of the Agit-Prop?"

"You are working on behalf of grammar, syntax and spelling, none of which is either diabolical or sectarian."

Don Camillo put on his spectacles, grasped a pencil and set to work on the tottering periods of the speech that Peppone was to make on the following day. Peppone read it through intently.

"Good," he approved. "There is only one thing that I do not understand. Where I had said: '*It is our intention to extend the schools and to rebuild the bridge over the Fossalto,*' you have substituted: '*It is our intention to extend the schools, repair the church tower and rebuild the bridge over the Fossalto.*' Why is that?"

"A mere matter of syntax," explained Don Camillo gravely.

"Blessed are those who have studied Latin and who are able to understand niceties of language," sighed Peppone. "And so," he added, "we are to lose even the hope that the tower may collapse on to your head!"

Don Camillo raised his arms. "We must all bow before the will of God!"

When he returned from accompanying Peppone to the door, Don Camillo came to say good night to the Lord.

"Well done, Don Camillo," said the Lord with a smile. "I was unjust to you and I am sorry you destroyed your last cigar. It was a penance that you did not deserve.

Nevertheless, we may as well be frank about it: Peppone was a skunk not to offer you even a cigar, after all the trouble you took!"

"Oh, all right," sighed Don Camillo, fishing a cigar from his pocket and preparing to crush it in his big hand.

"No, Don Camillo," smiled the Lord. "Go and smoke it in peace. You have earned it."

"But . . ."

"No, Don Camillo; you didn't steal it. Peppone had two cigars in his pocket. Peppone is a Communist. He believes in sharing things. In skilfully relieving him of one cigar, you only took your fair share."

"You always know best," exclaimed Don Camillo with deep respect.

OUT OF BOUNDS

DON CAMILLO WAS IN the habit of going to measure the famous crack in the church tower, and every morning his inspection met with the same result: the crack had not increased in width, but neither had it diminished. Finally, he lost his temper and one day he dispatched the sacristan to the headquarters of the Commune.

"Go and tell the mayor to come at once and look at this damage. Explain that the matter is serious."

The sacristan went and returned.

"Peppone says that he will take your word for it that it is a serious matter. In any case, he also said that if you really want to show him the crack, you had better take the tower to him in his office. He will be available there until five o'clock."

Don Camillo did not bat an eyelid: all he said was: "If Peppone or any member of his gang has the courage to turn up at mass to-morrow we shall see something sensational. But they know it, and not one of them will put in an appearance."

The next morning there was no sign of a Red in church, but five minutes before mass was due to begin the sound of marching was heard upon the flags before the church door. In perfect formation all the Reds, not only those of the village but also those of neighbouring cells, every man jack of them including the cobbler, Bilò, who had a wooden leg, and Roldo dei Prati, who was shivering with fever, came marching proudly towards the church, led by Peppone. With perfect composure they took their seats in church, sitting in a solid phalanx with faces as ferocious as the cruiser *Potemkin*.

When Don Camillo had finished his sermon, a very cultured exposition of the parable of the good Samaritan, he followed it by a brief exhortation to the faithful.

"As you all know, a most dangerous crack is threatening the security of the church tower. I therefore appeal to you, my dear brethren in the faith, to come to the assistance of the house of God. In using the term 'brethren in the faith' I am addressing those decent folk who come here with a desire to draw near to God, and not certain individuals who come only in order to parade their militarism. To such as these it can matter nothing should the tower fall to the ground."

The mass over, Don Camillo settled himself at a table near the presbytery door and the congregation filed past him, but not a soul left the place. One and all, having made the expected donation, remained on the little *piazzetta* in front of the church to watch developments. And last of all came Peppone, followed by his battalion in perfect formation. They drew up to a defiant halt before the table.

Peppone stepped forward proudly.

"From this tower, in the past, the bells have hailed the dawn of freedom, and from it, tomorrow, they shall welcome the glorious dawn of the proletarian revolution," said Peppone to Don Camillo as he laid on the table before him three large red handkerchiefs full of money.

Then he turned on his heel and marched away, followed by his gang. And Roldo dei Prati was shaking with fever and could scarcely remain on his feet, but he held his head erect, and the crippled Bilò, as he passed Don Camillo, stamped his wooden leg defiantly in perfect step with his comrades.

When Don Camillo went to the Lord to show Him the basket containing the money and told Him that there was more than enough for the repair of the tower, the Lord smiled in astonishment.

"You were quite right, Don Camillo."

"Naturally," replied Don Camillo. "Because you understand humanity, but I know Italians."

Up to that moment Don Camillo had behaved well. But he made a mistake when he sent a message to Peppone to the effect that he had much admired the military smartness of his men, but that he advised him to give them more intensive drilling in right-about-turn and the double, of which they would have urgent need on the day of the proletarian revolution.

This was deplorable, and Peppone prepared to retaliate.

Don Camillo was an honest man, but in addition to an overwhelming passion for shooting he possessed a splendid double-barrelled gun and a good supply of cartridges. Moreover, Baron Stocco's private shoot lay only three miles from the village and constituted a permanent temptation, because not only game but even the neighbouring poultry had learned that they were in safety behind his fence of wire netting and once within it could thumb their noses at anyone who wished to wring their necks.

It was therefore not at all astonishing that on a certain evening Don Camillo, his skirts bundled into an enormous pair of breeches and his face partly concealed beneath the brim of an ancient felt hat, should find himself actually on the business side of the baron's fence. The flesh is weak and the flesh of the sportsman particularly so.

Nothing to be surprised at, therefore, if Don Camillo fired a shot that brought down a hare almost under his nose. He thrust it into his game-bag and was beating a retreat when he suddenly found himself face to face with another invader. Ramming his hat down over his eyes, he butted the stranger in the stomach with the intention of knocking him out, since it was undesirable that the countryside should learn that their parish priest had been caught poaching.

Unfortunately, his adversary conceived the same idea at precisely the same moment and the two heads met with a crash so tremendous that both parties found themselves sitting on the ground seeing stars.

"A pate as hard as that can only belong to our beloved mayor," muttered Don Camillo as his vision began to clear.

"A pate as hard as that can only belong to our beloved parish priest," replied Peppone, scratching his head. For Peppone also was poaching on forbidden ground and also had a hare in his game-bag, and his eyes gleamed as he surveyed Don Camillo.

"Never would I have believed," said Peppone, "that the very man who preaches respect for other people's property would be found breaking through the fences of a preserve in order to go poaching."

"Nor would I have believed that our chief citizen, our comrade mayor . . ."

"Citizen, yes, but also comrade," Peppone interrupted, "and therefore perverted by those diabolic theories that aim at the fair distribution of all property, and therefore acting more logically in accordance with his known views than the reverend Don Camillo, who, for his part . . ."

Someone was approaching them and had drawn so near that it was quite impossible to take to their heels without the risk of stopping a charge of shot, since on this occasion the intruder happened to be a gamekeeper.

"We've got to do something!" whispered Don Camillo. "Think of the scandal if we are recognized!"

"Personally, I don't care," replied Peppone with composure. "I am always ready to answer for my actions."

The steps drew nearer and Don Camillo melted against a large tree trunk. Peppone made no attempt to move, and when the gamekeeper appeared with his gun over his arm Peppone greeted him:

"Good evening."

"What are you doing here?" inquired the gamekeeper.

"Looking for mushrooms."

"With a gun?"

"As good a means as another."

The means whereby a gamekeeper can be rendered relatively innocuous are also fairly simple. If one happens to be standing behind him, it suffices to muffle his head unexpectedly in an overcoat and give him a good rap on the head. Advantage can then be taken of his moment of unconsciousness in order to reach the hedge and scramble over it. Once over, all is well.

Don Camillo and Peppone found themselves sitting behind a bush a good mile away from the Baron's estate.

"Don Camillo!" sighed Peppone. "We have committed a serious offence. We have raised our hands against one in authority! That is a felony."

Don Camillo, who had in point of fact been the one to raise them, broke out into a cold sweat.

"My conscience troubles me," pursued the tormentor. "I shall have no peace remembering so horrible a thing. How shall I dare present myself before a minister of God to ask forgiveness for such a misdeed? Accursed be the day when I lent an ear to the infamous lures of the Muscovite doctrine, forgetting the holy precepts of Christian charity!"

Don Camillo was so deeply humiliated that he wanted to cry. On the other hand, he also wanted desperately to land one good crack on the pate of his perverted adversary, and as Peppone was well aware of the fact, he left off.

"Accursed temptation!" he shouted suddenly, pulling the hare out of his bag and hurling it from him.

"Accursed indeed!" shouted Don Camillo, and, hauling out his own hare, he flung it far into the snow and walked away with bent head. Peppone followed him as far as the cross-road and then turned to the right.

"By the way," he asked, pausing for a moment, "could you tell me of a reputable parish priest in this neighbourhood to whom I could go and confess this sin?"

Don Camillo clenched his fists and walked straight ahead.

When he had gathered sufficient courage to present himself before the Lord above the altar, Don Camillo spread his arms wide.

"I didn't do it to save myself, Lord," he said. "I did it simply because, had it become known that I go poaching, the Church would have been the chief sufferer from the scandal." But the Lord remained silent, and in such cases Don Camillo acquired a quartan ague and put himself on a diet of bread and water for days and days, until the Lord felt sorry for him and said: "Enough."

This time, the Lord said nothing until the bread-and-water diet had continued for seven days. Don Camillo had reached the stage where he could only remain standing by leaning against a wall and his stomach was fairly bawling with hunger.

Then Peppone came to confession.

"I have sinned against the law and Christian charity," said Peppone.

"I know it," replied Don Camillo.

"Moreover, as soon as you were out of sight, I went back and collected both the hares and I have roasted one and jugged the other."

"Just what I supposed you would do," murmured Don Camillo. And when he passed the altar a little later, the Lord smiled at him, not so much on account of his prolonged fast as in consideration of the fact that Don Camillo, when he had murmured, "Just what I supposed you would do," had felt no desire to hit Peppone but had experienced profound shame at the remembrance that on that same evening he himself had had a momentary temptation to do exactly the same thing.

"Poor Don Camillo," whispered the Lord tenderly. And Don Camillo spread out his arms as though he wished to say that he did his best and that if he sometimes made mistakes it was not deliberately.

"I know, I know, Don Camillo," replied the Lord. "And now get along and eat your hare—for Peppone has left it for you, nicely cooked, in the presbytery kitchen."

THE TREASURE

ONE DAY SMILZO made his appearance at the presbytery. He was a young ex-partisan who had been Peppone's orderly during the fighting in the mountains and the latter had now taken him on as messenger to the Commune. He was the bearer of a handsome letter printed in Gothic lettering on hand-made paper and with the Party heading.

"Your honour is invited to grace with his presence a ceremony of a social nature which will take place tomorrow at ten o'clock a.m. in Piazza della Libertà. The Secretary of the Section, Comrade Bottazzi, Mayor, Giuseppe."

Don Camillo looked severely at Smilzo. "Tell Comrade Peppone Mayor Giuseppe that I have no wish to go and listen to the usual imbecilities against reaction and the capitalists. I already know them by heart."

"No," explained Smilzo. "This is no affair of political speeches. This is a question of patriotism and social activities. If you refuse it means that you know nothing of democracy."

Don Camillo nodded his head slowly. "If that is so," he said, "then I have nothing more to say."

"Very good. And the leader says you are to come in uniform and to bring all your paraphernalia."

"Paraphernalia?"

"Yes: the pail and the brush; there is something to be blessed."

Smilzo permitted himself to speak in such a manner to Don Camillo precisely because he was Smilzo—that is to say, the lean one, and so built that by virtue of his amazing swiftness of movement he had been able in the mountains to slip between bullet and bullet without coming to harm. By the time, therefore, that the heavy book flung at him by Don Camillo reached the spot where his head had been, Smilzo had already left the presbytery and was pedalling away for dear life.

Don Camillo got up, rescued the book and went to let off steam to the Lord at the altar.

"Lord," he said, "is it conceivable that I should be unable to find out what those people are planning to do to-morrow? I never knew anything so mysterious. What is the meaning of all these preparations? All those branches that they are sticking into the ground round the meadow between the pharmacy and the Baghetti's house? What kind of devilry can they be up to?"

"My son, if it were devilry, first of all they wouldn't be doing it in the open and secondly they wouldn't be sending for you to bless it. Be patient until to-morrow."

That evening Don Camillo went to have a look round but he saw nothing but branches and decorations surrounding the meadow and nobody appeared to know anything.

When he set out next morning, followed by two acolytes, his knees were trembling. He felt that something was not as it should be, that there was treachery in the air.

He returned an hour later, shattered and with a temperature.

"What has happened?" inquired the Lord from the altar.

"Enough to make one's hair stand on end," stammered Don Camillo. "A terrible thing. A band, Garibaldi's hymn, a speech from Peppone and the laying of the foundation stone of 'The People's Palace'! And I had to bless the stone while Peppone chuckled with joy. And the ruffian asked me to say a few words, and I had to make a suitable little address because, although it is a Party activity, the rascal dressed it up as a social undertaking."

Don Camillo paced to and fro in the empty church. Then he came to a standstill in front of the Lord. "A mere trifle," he exclaimed. "An assembly hall, reading-room, library, gymnasium, dispensary and theatre. A skyscraper of two floors with adjacent ground for sports and *bocce*. And the whole lot for the miserable sum of ten million lire."

"By no means dear, given the present prices," observed the Lord.

Don Camillo sank down upon a bench. "Lord," he sighed dolefully, "why have You done this to me?"

"Don Camillo, you are unreasonable."

"No: I am not unreasonable. For ten years I have been praying to You on my knees to find me a little money so that I could establish a library, an assembly hall for the young people, a playground for the children with a merry-go-round and swings and possibly a little swimming pool like they have at Castellino. For ten years I have lowered myself making up to swine of bloated landowners when I should have liked to box their ears every time I saw them. I must have got up quite two hundred lotteries and knocked at quite two thousand doors, and I have nothing at all to show for it. Then along comes this excommunicate mountebank, and behold ten million lire drop into his pockets from heaven."

The Lord shook His head. "They didn't fall from heaven," He replied. "He found them underground. I had nothing to do with it, Don Camillo. It is entirely due to his own personal initiative."

Don Camillo spread out his arms. "Then it is simple enough and the obvious deduction is that I am a poor fool."

Don Camillo went off to stamp up and down his study in the presbytery, roaring with fury. He must exclude the possibility that Peppone had got himself that ten million by holding people up on the roads or by robbing a bank. "That fellow, in the days of the liberation, when he came down from the mountains and it seemed as if the proletarian revolution might break out at any moment, must have played upon the funk of those cowards of gentry and squeezed their money out of them."

Then he reflected that at that time there had been no gentry in the neighbourhood, but that, on the other hand, there had been a detachment of the British Army which had arrived simultaneously with Peppone and his men. The British had taken possession of the gentry's houses, taking the place of the Germans, who, having spent some time in the countryside, had thoroughly cleared those houses of everything of any value. It was therefore out of the question that Peppone should have obtained his ten million by looting.

Possibly the money had come from Russia? He burst out laughing: was it likely that the Russians should give a thought to Peppone?

At last he returned to the church. "Lord," he begged from the foot of the altar, "won't You tell me where Peppone found the money?"

"Don Camillo," replied the Lord with a smile, "do you take Me for a private detective? Why ask God to tell you the truth when you have only to seek it within yourself? Look for it, Don Camillo, and meanwhile, in order to distract your mind, why not make a trip to the town?"

On the following evening, having returned from his excursion to the town, Don Camillo presented himself before the Lord in a condition of extreme agitation.

"What has upset you, Don Camillo?"

"Something quite crazy," exclaimed Don Camillo breathlessly. "I have met a dead man! Face to face in the street!"

"Don Camillo, calm yourself and reflect: usually the dead whom one meets face to face in the street are alive."

"This one cannot be!" shouted Don Camillo. "This one is dead as mutton, and I know it because I myself carried him to the cemetery."

"If that is the case," replied the Lord, "then I have nothing more to say. You must have seen a ghost."

Don Camillo shrugged his shoulders. "Of course not! Ghosts have no existence except in the foolish pates of hysterical women!"

"And therefore?"

"Well . . ." muttered Don Camillo.

Don Camillo collected his thoughts. The deceased had been a thin young man, not a native of the village, who had come down from the mountains with Peppone and his men. He had been wounded in the head and was in a bad state, and they had fixed him up in the former German headquarters, which had become the headquarters of the British Command. Peppone had established his own office in the room next to that of the invalid. Don Camillo remembered it all clearly: the villa was surrounded by sentries three deep and not a fly could leave it unperceived, because the British were still fighting nearby and were particularly careful of their own skins.

All this had happened one morning, and on the same evening the young man had died. Peppone had sent for Don Camillo towards midnight, but by the time he had got there the young man had been already in his coffin. The British didn't want the body in the house, and so, at about noon, the coffin, covered with the Italian flag, was carried out of the villa by Peppone and his most trusted men. A detachment of British soldiers had kindly volunteered to supply military honours.

Don Camillo recalled that the ceremony had been moving: all the village had walked behind the coffin, which had been placed on a gun carriage. He himself had made the address before the body was lowered into the grave, and people had actually wept. Peppone, in the front row, had sobbed.

"When I put my mind to it, I certainly know how to express myself !" said Don Camillo to himself complacently, recalling the episode. Then he returned to his original train of thought. "And in spite of all that, I am prepared to take my oath that the young man whom I met to-day in the town was the same as the one I followed to the grave." He sighed. "Such is life!"

The following day Don Camillo sought out Peppone at his workshop, where he found him lying on his back underneath a car.

"Good morning, Comrade Mayor. I have come to tell you that for the past two days I have been thinking over your description of your People's Palace!"

"And what do you think of it?" jeered Peppone.

"Magnificent! It has made me decide to start work on that scheme of a little place with a bathing-pool, garden, sports ground, theatre, etcetera, which, as you know, I have had in mind for twenty years past. I shall be laying the foundation stone next Sunday. It would give me great pleasure if you, as mayor, would attend the ceremony."

"Willingly: courtesy for courtesy."

"In the meanwhile, you might try to cut down the plans for your own place a bit. It looks like being too big for my personal taste."

Peppone stared at him in amazement. "Don Camillo, are you demented?"

"Not more than I was when I conducted a funeral and made a patriotic address over a coffin that can't have been securely closed, because only yesterday I met the corpse walking about the town."

Peppone ground his teeth. "What are you trying to insinuate?"

"Nothing: only that that coffin to which the British presented arms was full of what you found in the cellars of the Villa Dotti, where the German Command had hidden it. And that the dead man was alive and concealed in the attic."

"A-a-h!" howled Peppone. "The same old story! An attempt to malign the partisan movement!"

"Leave the partisans out of it. I take no interest in them!"

And he walked away while Peppone stood muttering vague threats.

That same evening, Don Camillo was awaiting him at the presbytery when he arrived accompanied by Brusco and two other prominent supporters—the same men who had acted as coffin-bearers.

"You," said Peppone, "can drop your insinuations. It was all of it stuff looted by the Germans—silver, cameras, instruments, gold, etcetera. If we hadn't taken it, the British would have had it. Ours was the only possible means of getting it out of the place. I have here witnesses and receipts: nobody has touched so much as a lira. Ten million was taken and ten million will be spent for the people."

Brusco, who was hot-tempered, began to shout that it was God's truth and that he, if necessary, knew well enough how to deal with certain people.

"So do I," Don Camillo replied calmly. He dropped the newspaper which he had been holding extended in front of himself and thus allowed it to be seen that under his right arm-pit he held the famous tommy-gun that had once belonged to Peppone.

Brusco turned pale and retreated hastily, but Peppone extended his arms. "Don Camillo, it doesn't seem to me that there is any need to quarrel."

"I agree," replied Don Camillo. "The more easily as I am entirely of your opinion. Ten million was acquired and ten million should be spent on the people. Seven on your People's Palace and three on my recreation centre for the people's children. Suffer the little children to come unto me. I ask only what is my due."

The four consulted together for a moment in undertones. Then Peppone spoke: "If you hadn't got that damnable thing in your hands, I should tell you that your suggestion is the filthiest blackmail in the universe."

On the following Sunday Peppone, together with all the village council, assisted at the laying of the foundation stone of Don Camillo's recreation centre. He also made a short speech. However, he found a means of whispering in Don Camillo's ear:

"It might be better to tie this stone round your neck and throw you into the Po."

That evening Don Camillo went to make his report to the Lord above the altar. "Well; what do You think about it?" he said in conclusion.

"Exactly what Peppone said to you. That if you hadn't got that damnable thing in your hands, I should say that it was the filthiest blackmail in the universe."

"But I have nothing at all in my hands except the cheque that Peppone has just given me."

"Precisely," whispered the Lord. "And with that three million you are going to do so many beautiful things, Don Camillo, that I haven't the heart to scold you."

Don Camillo genuflected and went off to bed to dream of a garden full of children—a garden with a merry-go-round and a swing, and seated on the swing Peppone's youngest son chirping joyfully like a fledgling.

RIVALRY

A BIG NOISE FROM the town was expected on a visit, and people were coming from all the surrounding cells. Therefore Peppone decreed that the ceremony should be held in the big square, and he not only had a large platform, decorated with red, set up, but he got hold of one of those trucks with four great loudspeakers and all the electric mechanism inside them for amplifying the voice. And so, on the afternoon of that Sunday, the big square was crammed to overflowing with people, and so also was the church square, which happened to be adjacent.

Don Camillo had shut all the doors and withdrawn into the sacristy, so as to avoid seeing or hearing anything which would work him up into a temper. He was actually dozing when a voice like the wrath of God roused him with a jerk as it bellowed: "*Comrades!* . . ."

It was as though the walls had melted away.

Don Camillo went to work off his indignation at the high altar. "They must have aimed one of their accursed loudspeakers directly at the church" he exclaimed. "This is nothing short of violation of domicile."

"What can you do about it, Don Camillo? It is progress," replied the Lord.

After a preface of generalizations, the voice had got down to business and, since the speaker was an extremist, he made no bones about it.

"*We must remain within the law and we shall do so! Even at the cost of taking up our weapons and of using the firing squad for all the enemies of the people!* . . ."

Don Camillo was pawing the ground like a restive horse. "Lord, only listen to him!"

"I hear him, Don Camillo. I hear him only too well."

"Lord, why don't You drop a thunderbolt among all that rabble?"

"Don Camillo, let us remain within the law. If, in order to drive the truth into the head of one who is in error, your remedy is to shoot him down, where was the use of My allowing Myself to be crucified?"

Don Camillo threw up his hands. "You are right, of course. We can do nothing but wait for them to crucify us also."

The Lord smiled. "If, instead of speaking first and then thinking over what you have said, you thought first and did the speaking afterwards, you might avoid having to regret the foolish things you have said."

Don Camillo bowed his head.

". . . as for those who, hiding in the shadow of the Crucifix, attempt with the poison of their ambiguous words to spread dissension among the masses of the workers . . ." The voice of the loudspeaker, borne on the wind, filled the church and shook the blue, red and yellow glass in the gothic windows. Don Camillo grasped a heavy bronze candlestick and, brandishing it like a club, strode with clenched teeth in the direction of the church door.

"Don Camillo, stop!" cried the Lord. "You will not leave the church until everyone has gone away."

"Oh, very well," replied Don Camillo, putting back the candlestick in its place. "I obey." He strode up and down the church and finally halted in front of the Lord. "But in here I can do as I please?"

"Naturally, Don Camillo; here you are in your own house and free to do exactly as you wish. Short of climbing up to a window and firing at the people below."

Three minutes later, Don Camillo, leaping and bounding cheerfully in the bell-chamber of the church tower, was performing the most infernal carillon that had ever been heard in the village.

The orator was compelled to interrupt his speech and turned to the local authorities who were standing with him on the platform. "He must be stopped!" he cried indignantly.

Peppone agreed gravely, nodding his head. "He must indeed," he replied, "and there are just two ways of stopping him. One is to explode a mine under the church tower and the other is to bombard it with heavy artillery."

The orator ordered him to stop talking nonsense. Surely it was easy enough to break in the door of the tower and climb the stairs.

"Well," said Peppone calmly. "One goes up by ladders from landing to landing. Look, comrade, do you see those projections just by the big window of the belfry? They are the steps that the bell-ringer has removed as he went up. By closing the trap-door of the top landing, he is cut off from the world."

"We might try firing at the windows of the tower!" suggested Smilzo.

"Certainly," agreed Peppone; "but we should have to be certain of knocking him out with the first shot, otherwise he also would begin firing, and then there might be trouble."

The bells ceased ringing and the orator resumed his speech and all went well only so long as he was careful to say nothing of which Don Camillo disapproved. If he did so, Don Camillo immediately began the counter-argument with his bells, leaving off only to resume as soon as the orator left the straight and narrow path again. And so on until the peroration was merely pathetic and patriotic and was therefore respected by the admonitory bells.

That evening Peppone met Don Camillo. "Take care, Don Camillo, that this baiting does not bring you to a bad end."

"There is no baiting involved," replied Don Camillo calmly. "You blow your trumpets and we ring our bells. That, comrade, is democracy. If, on the other hand, only one person is allowed to perform, that is a dictatorship."

Peppone held his peace, but one morning Don Camillo got up to find a merry-go-round, a swing, three shooting-galleries, an electric track, the "wall of death" and an indefinite number of other booths established within exactly half a yard of the line that divided the church square from the public square.

The owners of the "amusement park" showed him their permits, duly signed by the mayor, and Don Camillo retired without comment to his presbytery. That evening pandemonium broke out: barrel organs, loudspeakers, gunfire, shouting and singing, bells, whistling, roaring, braying and bellowing.

Don Camillo went to protest before the Lord. "This is a lack of respect towards the house of God."

"Is there anything about it that is immoral or scandalous!" asked the Lord.

"No—merry-go-rounds, swings, little motor cars, chiefly children's amusements."

"Well, then, it is simply democracy."

"But this infernal din?" protested Don Camillo.

"The din also is democracy, provided it remains within the law. Outside church territory, the mayor is in command, my son."

The presbytery stood some thirty yards further forward than the church, having one of its sides adjoining the square, and exactly underneath one of its windows a strange apparatus had been erected that immediately aroused Don Camillo's curiosity. It was a kind of small column about three feet high, topped by a sort of stuffed mushroom covered with leather. Behind it was another column, taller and more slender, upon which was a large dial bearing figures from 1 to 1000. It was an instrument for the trial of strength: a blow was struck at the mushroom and the dial recorded its force. Don Camillo, squinting through the cracks of the shutters, began to enjoy himself. By eleven o'clock in the evening the highest number recorded was 750, and that stood to the credit of Badile, the Gretti's cowman, who had fists like sacks of potatoes. Then quite suddenly Comrade Peppone made his appearance, surrounded by his satellites.

All the people came running to see, crying, "Go on, Peppone. Go to it!" And Peppone removed his jacket, rolled up his sleeves and took his stand opposite the machine, measuring the distance with his clenched fist. There was total silence and even Don Camillo felt his heart hammering.

Peppone's fist cleft the air and struck the mushroom.

"Nine hundred and fifty," yelled the owner of the machine. "Only once before have I seen any man get that score, and he was a longshoreman in Genoa." The crowd howled with enthusiasm.

Peppone put on his coat again, raised his head and looked at the window behind which Don Camillo was concealed. "To anyone whom it may concern," he remarked loudly, "I might say that a blow that registers nine hundred and fifty is no joke!"

Everyone looked up at Don Camillo's window and sniggered. Don Camillo went to bed with his legs shaking under him. On the next evening he was there again, watching from behind his window and waiting feverishly for the clock to strike eleven. Once again Peppone arrived with his staff, took off his coat, rolled up his sleeve and aimed a mighty blow at the mushroom.

"Nine hundred and fifty-one!" howled the crowd. And once again they looked up at Don Camillo's window and sniggered. Peppone also looked up.

"To anyone whom it may concern," he remarked loudly, "I might say that a blow that registers nine hundred and fifty-one is no joke!"

Don Camillo went to bed that night with a temperature.

Next day he went and knelt before the Lord. "Lord," he sighed. "I am being dragged over the precipice!"

"Be strong and resist, Don Camillo!"

That evening Don Camillo went to his peep-hole in the window as though he were on his way to the scaffold. Rumour had spread like wildfire and the whole countryside had come to see the performance. When Peppone appeared there was an audible whisper of "Here he is!" Peppone looked up, jeering, took off his coat, raised his fist and there was silence.

"Nine hundred and fifty-two!"

Don Camillo saw a million eyes fixed upon his window, lost the light of reason and hurled himself out of the room.

"To anyone whom . . ." Peppone did not have time to finish his remarks about a blow that registered nine hundred and fifty-two: Don Camillo already stood before him. The crowd bellowed, and then was suddenly silent.

Don Camillo threw out his chest, took a firm stance, threw away his hat and crossed himself. Then he raised his formidable fist and struck hard.

"One thousand!" yelled the crowd.

"To anyone whom it may concern, I might say that a blow that registers one thousand is no joke," remarked Don Camillo.

Peppone had grown rather pale, and his satellites were glancing at him doubtfully, hesitating between resentment and disappointment. Other bystanders were chuckling delightedly. Peppone looked Don Camillo straight in the eyes and took off his coat again. He stepped in front and raised his fist.

"Lord!" whispered Don Camillo hastily.

Peppone's fist cleft the air.

"A thousand," bawled the crowd and Peppone's bodyguard rejoiced.

"At one thousand all blows are formidable," observed Smilzo. "I think we will leave it at that."

Peppone moved off triumphantly in one direction while Don Camillo moved off triumphantly in the other.

"Lord," said Don Camillo when he knelt before the crucifix. "I thank You. I was scared to death."

"That you wouldn't make a thousand?"

"No; that that pig- headed fool wouldn't make it too. I should have had it on my conscience."

"I knew it; and it was lucky that I came to your help," replied the Lord, smiling. "Moreover, Peppone also, as soon as he saw you, nearly died of fear lest you shouldn't succeed in reaching nine hundred and fifty-two."

"Possibly!" muttered Don Camillo, who now and then liked to appear sceptical.

CRIME AND PUNISHMENT

ON EASTER MORNING, Don Camillo, leaving his home at an early hour, was confronted at the door of the presbytery by a colossal chocolate egg tied up with a handsome riband of red silk. Or, rather, by a formidable egg that resembled a chocolate one, but was merely a two-hundred-pound bomb shorn of its fins and painted a rich brown.

The war had not omitted to pass over Don Camillo's parish, and planes had visited it on more than one occasion, dropping bombs. A number of these had remained unexploded, half buried in the ground or actually lying on the surface, since the planes had flown low. When all was over, a couple of engineers had arrived from somewhere or other, exploded the bombs lying far from any building and dismantled those too close to occupied places. These they had collected to be disposed of later. One bomb had fallen upon the old mill, destroying the roof and remaining wedged between a wall and a main beam and it had been left there because the house was derelict and the dismantled bomb no longer dangerous. It was this bomb that had been transformed into an Easter egg by unknown hands.

"Unknown," let us say, as a figure of speech, since there was the inscription: "Happy Eester," (with two e's) and there was also the red riband. The business had been carefully organized, because when Don Camillo turned his eyes away from the strange egg, he found the church square thronged with people. These scoundrels had all conspired to be present in order to enjoy Don Camillo's discomfiture.

Don Camillo felt annoyed and allowed himself to kick the object, which, naturally, remained immovable.

"It's pretty heavy!" someone shouted.

"Needs the bomb-removal squad!" suggested another voice.

There was a sound of sniggering.

"Try blessing it and see if it doesn't walk off of its own accord!" cried a third voice.

Don Camillo went pale and his knees began to tremble. Slowly he bent down and with his immense hands grasped the bomb at its two extremities. There was a deathly silence. The crowd gazed at Don Camillo, holding their breaths, their eyes staring in something akin to fear.

"Lord!" whispered Don Camillo desperately.

"Heave ho, Don Camillo!" replied a quiet voice that came from the high altar.

The bones of that great frame literally cracked. Slowly and implacably Don Camillo straightened his back with the enormous mass of iron welded to his hands. He stood for a moment contemplating the crowd and then he set out. Every step fell like a ton weight. He left the church square and step by step, slow and inexorable as Fate, Don Camillo crossed the big square. The crowd followed in silence, amazed. On reaching the far end of the square, opposite the Party headquarters, he stopped. And the crowd also stopped.

"Lord," whispered Don Camillo desperately.

"Heave ho, Don Camillo!" came a rather anxious voice from the now-distant high altar of the church.

Don Camillo collected himself, then in one sudden movement he brought the great weight up to the level of his chest. Another effort and the bomb began slowly to rise higher, watched by the now-frightened crowd.

Now Don Camillo's arms were fully extended and the bomb poised above his head. For one moment he held it there, then he hurled it from him and it landed on the ground exactly in front of the door of the Party headquarters.

Don Camillo looked at the crowd: "Returned to sender," he observed in a ringing voice. "Easter is spelt with an A. Correct and re-deliver."

The crowd made way for him and Don Camillo returned triumphantly to the presbytery.

Peppone did not re-deliver the bomb. With two helpers he loaded it on to a cart and it was removed and thrown down a disused quarry at a distance from the village. The bomb rolled down a slope but did not reach the bottom, because it was arrested by a tree stump and remained wedged in an upright position.

Three days later it happened that a goat approached the quarry and discovered an alluring patch of fresh grass at the roots of the tree stump. In cropping the grass, it pushed the bomb which resumed its descent and, having travelled some two yards, struck a stone and exploded with terrific violence. In the village, at a considerable distance, the windows of thirty houses were shattered.

Peppone arrived at the presbytery a few moments later, gasping, and found Don Camillo going upstairs.

"And to think," groaned Peppone, "that I spent an entire evening hammering at those fins!"

"And to think that I . . ." moaned Don Camillo, and could get no further because he was visualizing the scene in the square.

"I'm going to bed . . ." gasped Peppone.

"I was on my way there . . ." gasped Don Camillo.

He had the crucifix from the high altar brought to him in his bedroom.

"Forgive me if I put You to this inconvenience," murmured Don Camillo, whose temperature was raging, "but I had to thank You on behalf of the whole village."

"No need of that, Don Camillo," replied the Lord with a smile. "No need of that."

One morning shortly after this, on leaving the house, Don Camillo discovered that during the night someone had defaced the white wall of the presbytery by writing upon it in red letters two feet high the words: *Don Camàlo,* which means stevedore, and undoubtedly referred to his recent feat of strength.

With a bucket of whitewash and a large brush Don Camillo set to work to efface the inscription, but in view of the fact that it was written in aniline red, the application of whitewash was completely useless and the letters only glared more balefully through any number of coats. Don Camillo had to resort to scraping, and the job took him quite half the day.

He made his appearance before the Lord above the altar as white as a miller all over but in a distinctly black frame of mind. "If I can only find out who did it," he said, "I shall thrash him until my stick is worn away."

"Don't be melodramatic, Don Camillo," the Lord advised him. "This is some urchin's doing. After all, no one has really insulted you."

"Do you think it seemly to call a priest a stevedore?" protested Don Camillo. "And then, it's the kind of nickname that, if people get hold of it, may stick to me all my life."

"You've got broad shoulders, Don Camillo," the Lord consoled him with a smile. "I never had shoulders like yours and yet I bore the Cross without beating anybody."

Don Camillo agreed that the Lord was in the right. But he was not satisfied, and that evening, instead of going to his bed, he took up his station in a strategic position and waited patiently. Towards two o'clock in the morning an individual made his appearance in the church square and, having placed a small pail on the ground beside him, set to work carefully upon the wall of the presbytery. But without giving him time even to complete the letter D, Don Camillo overturned the pail on his head and sent him flying with a terrific kick in the pants.

Aniline dye is an accursed thing, and Gigotto (one of Peppone's most valued henchmen), on receiving the baptism of red paint, remained for three days concealed in his house scrubbing his face with every conceivable concoction, after which he was compelled to go out and work. The facts had already become generally known and he found himself greeted with the nickname of "Redskin." Don Camillo fanned the flames until a day came when, returning from a visit to the doctor, he discovered too late that the handle of his front door had received a coating of red. Without uttering so much as one word, Don Camillo went and sought out Gigotto at the tavern and with a blow that was enough to blind an elephant liberally daubed his face with the paint collected from the door handle. Naturally, the occurrence immediately took on a political aspect and, in view of the fact that Gigotto was supported by half a dozen of his own party, Don Camillo was compelled to use a bench in self-defence.

The six routed by the bench were seething with fury. The tavern was in an uproar and the same evening some unknown person serenaded Don Camillo by throwing a firework in front of the presbytery door.

People were getting anxious and it needed but a spark to set fire to the tinder. And so, one fine morning, Don Camillo received an urgent summons to the town because the bishop wished to speak to him.

The bishop was old and bent, and in order to look Don Camillo in the face he had to raise his head considerably. "Don Camillo," said the bishop, "you are not well. You need to spend a few months in a beautiful mountain village. Yes, yes; the parish priest at Puntarossa has died recently, and so we shall kill two birds with one stone: you will be able to reorganize the parish for me and at the same time you will re-establish your health. Then you will come back as fresh as a rose. You will be supplied by Don Pietro, a young man who will make no trouble for you. Are you pleased, Don Camillo?"

"No, Monsignore; but I shall leave as soon as Monsignore wishes."

"Good," replied the bishop. "Your discipline is the more meritorious inasmuch as you accept without discussion my instructions to do something that is against your personal inclinations."

"Monsignore, you will not be displeased if the people of my parish say that I have run away because I was afraid?"

"No," replied the old man, smiling. "Nobody on this earth could ever think that Don Camillo was afraid. Go with God, Don Camillo, and leave benches alone; they can never constitute a Christian argument."

The news spread quickly in the village. Peppone had announced it in person at a special meeting. "Don Camillo is going," he proclaimed, "transferred to some God-forsaken mountain village. He is leaving to-morrow afternoon at three o'clock."

"Hurrah!" shouted the entire meeting. "And may he croak when he gets there. . . ."

"All things considered, it's the best way out," said Peppone. "He was beginning to think he was the King and the Pope rolled into one, and if he had stayed here we should have had to give him a super dressing-down. This saves us the trouble."

"And he should be left to slink away like a whipped cur," howled Brusco. "Make the village understand that there will be trouble for anyone who is seen about the church square from three to half-past."

The hour struck and Don Camillo went to say goodbye to the Lord above the altar. "I wish I could have taken You with me," sighed Don Camillo.

"I shall go with you just the same," replied the Lord. "Don't you worry."

"Have I really done anything bad enough to deserve being sent away?" asked Don Camillo.

"Yes."

"Then they really are all against me," sighed Don Camillo.

"All of them," replied the Lord. "Even Don Camillo himself disapproves of what you have done."

"That is true enough," Don Camillo acknowledged. "I could hit myself."

"Keep your hands quiet, Don Camillo, and a pleasant journey to you."

In a town fear can affect 50 per cent. of the people, but in a village the percentage is doubled. The roads were deserted. Don Camillo climbed into the train, and when he watched his church tower disappear behind a clump of trees he felt very bitter indeed. "Not even a dog has remembered me," he sighed. "It is obvious that I have failed in my duties and it is also obvious that I am a bad lot."

The train was a slow one that stopped at every station, and it therefore stopped at Boschetto, a mere cluster of four houses three or four miles from Don Camillo's own village. And so, quite suddenly, Don Camillo found his compartment invaded; he was hustled to the window and found himself face to face with a sea of people who were clapping their hands and throwing flowers.

"Peppone's men had said that if anyone in the village showed up at your departure it meant a hiding," the steward from Stradalunga was explaining, "and so, in order to avoid trouble, we all came on here to say goodbye to you."

Don Camillo was completely dazed and felt a humming in his ears, and when the train moved off the entire compartment was filled with flowers, bottles, bundles and parcels of all sizes, while poultry with their legs tied together clucked and protested from the baggage nets overhead.

But there was still a thorn in his heart. "And those others? They must really hate me to have done such a thing! It wasn't even enough for them to get me sent away!"

A quarter of an hour later the train stopped at Boscoplanche, the last station of the Commune. There Don Camillo heard himself called by name, and going to the window beheld Mayor Peppone and his entire *giunta*. Mayor Peppone made the following speech:

"Before you leave the territory of the Commune, it seems to us proper to bring you the greetings of the population and good wishes for a rapid recovery, the which will enable a speedy return to your spiritual mission."

Then, as the train began to move, Peppone took off his hat with a sweeping gesture and Don Camillo also removed his hat and remained standing at the window with it posed in the air like a statue of the Risorgimento.

The church at Puntarossa sat on the top of the mountain and looked like a picture postcard. When Don Camillo reached it he inhaled the pine-scented air deeply and exclaimed with satisfaction:

"A bit of rest up here will certainly do me good, the which will enable a speedy return to my spiritual mission."

And he said it quite gravely, because to him that "the which" was of more value than the sum of all Cicero's orations.

RETURN TO THE FOLD

THE PRIEST WHO HAD been sent to supply the parish during Don Camillo's political convalescence was young and delicate. He knew his business and he spoke courteously, using lovely, polished phrases that appeared to be newly minted. Naturally, even though he knew that he was only in temporary occupation, this young priest established some small changes in the church such as any man feels to be necessary if he is to be tolerably at his ease in strange surroundings.

We are not making actual comparisons, but it is much the same when a traveller goes to an hotel. Even if he is aware that he will remain there only for one night, he will be inclined to move a table from left to right and a chair from right to left, because each one of us has a strictly personal concept of aesthetic balance and colour and experiences discomfort on every occasion when, being at liberty to do so, he does not exert himself to create such harmony as he desires.

It therefore happened that on the first Sunday following the new priest's arrival the congregation noticed two important innovations: the great candlestick that supported the big paschal candle with its floral decorations and which had always stood on the second step at the Gospel side of the altar had been shifted to the Epistle side and placed in front of a small picture representing a saint—a picture which had previously not been there.

Out of curiosity, together with respect to the new parish priest, the entire village was present, with Peppone and his henchmen in the foremost ranks.

"Have you noticed," muttered Brusco to Peppone with a stifled snigger, pointing out the candlestick, "changes!"

"M-m-m," mumbled Peppone irritably. And he remained irritable until the priest came down to the altar rails to make the customary address.

Then Peppone could bear no more, and just as the priest was about to begin, he detached himself from his companions, marched steadily towards the candlestick, grasped it firmly, carried it past the altar and placed it in its old position upon the second step to the left. Then he returned to his seat in the front row and with knees wide apart and arms folded stared arrogantly straight into the eyes of the young priest.

"Well done!" murmured the entire congregation, not excepting Peppone's political opponents.

The young priest, who had stood open-mouthed watching Peppone's behaviour, changed colour, stammered somehow through his brief address and returned to the altar to complete his mass.

When he left the church he found Peppone waiting for him with his entire staff. The church square was crowded with silent and surly people.

"Listen here, Don—Don whatever you call yourself," said Peppone in an aggressive voice, "who is this new person whose picture you have hung on the pillar to the right of the altar?"

"Santa Rita da Cascia," stammered the little priest.

"Then let me tell you that this village has no use for Santa Rita da Cascia or anything of the kind. Here everything is better left as it was before."

The young priest spread out his arms. "I think I am entitled . . ." he began, but Peppone cut him short.

"Ah, so that's how you take it? Well, then let us speak clearly: this village has no use for a priest such as you."

The young priest gasped. "I cannot see that I have done anything . . ."

"Then I'll tell you what you have done. You have committed an illegal action. You have attempted to change an order that the permanent priest of the parish had established in accordance with the will of the people."

"Hurrah!" shouted the crowd, including the reactionaries.

The little priest attempted a smile. "If that is all the trouble, everything shall be put back exactly as it was before. Isn't that the solution?"

"No," thundered Peppone, flinging his hat behind him and placing his enormous fists on his hips.

"And may I be allowed to ask why?"

Peppone had reached the end of his supplies of diplomacy. "Well," he said, "if you really want to know, it is not a solution because if I give you one on the jaw I shall send you flying at least fifteen yards, while if it were the regular incumbent he wouldn't move so much as an inch!"

Peppone stopped short of explaining that in the event of his hitting Don Camillo once, the latter would have hit him half a dozen times in return. He left it at that, but his meaning was clear to all his hearers with the exception of the little priest, who stared at him in amazement.

"But, excuse me," he murmured. "Why should you have any wish to hit me?"

Peppone lost patience. "Who in the world wants to hit you? There you are again, running down the left-wing parties! I used a figure of speech merely in order to explain our views. Is it likely that I should waste my time hitting a scrap of a priest like you!"

On hearing himself termed a "scrap of a priest," the young man drew himself up to his full five feet four inches and his face grew purple till the very veins in his neck swelled.

" 'Scrap of a priest' you may call me," he cried in a shrill voice, "but I was sent here by ecclesiastical authority and here I shall remain until ecclesiastical authority sees fit to remove me. In this church you have no authority at all! Santa Rita will stay where she is and, as for the candlestick, watch what I am going to do!"

He went into the church, grasped the candlestick firmly and after a considerable struggle succeeded in removing it again to the Epistle side of the altar in front of the new picture.

"There!" he said triumphantly.

"Very well!" replied Peppone, who had observed his actions from the threshold of the church door. Then he turned to the crowd which stood in serried ranks in the church square, silent and surly, and shouted: "The people will have something to say to this! To the town hall, all of you, and we will make a demonstration of protest."

"Hurray!" howled the crowd.

Peppone elbowed his way through them so that he could lead them, and they formed up behind him yelling and brandishing sticks. When they reached the town hall, the yells increased in volume, and Peppone yelled also, raising his fist and shaking it at the balcony of the council chamber.

"Peppone," shouted Brusco in his ear, "are you crazy? Stop yelling! Have you forgotten that you yourself are the mayor?"

"Hell! . . ." exclaimed Peppone. "When these accursed swine make me lose my head I remember nothing!" He ran upstairs and out on to the balcony, where he was cheered by the crowd including the reactionaries.

"Comrades, citizens," shouted Peppone. "We will not suffer this oppression that offends against our dignity as free men! We shall remain within the bounds of the law so long as may be possible, but we are going to get justice even if we must resort to gunfire! In the meantime I propose that a committee of my selection shall accompany me to the ecclesiastical authorities and impose in a democratic manner the desires of the people!"

"Hurrah!" yelled the crowd, completely indifferent to logic or syntax. "Long live our Mayor Peppone!"

When Peppone and his committee stood before the bishop he had some difficulty in finding his voice, but at last he got going.

"Excellence," he said, "that priest that you have sent us is not worthy of the traditions of the leading parish of the district."

The bishop raised his head in order to see the top of Peppone. "Tell me now: what has he been doing?"

Peppone waved his arms. "For the love of God! Doing? He hasn't done anything serious. . . . In fact, he hasn't done anything at all. . . . The trouble is that . . . Oh, well, Eminence, he's only a half man . . . you know what I mean, a priestling; when the fellow is all dressed up—your Eminence must excuse me, but he looks like a coat-hanger loaded with three overcoats and a cloak!"

The old bishop nodded his head gravely. "But do you," he inquired very graciously, "establish the merits of priests with a tape measure and a weighing machine?"

"No, Excellence," replied Peppone. "We aren't savages! But all the same, how shall I put it—even the eye needs some satisfaction, and in matters of religion it's the same as with a doctor, there's a lot to be said for personal sympathies and moral impressions!"

The old bishop sighed. "Yes, yes. I understand perfectly. But all the same, my dear children, you had a parish priest who looked like a tower and you yourselves came and asked me to remove him!"

Peppone wrinkled his forehead. "Monsignore," he explained solemnly, "it was a question of a *casus belli*, an affair *sui generis*, as they say. Because that man was a multiple offence in the way he exasperated us by his provocative and dictatorial poses."

"I know, I know," said the bishop. "You told me all about it when you were here before, my son, and, as you see, I removed him. And that was precisely because I fully understood that I had to deal with an unworthy man. . . ."

"One moment, if you will excuse me," Brusco interrupted. "We never said that he was an unworthy man! . . ."

"Well, well; if not 'an unworthy man,' " continued the bishop, "at any rate an unworthy priest inasmuch as . . ."

"I beg your pardon," said Peppone, interrupting him. "We never suggested that as a priest he had failed in his duty. We only spoke of his serious defects, of his very serious misdeeds as a man."

"Exactly," agreed the old bishop. "And as, unfortunately, the man and the priest are inseparable, and a man such as Don Camillo represents a danger to his neighbours, we are at this very moment considering the question of making his present appointment a permanent one. We will leave him where he is, among the goats at Puntarossa. Yes, we will leave him there, since it has not yet been decided whether he is to be allowed to continue in his functions or whether we shall suspend him *a divinis*. We will wait and see."

Peppone turned to his committee and there was a moment's consultation, then he turned again to the bishop.

"Monsignore," he said in a low voice, and he was sweating and had gone pale, as though he found difficulty in speaking audibly, "if the ecclesiastical authority has its own reasons for doing such a thing, of course that is its own affair. Nevertheless, it is my duty to warn your Excellency that until our regular parish priest returns to us, not a soul will enter the church."

The bishop raised his arms. "But, my sons," he exclaimed, "do you realize the gravity of what you are saying? This is coercion!"

"No, Monsignore," Peppone explained, "we are coercing nobody, because we shall all remain quietly at home, and no law compels us to go to church. Our decision is simply a question of availing ourselves of democratic liberty. Because we are the only persons qualified to judge whether a priest suits us or not, since we have had to bear with him for nearly twenty years."

"*Vox populi vox Dei*," sighed the old bishop. "God's will be done. You can have your reprobate back if you want him. But don't come whining to me later on about his arrogance."

Peppone laughed. "Eminence! The rodomontades of a type such as Don Camillo don't really break any bones. We came here before merely as a matter of simple political and social precaution, so as to make sure that Redskin here didn't lose his head and throw a bomb at him."

"Redskin yourself!" retorted the indignant Gigotto, whose face Don Camillo had dyed with aniline red and whose head had come in contact with Don Camillo's bench. "I never meant to throw any bombs. I simply threw a firework in front of his house to make him realize that I wasn't standing for being knocked on the head even by the reverend parish priest in person."

"Ah! Then it was you, my son, who threw the firework?" inquired the old bishop indifferently.

"Well, Excellence," mumbled Gigotto, "you know how it is. When one has been hit on the head with a bench one may easily go a bit too far in retaliation."

"I understand perfectly," replied the bishop, who was old and knew how to take people in the right way.

Don Camillo returned ten days later.

"How are you?" inquired Peppone, meeting him just as he was leaving the station. "Did you have a pleasant holiday?"

"Well, it was a bit dreary up there. Luckily, I took my pack of cards with me and worked off my restlessness playing patience," replied Don Camillo. He pulled a pack of cards from his pocket. "Look," he said. "But now I shan't need them any more." And delicately, with a smile, he tore the pack in two as though it were a slice of bread.

"We are getting old, Mr. Mayor," sighed Don Camillo.

"To hell with you and with those who sent you back here!" muttered Peppone, turning away, the picture of gloom.

Don Camillo had a lot to tell the Lord above the altar. Then at the end of their gossip he inquired, with an assumption of indifference:

"What kind of a fellow was my supply?"

"A nice lad, cultured and with a nice nature. When anyone did him a good turn, he didn't bait them by tearing up a pack of cards under their noses."

"Lord!" exclaimed Don Camillo, raising his arms. "I don't suppose anyone here ever did him a good turn, anyway. And then there are people who have to be thanked like that. I'll bet You that now Peppone is saying to his gang: 'And he tore the whole pack across, zip, the misbegotten son of an ape!' And he is thoroughly enjoying saying it! Shall we have a wager?"

"No," replied the Lord with a sigh, "because that is exactly what Peppone is saying at this moment."

THE DEFEAT

THE WAR TO THE knife that had now been in process for nearly a year was won by Don Camillo, who managed to complete his recreation centre while Peppone's People's Palace still lacked all its locks.

The recreation centre proved to be a very up-to-date affair: a hall for social gatherings, dramatic performances, lectures and suchlike activities, a library with a reading and writing room and a covered area for physical training and winter games. There was in addition a magnificent fenced sports ground with a gymnasium, running track, bathing pool and a children's playground with giant-stride, swings, etcetera. Most of the paraphernalia was as yet in an embryonic stage, but the important thing was to have made a start.

For the inauguration ceremony Don Camillo had prepared a most lively programme: choral singing, athletic competitions and a game of football. For the latter Don Camillo had succeeded in mustering a really formidable team, a task to which he had brought so impassioned an enthusiasm that in the course of the team's eight months of training the kicks administered by him alone to the eleven players were far more numerous than those that all those players put together had succeeded in giving to the ball.

Peppone knew all this and was deeply embittered. He could not endure the thought that the party that genuinely represented the people must play second fiddle in the celebration organized by Don Camillo on the people's behalf. And when Don Camillo sent to inform him that in order to demonstrate his "sympathetic understanding of the more ignorant social strata of the village" he was willing to allow a match between their Dynamos football team and his own Galliards, Peppone turned pale, summoned the eleven lads of the local sports squadron and made them stand to attention against the wall while he made them the following address: "You are to play against the priest's team. You have got to win or I shall smash in every one of your faces. The Party orders it for the honour of a downtrodden people!"

"We shall win!" replied the eleven, sweating with terror.

As soon as this scene was reported to him Don Camillo mustered the Galliards and addressed them as follows:

"We are not here among uncouth savages such as your opponents," he said, smiling pleasantly. "We are capable of reasoning like sensible and educated gentlemen. With the help of God, we shall beat them six goals to none. I make no threats; I merely remind you that the honour of the parish is in your hands. Also in your feet.

"Therefore let each of you do his duty as a good citizen. Should there be some Barabbas among you who is not ready to give his all even to the last drop of his blood, I shall not indulge in Peppone's histrionics with regard to the smashing of faces. I shall merely kick his backside to a jelly!"

The entire countryside attended the inauguration, led by Peppone and his satellites with blazing red handkerchiefs round their necks. In his capacity as *mayor*, he expressed his satisfaction at the event and as *personal representative of the people* he emphasized his confident belief that the occasion they were celebrating would not be made to serve "unworthy ends of political propaganda such as were already being whispered of by ill-intentioned persons."

During the performance of the choral singers, Peppone was able to point out to Brusco that, as a matter of fact, singing was also a sport, inasmuch as it developed the expansion of the lungs, and Brusco, with seeming amiability, replied that in his opinion the exercise would prove even more efficacious as a means of physical development for Catholic youth if they were taught to accompany it with gestures adapted to the improvement not only of their lung power, but also of the muscles of their arms.

During the game of basket-ball, Peppone expressed a sincere conviction that the game of ping-pong had also not only an undeniable athletic value, but was so graceful that he was astonished not to find it included in the programme.

In view of the fact that these comments were made in voices that were easily audible half a mile away, the veins of Don Camillo's neck were very soon swelled to the size of cables. He therefore awaited with indescribable impatience the hour of the football match, which would be that of his reply.

At last it was time for the match. White jerseys with a large "G" on the breast for the eleven Galliards. Red jerseys bearing the hammer, sickle and star combined with an elegant "D" adorned the eleven Dynamos.

The crowd cared less than nothing for symbols, anyway, and hailed the teams after their own fashion: "Hurrah for Peppone!" or "Hurrah for Don Camillo!" Peppone and Don Camillo looked at one another and exchanged slight and dignified bows.

The referee was a neutral: the clockmaker Binella, a man without political opinions. After ten minutes' play the sergeant of carabinieri, pale to the gills, approached Peppone, followed by his two equally pallid subordinates.

"Mr. Mayor," he stammered, "don't you think it would be wise for me to telephone to the town for reinforcements?"

"You can telephone for a division for all I care, but if those butchers don't let up, nobody will be able to avoid there being a heap of corpses as high as the first-floor windows! Not His Majesty the King himself could do a thing about it, do you understand," howled Peppone, forgetting the very existence of the republic in his blind fury.

The sergeant turned to Don Camillo, who was standing a few feet away. "Don't you think . . .?" he stuttered, but Don Camillo cut him short.

"I," he shouted, "simply think that nothing short of the personal intervention of the United States of America will prevent us all from swimming in blood if those accursed bolsheviks don't stop disabling my men by kicking them in the shins!"

"I see," said the sergeant, and went off to barricade himself into his quarters, although perfectly aware that the common sequel of such behaviour is a general attempt to close the festivities by setting fire to the barracks of the carabinieri.

The first goal was scored by the Galliards and raised a howl that shook the church tower. Peppone, his face distorted with rage, turned on Don Camillo with clenched fists as though about to attack him. Don Camillo's fists were already in position. The two of them were within a hair's-breadth of conflict, but Don Camillo observed out of the tail of his eye that all other eyes present were fixed upon them.

"If we begin fighting, there'll be a free-for-all," he muttered through clenched teeth to Peppone.

"All right, for the sake of the people."

"For the sake of the faith," said Don Camillo.

Nothing happened. Nevertheless, Peppone, when the first half ended a few moments later, mustered the Dynamos. "Fascists!" he said to them in a voice thick with contempt. Then, seizing hold of Smilzo, the centre-forward: "As for you, you dirty traitor, suppose you remember that when we were in the mountains I saved your worthless skin no less than three times. If in the next five minutes you haven't scored a goal, I'll attend to that same skin of yours!"

Smilzo, when play was resumed, got the ball and set to work. And work he did, with his head, with his legs and with his knees. He even bit the ball, he spat his lungs out and split his spleen, but at the fourth minute he sent the ball between the posts.

Then he flung himself on to the ground and lay motionless. Don Camillo moved over to the other side of the ground lest his self-control should fail him. The Galliards' goalkeeper was in a high fever from sheer funk.

The Dynamos closed up into a defensive phalanx that seemed impregnable. Thirty seconds before the next break, the referee whistled and a penalty was given against the Galliards. The ball flew into the air. A child of six could not have muffed it at such an angle. Goal!

The match was now over. The only task remaining for Peppone's men was that of picking up their injured players and carrying them back to their pavilion. The referee had no political views and left them to it.

Don Camillo was bewildered. He ran off to the church and knelt in front of the altar. "Lord," he said, "why did You fail to help me? I have lost the match."

"And why should I have helped you rather than the others? Your men had twenty-two legs and so had they, Don Camillo, and all legs are equal. Moreover, they are not My business. I am interested in souls. *Da mihi animam, caetera tolle.* I leave the bodies on earth. Don Camillo, where are your brains?"

"I can find them with an effort," said Don Camillo. "I was not suggesting that You should have taken charge of my men's legs, which in any case were the best of the lot. But I do say that You did not prevent the dishonesty of one man from giving a foul unjustly against my team."

"The priest can make a mistake in saying mass, Don Camillo. Why must you deny that others may be mistaken while being in good faith?"

"One can admit of errors in most circumstances, but not when it is a matter of arbitration in sport! When the ball is actually there . . . Binella is a scoundrel . . ." He was unable to continue because at that moment the sound of an imploring voice became progressively audible and a man came running into the church, exhausted and gasping, his face convulsed with terror.

"They want to kill me," he sobbed. "Save me!"

The crowd had reached the church door and was about to irrupt into the church itself. Don Camillo seized a candlestick weighing half a quintal and brandished it menacingly.

"Back, in God's name, or I strike!" he shouted. "Remember that anyone who enters here is sacred and immune!"

The crowd hesitated.

"Shame on you, you pack of wolves! Get back to your lairs and pray God to forgive you your savagery."

The crowd stood in silence, heads were bowed, and there was a general movement of retreat.

"Make the sign of the cross," Don Camillo ordered them severely, and as he stood there brandishing the candlestick in his huge hand he seemed a very Samson.

Everyone made the sign of the cross.

"Between you and the object of your brutality is now that sign of the cross that each one of you has traced with his own hand. Anybody who dares to violate that sacred barrier is a blasphemer. *Vade retro!* " He himself stood back and closed the church door, drawing the bolt, but there was no need. The fugitive had sunk on to a bench and was still panting. "Thank you, Don Camillo," he murmured.

Don Camillo made no immediate reply. He paced to and fro for a few moments and then pulled up opposite the man. "Binella!" said Don Camillo in accents of fury. "Binella, here in my presence and that of God you dare not lie! There was no foul! How much did that reprobate Peppone give you to make you call a foul in a drawn game?"

"Two thousand five hundred lire."

"M-m-m-m!" roared Don Camillo, thrusting his fist under his victim's nose.

"But then . . ." moaned Binella.

"Get out," bawled Don Camillo, pointing to the door.

Once more alone, Don Camillo turned towards the Lord. "Didn't I tell you that the swine had sold himself? Haven't I a right to be enraged?"

"None at all, Don Camillo," replied the Lord. "You started it when you offered Binella two thousand lire to do the same thing. When Peppone bid five hundred lire more, Binella accepted the higher bribe."

Don Camillo spread out his arms. "Lord," he said, "but if we are to look at it that way, then I emerge as the guilty man!"

"Exactly, Don Camillo. When you, a priest, were the first to make the suggestion, he assumed that there was no harm in the matter, and then, quite naturally, he took the more profitable bid."

Don Camillo bowed his head. "And do you mean to tell me that if that unhappy wretch should get beaten up by my men, it would be my doing?"

"In a certain sense, yes, because you were the first to lead him into temptation. Nevertheless, your sin would have been greater if Binella, accepting your offer, had agreed to cheat on behalf of your team. Because then the Dynamos would have done the beating up and you would have been powerless to stop them."

Don Camillo reflected awhile. "In fact," he said, "it was better that the others should win."

"Exactly, Don Camillo."

"Then, Lord," said Don Camillo, "I thank you for having allowed me to lose. And if I tell you that I accept the defeat as a punishment for my dishonesty, You must believe that I am really penitent. Because, to see a team such as mine who might very well—and I am not bragging—play in Division B, a team that, believe me or not, could swallow up and digest a couple of thousand Dynamos in their stride, to see them beaten . . . is enough to break one's heart and cries for vengeance to God!"

"Don Camillo!" the Lord admonished him, smiling.

"You can't possibly understand me," sighed Don Camillo. "Sport is a thing apart. Either one cares or one doesn't. Do I make myself clear?"

"Only too clear, my poor Don Camillo. I understand you so well that . . . Come now, when are you going to have your revenge?"

Don Camillo leaped to his feet, his heart swelling with delight. "Six to nothing!" he shouted. "Six to nought that they never even see the ball! Do You see that confessional?"

He flung his hat into the air, caught it with a neat kick as it came down and drove it like a thunderbolt into the little window of the confessional.

"Goal!" said the Lord, smiling.

THE AVENGER

Smilzo rode up on his racing bicycle and braked it in the American manner, which consists of letting the backside slip off the seat backwards and sit astride the wheel.

Don Camillo was reading the newspaper, seated upon the bench in front of the presbytery. He raised his head. "Does Stalin hand you down his trousers?" he inquired placidly.

Smilzo handed him a letter, touched his cap with a forefinger, leaped on to his bicycle and was just about to disappear round the corner of the presbytery when he slowed down for an instant. "No, the Pope does that," he bawled, then stood on his pedals and was gone in a flash.

Don Camillo had been expecting the letter. It contained an invitation to the inauguration ceremony of the People's Palace with a programme of the festivities enclosed. Speeches, reports, a band and refreshments. Then, in the afternoon: *"Great Boxing Match between the Heavyweight Champion of the Local Section, Comrade Bagotti Mirco, and the Heavyweight Champion of the Provincial Federation, Comrade Gorlini Anteo."*

Don Camillo went off to discuss the event with the Lord above the altar. "Lord!" he exclaimed when he had read the programme aloud. "If this isn't vile! If Peppone hadn't been an utter boor, he would have staged the return match between the Galliards and the Dynamos instead of this pummelling bout! And so I shall . . ."

"And so you will not even dream of going to tell him one word of what you would like to say; and in any case you're entirely wrong," the Lord interrupted him. "It was perfectly logical of Peppone to try to do something different. Secondly, it was also logical that Peppone should not expose himself to inaugurating his venture with a defeat. Even if we suppose that his champion may lose, he would be none the worse: one comrade fights another; it all remains in the family. But a defeat of his team by yours would be detrimental to the prestige of his party. Don Camillo, you must admit that Peppone couldn't possibly have staged a return match against your team."

"And yet," exclaimed Don Camillo, "I did stage a match against his team, and what's more, I lost it!"

"But, Don Camillo," put in the Lord gently, "you don't represent a party. Your lads were not defending the colours of the Church. They were merely defending the prestige of a sporting team, of a pleasant combination that had been organized under the patronage of the parish church. Or do you perhaps think that that Sunday afternoon defeat was a defeat for the Catholic faith?"

Don Camillo began laughing. "Lord," he protested, "You wrong me if you accuse me of any such idea. I was only saying, as a sportsman, that Peppone is a boor. And so you will forgive me if I can't help laughing when his famous champion gets such a drubbing that by the third round he won't know his own name."

"Yes, I shall forgive you, Don Camillo. But I shall find it less easy to forgive your taking pleasure in the spectacle of two men belabouring each other with their fists."

Don Camillo raised his arms. "I have never done anything of the kind and would never lend my presence to countenance such manifestations of brutality as serve only to foster that cult of violence which is already too deeply rooted in the minds of the masses. I am in full agreement with You in condemning any sport in which skill is subordinated to brute force."

"Bravo, Don Camillo," said the Lord. "If a man feels the need to limber his muscles, it is not necessary to fight with his neighbour. It suffices if, having put on a pair of well-padded gloves, he takes it out on a sack of sawdust or a ball suspended somewhere."

"Exactly," agreed Don Camillo, crossing himself hastily and hurrying away.

"Will you satisfy my curiosity, Don Camillo?" exclaimed the Lord. "What is the name of that leather ball which you have had fixed with elastic to the ceiling and the floor of your attic?"

"I believe it is called a 'punching ball,' " muttered Don Camillo, halting for a moment.

"And what does that mean?"

"I don't know any English," replied Don Camillo, making good his escape.

Don Camillo attended the inaugural ceremony of the People's Palace and Peppone accompanied him personally upon a tour of the entire concern: it was all obviously thoroughly up-to-date.

"What do you think of it?" asked Peppone, who was burbling with joy.

"Charming!" replied Don Camillo, smiling cordially. "To tell you the truth, I should never have thought that it could possibly have been designed by a simple builder such as Brusco."

"True enough!" muttered Peppone, who had spent God only knew how much in order to have his project realized by the best architect in the town.

"Quite a good idea to make the windows horizontal instead of perpendicular," observed Don Camillo. "The rooms can be less lofty without its being too obvious. Excellent. And this I suppose is the warehouse."

"It is the assembly room," Peppone explained.

"Ah! And have you put the armoury and the cells for dangerous adversaries in the basement?"

"No," replied Peppone. "We haven't any dangerous adversaries; they are all harmless little folk that can remain in circulation. As for an armoury, we thought that in case of need we could make use of yours."

"An admirable idea," agreed Don Camillo politely. "You have been able to see for yourself how well I look after the tommy-gun which you entrusted to my care, Mr. Mayor."

They had pulled up in front of a huge picture representing a man with a heavy walrus moustache, small eyes and a pipe. "Is that one of your dead leaders?" inquired Don Camillo respectfully.

"That is someone who is among the living and who when he comes will drive you to sit on the lightning conductor of your own church," explained Peppone, who had reached the end of his tether.

"Too high a position for a humble parish priest. The highest position in a small community always pertains to the mayor, and from now onwards I put it at your complete disposal."

"Are we to have the honour of your presence among us at the boxing match to-day, reverend sir?" asked Peppone, thinking it best to change the subject.

"Thank you, but you had better give my seat to someone who is better qualified than I am to appreciate the innate beauty and deeply educational significance of the performance. But I shall at any rate be available at the presbytery in the event of your champion requiring the Holy Oils. You have only to send Smilzo, and I can be with you within a couple of minutes."

During the afternoon Don Camillo chatted for an hour with the Lord and then asked to be excused: "I am sleepy and I shall take a nap. And I thank You for making it rain cats and dogs. The crops needed it."

"And, moreover, according to your hopes, it will prevent many people coming from any distance to see Peppone's celebrations," added the Lord. "Am I right?"

Don Camillo shook his head.

The rain, heavy though it was, had done no harm at all to Peppone's festivities: people had flocked from every section of the countryside and from all the nearer communes, and the gymnasium of the People's Palace was as full as an egg. "Champion of the Federation" was a fine title, and Bagotti was undeniably popular in the region. And then it was also in some sense a match between town and country and that aroused interest.

Peppone, in the front row close under the ring, surveyed the crowd triumphantly. Moreover, he was convinced that, at the worst, Bagotti could only lose on points, which, in such circumstances, would be almost as good as a victory.

On the stroke of four o'clock, after an outburst of applause and yelling sufficient to bring down the roof, the gong was sounded and the audience began to get restless and excitable.

It became immediately apparent that the provincial champion surpassed Bagotti in style, but on the other hand Bagotti was quicker, and the first round left the audience breathless. Peppone was pouring with sweat and appeared to have swallowed dynamite.

The second round began well for Bagotti, who took the offensive, but quite suddenly he went down in a heap and the referee began the count.

"No," bawled Peppone leaping to his feet. "It was below the belt!"

The federal champion smiled sarcastically at Peppone. He shook his head and touched his chin with his glove.

"No!" bellowed Peppone in exasperation, drowning the uproar of the audience. "You all saw it! First he hit him low and when the pain made him double up he gave him the left on the jaw! It was a foul!"

The federal champion shrugged his shoulders and sniggered, and meanwhile the referee, having counted up to ten, was raising the victor's hand to show that he had won when the tragedy occurred.

Peppone flung away his hat and in one bound was in the ring and advancing with clenched fists upon the federal champion: "I'll show you," he howled.

"Give it to him, Peppone," yelled the infuriated audience.

The boxer put up his fists and Peppone fell upon him like a Panzer and struck hard. But Peppone was too furious to retain his judgment, and his adversary dodged him easily and landed him one directly on the point of the jaw. Nor did he hesitate to put all his weight into it, as Peppone stood there motionless and completely uncovered: it was like hitting a sack of sawdust.

Peppone slumped to the ground and a wave of dismay struck the audience and smote them to a frozen silence. But just as the champion was smiling compassionately at the giant lying prone on the mat, there was a terrific yell from the crowd as a man entered the ring. Without even troubling to remove a drenched waterproof or his cap, he seized a pair of gloves lying on a stool in the corner, pulled them on without bothering to secure them and, standing on guard squarely before the champion, aimed a terrific blow at him. The champion dodged it, naturally, but failed to get in a return, as his opponent was ready for him. The champion danced round the man, who did no more than revolve slowly, and at a given moment the champion launched a formidable blow. The other seemed barely to move, but with his left he parried while his right shot forward like a thunderbolt. The champion was already unconscious as he fell and lay as if asleep in the middle of the ring.

The audience went crazy.

It was the bell-ringer who brought the news to the presbytery and Don Camillo had to leave his bed in order to open the door because the sacristan appeared to be insane and, had he not been allowed to pour out the whole story from A to Z, there seemed every reason for fearing that he might blow up. Don Camillo went downstairs to report to the Lord.

"Well?" the Lord inquired. "And how did it go off?"

"A very disgraceful brawl; such a spectacle of disorder and immorality as can hardly be imagined!"

"Anything like that business when they wanted to lynch your referee?" asked the Lord indifferently.

Don Camillo laughed. "Referee, my foot! At the second round Peppone's champion slumped like a sack of potatoes. Then Peppone himself jumped into the ring and went for the victor. Naturally, since, although he is strong as an ox, he is such a dunderhead that he pitches in without judgment, like a Zulu or a Russian, the champion gave him one on the jaw that laid him out like a ninepin."

"And so this is the second defeat his section has suffered."

"Two for the section and one for the federation," chuckled Don Camillo. "Because that was not the end! No sooner had Peppone gone down than another man jumped into the ring and fell upon the victor. Must have been somebody from one of the neighbouring communes, I imagine, a fellow with a beard and a moustache who put up his fists and struck out at the federal champion."

"And I suppose the champion dodged and struck back and the bearded man went down also and added his quotum to the brutal exhibition," the Lord remarked.

"No! The man was as impregnable as an iron safe. So the champion began dodging round trying to catch him off-guard, and finally, zac! he puts in a straight one with his right. Then I feinted with the left and caught him square with the right and left the ring!"

"And what had you to do with it?"

"I don't understand."

"You said: 'I feinted with the left and caught him square with the right.' "

"I can't imagine how I came to say such a thing."

The Lord shook His head. "Could it possibly be because you yourself were the man who struck down the champion?"

"It would not seem so," said Don Camillo gravely, "I have neither beard nor moustache."

"But those, of course, could be assumed so that the crowd should not suspect that the parish priest is interested in the spectacle of two men fighting in public with their fists!"

Don Camillo shrugged. "All things are possible, Lord, and we must also bear in mind that even parish priests are made of flesh and blood."

The Lord sighed.

"We are not forgetting it, but we should also remember that if parish priests are made of flesh and blood they themselves should never forget that they are also made of brains. Because if the flesh-and-blood parish priest wishes to disguise himself in order to attend a boxing match, the priest that is made of brains prevents him from giving an exhibition of violence."

Don Camillo shook his head. "Very true. But You should also bear in mind that parish priests, in addition to flesh and blood and brains, are also made of yet another thing. And so, when that other thing sees a mayor sent flat on the mat before all his own people by a swine from the town who has won by striking below the belt (which is a sin that cries to heaven for vengeance), that other thing takes the priest of flesh and blood and the priest of brains by the throat and sends the lot of them into the ring."

The Lord nodded. "You mean to say that I should bear in mind that parish priests are also made of heart?"

"For the love of heaven," exclaimed Don Camillo. "I should never presume to advise You. But I would venture to point out that none of those present is aware of the identity of the man with the beard."

"Nor am I aware of it," replied the Lord with a sigh; "but I should like to know whether you have any idea of the meaning of those words 'punching ball'?"

"My knowledge of the English language has not improved, Lord," replied Don Camillo.

"Well, then we must be content without knowing even that," said the Lord, smiling. "After all, culture in the long run often seems to do more harm than good. Sleep well, federal champion."

NOCTURNE WITH BELLS

FOR SOME TIME Don Camillo had felt that he was being watched. On turning round suddenly when he was walking along the street or in the fields he saw no one, but felt convinced that if he had looked behind a hedge or among the bushes he would have found a pair of eyes and all that goes with them.

When leaving the presbytery on a couple of evenings he not only heard a sound from behind the door, but he caught a glimpse of a shadow.

"Let it be," the Lord had replied from above the altar when Don Camillo had asked Him for advice. "Eyes never did anyone any harm."

"But it would be useful to know whether those two eyes are going about alone or accompanied by a third, for instance one of 9-calibre," sighed Don Camillo. "That is a detail not without its own importance."

"Nothing can defeat a good conscience, Don Camillo."

"I know, Lord," sighed Don Camillo once more, "but the trouble is that people don't usually fire at a conscience, but between the shoulders."

However, Don Camillo did nothing about the matter and a little time elapsed, and then late one evening when he was sitting alone in the presbytery reading, he unexpectedly "felt" the eyes upon him.

There were three of them, and raising his head slowly he saw first of all the black eye of a revolver and then those of Biondo.

"Do I lift my hands?" inquired Don Camillo quietly.

"I don't want to do you any harm," replied Biondo, thrusting the revolver into his jacket pocket. "I was afraid you might be scared when I appeared unexpectedly and might start shouting."

"I understand," replied Don Camillo. "And did it never strike you that by simply knocking at the door you could have avoided all this trouble?"

Biondo made no reply; he went and leaned over the windowsill. Then he turned round suddenly and sat down beside Don Camillo's little table. His hair was ruffled, his eyes deeply circled and his forehead was damp with sweat.

"Don Camillo," he muttered from behind clenched teeth, "that fellow at the house near the dyke; it was I that did him in."

Don Camillo lighted a cigar. "The house near the dyke?" he said quietly. "Well, that's an old story; it was a political affair and came within the terms of amnesty. What are you worrying about? You're all right under the law."

Biondo shrugged his shoulders. "To hell with the amnesty," he said furiously. "Every night when I put my light out I can feel him near my bed, and I can't understand what it means."

Don Camillo puffed a cloud of blue smoke into the air. "Nothing at all, Biondo," he replied with a smile. "Listen to me: go to sleep with the light on."

Biondo sprang to his feet. "You can go and jeer at that fool Peppone," he shouted, "but you can't do it to me!"

Don Camillo shook his head. "Firstly, Peppone is not a fool; and, secondly, where you are concerned there is nothing that I can do for you."

"If I must buy candles or make an offering to the church, I'll pay," shouted Biondo, "but you've got to absolve me. And in any case I'm all right legally!"

"I agree, my son," said Don Camillo mildly. "But the trouble is that no one has ever yet made an amnesty for consciences. Therefore, so far as we are concerned, we muddle along in the same old way, and in order to obtain absolution it is necessary to be penitent and then to act in a manner that is deserving of forgiveness. It's a lengthy affair."

Biondo sniggered. "Penitent? Penitent of having done in that fellow? I'm only sorry I didn't bag the lot!"

"That is a province in which I am completely incompetent. On the other hand, if your conscience tells you that acted rightly, then you should be content," said Don Camillo, opening a book and laying it in front of Biondo. "Look, we have very clear rules that do not exclude the political field. Fifth: thou shalt not kill. Seventh: thou shalt not steal."

"What has that got to do with it?" inquired Biondo in a mystified voice.

"Nothing," Don Camillo reassured him, "but I had an idea that you told me that you had killed him, under the cloak of politics, in order to steal his money."

"I never said so!" shouted Biondo, pulling out his pistol and thrusting it into Don Camillo's face. "I never said so, but it's true! And if it's true and you dare to tell a living soul I shall blow you to pieces!"

"We don't tell such things even to the Eternal Father," Don Camillo reassured him; "and in any case He knows them better than we do."

Biondo appeared to quiet down. He opened his hand and looked at his weapon. "Now look at that!" he exclaimed, laughing. "I hadn't even noticed that the safety catch was down."

He raised the catch with a careful finger.

"Don Camillo," said Biondo in a strange voice, "I am sick of seeing that fellow standing near my bed. There are only two ways for it: either you absolve me or I shoot you." The pistol shook slightly in his hand and Don Camillo turned rather pale and looked him straight in the eyes.

"Lord," said Don Camillo mentally, "this is a mad dog and he will fire. An absolution given in such conditions is valueless. What do I do?"

"If you are afraid, give him absolution," replied the voice of the Lord.

Don Camillo folded his arms on his breast.

"No, Biondo," said Don Camillo.

Biondo set his teeth. "Don Camillo, give me absolution or I fire."

"No."

Biondo pulled the trigger and the trigger yielded, but there was no explosion.

And then Don Camillo struck, and his blow did not miss the mark, because Don Camillo's punches never misfired.

Then he flung himself up the steps of the tower and rang the bells furiously for twenty minutes. And all the countryside declared that Don Camillo had gone mad, with the exception of the Lord above the altar, who shook His head, smiling, and Biondo, who, tearing across the fields like a lunatic, had reached the bank of the river and was about to throw himself into its dark waters. Then he heard the bells.

So Biondo turned back because he had heard a Voice that he had never known. And that was the real miracle, because a pistol that misfires is a material event, but a priest who begins to ring joybells at eleven o'clock at night is quite another matter.

MEN AND BEASTS

LA GRANDE WAS AN enormous farm with a hundred cows, steam dairy, orchards and all the rest of it. And everything belonged to old Pasotti, who lived alone at the Badia with an army of retainers. One day these retainers set up an agitation and, led by Peppone, went *en masse* to the Badia and were interviewed by old Pasotti from a window.

"May God smite you," he shouted, thrusting out his head. "Can't a decent man have peace in this filthy country."

"A decent man, yes," replied Peppone, "but not profiteers who deny their workmen what is their just due."

"I only admit of dues as fixed by the law," retorted Pasotti, "and I am perfectly within the law."

Then Peppone told him that so long as he refused to grant the concessions demanded, the workers of La Grande would do no work of any kind or description. "So you can feed your hundred cows yourself!" Peppone concluded.

"Very well," replied Pasotti. He closed the window and resumed his interrupted slumbers.

This was the beginning of the strike at La Grande, and it was a strike organized by Peppone in person, with a squad of overseers, regular watches, pickets and barricades. The doors and windows of the cowsheds were nailed up and seals placed upon them.

On the first day the cows lowed because they had not been milked. On the second day they lowed because they had not been milked and because they were hungry and on the third day thirst was added to all the rest and the lowing could be heard for miles around. Then Pasotti's old servant came out by the back door of the Badia and explained to the men on picket duty that she was going into the village to the pharmacy to buy disinfectants. "I have told the master that he can't possibly want to get cholera from the stench when all the cows have died of starvation."

This remark caused quite a lot of head-shaking among the older labourers, who had been working for more than fifty years for Pasotti and who knew that he was incredibly pig-headed. And then Peppone himself stepped in to say, with the support of his staff, that if anyone dared to go near the cowshed he would be treated as a traitor to his country.

Towards the evening of the fourth day, Giacomo, the old cowman from La Grande, made his appearance at the presbytery.

"There is a cow due to calve and she is crying out fit to break your heart, and she will certainly die unless someone goes to help her; but if anyone attempts to go near the cowshed they will break every bone in his body."

Don Camillo went and clung to the altar rails. "Lord," he said to the crucified Lord, "You must hold on to me or I shall make the march on Rome!"

"Steady, Don Camillo," replied the Lord gently. "Nothing is ever gained by violence. You must try to calm these people so that they will hear reason, and avoid exasperating them to acts of violence."

"Very true," sighed Don Camillo. "One must make them listen to reason. All the same, it seems a pity that while one is preaching reason the cows should die."

The Lord smiled. "If, by the use of violence, we succeed in saving a hundred beasts and kill one man and if, on the other hand, by using persuasion we lose the beasts, but avoid the loss of that man, which seems to you preferable: violence or persuasion?"

Don Camillo who, being filled with indignation, was loath to renounce his idea of a march on Rome, shook his head. "Lord, You are confusing the issue: this is not only a question of the loss of a hundred beasts, but also of the public patrimony; and the death of those beasts is not simply a personal disaster for Pasotti: it is also a loss for every one of us, good and bad. And it may also easily have repercussions such as may further exacerbate existing differences and create a conflict in which not only one man may die, but twenty."

The Lord was not of his opinion. "But if, by reasoning, you avoid one man being killed to-day, couldn't you also, by reasoning, avoid others being killed to-morrow? Don Camillo, have you lost your faith?"

Don Camillo went out for a walk across the fields because he was restless, and so it happened that quite by chance his ears began to be assailed more and more painfully by the lowing of the hundred cows at La Grande. Then he heard the voices of the men on picket duty at the barricades and at the end of ten minutes he found himself crawling inside and along the great cement irrigation pipe that passed underneath the wire netting at the boundaries of La Grande, and which was fortunately not in use at the moment.

"And now," thought Don Camillo, "it only remains for me to find someone waiting at the end of this pipe to knock me on the head." But there was nobody there and Don Camillo was left in peace to make his way cautiously along the entire length of the pipe in the direction of the farm.

"Halt!" said a voice presently, and Don Camillo made one leap out of the end of his pipe to shelter behind a tree trunk.

"Halt or I fire!" repeated the voice which came from behind another tree trunk on the further side of the pipe.

It was an evening of coincidences, and Don Camillo, quite by chance, found himself grasping an appliance made of steel. He manipulated a certain movable gadget and replied:

"Be careful, Peppone, because I also shall fire."

"Ah!" muttered the other. "I might have known that I should find you mixed up in this business."

"Truce of God," said Don Camillo; "and if either of us breaks it he is damned. I am now going to count and when I say 'three' we both jump into that ditch."

"You wouldn't be a priest if you weren't so mistrustful," replied Peppone, and at the count of three he jumped and they found themselves sitting together at the bottom of the ditch.

From the cowshed came the desperate lowing of the cows, and it was enough to make one sweat with anguish. "I suppose you enjoy such music," muttered Don Camillo. "A pity that it will stop when all the cows have died. You're a fine fellow to hold on, aren't you? Why not persuade the labourers to burn the crops and also the barns that contain them. Just think now of poor Pasotti's fury if he were driven to take refuge in some Swiss hotel and to spend those few millions that he has deposited over there."

"He would have to reach Switzerland first!" growled Peppone threateningly.

"Exactly!" exclaimed Don Camillo. "It's about time we did away with that old Fifth Commandment which forbids us to kill! And when one comes eventually face to face with Almighty God one will only have to speak out bluntly: 'That's quite enough from you, my dear Eternal Father, or Peppone will proclaim a general strike and make everyone fold their arms!' By the way, Peppone, how are you going to get the cherubim to fold their arms? Have you thought of that?"

Peppone's roar vied with that of the expecting cow, whose complaints were heartrending. "You are no priest!" he vociferated. "You are the chief of the *Ghepeù!*"

"The *Gestapo*," Don Camillo corrected him. "The *Ghepeù* is your affair."

"You go about by night, in other people's houses, clutching a tommy-gun like a bandit!"

"And what about you?" inquired Don Camillo mildly.

"I am in the service of the people!"

"And I am in God's service!"

Peppone kicked a stone. "No use trying to argue with a priest! Before you have uttered two words they have dragged in politics!"

"Peppone," began Don Camillo gently, but the other cut him short:

"Now don't you begin jawing about the national patrimony and rubbish of that kind or as there is a God above I shall shoot you!" he exclaimed.

Don Camillo shook his head. "No use trying to argue with a Red. Before you have uttered two words they drag in politics!"

The cow that was about to calve complained loudly.

"Who goes there?" came a sudden voice from someone very close to the ditch. Then Brusco, Il Magro and Il Bigio made their appearance.

"Go and take a walk along the road to the mill," Peppone ordered them.

"All right," replied Brusco; "but who are you talking to."

"To your damned soul," roared Peppone furiously.

"That cow that is going to calve is fairly bellowing," muttered Brusco.

"Go and tell the priest about it!" bawled Peppone. "And let her rot! I am working for the interests of the people, not of cows!"

"Keep your hair on, chief," stammered Brusco, making off hastily with his companions.

"Very well, Peppone," whispered Don Camillo; "and now we are going to work for the interests of the people."

"What do you intend to do?"

Don Camillo set out quietly along the ditch towards the farm and Peppone told him to halt or he would get what he was asking for between the shoulders.

"Peppone is as stubborn as a mule," said Don Camillo calmly, "but he doesn't shoot at the backs of poor priests who are doing what God has commanded them to do."

Then Peppone swore blasphemously and Don Camillo turned on him in a flash. "If you don't stop behaving like a balky horse, I shall give you one on the jaw exactly as I did to your celebrated federal champion. . . ."

"You needn't tell me: I knew all along that it could only be you. But that was quite another matter."

Don Camillo walked along quietly, followed by the other muttering and threatening to shoot. As they approached the cowshed another voice called to them to halt.

"Go to hell!" replied Peppone. "I am here myself now, so you can get along to the dairy."

Don Camillo did not even vouchsafe a glance at the cowshed door with its seals. He went straight up the stairs to the hay-loft above it and called in a low voice: "Giacomo."

The old cowman who had come to see him earlier and had related the story of the cow rose out of the hay. Don Camillo produced an electric torch and, shifting a bale of hay, revealed a trap-door.

"Go down," said Don Camillo to the old man, who climbed down and disappeared for a considerable time.

"She's had her calf all right," he whispered when he returned. "I've seen a thousand of them through it and I know more than any vet."

"Now go along home," Don Camillo told the old man, and the old man went.

Then Don Camillo opened the trap-door again and sent a bale of hay through the opening.

"What do you think you are doing?" asked Peppone, who had so far remained hidden.

"Help me to throw down these bales and then I'll tell you."

Grumbling as he did so, Peppone set to work chucking down the bales, and when Don Camillo had let himself down after them into the cowshed, Peppone followed him.

Don Camillo carried a bale to a right-hand manger and broke its lashings. "You'd better attend to the left-hand mangers," he said to Peppone.

"Not if you murder me!" shouted Peppone, seizing a bale and carrying it to the manger.

They worked like an army of oxen. Then there was the business of making the beasts drink and, since they were dealing with a modern cowshed with its drinking troughs placed along its outer walls, it was a matter of making one hundred cows right-about-turn and then belabouring their horns to stop them from drinking themselves to death.

When all was finished it was still pitch dark in the cowshed, but that was merely because all the shutters of the windows had been sealed from the outside.

"It's three o'clock in the afternoon," said Don Camillo, looking at his watch. "We shall have to wait until evening before we can get out!"

Peppone was biting his own fists with fury, but there was nothing for it but patience. When evening fell, Peppone and Don Camillo were still playing cards by the light of an oil lamp.

"I'm so hungry I could swallow a bishop whole!" exclaimed Peppone savagely.

"Hard on the digestion, Mr. Mayor," replied Don Camillo quietly, though he himself was faint with hunger and could have devoured a cardinal. "Before saying you are hungry, you should wait until you have fasted for as many days as these beasts."

Before leaving they again filled all the mangers with hay. Peppone tried to resist, saying that it was betraying the people, but Don Camillo was inflexible.

And so it happened that during the night there was a deathly silence in the cowshed, and old Pasotti, hearing no more lowing from the cows, became afraid that they must be so far gone that they had not even the strength to complain. In the morning he made a move to treat with Peppone, and with a little give and take on both sides the strike was settled and things resumed their normal course.

In the afternoon Peppone turned up at the presbytery.

"Well," said Don Camillo in honeyed tones, "you revolutionaries should always listen to advice from your old parish priest. You really should, my dear children."

Peppone stood with folded arms, struck speechless by such shameless audacity. Then he blurted out: "But my tommy-gun, reverendo!"

"Your tommy-gun?" replied Don Camillo with a smile. "I'm afraid I don't understand. You had it yourself."

"Yes, I did have it when we were leaving the cowshed, but then you took advantage of my exhaustion and stole it from me."

"Now that you mention it, I believe you're right," replied Don Camillo with disarming candour. "You must forgive me, Peppone, but the truth is that I am getting old and I don't seem able to remember where I've put it."

"Reverendo!" exclaimed Peppone indignantly. "But that's the second you've filched from me!"

"Never mind, my son. Don't worry. You will easily find another. Who knows how many you have even now lying about your house!"

"You are one of those priests that, one way or another, compel a decent man to become a Mohammedan!"

"Very possibly," replied Don Camillo, "but then you, Peppone, are not a decent man." Peppone flung his hat on the ground.

"If you were a decent man," the priest went on, "you would be thanking me for what I have done for you and for the people."

Peppone picked up his hat, jammed it on to his head and turned away. From the threshold he spoke: "You can rob me of not only two but two hundred thousand tommy-guns, but when the time comes I shall always have a .75 to train on this infernal house!"

"And I shall always find an 81 mortar with which to retaliate," replied Don Camillo calmly.

As he was passing the open door of the church and could see the altar, Peppone angrily pulled off his hat and then crammed it on again hastily lest anyone should see him.

But the Lord had already seen and when Don Camillo came into the church He said gaily: "Peppone went by just now and took off his hat to Me."

"You be careful, Lord," replied Don Camillo. "Remember there was someone before who kissed You and then sold You for thirty pieces of silver. That fellow who took off his hat had told me only three minutes earlier that when the time came he would always find a .75 with which to fire upon the house of God!"

"And what did you reply?"

"That I would always manage to find an 81 mortar with which to fire on his headquarters."

"I understand, Don Camillo. But the trouble is that you are already in posses-sion of that mortar."

Don Camillo spread out his arms. "Lord," he said. "There are so many odds and ends that a man hesitates to throw away because of associations. We are all of us a bit sentimental. And then, in any case, isn't it better that such a thing should be in my house than in someone else's?"

"Don Camillo is always in the right," smiled the Lord, "just as long as he plays fair."

"No fear about that; I have the best Adviser in the universe," replied Don Camillo, and to that the Lord could make no reply.

THE PROCESSION

EVERY YEAR, AT THE time of the blessing of the village, the crucified Lord from above the altar was carried in procession as far as the river bank, where the river also was blessed in order that it should refrain from excesses and behave decently.

Once again it seemed as though everything would take place with the customary regularity and Don Camillo was thinking over the final touches to be given to the programme of the celebrations when Brusco made his appearance at the pres-bytery.

"The secretary of our local section," said Brusco, "sends me to inform you that the entire section will take part in the procession complete with all its banners."

"Convey my thanks to Secretary Peppone," replied Don Camillo. "I shall be only too happy for all the men of the section to be present. But they must be good enough to leave their banners at home. Political banners have no place in religious processions and must not appear in them. Those are the orders that I have received."

Brusco retired, and very soon Peppone arrived, red in the face and with his eyes popping out of his head.

"We are just as much Christians as all the rest of them!" he shouted, bursting into the presbytery without even knocking on the door. "In what way are we differ-ent from other folk?"

"In not taking off your hats when you come into other people's houses," said Don Camillo quietly.

Peppone snatched his hat from his head.

"Now you are just like any other Christian," said Don Camillo.

"Then why can't we join the procession with our flag?" shouted Peppone. "Is it the flag of thieves and murderers?"

"No, Comrade Peppone," Don Camillo explained, lighting his cigar. "But the flag of a party cannot be admitted. This procession is concerned with religion and not with politics."

"Then the flags of Catholic Action should also be excluded!"

"And why? Catholic Action is not a political party, as may be judged from the fact that I am its local secretary. Indeed, I strongly advise you and your comrades to join it."

Peppone sniggered. "If you want to save your black soul, you had better join our party!"

Don Camillo raised his arms. "Supposing we leave it at that," he replied, smiling. "We all stay as we are and remain friends."

"You and I have never been friends," Peppone asserted.

"Not even when we were in the mountains together?"

"No! That was merely a strategic alliance. For the triumph of our arms, it is allowable to make an alliance even with priests."

"Very well," said Don Camillo calmly. "Nevertheless, if you want to join in the procession, you must leave your flag at home."

Peppone ground his teeth. "If you think you can play at being Duce, reverendo, you're making a big mistake!" he exclaimed. "Either our flag marches or there won't be any procession!"

Don Camillo was not impressed. "He'll get over it," he said to himself. And in fact, during the three days preceding the Sunday of the blessing, nothing more was said about the argument. But on the Sunday, an hour before mass, scared people began to arrive at the presbytery. Early that morning Peppone's satellites had called at every house in the village to warn the inmates that anyone who ventured to take part in the procession would do so at the risk of life and limb.

"No one has said anything of the kind to me," replied Don Camillo, "I am therefore not interested."

The procession was to take place immediately after mass, and while Don Camillo was vesting for it in the sacristy he was interrupted by a group of parishioners.

"What are we going to do?" they asked him.

"We are going in procession," replied Don Camillo quietly.

"But those ruffians are quite capable of throwing bombs at it," they objected. "You cannot expose your parishioners to such a risk. In our opinion, you ought to postpone the procession, give notice to the public authorities of the town, and have the procession as soon as there are sufficient police on the spot to protect the people."

"I see," remarked Don Camillo. "And in the meantime we might explain to the martyrs of our faith that they made a big mistake in behaving as they did and that, instead of going off to spread Christianity when it was forbidden, they should have waited quietly until they had police to protect them."

Then Don Camillo showed his visitors the way to the door, and they went off, muttering and grumbling.

Shortly afterwards a number of aged men and women entered the church. "We are coming along, Don Camillo," they said.

"You are going straight back to your houses!" replied Don Camillo. "God will take note of your pious intentions, but this is decidedly one of those occasions when old men, women and children should remain at home."

A number of people had lingered in front of the church, but when the sound of firing was heard in the distance (occasioned by Brusco letting off a tommy-gun into the air as a demonstration), even the group of survivors melted away, and Don Camillo, appearing upon the threshold of the sacristy, found the square as bare as a billiard table.

"Are we going now, Don Camillo?" inquired the Lord from above the altar. "The river must be looking beautiful in this sunshine and I shall really enjoy seeing it."

"We are going all right," replied Don Camillo. "But I am afraid that this time I shall be the entire procession. If You can put up with that . . ."

"Where there is Don Camillo, he is sufficient in himself," said the Lord, smiling.

Don Camillo hastily put on the leather harness with the support for the foot of the Cross, lifted the enormous crucifix from the altar and adjusted it in the socket. Then he sighed: "All the same, they need not have made this cross quite so heavy."

"You're telling Me!" replied the Lord, smiling. "Didn't I carry it to the top of the hill, and I never had shoulders such as yours."

A few moments later Don Camillo, bearing his enormous crucifix, emerged solemnly from the door of the church.

The village was completely deserted; people were cowering in their houses and watching through the cracks of the shutters.

"I must look like one of those friars who used to carry a big black cross through villages smitten by the plague," said Don Camillo to himself. Then he began a psalm in his ringing baritone, which seemed to acquire volume in the silence.

Having crossed the square, he began to walk down the main street, and here again there was emptiness and silence. A small dog came out of a side street and began quietly to follow Don Camillo.

"Get out!" muttered Don Camillo.

"Let it alone," whispered the Lord from His Cross; "and then Peppone won't be able to say that not even a dog walked in the procession."

The street curved at its end and then came the lane that led to the river bank. Don Camillo had no sooner turned the bend when he found the way unexpectedly obstructed. Two hundred men had collected and stood silently across it with straddled legs and folded arms. In front of them stood Peppone, his hands on his hips.

Don Camillo wished he were a tank. But since he could only be Don Camillo, he advanced until he was within a yard of Peppone and then halted. Then he lifted the enormous crucifix from its socket and raised it in his hands, brandishing it as though it were a club.

"Lord," said Don Camillo. "Hold on tight; I am going to strike!"

But there was no need, because, having in a flash grasped the situation, the men withdrew to the sides of the road, and as though by enchantment the way lay open before him.

Only Peppone, his arms akimbo and his legs wide apart, remained standing in the middle of the road. Don Camillo replaced the crucifix in its socket and marched straight at him, and Peppone moved to one side.

"I'm not shifting myself for your sake, but for His," said Peppone, pointing to the crucifix.

"Then take that hat off your head!" replied Don Camillo without so much as looking at him.

Peppone pulled off his hat and Don Camillo marched solemnly through two rows of Peppone's men.

When he reached the river bank he stopped. "Lord," said Don Camillo in a loud voice, "if the few decent people in this filthy village could build themselves a Noah's Ark and float safely upon the waters, I would ask You to send such a flood as would break down this bank and submerge the whole countryside. But as these few decent folk live in brick houses exactly similar to those of their rotten neighbours, and as it would not be just that the good should suffer for the sins of scoundrels such as the Mayor Peppone and his gang of Godless brigands, I ask You to save this countryside from the waters and to give it every prosperity."

"Amen," came Peppone's voice from just behind him.

"Amen," came the response from behind Peppone of all the men who had followed the crucifix.

Don Camillo set out on the return journey and when he reached the threshold of the church and turned round so that the Lord might bestow a final blessing upon the distant river, he found standing before him: the small dog, Peppone, Peppone's men and every inhabitant of the village, not excluding the chemist, who was an atheist, but who felt that never in his life had he dreamed of a priest such as Don Camillo who could make even the Eternal Father quite tolerable.

THE MEETING

As soon as Peppone read a notice pasted up at the street corners to the effect that a stranger from the town had been invited by the local section of the Liberal Party to hold a meeting in the square, he leaped into the air.

"Here, in the Red stronghold! Are we to tolerate such a provocation?" he bawled. "We shall very soon see who commands here!"

Then he summoned his general staff and the stupendous occurrence was studied and analysed. The proposal to set fire immediately to the headquarters of the Liberal Party was rejected. That of forbidding the meeting met with the same fate.

"There you have democracy!" said Peppone sententiously. "When an unknown scoundrel can permit himself the luxury of speaking in a public square!"

They decided to remain within the bounds of law and order: general mobilization of all their members, organization of squads to supervise things generally and avoid any ambush. Occupation of strategic points and protection of their own headquarters. Pickets were to stand by to summon reinforcements from neighbouring sectors.

"The fact that they are holding a public meeting here shows that they are confident of overpowering us," said Peppone. "But in any case they will not find us unprepared."

Scouts placed along the roads leading to the village were to report any suspicious movement, and were already on duty from early Saturday morning, but they failed to sight so much as a cat throughout the entire day. During the night Smilzo discovered a questionable cyclist, but he proved to be only a normal drunk. The meeting was to take place in the course of Sunday afternoon, and up to three o'clock not a soul had put in an appearance.

"They will be coming by the three-fifty-five train," said Peppone. And he placed a large contingent of his men in and around the railway station. The train steamed in and the only person who got out was a thin little man carrying a small fibre suitcase.

"It's obvious that they got wind of something and didn't feel strong enough to meet the emergency," said Peppone.

At that moment the little man came up to him and, taking off his hat, politely inquired whether Peppone would be so kind as to direct him to the headquarters of the Liberal Party.

Peppone stared at him in amazement. "The headquarters of the Liberal Party?"

"Yes," explained the little man. "I am due to make a short speech in twenty minutes' time, and I should not like to be late."

Everybody was looking at Peppone and Peppone scratched his head. "It is really rather difficult to explain, because the centre of the village is over a mile away."

The little man made a gesture of anxiety. "Will it be possible for me to find some means of transport?"

"I have a lorry outside," muttered Peppone, "if you care to come along."

The little man thanked him. Then, when they got outside and he saw the lorry full of surly faces, red handkerchiefs and Communist badges, he looked at Peppone.

"I am their leader," said Peppone. "Get up in front with me."

Halfway to the village Peppone stopped the engine and examined his passenger, who was a middle-aged gentleman, very thin and with clear-cut features.

"So you are a Liberal?"

"I am," replied the gentleman.

"And you are not alarmed at finding yourself alone here among fifty Communists?"

"No," replied the man quietly. A threatening murmur came from the men in the lorry.

"What have you got in that suitcase?"

The man began to laugh and opened the case.

"Pyjamas, a pair of slippers and a tooth-brush," he exclaimed.

Peppone pushed his hat on to the back of his head and slapped his thigh.

"You must be crazy!" he bellowed. "And may one be allowed to inquire why you aren't afraid?"

"Simply because I am alone and there are fifty of you," the little man explained quietly.

"What the hell has that got to do with it?" howled Peppone. "Doesn't it strike you that I could pick you up with one hand and throw you into that ditch?"

"No; it doesn't strike me," replied the little man as quietly as before.

"Then you really must either be crazy or irresponsible, or deliberately out to gull us."

The little man laughed again. "It is much simpler than that," he said. "I am just an ordinary, decent man."

"Ah, no, my good sir!" exclaimed Peppone, leaping to his feet. "If you were an ordinary, decent man, you wouldn't be an enemy of the people! A slave of reaction! An instrument of capitalism!"

"I am nobody's enemy and nobody's slave. I am merely a man who thinks differently from you."

Peppone started the engine and the lorry dashed forward. "I suppose you made your will before coming here?" he jeered as he jammed his foot on the accelerator.

"No," replied the little man unperturbed. "All I have is my work, and if I should die I couldn't leave it to anyone else."

Before entering the village Peppone pulled up for a moment to speak to Smilzo, who was acting as orderly with his motor-bike. Then, by way of several side streets, they reached the headquarters of the Liberal Party. Doors and windows were closed.

"Nobody here," said Peppone gloomily.

"They must all be in the square, of course. It is already late," retorted the little man.

"I suppose that's it," replied Peppone, winking at Brusco.

When they reached the square Peppone and his men got out of the lorry and surrounded the little man and thrust a way through the crowd to the platform. The little man climbed on to it and found himself face to face with two thousand men, all wearing the red handkerchief.

The little man turned to Peppone, who had followed him on to the platform. "Excuse me," he inquired, "but have I by chance come to the wrong meeting?"

"No,' Peppone reassured him. "The fact is that there are only twenty-three Liberals in the whole district, and they don't show up much in a crowd. To tell you the truth, if I had been in your place, it would never have entered my head to hold a meeting here."

"It seems obvious that the Liberals have more confidence in the democratic discipline of the Communists than you have," replied the little man.

Peppone looked disconcerted for a moment, then he went up to the microphone. "Comrades," he shouted, "I wish to introduce to you this gentleman who will make you a speech that will send you all off to join the Liberal Party."

A roar of laughter greeted this sally, and as soon as it died down the little man began speaking.

"I want to thank your leader for his courtesy," he said, "but it is my duty to explain to you that his statement does not tally with my wishes. Because if, at the end of my speech, you all went to join the Liberal Party, I should feel it incumbent upon me to go and join the Communist Party, and that would be against all my principles."

He was unable to continue, because just at that moment a tomato whistled through the air and struck him in the face.

The crowd began jeering and Peppone went white. "Anyone who laughs is a swine!" he shouted into the microphone, and there was immediate silence.

The little man had not moved, and was trying to clean his face with his hand. Peppone was a child of instinct, and quite unconsciously was capable of magnificent impulses; he pulled his handkerchief from his pocket, then he put it back again and unknotted the vast red handkerchief from his neck and offered it to the little man.

" I wore it in the mountains," he said. "Wipe your face."

"Bravo, Peppone!" thundered a voice from the first-floor window of a neighbouring house.

"I don't need the approval of the clergy," replied Peppone arrogantly, while Don Camillo bit his tongue with fury at having let his feelings get the better of him.

The little man shook his head, bowed and approached the microphone.

"There is too much history attached to that handkerchief for me to soil it with the traces of a vulgar episode that belongs to the less heroic chronicles of our times," he said. "A handkerchief such as we use for a common cold suffices for such a purpose."

Peppone flushed scarlet and also bowed, and then a wave of emotion swept the crowd and there was vigorous applause while the hooligan lad who had thrown the tomato was kicked off the square.

The little man resumed his speech calmly. He was quiet, without any trace of bitterness; smoothing off corners, avoiding contentious arguments, being fully aware that should he let himself go, he could do so with impunity and would therefore be guilty of taking a cowardly advantage of the situation. At the end, he was applauded, and when he stepped down from the platform a way was cleared before him.

When he reached the far end of the square and found himself beneath the portico of the town hall, he stood helplessly with his suitcase in his hand, not knowing where to go or what to do. At that moment Don Camillo hurried up and turned to Peppone, who was standing just behind the little man. "You've lost no time, have you, you Godless rascal, in making up to this Liberal priest-eater."

"What?" gasped Peppone, also turning towards the little man. "Then you are a priest-eater?"

"But . . ." stammered the little man.

"Hold your tongue," Don Camillo interrupted him. "You ought to be ashamed, you who demand a free church in a free state!"

The little man attempted to protest, but Peppone cut him short before he could utter a word. "Bravo!" he bawled. "Give me your hand! When a man is a priest-eater he is my friend, even if he is a Liberal reactionary!"

"Hurrah!" shouted Peppone's satellites.

"You are my guest!" said Peppone to the little man.

"Nothing of the kind," retorted Don Camillo.

"This gentleman is my guest. I am not a boor who fires tomatoes at his adversaries!"

Peppone pushed himself menacingly in front of Don Camillo.

"I have said that he is my guest," he repeated fiercely.

"And as I have said the same thing," replied Don Camillo, "it means that if you want to come to blows with me about it, you can also have those that are due to your ruffianly Dynamos!"

Peppone clutched his fists.

"Come away," said Brusco. "In another minute you'll be at fisticuffs with the priest in the public square!"

In the end, the matter was settled in favour of a meeting on neutral territory. All three of them went out into the country to luncheon with Gigiotto, a host completely indifferent to politics, and thus even the democratic encounter led to no results of any kind.

ON THE RIVER BANK

BETWEEN ONE AND three o'clock of the afternoon in the month of August, the heat in these districts that lie under hemp and buckwheat is something that can be both seen and felt. It is almost as though a great curtain of boiling glass hung at a few inches from one's nose. If you are crossing a bridge and you look down into the canal, its bed is dry and cracked with here and there a dead fish, and when from the road along the river bank you look at a cemetery you almost seem to hear the bones rattling beneath the boiling sun.

Along the main road you will meet an occasional wagon piled high with sand, with the driver sound asleep lying face downwards on top of his load, his stomach cool and his spine incandescent, or sitting on the shaft fishing out pieces from half a water melon that he holds on his knees like a bowl. Then when you come to the big bank, there lies the great river, deserted, motionless and silent, and it seems not so much a river as a cemetery of dead waters.

Don Camillo was walking in the direction of the big river, with a large white handkerchief inserted between his head and his hat. It was half-past one of an

August afternoon and, seeing him thus, alone upon the white road under the burning rays of the sun, it was not possible to imagine anything blacker or more blatantly priest-like.

"If there is at this moment anyone within a radius of twenty miles who is not asleep, I'll eat my hat," said Don Camillo to himself. Then he climbed over the bank and sat down in the shade of a thicket of acacias and watched the water shining through the interstices of the foliage. Presently he took off his clothes, folding each garment carefully, and, rolling them all into a bundle that he hid among the bushes and wearing only his drawers, went and flung himself into the water.

Everything was perfectly quiet; no one could possibly have seen him, because, in addition to selecting the hour of siesta, he had also chosen the most secluded spot. In any case, he was prudent and at the end of half an hour he climbed out of the water among the acacias and reached the bush where he had hidden his clothes, only to discover that the clothes were no longer there.

Don Camillo felt his breath fail him.

There could be no question of theft: nobody could possibly covet an old and faded cassock. It must mean that some devilry was afoot. And in fact at that very moment he heard voices approaching from the top of the bank. As soon as Don Camillo was able to see something he made out a crowd of young men and girls, and then he recognized Smilzo as their leader and was seized with an almost uncontrollable desire to break a branch from the acacias and use it on their backs. But he fully realized that he would only be gratifying his adversaries: what they were playing for was to enjoy the spectacle of Don Camillo in his drawers.

So he dived back into the water and, swimming beneath the surface, reached a little island in the middle of the river. Creeping ashore, he disappeared among the reeds.

But although his enemies had been unable to see him land they had become aware of his retreat and had now flung themselves down along the bank and lay waiting for him, laughing and singing.

Don Camillo was in a state of siege.

How weak is a strong man when he feels himself to be ridiculous! Don Camillo lay among the reeds and waited. Lying there unseen and yet able to see, he beheld the arrival of Peppone followed by Brusco, Bigio and his entire staff. Smilzo explained the situation with many gestures and there was much laughter. Then came more people and Don Camillo realized that the Reds were out to make him pay dearly for all past and present accounts and that they had hit upon the best of all systems because, when anyone has made themselves ridiculous, nobody is ever afraid of them again, not even if their fists weigh a ton and they represent the Eternal Father. And in any case it was all grossly unfair because Don Camillo had never wished to frighten anyone except the devil. But somehow politics had contrived so to distort facts that the Reds had come to consider the parish as their enemy and to say that if things were not was they wished it was all the fault of the priests. When things go wrong it always seems less important to seek a remedy than to find a scapegoat.

"Lord!" said Don Camillo. "I am ashamed to address You in my drawers, but the matter is becoming serious and if it is not a mortal sin for a poor parish priest who is dying of the heat to go bathing, please help me, because I am quite unable to help myself."

The watchers had brought flasks of wine, parcels of food and an accordion. The river bank had been transformed into a beach and it was obvious that they had not the faintest intention of raising the siege. Indeed, they had extended it to beyond the celebrated locality of the ford, two hundred yards of shore consisting of shrubs and undergrowth. Not a soul had set foot in this area since 1945, because the retreating Germans had destroyed all the bridges and mined both banks at the ford. After a couple of disastrous attempts, the mine-removal squads had merely isolated the area with posts and barbed wire.

There were none of Peppone's men in that region: they were unnecessary, as no one but a lunatic would think of going near the mine-field. There was thus nothing to be done, because should he attempt to land beyond the watchers downstream, Don Camillo would find himself in the middle of the village and any attempt to get ashore upstream would lead him into the mine-field. A priest wearing only his drawers could not permit himself such luxuries.

Don Camillo did not move: he remained lying on the damp earth, chewing a reed and following his own train of thought.

"Well," he concluded, "a respectable man remains a respectable man even in his drawers. The important thing is that he should perform some reputable action and then his clothing ceases to have any importance."

The daylight was now beginning to fail and the watchers on the bank were lighting torches and lanterns. As soon as the green of the grass became black, Don Camillo let himself down into the water and made his way cautiously upstream until his feet touched bottom at the ford. Then he struck out for the bank. No one could see him, as he was walking rather than swimming, only lifting his mouth out of the water at intervals to get his breath.

Here was the shore. The difficulty was to leave the water without being seen; once among the bushes, he could easily reach the bank and by running along it duck under the rows of vines and through the buckwheat and so gain his own garden.

He grasped a bush and raised himself slowly, but just as he had almost achieved his end, the bush came up by the roots and Don Camillo fell back into the water. The splash was heard and people came running. But in a flash Don Camillo had leaped ashore and had vanished among the bushes.

There were loud cries and the entire crowd surged towards the spot just as the moon rose to give its light to the spectacle.

"Don Camillo!" bawled Peppone, thrusting his way to the front of the crowd. "Don Camillo!" There was no reply and a deathly silence fell upon all those present.

"Don Camillo!" yelled Peppone again. "For God's sake don't move! You are in the mine-field!"

"I know I am," replied the voice of Don Camillo quietly from behind a shrub in the midst of the sinister shrubbery.

Smilzo came forward carrying a bundle. "Don Camillo," he shouted. "It was a rotten joke. Keep still and here are your clothes."

"My clothes? Oh, thank you, Smilzo. If you will be so kind as to bring them to me."

A branch was seen to move at the top of a bush some distance away. Smilzo's mouth fell open and he looked round at those behind him. The silence was broken only by an ironical laugh from Don Camillo.

Peppone seized the bundle from Smilzo's hand. "I'll bring them, Don Camillo," said Peppone, advancing slowly towards the posts and the barbed wire. He had already thrown a leg over the barrier when Smilzo sprang forward and dragged him back.

"No, chief," said Smilzo, taking the bundle from him and entering the enclosure. "He who breaks, pays."

The people shrank back, their faces were damp with sweat, and they held their hands over their mouths. Amid a leaden silence Smilzo made his way slowly towards the middle of the enclosure, placing his feet carefully.

"Here you are," said Smilzo, in the ghost of a voice as he reached Don Camillo's bush.

"Good!" muttered Don Camillo. "And now you can come round here. You have earned the right to see Don Camillo in his drawers." Smilzo obeyed him.

"Well? And what do you think of a parish priest in drawers?"

"I don't know," stammered Smilzo. "I've stolen trifles and I've hit a fellow now and again, but I've never really done any harm to anyone."

"*Ego te absolvo*," replied Don Camillo, making the sign of the cross on his forehead. They walked slowly towards the bank and the crowd held its breath and waited for the explosion.

They climbed over the barbed wire and walked along the road, Don Camillo leading and Smilzo, at his heels, still walking on tiptoe as though he had not left the mine-field, because he no longer knew what he was doing. Suddenly he collapsed on to the ground. Peppone, who at twenty paces distance was leading the rest of the people, picked up Smilzo by the collar as he went by and dragged him along like a bundle of rags, without once taking his eyes from Don Camillo's back. At the church door Don Camillo turned round for a moment, bowed politely to his parishioners and went into the church.

The others dispersed in silence and Peppone remained standing alone before the church, staring at the closed door and still clutching the collar of the unconscious Smilzo. Then he shook his head, and he also turned and went his way, still dragging his burden.

"Lord," whispered Don Camillo to the crucified Lord, "one must serve the Church, even by protecting the dignity of a parish priest in his drawers."

There was no reply.

"Lord," whispered Don Camillo anxiously. "Did I really commit a mortal sin in going to bathe?"

"No," replied the Lord; "but you did commit a mortal sin when you dared Smilzo to bring you your clothes."

"I never thought he would do it. I was thoughtless, but not deliberately wicked."

From the direction of the river came the sound of a distant explosion. "Every now and then a hare runs through the mine-field, and then . . ." Don Camillo explained in an almost inaudible voice. "So we must conclude that You . . ."

"You must conclude nothing at all, Don Camillo," the Lord interrupted him with a smile. "With the temperature you are running at this moment your conclusions would scarcely be of any value."

Meanwhile, Peppone had reached the door of Smilzo's home. He knocked, and the door was opened by an old man who made no comment as Peppone handed over his hurden. And it was at that moment that Peppone also heard the explosion, shook his head and remembered many things. Then he took Smilzo back from the old man for a moment and boxed his ears until his hair stood on end.

"Forward!" murmured Smilzo in a faraway voice as the old man once more took charge of him.

RAW MATERIAL

ONE AFTERNOON DON CAMILLO, who for a week past had been in a chronic state of agitation and had done nothing but rush to and fro, was returning from a visit to a neighbouring village. As soon as he reached his own parish he was compelled to alight from his bicycle because some men had appeared since his departure and were digging a ditch right across the road.

"We are putting in a new drain," a workman explained, "by the mayor's orders."

Then Don Camillo went straight to the village hall, and when he found Peppone he lost his temper.

"Are we all going off our heads?" he exclaimed. "Here you are, digging this filthy ditch and don't you know that this is Friday?"

"Well!" replied Peppone with every appearance of astonishment. "And is it forbidden to dig a ditch on a Friday?"

Don Camillo roared: "But have you realized that we are within less than two days of Sunday?"

Peppone looked worried. He rang a bell, and it was answered by Bigio. "Listen, Bigio," said Peppone. "The reverendo says that since to-day is Friday, it lacks less than two days to Sunday. What do you think about it?"

Bigio appeared to reflect very gravely. Then he pulled out a pencil and made calculations on a piece of paper. "Why," he said presently, "taking into consideration that it is now four o'clock in the afternoon and therefore within eight hours of midnight, it will actually be Sunday within thirty-two hours from the present time."

Don Camillo had watched all these manoeuvres and was by now almost foaming at the mouth. "I understand!" he shouted. "This is all a put-up job in order to boycott the bishop's visit."

"Reverendo," replied Peppone, "where is the connection between our local sewage and the bishop's visit? And also, may I ask what bishop you are speaking of and why he should be coming here?"

"To the devil with your black soul!" bawled Don Camillo. "That ditch must be filled in at once, or else the bishop will be unable to pass on Sunday!"

Peppone's face looked completely blank. "Unable to pass? But then how did you pass? There are a couple of planks across the ditch, if I am not mistaken."

"But the bishop is coming by car," exclaimed Don Camillo. "We can't ask a bishop to get out of his car and walk!"

"You must forgive me. I didn't know that bishops were unable to walk," retorted Peppone. "If that is so, then it is quite another matter. Brusco, call up the town and tell them to send us a crane immediately. We'll put it near the ditch, and as soon as the bishop's car arrives the crane can grapple on to it and lift it over the ditch without the bishop having to leave it. Have you understood?"

"Perfectly, chief. And what colour crane shall I ask for?"

"Tell them chromium or nickel-plated; it will look better."

In such circumstances even a man who lacked Don Camillo's armour-plated fists might have been tempted to come to blows. But it was precisely in such cases as these that Don Camillo, on the contrary, became entirely composed. His argument was as follows: "If this fellow sets out so blatantly and deliberately to provoke me it is because he hopes that I shall lose my temper. Therefore, if I give him one on the jaw I am simply playing his game. As a fact, I should not be striking Peppone, but a mayor in the exercise of his functions, and that would make an infernal scandal and create an atmosphere not only hostile to me personally, but also to the bishop."

"Never mind," he said quietly. "Even bishops can walk."

Speaking in church that evening, he literally implored all his congregation to remain calm and to concentrate upon asking God to shed light upon the mind of their mayor in order that he might not attempt to ruin the impending ceremony, breaking up the procession and compelling the faithful to pass one at a time over a couple of insecure boards. And they must also pray God to prevent this improvised bridge from breaking under the undue strain and thus turning a day of rejoicing into one of mourning.

This diabolical address had its calculated effect upon all the women of the congregation who, on leaving the church, collected in front of Peppone's house and carried on to such effect that at last Peppone came to a window and shouted that they could all go to hell and that the ditch would be filled in.

And so all was well, but on Sunday morning the village streets were adorned with large printed posters:

"*Comrades!*

"*Alleging as a pretext of offence the initiation of work of public utility, the reactionaries have staged an unseemly agitation that has offended our democratic instincts. On Sunday our borough is to receive a visit from the representative of a foreign power, the same in fact who has been, indirectly, the cause of the afore-mentioned agitation. Bearing in mind your just resentment and indignation, we are anxious to avoid, on Sunday, any demonstration which might complicate our relations with strangers. We therefore categorically exhort you to keep your reception of this representative of a foreign power within the limits of a dignified indifference.*

"Hurrah for the Democratic Republic! Hurrah for the Proletariat! Hurrah for Russia!"

This exhibition was further enlivened by a throng of Reds, who, it was easy to understand, had been specially mobilized with orders to parade the streets with *"dignified indifference,"* wearing red handkerchiefs or red ties.

Don Camillo, very white about the gills, went for a moment into the church, and was about to hurry away when he heard the Lord calling him. "Don Camillo, why are you in such a hurry?"

"I have to go and receive the bishop along the road," Don Camillo explained. "It is some distance, and then there are so many people about wearing red handkerchiefs that if the bishop does not see me immediately he will think that he has come to Stalingrad."

"And are these wearers of red handkerchiefs foreigners or of another religion?" asked the Lord.

"No; they are the usual rascals that You see before You from time to time, here in the church."

"Then if that is the case, Don Camillo, it would be better for you to take off that affair that you have strapped on under your cassock and to put it back in the cupboard." Don Camillo removed the tommy-gun and went to put it away in the sacristy.

"You can leave it there until I tell you to take it out again," commanded the Lord, and Don Camillo shrugged his shoulders.

"If I am to wait until You tell me to use a tommy-gun, we shall be in the soup!" he exclaimed. "You aren't likely ever to give the word, and I must confess that in many instances the Old Testament . . ."

"Reactionary!" smiled the Lord. "And while you are wasting time in chattering, your poor old defenceless bishop is the prey of savage Russian Reds!"

This was a fact: the poor old defenceless bishop was indeed in the hands of the Red agitators. From as early as seven o'clock in the morning, the faithful had flocked to both sides of the main road, forming two long and impressive walls of enthusiasm, but a few minutes before the bishop's car was sighted Peppone, warned by a rocket fired by his outpost to signal the passing by of the enemy, gave the order to advance and by a lightning manoeuvre the Red forces rushed forward half a mile, so that, upon his arrival, the bishop found the entire road a mass of men wearing red handkerchiefs. People wandered to and fro and clustered into gossiping groups, displaying a sublime indifference towards the difficulties of the bishop's driver, who was compelled to proceed at a foot's pace, clearing a passage by continuous use of his horn.

This was in fact the *"dignified indifference"* ordained by the headquarters staff. Peppone and his satellites, mingling with the crowd, were chuckling with delight.

The bishop (that celebrated and very aged man, white-haired and bent, whose voice, when he spoke, appeared to come not from his lips, but from another century) immediately understood the *"dignified indifference"* and, telling his driver to stop the car (which was an open tourist model), made an abortive movement to open the door, allowing it to seem as if he lacked the necessary strength. Brusco, who was standing nearby, fell into the trap and when he realized his mistake, because of the kick Peppone had landed on his shin, it was too late and he had already opened the door.

"Thank you, my son," said the bishop. "I think it would be better if I walked to the village."

"But it is some distance," muttered Bigio, also receiving a kick on the shin.

"Never mind," replied the bishop, laughing, "I shouldn't like to disturb your political meeting."

"It is not a political meeting," explained Peppone gloomily. "They are only workers quietly discussing their own affairs. You'd better stay in your car."

But by now the bishop was standing in the road and Brusco had earned another kick because, realizing that he was unsteady on his feet, he had offered the support of his arm.

"Thank you, thank you so much, my son," said the bishop, and he set out, having made a sign to his secretary not to accompany him, as he wished to go alone.

And it was in this manner, at the head of the entire Red horde, that he reached the zone occupied by Don Camillo's forces and beside the bishop were Peppone, his headquarters staff, and all his most devoted henchmen, because, as Peppone had very wisely pointed out, the slightest gesture of discourtesy shown by any hot-headed fool to the representative of a foreign power would have given the reactionaries the opportunity of their lives.

"The order remains and will remain unchanged," concluded Peppone. "*Dignified indifference.*"

The instant he sighted the bishop Don Camillo rushed towards him. "Monsignore," he exclaimed with great agitation, "forgive me, but it was not my fault! I was awaiting you with all the faithful, but at the last moment . . ."

"Don't worry," smiled the bishop. "The fault has been entirely my own, because I took it into my head to leave the car and take a walk. All bishops, as they get old, become a little crazy!"

The faithful applauded, the bands struck up and the bishop looked about him with obvious enjoyment. "What a lovely village!" he said as he walked on. "Really lovely, and so beautifully neat and clean. You must have an excellent local administration."

"We do what we can for the good of the people," replied Brusco, receiving his third kick from Peppone.

The bishop, on reaching the square, immediately noticed the fountain and halted.

"A fountain in a village of the Bassa!" he exclaimed. "That must mean that you have water!"

"Only a matter of bringing it here, Eminence," replied Bigio, to whom belonged the chief credit of the enterprise. "We laid three hundred yards of pipes and there, with God's help, was the water."

Bigio got his kick in due time and then, as the fountain was situated opposite the

People's Palace, the bishop noticed the large new edifice and was interested. "And what is that handsome building?"

"The People's Palace," replied Peppone proudly.

"But it is really magnificent!" exclaimed the bishop.

"Would you care to go over it?" said Peppone on an impulse, while a terrible kick on the shins made him wince. That particular kick had come from Don Camillo.

The bishop's secretary, a lean young man with spectacles perched upon a big nose, had hurried forward to warn him that this was an unsuitable departure from routine, but the bishop had already entered the building. And they showed him everything: the gymnasium, the reading-room, the writing-room, and when they reached the library he went up to the book-shelves and studied the titles of the books. Before the book-case labelled "Political," which was filled with propagandist books and pamphlets, he said nothing but only sighed, and Peppone, who was close to him, noticed that sigh.

"Nobody ever reads them, Monsignore," whispered Peppone.

He spared his visitor the inspection of the offices, but could not resist the temptation to show off the tea-room, which was the object of his special pride, and thus the bishop, on his way out, was confronted by the enormous portrait of the man with the big moustache and the small eyes.

"You know how it is in politics," said Peppone in a confidential voice. "And then, you may believe me, he isn't really such a bad fellow."

"May God in His mercy shed light upon his mind also," replied the bishop quietly.

Throughout all this business Don Camillo's psychological position was peculiar. Because, while he was foaming at the mouth with indignation at the presumption upon the bishop's kindness that dared to inflict upon him an inspection of the People's Palace, which was a foundation that surely cried to God for vengeance, on the other hand he was proud that the bishop should know how progressive and up-to-date a village he had come to visit. Moreover, he was not displeased that the bishop should realize the strength of the local leftist organization, since it could only enhance the merits of his own recreation centre in the bishop's eyes.

When the inspection was at an end Don Camillo approached the bishop. "It seems a pity, Monsignore," he said, so loudly that Peppone could not fail to hear him, "it seems a pity that our mayor has not shown you the arsenal. It is believed to be the most fully supplied of the entire province."

Peppone was about to retort, but the bishop forestalled him. "Surely not so well supplied as your own," he replied, laughing.

"Well said!" exclaimed Bigio.

"He even has an S.S. mortar buried somewhere," added Brusco.

The bishop turned towards Peppone's staff. "You would insist on having him back again," he said; "and now you can keep him. Didn't I warn you that he was dangerous?"

"He doesn't manage to scare us," said Peppone with a grin.

"Keep an eye on him, all the same," the bishop advised him.

Don Camillo shook his head. "You will always have your joke, Monsignore!" he exclaimed. "But you can have no idea what these people are like!"

On his way out, the bishop passed the news-board, saw the poster and paused to read it.

"Ah," he remarked, "you are expecting a visit from the representative of a foreign power! And who may that be, Don Camillo?"

"I know very little of politics," replied Don Camillo. "We must ask the gentleman who is responsible for the poster. Mr. Mayor, Monsignore wishes to know who is the representative of a foreign power who is mentioned in your manifesto?"

"Oh," said Peppone, after a moment's hesitation. "The usual American."

"I understand," replied the bishop. "One of those Americans who are looking for oil in these parts. Am I right?" .

"Yes," said Peppone. "It's a downright scandal: any oil there may be belongs to us."

"I quite agree," said the bishop with the utmost gravity. "But I think you were wise to tell your people to limit their reactions to a dignified indifference. In my view, we should be foolish to quarrel with America. Don't you agree?"

Peppone spread out his arms. "Monsignore," he said, "you know how it is: one puts up with as much as can be borne and then comes the final straw!"

When the bishop arrived in front of the church he found all the local children from Don Camillo's recreation centre mustered in a neat formation, singing a song of welcome. Then an immense bouquet of flowers was seen to detach itself from the formation, and when it came to a halt in front of the bishop the flowers moved upwards and revealed a tiny child, so lovely and with such beautiful curls and clothes that all the women present went nearly out of their minds. There was complete silence while the infant, without pause or punctuation and in a voice as clear and pure as a little spring of water, recited a poem in the bishop's honour. After which everyone present applauded the child vociferously, exclaiming that he was adorable.

Peppone went up to Don Camillo. "Dastard!" he hissed in his ear. "You have taken advantage of a child's innocence in order to make me ridiculous before everybody! I shall break every bone in your body. And as for that brat, I shall show him where he gets off. You have contaminated him, and I shall chuck him into the river!"

"Good hunting!" replied Don Camillo. "He's your own son, and you can do as you like with him."

And it really was a shocking episode, because Peppone, carrying off the poor child to the river like a bundle, compelled him after fearful threats to recite three times over the poem in honour of the bishop . . . of that poor old weak and ingenious bishop who, being the "*representative of a foreign power*" (the Vatican), had been received, according to plan, with "*dignified indifference.*"

THE BELL

DON CAMILLO, AFTER a week during which he had attacked Bigio at least three times daily wherever he met him, shouting that he and all his breed of house-painters were highway robbers and lived only by extortion, had at last succeeded in agreeing with him on a price for whitewashing the outside walls of the presbytery. And now, from time to time, he went to sit for a while upon the bench in the church square so that he might enjoy the spectacle of those gleaming white walls that, together with the newly painted shutters and the climbing jasmine over the doorway, made a really beautiful effect.

But after each gratifying contemplation, Don Camillo turned to look at the church tower and sighed heavily, thinking of Geltrude. Geltrude had been carried off by the Germans, and Don Camillo had therefore now been fretting for her for nearly three years. For Geltrude had been the largest of the church bells, and only God could provide the necessary cash for the purchase of another bell of her lordly proportions.

"Stop brooding, Don Camillo," said the Lord above the altar one day. "A parish can get along very nicely even if the church tower lacks one of its bells. In such a matter, noise is not everything. God has very sharp ears and can hear perfectly well even if He is called by a bell the size of a hazel nut."

"Of course He can," replied Don Camillo with a sigh. "But men are hard of hearing, and it is chiefly to call them that bells are needed: the masses do listen to those who make the loudest noise."

"Well, Don Camillo, peg away and you'll succeed."

"But, Lord, I have tried everything. Those who would like to give haven't the money, and the rich won't shell out even if you put a knife to their throats. I've been very near success a couple of times with the football pools. . . . A pity! If only someone had given me the shadow of a tip—just one name and I could have bought a dozen bells. . . ."

The Lord smiled. "You must forgive My carelessness, Don Camillo. You want Me in the coming year to keep My mind on the football championship? Are you also interested in the lottery?"

Don Camillo blushed. "You have misunderstood me," he protested. "When I said 'someone' I hadn't the faintest intention of alluding to You! I was speaking in a general sense."

"I am glad of that, Don Camillo," said the Lord with grave approval. "It is very wise, when discussing such matters, always to speak in a general sense."

A few days later Don Camillo received a summons to the villa of the Signora Carolina, the lady of Boscaccio, and when he came home he was fairly bursting with joy: "Lord!" exclaimed Don Camillo, halting breathlessly before the altar. "To-morrow You will see before You a lighted candle of twenty pounds' weight.

I am going now to the town to buy it, and if they haven't got one, I shall have it specially made."

"But, Don Camillo, where will you get the money?"

"Don't You worry, Lord. You shall have Your candle if I have to sell the mattress off my bed to pay for it! Look what You have done for me!"

Then Don Camillo calmed down a little. "The Signora Carolina is giving an offering to the church of all the money needful for casting a new Geltrude!"

"And how did she come to think of it?"

"She said she had made a vow," explained Don Camillo, "to the effect that if the Lord helped her to bring off a certain business deal she would give a bell to the church. Thanks to Your intervention, the deal was successful, and within a month's time Geltrude will once more lift up her voice to Heaven! I am going now to order the candle!"

The Lord checked Don Camillo just as he was making off under full steam.

"No candles, Don Camillo," said the Lord severely. "No candles."

"But why?" demanded Don Camillo in amazement.

"Because I do not deserve them," replied the Lord. "I have given the Signora Carolina no help of any kind in her affairs. I take no interest in competition or in commerce. If I were to intervene in such matters, the winner would have reason to bless Me, while the loser would have cause to curse Me. If you happen to find a purse of money, I have not made you find it, because I did not cause your neighbour to lose it. You had better light your candle in front of the middleman who helped the Signora Carolina to make a profit of nine million. I am not myself a middleman."

The Lord's voice was unusually severe and Don Camillo was filled with shame.

"Forgive me," he stammered. "I am a poor, obtuse, ignorant country priest and my brain is filled with fog and foolishness."

The Lord smiled. "Don't be unjust to Don Camillo," He exclaimed. "Don Camillo always understands Me, and that is clear proof that his brain is not filled with fog. Very often it is precisely the intellect that fogs the brain. It is not you who have sinned; indeed, your gratitude touches Me because in any small matter that gives you pleasure you are always ready to perceive the kindness of God. And your joy is always honest and simple, as it is now in the thought of once more having your bell. And as it is also in your desire to thank Me for having enabled you to have it. But the Signora Carolina is neither simple nor honest when she sets out to acquire money by enlisting God's help in her shady financial transactions."

Don Camillo had listened silently and with his head bowed. Then he looked up. "I thank You, Lord. And now I shall go and tell that usurer that she can keep her money! My bells must all be honest bells. Otherwise it would be better to die without ever again hearing Geltrude's voice!"

He wheeled round, proud and determined, and the Lord smiled as He watched him walk away. But as Don Camillo reached the door, the Lord called him back.

"Don Camillo," said the Lord. "I am perfectly aware of all that your bell means to you, because I can always read your mind at any moment, and your renunciation is so fine and noble that in itself alone it would suffice to purify the bronze of a statue of Antichrist. *Vade retro, Satana!* Get out of here quickly or you will compel Me to grant you not only your bell, but who knows what other development."

Don Camillo stood quite still. "Does that mean I can have it?"

"It does. You have earned it."

In such contingencies Don Camillo invariably lost his head. As he was standing before the altar he bowed, spun on his heel, set off at a run, pulled himself up halfway down the nave and finally skidded as far as the church door. The Lord looked on with satisfaction, because even such antics may at given moments be a manner of praising God.

And then a few days later there occurred an unpleasant incident. Don Camillo surprised an urchin busily engaged in adorning the newly whitened walls of the presbytery with a piece of charcoal and saw red. The urchin made off like a lizard, but Don Camillo was beyond himself and gave chase.

"I shall collar you if I burst my lungs!" he yelled.

He set off on an infuriated pursuit across the fields and at every step his ire increased. Then suddenly the boy, finding his escape blocked by a thick hedge, stopped, threw up his arms to shield his head and stood still, too breathless to utter word.

Don Camillo bore down on him like a tank and, grasping the child's arm with his left hand, raised the other, intending dire punishment. But his fingers closed on an arm so slender and emaciated that he let go and both his own arms fell to his sides.

Then he looked more attentively at the boy and found himself confronted by the white face and terrified eyes of Straziami's son.

Straziami was the most unfortunate of all Peppone's faithful satellites, and this not because he was an idler: he was in fact always in search of a job. The trouble lay in the fact that, having secured one, he would stick to it quietly for one day and on the second he would have a row with his employer, so that he seldom worked more than five days a month.

"Don Camillo," the child implored him, "I'll never do it again!"

"Get along with you," said Don Camillo abruptly.

Then he sent for Straziami, and Straziami strode defiantly into the presbytery with his hands in his pockets and his hat on the back of his head.

"And what does the people's priest want with me?" he demanded arrogantly.

"First of all that you take off your hat or else I knock it off for you; and, secondly, that you stop hectoring, because I won't put up with it."

Straziami himself was as thin and as colourless as his son and a blow from Don Camillo would have felled him to the ground. He threw his hat on to a chair with an elaborate assumption of boredom.

"I suppose you want to tell me that my son has been defacing the Archbishop's Palace? I know it already; someone else told me. Your grey Eminence need not worry: this evening the boy shall have his hiding."

"If you dare so much as to lay a finger on him, I'll break every bone in your body," shouted Don Camillo. "Suppose you give him something to eat! Haven't you realized that the wretched child is nothing but a skeleton?"

"We aren't all of us the pets of the Eternal Father," began Straziami sarcastically.

But Don Camillo interrupted him: "When you do get a job, try to keep it instead of getting thrown out on the second day for spouting revolution!"

"You look after your own bloody business!" retorted Straziami furiously. He turned on his heel to go, and it was then that Don Camillo caught him by the arm. But that arm, as his fingers grasped it, was as wasted as that of the boy and Don Camillo let go of it hastily.

Then he went off to the Lord above the altar. "Lord," he exclaimed, "must I always find myself taking hold of a bag of bones?"

"All things are possible in a country ravaged by so many wars and so much hatred," replied the Lord with a heavy sigh. "Suppose you tried keeping your hands to yourself?"

Don Camillo went next to Peppone's workshop and found him busy at his vice.

"As mayor it is your duty to do something for that unhappy child, Straziami's," said Don Camillo.

"With the funds available to the commune, I might possibly be able to fan him with the calendar on that wall," replied Peppone.

"Then do something as chief of your beastly Party. If I am not mistaken, Straziami is one of your star scoundrels."

"I can fan him with the blotter from my desk."

"Heavens above! And what about all the money they send you from Russia?"

Peppone worked away with his file. "The Red Tzar's mails have been delayed," he remarked. "Why can't you lend me some of the cash you get from America?"

Don Camillo shrugged his shoulders. "If you can't see the point as mayor or as Party leader, I should have thought you might understand as the father of a son (whoever may be his mother!) the need for helping that miserable child who comes and scribbles on the presbytery wall. And by the way, you can tell Bigio that unless he cleans my wall free of charge I shall attack your Party from the Demo-Christian news-board."

Peppone carried on with his filing for a bit; then he said: "Straziami's boy isn't the only one in the commune who needs to go to the sea or to the mountains. If I could have found the money, I should have established a colony long ago."

"Then go and look for it!" exclaimed Don Camillo. "So long as you stay in this office and file bolts, mayor or no mayor, you won't get hold of money. The peasants are stuffed with it."

"And they won't part with a cent, reverendo. They'd shell out fast enough if we suggested founding a colony to fatten their calves! Why don't you go yourself to the pope or to Truman?"

They quarrelled for two hours and very nearly came to blows at least thirty times. Don Camillo was very late in returning to the presbytery.

"What has happened?" asked the Lord. "You seem upset?"

"Naturally," replied Don Camillo. "When an unhappy priest has had to argue for two hours with a Communist mayor in order to make him understand the necessity for founding a seaside colony, and for another two hours with a miserly woman capitalist to get her to fork out the money required for that same colony, he may justly feel a bit gloomy."

"I understand you," replied the Lord.

Don Camillo hesitated. "Lord," he said at last, "You must forgive me if I have dragged even You into this business of the money."

"Me?"

"Yes, Lord. In order to compel that usurer to part with her cash, I had to tell her that I saw You in a dream last night and that You told me You would rather her money went for a work of charity than for the buying of the new bell."

"Don Camillo! And after that you have the courage to look Me in the eyes?"

"Yes," replied Don Camillo calmly. "The end justifies the means."

"Machiavelli doesn't strike me as being one of those sacred scriptures upon which you should base your actions," exclaimed the Lord.

"Lord," replied Don Camillo, "it may be blasphemy to say so, but even he can sometimes have his uses."

"And that is true enough," agreed the Lord.

Ten days later when a procession of singing children passed by the church on their way to the colony, Don Camillo hurried out to say goodbye and to bestow stacks of little holy pictures. And when he came to Straziami's boy at the end of the procession, he frowned at him fiercely. "Wait until you are fat and strong and then we shall have our reckoning!" he threatened.

Then, seeing Straziami, who was following the children at a little distance, he made a gesture of disgust. "Family of scoundrels," he muttered as he turned his back and went into the church.

That night he dreamed that the Lord appeared to him and said that He would sooner the Signora Carolina's money were used for charity than for the purchase of a bell.

"It is already done," murmured Don Camillo in his sleep.

FEAR

PEPPONE FINISHED READING the newspaper that had come by the afternoon post and then spoke to Smilzo, who was awaiting orders perched on a high stool in a corner of the workshop.

"Go and get the car and bring it here with the squadron in an hour's time."

"Anything serious?"

"Hurry up!" shouted Peppone.

Smilzo started up the lorry and was off, and within three-quarters of an hour he was back again with the twenty-five men of the squadron. Peppone climbed in and they were very soon at the People's Palace.

"You stay here and guard the car," Peppone ordered Smilzo, "and if you see anything odd, shout."

When they reached the assembly room Peppone made his report. "Look here," he said, thumping with his big fist upon the news-sheet, which bore enormous headlines, "matters have reached a climax: we are for it. The reactionaries have broken loose, our comrades are being shot at and bombs are being thrown against all the Party headquarters." He read aloud a few passages from the paper, which was in point of fact the *Milano Sera*, a Milanese evening publication.

"And note that we are told these things not by one of our Party papers! This is an independent newspaper and it is telling the truth, because you can read it all clearly printed under the headlines!"

"Just think of it!" growled Brusco. "If one of those independent papers that always favour the right so damnably and oppose us whenever they can, is compelled to publish such things, only think how much worse the reality must be! I can't wait to read to-morrow's *Unità*!"

Bigio shrugged his shoulders. "It'll probably be tamer than this," he said. "*Unità* is run by comrades who are active, but all of them educated persons of culture who are learned in philosophy, and they always tend to minimize such matters, so as to avoid exciting the people."

"Yes; educated folk who are careful to observe rules and to do nothing illegal," added Pellerossa.

"More like poets than anything else!" concluded Peppone. "But all the same they are people who, once they do pick up a pen, strike so hard that they would knock out the Eternal Father!"

They continued to discuss the situation, reading over again the principal statements in the Milanese paper and commenting upon what they had read. "It is obvious that the Fascist revolution has already begun," said Peppone. "At any moment, here where we stand, we may expect the flying squads to burn the Co-operatives and the people's houses and beat folk up and purge them. This paper mentions 'Fascist cells' and 'storm-troopers'; there is nothing equivocal about it. If it were a case of simple *qualunquismo*,[1] capitalism or monarchism they would speak of reactionaries, of 'nostalgists,' etcetera. But here they put it perfectly clearly and bluntly as 'fascism' and 'flying squads.' And bear in mind that it's an independent paper. We must be ready to face up to any eventuality."

Lungo gave it as his opinion that they ought to move first before the others got going: they knew perfectly well every individual reactionary in the commune. "We should go to every house in turn and pull them out and beat them up, and we should do it without any further talk."

"No," Brusco objected. "It seems to me that we should be putting ourselves in the wrong from the start. Even this paper says that we should reply to provocation, but not invite it. Because if we give provocation, we give them the right to retaliate."

Peppone agreed. "If we are to beat up anybody we should do it with justice and democratically."

They went on talking more quietly for another hour and were suddenly roused by an explosion that shook the windows. They all rushed out of the building and found Smilzo lying full length behind the lorry, as though he were dead, with his

[1] Italian party entitled "L'Uomo Qualunque": equivalent to "The Man in the Street."

face covered with blood. They handed over the unconscious man to his wife's care and leaped into the lorry.

"Forward!" bawled Peppone as Lungo bent to the wheel. Off went the lorry at full tilt and it was not until they had covered a couple of miles that Lungo turned to Peppone.

"Where are we going?"

"That's just it," muttered Peppone. "Where are we going?"

They stopped the car and collected themselves. Then they turned round and went back to the village and drew up in front of the Demo-Christian headquarters. There they found a table, two chairs and a picture of the pope, and all these they threw out of the window. Then they climbed into the lorry again and set out firmly for Ortaglia.

"Nobody but that skunk Pizzi would have thrown the bomb that killed Smilzo," said Pellerossa. "He swore vengeance on us that time when we quarrelled over the labourers' strike. 'We shall see!' he said."

They surrounded the house, which was isolated, and Peppone went in. Pizzi was in the kitchen stirring the *polenta*. His wife was laying the table and his little boy was putting wood on the fire.

Pizzi looked up, saw Peppone and immediately realized that something was wrong. He looked at the child, who was now playing on the floor at his feet. Then he looked up again.

"What do you want?" he asked.

"They have thrown a bomb in front of our headquarters and killed Smilzo!" shouted Peppone.

"Nothing to do with me," replied Pizzi. The woman caught hold of the child and drew back.

"You said that you would make us pay dearly when we came up against you over the labourers' strike. You are a reactionary swine, anyway." Peppone bore down on him menacingly, but Pizzi stepped back a pace and, catching up a revolver that lay on the mantelpiece, he pointed it at Peppone.

"Hands up, Peppone, or I shoot you!"

At that moment somebody who was hiding outside threw open the window, fired a shot and Pizzi fell to the ground. As he fell his revolver went off and the bullet lost itself among the ashes on the hearth. The woman looked down at her husband's body and put her hand in front of her mouth. The child flung himself on his father and began screaming.

Peppone and his men climbed hastily into the lorry and went off in silence. Before reaching the village, they stopped, got out and proceeded separately on foot.

There was a crowd in front of the People's Palace, and Peppone met Don Camillo coming out of it. "Is he dead?" Peppone asked.

"It would take a lot more than that to kill a fellow of his stamp," replied Don Camillo chuckling. "Nice fool you've made of yourself destroying the table at the Demo-Christian headquarters. They won't half laugh at you!"

Peppone looked at him gloomily. "There isn't much to laugh at, when people begin throwing bombs."

Don Camillo looked at him with interest. "Peppone," he said. "One of two things: either you are a scoundrel or a fool."

In point of fact, Peppone was neither. He quite simply did not know that the explosion had not been caused by a bomb, but by one of the retreaded tyres of the lorry from which a piece of rubber had struck the unfortunate Smilzo in the face.

He went to look underneath the lorry and saw the disembowelled tyre and then thought of Pizzi lying stretched out on the kitchen floor, of the woman who had put her hand to her mouth to stifle her screams and of the screaming child.

And meanwhile people were laughing. But within an hour the laughter died down because a rumour had spread through the village that Pizzi had been wounded.

He died next morning, and when the police went to question his wife the woman stared at them with eyes that were blank with terror.

"Didn't you see anyone?"

"I was in the other room; I heard a shot and ran in and found my husband lying on the ground. I saw nothing else."

"Where was the boy?"

"He was already in bed."

"And where is he now?"

"I've sent him to his grandmother."

Nothing more could be learned. The revolver was found to have one empty chamber, the bullet that had killed Pizzi had hit him in the temple and its calibre was identical with that of those remaining in the revolver. The authorities promptly decided that it was a case of suicide.

Don Camillo read the report and the statements made by various persons to the effect that Pizzi had been worried for some time past by the failure of an important deal in seeds, and had been heard to say on several occasions that he would like to make an end of it all. Then Don Camillo went to discuss the matter with the Lord.

"Lord," he said unhappily, "this is the first time in my parish that someone has died to whom I cannot give Christian burial. And that is right enough, I know, because he who kills himself kills one of God's children and loses his soul, and, if we are to be severe, should not even lie in consecrated ground."

"That is so, Don Camillo."

"And if we decide to allow him a place in the cemetery, then he must go there alone, like a dog, because he who renounces his humanity lowers himself to the rank of a beast."

"Very sad, Don Camillo, but so it is."

The following morning (it happened to be a Sunday) Don Camillo, in the course of his mass, preached a terrible sermon on suicide. It was pitiless, terrifying and implacable.

"I would not approach the body of a suicide," he said in his peroration, "not even if I knew that my doing so would restore him to life!"

Pizzi's funeral took place on that same afternoon. The coffin was pushed into a plain third-class hearse which set out jerkily followed by the dead man's wife and child and his two brothers in a couple of two-wheeled carts. When the convoy entered the village people closed their shutters and peeped through the cracks.

Then suddenly something happened that struck everybody speechless. Don Camillo unexpectedly made his appearance, with two acolytes and the cross, took up his station in front of the hearse and preceded it on foot, intoning the customary psalms.

On reaching the church square, Don Camillo beckoned to Pizzi's two brothers, and they lifted the coffin from the hearse and carried it into the church, and there Don Camillo said the office for the dead and blessed the body. Then he returned to his position in front of the hearse and went right through the village, singing. Not a soul was to be seen.

At the cemetery, as soon as the coffin had been lowered into the grave, Don Camillo drew a deep breath and cried in a stentorian voice: "May God reward the soul of his faithful servant, Antonio Pizzi."

Then he threw a handful of earth into the grave, blessed it and left the cemetery, walking slowly through the village depopulated by fear.

"Lord," said Don Camillo when he reached the church, "have You any fault to find with me?"

"Yes, Don Camillo, I have: when one goes to accompany a poor dead man to the cemetery one should not carry a pistol in one's pocket."

"I understand, Lord," replied Don Camillo, "You mean that I should have kept it in my sleeve so as to be more accessible."

"No, Don Camillo, such things should be left at home, even if one is escorting the body of a . . . suicide."

"Lord," said Don Camillo after a long pause, "will You have a bet with me that a commission composed of my most assiduous bigots will write an indignant letter to the bishop, to the effect that I have committed a sacrilege in accompanying the body of a suicide to the cemetery?"

"No," replied the Lord. "I won't bet, because they are already writing it."

"And by what I have done I have drawn upon myself the hatred of everyone: of those who killed Pizzi, of those who, while well aware, like everybody else, that Pizzi had been murdered, found it inconvenient that doubts should be raised regarding his suicide. Even of Pizzi's own relations who would have been glad to have it believed that there was no suspicion that he had not killed himself. One of his brothers asked me: 'But isn't it forbidden to bring a suicide into the church?' Even Pizzi's own wife must hate me, because she is afraid, not for herself, but for her son, and is lying in order to defend his life."

The little side door of the church creaked and Don Camillo looked round as Pizzi's small son entered. The boy came forward and halted in front of Don Camillo.

"I thank you on behalf of my father," he said in the grave, hard voice of a fully grown man. Then he went away as silent as a shadow.

"There," said the Lord, "goes someone who does not hate you, Don Camillo."

"But his heart is filled with hatred of those who killed his father, and that is another link in an accursed chain that no one succeeds in breaking. Not even You, who allowed Yourself to be crucified for these mad dogs."

"The end of the world is not yet," replied the Lord serenely. "It has only just begun, and up There time is measured by millions of centuries. You must not lose your faith, Don Camillo. There is still any amount of time."

THE FEAR CONTINUES

AFTER THE PUBLICATION of his parish magazine, Don Camillo found himself quite alone.

"I feel as though I were in the middle of a desert," he confided to the Lord. "And it makes no difference even when there are a hundred people around me, because although they are all there, within half a yard of me, there seems to be a thick wall of glass that divides us. I hear their voices, but as though they came from another world."

"It is fear," replied the Lord. "They are afraid of you."

"Of me!"

"Of you, Don Camillo. And they hate you. They were living warmly and comfortably in their cocoon of cowardice. They were perfectly aware of the truth, but nobody could compel them to recognize it, because nobody had proclaimed it publicly. You have acted and spoken in such a manner that they are now forced to face up to it, and it is for that reason that they hate and fear you. You see your brothers who, like sheep, are obeying the orders of a tyrant and you cry: 'Wake up out of your lethargy and look at those who are free; compare your lives with those of people who enjoy liberty!' And they will not be grateful to you but will hate you, and if they can they will kill you, because you compel them to face up to what they already knew but for love of a quiet life pretended not to know. They have eyes, but they will not see. They have ears, but they will not hear. You have given publicity to an injustice and have placed these people in a serious dilemma: if you hold your tongue you condone their imposition; if you don't condone it you must speak out. It was so much easier to ignore it. Does all this surprise you?"

Don Camillo spread out his arms. "No," he said. "But it would have surprised me had I not known that You were crucified for telling people the truth. As it is, it merely distresses me."

Presently there came a messenger from the bishop. "Don Camillo," he explained, "Monsignore has read your parish magazine and is aware of the reactions it has aroused in the parish. The first number has pleased him, but he is exceedingly anxious that the second number shouldn't contain your obituary. You must see to it."

"That matter is independent of the will of the publishers," replied Don Camillo, "and therefore any request of the kind should be addressed not to me, but to God."

"That is exactly what Monsignore is doing," explained the messenger, "and he wished you to know it."

The sergeant of police was a man of the world: he met Don Camillo by chance in the street. "I have read your magazine and the point you make about the tyre tracks in the Pizzi's yard is very interesting."

"Did you make a note of them?"

"No," replied the sergeant. "I didn't make a note of them because directly I saw them I had casts taken of them then and there and happened to discover, quite by chance, when I was comparing the casts with the wheels of various local cars, that those tracks had been made by the mayor's lorry. Moreover, I observed that Pizzi had shot himself in the left temple when he was holding the revolver in his right hand. And when I hunted among the ashes in the fireplace I found the bullet that left Pizzi's revolver when Pizzi fell, after the other bullet had been fired at him through the window."

Don Camillo looked at him sternly. "And why have you not reported all this?"

"I have reported it in the proper quarter, reverendo. And I was told that if, at such a moment, the mayor was arrested, the matter would immediately assume a political significance. When such things get mixed up with politics there are complications. It is necessary to wait for an opportunity, and you, Don Camillo, have supplied it. I have no wish to shift my responsibility on to other shoulders; I merely want to avoid the danger that the whole business should get bogged because there are people who wish to make a political issue of it."

Don Camillo replied that the sergeant had acted most correctly.

"But I can't detail two constables to guard your back, Don Camillo."

"It would be a blackguardly attack!"

"I know it; but all the same I would surround you with a battalion if it were in my power," muttered the sergeant.

"It isn't necessary, sergeant. Almighty God will see to it."

"Let's hope He'll be more careful than He was of Pizzi," the sergeant retorted.

The following day the inquiries were resumed and a number of landowners and leaseholders were interrogated. As Verola, who was among those questioned, protested indignantly, the sergeant replied very calmly.

"My good sir: given the fact that Pizzi had no political views and that nobody robbed him of anything, and given also the fact that certain new evidence tends to suggest a murder rather than a suicide, we must exclude the supposition that we are dealing with either a political crime or a robbery. We must therefore direct our inquiries towards those with whom Pizzi had business or friendly relations and who may have borne him a grudge."

The matter proceeded in this manner for several days and the persons questioned were furiously angry.

Brusco also was infuriated, but he held his tongue.

"Peppone," he said at last. "That devil is playing with us as though we were kids. You'll see. When he has questioned everybody he can think of, including the midwife, in a couple of weeks' time he'll be coming to you with a smile to ask whether you have any objection to his questioning one of our people. And you won't be able to refuse, and he will begin his questioning and out will come the whole business."

"Don't be ridiculous," shouted Peppone. "Not even if they tore out my nails."

"It won't be you that they'll question, or me, or the others we are thinking of. They'll go straight for the one who will spill everything. They'll tackle the man who fired the shot."

Peppone sniggered. "Don't talk rubbish! When we ourselves don't know who did it!"

And thus it was. Nobody had seen which of the twenty-five men of the squadron had done the deed. As soon as Pizzi had fallen, they had all of them climbed into the lorry and later on had separated without exchanging a single word. Since then nobody had even mentioned the matter.

Peppone looked Brusco straight in the eyes. "Who was it?" he asked.

"Who knows. It may have been you yourself."

"I," cried Peppone. "And how could I do it when I wasn't even armed?"

"You went alone into Pizzi's house and none of us could see what you did there."

"But the shot was fired from outside, through the window. Someone must know who was stationed at that window."

"At night all cats are grey. Even if someone did see, by now he has seen nothing at all. But one person did see the face of the man who fired, and that was the boy. Otherwise his people wouldn't have said that he was in bed. And if the boy knows it then Don Camillo also knows it. If he hadn't known he wouldn't have said or done what he has said and done."

"May those who brought him here roast in Hell!" bawled Peppone.

Meanwhile, the net was being drawn closer and closer and every evening, as a matter of discipline, the sergeant went off to inform the mayor of the progress of the inquiries.

"I can't tell you more at the moment, Mr. Mayor," he said one evening, "but we know where we are at last; it seems that there was a woman in the case."

Peppone merely replied, "Indeed!" but he would gladly have throttled him.

It was already late in the evening and Don Camillo was finding jobs for himself in the empty church. He had set up a pair of steps on the top step of the altar, for he had discovered a crack in the grain of the wood of one arm of the crucifix and having filled it up was now applying a little brown paint to the white plaster of the stopping.

At a certain moment he sighed and the Lord spoke to him in an undertone. "Don Camillo, what is the matter? You haven't been yourself for several days past. Are you feeling unwell? Is it perhaps a touch of influenza?"

"No, Lord," Don Camillo confessed without raising his head. "It is fear."

"You are afraid? But of what, in heaven's name?"

"I don't know. If I knew what I was afraid of I shouldn't be frightened," replied Don Camillo. "There is something wrong, something in the air, something against which I can't defend myself. If twenty men came at me with guns I shouldn't be afraid. I should only be angry because they were twenty and I was alone and had no gun. If I found myself in the sea and didn't know how to swim I'd think: 'There now, in a few moments I shall drown like a kitten!' and that would annoy me very much but I should not be afraid. When one understands a danger one isn't frightened. But fear comes with dangers that are felt but not understood.

It is like walking with one's eyes bandaged on an unknown road. And it's a beastly feeling."

"Have you lost your faith in your God, Don Camillo?"

"*Da mihi animam, caetera tolle.* The soul is of God, but the body is of the earth. Faith is a great thing, but this is a purely physical fear. I may have immense faith, but if I remain for ten days without drinking I shall be thirsty. Faith consists in enduring that thirst in serenity as a trial sent by God. Lord, I am willing to suffer a thousand fears such as this one for love of You. But nevertheless I am afraid."

The Lord smiled.

"Do You despise me?"

"No, Don Camillo; if you were not afraid, what value would there be in your courage?"

Don Camillo continued to apply his paint-brush carefully to the wood of the crucifix and his eyes were fixed upon the Lord's hand, pierced by the nail. Suddenly it appeared to him that this hand came to life, and at exactly that moment a shot resounded through the church.

Somebody had fired through the window of the little side chapel.

A dog barked, and then another; from far away came the brief burst of a tommy-gun firing. Then there was silence once more. Don Camillo gazed with scared eyes into the Lord's face.

"Lord," he said, "I felt Your hand upon my forehead."

"You are dreaming, Don Camillo."

Don Camillo lowered his eyes and fixed them upon the hand pierced by the nail. Then he gasped and the brush and the little pot of paint fell from his fingers.

The bullet had passed through the Lord's wrist.

"Lord," he said breathlessly, "You pushed back my head and Your arm received the bullet that was meant for me!"

"Don Camillo!"

"The bullet is not in the wood of the crucifix!" cried Don Camillo. "Look where it went!"

High up to the right and opposite the side chapel hung a small frame containing a silver heart. The bullet had broken the glass and had lodged itself exactly in the centre of the heart.

Don Camillo ran to the sacristy and fetched a long ladder. He stretched a piece of string from the hole made by the bullet in the window to the hole made in the silver heart. The line of the string passed at a distance of about twelve inches from the nail in the Lord's hand.

"My head was just there," said Don Camillo, "and Your arm was struck because You pushed my head backwards. Here is the proof!"

"Don Camillo, don't get so excited!"

But Don Camillo was beyond recovering his composure, and had he not promptly developed a fierce temperature the Lord only knew what he might have done. And the Lord obviously did know it, because He sent him a fever that laid him low in his bed as weak as a half-drowned kitten.

The window through which the shot had been fired gave on to the little enclosed plot of land that belonged to the church, and the police sergeant and Don Camillo stood there examining the church wall.

"Here is the proof," said the sergeant, pointing to four holes that were clearly visible upon the light distemper just below the window-sill. He took a penknife from his pocket, dug into one of the holes and presently pulled out some object.

"In my opinion, the whole business is quite simple," he explained. "The man was standing at some distance away and fired a round with his tommy-gun at the lighted window. Four bullets struck the wall and the fifth hit the glass and went through it."

Don Camillo shook his head. "I told you that it was a pistol shot and fired at close range. I am not yet so senile as to be unable to distinguish a pistol shot from a round of machine-gun fire! The pistol shot came first and was fired from where we are standing. Then came the burst from the tommy-gun from further away."

"Then we ought to find the cartridge case nearby," retorted the sergeant; "and it isn't anywhere to be seen!"

Don Camillo shrugged his shoulders. "You would need a musical critic from La Scala to distinguish by the key tone whether a shot comes from an automatic or from a revolver! And if the fellow fired from a pistol he took the cartridge case with him."

The sergeant began to nose round and presently he found what he was looking for on the trunk of one of the cherry trees that had been planted in a row some five or six paces from the church.

"One of the bullets has cut the bark," he said. And it was obvious that he was right. He scratched his head thoughtfully.

"Well," he said, "we may as well play the scientific detective!"

He fetched a pole and stuck it into the ground close to the church wall, in front of one of the bullet holes. Then he began to walk to and fro with his eyes fixed on the damaged cherry tree, moving to right or left until the trunk was in a direct line covering the pole by the wall. Thus he ultimately found himself standing in front of the hedge and beyond the hedge were a ditch and a lane.

Don Camillo joined him and, one on either side of the hedge, they carefully examined the ground. They went on searching for a while, and after about five minutes Don Camillo said: "Here it is," and held up a tommy-gun cartridge case. Then they found the other three.

"That proves I was right," exclaimed the sergeant. "The fellow fired from here through the window."

Don Camillo shook his head. "I've never used a tommy-gun," he said, "but I know that with other guns bullets never describe a curve. See for yourself."

Just then a constable came up to inform the sergeant that everyone in the village was quite calm.

"Many thanks!" remarked Don Camillo. "Nobody fired at any of them! It was me that they shot at!"

The sergeant borrowed the constable's rifle and lying flat on the ground aimed in the direction of the upper pane of the chapel window where, so far as his memory served him, he thought the bullet had struck it.

"If you fired now, where would the bullet go?" asked Don Camillo.

It was an easy reckoning, mere child's play: a bullet fired from where they were and passing through the chapel window would have hit the door of the first confessional on the right-hand side, at about three yards' distance from the church door.

"Unless it was a trained bullet, it couldn't have gone past the altar, not if it split itself!" said the sergeant. "Which only goes to show," he went on, "that any matter in which you are mixed up is always enough to make one tear out one's hair! You couldn't be contented with one assailant! No, sir: you must have two of them. One that fires from behind the window and another that fires from behind a hedge a hundred and fifty paces away."

"Oh well, that's how I'm made," replied Don Camillo. "I never spare expense!"

That same evening Peppone summoned his staff and all the local Party officials to headquarters.

Peppone was gloomy. "Comrades," he said, "a new event has occurred to complicate the present situation. Last night some unknown person shot at the so-called parish priest and the reaction is taking advantage of this episode in order to raise its head and throw mud at the Party. The reaction, cowardly as always, has not the courage to speak out openly, but, as we would expect, is whispering in corners and trying to saddle us with the responsibility for this attack."

Lungo held up his hand and Peppone signed to him that he could speak.

"First of all," said Lungo, "we might tell the reactionaries that they had better offer proof that there really has been an attempt on the priest's life. Since there seem to have been no witnesses, it might easily be that the reverend gentleman himself fired off a revolver in order to be able to attack us in his filthy periodical! Let us first of all obtain proof!"

"Excellent!" exclaimed his audience. "Lungo is perfectly right!"

Peppone intervened. "One moment! What Lungo says is fair enough, but we should not exclude the possibility that what we have heard is the truth. Familiar as we all are with Don Camillo's character, it can hardly be said, honestly, that he is in the habit of using underhand methods . . ."

Peppone was in his turn interrupted by Spocchia, the leader of the cell at Milanetto. "Comrade Peppone, do not forget that once a priest always a priest! You are letting yourself be carried away by sentimentality. Had you listened to me, his filthy magazine would never have seen the light and to-day the Party would not have had to endure all the odious insinuations with regard to Pizzi's suicide! There should be no mercy for the enemies of the people! Anyone who has mercy on the people's enemies betrays the people!"

Peppone crashed his fist down on the table. "I don't require any preaching from you!" he bawled.

Spocchia seemed unimpressed. "And, moreover, if instead of opposing us you had let us act while there was still time," he shouted, "we shouldn't now be held up by a crowd of accursed reactionaries! I . . ."

Spocchia was a thin young man of twenty-five and sported an immense head of hair. He wore it brushed back, waved on top of his head and smooth at the sides, forming a kind of upstanding crest such as is affected by louts in the north and by the boors of Trastevere. He had small eyes and thin lips.

Peppone strode up to him aggressively. "You are a half-wit!" he said, glaring at him. The other changed colour, but made no reply.

Returning to the table, Peppone went on speaking. "Taking advantage of an episode that is based only upon the statement of a priest," he said, "the reaction is putting forward fresh speculations to the discredit of the people. The comrades need to be more than ever determined. To such ignoble suggestions they . . ."

Quite suddenly something happened to Peppone that had never happened to him before: Peppone began *listening to himself*. It seemed to him as though Peppone were among his audience listening to what Peppone was saying:

" . . . *and their bodies sold, the reaction paid by the enemies of the proletariat, the labourers starved . . .*" Peppone listened and gradually he seemed to be listening to another man. "*. . . the Savoy gang . . . the lying clergy . . . the black government . . . America . . . plutocracy . . .*"

"What in the world does plutocracy mean? Why is that fellow spouting about it when he doesn't even know what it means?" Peppone was thinking. He looked round him and saw faces that he barely recognized. Shifty eyes, and the most treacherous of all were those of young Spocchia. He thought of the faithful Brusco and looked for him, but Brusco stood at the far end of the room, with folded arms and bent head.

"*But let our enemies learn that in us the Resistance has not weakened. . . . The weapons that we took up for the defence of our liberty . . .*" And now Peppone heard himself yelling like a lunatic, and then the applause brought him back to himself.

"Splendid!" whispered Spocchia in his ear as they went downstairs. "You know, Peppone, it only needs a whistle to set them going. My lads could be ready in an hour's time."

"Good! excellent!" replied Peppone, slapping him on the shoulder. But he would gladly have knocked him down. Nor did he know why.

He remained alone with Brusco and at first they were silent. "Well!" exclaimed Peppone at last. "Have you lost your wits? You haven't even told me whether I spoke well or not?"

"You spoke splendidly," replied Brusco, "wonderfully. Better than ever before." Then the curtain of silence fell back heavily between them.

Peppone was doing accounts in a ledger. Suddenly he picked up a glass paper-weight and threw it violently on to the ground, bellowing a long, intricate and infuriated blasphemy. Brusco stared at him.

"I made a blot," explained Peppone, closing the ledger.

"Another of that old thief Barchini's pens," remarked Brusco, being careful not to point out to Peppone that, as he was writing in pencil, the explanation of the blot did not hold water.

When they left the building and went out into the night they walked together as far as the cross-roads and there Peppone pulled up as though he had something that he wished to tell Brusco. But he merely said: "Well; see you to-morrow."

"To-morrow then, Chief. Good night."

"Good night, Brusco."

MEN OF GOODWILL

CHRISTMAS WAS APPROACHING, and it was high time to get the figures of the Crib out of their drawer so that they might be cleaned, touched up here and there and any stains carefully removed. It was already late, but Don Camillo was still at work in the presbytery. He heard a knocking on the window and on seeing that it was Peppone went to open the door.

Peppone sat down while Don Camillo resumed his work and neither of them spoke for quite a long time.

"Hell and damnation!" exclaimed Peppone suddenly and furiously.

"Couldn't you find a better place to blaspheme in than my presbytery?" inquired Don Camillo quietly. "Couldn't you have got it off your chest at your own headquarters?"

"One can't even swear there any longer," muttered Peppone. "Because if one does, someone asks for an explanation."

Don Camillo applied a little white lead to St. Joseph's beard. "No decent man can live in this filthy world!" exclaimed Peppone after a pause.

"How does that concern you?" inquired Don Camillo. "Have you by any chance become a decent man?"

"I've never been anything else."

"There now! And I should never have thought it." Don Camillo continued his retouching of St. Joseph's beard. Then he began to tidy up the saint's clothing.

"How long will you be over that job?" asked Peppone angrily.

"If you were to give me a hand, it would soon be done."

Peppone was a mechanic and he possessed hands as big as shovels and enormous fingers that gave an impression of clumsiness. Nevertheless, when anybody wanted a watch repaired, they never failed to take it to Peppone. Because it is a fact that it is precisely such bulky men that are best adapted to the handling of minute things. Peppone could streamline the body of a car or the spokes of a wheel like a master painter.

"Are you crazy! Can you see me touching up saints!" he muttered. "You haven't by any chance mistaken me for a sacristan?"

Don Camillo fished in the bottom of the open drawer and brought forth a pink-and-white object about the size of a sparrow: it was in fact the Holy Infant Himself.

Peppone hardly knew how he came to find it in his hands, but he took up a little brush and began working carefully. He and Don Camillo sat on either side of the table, unable to see each other's faces because of the light of the lamp between them.

"It's a beastly world," said Peppone. "If you have something to say you daren't trust anyone. I don't even trust myself."

Don Camillo appeared to be absorbed in his task: the Madonna's whole face required repainting.

"Do you trust me?" he asked casually.

"I don't know."

"Try telling me something and then you will know."

Peppone completed the repainting of the Baby's eyes, which were the most difficult part. Then he touched up the red of the tiny lips. "I should like to give it all up," said Peppone, "but it can't be done."

"What prevents you?"

"Prevents me? With an iron bar in my band, I could stand up to a regiment!"

"Are you afraid?"

"I've never been afraid in my life!"

"I have, Peppone. Sometimes I am frightened."

Peppone dipped his brush in the paint. "Well, so am I, sometimes," he said, and his voice was almost inaudible.

Don Camillo sighed. "The bullet was within four inches of my forehead," said Don Camillo. "If I hadn't drawn my head back at that exact moment I should have been done for. It was a miracle."

Peppone had completed the Baby's face and was now working with pink paint on His body.

"I'm sorry I missed," he mumbled, "but I was too far off and the cherry trees were in the way." Don Camillo's brush ceased to move.

"Brusco had been keeping watch for three nights round the Pizzi house to protect the boy. The boy must have seen who it was that fired at his father through the window, and whoever did it knows that. Meanwhile I was watching your house. Because I was certain that the murderer must know that you also knew who killed Pizzi."

"The murderer: who is he?"

"I don't know," replied Peppone. "I saw him from a distance creeping up to the chapel window. But I wasn't in time to fire before he did. As soon as he had fired I shot at him and I missed."

"Thank God," said Don Camillo. "I know how you shoot, and we may say that there were two miracles."

"Who can it be? Only you and the boy can tell."

Don Camillo spoke slowly. "Yes, Peppone, I do know; but nothing in this world could make me break the secrecy of the confessional."

Peppone sighed and continued his painting.

"There is something wrong," he said suddenly. "They all look at me with different eyes now. All of them, even Brusco."

"And Brusco is thinking the same thing as you are, and so are the rest of them," replied Don Camillo. "Each of them is afraid of the others and every time any one of them speaks he feels as if he must defend himself."

"But why?"

"Shall we leave politics out of it, Peppone?"

Peppone sighed again. "I feel as if I were in gaol," he said gloomily.

"There is always a way out of every gaol in this world," replied Don Camillo. "Gaols can only confine the body, and the body matters so little."

The Baby was now finished and it seemed as if His clear, bright colouring shone

THE LITTLE WORLD OF DON CAMILLO   103

in Peppone's huge dark hands. Peppone looked at Him and he seemed to feel in his palms the living warmth of that little body. He forgot all about being in gaol.

He laid the Baby delicately upon the table and Don Camillo placed the Madonna near Him.

"My son is learning a poem for Christmas," Peppone announced proudly. "Every evening I hear his mother teaching it to him before he goes to sleep. He's a wonder!"

"I know," agreed Don Camillo. "Look how beautifully he recited the poem for the bishop!"

Peppone stiffened. "That was one of the most rascally things you ever did!" he exclaimed. "I shall get even with you yet."

"There is plenty of time for getting even, or for dying," Don Camillo replied.

Then he took the figure of the ass and set it down close to the Madonna as she bent over Her Child. "That is Peppone's son, and that is Peppone's wife, and this one is Peppone," said Don Camillo, laying his finger on the figure of the ass.

"And this one is Don Camillo!" exclaimed Peppone, seizing the figure of the ox and adding it to the group.

"Oh well! Animals always understand one another," said Don Camillo.

And though Peppone said nothing he was now perfectly happy, because he still felt in the palm of his hand the living warmth of the pink Baby; and for a time the two men sat in the dim light looking at the little group of figures on the table and listening to the silence that had settled over the Little World of Don Camillo, and that silence no longer seemed ominous but instead full of peace.

DON CAMILLO
AND THE
PRODIGAL SON

THE THIRTEENTH-CENTURY ANGEL

WHEN OLD BASSINI DIED they found written in his will: "I bequeath everything I have to the parish priest, Don Camillo, to be spent for gilding the angel on the church tower so that I can see it shining all the way from Heaven and recognize the place where I was born."

The angel was at the top of the bell tower and, from below, it did not appear to be very large. But when they had erected scaffolding and climbed up to see, they found it was almost the size of a man and would require quite an amount of gold leaf to cover it. An expert came from the city to examine the statue at close hand, and he came down a few minutes later in a state of great agitation.

"It's the Archangel Gabriel in beaten copper," he explained to Don Camillo. "A beautiful thing, straight from the thirteenth century."

Don Camillo looked at him and shook his head.

"Neither the church nor the tower is more than three hundred years old," he objected.

But the expert insisted that this didn't matter.

"I've been in business forty years, and I've gilded I can't tell you how many statues. If it isn't thirteenth-century, I'll do the job for you free."

Don Camillo was a man who preferred to keep his feet firmly on the ground, but curiosity drove him to climb with the expert to the top of the tower and look the angel in the face. There he gaped in astonishment, for the angel was very beautiful indeed. He, too, was agitated when he came down, because he couldn't imagine how such a work of art had come to be on the bell tower of a humble country church. He dug into the parish archives, but found no account of it whatsoever. The next day the expert came back from the city with two gentlemen who went with him to the top of the tower, and they backed up his opinion that the statue was beyond a shadow of doubt thirteenth-century. They were two professors in the line of art, two important names, and Don Camillo could not find words with which to thank them.

"It's quite wonderful!" he exclaimed. "A thirteenth-century angel on the tower of this poor little church! It's an honour for the whole village."

That afternoon a photographer came to take pictures of the statue from every possible angle. And the next morning a city newspaper carried an article, with three illustrations, which said it was a crime to leave such a treasure exposed to the four winds, when it was part of the nation's cultural heritage and should be kept under shelter. Don Camillo's ears turned crimson as he read.

"If those city rascals think we'll let them take our angel away, then they can think again," he said to the masons who were strengthening the scaffolding.

"That's right," said the masons. "It's ours, and nobody has a right to touch it."

Then some more important people arrived upon the scene, including representatives of the bishop, and as soon as they came down from looking at the angel they all told Don Camillo that it was a shame to leave it there, exposed to the weather.

"I'll buy him a raincoat," Don Camillo said in exasperation, and when they protested that this was an illogical thing to say he retorted with considerable logic: "In public squares all over the world statues have stood for centuries amid the raging elements and no one has dreamed of putting them under shelter. Why should we have to tuck our angel away? Just go and tell the people of Milan that the Madonnina on that cathedral of theirs is falling to pieces and they ought to take it down and put it under cover. Don't you know that they'd give you a good, swift kick if you suggested anything of the kind?"

"The Madonnina of Milan is a very different matter," said one of the important visitors.

"But the kicks they give in Milan are very much like those we give here!" Don Camillo answered, and because the villagers crowding around him on the church square punctuated his last remark with a "That's right!" no one pursued the subject further.

Some time later the city newspaper returned to the attack. To leave a beautiful thirteenth-century angel on the church tower of a valley village was a crime. Not because anyone wanted to take the angel away, but because the village could make good money from tourists if only it were in a more accessible place. No art-lover was going to travel so far, simply in order to stand in the square and gape up at a statue on top of a tower. They ought to bring the angel down into the church, have a cast made, and then an exact copy which they could gild and put in its place.

After people in the village had read that newspaper article, they began to mumble that there was something to it, and the local Communists, under the leadership of Mayor Peppone, couldn't very well miss the opportunity to comment on "a certain reactionary who should have been born in the Middle Ages." As long as the angel stayed up on the tower, no one could appreciate its beauty. Down in the church it would be in plain sight, and there would be no loss to the tower if another angel were to replace it. Don Camillo's most prosperous parishioners talked it over with him, and eventually he admitted that he might have been in the wrong. When the angel was taken down the whole village gathered in the square, and it had to be left there for several days because people wanted to see and touch it. They came from miles around, for word had spread that the angel had miraculous powers. When the time came to make the cast, Don Camillo said stubbornly: "The angel's not to budge. Bring your tools and do the job here."

After the settlement of old Bassini's estate, it was found that he had left enough money to gild a dozen angels, and so there was plenty to spend on the bronze copy. The copy itself finally arrived from the city, all covered with gold, and everyone proclaimed it a masterpiece. People compared the measurements, inch by inch, and found that they tallied exactly.

"If the original were gilded too," they said, "no one could tell them apart."

However, Don Camillo felt some scruples about his failure to carry out the terms of old Bassini's will.

"I'll have the original gilded, then," he said. "There's plenty of money."

But the people from the city intervened and said the original mustn't be tampered with. They presented a number of arguments, but Don Camillo had ideas of his own.

"It isn't a question of art," he insisted. "Bassini left me the money for the express purpose of gilding the angel on the tower. This is the angel he meant, and if I don't have it gilded, then I'm betraying his trust."

The new angel was hoisted to the top of the tower, and the experts proceeded to gild the old one. It was placed in a niche near the door, and everyone gaped at it in its shiny new dress.

The night before the unveiling of both statues, Don Camillo could not sleep. Finally he got up and went over to the church to look at the original angel.

"Thirteenth-century," he said to himself, "and this little church no more than three hundred years old! You existed four hundred years before the tower was built. How did you ever get up there?"

Don Camillo stared at the great wings of the Archangel Gabriel and ran his big hand over his perspiring face. How could a heavy copper angel like this one have flown up to the top of a tower? Now he stood in a niche, behind a glass door that could be opened and shut for protection. Impulsively Don Camillo took a key out of his pocket and opened the door. How could an angel that had lived on top of a tower stay shut up in a box? Surely he must be suffocating for want of air. And Don Camillo remembered the text of old Bassini's will: 'I bequeath everything I have to the parish priest, Don Camillo, to be spent for gilding the angel on the church tower so that I can see it shining all the way from Heaven and recognize the place where I was born."

"And now he doesn't see his angel at all," Don Camillo reflected. "He sees a false angel in its place. That isn't what he wanted."

Don Camillo was very troubled, and when that happened he went to kneel at the feet of Christ on the big cross over the altar.

"Lord," he said, "why did I cheat old Bassini? What made me give in to those rascals from the city?"

The Lord did not answer, and so Don Camillo went back to the angel.

"For three hundred years you've watched over this valley and its people. Or perhaps for seven hundred years. Who knows? For this church may have been built on the ruins of one much older. You have saved us from famine and plague and war. Who can say how many gales and bolts of lightning you have turned away? For three, or perhaps seven hundred years, you have given the village's last farewell to the souls of the dead as they rose up into Heaven. Your wings have vibrated to the sound of the bells, whether they called men to rejoice or to mourn. Yes, centuries of joy and sorrow are in your wings. And now you are shut up in a gilded cage, where you will never see the sky or the sun again. Your place has been usurped by a false city angel, whose only memories are the swear words of unionized foundry workers. You took shape from an unknown thirteenth-century craftsman with faith to inspire his hammer, while the usurper was turned out by some monstrously unholy machine. How can a pitiless, mechanical creature like that protect us? What does he care for our land and its people?"

It was eleven o'clock at night and the village lay wrapped in silence and fog from the river when Don Camillo went out of the church and into the darkness.

Peppone was not in a good humour when he answered the knock at his door.

"I need you," said Don Camillo. "Put on your coat and follow me."

When they were inside the church the priest pointed to the captive angel.

"He protected your father and mother and their fathers and mothers before them. And he must watch over your son. That means going back to where he was before."

"Are you mad?" asked Peppone.

"Yes," said Don Camillo. "But I can't do it alone. I need the help of a madman like you."

The scaffolding was still up all around the tower. Don Camillo tucked his cassock into his trousers and began to climb, while Peppone followed him with a rope and pulley. Their madness lent them the strength of a dozen men. They lassooed the angel, detached it from its pedestal and lowered it to the ground. Then they carried it into the church, took the original angel out of the niche and put the false one in its place.

Five men had worked at hoisting the false angel up to the top of the tower, but now the two of them managed to do it alone. They were soaked with fog and perspiration and their hands were bleeding from the rope.

It was five o'clock in the morning. They lit a fire in the rectory and downed two or three bottles of wine in order to collect their thoughts. At this point they began to be afraid. There was the angel, high above them, on top of the tower.

"It's impossible," said Peppone.

Suddenly he grew angry and turned upon Don Camillo.

"Why did you rope me into it?" he asked him. "What damned business is it of mine?"

"It isn't damned business at all," Don Camillo answered. "There are too many false angels loose in the world working against us already. We need true angels to protect us."

Peppone sneered.

"Silly religious propaganda!" he said, and went away without saying goodbye.

In front of his own door, something made him turn round and look up into the sky. There was the angel, shining in the first light of dawn.

"Hello there, Comrade!" Peppone mumbled serenely, taking off his cap to salute him.

Meanwhile Don Camillo knelt before the crucifix at the altar and said:

"Lord, I don't know how we did it!"

The Lord did not answer, but he smiled, because He knew very well how.

THE DANCE OF THE HOURS

LA ROCCA, THE TOWER which was the centre of the township and the seat of the Town Hall, was in a sad state of disrepair. When one day a squad of masons appeared upon the scene and began to throw up scaffolding round the tower, everybody said: "It's about time!"

It wasn't a question of looks, because in the Po River valley aesthetics matter very little, and a thing is beautiful when it is well made and serves its purpose. But everybody had occasion at one time or another to go to the Town Hall, and they didn't like the prospect of having a brick or a fragment of cornice fall upon their heads.

When the scaffolding was up, the masons swathed the façade with cloth so that no plaster would fall on the passers-by and then began the repairs. These went on for about a month, until one night everything was taken down, and the next morning the people of the village, along with a number of strangers who had come to the weekly market-day, found the tower completely restored. The masons knew their trade and had done a good job. Of course, they couldn't leave politics out of it and so they had hung up a big sign, near the top, which said: "*This public work was NOT financed by the Marshall Plan.*"

Don Camillo was among the crowd that had gathered in the square and when Peppone saw him he edged up behind his back and sprang on him the question: "Well, what have you got to say?"

Don Camillo did not even turn round. "A good job," he said. "Too bad that the looks of it should be ruined by that sign."

Peppone turned to a group of his gang, who just happened to be standing by.

"Did you hear? He says that the looks of the thing are ruined by the sign. Do you know, I very nearly agree!"

"Where artistic matters are concerned, the priest's word carries a lot of weight," Smilzo put in. "I think he's right."

They discussed it further, and finally Peppone said:

"Someone go and tell them to take down that sign. That'll prove we're not like certain people who claim to be infallible."

A couple of minutes later, someone loosened a rope, and the sign came down. And then appeared the real surprise: a magnificent new clock. For years and years the clock on the bell tower of the church had been the only public timepiece in the village, but now there was another on the Town Hall.

"You can't appreciate it fully in the daytime," Peppone explained. "But the dial is transparent and lighted from inside, so that by night you can read the time from a mile away."

Just then there was a vague noise from the top of La Rocca and Peppone shouted:

"Silence!"

The square was full of people, but they all fell silent to hear the new clock strike ten. Hardly had the echoes died away, when the clock on the church tower began to ring out the same hour.

"Wonderful," said Don Camillo to Peppone. "Only your clock is nearly two minutes fast."

Peppone shrugged his shoulders.

"One might just as well say that your clock is nearly two minutes slow."

Don Camillo did not lose his aplomb.

"One might just as well say so, but it's inadvisable. My clock is exact to the second, just as it has been for the last thirty or forty years, and there was no use in squandering public funds for a new one on the Town Hall."

Peppone wanted to say any number of things, but there so many he choked, and the veins of his neck stood out like ropes. Smilzo rushed into the breach, raising one finger.

"You're angry because you wanted to have a monopoly on time! But time doesn't belong exclusively to the clergy! It belongs to the people!"

The new clock struck a quarter past the hour, and once more the square was silent. First one and then two minutes went by.

"It's more inaccurate than before!" exclaimed Don Camillo. "Now it's a full two minutes fast."

People took big silver watches out of their vest pockets and began to argue. It was all very strange, because before this none of them had ever cared about minutes at all. Minutes and seconds are strictly city preoccupations. In the city people hurry, hurry so as not to waste a single minute, and fail to realize that they are throwing a lifetime away.

When the Town Hall clock struck half-past ten, and the bell tower followed, two minutes later, there were two schools of opinion. The conflict was not a violent one, because it remained within the circumference of the opposing parties' vest pockets. But Smilzo had warmed up to all the implications, and shouted:

"On the day when La Rocca clock strikes the hour of the people's revolution, some people are going to find out that they're not two minutes but two centuries behind!"

Smilzo always talked like that, but this time he made the mistake of shaking a threatening finger under Don Camillo's nose. And Don Camillo made an unequivocal answer. He stretched out his hand, pulled Smilzo's cap down over his eyes and then did the classical turn of the screw, leaving the visor at the back of his neck. Peppone stepped forward.

"What would you say if anyone played that trick on you?" he asked through his teeth.

"Try and see!" said Don Camillo. "No one's ever tried so far!"

Twenty hands dragged Peppone back.

"Don't do anything rash," they said. "The Mayor mustn't get into trouble."

The gang of Reds closed in on Don Camillo and began to shout. Don Camillo felt an urge to create some fresh air about him and a bench was the first fan that came into his hand. With his steam up and a bench in his grasp, Don Camillo was a cyclone. In a second there was an empty space around him, but since the square was packed with people and market-stands, an empty space at one point meant increased density at some other. A chicken cage was trampled, a horse reared, and there was a chorus of shouts, moos and whinnies. The Red gang was routed, but Peppone, who was squashed into the entrance of the Town Hall by people who didn't want him to get into trouble, managed to seize a bench in his turn. And Peppone, too, when his motor was running at high speed and he had a bench in his grasp, was a tornado that knew neither friend nor foe. The crowd stepped back, while Peppone slowly and fatefully advanced towards Don Camillo, who stood his ground, bench in hand. The crowd had retreated to the periphery of the square, and only Smilzo kept his head and threw himself in Peppone's way.

"Forget it, Chief! Don't behave like a donkey!"

But Peppone implacably advanced towards the centre of the square, and Smilzo had to back away as he delivered his warning. Suddenly he found himself between the two benches, but he stood firm and awaited the shock of the earthquake. The crowd was silent. The most desperate of the Reds had grouped themselves behind Peppone, and Don Camillo was backed up by a group of old peasants, who had a nostalgic longing for the blackjack, and now shook their stout cherry sticks at their opponents. There seemed to be a tacit agreement between both sides. As soon as Peppone and Don Camillo let go with their benches, there would be a free-for-all fight. There was a moment of deathly silence while the two protagonists brandished their weapons, and then something extraordinary happened. The old clock and the new both both started to strike eleven, and their strokes were in perfect synchronization.

The benches fell, and the empty middle of the square filled up with people. As if they were coming out of a dream, Don Camillo and Peppone found themselves in a busy market-place, where vendors were crying their wares. Peppone went off to the Town Hall and Don Camillo to the presbytery. Smilzo was left alone in the middle of the square, trying to puzzle out what had happened. Finally he gave up his attempt to understand, and since all the Reds had melted away he went over to a nearby stand and drank a Coca-cola.

RHADAMES

RHADAMES WAS THE SON of Badile, the locksmith, whose real name was Hernani Gniffa. Obviously an operatic family. Badile had a good ear, and when he had tucked away a bottle or two of wine he sang with a powerful voice that was a pleasure to hear. When Badile's son, Rhadames, was six years old, his father brought him to Don Camillo and asked to have him taken into the choir. Don Camillo tested the boy's voice and then said:

"The only thing I can do is set him to blowing the organ bellows." For Rhadames had a voice as hard and cutting as a splinter of stone.

"He's my son," said Badile, "so he must have a voice. It's still tight, that's all. What it needs is loosening up."

To say no would have meant giving Badile the worst disappointment of his life, and so the priest sighed and said, "I'll do my best."

Don Camillo did everything he could, but after two years Rhadames' voice was worse than ever. Besides being even harsher than before, it stuck in his throat. Rhadames had a magnificent chest, and to hear a miserable squeak come out of it was really infuriating. One day Don Camillo lost patience, got up from the organ and gave Rhadames a kick that landed him against the wall. Where singing is concerned, a kick may be more effective than three years' study of harmony: Rhadames went back to the choir and produced a voice that seemed to come straight from La Scala. When people heard him they said that it would be a crime for him to discontinue his studies.

This is the way they are in a village. If a fellow is disagreeable and unattractive they'll let him die of starvation. But if they take a liking to a fellow, they'll put together the money to get him singing lessons. In this case, they collected enough to send Rhadames to the city. Not to live like a gentleman—that couldn't be expected—but with his singing lessons paid for. And for the rest, Rhadames had to earn his board and keep by sawing wood, delivering parcels, and so on. Every now and then Badile went to see him and brought back the news: "He's not doing too badly. He's making progress."

Then the war came along and Rhadames was lost from sight. One day when it was all over he turned up in the village. Peppone was Mayor and, when Don Camillo told him that Rhadames' musical education must go on, he found the money to send him back to the city. A year or two later, Rhadames turned up again.

"They're letting me sing in *Aïda*," he said.

Things were tense in the village for political reasons, and violence was in the air, but because of this news hostilities were suspended. Peppone held a meeting at the Town Hall, and Don Camillo attended it. The first question that came up was how to raise funds.

"The honour of the village is at stake," Peppone explained.

"Rhadames mustn't cut a poor figure before those big shots in the city."

And the committee agreed.

"If anyone can get money out of those that have it," said Peppone, "I can guarantee the support of the common people."

Don Camillo understood that this was a gentle hint, and answered. "Somebody will do it."

Then Rhadames gave a detailed account of his needs, which was found quite satisfactory.

"Here there's no question of corruption or special favours," Peppone said proudly. "This is definitely a proletarian victory."

Don Camillo turned to Rhadames.

"What is your stage name?" he asked him.

"His stage name?" shouted Peppone. "His own, of course! Do you want him to assume yours?"

Don Camillo did not lose his temper.

"Rhadames Gniffa isn't the kind of name you can put on an opera programme.

It's a most unfortunate name, because it's bound to make people laugh."

Then Rhadames' father came into the discussion.

"My name is Hernani Gniffa, and I've borne it for sixty-five years without anyone's laughing!"

"That's all very well, but you're a locksmith, not a tenor!" Don Camillo answered. "Around here nobody cares, but in the theatrical world it's a different matter. There you need a name that sounds well and is sure to be popular."

"How ridiculous!" exclaimed Peppone. "Middle-class stupidity!"

Don Camillo looked at him hard.

"If Giuseppe Verdi had been called Rhadames Gniffa, do you think he would have won such fame as a composer?"

Peppone stopped to think, and Don Camillo gave him another example. "If Joseph Stalin had happened to be called Euripides Bergnocioni, would he have left the same mark on history?"

"The very idea!" stammered Peppone. "Think of Stalin under the name of Bergnocioni! Impossible!"

The committee sat until late at night, and finally made a unanimous choice of the name Franco Santalba.

"It's a queer world!" they all said.

Rhadames shrugged his shoulders. "Whatever you decide suits me all right," he said.

The great day came at last, and the committee met in the village square to read the announcement of the opera in the newspaper that had just arrived from the city. Rhadames' photograph was there, and under it the caption: "Franco Santalba, tenor." They couldn't resist going to hear him.

"There's room in the truck for all of us," said Peppone. "And we'd better make an early start in order to get seats. We'll meet here in the square at four o'clock."

"Somebody must tell the priest," one of the men observed. "He won't be able to come, but he ought to know about it."

"Priests don't interest me," said Peppone.

But they went to the presbytery in a body.

"I can't go, you know that," Don Camillo said sadly. "It wouldn't do for a priest to go to the opera, especially on the opening night. You'll have to tell me all about it."

When the committee had gone, Don Camillo went to confide his sorrow to Christ on the altar.

"I'm distressed that I can't go," he said with a sigh. "Rhadames is almost like a son to us all. But of course duty is duty. My place is here, and not amid the worldly frivolities of a theatre. . . ."

"Quite right, Don Camillo. One of those small sacrifices that you must accept cheerfully."

"Yes, of course from a general or absolute point of view, it's a small sacrifice," said Don Camillo. "But to the person concerned, it's a large one. Of course, the greater the sacrifice, the more cheerfully it should be accepted. Complaints take all the value of a sacrifice away. In fact, if a sacrifice brings out a complaint, it doesn't count as a sacrifice at all."

"Naturally," the Lord answered.

Don Camillo paced up and down the empty church.

"I developed the boy's voice," he explained, stopping in front of the altar. "He came not much higher than my knees, and he couldn't sing; he squeaked like a rusty chain. And now he's singing in *Aïda*. Rhadames in *Aïda*! And I can't hear him. Surely that's a tremendous sacrifice. But I'm bearing up very cheerfully."

"Certainly you are," the Lord whispered gently.

Peppone and his gang sat in the front row of the gallery with their heads whirling. To gain admission to the gallery, it's not sufficient to pay for a ticket; one has to fight for a seat as well. And when *Aïda*'s on the boards, the gallery is a mad-house. That evening, however, a burly man made his way through the crowd at the last minute and came in just behind Peppone. He was wearing a green coat, and Peppone seemed to know him, because he squeezed over on the bench and made a place for him.

"If Rhadames loses his nerve, he's out of luck," Peppone mumbled. "This is a merciless crowd."

"Here's hoping," said the burly man in the green coat.

"If they hiss him, I'll kill somebody," said Peppone excitedly, and the man in the green coat motioned to him to keep his head.

But they didn't whistle; they were kind enough simply to snigger. Towards the end of the first act, things got worse and worse. Rhadames grew really scared and sang off key. The gallery howled, vigorously enough to make the curtain tremble. Peppone clenched his teeth, and his stalwarts were ready to sow murder round them. But the burly man took Peppone by the collar and dragged him outside. They walked up and down in the fresh air, and, when they heard a howl, they knew that Rhadames had hit still another false note. Then at the sound of the triumphal march the audience began to calm down. Shortly before the third act, the burly man said to Peppone: "Let's go."

The attendants didn't want to admit them behind the scenes. But before two strapping men with the combined strength of an armoured division, there was nothing to do. They found Rhadames waiting in terror to be howled off the stage for the third and last time. When he saw the two men, his jaw fell open. The man in the green coat went behind and gave him a kick powerful enough to launch a Caruso.

Rhadames practically sailed through the air on to the stage, but he was completely transformed when he got there. When he sang the great aria "*Io son disonorato!*" the theatre almost broke down under the applause.

"You've got to know a singer down to the bottom," the burly man said triumphantly to the hysterical Peppone.

"Yes, Don . . ." Peppone started to reply, but at one look from the burly man he broke his sentence off in the middle.

THE STUFF FROM AMERICA

THE PARTY DELEGATE was one of those gloomy, tight-lipped persons who seem to have been just made for wearing a red scarf round the neck and a tommy-gun slung from one shoulder. The reason for his visit to the village was to *galvanize* and *activate* the local section of the Party. He made endless speeches to the cell leaders, for when these gloomy, tight-lipped fellows start talking politics they are as long-winded as the late Adolf Hitler. He stayed three whole days, and on the morning of the third day, when he had finished laying down the latest Party line, he said to Peppone:

"On Saturday you're to call a meeting of the village Council and announce that you're resigning from the post of Mayor."

"Have I done so badly?" stammered Peppone.

"No, Comrade; you've done so well that you're to be promoted. You're to run for Parliament on the People's Front programme."

"Me run for Parliament?"

"Yes, that's what I said."

"But I haven't any education . . ."

"You know how to obey, Comrade, don't you? All a deputy to Parliament needs to know is how to obey Party orders. And you're sure to attract votes. You're known all over the province for the way you hustle round and get things done."

Peppone threw out his arms.

"But what about my own village?"

"Do you care more for the community than for Communism?"

Peppone bowed his head.

"Of course you'll have to make some campaign speeches. But we'll send you those, don't worry. You can just learn them by heart."

While the delegate was giving him further instructions as to how to conduct his campaign, Smilzo burst breathlessly into the room.

"The stuff from America is here!" he shouted. "I mean the foodstuff. There are posters up to announce that the needy can call at the presbytery for relief parcels. Spaghetti, tinned milk, preserves, butter and sugar. The posters have created quite a sensation."

"What's the exact wording of the announcement?" the delegate asked him.

"*The fatherly heart of His Holiness . . . etc.. . . . etc.. . . . parcels which all the needy are entitled to receive upon application to the parish priest, Don Camillo . . . etc.. . . . etc.. . .*"

"*All* the needy, did you say?"

"Yes, all of them, without distinction."

Peppone clenched his fists.

"I knew that devil was cooking up something," he said. "They speculate in human misery, the filthy cowards. We'll have to deal with it somehow."

"Yes, Comrade, deal with it!" the delegate ordered. "Call a meeting of the cell leaders."

When the cell leaders had hastened to answer the call, Peppone told them of the latest reactionary manoeuvre.

"Within half an hour the comrades must hear that if one of them accepts so much as a safety-pin I'll strangle him for it. Smilzo, you stand guard in front of the presbytery. Keep your eyes peeled every minute and take down the names of all those who go to pick up parcels."

"Well spoken," the delegate said approvingly. "A case like this requires decisive action."

All day long there was a line in front of the presbytery. The priest was jubilant, because the parcels were plentiful and well filled and people were happy to get them.

"Tell me if the so-called People's Party gives you anything better," he said, laughing.

"They give nothing but tall talk," everyone answered.

Some of the Reds were needy enough, but they didn't come. This was the only fly in the priest's ointment, because he had prepared a special homily for their benefit. "You haven't any right to this, since you have Stalin to look after you. But take a parcel just the same, Comrade, and here's luck to you!" When none of the Reds put in an appearance and the priest was told that Smilzo was standing behind a bush, taking down the name of everyone that went away with a parcel, he realized that he would have to keep his homily to himself. By six o'clock in the evening all the "regular" needy had been taken care of and there were left only the parcels meant for "special cases." Don Camillo went into the church to talk to the Lord.

"See here, Lord, what do You think of that?"

"I see, Don Camillo, and I must admit I find it touching. Those people are just as poor as the rest, but they're putting Party loyalty above their hunger. And so Don Camillo has lost a chance to deliver some sarcastic remarks at their expense."

Don Camillo lowered his head.

"Christian charity doesn't mean giving the crumbs from your table to the poor; it means dividing with them something that you need yourself. When Saint Martin divided his cloak with a beggar, that was Christian charity. And even when you share your last crust of bread with a beggar, you mustn't behave as if you were throwing a bone to a dog. You must give humbly, and thank him for allowing you to have a part in his hunger. To-day you simply aped the part of an altruist and the crumbs you distributed were from someone else's table. You had no merit. And instead of being humble, you had poison in your heart."

Don Camillo shook his head. "Lord," he whispered, "just send some of those poor Reds to me. I won't say a thing. I don't think I'd really have said anything before, either. You'd have shown me the light before I could say it."

Then he went back to the presbytery and waited. After an hour had gone by, he closed the door and the front window. But after another hour he heard a knock at the door. The priest ran to open it, and there was Straziami, one of Peppone's most loyal followers, looking just as frowning and glum as ever. He stood silently at the entrance for a moment and then said:

"I don't think any better of you and your friends, and I intend to vote as I please. So don't pretend I misled you."

The priest barely nodded. Then he took one of the remaining parcels out of the cupboard and handed it to him. Straziami took it and tucked it away under his coat.

"Tell me the truth, Father," he said ironically. "You might very well make a good joke out of the sight of Comrade Straziami sneaking in for a relief parcel from America."

"Go out through the garden," was all the priest said in reply, and he lit the butt of his cigar.

Peppone and the Party delegate were having supper when Smilzo came to report.

"It's quarter past eight, and the priest has gone to bed."

"Is everything in good order?" asked Peppone.

"On the whole, yes," Smilzo said with some hesitation.

"Speak up, Comrade," said the delegate harshly. "Tell us the entire story."

"Well, all day long there was just the usual crowd, and I got all the names. Then just a quarter of an hour ago, a latecomer went into the rectory and it was too dark for me to see who he was."

Peppone clenched his fists.

"Out with it, Smilzo! Who was he?"

"It looked like one of our people to me . . ."

"Which one?"

"It looked like Straziami. But I can't swear to it."

They finished their supper in silence, and then the delegate stood up. "Let's investigate," he said. "Such things need prompt attention."

Straziami's little boy was pale and thin, with big eyes and hair that tumbled over his forehead. Small for his age, he looked a lot and said little. Now he sat at the kitchen table and stared with wide-open eyes at his father, who was glumly opening a jar of fruit.

"That's for dessert," said his mother. "First have your spaghetti and tinned milk."

She brought the bowl to the table and stirred its steaming contents, while Straziami went to sit down by the wall, between the fireplace and the cupboard. From this vantage-point he gazed with a kind of wonder at his son, whose eyes roved in bewilderment from his mother's hands to the jar of fruit and then to the tin of milk on the table.

"Aren't you coming to supper?" the woman said to Straziami.

"I don't want anything to eat," he mumbled.

She sat down opposite the boy and was just about to fill his plate with spaghetti when Peppone and the Party delegate threw open the door. The delegate looked at the spaghetti and examined the label on the milk and the jar of fruit.

"Where did you get this stuff?" he said harshly to Straziami, who had risen hesitatingly to his feet.

He waited in vain for an answer. Then he calmly gathered the four corners of the tablecloth into his hand, picked it up and threw it out of the window. The little boy trembled, holding both hands in front of his mouth and staring at the delegate with terror. The woman had taken refuge against the wall and Straziami stood in the middle of the room with his arms hanging at his sides, as if he had been turned into stone. The delegate closed the window, walked over to Straziami and struck him across the face. A thread of blood trickled out of one corner of Straziami's mouth, but he did not move. The delegate went to the door and then turned round to say:

"That's Communism for you, Comrade. And if you don't like it, you can leave it."

His voice aroused Peppone, who had been gaping from one corner of the room as if the whole thing were a dream. They walked away in silence through the dark countryside, and Peppone could hardly wait to get home. In front of the inn the delegate held out his hand.

"I'm leaving at five o'clock to-morrow morning," he said. "You've got everything straight, haven't you? On Saturday you resign and put Brusco in your place. You're to make your first speech at Castellino, and to-morrow you'll receive the main body of the text. You can insert references to local conditions in the blank spaces. Good night, Comrade."

"Good night."

Peppone went straight to Smilzo's.

"I'll beat him up," he said to himself, but when he reached the door he hesitated and retraced his steps. He found himself in front of the presbytery, but there he did not linger either.

"That's Communism for you, Comrade. And if you don't like it, you can leave it." The delegate's words were imprinted on his mind. At home he found his own son still awake in his crib, smiling and holding out his arms.

"Go to sleep," Peppone said brusquely. He spoke in so harsh and threatening a voice that no one, not even he himself, could have suspected that he was thinking of the wide-open eyes of Straziami's son.

In the room at the inn the Party delegate's mind was quite empty. He was fast asleep, satisfied with both himself and his Communism. But there was still a frown on his face, because Communists are on duty even when they are sleeping.

A MATTER OF CONSCIENCE

For some time Peppone had been bringing the hammer down on the anvil, but no matter how accursedly hard he struck it, he could not get a certain tormenting thought out of his mind.

"The fool!" he mumbled to himself. "He's going to make things worse!"

Just then he raised his eyes and saw the fool standing before him.

"You scared my boy," Straziami said gloomily. "He was restless all night long, and now he's in bed with fever."

"It's your own fault," said Peppone, hammering away, with his eyes on his work.

"Is it my fault that I'm poor?"

"You had orders, and Party orders have to be obeyed without discussion."

"Hungry children come before the Party."

"No, the Party comes before everything."

Straziami took something out of his pocket and laid it on the anvil.

"I'm turning in my card. It doesn't stand for Party membership any more; it just means that I'm under special surveillance."

"Straziami, I don't like your way of talking."

"I'll talk as I choose. I won my freedom at the risk of my own skin, and I'm not going to give it up so lightly."

Peppone put down the hammer and wiped his forehead with the back of one hand. Straziami was one of the old guard; they had fought side by side, sharing the same hunger and hope and despair.

"You're betraying the cause," said Peppone.

"Isn't the cause freedom? If I give up my freedom, then I'm betraying the cause."

"We'll have to throw you out, you know. You're not allowed to resign. If you turn in your card, you'll be thrown out."

"I know it. And anyone that cheats too much is thrown out three months before he does it. To think that we have the face to call other people hypocrites! So long, Peppone. I'm sorry that you'll have to consider me your enemy when I'll still look on you as a friend."

Peppone watched Straziami walk away. Then he took hold of himself, threw the hammer into the corner with a loud curse, and went to sit in the garden at the back of the workshop. He couldn't get used to the idea that Straziami had to be thrown out of the Party. Finally he jumped to his feet.

"It's all the fault of that damned priest," he decided. "Here's where I get him."

The "damned priest" was in the presbytery leafing through some old papers, when Peppone came in.

"I hope you're happy!" Peppone said angrily. "At last you've managed to hurt one of our people."

Don Camillo shot him a curious glance.

"Is the election affecting your mind?" he asked.

"Proud of yourself, aren't you? Just to have ruined a fellow's reputation, when this social system of yours has given him nothing but trouble."

"Comrade Mayor, I still don't understand."

"You'll understand well enough when I tell you that it's all your fault if Straziami is thrown out of the Party. You took advantage of the fact that he's so poor and lured him to accept a filthy food parcel from America. Our Party delegate got wind of it and caught him at his own house, red-handed. He threw the food out of the window and struck him across the face."

It was clear that Peppone was highly excited.

"Calm yourself, Peppone," said the priest.

"Calm yourself, my foot! If you'd seen Straziami's boy when the food was prac-tically taken off his plate and he watched his father being struck, you wouldn't be calm. That is, not if you had any feelings."

Don Camillo turned pale and got up. He asked Peppone to tell him again exactly what the Party delegate had done. Then Don Camillo shook an accusing finger in Peppone's face.

"You swindler!" he exclaimed.

"Swindler yourself, for trying to take advantage of poor people's hunger and get them to vote for you!"

Don Camillo picked up an iron poker standing up in one corner of the fire-place.

"If you open your mouth again, I'll slaughter you!" he shouted. "I haven't speculated on anybody's starvation. I have food parcels to distribute and I haven't denied them to anyone. I'm interested in poor people's hunger, not their votes. You're the swindler! Because you have nothing to give away except printed papers full of lies, you won't let anyone have anything else. When somebody gives people things they need you accuse him of trying to buy votes, and if one of your followers accepts, you brand him as a traitor to the people. You're the traitor, I say, because you take away what someone else has given. So I was playing politics, was I? Making propaganda? Straziami's boy and the children of your other poor comrades who haven't the courage to come for food parcels don't know that they come from America. These children don't even know that there is such a place. All they know is that you're cheating them of the food they need. You'd say that if a man sees that his children are hungry he's entitled to steal a crust of bread for them to eat, but you wouldn't let him take it from America. And all because the prestige of Russia might suffer! But tell me, what does Straziami's boy know about America and Russia? He was just about to tuck away the first square meal he's seen for some time when you snatched it out of his mouth. I say that you're the swindler."

"I didn't say or do a thing."

"You let another man do it. And then you stood by while he did something even worse, while he struck a father in the presence of his child. A child has complete confidence in his father; he thinks of him as all-powerful and untouchable. And you let that double-faced delegate destroy the only treasure of Straziami's unfortunate boy. How would you like it if I were to come to your house this evening and beat you in front of your son?"

Peppone shrugged his shoulders. "You may as well get it out of your system," he said.

"I will!" shouted Don Camillo, livid with rage. "I'll get it out of my system, all right." He grasped both ends of the poker, clenched his teeth and with a roar like a lion's bent it double.

"I can throw a noose around you and your friend Stalin as well," he shouted. "And after I've got you in it, I can pull it tight, too."

Peppone watched him with considerable concern and made no comment. Then

Don Camillo opened the cupboard and took out of it a parcel which he handed to Peppone.

"If you're not a complete idiot, take this to him. It doesn't come from America, or England, or even Portugal, for that matter. It's a gift of Divine Providence, which doesn't need anybody's vote to rule over the universe. If you want to, you can send for the rest of the parcels and distribute them yourself."

"All right. I'll send Smilzo with the truck," muttered Peppone, hiding the parcel under his coat. When he reached the door he turned round, laid the parcel on a chair, picked up the bent poker and tried to straighten it out.

"If you can do it, I'll vote for the 'People's Front,' " leered Don Camillo.

Peppone's effort made him red as a tomato. The bar would not return to its original shape, and he threw it down on the floor.

"We don't need your vote to win," he said, picking up the parcel and going out.

Straziami was sitting in front of the fire reading the paper, with his little boy crouched beside him. Peppone walked in, put the parcel on the table and untied it.

"This is for you," he said to the boy, "straight from the Almighty." Then he handed something to Straziami: "And here's something that belongs to you," he added. "You left it on my anvil."

Straziami took his Party membership card and put it into his wallet.

"Is that from the Almighty too?" he asked.

"The Almighty sends us everything," muttered Peppone, "the good along with the bad. You can't ever tell who's going to get what. This time we're lucky."

The little boy had jumped to his feet and was admiring the profusion of good things spilled out on the tablle.

"Don't worry; no one will take it away from you," Peppone said reassuringly.

Smilzo came with the truck in the afternoon.

"The chief sent me to pick up some stuff," he said to Don Camillo, who pointed out the parcels waiting stacked up for him in the hall.

When Smilzo came to pick up the last lot of them, Don Camillo followed him as he staggered under his loads and gave him a kick so hearty that both Smilzo and half of his parcels landed in the truck.

"Make a note of this along with the list of names you gave to the Party delegate," Don Camillo explained.

"We'll settle with you on election day," said Smilzo, extricating himself from the confusion. "Your name is at the head of another list of ours."

"Anything more I can do for you?"

"No. But I still don't understand. I've had the same treatment from Peppone and Straziami already. And all because I carried out an order."

"Wrong orders shouldn't be carried out," Don Camillo warned him.

"Right. But how can one know ahead of time that they're wrong?" asked Smilzo with a sigh.

WAR TO THE KNIFE

DON CAMILLO HAD SOMETHING on his mind that would give him no peace. It all began the day he met the "live corpse," a young man who had supposedly died after fighting in the mountains with Peppone and his men during the Resistance. Don Camillo himself had officiated at the funeral and followed the coffin to the cemetery. Then one day in the city after the war was over, Don Camillo caught a glimpse of this same young man who was far from being dead as mutton.

But it wasn't the walking corpse that bothered Don Camillo. He discovered that the coffin had contained, not a dead body, but a collection of loot seized from the Germans. He also knew that Peppone and his men had used the loot to finance the building of their People's Palace; and just because he had run across this useful bit of information, as well as the walking corpse, he had been able to persuade Peppone and his followers to make a modest contribution to the building of a Recreation Centre for the children of the village. And there the matter rested. The People's Palace was built and the Recreation Centre had a swing which was the delight of the children—especially Peppone's son, who played on it by the hour, chirping joyfully like a fledgling. But the question that troubled Don Camillo was how Peppone's men had managed to smuggle the coffin containing the loot out of the cemetery in the first place without attracting attention.

The cemetery served the whole township and was therefore fairly large. It lay outside the village and was built on the conventional plan—that is, enclosed by four walls, one of which had an entrance gate. These walls were bare and plain on the outside, while on the inside they formed an arcade over rows of tombs.

In order to solve the mystery, Don Camillo took upon himself the role of Sherlock Holmes. He went to examine the cemetery. Halfway down the left-hand arcade, in the second row, he found the famous niche, bearing a marble tablet on which was carved the fake name of the fake corpse. He turned his back on the niche and proceeded to walk straight through the grassy plot, studded with crosses, until he came to the central aisle. There he wheeled round in the direction of the gate and counted the number of steps it took him to reach it. The next day he walked inconspicuously along the path running parallel to the outside of the left wall, once more counting his steps, and when he had counted enough of them he stopped to light the butt of a cigar. The wall was overgrown with vines, but an attentive eye could see that about three feet above the ground, at a point corresponding to the niche the priest had inspected the day before, there was a section of plaster of a lighter colour than the rest. And Don Camillo's eye was an attentive one.

"This is the way the treasure came out, and where one object came out another can go in. The thing about holes is that they allow two-way traffic."

He continued his walk, stopping in front of the police station to chat with the sergeant. That night the police quietly made a hole in the cemetery wall, at the point where Don Camillo had noticed the different shade of plaster, and out of the niche they took one machine-gun, thirty-eight tommy-guns, and twenty-three pistols, all of them so shiny and carefully oiled that they would have tempted any hot-head to launch the "second phase of the revolution" then and there. The news created quite a stir and even got into the big-city papers, but no one came to claim the guns. At that point the story had seemed to fizzle out, because Don Camillo took care to make no reference to anything that had happened.

"When God gives you an inch, don't take a mile," he said to the police sergeant, when the latter tried to get something more out of him. "You ought to be glad you've got the guns."

"I can't be so easily satisfied. Now that I've found them I feel I must find the dead man whose place they were taking."

"I understand, but I wouldn't worry about him, Sergeant," Don Camillo advised him. "The guns are more important. After all, they can shoot, and that's more than a dead man can do."

Peppone, of course, had no comment to make, but he was about as easy in his mind as a man who has swallowed a mouse.

"*He* must have done it," he shouted to Brusco. "No one would dig a hole in a tomb unless he was sure there was nobody in it. But I'll make him pay."

He, of course, was Don Camillo, who continued to be extremely discreet. All he did was to plaster the walls of the "People's Palace" and Peppone's workshop with signs reading:

FOUND

Near the local cemetery, the corpse of the "second phase of the Revolution." Claimants apply to the police.

Five days later the village woke up to find itself covered with big yellow posters bearing the following notice:

LOST

Six hundred pounds of dried foods and tinned groceries consigned by the Regional Relief Committee to the priest, Don Camillo for distribution to the needy. If Don Camillo finds these goods, will he please turn them over to their rightful owners.
                                                    Signed: *The Village Needy.*
                              Death to all thieves!

Don Camillo rushed indignantly to the police station.

"I'll report them!" he shouted. "I'll report and accuse them, every one! This is an outrage!"

"Who's to be accused?" asked the sergeant. "The notice is signed 'the village needy'."

" 'Needy' indeed! The village riffraff! Peppone and his gang are at the bottom of this."

"That may be. But we have only your word for it. Go ahead and file your complaint, and then we'll investigate."

Don Camillo started to go home, but in the square he pulled down the first poster that caught his eye and tore it into small pieces.

"Go on! Tear it up!" a man shouted to him from a bicycle. "But truth will out!"

And a ragged and dishevelled woman added her cries to his:

"Look at the priest's bulk!" she jeered. "He's grown fat on the food he stole from the poor!"

Don Camillo went his way, and a little farther on he met Filotti.

"Do you see what I see, Signor Filotti?" he asked him.

"Yes, I see," answered Filotti calmly. "But you mustn't let it bother you. I'm sure you can clear yourself. If I were you, I'd put up a poster reproducing your receipts for the groceries and the list of the persons to whom you distributed them."

"What receipts? What groceries?"

"The groceries from the Regional Relief Committee."

"But I didn't receive anything!" Don Camillo shouted. "And I didn't know such a committee existed!"

"Good Heavens! Is that possible?"

"It's more than possible; it's the literal truth! I never received a single thing!"

"How's that? It's unbelievable that anyone should make up a story of the kind. But if you say so, it must be true . . ."

Farther along the way Don Camillo ran into Signor Borghetti, who was reading the poster through spectacles perched on the end of his nose.

"This is a wicked world, Don Camillo," he said, shaking his head.

Old Barchini, the printer, was standing at the door of his shop.

"I didn't print it," he explained. "If they'd given me the job, I'd have told you about it. What about these groceries, Don Camillo? Are these the goods we were supposed to get from the Bishop?"

Just then Peppone's truck went by with Smilzo at the wheel.

"Here's a good appetite to you!" he called out, and everyone laughed.

Don Camillo ate no lunch. At three o'clock he was still lying on his bed and staring up at the beams of the ceiling. At four o'clock an infernal clamour rose from the church square and he looked out to see what was happening. There was an enormous crowd below, and, as might have been expected, the front ranks were filled by women. Don Camillo found most of their faces unfamiliar, and he thought of Smilzo and the truck.

"They've picked up roughnecks from all the surrounding villages," he said to himself. "They know how to organize. I'll grant them that."

"We want our groceries!" the women and children shouted. "Down with the exploiters of the people!"

"I've nothing to give you," shouted back Don Camillo from the window. "Because no one gave anything to me. It's a miserable lie!"

"We want to see for ourselves," a woman shouted, shaking her fists at him. "If you have nothing to hide, let us see!"

The crowd surged against the presbytery door, and Don Camillo withdrew from the window and took his shotgun down from the wall. Then he laid it on the bed and went to look again. The police sergeant and six of his men were standing guard at the presbytery door. But the crowd seemed to have gone wild and was still clamouring to get in. At this point Peppone stepped forward.

"Quiet," he shouted. "I have something to say."

The crowd kept silence, and Peppone looked up at the window.

"Don Camillo," said Peppone, "I am speaking as Mayor. This is no time to argue about whether what the poster says is false or true. These people feel that they have been cheated and they are justified in protesting. In order to avoid bloodshed, you must allow a committee to inspect the presbytery. The committee will include myself and the village Council and also the police sergeant with his men."

"Bravo!" shouted the crowd.

Don Camillo shook his head.

"There's nothing to see," he said. "This is my house, and I won't have it invaded. The poster was a lie from beginning to end; I'll swear to that on the Gospel."

"Swear to it on the cupboard where you've stowed away six hundred pounds of our groceries!" the crowd shouted. "You're not going to get away with it so easily."

Don Camillo shrugged his shoulders and stepped back. The crowd threw itself against the policemen and threatened to engulf them. But the sergeant kept his presence of mind and fired a shot into the air. The crowd retreated far enough for the police to pull themselves together and take a new position of defence.

"Stay where you are, or I'll have to use force of arms!" shouted the sergeant.

The crowd hesitated, then moved slowly but resolutely forward. The policemen paled, clenched their teeth and loaded their guns. Just as it looked as if events might take a tragic turn, Don Camillo raised his hand.

"Stop!" he shouted. "I'm coming to open the door."

When he came to open it the committee was ready. There were thirty members in all—Peppone and his Councillors and the police sergeant with four of his men. They made a mercilessly thorough search, opening every chest of drawers and cupboard and cabinet, tapping the walls and floors, sounding every bottle and barrel in the cellar and exploring under the eaves, up the chimney, and in the woodshed. Even if anything so small as a needle had been the object of their search, they would surely have found it. All the food they discovered in the kitchen amounted to three eggs, a loaf of bread, and a rind of cheese. And in the cellar, two salami sausages and two gourds full of lard hung from the ceiling. Don Camillo stood by with folded arms and an indifferent air. After they had fingered the mattresses they said they wanted to examine the bell tower and the church. The sergeant turned pale, but Don Camillo led the way, and let the committee look into the sacristy and the confessionals and under the altar. They did not touch anything, but insisted upon nosing everywhere. Finally, with nothing to show for their pains, they left the house, with their heads hanging. They conferred for a while with the crowd, and finally the latter melted away.

Don Camillo ate no supper either. He lay for a while on his bed, gazing up at the beams of the ceiling, then when he could see them no longer he went into the church and knelt before the altar.

"Lord, I thank you," he murmured.

But there was no reply. Now whenever this happened Don Camillo acquired a fever and went on a diet of bread and water for days and days, until the Lord felt sorry for him and said: "Enough." But this time he hadn't had even bread and water so he went back to his room. There were two windows in this room; one looked out on the village square and the other on the presbytery garden. The latter was still wide open, and hanging out of it was a blanket that had been put there to dry earlier in the day. He pulled the blanket in, revealing three nails in the outside wall of the house, each one with a tommy-gun strung to it. He pulled in the guns and put them in a sack. Then he went to the cellar and took down one of the two sausages and the gourds. Only one of the sausages was stuffed with pork, and both gourds contained heavy yellow grease with cartridges embedded in it. He added a sausage and both gourds to his sack, climbed over the garden hedge and walked across the fields until he came to the river. There he got into a boat, rowed out past that spit of land known locally as the Island and threw the sack into the water. After that, he went back to kneel in front of the altar.

"I thank You, Lord," he whispered again. "I thank You for not having let them find the things I have just thrown away. Those are what they were after. They wanted to make a sensational story out of their discovery. I thank You not for my sake, but for having saved the reputation of the Church."

"Very well, Don Camillo. But I told you many times before to throw those things away."

Don Camillo sighed.

"Here I am, stripped of everything, with only an old shotgun that would scare nothing bigger than an owl for a weapon. How am I to defend myself?"

"With your honesty, Don Camillo."

"No," said the priest. "You saw to-day for Yourself that honesty is no defence. Peppone and his gang knew what they were really looking for, but the others shouted against me just because of a false accusation intended to persuade them that I was a thief. My honesty was no help at all. And it won't do any good in the future. They don't know I've got rid of the guns, and because they were thwarted in their plan to disgrace me they'll continue their war to the knife against me. But I'll . . ."

He threw out his chest and clenched his big fists. Then he relaxed, lowered his head and bowed low.

"I'll do nothing at all. The lie has been sown by now, and I'm known as 'the priest who grows fat on the food of the poor.' "

As he said this, the thought came to him that he hadn't eaten all day and so he closed the church for the night and went to the presbytery cellar. There he reached for the sausage with the intention of eating a slice or two for a late supper. But his knife struck something hard.

"I threw the good salami away with the guns, and here I am with one full of cartridges," he said to himself with a melancholy smile.

After a sad meal consisting of a rind of cheese he went to bed. Meanwhile, in the darkness of his own room, Peppone was thinking of the meagre contents of Don Camillo's cupboard: three eggs, a loaf of bread, and a piece of cheese. He turned over and over in his bed, unable to close his eyes. Then he remembered the two sausages hanging in the cellar. "Well, he'll have a bite of sausage," he muttered to himself, and went to sleep with an easy conscience.

THE POLAR PACT

THOSE WERE THE DAYS when there was a great deal of argument about that piece of international political machinery known as the "Atlantic Pact," which may have owed its name to the fact that between words and deeds there lies the breadth of an ocean. Peppone took the whole proposition as a personal insult. He was so thoroughly incensed by the American "saboteurs of peace" that if it had been within his power he would have declared war upon the United States without an instant's delay. He was in this state of boiling frenzy when he saw Don Camillo pass by with his nose in his breviary, and from the workshop door threw at him an oath violent enough to make anyone's hair stand up on end.

Don Camillo stopped and raised his eyes. "Did you call me?" he asked mildly.

"I was speaking to God," said Peppone threateningly. "Do you think you are the Deity in person?"

"No, I don't. But since God hasn't time to listen to you, say what you have to say to me."

Although Peppone could hardly wait to declare war on the United States, he didn't want to open hostilities with an attack upon Don Camillo, who stood all too close by and held in one hand a piece of steel cable he had just picked up from the ground. There was no point in being blessed by a priest who wielded an aspergillum like that, and so he contented himself with shrugging his shoulders. Fortunately, at this very moment, a tractor clanked up and came to a halt between them, and Peppone turned his attention to the driver's tale of woe.

"There's something wrong," said the driver. "The motor spits and kicks back. It must be the timing."

Now Peppone, in addition to being Mayor, was the village mechanic—in fact he was the best mechanic within miles. He could work wonders with machinery of all kinds, but in this case the tractor was a Fordson and Peppone looked at it with distaste, pointing the handle of his hammer at the plate bearing the words "Made in U.S.A."

"The U.S.A. and I are through with each other," he said. "If you want to get this piece of junk fixed, go and see the priest. He's the one that's in with the Americans."

Don Camillo had just resumed his walk, but he turned back slowly. He peeled off his overcoat and gave it, along with his hat and breviary, to the driver. Then he rolled up his sleeves and began to tinker with the motor.

"Give me a pair of pincers," he said and the driver got one out of his tool-box. Don Camillo worked for a few minutes longer and then stood up straight. "Start it going," he said.

The man stepped on the starter.

"Like clockwork," he said happily. "How much do I owe you, Father, for your trouble?"

"Not a penny," said Don Camillo. "It's included in the Marshall Plan!"

A moment later the tractor pulled away. Peppone was left gaping, and Don Camillo opened his breviary under his nose.

"Read this and tell me what it means," he said, pointing to a sentence on the page.

Peppone shrugged his shoulders.

"My Latin won't take me that far," he mumbled.

"Then you're a donkey," Don Camillo said calmly, continuing his walk. He had got grease up his nose, but he was proud of it.

This incident was a trifling matter, but it put Peppone in a very bad humour. That evening, when he had gathered his stalwarts together in the People's Palace, he shouted that something must be done to show the indignation of the masses over the signing of the infamous Atlantic Pact.

"We must take over and occupy some important place," he exclaimed in conclusion. "It's got to be a spectacular protest."

"Chief," said Smilzo, "we already occupy the People's Palace and the Town Hall. Our children occupy the school and our dead the cemetery. All that's left for us to occupy is the church."

"Thanks!" said Peppone. "And if we occupy it, what do we do next? Say Masses to compete with those of the Vatican? No, we must occupy a place that will benefit the whole people. Brusco, do you get what I mean?"

Brusco caught on at once.

"Good," he said. "When do we start moving?"

"Right away. Before midnight all our people must be put on the alert. They must move in waves, beginning at two o'clock, and by five the whole Island must be ours."

Just at the village the river broadened to such an extent that it seemed like a patch of sea, and there lay the place known as the Island. It was not an island, really, but a strip of land fifty feet offshore running parallel for about half a mile to the mainland, and attached to it at the lower end by a spit or tongue of muddy earth almost submerged by water. The Island was not cultivated, but was given over to a grove of poplars. That is, the poplars grew of their own accord, and every now and then the owner, Signor Bresca, came to mark with a knife those which were to be cut down and sold.

Peppone and his followers had said for some time that this was a typical example of abandoned and neglected private property and that it ought to be turned over to the workers for development as a co-operative farm. Its occupation had been put off from one day to another, but now the time had come.

"We'll oppose the 'Atlantic Pact' with a 'Polar Pact' of our own!" Peppone exclaimed on the evening of this historic decision.

It seems that, in spite of appearances, the word "Polar" in this case was derived from the River Po. It was a strictly local and proletarian term, with no reactionary

Latin pedigree. Surely it was time to do away with Julius Caesar, and the ancient Romans, who together with the clergy used Latin to pull the wool over the people's eyes. At least, this was Peppone's answer to someone who objected on etymological grounds to his idea of giving a Party newspaper the name of "The Polar Call."

"The days of etymology are over," Peppone told him. "Every word is making a fresh start."

In any case, the "Polar Pact" was put into action, and at seven o'clock the next morning Don Camillo was warned that Peppone and his men had occupied the Island. The "men" were actually for the most part women, but, be that as it may, they were cutting down poplars as fast as they could, one after another. One tree, higher than the rest, had been plucked like a chicken neck and now served as a pole from which the Red Flag fluttered happily in the April breeze.

"There's going to be trouble," the messenger told Don Camillo. "Someone's called for special police from the city. Peppone has started to cut the connecting spit of land and says he'll hold out there indefinitely. If you don't do something there's no telling where the trouble will end."

Don Camillo pulled on a pair of rough twill trousers, rubber boots and a hunter's jacket, for he knew that the Island was a sea of mud.

Peppone was on the spot, standing with his legs far apart, directing the cutting of the channel. At first he failed to recognize Don Camillo; then he pretended not to; but in the end he couldn't help bursting out with: "Did you disguise yourself so as to spy on the enemy's camp?"

Don Camillo came down from the river bank, plunged halfway up his legs into the mud, crossed the channel and arrived in front of Peppone.

"Drop all that, Peppone," he pleaded; "the police are on their way from the city."

"Let them come!" Peppone answered. "If they want to get over here, they'll have to borrow the United States Navy!"

"Peppone, it's only fifteen yards from the shore to the Island, and bullets can travel."

"It's only fifteen yards from the Island to the shore, for that matter," said Peppone sombrely, "and we have bullets too."

Peppone was really in a bad fix, and Don Camillo knew it.

"Listen," he said, pulling him to one side, "you have a right to be a fool and behave like one if you want to. But you have no right to involve these other poor devils in your folly. If you want to be sent to prison, stand your ground and shoot. But you can't compel the rest of them to be sent along with you."

Peppone thought for a minute or two and then shouted: "The others can do as they please. I'm not forcing anybody. Those who want to stick it out can stay."

The men who were digging the channel stopped and leaned on their shovels. They could hear a roar of motors from the main road.

"The jeeps of the special police," Don Camillo said in a loud voice. And the men looked at Peppone.

"Do as you please," Peppone muttered. "Democracy allows every man to follow his own will. And here on the Island we have democracy!"

Just then Smilzo and the other Comrades arrived upon the scene. Smilzo shot a curious glance at Don Camillo.

"Is the Vatican sticking its nose into things again?" he asked. "You'd better make yourself scarce, Father; it's going to be hot around here."

"Heat doesn't bother me," Don Camillo answered.

A cloud of dust rose from the road.

"They're here," said the shovellers. With which they threw down their shovels and made their way ashore. Peppone looked at them with scorn.

There were six jeeps in all, and the police inspector stood up and called out to the men who were hacking at the underbrush on the Island: "Move on!"

They went on hacking, and the inspector turned to one of his aides.

"Perhaps they didn't hear," he said. "Play some music!"

His aide fired a volley of shots into the air, and the Islanders raised their heads.

"Get moving!" the inspector shouted.

Peppone and his henchmen grouped themselves at one end of the channel. Some of the men who had been working behind them crossed over. When they reached the shore they scattered to right and left, skirting the jeeps that were in their way. About a dozen die-hards continued to cut down the underbrush. Peppone and his men fell into line, forming a wall along the canal, and stood there with folded arms, waiting.

"Move on! Clear out!" came a shout from the bank.

No one budged, and the police got out of their jeeps and started down the river bank.

The veins of Peppone's neck were swollen and his jaw was set. "The first one to lay hands on me will get strangled," he said darkly.

Don Camillo was still there beside him, forming part of the living wall.

"For the love of God, Peppone," he murmured, "don't do anything rash."

"What are you doing here?" Peppone asked him, startled.

"Doing my duty. I'm here to remind you that you're a thinking being and therefore have got to think things out clearly. Come on, let's go!"

"Go ahead! I've never run away in my life, and I never will."

"But this is the law!"

"It's your law, not mine. Go on and obey it."

The police were down beside the river, just opposite the Island.

"Clear out!" they shouted.

Don Camillo tugged at Peppone's sleeve.

"Let's go!"

"I won't move out of here alive. And the first one to lay hands on me gets his skull cracked!"

The police repeated their injunction and then began walking through the mud. When they came up against the wall of men they repeated it again, but no one moved or gave any answer.

A sergeant grabbed hold of Peppone's jacket and would have come to a very bad end if Don Camillo hadn't pinned Peppone's arms down from behind.

"Let go!" he muttered between his clenched teeth.

Don Camillo had on the same sort of trousers and boots and jacket as the rest, and when the police started laying about them he got one of the first blows and was sorely tempted to let Peppone go, and to pitch some of the attackers into the water. Instead, he took it without batting an eyelash. More blows fell on his head and on those of Smilzo and the others. But no one said a word. They held on to each other and took it in silence. Finally, they had to be hauled away like rocks, but none of them had opened his mouth or moved a finger in revolt.

"They're crazy in this village," the inspector grumbled. By now the Island was empty, because the few men who were left had escaped in boats. The police got into their jeeps and drove away.

Don Camillo, Peppone, and the others sat silently on the shore, gazing into the water and at the Red Flag waving from the plucked poplar.

"Father, you've got a bump as big as a walnut on your forehead," said Smilzo.

"You don't need to tell me," said Don Camillo. "I can feel it."

They got up and went back to the village, and that was the end of the "Polar Pact."

THE PETITION

DON CAMILLO WAS WALKING quietly along the Low Road toward the village, smoking his usual cigar when, just round a curve, he came upon Peppone's gang. There were five of them, and Smilzo was in charge. Don Camillo looked at them with frank curiosity.

"Are you planning to attack me?" he asked them. "Or have you some better plan in mind?"

"Don't you dare incite us to violence!" said Smilzo, taking a sheet of paper out of an envelope and unfolding it before him.

"Is this for the last wishes of the condemned man?"

"It's for everyone to sign who wants peace," said Smilzo. "If you don't sign, then you don't want peace. From now on, honest men and warmongers are going to be clearly divided."

"Don Camillo examined the dove printed at the top of the paper.

"I'm an honest man," he said, "but I'm not signing. A man who wants peace doesn't have to testify to it with his signature."

Smilzo turned to Gigo, who was standing beside him.

"He thinks this is a political move," he said. "According to him, everything we do is tied up with politics."

"Look, there's no politics in this," put in Gigo. "It's just a question of preserving peace. Peace is good for all political parties. It will take plenty of signatures to get us out of the Alantic Pact, and if we don't get out, it's going to land us in war, as sure as shooting."

Don Camillo shook the ashes off the end of his cigar.

"You'd better make yourselves busy," he said. "If I'm not mistaken, you haven't even started."

"Of course not. We wanted you to have the honour of being the first name on the list. That's only natural. When peace is at stake, the clergy ought to take the lead."

Don Camillo threw out his arms. "It can be taken for granted that the clergy's in favour of peace, so it's just as if my signature were there."

"Then you're not going to sign?"

Don Camillo shook his head and walked away.

"If we're saddled with a clergy of this kind, then we'll have to fight not one war, but two," Smilzo said bitterly, putting the paper back in the envelope.

A little later, Peppone arrived at the presbytery door.

"No politics involved," he declared. "I'm here in the capacities of Mayor, citizen, father of a family, Christian, and honest man."

"Too many people!" exclaimed Don Camillo. "Too big a crowd! Come in just as Peppone, and leave the rest outside."

Peppone came in and sat down.

"We've come to the ragged edge," he began. "If honest men don't stick together, the world's headed for a smash-up."

"Sorry to hear it," Don Camillo answered seriously. "Is there anything new?"

"Only that if we don't safeguard peace, everything's going to ruin. Let's leave politics and parties out of it and all get together."

Don Camillo nodded. "That's the way I like to hear you talk," he said. "It's about time you cut loose from that brood of Satan."

"I said we'd leave politics out of it," retorted Peppone. "This is a time for thinking in world-wide terms."

Don Camillo looked at him with astonishment, for he had never heard him mouth such big ideas.

"Do you want peace or don't you?" asked Peppone. "Are you with Jesus Christ or against Him?"

"You know the answer."

Out of his pocket Peppone took the envelope and paper that Don Camillo had seen earlier in the day.

"When it comes to fighting for peace, the clergy must be in the front line," he asserted.

Don Camillo shook his head. "You're changing the rules of the game. Didn't you say politics weren't in it?"

"I'm here as a plain citizen," Peppone insisted.

"Very well then, as one citizen to another, I tell you I'm not caught." And as Peppone started to rise excitedly to his feet, he added: "You know very well that if I sign your paper, a lot of other signatures will follow. Without me, you can only hope for those of your own people, and many of them can't write their own names. Since you see that I'm not to be taken in, put that pigeon back in your pocket and hand me two glasses from the sideboard. Otherwise, you and your pigeon and your cause of peace may as well all go back where you came from."

Peppone tucked the paper away.

"Since you're giving yourself such airs," he said proudly, "I'll show you that I can get all the signatures I want without yours as an attraction."

Smilzo and the rest of the "peace gang" were waiting outside.

"Start making the rounds," said Peppone. "But go to our people last. Everyone's got to sign. Peace must be defended; with blows if necessary."

"Chief, if I go jail, what will happen?" Smilzo asked him.

"Nothing will happen. A man can serve the cause perfectly well in jail."

These words were not exactly comforting. But Smilzo set out, with the gang at his heels, strengthened by some reinforcements from the People's Palace.

Now when people have haystacks and vineyards and fields, it's almost impossible for them to say no to a fellow who asks them to sign for peace and swears that politics don't enter into it. And in a village the first five or six signatures are what count. It took several evenings to cover the whole area. But there were no arguments, except from Tonini, who shook his head when they showed him the paper.

"Don't you want peace?"

"No," said Tonini, who was a fellow with hands as big as shovels. "I happen to like war. It kills off a lot of rascals and clears the air."

Here Smilzo made a very sensible observation.

"Still you know, of course, that more honest men are killed off than rascals."

"But I care even less for honest men."

"And what if you get killed yourself?"

"I'd rather be killed than sign a paper. At least, when you die, you know where you're going."

The gang started to come forward, but Tonini picked up his shotgun, and Smilzo said he needn't bother.

Everything else went smoothly, and when Peppone saw the sheets full of signatures, he was so happy that he brought his fist down on the table hard enough to make the People's Palace tremble. He compared the peace list with the village census and found that they tallied. The mayors of the neighbouring villages complained that they couldn't get people to sign because the reactionaries obstructed them. There had been shooting at Castelina and fisticuffs at Fossa for a whole day. And to think that Smilzo, after taking an hour to persuade each of the first five or six signatories, had won over the rest without a murmur.

"It's the prestige I enjoy as Mayor," said Peppone, and he gathered together the papers and went to savour his triumph.

Don Camillo was reading a book when Peppone appeared before him.

"The power of the clergy is on the decline!" Peppone announced to him. "I thank you in the name of the world's democracies for not having signed. Your signature wouldn't have brought in half as many others. It's too bad for the Pope, that's all." And he added, spreading his papers out on the table, "America's done for! The Atlantic Pact is no good, because we have a totality of votes against it. And everywhere else it's going to go the same way."

Don Camillo scrutinized the lists carefully. Then he threw out his arms. "I'm sorry to tell you, but one signature is missing. Tonini's. So you can't claim a 'totality.'"

Peppone laughed.

"I have all the rest," he said. "What's one against eight hundred?"

Don Camillo opened a drawer, took out some papers, and scattered them in front of Peppone.

"You have signatures against the Pact and I have signatures in its favour."

Peppone opened his eyes wide.

"Russia's done for," said Don Camillo. "Because I have Tonini's signature along with the rest."

Peppone scratched his head.

"There's nothing so remarkable about it," Don Camillo pointed out. "I worked by day, and your men went around by night, when people were already softened up. As a matter of fact, they were glad to sign for you, because that cancelled their signing for me. The only one who didn't like it was Tonini, because I had to knock his head against a wall. But I advise you not to go after him, because he says that before he'll sign another petition he'll shoot to kill."

Peppone took his papers away. And so it was that in Don Camillo's village America triumphed by a majority of one, all on account of Tonini.

A SOLOMON COMES TO JUDGMENT

ONE DAY, AFTER DON CAMILLO and Peppone had settled a slight misunderstanding to the mutual satisfaction of both, the Mayor turned to the priest and said, "There's no sense in turning everything in life into a tragedy. If we reason things out, we can always compromise."

"Right you are," said Don Camillo warmly. "Why did God give us brains if He didn't expect us to reason?"

The two men parted on this note, and a few days later something happened in the valley which clearly proves that man is a reasoning creature, especially when it comes to living peacefully with his neighbour. First, however, you need to know the local geography of the little world or you won't understand a thing about it.

The Po River rolls on its mighty way without so much as an if-you-please and on either side it is fed by countless streams and tributaries. The Tincone is one of these little streams. Now the Molinetto road, running parallel to the Po, connects the tiny communities of Pieve and La Rocca. At a certain point the road crosses the Tincone. Here there is a bridge; it is, in fact, a structure of some size because at this point the Tincone is fairly wide, being only a mile or so away from where it flows into the big river. Pieve and La Rocca are each about three miles from the bridge over the Tincone, which is, indeed, the boundary line between them.

This is the topography of the story, and its point of departure is the problem of public education. The school that served both communities was at La Rocca, and for the people of Pieve this was a serious matter. Every day their children had to travel six miles, and six miles are thirty thousand feet, even in the flat river valley. Children can't resist taking short-cuts, and since the road they travelled was straight as an arrow, the short-cuts always led them a longer way round.

One day a committee of women from Pieve came to the Mayor of the whole township, Peppone, and announced that unless they were given a schoolhouse of their own they wouldn't send their children to school. Now the township was about as rich as a travelling rabbit and a new school would have entailed not only building costs, but double the amount of teachers' salaries as well. So, having by hook or crook raised some funds, Peppone decided to build the new schoolhouse at the bridge over the Tincone, halfway between Pieve and La Rocca, and send the children from both communities there. But at this point the problem became thorny.

"That's all very well," they said at La Rocca, "as long as it's on our side of the bridge."

"All well and good," they said at Pieve, "but of course it must be on our side."

To be exact, both of them were in the wrong (or in the right, as you prefer), because the real halfway point was not on either side of the bridge, but in the middle.

"You don't want the school built on the bridge, do you?" Peppone shouted, after a long discussion with committees from both villages.

"You're the Mayor," they answered, "and it's up to you to find a fair solution."

"The only real solution would be to lead you all to the bridge, tie millstones round your necks and throw you into the water," said Peppone. And he wasn't so wrong either.

"It's not a question of a hundred yards one way or the other," they told him. "Social justice is at stake." And that silenced the Mayor very effectively, because whenever he heard the phrase "social justice," Peppone drew himself up as if he were witnessing the miracle of creation.

Meanwhile trouble began to brew. Some boys from La Rocca went by night to the bridge and painted a red line across the middle. Then they announced that anyone from Pieve would find it healthier to stay on his own side. The next evening, boys from Pieve painted a green line parallel to the red one and intimated that anyone from La Rocca would be better off at home. The third evening, boys from both villages arrived at the middle of the bridge at the same time. One of those from La Rocca spat over the green line and one of those from Pieve spat over the red one. A quarter of an hour later, three boys were in the river and five had severe wounds on the head. The worst of it was that of the three boys in the river, two were from Pieve and only one was from La Rocca, so to even up the score another boy from La Rocca would have to be thrown in. And of the five boys with head wounds, three were from La Rocca and two from Pieve and so another boy from Pieve needed a beating. All, of course, for the sake of social justice.

The number of head wounds and boys thrown into the river increased daily, and soon the numbers were swelled by grown men, both old and young. Then one day Smilzo, who hung about the bridge as an observer, brought Peppone a piece of really bad news.

"There's been a fist fight between a woman from Pieve and a woman from La Rocca."

Now when women get mixed up in an affair of this kind, the trouble really starts. Women are always the ones to stick a gun into the hand of husband, brother, lover, father or son. Women are the plague of politics, and alas, politics are about ninety-five per cent of the world's occupation. So it was that knives were drawn and shots began to fly.

"Something's got to be done," said Peppone, "or else we shan't need a school, but a cemetery."

Apart from the fact that there's more to be learned in the cool grave than in a schoolroom, this was no joking matter, and Peppone handled it in masterful fashion. Out on the Po there had lain for years an old floating water mill, made of two big hulks with the millwheel between and a cabin bridging them over. Peppone had these towed under the central arch of the bridge across the Tincone. He chained them to the supporting columns and then remodelled them in such a way as to make them into one, joined by gangplanks to both banks of the river. So it was that one day there was a solemn opening of the new floating school. A large crowd was present, including a group of newspapermen from the big city.

The only accident ever recorded took place when Beletti, a boy who had to repeat the third grade for six years in succession, threw his teacher into the water. But this did not upset Peppone.

"Italy is in the middle of the Mediterranean," he said, "and everybody must know how to swim."

THUNDER ON THE RIGHT

PEPPONE'S PASSION TO show moving-pictures was inherited straight from his father. His father, too, was mechanically minded, and he had brought the first threshing-machine to the Valley, as all the old inhabitants remembered very well. Young people may laugh because they fail to see any connection between moving pictures and a threshing-machine. But the young people of to-day are benighted creatures born with their telephone numbers imprinted on their brains, and where passion is concerned they have about as much grace as a pig in a cornfield.

In the old days electric power was a luxury confined to the city, and since a moving-picture projector has to be run electrically, country people had no chance to see any pictures. But Peppone's father mounted a dynamo on the steam engine that powered the thresher, and when his machine wasn't needed in the fields he hitched two oxen to it and went from village to village, giving picture shows. So many years have gone by that the young people of to-day can't possibly visualize a steam engine drawn by two oxen. It was painted green with magnificent bands of shiny brass around it and had an enormous fly-wheel and a tall chimney, which was lowered while it was travelling from one place to another. It didn't smell or make any noise, and it had a very wonderful whistle.

So Peppone's ambition to show moving-pictures was quite legitimately in his blood. As soon as the auditorium of the newly built "People's Palace" was at his disposal, this was the first thing that came into his mind. One fine morning the village awoke to find itself plastered with posters announcing the opening of the moving-picture season at the People's Palace the next Sunday.

Now Don Camillo's father had never even thought about going round the countryside to show moving-pictures, but for some time Don Camillo had been set upon the idea of acquiring a projector for his Recreation Centre and Peppone's announcement made his stomach turn over. He was somewhat consoled on Sunday by a fierce storm and a flood-like downpour of rain. At ten o'clock in the evening he was still waiting to hear what had happened when his friend Barchini, dripping but happy, appeared at the door.

"There were only a few waifs and strays at the People's Palace," Barchini told him. "The rain kept the people from the outskirts away. What's more, the lights kept going on and off, and finally they had to stop the show. Peppone was fit to burst."

Don Camillo went to kneel before the Lord on the altar.

"Lord, I thank You . . ." he began.

"What for, Don Camillo?"

"For sending a storm and disrupting the electric current."

"Don Camillo, I had nothing to do with the lights going off. I'm a carpenter, not an electrician. And as for the storm, do you really think that Almighty God would inconvenience winds, clouds, lightning and thunder simply in order to prevent Peppone from showing his pictures?"

Don Camillo lowered his head.

"No, I don't really think so," he stammered. "We men have a way of thanking God for anything that falls in with our plans, as if it had come to pass just for our pleasure."

At midnight the storm died down, but at three o'clock in the morning it came back more fiercely than before, and an unearthly noise awakened Don Camillo. He had never heard a crash so loud and so close, and when he reached the window and looked out he was left gaping. The spire of the church tower had been struck by lightning and cleft with jagged rents. It was just as simple as all that, but to Don Camillo it was so incredible that he rushed to tell the Lord about it.

"Lord," he said in a voice shaky with emotion, "the church spire has been struck by lightning."

"I understand, Don Camillo," the Lord answered calmly. "Buildings are often struck that way in the course of a storm."

"But this was the church!" Don Camillo insisted.

"I heard you, Don Camillo."

Don Camillo looked up at the crucified Christ and threw out his arms in dismay.

"Why did it have to happen?" he asked bitterly.

"A church spire has been struck by lightning in the course of a storm," said the Lord. "Does God have to justify Himself for this in your sight? A short time ago you thanked Him for sending a storm that damaged your neighbour, and now you reproach Him because the same storm has damaged you."

"It hasn't damaged me," said Don Camillo. "It has damaged the house of God."

"The house of God is infinite and eternal. Even if every planet in the universe were to be reduced to dust, the house of God would still stand. A church spire has been struck by lightning; that is all anyone is entitled to think or say. The lightning had to strike somewhere."

Don Camillo was talking to the Lord, but during the conversation the thought of the mutilated tower was uppermost in his mind.

"Surely that particular stroke could have stayed away," he said. And the Lord took pity on his sorrow and continued to reason gently with him:

"Calm yourself, Don Camillo, and think it out clearly. God created the universe, and the universe is a perfect and harmonious system, in which every element is indissolubly bound, whether directly or indirectly, to all the rest. Everything that happens in the universe is necessary and fore-ordained, and if this stroke of lightning had not fallen exactly where and when it did, the harmony of the universe would have been troubled. This harmony is perfect, and if the lightning struck at this time and place, then it is a meet and right thing and we must thank God for it. We must thank Him for everything that takes place in the universe, for everything is a proof of His infallibility and the perfection of His creation. The stroke of lightning had to fall just where it did and not an inch in any other direction. The fault is man's, for having chosen to build the tower in that place. He could quite as well have built it a couple of yards farther off."

Don Camillo thought of his mutilated tower and there was bitterness in his heart.

"If everything that happens in the universe is fore-ordained and a manifestation of God's will, and otherwise the system would not be perfect, then the church tower had to be built where it is and not a couple of yards farther off."

"Yes, it could have been built a couple of yards farther off," the Lord assured him, "but then man would unconsciously have violated God's law. And that God didn't allow."

"Then there's no free will," protested Don Camillo.

The Lord continued to speak with great gentleness.

"Woe to the man who out of anger or grief or sensual excitement forgets those things that deep down inside he cannot help but know. God points out the right way, but man has a choice of whether to follow it or not. In His infinite kindness, God leaves man free to choose the wrong way and yet, by repentance and recognition of his mistake, to save his soul. A church spire has been struck by lightning in the course of a storm. The lightning had to strike there, and so the man who built the tower is to blame. Yet the tower had to be built where it is and man must thank God for it."

Don Camillo sighed.

"Lord, I thank You. But if with Your help I manage to put up another spire, I am going to arm it with a lightning conductor."

"Yes, Don Camillo, if it is fore-ordained that you are to put a lightning conductor on the tower, then you will surely do so."

Don Camillo bowed his head. Then in the first light of dawn he climbed up to examine the damaged tower more closely.

"Exactly," he said to himself at last. "The tower had to be built just where it is!"

Soon people began to crowd into the square to see the tower. They stood there in the torrential rain and looked at it in bewilderment, without speaking. When the square was full, Peppone and his crew appeared on the scene. He pushed his way to the front of the crowd and stood there for some time staring at the sight. Then he solemnly pointed one finger to the sky.

"Here is a proof of God's wrath!" he exclaimed. "This is God's answer to your boycott. Lightning strikes where God wills, and God wills it to accomplish a purpose."

Don Camillo listened from the presbytery window. Peppone spied him there and pointed him out to the crowd.

"The priest is silent," he shouted, "because the lightning struck his church. If it had struck our People's Palace, he'd have plenty to say."

Smilzo looked up at Don Camillo too.

"This is God's answer to the warmongers!" he shouted. "Hurrah for Mao Tse-tung!"

"Hurrah for peace and the Confederation of Labour!" chorused his followers.

Don Camillo counted to fifty-two before saying what was boiling up inside him. Then he said nothing. He took a half-smoked cigar out of his pocket and lit it.

"Look at that!" shouted Peppone. "Nero fiddling while Carthage burns!"

With which slightly garbled historical reference, he and his gang stalked proudly away.

Toward evening Don Camillo took his bitterness to the altar.

"Lord," he said at the end of his prayer, "what maddens me is to hear those scoundrels speak of Your divine wrath. I wouldn't dream of destroying the harmony of the universe, but after the blasphemous things they said this morning it would serve them right if lightning were to strike their People's Palace. Their blasphemies were enough to provoke divine wrath in earnest!"

"You're indulging in somewhat loose talk yourself, Don Camillo," said the Lord mildly. "Have you the face to inconvenience God in all His majesty just in order to knock down the four walls of a village shack? You must respect your God more than that, Don Camillo!"

Don Camillo went back to the presbytery. The distance was a short one, but at night, even within the space of a few steps, there's no telling what may happen. It was still raining, and at midnight the rain was coming down harder than ever. At one o'clock the stormy cacophony of the night before was repeated, and at two a clap of thunder aroused the whole village. By 2.10 everyone was awake, because a building in the square was afire, and the building was the People's Palace. When Don Camillo arrived the square was crowded with people, but Smilzo and his followers had already extinguished the flames. The roof had caved in, most of the framework was destroyed and the rest was a heap of smouldering ashes. Don Camillo edged up as if by accident to Peppone.

"A neat job," he observed casually. "Lightning seems to have a conscience."

Peppone wheeled around.

"Have half a cigar?" said Don Camillo.

"I don't smoke," answered Peppone darkly.

"You're quite right. The People's Palace is doing enough smoking. But I'm sorry. If you don't smoke, how can I say 'Nero fiddling while Carthage burns'? Only, for your information, it wasn't Carthage, it was Rome."

"That's good news! With every priest in it, I trust!"

Don Camillo shook his head and said gravely and in a loud voice: "You mustn't provoke God's wrath. Don't you see what you've brought upon yourself with the sacrilegious words you uttered this morning?"

Peppone almost jumped out of his skin with rage.

"Don't lose your temper," Don Camillo advised him. "The Marshall Plan might help you out."

Peppone stood face to face with Don Camillo, his fists clenched.

"The roof will be repaired in a few days," he shouted. "We don't need any plans; we'll take care of it ourselves."

"Good for you, Mr. Mayor," said Don Camillo, dropping his voice. "That way you can kill two birds with one stone. When you get the Council to appropriate money for the People's Palace, you can allot something for the repair of the church tower as well."

"Over my dead body!" said Peppone. "Ask your Americans for that. The People's Palace is a public utility, and the church is a private corporation."

Don Camillo lit the butt of his cigar.

"It was a fine stroke of lightning," he observed; "much more powerful than mine. It made a magnificent noise and did quite a bit of damage. Someone really ought to study it from a scientific point of view. I think I'll speak to the police sergeant about it."

"Keep your nose in your own dirty business," said Peppone.

"My business is to get you to repair the church tower."

Peppone shot him a sombre look.

"All right," he said between clenched teeth. "But some day I'll settle accounts with you."

Don Camillo started back to the presbytery. There was nothing more to see or to say. He meant to go straight home, but he knew that the Lord was waiting for him.

"Don Camillo," said the Lord severely, when the priest stood before him in the half-dark church. "Aren't you going to thank Me because the People's Palace was struck by lightning?"

"No," said Don Camillo, with his head hanging. "A stroke of lightning is part of the natural order created by God. Surely God wouldn't inconvenience winds, clouds, lightning and thunder simply in order to please a poor devil of a country priest and knock down the walls of a village shack."

"Exactly," said the Lord. "and how could God take advantage of a storm to throw a bomb on to the roof of the People's Palace? Only a poor devil of a country priest could think of a thing like that."

Don Camillo held out his arms.

"Yes, Lord, but even in this shameful deed there is evidence of God's mercy. If the poor devil of a country priest, tempted by Satan himself, hadn't tossed a bomb on to the roof of the People's Palace, then the case of dynamite hidden in the Palace attic wouldn't have exploded, and its presence there was a menace. Now the menace has been eliminated and the poor devil of a country priest has found a way to have the spire of his church tower properly replaced. Moreover, an individual who took the Lord's name in vain has received the punishment he deserved."

"Don Camillo," said the Lord, "are you sure you did the right thing?"

"No," Don Camillo replied. "God leaves man free to choose between right and wrong. I did wrong, I admit it, and I shall repent."

"Aren't you repentant already?"

"No, Lord," whispered Don Camillo. "It's still too early. I must ask for an extension."

The Lord sighed, and Don Camillo went off to bed. In spite of his guilty conscience, he slept like a log and dreamed that there was a gleaming gold spire on the church tower. When he woke up, he thought happily of his dream. But he realized that he had forgotten one very important thing. So he dropped off to sleep again and dreamed that on the gleaming spire there was a wonderful lightning conductor.

RED-LETTER DAY

BARCHINI, THE VILLAGE printer and stationer, had been ill for some time, and there was no one to replace him in the shop, for his was the sort of business where "boss" and "workers" are combined in one and the same person. So it was that Don Camillo had to hire someone in the city to print his parish magazine, and when he went back to read the proofs he amused himself by poking about among the machines.

The devil is a rascal who has no respect for anything or anybody, and plays his tricks not only in night-clubs and other so-called resorts of perdition, but also in places where honest men are at work. In this case, the devil was lurking near the machine where a man was printing letterheads, and when Don Camillo got out to the street he found himself in a pretty pickle. Since the flesh is notoriously weak and even the most honourable of parish priests has some flesh and blood in his make-up, what was Don Camillo to do when, upon his return to the village, he found his pockets stuffed with five or six sheets of writing paper bearing the address of the provincial headquarters of a certain political party?

A few days later Peppone was surprised to receive a registered letter with a city postmark and on the back the name Franchini, which he had never heard before. Inside there was a letterhead which made him instinctively draw himself to attention.

DEAR COMRADE,—Of course, you are already acquainted with the latest American betrayal, a secret clause in the nefarious Atlantic Pact which compels the other conspiring nations to watch over their democratic parties and sabotage any efforts on behalf of peace. Since we are under watch by the police, it is folly to put our Party name on our envelopes, that is, except when we actually want the police to find out about something. When the time comes you will receive detailed rules for the conduct of your correspondence.

We are writing to you to-day about a delicate and stricty confidential matter. Comrade, the capitalists and clergy are working for war. Peace is under attack, and the Soviet Union, which alone has the benevolent power to defend it, needs the help of active friends.

The Soviet Union must be ready to bear the onslaught which the Western world is preparing to launch against it. The sacred cause of Peace needs men of unshakeable faith and professional ability, ready to discipline themselves for action. We are so sure of you, Comrade, that the Special Committee for Political Action has unanimously decided to admit you to the inner sanctum. Here is a piece of news that should fill you with pride and joy: you are to be sent to the Soviet Union, where your mechanical talents will be put to work in the cause of Peace.

The Socialist Homeland will accord to the members of the Peace Brigade the rights and privileges of a Soviet citizen. We call this to your attention as one more sign of our Soviet comrades' generosity.

Instructions as to the day of departure and the equipment you should take with you will follow. You will travel by air. In view of the delicacy of this matter, we order you to destroy this letter and to send your reply to the comrade whose name and address are on the envelope. Take good care. To-day, more than ever, the sacred cause of Peace is in your hands. In the expectation of a prompt reply . . .

For the first time in his life Peppone disobeyed a Party order. He did not burn the letter. "This is the most eloquent testimonial I have ever received from the Party," he said to himself. "I can't part with an historical document of this kind. If some fool should ever question my merits I'll wave this in his face and make him bite the dust. There's nothing more powerful than the printed word."

He read the letter over any number of times, and when he knew it by heart he added: "I've worked hard, certainly, but this is a great reward!" His only regret was that he could not exhibit the letter. "Now," he said, "I must write an answer in equally historic terms, an answer that will bring tears to their eyes. I'll show them what kind of feelings I have in my heart, even if I never went past the third grade in school." That evening he sat down in the cellar to work over his reply.

COMRADE,—I overflow with pride to be chosen for the Peace Brigade and awate further Party orders. Let me anser with the Socialist cry, "I obey!" like the red-shirt Garibaldi, even if my first impulze is to go rite away. I never asked a favor befor, but now I ask to be alowed to be the first to go.

Peppone read this over and saw that it needed a bit of polish and punctuation. But for a first draft it would do very well. There would be time enough to make a second draft the next day. No need to hurry. It was more important to write the kind of a letter that would be published in the Party papers with a note from the Editor above it. And he calculated that three drafts would do the job.

As Don Camillo was smoking his cigar and admiring the beauties of spring one evening on the road that led to the mill, he found Peppone in his path. They talked about the time of day and the weather, but it was obvious that there was something Peppone wanted to get off his chest and finally he came out with it.

"Look here, I'd like to talk to you for a minute as man to man instead of as man to priest."

Don Camillo stopped and look at him hard.

"You've made an unhappy start," he observed, "by talking like a donkey!"

Peppone made an impatient gesture.

"Don't let's talk politics," he said. "I'd like you to tell me, as man to man, what you think of Russia."

"I've told you that eighty thousand times," said Don Camillo.

"We're quite alone, and no one can overhear us," Peppone insisted. "For once you can be sincere and leave political propaganda out of it. What's it like in Russia, anyhow?"

Don Camillo shrugged him shoulders.

"How should I know, Peppone?" he said. "I've never been there. All I know is what I've read about it. In order to tell you anything more, I'd have to go and see for myself. But you ought to know better than I."

"Of course I do," Peppone retorted. "Everyone's well off in Russia; everyone has a job. The Government is run by the people, and there's no exploitation of the poor. Anything the reactionaries say to the contrary is a lie."

Don Camillo looked at him sharply.

"If you know all that, why do you ask me about it?"

"Just to get your man-to-man opinion. So far I've always heard you talk strictly as a priest."

"And I've always heard you talk as a *comrade*. May I hear your man-to-man opinion as well?"

"To be a comrade means to be a man. And I think as a man just the same that I think as a comrade."

They walked on for a while, and then Peppone returned to the attack.

"In short, you'd say a fellow's just about as well off in Russia as he is here."

"I said nothing of the sort, but since you say it, I'll admit that's more or less my opinion. Except, of course, for the religious angle."

Peppone nodded.

"We agree then," he said. "But why do you suppose people speak and write so much against it?"

Don Camillo threw out his arms. "Politics . . ."

"Politics! . . . Politics! . . ." muttered Peppone. "America is all mixed up with politics in the same way. But no one talks about America quite so violently as about Russia."

"Well, the fact is that people can go to see America for themselves, while very few of them have ever set foot in Russia."

Peppone explained that Russia had to be careful. Then he grasped Don Camillo's sleeve and stopped him.

"Listen . . . as man to man, of course. If a fellow had a chance to take a good job in Russia, what would you advise him to do.?"

"Peppone, you're asking me quite a hard . . ."

"Man to man, Father. . . . I'm sure you have the courage to be frank."

Don Camillo shook his head.

"To be frank, then, I'll say that if it were a question of taking a good job I might advise him to go."

Life is a queer sort of proposition. Logically, Peppone ought to have leaped into the air with joy. But Don Camillo's reply did not make him at all happy. He touched his hat and started to go away. After he had taken a few steps he turned round.

"How can you conscientiously advise a fellow to go to a place where you've never been yourself ?" he asked.

"I know more about it than you think," Don Camillo said. "You may not realize it, but I read your newspapers. And some of the people that write for them have been to Russia."

Peppone wheeled abruptly.

"Oh, the newspapers! . . ." he grunted as he walked away.

Don Camillo was jubilant and he hurried back to the church to tell the Lord the whole story.

"Lord, he's got himself into a real tangle! He'd like to say he won't go, but in view of his position he doesn't dare to refuse the honour. And he came to me in the hope that I'd bolster up his resistance. Now he's caught worse than ever and doesn't see how he can get out of it. I shouldn't like to be in his shoes, I can tell you!"

"And I shouldn't like to be in yours—that is, if God would allow it," the Lord answered. "For they're the shoes of a wicked man."

Don Camillo's mouth dropped open.

"I played a good joke on him, that's all," he stammeringly protested.

"A joke's a joke only so long as it doesn't cause or rejoice in pain," the Lord rebuked him.

Don Camillo hung his head and left the church. Two days later Peppone received another letter.

DEAR COMRADE,—We are sorry to say that, on account of unexpected complications, neither you nor any of the others chosen as members of the Peace Brigade will be able to go to the Soviet Union at this time. Forgive us for causing you this disappointment, but for the moment you can best serve the cause of Peace by staying where you are.

No one ever knew who it was that brought an enormous candle into the church under the cover of darkness that evening. But Don Camillo found it burning near the crucifix when he went that night to say his prayers.

THE STRIKE

Don Camillo walked into Peppone's workshop and found the owner sitting in a corner, reading his paper.

"Labour ennobles man," Don Camillo observed. "Take care not to overdo it."

Peppone raised his eyes, turned his head to one side in order to spit, and went on with his reading. Don Camillo sat down on a box, took off his hat, wiped the perspiration away from his forehead and remarked calmly: "Good sportsmanship is all that really matters."

Just then Smilzo came in, out of breath from having ridden his racing bicycle so fast. At the sight of Don Camillo, he raised a finger to his cap.

"Greetings, Your Eminence," he said. "The influence exercised by the clergy upon minds still beclouded by the Dark Ages is a brake upon social progress."

Peppone did not stir, and Don Camillo continued to fan himself with his handkerchief, only imperceptibly turning his head so as to look at Smilzo out of the corner of one eye.

Smilzo sat down on the floor, leaned up against the wall, and said no more. A few minutes later, Straziami came in with his jacket over one shoulder and his hat pushed back on his head. Taking in the situation at a glance, he stood against the door-post and gazed at the world outside. The next to arrive was Lungo, who pushed some tools to one side of the work-bench and sat down on it. Ten minutes went by, and the only sign of life among the five of them was the fanning motion of Don Camillo's hand. Suddenly Peppone crumpled up his paper and threw it away.

"Devil take it!" he exclaimed angrily. "Hasn't anyone got a cigarette?"

Nobody moved, except for Don Camillo, who went on fanning.

"Haven't *you* one?" Peppone asked him maliciously. "I haven't smoked since early this morning."

"And I haven't even smelled tobacco for two whole days," Don Camillo answered. "I was counting on *you.*"

Peppone kicked an empty can.

"You asked for it," he shouted. "I hope you're enjoying your De Gasperi Government."

"If you were to work instead of reading your paper, you'd have some cigarette money," Don Camillo said calmly.

Peppone threw his cap on the ground.

"Work! Work!" he shouted. "How can I work if no one brings me anything to do? Instead of having their mowers repaired, people are cutting their hay with a scythe. And my truck hasn't been called out for two months. How am I supposed to get along?"

"Nationalize your business," Don Camillo said calmly.

Smilzo raised a finger.

"The Marshall Plan is the enemy of the people," he began gravely. "And the proletariat needs social reforms, not just a lot of talk."

Peppone got up and stood with his legs wide apart in front of Don Camillo.

"Stop raising a breeze with that damned handkerchief, will you?" he shouted. "And tell us what that Government of your choice is doing about the general strike."

"Don't ask me," said Don Camillo. "I can't fit newspapers into my budget. This last month I haven't read anything but my missal."

Peppone shrugged his shoulders.

"It suits you not to know what's going on," he said. "The fact is that you've betrayed the people."

Don Camillo stopped fanning.

"Do you mean me?" he asked gently.

Peppone scratched his head and went back to sit in his corner with his face buried in his hands. In the half-dark workshop silence once more reigned. Each returned to his thoughts on the general strike which had been called from the national headquarters of the Party. Bulletins had been issued, pamphlets distributed and posters put up to explain what the Party leaders were accomplishing for the people, with the result that in the little world of Don Camillo the people were hungry and life in the village was at a standstill. As the days seemed to grow longer and the tempers shorter, Don Camillo had begun to worry.

"To think that on the other side of the river there are people who might work and choose to strike instead!" Don Camillo exclaimed. "At a time like this, I call that a crime!"

He had diplomatically referred to the neighbouring township, which was outside Peppone's jurisdiction. It was an important agricultural centre and there, as everywhere in the valley, the farmers, unable to get labour, were forced to tighten their belts and watch their harvests rot.

Peppone raised his head.

"The strike is the workers' only weapon," he shouted. "Do you want to take it away? What did we fight for in the Resistance movement?"

"To lose the war faster."

So they began to discuss who should pay for the war, and that argument took a long time. Then they emptied some tins of petrol into the tank of Lungo's motorcycle, and Smilzo and Lungo rode away, while Don Camillo returned to the presbytery.

At midnight a boat shot silently out over the river. In it were five men in overalls, with grease all over their faces, looking like mechanics of some kind; three of them were fellows with especially broad shoulders. They landed on the opposite bank, quite a long way downstream, and after walking a mile through empty fields found a truck waiting to take them to a big commercial farm. They proceeded to clean the stable and then to milk the cows. Although there were only five of them, they worked like a whole battalion. Just as they were finishing with the cows, someone breathlessly spread the alarm: "The squad!"

The five barely had time to get out of the stable by one door before the squad appeared at another, where cans of milk were lined up ready for delivery. The squad leader kicked over one of the cans and said: "I'll give you a lesson in making butter!" Then, turning to his followers, he added: "Some of you take care of the rest of the cans, and the others come with me to give a lesson to the strike-breakers."

He advanced threateningly towards the five, but the iron bars wielded by the three with the broad shoulders did the work of eight, and their two smaller companions were as slippery as eels and gave just as much trouble. Before long the squad retired, licking its wounds. But, three hours later, a veritable army came to reinforce it. The five picked up pitchforks and awaited the attack, while their new enemies stopped some sixty feet away.

"We don't want to hurt you," shouted their leader. "We're after the farmer that got you out from the city. You go on about your business, and we'll settle accounts with him."

The women of the family began to cry, and the farmer and his two sons were white with fear.

"No, we can't let you do that," mumbled one of the five, and they held their ground, while the others, waving sticks, advanced towards them.

"Look out!" said one of the giants. And he threw the pitchfork in the direction of the advancing enemy, who drew back while the pitchfork went into the vacated ground. Then he ran into the stable and reappeared just in time to face the enemy's regrouped forces with a tommy-gun in his hand.

A tommy-gun is no laughing matter, but what is even more frightening is the face of the man who bears it, which reveals from the start whether he intends to shoot or not. In this instance the bearer's face made it very clear that if the enemy didn't desist and retire, he would mow them down. They made another attempt late at night to besiege the stable, but a volley of shots decided them to keep their distance. The strike-breakers stayed on the job twelve days, until it was all over, and when they went away they were loaded down with foodstuffs and money.

No one ever knew exactly who the strike-breakers were. But for some time Peppone, Smilzo, Lungo, and Straziami were very quite. When Don Camillo discussed the matter at the altar, the Lord reproached him for having carried a tommy-gun, but Don Camillo insisted it had been Peppone. Finally, however, he threw out his arms and gave in.

"What do you expect, Lord?" he said. "How can I explain it to You? We were so alike that no one could say which was me and which Peppone. All strike-breakers look the same by night."

And when the Lord insisted that the tommy-gun had been carried by broad daylight, Don Camillo only threw out his arms again and said: "There are circumstances that cause a man to lose all notion of time!"

THUNDER

Two days before the opening of the hunting season, Lightning died. He was as old as the hills and had every reason to be sick and tired of playing the part of a hunting dog when he wasn't born one. Don Camillo could do nothing but dig a deep hole beside the acacia tree, toss in the body and heave a long sigh. For a whole fortnight he was depressed, but finally he got over it, and one morning he found himself out in the fields with a shotgun in his hands. A quail rose out of a nearby meadow, and Don Camillo shot at him, but the quail flew on as calmly as before. Don Camillo nearly yelled, "You wretched dog!" but he remembered that Lightning wasn't there, and felt depressed all over again. He wandered about the fields, over the river bank and under grape arbours, discharged as many volleys as a machine-gun, but never made a single hit. Who could be lucky without a dog beside him?

With the one cartridge he had left, he aimed at a quail flying low over a hedge. He couldn't have missed, but there was no way to be sure. The quail might have fallen either into the hedge or into the field on the other side. But to search for it would be like looking for a needle in a haystack. Better give the whole thing up. He blew into the barrels of his gun and was looking round to see where he was and which was the shortest way to go home when a rustle made him turn his head. Out of the hedge jumped a dog, holding a hare in his mouth, which he proceeded to drop at Don Camillo's feet.

"Heaven help us!" Don Camillo exclaimed. "I shoot a quail, and this dog brings me a hare!"

He picked the hare up and found that it was soaking wet, and so was the dog. Obviously he had swum across from the opposite side of the river. Don Camillo slipped the hare into his bag and started home, with the dog following. When he reached the presbytery, the dog crouched outside the door. Don Camillo had never seen a dog like him. He was a fine animal and seemed to be in the pink of condition. Perhaps he was a dog with a pedigree like that of a count or a marquis, but he had no identification papers on him. He wore a handsome collar, but there was no plate or tag attached to it.

"If he doesn't come from another world but has a rightful owner in this one, surely someone will turn up to look for him," Don Camillo thought to himself. And he let the dog in. That evening before going to bed, he thought about the dog and finally put his conscience at rest by saying to himself: "I'll mention him in church on Sunday." The next morning, when he got up to say Mass, he forgot all about the dog until he found him at the church door.

"Stay there and wait for me," Don Camillo shouted.

And the dog curled up in front of the sacristy door, where after Mass he gave the priest an enthusiastic greeting. They breakfasted together, and when the dog saw Don Camillo take his shotgun out of the corner where he had left it and hang it on a nail, he barked, ran to the door, returned to see if Don Camillo were following and, in short, would give him no peace until Don Camillo slung the gun over his shoulder and made for the fields. He was an extraordinary dog, one of the kind that puts a hunter on his mettle and makes him think: "If I miss my aim, *I'm* a dirty dog." Don Camillo concentrated as if he were under examination and showed himself to be a worthy master. On his way home with a bag full of game, he said to himself: "I'll call him Thunder." Now that the dog had done his work, he was amusing himself by chasing butterflies in a meadow.

"Thunder!" Don Camillo shouted.

It seemed as if from the far side of the meadow someone had launched a torpedo. The dog streaked along with his belly close to the ground, leaving the long grass parted in his wake. He arrived in front of Don Camillo with six inches of tongue hanging out, ready for orders.

"Good dog!" said Don Camillo, and Thunder danced and barked with such joy that Don Camillo thought: "If he doesn't leave off, I'll find myself dancing and barking."

Two days went by, and Satan tagged at Don Camillo's heels, whispering to him that he should forget to say anything about the dog in church on Sunday. On the afternoon of the third day, when Don Camillo was on his way home with a bag of game and Thunder frisking ahead of him, he ran into Peppone. Peppone was in a gloomy mood; he had been hunting too, but his bag was empty. Now he looked at Thunder, took a newspaper out of his pocket and opened it.

"That's funny," he said. "He looks just like the dog they've advertised as lost."

Don Camillo took the paper from him and found what he had hoped he would not find. Someone from the city was offering a reward to anyone who found a hunting dog with such and such marks upon him, lost three days before along the river.

"Very well, then," said Don Camillo. "I needn't make any announcement in church. Let me keep this paper. I'll give it back to you later."

"It's really too bad," said Peppone. "Everyone says he's an extraordinary dog. And they must be right, because when you had Lightning you never brought home a haul like that one. If I were in your shoes . . ."

"And if I were in yours . . ." Don Camillo interrupted. "But I happen to be in my own, and as an honest man I must restore the dog to his rightful owner."

When they reached the village Don Camillo sent a telegram to the man in the city. Satan had been working out a new argument to use on Don Camillo, but he was too slow, because he had counted on Don Camillo's sending a letter rather than a telegram. That would have taken fifteen or twenty minutes, time enough for anyone so persuasive as Satan to win a point reluctantly defended. But a five-word telegram was so quickly despatched that Satan was left at a standstill. Don Camillo went home with his conscience in good order, but with a feeling of deep depression. And he sighed even more deeply than when be had buried Lightning.

The city man drove up the next day in a low-slung sports model. He was vain and unpleasant, as might have been expected from his flashy taste in cars; what is called a city slicker.

"Where is my dog?" he asked.

"A dog has been found that must belong to somebody," said Don Camillo. "But you'll have to prove your ownership."

The man described the dog from stem to stern.

"Is that enough?" he asked. "Or do I have to describe his insides as well?"

"That's enough," said Don Camillo glumly, opening the cellar door.

The dog lay on the floor without moving.

"Thunder!" called the city slicker.

"Is that really his name?" asked Don Camillo.

"Yes."

"That's funny."

Still the dog did not move and the man called again:

"Thunder!"

The dog growled and there was an ugly look in his eyes.

"He doesn't seem to be yours," observed Don Camillo.

The claimant went and took the dog by the collar in order to drag him up from the cellar. Then he turned the collar inside out, revealing a brass plate with a name on it.

"Just read this, Father. Here are my name and address and telephone number. Appearances to the contrary, the dog is mine."

Then he pointed to the car.

"Get in!" he ordered.

The dog obeyed, with his head hanging low and his tail between his legs, and curled up on the back seat. His owner held out a five-thousand lire note.

"Here's for your trouble," he said.

"It's no trouble to restore something lost to its rightful owner," said Don Camillo, proudly pushing the money away.

"I'm truly grateful," said the city slicker. "He's a very expensive dog, a thoroughbred from one of the best English kennels, with three international blue ribbons to his credit. I'm an impulsive sort of fellow, and the other day, when he caused me to miss a hare, I gave him a kick. And he resented it."

"He's a dog with professional dignity," said Don Camillo. "And you didn't miss the hare, because he brought it to me."

"Oh well, he'll get over it," said the city slicker, climbing back into his car.

Don Camillo spent a restless night, and when he got up to say Mass the next morning he was immersed in gloom. It was windy and pouring rain, but Thunder was there. He was covered with mud and soaked like a sponge, but he lay in front of the sacristy door and gave Don Camillo a welcome worthy of the last act of an opera. Don Camillo went in and spoke to the Lord.

"Lord, Your enemies are going to say that Christians are afraid of wind and water, because not a single one of them has come to church this morning. But if You let Thunder in, they'll be confounded."

Thunder was admitted to the sacristy, where he waited patiently, except when he stuck his nose through the door near the altar, causing Don Camillo to stumble over his prayers. They went back to the presbytery together, and the priest sank into his former melancholy.

"No use fooling myself," he said with a sigh. "He knows the way, and he'll come back for you."

The dog growled as if he had understood. He let Don Camillo brush him and then sat down by the fire to dry. The owner returned in the afternoon. He was in a very bad humour, because he had got his car muddy. There was no need for explanations; he walked into the presbytery and found Thunder in front of the spent fire.

"Sorry to have given you more trouble," he said, "but it won't happen again. I'll take him to a place of mine in the next province, and he couldn't find his way back from there even if he were a carrier pigeon."

When his master called this time, Thunder gave an angry bark. He would not get into the car of his own accord, but had to be lifted on to the seat. He tried to escape, and when the door was closed he scratched and barked without ceasing.

The next morning Don Camillo left the presbytery with his heart pounding. Thunder was not there either that day or the next, and little by little the priest resigned himself to his absence. A fortnight went by, and on the fifteenth night, at about one o'clock, Don Camillo heard a cry from below and knew that it was Thunder. He ran downstairs and out on the church square, quite forgetting that he was in his nightshirt. Thunder was in a very bad condition: starved, dirty, and so tired that he could not hold up his tail. It took three days to restore him to normal, but on the fourth day, after Mass, Thunder pulled him by his cassock to where the shotgun was hanging and made such a scene that Don Camillo took his gun, bag and cartridge belt and set out for the fields. There followed a rare and wonderful week, when Don Camillo's catches made the most seasoned hunters green with envy. Every now and then someone came to see the dog, and Don Camillo explained:

"He's not mine. A man from the city left him here to be trained to chase hares."

One fine morning Peppone came to admire him. He stared at him for some time in silence.

"I'm not going to hunt this morning," said Don Camillo. "Do you want to try him?"

"Will he come?" said Peppone incredulously.

"I think he will. After all, he doesn't know you're a Communist. Seeing you in my company, he probably takes you for a perfectly respectable person."

Peppone was so absorbed by the prospect of trying the dog that he did not answer. Don Camillo turned his gun and bag and cartridge-belt over to Peppone. Thunder had been excited to see Don Camillo take down his gun, but now he seemed taken aback.

"Go along with the Mayor," said Don Camillo. "I'm busy to-day."

Peppone put on the belt and hung the gun and bag over his shoulder. Thunder looked first at one man and then the other.

"Go on," Don Camillo encouraged him. "He's ugly, but he doesn't bite."

Thunder started to follow Peppone, but then he stopped in perplexed fashion and turned round.

"Go, go," Don Camillo repeated. "Only watch out that he doesn't enlist you in the Party."

Thunder went along. If Don Camillo had turned over his hunting equipment to this man, he must be a friend. Two hours later he bounded back into the presbytery and laid a magnificent hare at Don Camillo's feet. Soon, panting like a locomotive, Peppone arrived upon the scene.

"Devil take you and your dog!" he exclaimed. "He's a perfect wonder, but he eats the game. He stole a hare a yard long. After he had brought me the quails and the partridges, he had to steal a hare."

Don Camillo picked up the hare and held it out to Peppone.

"He's a thinking dog," he answered. "He thought that if the gun and the cartridges were mine, I was entitled to part of the kill."

It was plain that Thunder had acted in good faith, because he did not run away from Peppone, but greeted him with affection.

"He's an extraordinary animal," said Peppone, "and I wouldn't give him back to that man even if he came with a regiment of militia."

Don Camillo sighed.

The owner turned up a week later. He wore a hunting outfit and carried a feather-weight Belgian shotgun.

"Well, he got away from up there, too. I've come to see whether he landed here again."

"He arrived yesterday morning," said Don Camillo glumly. "Take him away."

Thunder looked at his master and growled.

"I'll settle accounts with you this time," said the city slicker to the dog.

Thunder growled again, and the city slicker lost his head and gave him a kick.

"You cur! I'll teach you! Lie down!"

The dog lay down, growling, and Don Camillo stepped in.

"He's a thoroughbred, and you can't handle him with violence. Let him quieten down while you drink a glass of wine."

The man took a seat, and Don Camillo went down to get a bottle from the cellar. While he was there he found time to scribble a note which he gave to the bell-ringer's son.

"Take it to Peppone at his workshop, and hurry."

The note contained only a few words: "*The fellow's here again. Lend me twenty thousand lire so that I can try to buy the dog. And get them here fast.*"

The city slicker drank several glasses of wine, talked idly to Don Camillo, then looked at his watch and stood up.

"I'm sorry, but I must go. Friends are expecting me for the hunt, and I've just time to get there."

Thunder was still crouching in a corner, and as soon as he saw his master looking at him he began to growl. He growled louder when the man came near. Just then there came the roar of a motorcycle and Don Camillo saw Peppone dismount from it. He made an interrogative gesture and Peppone nodded an affirmative answer. He held up two open hands, then one, and finally one finger. Then with his right hand he made a horizontal cut through the air. Which signified that he had sixteen thousand five hundred lire. Don Camillo sighed with relief.

"Sir," he said to the visitor. "You can see that the dog has taken a dislike to you. Thoroughbreds don't forget, and you'll never make him put it behind him. Why don't you sell him to me?"

Then he made a mental calculation of all his resources.

"I can pay you eighteen thousand eight hundred lire. That's all I possess."

The city slicker sneered.

"Father, you must be joking. The dog cost me eighty thousand and I wouldn't sell him for a hundred. He may have taken a dislike to me, but I'll make him get over it."

Heedless of Thunder's growling, he seized him by the collar and dragged him over to the car. As he tried to lift him in, the struggling dog clawed some paint off the mudguard. The city slicker lost his head and with his free hand beat him over the back. The dog continued to struggle, caught the hand that held his collar and bit it. The owner let go, and the dog went to lie against the presbytery wall, growling. Don Camillo and Peppone stared from where they stood and did not have time to say a word. The city slicker, as pale as a corpse, pulled his shotgun out of the car and aimed it at the animal.

"You bastard!" he said between his teeth as he fired.

The wall of the rectory was stained with blood. After a piercing howl, Thunder lay motionless on the ground. The city slicker got into his car and drove off at top speed. Don Camillo took no heed of his departure and did not notice that Peppone had followed on his motorcycle. He knelt beside the dog, with all his attention concentrated upon him. The dog groaned as Don Camillo stroked his head, and then suddenly licked his hand. Then he got up and barked happily.

After twenty minutes, Peppone returned. He was red in the face and his fists were clenched.

"I caught up with him at Fiumaccio, where he had to stop at the level crossing. I dragged him out of the car and boxed his ears until his head was as big as a water-melon. He reached for his gun, and I broke it over his back."

They were in the hall, and now a howl came from farther inside.

"Isn't he dead yet?" asked Peppone.

"Only his flank was grazed," said Don Camillo. "In a week he'll be livelier than ever."

Peppone ran a big hand doubtfully over his chin.

"Morally speaking," said Don Camillo, "he killed the dog. When he shot that was his intention. If Saint Anthony deflected his aim, that doesn't take away from the vileness of the deed. You were wrong to box his ears, because violence is never a good thing. But in any case . . ."

"In any case . . . he won't show his face here again," said Peppone, "and you have acquired a dog."

"Half a dog," declared Don Camillo. "Because I'm morally indebted to you for the money you were ready to lend me. So half the dog is yours."

Peppone scratched his head.

"Well, by all that's wonderful!" he exclaimed. "An honest priest, and one that doesn't defraud the people!"

Don Camillo gave him a threatening look.

"Listen, if you bring politics into it, I'll change my mind and keep the dog to myself!"

"Consider it unsaid!" exclaimed Peppone, who underneath it all was a man and a hunter and cared more for Thunder's esteem than for that of Marx, Lenin and company. And Thunder, with a bandage around his hips, came barking in to seal the pact of non-aggression.

THE WALL

PEOPLE CALLED IT Manasca's Garden, but it was just a quarter of an acre of underbrush, with weeds as tall as poplars, surrounded by a ten-foot wall. A forgotten plot with a hundred and fifty feet of frontage on the square and ninety feet on the tree-lined street leading into it. Because it was the only vacant site in the square old Manasca had been offered any amount of money for it, but he had never been willing to sell. For years and years it lay there, just as fallow and uncultivated as its owner, until finally the old man died and it was inherited by his son, together with a pile of thousand-lire notes and other pieces of property here and there on both sides of the river. Young Manasca thought it was a shame not to put the plot to use, and finally he went to see the Mayor.

"Men are starving because they can't find work," he said very directly, "but you proletarians, as you call yourselves, with all your red kerchiefs, are such a filthy bunch that it's a sin to give you anything to do."

"We're not as filthy as you fine gentlemen," Peppone answered peacefully. "The best of you deserves to be strung up on a rope made of the guts of the most miserable of us."

Young Manasca and Peppone had had a fist-fight every day until they were twenty; as a result they were very good friends and understood one another perfectly. So now Peppone asked what he was driving at.

"If you promise you won't trip me up with trade unions, Party, vice-Party, victims of the Resistance movement, social justice, rightful claims, sympathy strikes and all the rest of your revolutionary paraphernalia, I'll provide work for half the men in the village," Manasca told him.

Peppone put his fists on his hips.

"Do you want me to help you to exploit the worker? To convince him he ought to toil for a dish of spaghetti and a kick in the pants?"

"I don't intend to cheat anybody. I'll pay regular wages and old-age insurance and give you a barrel of wine into the bargain if you promise me that those stupid fools won't walk out in the middle of the job and try to blackmail me. It's a big project, and if it doesn't come off I'm a ruined man."

Peppone told him to lay his cards on the table.

"I propose to put up a five-storey building in the garden," said Manasca. "Big-city stuff, with a hundred-foot arcade on to the square, shops, a café, a restaurant with rooms to let above it, a garage, a petrol pump and so on. If all goes well, I'll let you run the petrol pump. However much of a nuisance you are, you know how to get things done. With a building like that we'll make this into an important market centre and turn our yokels into sophisticates."

Peppone had never laid eyes on Paris or London or New York, but he imagined the new building as equal to any of theirs. And he could see a red-and-yellow petrol pump in front of his workshop, with a pump for compressed air as well.

"A complete filling-station needs a hydraulic machine to lift cars up for greasing," he murmured.

"There'll be a hydraulic machine and all the other gadgets you can think of," said Manasca. "But you've got to make me a promise."

"What if I'm not re-elected Mayor?" Peppone said anxiously.

"So much the better! The new Mayor will be afraid of you and your gang. And that's more than you can say for yourself!"

Peppone brought a fist down on his desk.

"That's a bargain! And I'll kill the first man that gives you trouble. The future of the village is concerned, and anyone that doesn't do a good job will get a swift kick. Tell me what you need and I'll find you the right people."

"Let's have a clear understanding," said Manasca. "You're not to hire only people from your own Party. I want men that are willing to work and have the know-how."

"That's right; all men are equal when they're hungry," Peppone said sententiously.

And that evening, with due solemnity, he gave the news to his Party stalwarts.

"Tell people that, while others chatter, we actually do something. We're building a skyscraper."

A week later, a crew of wreckers began to tear down the wall. And then it was that trouble began. The wall was a mass of stones and rubble and mortar, at least three hundred years old, which was easy enough to smash; but there was something on the wall that everyone had forgotten. On the street side, just a yard before the corner, there was a niche, with a rusty grating over it to protect a Madonna painted inside.

The Madonna was a thing of no artistic value, painted by some poor devil two or three hundred years before, but everyone knew her; everyone had greeted her a thousand times and stopped to put a flower in the tin can at her feet. And if the wall around her were torn down, the Madonna would fall to pieces. Manasca sent for an expert from the city, one of those fellows who can peel a painting off a wall. But after studying the situation he declared that there was nothing to do.

"If we so much as touch the painting, it will crumble into dust."

Meanwhile the wreckers were advancing, and when they were a couple of yards away on either side, they stopped. Peppone came to look at the Madonna clinging to the last bit of wall and shook his head.

"Nonsense!" he said. "This isn't religion; it's superstition. There's no intention of hurting anybody's feelings. For the sake of this painting, are we to give up a plan that's providing work for a lot of people and doing something for the village as well?"

The wreckers were tough fellows, who would just as soon have demolished their own mothers. And there they stood in front of the remaining scrap of wall. Their chief, Bago, spat out a cigarette butt and shook his head.

"I wouldn't destroy it even on orders from the Pope!" he exclaimed, and the others looked as if they felt as he did.

"No one said anything about destroying it," shouted Peppone. "That's all sentimentality, traditionalism, childishness and so on. There's only one thing to do, to tear down as much of the wall as possible, then to prop up and protect what's left, lift it away and put it somewhere else. In Russia they move fifteen-storey buildings from one street to another, and no matter how far we may be behind them, we ought to be able to pull off a trick like this one."

Bago shrugged his shoulders.

"In Russia they may move buildings, but they haven't any Madonnas to move," he mumbled.

Brusco took a good look and then threw out his arms in despair.

"There's a crack at the back of the niche, and it's a miracle that the whole thing hasn't fallen apart years ago. The wall's made of mud and stones, and if you try to lift a piece of it out you'll be left with a fistful of sand."

Peppone strode up and down, and half the village gathered to look on.

"Well then, what have you got to say, all of you?" Peppone snarled. "You can see the situation for yourselves. Are we to stop work or not? Say something, or may God strike you dead!"

But no one seemed to have any answer.

"We'd better go and see the priest about it," was their conclusion.

Peppone jammed his cap down on his head.

"All right. Since the future of the village is at stake, I suppose we'll have to call upon the priest."

Don Camillo was transplanting some vegetables in his garden when Peppone and the rest of them looked over the hedge. Manasca explained the problem, and Peppone put the question:

"What shall we do?"

Don Camillo asked for further details and prolonged the discussion. Of course, he already knew what it was all about and only wanted to gain time.

"It's late now," he said at last. "We'll decide to-morrow."

"In the city I've seen any number of churches that have been de-consecrated and taken over by coal merchants or cabinet-makers," said Peppone. "If a church can be transformed in that way, why can't we do the same thing with a picture painted on a wall?"

"The very fact that you've come to consult me shows that there are some difficulties in your minds," said Don Camillo.

That night the priest could not sleep for worry. But the next morning, when Peppone and his gang appeared before him, he had a solution.

"If you are quite sure in your consciences that there is no way of saving the picture, then go ahead and tear down the wall. It's for the good of the whole community, and a poor old painted Madonna wouldn't want to take bread out of men's mouths and stand in the way of progress. God be with you! But go at it gently."

"Very well," said Peppone, touching his cap, and marching off with his men to the square.

When they reached the Madonna he turned and said to Bago:

"You heard what the priest told us, didn't you? We're not giving offence to anyone."

Bago twisted the visor of his cap to one side of his head, spat into his hands and grasped the handle of his pick. He raised the pick in the air, left it suspended there for several minutes, and then said: "Not me! I'll not be the one to do it."

Peppone stormed and shouted, but none of the men was willing to deliver the fatal blow. Finally he seized the pick himself and advanced towards the wall. He raised it above his head, but when through the grating he saw the Madonna's eyes upon him, he threw it down on the ground.

"Devil take it!" he exclaimed. "Why should this be the Mayor's job? What has a Mayor to do with the Madonna? The priest ought to be good for something. Let him do it! Everyone to his own trade, I say."

And he went angrily back to the presbytery.

"All done?" Don Camillo asked him.

"The devil it's done!" shouted Peppone. "It's no use."

"Why?"

"Because the Madonna and saints are your racket. I've never called on you to smash a bust of Marx or Lenin, have I?"

"No, but if you want me to, I'd be glad to oblige," said Don Camillo.

Peppone clenched his fists.

"Do what you see fit," said Peppone. "But remember that as long as the Madonna's there, we can't go on with the work, and you'll be responsible for the resulting unemployment. I'm a Mayor by profession, not a destroyer of Madonnas. And I don't want to be told that we're a bunch of sacrilegious Reds, smashing up saints wherever we find them."

"Very well, then," said Don Camillo. "The rest of you can go along, while I talk to the Mayor."

When the two men were left alone together, they said nothing for several minutes. Then Don Camillo broke the silence.

"Peppone, it's no good, I can't tear it down."

"Neither can I," said Peppone. "If you, who specialize in saints, haven't got the nerve . . ."

"It's not a question of nerve," said Don Camillo. "It's like it was with the angel in the bell tower, that for hundreds of years had looked down on the village. The eyes of this Madonna have seen all our beloved dead, they have reflected the hope and despair, the joys and sorrows of centuries past. Do you remember, Peppone, when we came back from the war in 1918? I gave the Madonna flowers, and you put them in your tin cup."

Peppone grunted, and Don Camillo ran his hand over his chin. Then he threw his coat around him and put on his hat. When they arrived in front of the

Madonna, they found half the village waiting there. There was a stranger also, a young man who had come in a car, and from the manner in which Peppone ran to greet him, it was clear that he was a Party bigwig from the city. Now he stepped forward and looked at the Madonna.

"Well," he said, "if things are as you tell me and the priest agrees that you can't give up a project that's so good for the community and the working-man, then I'll be the one to cut through your middle-class sentimentality. I'll do the job myself."

He took a pick and started over to the wall. But Don Camillo laid a hand on his shoulder and pulled him back.

"It's not necessary," he said roughly.

There was a deep silence, while everyone looked expectantly at the wall. Suddenly the wall quivered and then slowly cracked open. The wall did not fall to the ground; it crumbled into a heap of stones and plaster. On top of the heap, free of the rusty grating and the shadows of the niche in which it had dwelt for so long, stood the Madonna, completely unscathed. Although she had been painted two or three hundred years before, she was as fresh as a rose.

"She can go back to the same place in the new wall," said Manasca.

"Motion carried by unanimous applause!" shouted Peppone. And he thought of his old Army tin cup, with the offering of flowers from Don Camillo.

THE SUN ALSO RISES

ONE AFTERNOON AN OLD woman by the name of Maria Barchini came to confession. Don Camillo listened to her quietly, but toward the end he was startled almost out of his skin to hear her say hesitantly: "Father, I'm going to vote for the Communists."

He came out of the confessional and said to her: "Come along over to the presbytery." And when they had sat down in his study, he asked if there were anything wrong with her head. "I thought I'd explained all these things any number of times," he told her. "Didn't you understand me?"

"Yes, I understood," said the old woman. "I'm willing to do whatever penance you prescribe, to fast or make a pilgrimage to the Sanctuary. . . . But I'm voting for the Communists."

"There's no use in my wasting breath to explain something you say you already understand," Don Camillo said brusquely. "If you vote for those people, I can't give you absolution."

She spread out her arms in a gesture of resignation.

"God will forgive me," she said, "and I'll pay whatever the price may be. The main thing is for my boy to come home. A mother must be ready to sacrifice herself for her son."

Don Camillo looked at her in bewilderment and asked her what her son had to do with the election.

"Two ladies came from the city the other day," she explained, "and promised that if I voted for the right candidates my boy would be sent back from Russia. These people are friendly to the Russians, and if they win they'll bring back the prisoners of war. They took down my name and put it high on their list. And I gave them the boy's picture. I can understand why you can't give me absolution, but I still say a mother must sacrifice herself for her child."

Don Camillo shook his head.

"I see," he muttered. "But you've got to be sure your boy will really come."

"I had lost all hope until they gave it back to me. When you're drowning, you know, you'll clutch at any straw."

"I see," said Don Camillo. "But what if the Communists don't win?"

"Ah well . . ." the old woman sighed. "I have to do all I can. They put his name at the head of the list. I saw them write it down. And they were respectable people, educated people. They said they knew how things are, but a mother has to do everything she can for her son. I'll have to vote for the 'People's Front.'"

Don Camillo stood up and traced a cross in the air.

"*Ego te absolvo*," he said. "Say four Our Fathers, four Hail Marys and four Glorias for penance. And God be praised."

And when from his window he saw the old woman leave the church, he went to talk to the Lord on the altar.

"Lord," Don Camillo said impetuously, "if a woman is willing to sacrifice herself in the hope of saving her son, Don Camillo has no right to take her hope away. If I had refused her absolution it would have been like saying: 'You're willing to make any sacrifice for your boy, but God is against you.' And that would have been a wicked thing to say, for even when hope is based on material things, its origin is divine. In Your divine wisdom You know how to turn evil means to a good end, and You chose to speak through sacrilegious mouths in order to restore hope to a mother's heart. To refuse her absolution would have meant telling her she had no right to hope, and to deny hope means to deny You."

The Lord smiled.

"What have you in mind, Don Camillo?" he asked. "Do you want me to vote for the 'People's Front'?"

"I merely wanted to explain why I gave old Maria Barchini absolution in spite of the fact that she's voting for the Communists."

"And why must you explain, Don Camillo? Did I ask for any explanation? Aren't you at peace with your own conscience?"

"I'm not, Lord, that's just the trouble. I should have taken away from Your enemies the vote they have extorted from that poor woman."

"But her illusions have been turned into hope, and you have just said that hope is divine, Don Camillo."

Don Camillo ran his big hands over his face.

"That's equally true," he admitted. "What's to be done?"

"I can't tell you," the Lord said. "I don't go in for politics."

Peppone was in his workshop, busy repainting a mudguard on his truck, when Don Camillo accosted him.

"Some of your filthy propagandists are going round telling poor people whose boys are still in Russia that if they vote for the Communists the Russians will send all the prisoners home."

"I don't believe it," muttered Peppone. "Give me the names of some of the people."

"That would be violating the secrecy of the confessional. But I swear to you it's true."

Peppone shrugged his shoulders.

"I didn't send anybody out on such a mission. It must be an idea from the city. Anyhow, we're at war, aren't we? And each side must use whatever cards he has in his hand."

"Exactly," said Don Camillo gloomily.

"You have a trick up your sleeve, for that matter. If someone votes for us, you won't grant him absolution."

"I shan't refuse absolution to anyone who's been given the false hope of recovering a son. But when the time comes, God will refuse absolution to you. You're damning your own soul!"

Don Camillo spoke very calmly and then went away. Peppone stared after him, open-mouthed, for he had never heard Don Camillo speak just like that before, in a cold, far-away voice that seemed to come from another world. He thought of it several times both that day and the next. Then posters appeared on the walls announcing a meeting of the Socialist Unity Party and, in accordance with directives from headquarters, he had to organize a counter-demonstration. On Sunday the village was packed with people.

"In the front row, just below the platform, put the comrades from Molinetto and Torricella," ordered Peppone. "At the first slip made by one of the Socialist speakers they're to go into action. Our own people are all going to Molinetto and Torricella to do the same job at the Christian Democrat and Nationalist rallies. Brusco and I and the rest of the local leaders will stay in the Town Hall. We're not to appear on the scene unless there's trouble."

The Socialist speaker was about thirty-five years old, a well-bred man and a born orator. As soon as Peppone heard the voice he jumped up on a chair and peered out of the window.

"It's him!" he stammered. And Brusco and Bigio and Smilzo and all the rest agreed that it was he indeed, and had nothing more to say.

A few minutes later, the nuisance squad went into action. The speaker made telling answers to their insults and accusations, and finally they lost control of themselves and made a rush for the platform. Peppone signalled to them from the window, but it was too late. The crowd gathered in front of the house where the speaker had been rushed to safety. Peppone and his seconds made their way through to the door. The speaker was sitting on a sofa inside, while a woman bandaged his hand. He had blood on his face because someone had struck him with a key across the forehead. Peppone looked at him, gaping.

"Hello there, Peppone," said the wounded man, raising his head. "Did you organize this little party?"

Peppone did not answer, and the wounded man smiled again.

"Ah, so Brusco's here, and Smilzo, and Straziami, and Lungo. Well, I'm here too. Our old group is together again, all except for Rosso and Giacomino, who died in our mountain encampment. Who could have imagined that Peppone was going to organize a party like this for his old commander? . . ."

Peppone spread out his arms.

"Chief, I didn't know . . ." he stammered.

"Oh, don't let that bother you," the wounded man interrupted him. "We're at war, and everyone plays the cards he can. I quite see your point of view." The bandage was finished, and he got up to go. "So long, Comrade Peppone," he said with a smile. "We saved our skins from the Germans; now let's hope we can save them from the Communists, too. Rosso and Giacomino are lucky to have died when they did, up in the mountains."

He got into a waiting car, and Peppone heard the hooting and shouting that accompanied its departure. When the "chief" had spoken that last sentence, his voice had been as cold and far-away and other-worldly as Don Camillo's when he said: "You're damning your own soul!"

That evening, the leaders of the squads that had done a job at Molinetto and Torricella came to report. At Molinetto the Christian Democrat speaker had been forced to stop halfway through his address, and nothing serious had happened. At Torricella the Nationalist had received a slap in the face. Peppone knew them both. The first was a university professor and the second had been in a German labour camp.

"They gave them an even rougher time in the city," the leader of the Molinetto squad was saying. "They trampled down some students and gave a police sergeant a black eye."

"Good," said Peppone, getting up to leave the room.

The sun was setting as he walked slowly along the road leading down to the river. On the bank someone was smoking a cigar and looking into the water. It was Don Camillo. They said nothing for a while, until Peppone observed that it was a fine evening.

"Very fine," Don Camillo answered.

Peppone lit the butt of a cigar, inhaled a few mouthfuls of smoke, then put it out with his shoe. He spat angrily.

"Everybody's against us," he said glumly. "Even my old Partisan commander. Everybody, including God."

Don Camillo went on quietly smoking. "Everybody's not against you. You're against everybody, God included."

Peppone crossed his arms on his chest. "Why did you say I was damning my own soul? Just because old Maria Barchini's going to give us her vote?"

"Maria Barchini? Who's she?"

"I went yesterday to see all the families whose boys are prisoners in Russia, and she told me that two women had called upon her on behalf of the People's Front. I told her that they were fakers and that even if she were to vote as they said she'd never see her son again."

Don Camillo threw away his cigar.

"And what did she say?"

"She asked how she was to vote in order to get back her son. I told her I didn't know, and she said if no party could bring him back there was no use in voting at all."

"You're an idiot," said Don Camillo.

He said it solemnly, but not in that cold far-away voice. Peppone felt better. When he thought of the blood on his former commander's face and the slap given to the former labour-camp inmate at Molinetto and the old professor at Torricella who couldn't finish his address because of the shouts, he felt like crying. But he took hold of himself and called out fiercely:

"We're going to win!"

"No," Don Camillo said calmly but firmly.

For a moment they just stood there silently, each one looking straight ahead. The valley stretched out peacefully under the evening sky and the river was just the same as it had been a hundred thousand years before. And so was the sun. It was about to set, but the next morning it would rise again from the opposite direction. Peppone—who can say why?—found himself thinking of this extraordinary fact and privately came to the conclusion that, to tell the truth, God knows His business.

TECHNIQUE OF THE *COUP D'ETAT*

AT TEN O'CLOCK ON Tuesday evening the village square was swept with wind and rain, but a crowd had been gathered there for three or four hours to listen to the election news coming out of a radio loudspeaker. Suddenly the lights went out and everything was plunged into darkness. Someone went to the control box but came back saying there was nothing to be done. The trouble must be up the line or at the power plant, miles away. People hung around for a half-hour or so, and then, as the rain began to come down even harder than before, they scattered to their homes, leaving the village silent and deserted. Peppone shut himself up in the People's Palace, along with Lungo, Brusco, Straziami and Gigio, the lame leader of the "Red Wing" squad from Molinetto. They sat around uneasily by the light of a candle stump and cursed the power and light monopoly as an enemy of the people, until Smilzo burst in. He had gone to Roccaverde on his motorcycle to see if anyone had news, and now his eyes were popping out of his head and he was waving a sheet of paper.

"The Front has won!" he panted. "Fifty-two seats out of a hundred in the Senate and fifty-one in the Chamber. The other side is done for. We must get hold of our people and have a celebration. If there's no light, we can set fire to a couple of haystacks nearby."

"Hurrah!" shouted Peppone. But Gigio grabbed hold of Smilzo's jacket.

"Keep quiet and stay where you are!" he said grimly. "It's too early for anyone to be told. Let's take care of our little list."

"List? What list?" asked Peppone in astonishment.

"The list of reactionaries who are to be executed first thing. Let's see now . . ."

Peppone stammered that he had made no such list, but the other only laughed.

"That doesn't matter. I've a very complete one here all ready. Let's look at it together, and once we've decided, we can get to work."

Gigio pulled a sheet of paper with some twenty names on it out of his pocket and laid it on the table.

"Looks to me as if all the reactionary pigs were here," he said. "I put down the worst of them, and we can attend to the rest later."

Peppone scanned the names and scratched his head.

"Well, what do you say?" Gigio asked him.

"Generally speaking, we agree," said Peppone. "But what's the hurry? We have plenty of time to do things in the proper style."

Gigio brought his fist down on the table.

"We haven't a minute to lose, that's what I say," he shouted harshly. "This is the time to put our hands on them, before they suspect us. If we wait until tomorrow, they may get wind of something and disappear."

At this point Brusco came into the discussion.

"You must be crazy," he said. "You can't start out to kill people before you think it over."

"I'm not crazy, and you're a very poor Communist, that's what you are! These are all reactionary pigs; no one can dispute that, and if you don't take advantage of this golden opportunity then you're a traitor to the Party!"

Brusco shook his head.

"Don't you believe it! It's jackasses that are traitors to the Party! And you'll be a jackass if you make mistakes and slaughter innocent people."

Gigio raised a threatening finger.

"It's better to eliminate ten innocents than to spare one individual who may be dangerous to the cause. Dead men can do the Party no harm. You're a very poor Communist, as I've said before. In fact, you never were a good one. You're as weak as a snowball in Hell, I say; you're just a *bourgeois* in disguise!"

Brusco grew pale, and Peppone intervened.

"That's enough," he said. "Comrade Gigio has the right idea, and nobody can deny it. It's part of the groundwork of Communist philosophy. Communism gives us the goal at which to aim and democratic discussion must be confined to the choice of the quickest and surest ways to attain it."

Gigio nodded his head in satisfaction, while Peppone continued: "Once it's been decided that these persons are or may be dangerous to the cause and therefore we must eliminate them, the next thing is to work out the best method of elimination. Because if by our carelessness we were to allow a single reactionary to escape, then we should indeed be traitors to the Party. Is that clear?"

"Absolutely," the others said in chorus. "You're dead right."

"There are six of us," Peppone went on, "and twenty names on the list, among them Filotti, who has a whole regiment in his house and a cache of arms in the cellar. If we were to attack these people one by one, at the first shot the rest would run away. We must call our forces together, and divide them up into twenty squads, each one equipped to deal with a particular objective."

"Very good," said Gigio.

"Good, my foot!" shouted Peppone. "That's not the half of it! We need a twenty-first squad, equipped even better than the rest, to hold off the police. And mobile squads to cover the roads and the river. If a fellow rushes into action in the way you proposed, without proper precautions, running the risk of botching it completely, then he's not a good Communist, he's just a damned fool."

It was Gigio's turn to pale now, and he bit his lip in anger while Peppone proceeded to give orders. Smilzo was to transmit word to the cell leaders in the outlying settlements, and these were to call their men together. A green rocket would give the signal to meet in appointed places, where Falchetto, Brusco and Straziami would form the squads and assign the targets. A red rocket would bid them go into action. Smilzo went off on his motorcycle, while Lungo, Brusco, Straziami, and Gigio discussed the composition of the squads.

"You must do a faultless job," Peppone told them. "I shall hold you personally responsible for its success. Meanwhile, I'll see if the police are suspicious and find some way to put them off."

Don Camillo, after waiting in vain for the lights to go on and the radio to resume its mumble, decided to get ready for bed. Suddenly he heard a knock at the door, and when he drew it open cautiously, he found Peppone before him.

"Get out of here in a hurry!" Peppone panted. "Pack a bag and go! Put on an ordinary suit of clothes, take your boat and row down the river."

Don Camillo stared at him with curiosity.

"Comrade Mayor, have you been drinking?"

"Hurry!" said Peppone. "The People's Front has won, and the squads are getting ready. There's a list of people to be executed, and your name is the first one!"

Don Camillo bowed.

"An unexpected honour, Mr. Mayor! But I must say I never expected you to be the sort of rascal that draws up lists for murder."

"Don't be silly," said Peppone impatiently. "I don't want to murder anybody."

"Well then?"

"Gigio, the lame fellow from Molinetto, came out with the list and secret Party orders."

"You're the chief, Peppone. You could have sent him and his list to blazes."

Peppone rubbed his perspiring face.

"You don't understand these things. The Party always has the last word, and he was speaking for the Party. If I'd stood out against him he'd have added my name to the list, above yours."

"That's a good one! Comrade Peppone and the reactionary priest, Don Camillo, strung up together!"

"Hurry, will you?" Peppone repeated. "You can afford to joke because you're all alone in the world, but I have a mother, a wife, a son and a whole lot of other dependants. Move fast if you want to save your skin!"

Don Camillo shook his head.

"Why should I be saved? What about the others?"

"I can't very well go to warn them, can I? You'll have to do that yourself. Drop in on one or two of them on your way to the river, and tell them to pass on the alarm. And they'd better look lively! Here, take down the names."

"Very well," said Don Camillo when he'd taken them down. "I'll send the sexton's boy to call the Filotti family, and there are so many of them that they can take care of the rest. I'm staying here."

"But you've got to go, I tell you!"

"This is my place, and I won't budge, even if Stalin comes in person."

"You're crazy!" said Peppone, but before he could say anything else, there was a knock at the door and he had to run and hide in the next room.

The next arrival was Brusco, but he had barely time to say: "Don Camillo, get out of here in a hurry!" before someone knocked at the door again. Brusco, too, ran to hide, and a minute later Lungo burst in.

"Don Camillo," said Lungo, "I've only just been able to sneak away for a minute. Things are hotting up, and you'd better get out. Here are the names of the other people you ought to take with you."

And he rushed to hide, because there was another knock at the door. This time it was Straziami, as glum and pugnacious as ever. He had hardly stepped in, when Lungo, Brusco, and Peppone emerged to meet him.

"It's beginning to look like one of those old-fashioned comedies," said Don Camillo, laughing. "As soon as Gigio comes, the whole cast will be on the stage."

"He's not coming," muttered Peppone.

Then with a sigh, he slapped Brusco on the back.

"Notice anything?" he said reminiscently. "Here we are again, the way we were up in the mountains in the old days of the Resistance. And we can still get along together."

The others nodded.

"If Smilzo were only here the old guard would be complete," sighed Peppone.

"He *is* here," said Don Camillo. "In fact, he was the first to come."

"Good," said Peppone approvingly. "And now you'd better hustle."

But Don Camillo was a stubborn man.

"I told you once that my place is here," he said. "I'm quite happy enough to know that you're not against me."

Peppone lost patience. He twisted his hat about and then jammed it down on his head in the way that he did when he was ready to come to blows.

"You two take his shoulders, and I'll take his legs," he ordered. "It's too late to go by boat. We'll tie him to the seat of his cart and send him away. Straziami, go and harness the horse."

But before they could raise their arms the lights went on, and they stood there, dazzled. A moment later the radio began to mumble.

"Here are the results of the election of Deputies to Parliament, with 41,000 out of 41,168 electoral districts heard from: Christian Democrats, 12,000,257 votes; People's Front, 7,547,468 . . ."

They all listened in silence until the announcement was over. Then Peppone looked gloomily at Don Camillo.

"Some weeds are so tough that they overrun everything," he said angrily. "You had a lucky escape, that's all I can say."

"You had a lucky escape yourself," Don Camillo answered calmly, "for which God be praised."

One man didn't escape and that was Gigio. He was proudly waiting for orders to set off the green rocket and, instead, he got a volley of kicks that left him black and blue all over.

BENEFIT OF CLERGY

THE TIME HAS COME to speak of Smilzo, official messenger at the Town Hall and head of the "flying squad" of the local Communist Party, and to brand him for what he was, an example of flagrant immorality, a man without any sense of shame, because a man must be shameless to live openly with a woman to whom he is not married in a village of the Po Valley. And the woman who shared his bed and board was just as shameless as he.

People called Moretta a "kept woman," but in reality she was a girl quite capable of keeping herself. She was big-boned and as strong as any man, and farmers hired her to run a tractor, which she manoeuvred just as skilfully as Peppone. Although the women of the village referred to her as "that hussy," no man but Smilzo had ever made advances to her without getting a slap in the face that left him groggy. Nevertheless, it was a village scandal to see him carry her on the handlebars of his bicycle, which was where she rode when she didn't occupy the saddle and carry him.

Don Camillo had come into the world with a constitutional preference for calling a spade a spade and so it was that he spoke from the pulpit of "certain women who rode around on racing bicycles, flaunting their flanks as freely as their faces." From then on, Moretta wore blue dungarees and a red kerchief around her neck, which left the village even more shocked than before. Once Don Camillo managed to catch hold of Smilzo and say something to him about "legalizing the situation," but Smilzo only jeered in his face.

"There's nothing to 'legalize' about it. We do nothing more and nothing less than people who are idiotic enough to get married."

"Than decent men and women . . ." Don Camillo sputtered.

"Than idiots who spoil the beauty of affinity between two united souls by dragging a clumsy oaf of a mayor or a priest reeking of tobacco into it."

Don Camillo swallowed the aspersion on his tobacco and came back to the main point of what he was saying. But Smilzo continued to jeer at him.

"If God Almighty had intended men and women to be joined in matrimony, He'd have put a priest with Adam and Eve in the Garden of Eden! Love was born free and free it ought to remain! The day is coming when people will understand that marriage is like a jail sentence, and they'll get along without benefit of clergy. And when that day comes there'll be dancing in the churches."

Don Camillo found only a brick handy. He picked this up and threw it, but Smilzo had learned during the period of the Resistance movement to slip between one volley of machine-gun fire and another, and so the brick was wasted. But Don Camillo was not discouraged, and one day he lured Moretta to the presbytery. She came in her blue dungarees, with the red kerchief around her neck, and lit a cigarette as soon as she sat down before him. Don Camillo refrained from scolding her and spoke in the mildest tone of voice he could manage.

"You're a hard-working girl and a good housekeeper," he told her. "I know that you don't gossip or waste money. And I know too that you love your husband . . ."

"He isn't my husband," Moretta interrupted.

"That you love Smilzo, then," said Don Camillo patiently. "And so, although you've never come to confession, I'm convinced that you're a decent sort of woman. Why do you have to behave in such a way that people brand you as indecent?"

" 'People' can go straight to . . . where they belong," Moretta retorted.

Don Camillo was growing red in the face, but he went ahead with his plan and murmured something about getting married. But Moretta interrupted him.

"If God Almighty had intended men and women to be joined in matrimony. . . ."

"Never mind," said Don Camillo, interrupting her in his turn. "I know the rest already."

"Love was born free and free it ought to remain!" Moretta concluded gravely. "Marriage is the opium of love."

The village gossips did not give up so easily. They formed a committee and went to tell the Mayor that the affair was bringing shame upon the village and for the sake of public morals he must do something about it.

"I'm married myself," said Peppone, "and I have a right to perform a civil marriage, but I can't force people to marry when they don't want to. That's the law. Perhaps when the Pope comes into power things will be different."

But the old crones insisted.

"If you can't do anything as Mayor, then as head of the local section of the Party you can bring pressure on them. They're a disgrace to the Party, too."

"I'll try," said Peppone, and so he did.

"I'd rather join the *Socialist* Party than marry," was Smilzo's answer.

That was all there was to it, and with the passage of time the scandal abated, or rather politics took its place. But one day it came to the fore again and in a clamorous manner. For some time Comrade Moretta was not seen about, and then all of a sudden there was a startling piece of news. There were no longer two Comrades, but three, because, as the midwife told it, a little girl had been born to them, and one far prettier than they deserved. The old crones of the village began to wag their tongues again, and those who were politically-minded said:

"There are Communist morals for you. It's a hundred to one these godless parents will never have the child baptized."

The news and the comment reached Peppone's ears, and he rushed to the godless parents' home.   *

Don Camillo was reading when Smilzo came in.

"There's a baptizing job for you to do," Smilzo said abruptly.

"A fine job indeed," muttered Don Camillo.

"Must one obtain a *nihil obstat* before having a baby?" Smilzo asked him.

"The *nihil obstat* of your own conscience," said Don Camillo. "But that's strictly your affair. Only if Moretta arrives dressed in her blue dungarees, I'll chase you all away. You can come twenty minutes from now."

Moretta came with the baby in her arms and Smilzo at her side. Don Camillo received them along with Peppone and his wife at the door to the church.

"Take all that red stuff off," he said, without even looking to see if they really were wearing anything red. "This is the House of God and not the People's Palace."

"There's nothing red around here except the fog in your brain," muttered Peppone.

They went into the church and over to the baptismal font, where Don Camillo began the ceremony.

"What's the name?" he asked.

"Rita Palmira Valeria," the mother stated firmly.

There was a dead silence as the three names—every one of them of internationally famous Communists—echoed in the little church. Don Camillo replaced the cover on the font and was just about to say "then go and get her baptized in Russia" when he saw the Lord looking down at him from the Cross. So he just took a deep breath and counted to ten instead.

"Rita is for my mother, Palmira for his and Valeria for my grandmother," Moretta pointed out.

"That's their bad luck," said Don Camillo dryly. "I say Emilia Rosa Antonietta."

Peppone pawed the ground, while Smilzo sighed and shook his head, but Moretta seemed secretly pleased.

Afterwards they went to the presbytery to sign the register.

"Under the Christian Democrat Government, is Palmira a forbidden name?" Peppone asked sarcastically.

Don Camillo did not answer, but motioned to him and his wife to go home. Smilzo, Moretta and the baby were left standing in front of the table.

"*Enciclica rerarum novium,*" said Smilzo more cleverly than correctly, with the look of a man resigned to his fate.

"No. I'm not making a speech," Don Camillo said coldly. "I just want to give you a warning. By not getting married you are not hurting the Church. You're just two cockroaches trying to gnaw at one of the columns of Saint Peter's. Neither you nor your offspring are of the slightest interest to me."

At this moment the bundle in Moretta's arms stirred, and the "offspring" opened her eyes wide and smiled at Don Camillo. She had such a pink little face that Don Camillo paused and then his blood began to boil and he lost his temper.

"Miserable creatures!" he shouted. "You have no right to visit your foolish sins upon the head of this innocent baby. She's going to grow up to be a beautiful girl and when people are envious of her beauty they'll throw mud at her by calling her a 'kept woman's child.' If you weren't such wretches you wouldn't expose your daughter to people's jealous hypocrisy. You may not care what people say about you, but if on your account they slander her . . ."

Don Camillo had raised his fist and thrown out his chest so that he looked even taller and bigger than he was, and the two parents had taken refuge in a corner.

"Get married, you criminals!" the priest shouted.

Pale and perspiring, Smilzo shook his head.

"No; that would be the end of everything for us. We couldn't face people."

The baby seemed to enjoy the scene. She waved her hands and laughed, and Don Camillo was taken aback.

"Please, I'm begging you!" he exclaimed. "She's too beautiful!"

Strange things can happen in this world. A man may try with a crowbar to force a door open and not move it a single inch. Then when he is dead tired and hangs his hat on the knob in order to wipe the sweat off his brow, click, the door opens. Moretta was a stubborn woman, but when she saw that Don Camillo's anger was dying down as he looked at her baby, she threw herself on to a chair and began to cry.

"No, no," she sobbed. "We can't marry because we're married already. We did it three years ago, only nobody knows, because we chose somewhere far away. We've always liked free love. And so we've never told a soul."

Smilzo nodded.

"Marriage is the opium of love," he began. "Love was born free, and if God Almighty . . ."

Don Camillo went to douse his face in cold water. When he came back, Smilzo and his wife were quite calm, and Moretta was holding out a paper which was a marriage certificate.

"Under the secrecy of the confessional," she whispered.

Don Camillo nodded.

"So you've registered with your employer as 'single,' " he said to Smilzo, "and you don't get any of the benefits of being a family man."

"Exactly," said Smilzo. "There's nothing I wouldn't do for my ideals."

Don Camillo handed back the certificate.

"You're two donkeys," he said calmly. Then, when the baby smiled, he corrected himself: "Two donkeys and a half."

Smilzo turned round at the door and raised a clenched fist in salute.

"There'll always be a place on the gallows for those who run down the people," he said gravely.

"You'd better hang your hat on it then, so as to reserve a place for yourself!" answered Don Camillo.

"The election we lost was just a passing phase," said Smilzo. "We have come from very far and we still have far to go. Farewell, citizen priest."

OUT OF THE NIGHT

FOR SOME UNKNOWN reason Don Camillo had fallen into the habit of waking up in the middle of the night. He could hear nothing out of the ordinary, and yet he felt sure that there was something wrong. Finally, one night he heard a scuffling noise outside and, looking out of the window, he saw a shadow moving about near the small side door of the church, below the tower. He must have made a noise, for the shadow slipped away. But the next night Don Camillo was better prepared. He left the window slightly open and laid his shotgun on the sill. Then at the last minute he gave up this plan.

"If it's someone trying to break into the church, then he isn't after me. That is, unless he's trying to place a time bomb inside."

This was a possibility, but one shouldn't impugn a stranger's intentions, even in the valley. And so Don Camillo finally decided to keep watch in the church. For three nights he played sentry in vain, and on the fourth night, when he was just about to give the whole thing up, he heard someone scraping at the lock of the side door. He kept perfectly still, and in a few minutes the lock sprang and the door slowly opened. There was no light in the church other than that given by a feeble sanctuary lamp, but Don Camillo made out the hesitant figure of a skinny young man. The man looked about him, found a ladder and cautiously raised it against the wall to the right of the altar. High along this wall were many offerings, in the form of silver hearts mounted in frames and hung as tokens of gratitude for some mark of divine favour. "So that's what you're after!" Don Camillo said to himself.

He let the intruder climb halfway up the ladder before he came out of ambush, but Don Camillo was a big man and about as graceful in his movements as a division of armoured cars so he made a tremendous racket. The man leaped down and tried to reach the door, but Don Camillo seized him by the nape of the neck. Then, in order to get a better hold, he let go of the neck, caught the arms and raised them up in the air to make sure the fellow didn't carry a gun. The fellow had crumpled up completely, and even if he had had a revolver on him he wouldn't have had the strength to pull the trigger. Don Camillo carried his catch into the sacristy, where he switched on the light and looked him in the face. When he saw who it was, he let him drop like a bundle of rags to the floor and sat down in front of him.

"Smilzo, you're no good as a thief, either!"

Smilzo shrugged his shoulders.

"It's not my trade," he answered. "I didn't mean to steal."

Don Camillo laughed.

"I don't suppose it was in order to say your prayers that you let yourself into the church with a pass-key in the middle of the night and started climbing up a ladder."

"Everyone prays in his own way," Smilzo protested.

"Well, you can explain it to the police," said Don Camillo.

This last word caused Smilzo to leap up, but Don Camillo simply stretched out one paw and put him down.

"Don't you get me into trouble," said Smilzo. "Here everything is tied up with politics, and that means a mess."

"Don't worry," Don Camillo reassured him. "This is a strictly criminal affair, and the charge will be attempted burglary."

Then he yanked the limp Smilzo to his feet and searched his pockets.

"Actual burglary!" he correct himself. "This is the real thing!" And he held up what he had found.

"It isn't burglary at all," said Smilzo. "That belongs to me, and I paid for it with my own money."

The object was a votive offering, a frame with a silver heart inside. Obviously it was brand new, but Don Camillo found it difficult to believe Smilzo's story and dragged him over to the wall where the ladder was still standing. Sure enough, nothing was missing. The offerings formed a perfect rectangle and the absence of even a single one would have been noticed. Don Camillo examined the offering he had found in Smilzo's pocket. The heart was sterling silver and carefully framed.

"Well then, what's it all about?" he asked. "How can you explain?"

Smilzo shrugged his shoulders.

"Gratitude is a good thing, but politics are filthy. I promised that if a certain deal came off, I'd offer one of these things to God. But since the Party and the Vatican are at swords' points, I couldn't afford to be seen. People might talk, because everyone knows you priests start them talking. Yes, when you war-mongers . . ."

"Drop that," Don Camillo interrupted. "I know that whole rigmarole by heart. Let's stick to our present business. If you didn't want to be seen, you could have sent somebody. Why did you turn it into a detective story?"

Smilzo puffed up his chest.

"We who come from the people always keep our word, even in matters of religion. I had promised to offer this thing in person and so I brought it. Now I shall hand it over to you."

In the valley close to the shore of the river they're all a little queer in the head, and after a few moments of reflection, Don Camillo gave up and threw out his arms.

"Very well," he said, "here's a receipt, and let's forget about it."

Smilzo slipped away from the foot Don Camillo had ready for him and called from the door:

"If you priests get through another year without being swept away by the rising tide of the people's revolution, you can thank God with one of these things ten feet square!"

Don Camillo was left with the silver heart in his hand, and took it to the altar to show to the Lord.

"Lord, these people require understanding," he said. "They're less complex than one might think. They're simple, primitive souls, and even when they do something good they have to be violent about it. There are many things which we must forgive them."

"We must forgive them, indeed, Don Camillo," said the Lord with a sigh.

Don Camillo was sleepy.

"I'll hang this up and not think about it any more until tomorrow," he said to himself. And he climbed up on the ladder and hung it just under the bottom row. Then he pulled out the nail he had just driven in and changed the location. "I'd better place it beside the one given by his wife. Whom God has joined together let no man put asunder, either in God's house or the Devil's."

Three months before, Smilzo's wife, Moretta, had been very ill, and since it seemed that the Party couldn't heal her, she had turned to God. After an almost miraculous cure, she had brought an offering. Now Don Camillo leaned back and admired the two identical hearts.

"There's the same sinful soul in both bodies," he mumbled, shaking his head. After he had come down from the ladder he started to leave the church, but did not get as far as the door. He stopped short and went back to the altar.

"Lord, a man breaks into a church at two o'clock in the morning in order to hang up a votive offering. It simply doesn't make sense."

He paced up and down for a few minutes, then climbed up on the ladder again. He took down the two framed hearts and examined them under the light. Then he raised his head.

"We must indeed forgive them," commented the Lord.

Smilzo appeared at the presbytery the next evening.

"I'm here about the same old story," he said with an indifferent air. "My wife's got it into her head that she must add two silver flowers to the offering she made three months ago. If you give it to me, I'll bring it back tomorrow."

"That's a good idea," said Don Camillo. "I actually have it here. Last night, when I was hanging yours beside it, I saw that some dust had got under the glass and I took it down to clean it."

He opened a drawer of his desk and took out the offering given by Smilzo's wife. Then he reached for something else and showed it to Smilzo.

"Between the wooden frame and the velvet lining I found this object. I can't imagine how it got there. Is it yours?"

The object was Smilzo's Party membership card. Smilzo put out his hand, but Don Camillo slipped it back into the drawer.

"Well, what's the game?"

"It's not so funny," said Smilzo. "Moretta was about to die. She vowed she would give a silver heart and I promised a proletarian one. When she got well I put my Party card in with her offering, but at the last minute I didn't dare to get out of the Party, so I stayed in. Now Peppone wants to check all our cards. And it's no joking matter, as it would be in Church or big business circles, where anything can be condoned for a little bribe. I'd be in serious trouble. So that's why I've got to get my card back."

Don Camillo slowly lit his cigar.

"Now the story makes sense," he said. "You had an exact duplicate of

Moretta's offering made and sneaked into the church like a thief in order to switch them and rescue your Party card."

Smilzo shrugged his shoulders.

"I planned to return the offering the next day to take the place of the card, so you end up with two offerings instead of one," he said. "What use is a Party card to God, anyhow?"

Don Camillo raised his finger.

"A vow is a solemn obligation, and you vowed . . ." he said.

"I'll fulfil it when the time comes," said Smilzo. "But I can't do it just now."

He seemed to be the same limp bundle of rags as the night before. Don Camillo took out the card and gave it to him.

"This filthy thing has no place in church," he said with scorn.

Smilzo put the card carefully into his wallet.

"Render unto Caesar that which is Caesar's, unto God that which is God's, and unto the people that which is the people's," he said as a parting shot.

"And unto Smilzo that which is Smilzo's!" added Don Camillo, giving him a hearty kick in the pants.

Smilzo took it with dignity.

"Come the revolution, those who have lifted a hand against the defenceless people will be paid back with interest," he proclaimed, "even when the hand happens to be a foot!"

Don Camillo went to hang up the hearts, and as he passed the altar he threw out his arms. The Lord smiled upon him.

"There are many things which we must forgive them, Don Camillo," he said. "On the Judgment Day none of them will carry a Party card."

Meanwhile Smilzo was walking proudly toward the People's Palace with his card in his pocket, feeling at peace with both God and man. Perhaps because what he had called his "proletarian heart" wasn't in his wallet, as he imagined, but in the votive offering to the right of the altar.

THE BICYCLE

IN THIS SLICE OF LAND between the river and the highway it is hard to imagine a time when the bicycle did not exist. Here, in the valley, everyone from five years old to eighty rides a bicycle. Little boys make remarkable riders because they support themselves on bent legs in the middle of the frame, and their bicycles move in anything but a straight line, but they do move just the same. The peasants for the most part use women's models, and the paunchy landowners trundle along on old-fashioned contraptions with a high seat which they reach by means of a little step screwed on to the rear axle.

City people's bicycles are utterly laughable. With gleaming metal gadgets, electric batteries, gears, baskets, chain-guards, speedometers and so on, they are mere toys and leg-exercisers. A genuine bicycle should weigh at least sixty-five pounds; it should have lost most of its paint and at least one pedal. All that should be left of the remaining pedal is the shaft, rubbed smooth and shiny by the sole of the rider's shoe. Indeed, this should be its only shiny feature. The handlebars (with no rubber tips to them) should not be at the conventional right angle to the wheels, but inclined at least twelve degrees one way or the other. A genuine bicycle has no mudguard over the rear wheel, and hanging before the front mudguard there should be a piece of automobile tyre, preferably red, to ward off splashes of water. A rear mudguard may be allowed when the rider is excessively disturbed by the streak of mud that accumulates on his back during a rainstorm. But in this case the mudguard must be split open in such a way that the rider can brake in so-called "American style," that is by pressing his trouser turn-up against the rear wheel.

A Po Valley bicycle has no mechanical brakes and its tyres wear conspicuous patches, so protuberant as to impart to the wheels a spirited, jumping motion. In the little world a bicycle blends with the landscape; it would never try to be showy and, beside it, those dressed-up racing models are like third-rate chorus girls next to a substantial housewife. City people can't be expected to understand these things; where sentiments are concerned they are about as delicate as cows in clover. They live quite contentedly in their civil corruption, and never refer to their female poodles as bitches. They have what they call their "toilets" or "lavatories" right in the middle of the house, whereas every self-respecting countryman puts his honestly named "water-closet" in an outhouse at the far end of the courtyard. To locate this convenience next to one's eating or sleeping quarters is supposed to be a symbol of "Progress," but to leave it outdoors, where it is out of reach and lacking tiled walls and pavement, is to my mind cleaner and more truly civilized.

In the valley a bicycle is just as necessary as a pair of shoes, in fact more so. Because even if a man hasn't any shoes he can still ride a bicycle, whereas if he hasn't a bicycle he must surely travel on foot. This may hold true in the city as well, but in the city there are trams, while in the valley there are no rails of any kind, but only bicycle, motorcycle, and wagon tracks, cut every now and then by the trail of a snake that has slithered from one ditch to another.

Don Camillo had never been in business, unless it is business to buy a pound of beef or a couple of black cigars and the accompanying box of what are locally called "lightning bolts," that is, sulphur matches to be struck on the soles of one's shoes or the seat of one's trousers. But if Don Camillo had never been in business he enjoyed seeing it go on, and whenever Saturday was a fine day he mounted his bicycle and went to the weekly market at La Villa. He was interested in livestock, farm machinery, fertilizers, and sprays, and when he could buy a bag of copper sulphate with which to protect the grapevines behind the presbytery he felt just about as happy as Farmer Bidazzi with all his acres. There were all kinds of amusement stands in the market-place and the holiday atmosphere and bustling activity never failed to put him in a good humour.

On this particular Saturday, then, Don Camillo got on his old bicycle and gaily ate up the seven miles to La Villa. The market was unusually crowded and Don

Camillo got more fun out of it than if it had been the yearly fair at Milan. At half-past eleven he went to get his bicycle from the spot where he had left it. He pulled it out by the handlebars and, working his way through all the confusion, started towards the narrow street leading to the open country. Here the Devil came into the picture, because Don Camillo stopped at a shop to buy some trifle, and when he came out his bicycle, which he had left leaning against the wall, had disappeared.

Don Camillo was equipped with outsize bones and muscles. From his toes to the top of his head he was as tall as an ordinary man standing on a stool, and from the top of his head to his toes he was a hand's breadth taller, which means that although other people saw him as of one height he saw himself as of another; that is, his courage was a hand's breadth greater than his considerable physical stature. Even if someone were to have pulled a shotgun on him, his blood-pressure wouldn't have gone up a single degree. But if he stumbled over a stone in the road or someone played a trick upon him, he was unnerved by the humiliation. At such times he felt almost sorry for himself and positively melancholy.

Now, with his bicycle gone, he did not make a row. He asked an old man standing near by if he had seen anyone ride off on a woman's bicycle with a green basket. And when the man said no, he touched his hat and went away. He walked by the police station, but never thought of going in. The fact that a country priest, with twenty-five lire in his pocket, had been robbed of a bicycle was a private and moral problem, and not one to be introduced into the public domain. Your rich man, to whom it is all a matter of money, may rush to report a theft. But to the poor it is a personal injustice, in the same class as striking a cripple or knocking his crutch out from under him.

Don Camillo pulled his hat down over his eyes and started to walk home. Every time he heard a cart or wagon behind him, he ducked down at the side of the road. He wanted to go home under his own steam without having to talk to anybody. And he wanted to cover the whole seven miles on foot in order to underline the thief's guilt and his own sense of injury. He walked alone through the dust and heat for a solid hour without pause, brooding over the misfortunes of a Don Camillo who seemed to him to exist quite apart from himself. At a certain point a side road came into the one along which he travelled, and he stopped to lean on the wall of a small brick bridge. Leaning up against the same wall was his bicycle. He knew every inch of it, and there was no chance of any mistake. Immediately he looked round, but no one was in sight. He touched the bicycle and tapped the handlebars with his knuckles. Yes, they were of solid metal. The nearest house was at least half a mile away and the bushes were not yet covered with enough leaves to provide a hiding-place. Finally, he looked over the wall of the bridge and saw a man sitting in the dried-up bed of the stream. The man stared up at him enquiringly.

"This bicycle is mine," Don Camillo said with a little hesitation.

"What bicycle?"

"The one here against the wall of the bridge."

"Good," said the man. "If there's a bicycle on the bridge and it's your bicycle, that's not my business."

"I was just telling you," Don Camillo said with considerable perplexity. "I didn't want there to be any muddle about it."

"Are you sure it's yours?" the man asked.

"I should say I am! It was stolen from me while I was in a shop at La Villa an hour ago. I don't know how it got here."

The man laughed.

"It must have got bored waiting and gone on ahead of you," he said.

Don Camillo threw out his arms in uncertainty.

"Are you, as a priest, able to keep a secret?" the man asked him.

"Certainly."

"Then I can tell you that the bicycle got here, because I brought it here myself."

Don Camillo opened his eyes wide.

"Did you find it?"

"Yes, I found it in front of the shop. And I took it."

"Was that your idea of a joke?" asked Don Camillo, after another moment of hesitation.

"Don't be silly!" the man protested. 'Do you think that at my age I go around joking? I meant to take it for keeps. Then I thought better of it and pedalled after you. I followed you up to about a mile back, then I took a short-cut, got here before you and put it right under your nose."

Don Camillo sat down on the wall and looked at the fellow below him.

"Why did you take a bicycle that wasn't yours?" he asked.

"Everyone to his own trade. You deal in souls and I deal in bicycles."

"Has that been your trade for long?"

"No; just for the last two or three months. I operate at markets and fairs, and I usually do pretty well, because a lot of these peasants have stone jars full of banknotes. This morning I had no luck, and so I took your bicycle. Then I saw you come out of the shop and go your way without telling anybody. I began to be sorry and followed you, I still don't understand exactly why. Why did you duck down every time a wagon caught up with you? Did you know I was behind you?"

"No."

"Well, I was. And if you'd accepted a lift, I'd have turned back. But since you kept on walking I had to follow."

Don Camillo shook his head. "Where are you going now?" he asked.

"Back to see if there's anything doing at La Villa."

"To see if you can lay hands on another bicycle."

"Of course."

"Then keep this one."

The man looked up at him.

"Not on your life, Father. Not even if it were made of solid gold. It would be on my conscience and ruin my career. I prefer to stay clear of the clergy."

Don Camillo asked if he had had anything to eat, and the man said no.

"Then come and eat something with me."

A wagon came by, and in it rode a peasant called Brelli.

"Come along, you wretch!" said Don Camillo. "You take the bicycle and I'll go in the wagon."

Then he stopped Brelli and told him that he had a pain in his leg. The man came up from below the bridge. He was so angry that he threw his cap on the ground and cursed a large number of saints before he got on the bicycle.

Don Camillo had had the meal ready for ten minutes by the time the bicycle thief arrived at the presbytery.

"There's only bread, sausage, cheese, and a drop of wine," said the priest. "I hope that's enough for you."

"Don't worry, Father," said the man. "I've taken care of that." And he put a chicken on the table.

"The creature was crossing the road and I accidentally ran over it," he explained. "I didn't want to leave it to die there, and so I put an end to its pain. . . . Don't look at me like that, Father. I'm sure that if you cook it properly, God will forgive you."

Don Camillo cooked the chicken and brought out a bottle of special wine. After an hour or so, the man said he must be about his business, but there was a worried look on his face.

"I don't know how I can go back to stealing bicycles," he sighed. "You've demoralized me completely."

"Have you a family?" Don Camillo asked him.

"No, I'm all alone."

"Then I'll take you on as a bell-ringer. Mine just went away two days ago."

"But I don't know how to ring bells."

"A man who knows how to steal bicycles won't find that hard to learn."

And he was bell-ringer from that day on.

THE PRODIGAL SON

ONE DAY DON CAMILLO was in the church talking things over with the Lord, and at a certain point he said:

"Lord, too many things in this world are out of joint."

"I don't see it in that way," the Lord answered. "Man may be out of joint, but the rest of the universe works pretty well."

Don Camillo paced up and down and then stopped again in front of the altar.

"Lord," he said, "if I were to start counting: one, two, three, four, five, six, seven, and count for a million years, should I ever come to a point where there were no more numbers?"

"Never," said the Lord. "You remind me of the man who drew a big circle on the ground and began to walk round it, saying: 'I want to see how long it will take me to get to the end.' So I must tell you: 'No, you'd never come to such a point.' "

In his imagination, Don Camillo was walking round the circle and feeling the breathlessness that must stem from a first glance into infinity.

"I still say that numbers must be finite," he insisted "Only God is infinite and eternal, and numbers can't claim to have the attributes of God."

"What have you got against numbers?" the Lord asked him.

"Why, that numbers are what have put men out of joint. Having discovered numbers, they've proceeded to deify them."

When Don Camillo got an idea into his head, there was no easy exit for it. He locked the main door of the church for the night, paced up and down again, and then came back to the altar.

"Perhaps, Lord, men's reliance upon the magic of numbers is just a desperate attempt to justify their existence as thinking beings." He remained uneasily silent for a minute and then went on: "Lord, are ideas finite? Are there new ideas in reserve or have men thought of everything there is to be thought?"

"Don Camillo, what do you mean by ideas?"

"As a poor country priest, all I can say is that ideas are lamps shining through the night of human ignorance and lighting up some new aspect of the greatness of the Creator."

The Lord was touched.

"Poor country priest," He said, "you're not so far from right. Once a hundred men were shut into an enormous dark room, each one of them with an unlit lamp. One of them managed to light his lamp, and so they could all see one another and get to know one another. As the rest lit their lamps, more and more of the objects around them came into view, until finally everything in the room stood out as good and beautiful. Now, follow me closely, Don Camillo. There were a hundred lamps, only one idea; yet it took the light of all the lamps to reveal the details of everything in the room. Every flame was the hundredth part of one great idea, one great light, the idea of the existence and majesty of the Creator. It was as if a man had broken a statuette into a hundred pieces and given one piece to each of a hundred men. The hundred men groped for one another and tried to fit the fragments together, making thousands of misshapen figures until at last they joined them properly. I repeat, Don Camillo, that every man lit his own lamp and the light of the hundred lamps together was Truth and Revelation. This should have satisfied them. But each man thought that the beauty of the objects he saw around him was due to the light of his own lamp, which had brought them out of the darkness. Some men stopped to worship their own lamps, and others wandered off in various directions, until the great light was broken up into a hundred flames, each one of which could illuminate only a fraction of the truth. And so you see, Don Camillo, that the hundred lamps must come together again in order to find the true light. To-day men wander mistrustfully about, each one in the light of his own lamp, with an area of melancholy darkness all around him, clinging to the slightest detail of whatever object he can illuminate by himself. And so I say that ideas do not exist; there is only one Idea, one Truth with a hundred facets. Ideas are neither finite nor finished, because there is only this one and eternal Idea. But men must join their fellows again like those in the enormous room."

Don Camillo threw out his arms.

"There's no going back," he sighed. "To-day men use the oil of their lamps to grease their filthy machines and machine-guns."

"In the Kingdom of Heaven," the Lord said, "oil is so bountiful it runs in rivers."

In the presbytery Don Camillo found Brusco waiting. Brusco was Peppone's right-hand man, a big fellow who opened his mouth only when he had something important to say. His daily average of spoken words was perhaps the lowest in the village.

"Somebody must be dead. Who is it?" Don Camillo asked him.

"Nobody. But I'm in trouble."

"Did you kill somebody by mistake?"

"No, it's about my son."

"Which one? Giuseppe?"

"No, none of the eight that are here at home. The one that's been in Sicily all these years."

Don Camillo remembered that in 1938 one of Brusco's sisters, who had married a man with land holdings in Sicily, had come to visit him. Before going home she had lined up Brusco's nine children.

"Can I have one?" she asked him.

"Take whichever one you like best."

"I'll take the least dirty of the lot."

And her choice fell upon Cecotto, who happened to have just washed his face. He was about eight years old and somehow different from the rest.

"Let's be quite frank if we want to stay friends," said Brusco's sister. "I'll take him and bring him up and you'll never see him again."

Brusco's wife had just died, and to be relieved of responsibility for one of his nine children was a blessing from Heaven. He nodded assent and only when his sister was at the door did he tug at her sleeve and say:

"Do you mind taking Giuseppe instead?"

"I wouldn't have him even as a gift," she answered, as if she had paid hard cash for Cecotto.

Don Camillo remembered the whole story.

"Well then?" he asked.

"I haven't seen him for twelve years," said Brusco, "but he's always written to me, and now he says he's coming home for a visit."

Don Camillo looked at him hard.

"Brusco, has the Five-year Plan gone to your head? Is it such a misfortune to see your son? Are you Reds ashamed of your own children?"

"No, I'm not ashamed even of Giuseppe, who's one of the biggest cowards I've ever known. It's my fault, not his, if he's turned out the way he has. This is an entirely different matter. In Sicily they're all reactionaries of one kind or another: barons, landowners, priests and so on. Of course, a son's a son, no matter what he does. But if he comes here I'll fall into disgrace with the Party. I should have let the Party know about the whole situation. . . ."

Don Camillo could hold himself back no longer.

"Come on and let the cat out of the bag!" he exclaimed. "What has the poor fellow done?"

Brusco lowered his head.

"They sent him to school . . ." he muttered.

"Well, you're not ashamed of him for that, are you?"

"No, but he's studying for the priesthood."

Don Camillo couldn't help laughing.

"So your son's a priest! That's a good one! A priest!"

"Pretty nearly one. . . . But you needn't rub it in."

Don Camillo had never heard Brusco speak in just this tone of voice. He waited to hear more.

"If he comes here, and Peppone catches on, he'll kill me. And since the boy's a priest, or nearly, I don't want him to know that I'm on the other side. You priests understand one another. And if you can't think of something, I'm done for. He's arriving at eight o'clock to-morrow."

"All right. Let me sleep on it."

Brusco had never thanked anyone in his life.

"I'll make it up to you," he muttered. And he added, from the door: " I have the worst luck! With all the reactionaries there are around, why did I have to have a priest for a son?"

Don Camillo was not in the least discomfited.

"With all the rogues there are available, why should a poor priest be cursed with a Communist father?"

Brusco shook his head.

"Everyone has his own troubles," he said with a bitter sigh.

SHOTGUN WEDDING

WHENEVER DON CAMILLO saw old man Rocchi come to the church or the presbytery he grumbled to himself: "Here's the commissar." For old man Rocchi was the leader of the watchdogs who appoint themselves in every parish to scrutinize the conduct of the priest, in church and out of it, and to write letters of protest to the bishop when they find it shocking or even improper. Of course the old man never missed a single service, and since he and his family occupied one of the front pews he followed everything Don Camillo said and did, and would turn to his wife in the middle of Mass with: "He skipped something," or: "To-day he's not got his wits about him," or: "Don Camillo isn't what he used to be." And he would go to the presbytery afterwards to comment upon the sermon and give Don Camillo some sound advice.

Don Camillo wasn't the type to worry about such things, but it was a nuisance to feel old Rocchi's eyes constantly upon him, and whenever he had to blow his nose in the middle of Mass he raised his eyes to Christ on the cross above the altar and silently prayed: "Lord, help me blow my nose in a manner that will not cause a scandal!" For Rocchi was a great stickler for form. More than once he had remarked: "When the priest at Treville has to blow his nose in the middle of Mass, nobody knows it, but this one sounds like a trumpet call to the Last Judgment."

That is the kind of a man Rocchi was, and if such men exist in the world it must mean that they have a place to fill in it. He had three sons and one daughter, Paolina, who was the most virtuous and most beautiful girl in the village. And it was Paolina who startled Don Camillo almost out of his wits one day in the confessional.

"I can't grant you absolution before you do what you are supposed to," he told her.

"I know," said the girl.

This is the sort of thing that happens in every village, and in order to understand it one really has to have lived in one of the low houses in the broad valley and to have seen the moon rise like a great red ball over the bank of the river. There is no visible movement in the valley and a stranger may have the idea that nothing ever happens along the deserted river banks, that nothing *could* happen in the red and blue houses. Yet more things happen there than up in the mountains or in the big city. For the blazing summer sun gets into people's veins, and that big red moon is utterly unlike the pale satellite they see in other places; it blazes just like the sun, inflaming the imaginations of the living and the bones of the dead. Even in winter, when the valley is filled with cold and fog, the heat stored up during the summer is so great that people's imaginations aren't cooled off sufficiently to see things as they actually are. That is why every now and then a shotgun peeps out of a thicket or a girl does something she ought not to do.

Paolina went home, and when the family had finished saying the evening rosary she stepped up to her father.

"Father, I must have a talk with you," she said.

The others went their various ways and Paolina and her father were left beside the fire.

"What's it all about?" asked the old man suspiciously.

"It's time to think about my getting married."

"Don't you bother your head about that. When the time comes, we'll find the right sort of fellow."

"The time has already come, Father, and I've found him."

The old man opened his eyes wide.

"Go straight to bed, and don't let me hear you talk of such things again!" he ordered.

"Very well," said the girl, "but you'll hear other people talking about them."

"Have you given some cause for scandal?" asked the horrified father.

"No, but the scandal will come out. It's not something that can be concealed."

Rocchi took hold of the first thing that came to hand, which happened to be a broken broomstick. The girl crouched in a corner, hiding her head, and received a rain of blows upon her back. Luckily, the broomstick broke again and her father quietened down.

"If you're so unlucky as to be still alive, get up," he told her. "Does anyone know about it?"

"*He* knows . . ." murmured the girl, causing the old man to lose his head again and start to beat her with a stick taken from a bundle of faggots by the fire. "And so does Don Camillo," she added. "He wouldn't grant me absolution." Again the old man took it out on her. Finally she got in another word: "If you kill me, it will be an even worse scandal," she said, and that calmed him.

"Who's the man?" he asked.

"Falchetto," she answered.

She would have produced less of an effect if she had named Beelzebub in person. Falchetto was the nickname of Gigi Bariga, one of the most stalwart of Peppone's henchmen. He was the intellectual member of the gang, the one who wrote speeches, organized rallies and explained the Party directives. Because he understood more than the others, he was the unholiest of them all. The girl had taken so much punishment by now that the old man pushed her on to a couch and sat down beside her.

"You've beaten me enough," she said. "If you touch me again, I'll call for help and tell everybody. I have to protect the life of my child."

At eleven o'clock that night the old man gave in to his fatigue.

"I can't kill you, and in the state you're in, you can't very well enter a convent," he said. "Marry, then, and be damned, both of you."

When Falchetto saw the effects of Paolina's beating his jaw dropped.

"We must get married," she said, "or this will be the death of me."

"Of course!" said Falchetto. "That's what I've been asking you all along. Any moment, if you give the word, Paolina."

It was no use thinking of marriage at a quarter to one in the morning, but words exchanged at the garden gate, before the fields covered with snow, had a certain value and significance.

"Have you told your father everything?" Falchetto asked.

She did not answer, and Falchetto realized that it was a stupid question.

"I'll take my tommy-gun and shoot your entire family," he exclaimed. "I'll . . ."

"There's no need to shoot. All we have to do is to go and get the priest's permission."

Falchetto stepped back.

"You know I can't do that," he said. "Just think of my position. We can go to the Mayor."

The girl pulled her shawl around her.

"No, never," she said. "I don't care about what may happen. Either we are married like Christians or else I'll never see you again."

"Paolina! . . ." Falchetto implored her, but she had already slipped through the gate in the opposite direction from that which she had so often taken before.

Paolina stayed in bed for two days, and on the third day her father came up to her room.

"You saw him the other evening," he said. "I happen to know."

"So do I."

"Well, then?"

"There's no way out. He won't have a Christian wedding. And I say a Christian wedding or nothing at all."

The old man shouted and stamped his feet. Then he left his daughter, threw his overcoat over his shoulders and went out. And a few minutes later Don Camillo had a difficult problem before him.

"Father, you already know the story," said Rocchi.

"I do. Children need looking after. It's a parent's job to give them some moral principles."

Rocchi was properly put in his place, and he would gladly have strangled Don Camillo.

"I've consented to the marriage, but the rascal won't have anything to do with the Church."

"That doesn't surprise me."

"I've come to ask you this: is it more scandalous for a girl in my daughter's condition to marry outside the Church or not to marry at all?"

Don Camillo shook his head.

"This isn't a question of scandal. It's a question of good or evil. We must consider the unborn child."

"All I care about is to get them married and let them be damned!" said Rocchi.

"Then why do you ask for my advice? If all you care about is to get them married, let them marry as they please."

"But she says if she can't have a church wedding she'll have none at all," groaned the unhappy father.

Don Camillo smiled.

"You ought to be proud of your daughter. Two wrongs don't make a right. I say she has a head on her shoulders and you ought to be proud of her."

"I'll have to kill her, that's all," Rocchi shouted as he left the presbytery.

"You don't expect me to argue the girl out of a church wedding, do you?" Don Camillo shouted back after him.

During the night Paolina heard a hail of pebbles against her window and finally her resistance was overcome and she went down. Falchetto was waiting, and when she saw his face she burst into tears.

"I've left the Party," he told her. "To-morrow they'll get out an announcement of my expulsion. Peppone wanted me to write it myself."

The girl went closer to him.

"Did he beat you?" she asked.

"I thought he'd never stop," Falchetto admitted. "When are we going to get married?"

"Any moment, if you give the word," she said. And her impulse was just as foolish as his, because it was almost one o'clock in the morning and poor Falchetto had one eye as black as a lump of coal.

"I'll talk to the priest about it to-morrow," he said. "But I won't go near the Town Hall. I don't want to see Peppone."

He touched his black eye and Paolina put a hand on his shoulder.

"We'll go to the Mayor, too," she said. "I'll be there to stick up for you."

Paolina went early the next morning to Don Camillo.

"You can grant me absolution," she told him. "I didn't do any of the things I confessed to you. My only sin is to have told you a big lie."

Don Camillo was puzzled, but she quickly explained.

"If I hadn't made up that story, my father would never have let me marry Falchetto."

Don Camillo shook his head.

"Don't tell him the truth at this point," he advised her, secretly thinking that old man Rocchi had earned it.

"No, I won't tell him, not even after we're married," said the girl. "He beat me just as hard as if what I told him had been true."

"That's what I say," chimed in Don Camillo. "Such a beating shouldn't be given in vain."

As he passed by the altar, the Lord frowned down at him.

"Lord," said Don Camillo, "Whosoever shall exalt himself shall be humbled and he that shall humble himself shall be exalted."

"Don Camillo," said the Lord, "for some time now you've been skating on thin ice."

"With God's help, no ice is too thin," said Don Camillo. "This wedding will be worth a dozen of the usual kind."

And so it was.

SEEDS OF HATE

PEPPONE POPPED UP IN front of Don Camillo without any warning, followed by Smilzo, Bigio, Brusco, and Lungo. It looked like revenge or intimidation, and Don Camillo's first thought was of Falchetto, who had left the Party to marry Rocchi's daughter. "They're furious because they imagine I had something to do with it," he said to himself. But the gang wasn't thinking of Falchetto at all.

"There's no God in this, and no politics either," said Peppone, puffing like a steam engine on the Mulino Nuovo hill. "This is a patriotic matter. I'm here in my capacity of citizen Mayor and you in your capacity of citizen priest."

Don Camillo threw out his arms in welcome.

"Speak, citizen Mayor! The citizen priest is all ears."

Peppone stood in front of the table where Don Camillo was sitting, while his followers silently lined up behind him with their legs wide apart and their arms crossed over their chests.

"The Nemesis of History . . ." Peppone began, somewhat to Don Camillo's alarm, ". . . and not only the Nemesis of History but the Nemesis of Geography as well, and if that isn't enough . . ."

"I think it *is* enough," said Don Camillo, feeling reassured by the addition of Geography. "Just tell me what it's all about."

Peppone turned toward his followers with an indignant and ironical smile.

"They claim independence and home rule," he said, "and yet they don't know what's going on a mere fifty yards away."

"They're still living in the egotistical Middle Ages," said Smilzo unctuously. "*Cicero pro domo sua* and let the people eat cake!"

Don Camillo looked up at him.

"Are they teaching you Latin now?" he asked.

"Why not?" Smilzo retorted. "Do you think you have a monopoly on culture?"

But Peppone interrupted this exchange.

"They're a bunch of unpatriotic scoundrels, who want to usurp the sacred rights of the people by setting up an utterly unfounded claim to independence. I'm speaking of those wretched citizens of Fontanile, who want to secede from our township and set up a village administration of their own. We must nip their attempt in the bud by a manifesto outlining from A to Z the historical and geographical Nemesis which makes this town their capital city and their miserable village a mere suburb or dependency. . . ."

The discovery of what Peppone meant by "historical and geographical Nemesis" was not completely reassuring after all. Don Camillo knew his river valley and was aware of the fact that when two of its communities started to bicker, even on the basis of such a big word as "Nemesis," it was no laughing matter. Between these two in particular there were several old unsettled grudges. And for some time the inhabitants of Fontanile had had this home-rule bee in their bonnets. They had struck the first blow in 1902, when three or four groups of four houses each had put together the money to erect a public building, complete with arcade, sweeping stairway, clock tower and coat-of-arms over the door. This was to be the Town Hall. Then there was such high feeling about it that the police were called in and several citizens went to jail. That was as far as they got then. But the building remained and it was never put to any other use. They tried again in 1920, just after the First World War, but with no more success. And this was a third attempt. Don Camillo proceeded to feel his way cautiously.

"Have you tried talking to them about it?" he asked.

"Me talk to them?" shouted Peppone. "The only language I can make them understand is the tommy-gun."

"It doesn't seem as if negotiations would get very far on that basis," observed Don Camillo.

Peppone couldn't have been any angrier if his status had been lowered to that of a feudal serf.

"We'll act in strictly democratic fashion," he said with painful deliberation. 'We'll draw up a statement explaining the historical and geographical Nemesis, and if they're too dense to understand it. . . ."

Here Peppone paused, and Bigio, who was the best balanced of the gang, put in sombrely: "If they don't understand, we'll teach them a real lesson."

When the slow-going Bigio spoke in these terms, it meant that things were close to the boiling-point. Don Camillo tried another tack.

"If they want to secede, why not let them do it? What do you care?"

"It doesn't matter to me personally," shouted Peppone, "but it's an attack on the sovereignty of the people. This is the seat of the township. If we lose Fontanile and some of the territory beyond La Rocchetta, what's left? What sort of a one-horse place would this be? Are you by any chance unpatriotic?"

Don Camillo sighed.

"Why turn it into a tragedy? Fontanile has never been allowed to set itself up as an independent village, has it? Why should the authorities allow it to do so now? There's no change in the situation."

Peppone brought his fist down on the table.

"That's what *you* say!" he shouted ironically. "There's a political factor involved. Our Party is entrenched in the Town Hall and over at Fontanile they're all reactionaries. So the national Government would be glad to see some of our land and our people fall under a different administration!"

Don Camillo looked at him hard.

"You're the citizen Mayor and in politics up to your ears, so you ought to know. As a mere citizen priest, I'm in the dark."

Smilzo came forward and pointed an accusing finger at him. "You hireling of the Americans!" he said cuttingly.

Don Camillo shrugged his shoulders.

"Well, what are we going to do?" he asked Peppone.

"The first thing is to draw up a manifesto embodying our historical, geographical and economic arguments."

"And where am I to find them?" asked Don Camillo.

"That's up to you. Didn't they teach you anything at the seminary except how to make propaganda for America? . . . After that we'll see. If they drop their plan, all right; if they don't, we'll send them an *intimatum* to the effect that either they drop it or else . . . or else the will of the people shall decide!"

"God's will, you mean," Don Camillo corrected him.

"God doesn't come into this; we've said that already," replied Peppone. "But I'll take care of the *intimatum*, anyhow."

Don Camillo spent half the night putting together a manifesto of the reasons why Fontanile should not set itself up as an independent village. The hardest part was to reconcile the conflicting points of view and not to tread on anybody's toes. Finally, the manifesto was sent to the printer and then a group of young men went to paste it up at Fontanile.

At noon the next day a box was delivered to Peppone at the Town Hall. It contained one of the posters that had been pasted up at Fontanile the night before, and rolled up inside was something extremely unpleasant. Peppone wrapped it up again and hurried over to the presbytery, where he unfolded it in front of Don Camillo.

"Here is the answer from Fontanile," he said.

"Very well," said Don Camillo. "I wrote the statement, so that's meant for me. Leave it here and don't think about it any more."

Peppone shook his head. He folded it up again and started to go silently away. But at the door he turned round.

"Citizen priest," he said, "you'll soon have plenty of work to do."

Don Camillo was so taken aback that he could find nothing to answer. Peppone's words had transfixed him with fear.

"Lord," he said to the Lord at the altar. "Haven't war and politics put enough hate into these men's hearts?"

"Unfortunately, they can always find room for more," sighed the Lord.

WAR OF SECESSION

MESSENGERS WERE COMING and going at the Town Hall all day long, and Don Camillo could not guess what those devils were up to, especially as everybody claimed not to know. But toward nine o'clock in the evening, when he was preparing to go to bed, someone knocked at the shutter of the window on the church square. It was Smilzo, who said at once: "You've got to come to the Town Hall immediately. Hurry up, because the people have no time to wait upon the convenience of the clergy."

Smilzo was even more peremptory than usual. He felt that he could be so quite safely with the grating of the window between Don Camillo and himself, and furthermore his tone of voice made plain that he believed that he was entrusted with an unusually important mission.

"What do you mean by the people?" Don Camillo asked him. "People like yourself?"

"I didn't come here for a political discussion. If you're afraid to come out of your lair, that's another matter."

Don Camillo threw on his coat and picked up an umbrella, because just for a change it was raining.

"May I be told what's going on?" he asked on the way.

"It's not something that can be discussed in the street," said Smilzo. "That's just as if I were to ask you about the latest secret instructions sent you by the Pope."

"Leave the Pope alone," said Don Camillo, "or I'll break this umbrella over your head. The Pope has nothing to do with it."

"Whether he does or doesn't is something that we shall see about later, come the revolution," said Smilzo. "But never mind about that just now. You'll see what's going on when we reach the Town Hall."

Before they arrived a sentry halted them.

"Give the password," said a voice.

"*Venezia*," said Smilzo.

"*Milano*," came the reply.

Once they were past Don Camillo asked what was the meaning of all this nonsense, but Smilzo said that it wasn't nonsense at all.

"It's war," he maintained.

When they walked into the Council room, Don Camillo was very much surprised. The place was full of people, and not people to be dismissed as unimportant, either. All the notables of the village were there, representing all shades of political opinion, with nobody missing. There was a sepulchral silence, and evidently they were waiting for Don Camillo, for when he came in they made way before him. Then Peppone stood up and gave an explanation.

"Father," he said, "at this tragic time, when our country is in danger, you see here before you our most representative citizens, without distinction of party; farmers, workers, landowners, and shopkeepers, all joined in one faith. The attempt of an irresponsible group to trespass on our sacred rights must be defeated at any cost whatsoever . . . and so far I believe we all agree."

"Good," was the crowd's unanimous reply.

"In order to do away with any suspicion of party intrigue, the representatives of every faction have decided to choose someone who shall impartially pass opinion upon every decision made by the Committee for Public Safety for the defence of the village. By a secret ballot you were elected, and so, overcoming our political differences, we call upon you to be a member of the Committee in the role of neutral observer."

"I accept," said Don Camillo, looking around him, and the crowd applauded him loudly.

"We welcome your help. Here, then, is the situation. The people of Fontanile have answered our statement, duly approved by the representative of the Vatican here present, in an insulting and anti-democratic manner. In short, they have defied their capital city."

An angry murmur arose from the audience.

"Yes!" shouted Peppone. "On historical, geographical, and economic grounds we may call our village the spiritual 'capital' of the whole township, a capital one and indivisible forever."

"Well spoken!" called the crowd.

Peppone had now swung into top gear and was going full speed ahead:

"Strengthened by this gathering's lofty spirit of concord and comprehension, we say that we will not tolerate the "home-rulers' of Fontanile in their attempt to secede from our township and set up a village administration of their own. We suggest sending them an *intimatum* to say: Either drop the idea or we'll make you drop it. Because democracy is all very well, but when you're dealing with a bunch of people like those at Fontanile . . ."

Peppone was so swollen with rage that he looked even bigger and stronger than usual and his audience stared at him in fascination. Unfortunately, with the word "Fontanile" his vocabulary suddenly gave out and he could not find another word to say. He was standing on a two-inch-thick telephone book, and he seized upon this and slowly twisted it in his hands until it was torn in two. In the river valley an argument of this kind is invariably decisive. The assembly let out a yell of enthusiasm, and when Peppone threw the two parts of the book on the table before him, crying: "And this is our *intimatum*!" the applause threatened to bring down the ceiling. When quiet once more prevailed, Peppone turned to Don Camillo.

"Will the neutral observer give us the benefit of his opinion?"

Don Camillo got up and said calmly but in a loud voice: "My opinion is that you're all crazy."

His words were like an icy wind, and a heavy silence fell over the gathering.

"You've lost all sense of reality and proportion," Don Camillo continued. "It's as if you were building a skyscraper on a six-inch foundation, with the result that the whole thing will topple down on you. It isn't a question of sending ultimatums or tearing telephone books in two. We must use our heads, and if we do so it is clear that there's no use in even discussing the matter until the authorities give Fontanile permission to secede."

"But we're the authorities," shouted Peppone. "This is a matter for our concern."

Looking at the assembly, Don Camillo saw old man Rocchi rise from his seat in the front row.

"We agree, Father," said Rocchi, "that we should act calmly and not dramatize the situation. But if we wait for the authorities to give their permission, then our protest will be a revolt against the Government. We must, in orderly fashion of course, prevent Fontanile from putting in any request for home rule. I think the Mayor is wrong to speak of using force, but the substance of what he says is right."

"Good!" came voices from the assembly. "The Mayor has the right idea, even if we belong to different political parties. Politics don't come into this at all; it's the welfare of the village that's at stake. And let's be frank. We know what sort of people they are in Fontanile, and this is something we can't endure."

Peppone shot a triumphant glance at Don Camillo and Don Camillo threw out his arms in dismay.

"It's a sad fact," he said, "but people seem to agree only when it comes to doing something very foolish. But before carrying things too far, the two parties to the dispute must have a discussion. We must send a committee over to Fontanile."

"Of course," said Rocchi, and all the others nodded assent.

Peppone had no more telephone books to which he could give a "twister," but he took something out of the drawer of the table. This was the famous and insulting answer from Fontanile.

"How can you 'discuss' anything with people like these?" he asked.

At that the crowd became very restless.

"Even an *intimatum* would be too good for the likes of them," said Farmer Sacchini, shaking his big stick. "This is the only language they can understand."

Don Camillo felt himself entirely alone.

"It's no use my asking God to illuminate your minds," he cried, "because it's plain you haven't any. But I say that you simply can't do any of these things you propose."

"Who'll stop us?" asked Peppone.

"I will," said Don Camillo. He went resolutely to the door and then turned round while he put up his umbrella. "I'm going straight to the police sergeant," he said. "That may change your plans."

"You spy!" Peppone shouted, pointing an accusing finger at him from the platform. The crowd formed a wall between Don Camillo and Peppone, and the priest had no alternative but to go straight to the police station.

The forces of the law, consisting of the sergeant and four men, were put on watch, half at Fontanile and half in the "capital city." The sergeant, since he could not be split in two, rode on his bicycle to reinforce first one squad and then the other. Three days went by and nothing happened.

"It's clear that they've thought better of it," the sergeant said to Don Camillo. "They seem to have calmed down."

"Here's hoping God gave them minds and then illuminated them," Don Camillo replied without much conviction.

But on the afternoon of the fourth day an ugly incident took place at a big farm known as Case Nuove. A group of unemployed farm labourers swarmed over the place on bicycles, saying that they must be given work. Among other things, their claim was a stupid one, for it had rained for ten days in succession and the only work anyone could do in the fields was to walk a couple of yards and then sink up to the hips in mud. Obviously it was a trouble-making political manoeuvre. But for fear the farmer or some of his family might pull out a shotgun, the sergeant had to despatch his men to the spot. Toward evening Don Camillo went to look the situation over. The farm had been cleared of intruders, and these were wandering about in small groups not far away.

"If we leave, they'll be back in five minutes and start more trouble," said the sergeant. "Night is coming, and that's a tricky time where something like this is concerned."

Don Camillo ran into one of the groups on his way home and recognized among it the tailor from Molinetto.

"Have you changed your trade?" the priest asked him, "and turned into an unemployed farm labourer?"

"If people weren't so inquisitive, it would be a very fine thing," grumbled the tailor.

A little farther on Don Camillo met the old postman riding a bicycle, with a tool-box slung round his shoulder, which served him for his supplementary job as linesman for the telephone and telegraph systems. The priest was surprised to see him out so late, but the old man explained:

"I'm having a look round. The storm must have brought down a wire somewhere. Neither the telephone nor the telegraph is working."

Instead of going back to the presbytery, Don Camillo went to Brelli's house. He wrote a hurried note and gave it to the youngest boy to deliver.

"Take your motorcycle and get this to the parish priest at Villetta as fast as you can. It's a matter of life and death."

The boy was off like a flash. An hour later he came back to report:

"The priest said he'd telephone right away."

The river was swollen with rain and pressing against its banks. So were all the tributaries that poured into it across the plain. In normal weather these streams are ridiculous affairs. Either their beds are completely dry or else they contain only a few spoonfuls of water and one wonders why people with any sense should throw away money building up banks on either side. But they are not only ridiculous; they are unpredictable as well, like an ordinarily temperate man who once in a while goes out and gets . . . well, dead drunk is too mild a phrase for it. When these valley streams rise, they are so many Mississippis, with the water surging halfway up their banks and over. Now, after the prolonged storm, even the tiniest streams were frighteningly high and people went along the banks measuring their height with a stick. And the water continued to rise.

Fontanile was divided from the "capital" by just such a stream, and for twenty years no one had seen so much water in it. Night had fallen, but Don Camillo paced nervously up and down the road leading along the bank. His nervousness did not pass until he heard the brakes of a big car. The car was full of policemen, and with their arrival Don Camillo went back to the presbytery and hung his shotgun on the wall. After supper Peppone came to see him, looking very glum.

"Did you call the police?" he asked Don Camillo.

"Of course I did, after you staged that diversion at Case Nuove in order to have a free hand for your other mischief; yes, and after you cut the telephone and telegraph wires, too."

Peppone looked at him scornfully.

"You're a traitor!" he said. "You asked for foreign aid. A man without a country, that's what you are!"

This was such a wild accusation that Don Camillo was left gaping. But Peppone had still more to say.

"You're positively Godless!" he exclaimed. "But your police won't get anywhere. In two minutes God's justice will triumph!"

Don Camillo leaped to his feet, but before he could say a word there was a loud roar in the distance.

"The bank at Fontanile has given way," Peppone explained. "A concealed wire attached to a mine did the job. Now that Fontanile is flooded, they can found a little Venice if they want to!"

Don Camillo grabbed Peppone by the neck, but before he could squeeze it there came another roar, followed by a splash of water. A moment later the presbytery was flooded. When the water had reached the two men's belts it stopped rising.

"Do you see what murderers they are?" Peppone shouted. "So this was their little plan!"

Don Camillo looked sadly at the liquid mess, then shook his head and sighed.

"Dear God, if this is the beginning of the Great Flood, then I bless You for wiping this idiotic human race off the face of the globe."

But Peppone didn't see it the same way.

"*Navigare necessariorum est!*" he shouted, wading toward the door. "Italy's manifest destiny is on the seven seas!"

"Then all we have to do is wait for low tide," concluded Don Camillo philosophically.

There were three feet of water in the church, and when the candles were lit on the altar they cast the reflection of their flames into the water.

"Lord," said Don Camillo to the crucified Christ, "I beg Your forgiveness, but if I were to kneel down, I'd be up to my neck in water."

"Then remain standing, Don Camillo," the Lord answered, smiling.

BIANCO

NOWADAYS THE PEOPLE of the Po River Valley go to the city by bus, in one of those cursed modern machines where a human being travels like a trunk, and even if he is sick at his stomach he cannot budge from his seat. And during the winter, when there is a heavy fog or a treacherous coating of ice on the roads, he risks, at the very least, ending up in a ditch.

And to think that once upon a time there was a real steam train—even though it was only a very small one, with no more than a couple of carriages—which ran smoothly along its track through fog and ice! Until one fine day a city slicker discovered that it was out of date and substituted for its fidelity the fickleness of a vehicle supposedly more modern.

The steam train used to transport not only people, but sand, gravel, bricks, coal, wood, and vegetables as well. It was eminently practical and at the same time full of poetry. Then, one day, a dozen workmen wearing municipal badges appeared upon the scene and proceeded to tear up the tracks. And nobody protested; in fact, the general comment was: "It's about time." Because nowadays even old women who go to the city no more than once a year and spend the rest of their days just waiting for time to go by are in a hurry.

The train ran from the city to the river, and no farther, although this was not the end of the line. The largest villages of the region are strung out along the highway followed by the train, except for a particularly important one, two or three miles away, which it could not have reached except by making a long detour among the canals. On the road which linked this village to the highway, a special horse-drawn car carried passengers to and fro.

Bianco, the last horse to perform this service, was the handsomest of the lot, a beast so noble that he seemed to have stepped down from some public monument. On the village road the ties between the two rails of the line had been covered with tightly packed dirt and along this path Bianco trotted six times a day. A few minutes before the car came to a stop, that is, as soon as he heard the brake grinding, Bianco stepped out from between the rails and trotted alongside them. Then, as soon as the driver called: "Whoa!" he slowed down, without any danger of the car's bumping into his hindquarters.

Bianco was on the job for a number of years and knew it thoroughly. He had extraordinarily keen ears and could hear the train's steam whistle long before anyone knew that it was coming. He heard the whistle announcing the train's arrival at Trecaselli and pawed the stable floor to signify that it was time to hitch him to his car, pick up the village passengers, and start for the highway, in order to reach it with five minutes to spare. The first day that the whistle failed to sound because the train was no longer running, Bianco seemed to be bewitched. He stood tensely, with his ears sticking straight up into the air, and waited. For a whole week he behaved in the same way, until finally he set his mind at rest.

Yes, Bianco was a fine creature, and when he was put up at auction everyone wanted to buy him. Barchini was the highest bidder, and he hitched Bianco to a brand-new red wagon. Even between the wagon shafts, Bianco cut a handsome figure. This first time that he was hitched to the wagon, Bianco almost upset his new master, who was sitting on top of a load of beets. For when Barchini called out: "Whoa!" and pulled the reins, Bianco stepped to one side so abruptly that Barchini almost toppled over. But this was the only time that Bianco's memory tricked him; he caught on at once to the fact that the wagon was very different from a car running on rails. He had a touch of nostalgia every time he went along the road between the village and the highway. On the way out, nothing happened, but when he started home Bianco had a way of walking on the extreme left-hand side of the road, beside the ditch where the track had formerly been laid. The years went by, but, as he grew older, Bianco was such a good fellow that Barchini considered him one of the family, and even when he was no longer of much use no one dreamed of getting rid of him. He was given light work, and one day when Barchini caught a hired man beating him he went for him with a pitchfork, and if the fellow hadn't run up into the hayloft he would have found himself speared.

With the passage of the years, Bianco became increasingly weary and indifferent. There came a time when he did not swish his tail to scare off the flies, and he never had to be tied up because there was no likelihood that he would move from the place where anyone left him. He stood stock-still, with his head hanging, like a stuffed horse instead of a real one.

One Saturday afternoon Bianco was hitched to a light cart to take a bag of flour to Don Camillo. While the driver carried the bag into the presbytery on his shoulder, Bianco waited outside with his head hanging. All of a sudden he raised his head and pricked up his ears. The sight was so unexpected that Don Camillo, who was standing at the door lighting a cigar, let the match drop from his hand. Bianco stood tautly on the alert for several minutes, and then, wonder of wonders, bolted away. He galloped across the square, and it was sheer luck that nobody was run down. Then he turned into the road leading to the highway and disappeared, leaving a cloud of dust in his wake.

"Bianco's gone crazy," people shouted.

Peppone came by on his motorcycle, and Don Camillo tucked up his cassock and mounted behind him.

"Fast!" Don Camillo shouted, and Peppone threw out the clutch and went like the wind.

Bianco galloped down the road, with the cart swaying behind as if it were tossed on a stormy sea. If it didn't smash to pieces, it must have been because the patron saint of carts had his eye on it. Peppone drove his motorcycle at full speed, and halfway up the road the horse was overtaken.

"Run along beside him," said Don Camillo, "and I'll try to catch the rein near the bit."

Peppone steered close, and Don Camillo stretched out his hand toward the rein. For a moment Bianco seemed to remember that he was a very old nag and consented to being caught; then suddenly he speeded up and Don Camillo had to let go.

"Let him run!" Don Camillo shouted into Peppone's ear. "Go faster, and we'll wait for him at the highway."

The motorcycle shot ahead. When they reached the highway, Peppone braked. He tried to say something, but Don Camillo motioned to him to be silent. A few seconds later Bianco galloped into sight. Soon he threatened to join the highway traffic and Peppone had an impulse to give the alarm. But he didn't move in time, and then, after all, it turned out to be unnecessary. When Bianco reached the highway he came to a halt and dropped down on one side. He lay there sprawling in the dust, while the cart fell, with its shafts broken, into the ditch. Along the highway came the steam-roller, which was flattening out a coat of macadam. As the steam-roller passed by it whistled and then from the bag of bones—which was all that was left of Bianco—came a whinny. That was the end; now Bianco was a bag of bones indeed. Peppone stood looking down at the carcass, then he tore off his cap and threw it down on the ground.

"Just like the State!" he shouted.

"What do you mean, the State?" asked Don Camillo.

Peppone turned round with a fierce look on his face.

"The State! A man may say he's against it, but when the whistle calls him, he comes forward, and there he is."

"Where is he?" asked Don Camillo.

"Here! There! Everywhere!" shouted Peppone. "With his helmet on his head, his gun in hand and a knapsack over his shoulder. . . . And then it turns out that the call came not from the train, but from a steam-roller. But meanwhile he's a dead duck!"

Peppone wanted to say a great many things, but he didn't know where to begin. He picked up his cap, put it on his head and then lifted it again in salutation.

"A salute to the People!" he exclaimed.

Others began to arrive, in carts and on bicycles, and among them was Barchini.

"He heard the whistle of the steam-roller," Don Camillo explained, "and believed it was the train. That was plain from the way he stopped at the highway."

Barchini nodded. "The main thing is that he should have died believing," he said.

THE UGLY MADONNA

Don Camillo had a thorn in the flesh, one that had annoyed him intensely for a very long time. Once a year it was particularly painful, and that was during the procession in honour of the Assumption. For three hundred and sixty-four days the dim, shadowy chapel afforded concealment, but under the pitiless sun of

August fifteenth the true state of affairs was visible to everybody. And it was a serious matter.

She was known as the "ugly Madonna," a phrase which smacked of collective blasphemy. But actually no disrespect towards the Mother of God was intended; this was merely an accurate description of the statue which was the cause of Don Camillo's pain. The statue was a six-foot-tall terracotta affair, as heavy as lead, and painted in colours so offensive as to give anyone an eye-ache. The sculptor—God rest his soul!—appeared to have been one of the most miserable cheats the world has ever known. If an ignorant but honest man had done the job, no one would have called it ugly. Ignorance is not detrimental to a work of art, because a simple-minded craftsman may put his heart and soul into it and these count for infinitely more than his technical ability. But in this case the sculptor was obviously able and had turned all his skill to the creation of something ugly.

On that day long ago when Don Camillo set foot in the church for the first time, he was shocked by the statue's ugliness and he determined then and there to replace it with some more fitting image of God's Mother. He declared this intention on the spot, and was told to forget it. It was pointed out to him that the statue dated from 1693, and there was a date on the pedestal to prove it.

"I don't care about the date," Don Camillo objected. "It's downright ugly."

"Ugly, but venerably antique," they insisted.

"Venerably antique, but ugly," retorted Don Camillo.

"Historical, Father," they said, insisting upon having the last word.

For several years Don Camillo struggled in vain. If the statue had such historical importance, then it could be sent to a museum and replaced by one with a decent face. Or, if this wouldn't do, it could be moved into the sacristy and thus make way for a more suitable successor. Of course the purchase of another statue would require money. When Don Camillo started to make the rounds with fund-raising in view, he came upon more opposition.

"Replace the ugly Madonna? That statue is historical, and nothing can take its place. It wouldn't be right. Whoever heard of crowding out history?"

Don Camillo gave the project up, but the statue remained a thorn in his flesh, and every now and then he exploded to the Lord at the main altar about it.

"Lord, why don't You help me? Aren't You personally offended by the sight of Your Mother in such an unworthy guise? How can you bear it that people call her the 'ugly Madonna'?"

"Don Camillo," the Lord answered, "true beauty does not reside in the face. That, as we all know, must one day return to the dust from which it sprang. True beauty is eternal and does not die with the flesh. And the beauty of the Mother of God is in her soul and hence incorruptible. Why should I take offence because someone has carved a woman with an ugly face and set her up as a Madonna? Those who kneel before her aren't praying to a statue, but to the Mother of God in Heaven."

"Amen," said Don Camillo.

There was no other answer, but it still troubled him to hear people refer to the "ugly Madonna." He became accustomed to the thorn in his flesh, but every August fifteenth, when the statue was taken down and carried in the procession, the pain was more than he could bear. Once removed from the kindly shadows of the chapel and exposed to the sunlight, the face stood out all too clearly. It was not only an ugly face, but an evil one as well; the features were heavy and vulgar, and the eyes expressionless rather than ecstatic. And the Infant Jesus in the Madonna's arms was just a bundle of rags with an empty doll's head sticking out of them. Don Camillo had tried to mask the ugliness of the statue with a crown and necklace and veil, but these had served only to accentuate it. Finally, he removed all extraneous ornaments and let the vile colouring show for exactly what it was.

Then war came to the river valley, leaving in its wake death and destruction. Bombs fell upon churches and thieving, sacrilegious hands plundered their altars as they passed by. Don Camillo didn't dare admit it but he secretly hoped that someone would "liberate" him from the "ugly Madonna." When foreign soldiers first appeared upon the scene Don Camillo hurried to the proper authorities to say:

"Our ugly Madonna is a masterpiece dating from 1693, an object of both historical and artistic importance. Shouldn't it be evacuated to a safe place of storage for the duration?"

But they told him to set his mind at rest. Historically and artistically important as the Madonna might be, the fact remained that she was ugly, and this was her best defence. If she hadn't been ugly, she would never have stayed in place for so many years.

The war came to an end, and the first post-war years went by, and then a time came when the thorn in Don Camillo's flesh troubled him most acutely. He had painted the church walls, varnished the imitation marble columns and the wooden railings, and gilded the candlesticks on the various altars. As a result, the "ugly Madonna" simply didn't belong. A dark spot on a grey background is not too conspicuous, but on a white one it stands out like a black eye.

"Lord," said Don Camillo, on his knees before the Lord. "This time You simply must help me. I've spent all the money I had and some I didn't have on doing up the church. In order to pay my debts, I've rationed my food and given up cigars. And I rejoice not so much in the beauty of the church as in the God-given strength to sacrifice a few of my comforts. Now, won't You deliver me from the thorn in my flesh? Won't You do something to stop people from calling Don Camillo's church the 'Church of the Ugly Madonna'?"

"Don Camillo, do I have to tell you the same thing over and over?" the Lord answered. "Do I have to tell you again that true beauty does not reside in the face, that true beauty cannot be seen, because it is a thing of the spirit, which defies the erosion of time and does not return to the dust whence the body sprang?"

Don Camillo lowered his head without answering. And this was a bad sign.

The feast of the Assumption was drawing near, and one day Don Camillo summoned those who would carry the statue in the procession.

"This year the route followed by the procession will be longer than usual," he told them, "because we must go as far as the newly built houses along the south road."

It was a steaming hot August, and the idea of walking an extra mile over a freshly gravelled road was enough to make even a strong man flinch.

"We might carry the statue in two shifts," suggested old Giarola, who was in charge of arrangements.

"That's dangerous," said Don Camillo. "The sun beats down and the bearers' hands get sweaty and may slip just at the moment of changing. No, I think we might rig up Rebecci's small truck. As a matter of fact, that would add to the dignity of the whole thing, and I don't see any real objections."

In a way the bearers were half sorry, but when they thought of the length of the route and the heat of the sun, they felt relieved and gave their assent. Rebecci was glad to lend his truck, and the next day he brought it to the shed at the back of the presbytery. Don Camillo insisted on decorating it in person, and for a whole week he worked so hard that all over the village they could hear the sound of his hammer. He had built a platform on the back of the truck and then covered it with draperies and flowers, producing a truly magnificent effect. When Sunday came, the "ugly Madonna" was brought out of the church and hoisted up on to the platform. The pedestal was tied down with strong ropes and these were covered with garlands of flowers.

"You don't have to worry about the driving," Don Camillo said to Rebecci. "Even if you go at fifty miles an hour, I guarantee that it will hold fast."

"With all those decorations the Madonna is very nearly beautiful," people said when the truck started.

The procession began to wind its way towards the south road, with the truck moving at the speed of a man's walk. The freshly laid gravel was bumpy and suddenly the clutch went wrong, which jolted the truck so hard that if Don Camillo hadn't tied the pedestal securely to the platform the "ugly Madonna" would have been out of luck. Don Camillo saw that something was wrong and knew that Rebecci must be worried about it, so when they reached the south road he decided to change the route.

"The truck can't go so slowly over the gravel," he said, "so we'll cut across the fields to the highway. Rebecci will drive back at normal speed and wait for us at the bridge. There we'll re-form the procession and march on a smooth surface all the way back to the centre of the village."

Rebecci went dutifully back, and the "ugly Madonna" made the most uncomfortable trip of her long life. The procession re-formed at the bridge and moved smoothly along the paved road, although occasionally Rebecci's clutch caused the truck to leap forward as if someone had given it a kick from behind. The village was all decked out, especially the main street, with the arcades on either side, where every house was covered with streamers and people threw handfuls of flowers out of the windows. Unfortunately, this street was paved with cobblestones, and because the truck had hard tyres as well as a broken clutch, it bounced up and down as if it had St. Vitus's dance. But the "ugly Madonna" seemed to be glued to the platform, through Don Camillo's particular merit. Halfway down the main street, however, there was an especially rough bit of paving, punctuated by holes left from the construction of a sewer running below it.

"Once they're over that, there's no more danger," people said. Although they had complete faith in Don Camillo, they left a considerable space between themselves and the bouncing truck.

But the "ugly Madonna" did not get through the danger zone. She didn't fall, because Don Camillo's ropes held her fast, but on a particularly rough bump she just crumbled into pieces. The statue was not made of terracotta after all; it was some infernal mixture of brick dust or plaster or who knows what, and after two or three thousand death-dealing jars such as it had just received, an inevitable fate overtook it. But the shout which rose from the bystanders was not occasioned by the crumbling of the "ugly Madonna." It was a salute to the "fair Madonna," which as if by a miracle took its place.

On the pedestal, which was still roped securely to the truck, there emerged, like a butterfly coming out of its cocoon, a somewhat smaller statue of solid silver. Don Camillo stared at it in astonishment, and into his mind came the Lord's words: "True beauty does not reside in the face. . . . True beauty cannot be seen, because it is a thing of the spirit, which defies the erosion of time and does not return to the dust whence the body sprang. . . ." Then he turned round because an old woman was shouting:

"A miracle! A miracle!"

He shouted her down and then stooped over to pick up a fragment of the "ugly Madonna," a piece of one of the expressionless eyes which had once so annoyed him.

"We'll put you together again, piece by piece," he said in a loud voice, "even if it takes us ten years; yes, I'll do it myself, you poor 'ugly Madonna.' You concealed and saved this silver statue from one of the many barbarian invasions of the last three hundred years. Whoever hurriedly threw you together to cloak the Silver Madonna made you ugly on purpose. And so you did not attract an invader already on the march against this village or some distant city from which you may have originally come. When we have put you together, piece by piece, you shall stand side by side with your silver sister. Quite involuntarily, I brought you to this miserable end."

Don Camillo was telling the most shameless lie of his life. But he could not, in the face of his assembled parish, explained that he had chosen a roundabout and rocky route for the procession, blown up the truck tyres to the bursting-point, sabotaged the clutch and even abetted the destructive power of holes and gravel by driving a pointed tool into the terracotta and starting to crack it open, which last effort he had abandoned when he had seen that the material of which the ugly statue was made would crumble of its own accord. He meant to confess it to the Lord, who of course already knew about it. Meanwhile, he went on with his peroration.

"Poor 'ugly Madonna,' you saved the silver statue from one of the many waves of barbarian invaders. But who will save the silver Madonna from the barbarians of to-day as they press at our frontiers and eye with hatred the citadel of Christ? Is your appearance an omen? Does it mean that the new barbarians will not invade our valleys, or that if they do our strong faith and powerful arms will defend you? . . ."

Peppone, who was standing in the front row, in order to "observe the phenomenon more closely," turned to his lieutenant, Smilzo: "What's he mean by the 'new barbarians'?" he asked him.

Smilzo shrugged his shoulders. "Just a bit of unbridled clerical imagination."
There was a moment of silence and then the procession continued.

THE FLYING SQUAD

THAT YEAR AS USUAL the time came round for "Party Paper Promotion Day."
Peppone himself was supposed to go about hawking papers in order to give a good
example, but he didn't want to be made a fool of, and so three or four days before-
hand he stopped Don Camillo, who was coming back from a parochial call he had
made on his bicycle.

"Once is enough, Father, but twice is too much," Peppone said solemnly.

"What do you mean?" asked Don Camillo, putting one foot on the ground.

"Sunday is Party Paper Promotion Day, and I won't stand any of your joking.
You stick to your business and I'll stick to mine. An insult to me is an insult to the
Party."

Don Camillo shook his head.

"If I meet you on the street, I can at least buy a paper, can't I?"

"No; if a reactionary in uniform approaches the local leader of the People's
Party to buy the People's Party paper, it's an attempt to provoke violence. It's
almost as bad as if I were to force a paper on you. Each one of us should stick to his
own job: you dish out propaganda for the Pope and I dish it out for the Party."

"Good," said Don Camillo. "Then you admit that dishing out propaganda for
the Pope is within my rights."

"Of course, as long as you don't do it in an aggressive and provocative fashion.
Within your own province you can dish out propaganda for anything you damn
well please."

"That's a bargain!"

When Sunday morning came, Peppone had mapped out his strategy.

"We won't show our faces, because rather than buy a paper these people are
capable of staying away from Mass. Of course, their staying away is a Party
triumph, because it rescues them for once from the domination of the clergy. But
the Party paper doesn't profit. We'll spread word that we've gone to Castelletto,
and that way they'll be tricked into going to Mass. When they all come out at noon,
we'll blockade the square and see who has the nerve to refuse the paper!"

The plan worked well. People went to Mass, and a few minutes before noon
every street leading away from the square was covered. But when twelve o'clock
came nobody left the church.

"He's caught on to the trick and is dragging out the Mass so as to keep them
there longer," said Peppone. "But a lot of good that will do him!"

A few minutes later, they did pour out, but instead of scattering they stood
compactly together.

"What are those devils up to?" mumbled Peppone. "They must be waiting for
someone."

Just then there came a loud noise from the top of the church tower.

"He's set up a loud-speaker," Peppone shouted. "But if he makes a political speech there'll be hell to pay."

The noise from the loud-speaker increased, and became recognizable as the applause of a crowd. Then came a clear, powerful voice, that of the Pope speaking to two hundred and fifty thousand citizens of Rome. He spoke succinctly of the cardinal imprisoned by the Reds of Hungary, and when the loud-speaker had spilled the last wave of shouting and cheering down from the church tower, the village square was filled with people. They had come out of their houses, even the oldest and most infirm among them, from every direction, and Peppone's gang was disrupted and drowned in their surge. Some people were hurrying home, others talking excitedly to one another and feeling braced up by the two hundred and fifty thousand Romans gathered in St. Peter's Square. When the transcribed broadcast from Rome was over, Don Camillo turned on the gramophone, and a flood of music and singing kept the villagers' spirits high.

In the end, Peppone's gang found themselves still holding their papers in the middle of a deserted square. Smilzo tried offering them to a few stragglers, but they paid him no attention. Peppone was the last one to regain his self-control. He had such confusion in his head and such convulsions of rage in his stomach that he didn't know his left hand from his right. He began to see straight only when Don Camillo appeared at the church's open door. With lowered head, Peppone advanced toward him, and when he had come close he stood his ground and clenched his teeth. Don Camillo looked at him with a smile.

"As you see, I kept my part of our bargain," he said. "You advertised the Party and I advertised the Pope."

When you have a whole dictionary full of swear-words in your mind, it is useless even to begin to come out with them, so Peppone merely drew a sigh that had the volume of a cyclone. He stood there, with lowered head, wishing that he had horns like a bull and could disembowel Don Camillo and the whole of Christianity as well.

"Give me a copy of your paper," said a voice, and fifteen lire floated into Peppone's field of vision. Mechanically he held out the paper and took the money, but before slipping it into his pocket he remembered something, raised his head and saw Don Camillo standing there with the Communist paper in his hand. Then he really lost control. He raised the pile of papers above his head and threw them down to the ground with every ounce of strength the Creator had put into his muscles. It was a lovely crash. Then he wheeled about and walked away, while Smilzo picked up the papers and started to follow. But after he had gone a few feet, he turned to throw over his shoulder:

"When Stalin speaks from St. Peter's Square, then you'll hear something!"

Don Camillo showed considerable interest.

"Does your paper say when that's going to be?" he asked.

"No, it doesn't," Smilzo grudgingly admitted.

"Well, for a Russian paper, it's singularly ill-informed," Don Camillo said in a loud voice.

Peppone heard him, and wheeling about again he came back and stood in front of Don Camillo.

"Does the Vatican news-sheet say when the Pope will speak in Moscow's Red Square?" he asked him.

"No," said Don Camillo.

"Then we're even," Peppone shouted.

Don Camillo threw out his arms in mock despair.

"If that's so, why do you lose your temper so easily?" he asked.

"Because it's not so. And I'd like to see you and that Pope of yours hanging up there where you put the loud-speaker."

"Peppone, you know His Holiness can't travel so far from Rome."

"Then I'll take you there," shouted Peppone. "All I want is to see you swinging from the same gallows."

"You pay me too much honour, Peppone. I'm tempted to buy another copy of your informative paper."

At that Peppone walked away. He had a family and couldn't afford to get into real trouble.

It was a stormy February evening and the valley was full of melancholy and mud. Don Camillo was sitting in front of the fire, looking at some old newspapers, when he got news that something serious had happened. He threw down the papers, put on his black coat and hurried into the church.

"Lord," he said, "there's more trouble with that devil's son."

"Whose son do you mean?" asked the Lord.

"Peppone's. God the Father must have turned His back on him. . . ."

"How do you know, Don Camillo? Does God let you look into His books? And how can you intimate that He loves one human being less than another? God is the same for all men."

Don Camillo went behind the altar to search for something in a cabinet.

"Lord, I don't know anything," he said. "The fact is that Peppone's little boy is badly hurt and they've called me to give him Extreme Unction. A rusty nail did it . . . apparently just a trifle. . . . And now he's at death's door."

Having found what he was searching for, Don Camillo passed hastily in front of the altar, genuflected and started to hurry away. But he had only gone half the length of the church when he stopped and came back.

"Lord," he said, when he came to the altar, "I have a lot to say, but no time to say it. I'll explain to You on the way. Meanwhile, I'm not taking the Holy Oil with me. I'm leaving it here on the railing."

He walked hurriedly through the rain, and only when he arrived at Peppone's door did he realize that he was holding his hat in his hand. He wiped his head with his coat and knocked. A woman opened and led him down the hall until she stopped in front of a door to whisper something. The door was thrown open with a loud shout, and there was Peppone. Peppone's eyes were startled and bloodshot, and he raised his fists threateningly.

"Get out of here!" he shouted. "Go away!"

Don Camillo did not move. Peppone's wife and his mother were hanging on to him, but Peppone seemed half-mad and threw himself upon Don Camillo, grabbing hold of his chest.

"Get out! What do you want here? Did you come to liquidate him? Get out, or I'll strangle you!"

He shouted an oath strong enough to make the sky tremble, but Don Camillo did not blench. Pushing Peppone aside, he walked into the child's room.

"No!" shouted Peppone. "No Holy Oil! If you give him that it means he's done for."

"What Holy Oil are you talking about? I didn't bring any Holy Oil with me."

"Do you swear it?"

"I swear."

Then Peppone grew calm.

"You mean you really didn't bring the Holy Oil?"

"No. Why should I?"

Peppone looked at the doctor, then at Don Camillo and then at the child.

"What is the trouble?" Don Camillo asked the doctor.

"Father," the doctor answered, "only streptomycin can save him."

Don Camillo clenched his fists.

"Only streptomycin?" he shouted. "And what about God? Can't God do anything?"

The doctor shrugged his shoulders.

"I'm not a priest. I'm a doctor."

"I'm disgusted with you," said Don Camillo.

"Good," chimed in Peppone.

"And where is this streptomycin?" Don Camillo asked, beside himself.

"In the city," the doctor answered.

"Then we'll go and get it."

"It's too late, Father. It's only a matter of minutes now. And there's no way of reaching the city. The telephone and the telegraph are both cut off because of the storm. There's nothing we can do."

Don Camillo picked up the little boy and wrapped him in a blanket with a rubber sheet over it.

"Come on, you idiot," he shouted to Peppone. "Call out your squad!"

The squad was waiting in Peppone's workshop. It consisted for the moment of Smilzo and a few young loafers.

"There are half a dozen motorcycles in the village. I'll get Breschi's racer, and you round up the rest. If they won't give them to you, shoot."

Then all of them went off in various directions.

"If you don't lend me your motorcycle, this child is going to die," Don Camillo said to Breschi. "And if he dies, I'll wring your neck."

Breschi was speechless, although deep-down inside he wept at the idea of his brand-new machine being rattled about on a wet night. Ten minutes later the motorcycle squad was complete. A few of the owners had been knocked down, but Don Camillo said that didn't matter.

"With six of us starting, surely one will get to the city," said Don Camillo. He himself was astride the shining red racer and held the child to him under his coat.

Two ahead, two behind, with Don Camillo in the middle and Peppone ahead of them all on Brusco's big motorcycle, this was the formation of the "flying squad" as it shot along the deserted valley roads under the rain. The roads were slippery and every curve an unexpected menace. Skirting hedges and ditches, the "flying squad" went through gravel and mud to the paved highway. There the motors began to roar, and they raced in dead earnest. All of a sudden Don Camillo heard a pitiful moan from the bundle he pressed to him. He must go even faster.

"Lord," he implored through clenched teeth, "give me more speed! And you, you filthy machine, let's see if you have any real guts in you!" The racer seemed to leap ahead, passing all the rest, including Peppone, who didn't have Don Camillo's Lord to give him more speed!

Don Camillo could not remember the details of his arrival. They told him that he charged in with a child in his arms, took the hospital doorman by the neck, thrust a door open with one shoulder and threatened to strangle a doctor. The "flying squad" went home, leaving Peppone's boy in the hospital to recover. Don Camillo returned to the village blowing his horn like the last trump, and covered with glorious mud.

HORSES OF A DIFFERENT COLOUR

They called him Romagnolo, simply because he came from the province of Romagna. He had come to the village years ago, but he was still *romagnolo* to the core. And to explain what this means I must tell you that this man had the nickname of "Civil-and-with-the-band." In the course of a political rally, the platform under him gave way and he started to fall to the ground. Upon which he called out with alacrity: "Civil, and with the band!" to signify that he wanted a civil burial, and not a Church one, with the band playing the Hymn of Garibaldi in slow tempo for a funeral march. When they start a new town in Romagna, they first throw up a monument to Garibaldi and then build a church, because there's no fun in a civil funeral unless it spites the parish priest. The whole history of the province is concerned with spite of this kind.

Now, Romagnolo was a man with the gift of the gab and one who spoke with the big words that can be read in revolutionary papers. The fact that there was no more king had knocked the props from under his pet subject for an argument, so he had to concentrate his heavy artillery upon the clergy. He finished every speech with the sentence:

"When I die, I want a civil funeral and the band playing."

Don Camillo was acquainted with the whole story, but had never paid it any attention. And so one day Romagnolo button-holed him in order to say:

"For your information, remember that after having steered clear of you my whole life long, I intend to steer clear of you when I'm dead. I don't want any priest at my funeral."

"Very well," said Don Camillo calmly. "Only you're barking up the wrong tree. You ought to go to the veterinary surgeon. I look after Christian souls, not animals."

Romagnolo started to make a speech.

"When that Pope of yours . . ."

"Don't bother anyone so far away. Let's stick to present company. I'll have to pray God to grant you a long life so that you'll have plenty of time to think better of it."

When Romagnolo celebrated his ninetieth birthday the whole village turned out for the festivities, including Don Camillo, who walked up to him with a smile and said: "Congratulations!"

Romagnolo shot him a resentful look and shouted:

"You'd better pray to your God again. Some day or other He'll have to let me die. And then it will be my turn to laugh."

The strange business of the horses took place in the following year.

The business of the horses took place in a village on the other side of the river.

A seventy-four-year-old Red had died, and they held a civil funeral, with red flags, red carnations, red kerchiefs, and in short red everything. The coffin was placed on the hearse carriage, the band began to play the "Red Flag" in funeral tempo, and the horses started forward with their heads hanging low as they always did on such occasions. Behind them came the procession, with red flags flying. But when they reached the church, the horses came to a stop and no one could make them budge. Several men pulled them by their bridles and others pushed the hearse from behind, but the horses stood their ground. When someone took a whip and began to beat them over the back, the horses reared up and then fell on to their knees. Finally, they were set on their feet and walked along for a short distance, but when they got to the cemetery they reared up again and started to go backwards.

The old man himself hadn't refused to have a religious funeral, the newspapers explained; his sons had imposed their ideas upon him. The story travelled all over the countryside, and anyone who wanted to test the truth of it had only to cross the river to hear it first-hand. Whenever a little knot of people gathered to discuss it, Romagnolo would descend upon them, shouting: "Middle Ages. That's stuff for the Middle Ages!"

And he went on to say that there was nothing miraculous about it; there was a perfectly rational explanation. For years immemorial the horses had stopped in front of the church, and so they had followed their usual habit this time as well. People were impressed by this version of the story and went to Don Camillo about it.

"What do you say?"

Don Camillo threw out his arms.

"Divine Providence knows no limits, and may well choose the humblest flower or tree or stone to teach a lesson to men. The sad part of it is that men pay so little attention to those of their fellows whose job it is to explain God's word, and choose rather to heed the example given them by a horse or a dog."

Many people were disappointed with this way of speaking and some of Don

Camillo's most important parishioners brought their complaints to the presbytery.

"Father, this thing has created quite a sensation. Instead of dismissing it so lightly, you ought to interpret it and bring out its moral teaching."

"I can't say anything more than what I said before," answered Don Camillo. "When God decided to give men the Ten Commandments he did it, not through a horse, but through a man. Do you think that God is so badly off as to call upon horses? You know the facts; let each one of you take from them what lesson he may. If you don't like what I have said, go to the bishop and tell him to put a horse in my place."

Meanwhile, Romagnolo was sputtering with rage, because people shrugged their shoulders at his explanation.

"That's all very well," they said, "there's nothing extraordinary or miraculous involved, but . . ."

So it was that Romagnolo button-holed Don Camillo again.

"Father, you're just the man I wanted to see. What is the official interpretation of the horse story?"

"Barking up the wrong tree, as usual," Don Camillo replied with a smile. "Horses aren't my line. You ought to go to the vet."

Romagnolo made a long speech to explain the horses' behaviour, and at the end Don Camillo simply threw out his arms.

"I can see that the thing has made quite an impression upon you. If it has caused you to stop and think, then I say thank God for it."

Romagnolo raised a threatening skinny finger.

"I can tell you one thing," he said, "and that is, the horses won't stop when my coffin passes by!"

Don Camillo went to talk to the Lord on the altar.

"Lord, the foolish things he says are not meant to hurt You; they're just barbs directed at me. When he comes up for Judgment, remember that he hails from Romagna. The trouble is that's he's over ninety, and anyone could knock him over with a feather. If he were in his prime, it would be a different matter. I'd get after him."

"Don Camillo, the system of teaching Christian charity by knocking people over the head is one that doesn't appeal to me," the Lord answered severely.

"I don't approve of it myself," said Don Camillo humbly. "But the fact is that often the ideas people have in their heads aren't so bad; it's just that they're in bad order. And sometimes a good shaking-up will cause them to fall into place."

Romagnolo went to Peppone's office and declared with no preamble: "Take this piece of legal paper, call two of your jumping-jacks to bear witness, and write down what I say."

He threw the piece of paper on the Mayor's desk and sat down.

"Put the date on top and write clearly: 'I, the undersigned Libero Martelli, ninety-one years old, by profession a free-thinker, in full possession of all my faculties, desire that upon my death all my property and possessions be transferred to this township for the purpose of buying a motor hearse to take the place of the present horse-drawn vehicle. . . .' "

Peppone stopped writing.

"Well?" said Romagnolo. "Do you want me to leave all my worldly goods to the priest?"

"I accept, of course," Peppone stuttered. "But how are we to buy a motor hearse so soon? It would cost at least a million and a half liras, and we . . ."

"I have two millions in the bank. Just go ahead and buy it, and I'll pay."

Romagnolo came out of the Town Hall glowing with satisfaction and for the first time in his life went deliberately to the church square.

"Everything's settled, Father!" he shouted. "When I go by in my coffin, the horses won't stop. I've taken care of priests and horses alike."

Romagnolo got too excited, and drank more than was good for him. Not that wine hurt him, after having been good for him all his life long. Water was his downfall. Coming home one night, full to the gills with wine, he was so over-poweringly sleepy that he lay down in a ditch. At over ninety years of age, spending the night in a puddle of water isn't exactly healthy. Romagnolo caught pneumonia and died. But before closing his eyes he summoned Peppone.

"Is everything agreed?" he asked him.

"Yes. Your wishes will be faithfully observed."

Romagnolo was the motor hearse's first customer. And the whole village turned out to see its inauguration. The band struck up, and the hearse moved slowly and steadily along. But in front of the church it came to a sudden stop. The driver wriggled the gear lever frantically, but all in vain. He looked under the hood, but found the plugs, carburettor and points all in perfect order and the tank full of petrol. The church door was closed, but Don Camillo was looking through a crack. He saw men milling about the hearse, and the hearse standing, obviously stuck, among them. The band had stopped playing and the bystanders had fallen into an astonished silence. The minutes dragged by, until Don Camillo ran to the sacristy and pulled the bell rope.

"God have mercy on you," he panted; "God have mercy on you . . ."

And the bells tolled out in the silent air. People shook themselves and the driver shifted the gear. The motor started and the motor hearse pulled away. No one could follow it any longer, because the driver put it into second and then into third gear, and it disappeared in a cloud of dust in the direction of the cemetery.

BLUE SUNDAY

OLD MAN GROLINI TURNED up at the presbytery to show Don Camillo a letter. Under the watchful eye of his dog Thunder, Don Camillo was greasing cartridges for his shotgun. Even before he read the letter he threw a questioning look at Grolini.

"The usual thing," Grolini sputtered. "That little wretch is in hot water again."

The Headmaster of young Grolini's boarding-school was thoroughly dissatisfied with him and wanted his father to do something about it.

"You'd better go in my place," Grolini said. "If I go, I'm likely to hit him over the head. When you see him, Father, tell him that if he doesn't behave I'll kick him out of the house."

Don Camillo shook his head.

"That would be even more stupid than hitting him over the head," he muttered. "How can anyone kick a boy out of the house when he's only eleven years old?"

"If I can't kick him out of the house, then I'll send him to the reformatory," shouted Grolini. "I don't want to see him again!"

Seeing that the father was not to be appeased, Don Camillo finally said: "I'll go and talk to him on Sunday afternoon."

"Then I authorize you to kick him about the school grounds," Grolini shouted. "The worse you treat him the better pleased I'll be."

After Grolini had gone, Don Camillo turned the letter over and over in his hands. The matter troubled him, because he had been the one to advise Grolini to encourage the boy in his studies and send him away to school. Grolini was a rich man. He tilled the soil, but the soil was his own. Moreover, it was fertile soil, and he had livestock in his stable and as many tractors and other agricultural machines as he could desire. Giacomino, his youngest son, was a quick-witted fellow who had always done well at school, and his father was attracted by the idea of having a university graduate in the family. Not to mention his wife, who gave herself very great airs. So it was that as soon as Giacomino finished elementary school he was bundled off to the city. Don Camillo had filled in his application papers and escorted him there in person. Giacomino was one of the mildest and best boys Don Camillo had ever known. He had been an acolyte for years and never got himself into the least trouble. So now the priest could not understand why he had turned out so badly.

When Sunday came, Don Camillo appeared at the boarding-school at the visitors' hour. When the Headmaster heard the name of Grolini he held his head in his hands. Don Camillo threw out his arms in a gesture of hopelessness.

"I'm amazed," he said with mortification. "I always knew him to be a good, obedient boy. I can't understand why he should be so wild."

" 'Wild' isn't exactly the word for it," the Headmaster put in. "His conduct doesn't give us any worry. But we're more concerned about him than about the worst boys in the school."

He took an envelope out of his desk drawer and drew forth a sheet of paper.

"Look at this composition," he said.

Don Camillo found himself looking at a clean paper, bearing on it in neat writing: *Giacomino Grolini. Class IB. Theme: My favourite book. Exposition.*

Turning the page, he came upon a perfect blank.

"There you are," said the Headmaster, holding out the entire envelope to him. "All his class work follows the same pattern. He neatly puts down the theme subject or problem, then sits back with folded arms and waits for the time to go by."

When he's asked a question, he makes no answer. At first we thought he must be a perfect idiot. But we've watched him and heard him talk to his companions, and we find that he isn't an idiot at all. Quite the contrary."

"I'll talk to him," said Don Camillo. "I'll take him to some quiet place outside, and, if necessary, I'll give him a proper dressing-down."

The Headmaster looked at Don Camillo's big hands.

"If you can't bring him round that way, I'm afraid there's nothing more to do," he mumbled. "He has no right to leave the premises after the way he's behaved, but I'll give him permission to stay out with you until five o'clock."

When Giacomino arrived on the scene a few minutes later, Don Camillo did not even recognize him. Quite apart from his school uniform and closely clipped hair, there was something entirely new in his manner.

"Have no fear," Don Camillo said to the Headmaster. "I'll work on him."

They walked in silence through the empty streets, typical of a tedious Sunday afternoon, and beside the bulky priest Giacomino looked smaller and skinnier than ever. When they had reached the outskirts, Don Camillo looked round for a place where they could talk freely. He turned on to a thoroughfare leading out into the country and then fifty yards later on to an unprepared road running beside a canal. The sun was shining, and although the trees were bare the landscape was pleasant to the eye. Finally, Don Camillo sat down on a tree trunk. He had in mind the speech he intended to make to the boy, and it was ferocious enough to make an elephant quiver. Giacomino stood in front of him and suddenly said:

"May I have a run?"

"A run?" said Don Camillo severely. "Can't you run during recreation at school?"

"Yes, but not very far," the boy answered. "There's always a wall in the way."

Don Camillo looked at the boy's pale face and clipped hair.

"Have your run, then," he said, "and then come here. I want to talk to you."

Giacomino was off like a bolt of lightning, and Don Camillo saw him cross the field, duck under a fence and run parallel to it under some bare grapevines. A few minutes later he came back, with his eyes and cheeks glowing.

"Rest a minute and then we'll talk," mumbled Don Camillo.

The boy sat down, but a minute later he jumped to his feet and ran over to an elm near by. He climbed it like a squirrel and made for a vine among its top branches. He explored among the red leaves and then came down with something in his hand.

"Grapes!" he exclaimed to Don Camillo, showing him a cluster that had survived the autumn picking. He proceeded to eat the grapes one by one and when he had finished he sat down beside the trunk.

"May I throw a stone?" he asked.

Don Camillo continued to lie low. "Go ahead and amuse yourself," he was thinking, "and we'll talk business later."

The boy rose, picked up a stone, brushed the dirt off it and threw it with all his strength. Don Camillo had a feeling that the stone had flown behind the clouds, never to return. A cold wind had blown up, and Don Camillo began to think they had better repair to some quiet café, where he wouldn't have to shout in order to make the boy hear him. As they walked away Giacomino asked permission to race ahead, and found another cluster of grapes left from the autumn.

"That's just a small part of what there must have been on the vine!" he murmured as he ate them. "At home now, they must have hung up the grapes to dry . . ."

"Never mind about the grapes," Don Camillo mumbled.

The outskirts of the city were squalid and melancholy. As they walked along they met a man selling roast chestnuts and peanuts. Giacomino opened his eyes wide.

"Silly stuff," said Don Camillo ill-humouredly. "I'll get you a piece of cake when we sit down."

"No thanks," said the boy in a tone of voice that set Don Camillo's nerves on edge.

The nut-vendor knew his business and had stopped a few yards behind them. And the proof of his astuteness was that Don Camillo turned round and grudgingly tossed him a hundred-lire note.

"Mixed, Father?"

"Yes, mixed."

Don Camillo put the bag of silly stuff into the boy's hand, and they continued to walk along the deserted thoroughfare. The priest held out as long as he could, and then finally stuck his hand into the bag. The taste of the nuts called up memories of the melancholy Sunday afternoons of his own youth, and filled him with a sudden sadness. A church bell rang, and when Don Camillo pulled out his heavy gold watch he saw that it was twenty minutes to five.

"Hurry," he said to the boy. "You must be back promptly on the hour."

They quickened their pace, as the sun sank below the houses around them. When they arrived, without a minute to spare, the boy held the bag out to Don Camillo.

"When you come back from outside they take everything like this away," he explained in a low voice.

Don Camillo put the bag into his pocket.

"That's where I sleep," said the boy, pointing to a barred second-storey window with a box-like protuberance under it that blocked the sight of the ground below. Then he hesitated for a moment before pointing to a window on the ground floor, barred in the same way but affording a view of the world outside.

"In that hall are the cupboards where we hang our clothes," he said. "I'll try to walk along it on my way upstairs and in that way I'll be able to wave goodbye."

Don Camillo went with him to the heavy front door; then he came back and waited on the pavement outside the ground-floor window, which gave on to a side street. Nervously he lit a cigar. After what seemed like an endless time, he heard a whisper. Giacomino had opened a window and was waving to him from behind the bars. Don Camillo walked over and handed him the bag of nuts. Then he started to walk away, but something made him turn back. He could see nothing of Giacomino but a pair of eyes, but these were so filled with tears that Don Camillo broke out into a cold perspiration. By some mysterious process his dangerously powerful hands found themselves twisting the iron bars, and the iron bars bent and gave way. When the opening was large enough, Don Camillo stretched out an arm, grasped the boy's collar and pulled him through. It was dark by now, and no one saw anything strange in the sight of a priest and a schoolboy walking together.

"Wait for me," Don Camillo said, "while I get my motorcycle."

By eight o'clock they were back in the village, and Giacomino had eaten all the nuts on the way.

"Come into the presbytery by the back door," Don Camillo told him as they got off the motorcycle, "and don't let anyone see you."

By nine o'clock Giacomino was sleeping on a couch in the hall while Don Camillo finished his supper in the kitchen. At a quarter past nine Grolini turned up, waving a telegram in one hand.

"That rascal has run away from school," he shouted. "If I lay my hands on him, I'll kill him for sure."

"Then I hope you don't lay hands on him," Don Camillo murmured.

Grolini was beside himself with anger.

"At least you gave him a good scolding this afternoon," he added.

Don Camillo shook his head.

"No, not I. That boy was made to follow in your footsteps and live on the land. He simply can't stay away from the country. A good little fellow, too. . . . But perhaps he's dead by now."

"Dead?" Grolini shouted.

Don Camillo sighed.

"I found him in a very bad state of mind, and he talked to me in a most alarming way. . . . You'd more or less given him up for lost, hadn't you? I told him what you said, that rather than see his face again you'd send him to the reformatory."

Grolini sank on to a chair and finally managed to say:

"Father, if God brings him home safe and sound I'll foot the bill for repairs to the bell tower."

"That's not necessary," said Don Camillo gently. "God will be satisfied with your grief. Go back home, and don't lose heart. I'll go and look for your boy."

Giacomino came home the next day, and Don Camillo was with him. His family were gathered in the yard, but no one said a word. Only Flick, the old dog, barked and jumped like a kangaroo because he was so happy. Giacomino threw him his school cap and Flick ran off, holding it between his teeth with Giacomino running after him.

"The Headmaster called me up this morning," said old man Grolini. "He can't understand how the boy could have twisted two heavy iron bars."

"He's an able boy, I tell you," said Don Camillo. "He'll make a very good farmer. And it's better to farm for love than to study for fear of a beating."

And Don Camillo went away very fast, because he had just felt a peanut in his pocket and couldn't wait to eat it.

DON CAMILLO GETS INTO TROUBLE

SAINT MARTIN'S SUMMER brought some strangers to the village, among them a certain Marasca, who might better have stayed away. Marasca had a little boy and when he took him to school for the first time he said to the teacher:

"I hear that the priest comes every Wednesday to give religious instruction. When he arrives, will you kindly send my boy home?"

And since the teacher told him that was impossible, every Wednesday Marasca kept the boy away from school. Don Camillo stayed out of it as long as he could, then one Wednesday afternoon he went to Olmetto, the farm where Marasca was a tenant. He meant to make a joke of it rather than to stir up trouble, but at first sight Marasca showed signs of resentment at his visit.

"This is my land," he said. "You must have crossed the wrong bridge."

"No; I didn't cross the wrong bridge," said Don Camillo. "I hear that on Wednesdays your boy can't come to school, and so I thought I'd give him a little religious instruction at home."

Marasca came out with an oath that was really more than Don Camillo deserved.

"I see you need a little religious instruction yourself," said the priest, "and I'm ready to give it to you."

Marasca's brother came out of the house and looked threateningly at the visitor.

"Get out of here and don't let me see you again, you cursed black crow!" shouted Marasca.

Don Camillo did not say a word. He retraced his steps, and when he was across the bridge and back on the road, he called out.

"Now I'm off your land," he said. "But you'll have to come and repeat your words, because I didn't understand you."

The two brothers looked at one another; then they crossed the bridge and planted themselves defiantly in front of Don Camillo. And there they found that the priest had quite a bag of tricks up his sleeve. While he was slapping the dust off the face of the first Marasca, the brother, who had already had a taste of the same medicine, ran back to the yard and returned with a pitchfork. The pitchfork was of an ordinary kind, and had a handle. But this was where the trouble began, for in Don Camillo's powerful hands the handle turned into a regular earthquake. The two Marascas found this out to their sorrow, because the handle was broken on their backs.

The whole village was turned upside down, and the Communist newspaper sent a special correspondent who painted Don Camillo as a dangerously aggressive and violent man. As a result, Don Camillo was called up before the old Bishop, and before he could say any more than: "Self-defence . . ." the Bishop interrupted him gently.

"Monterana is without a priest. Go up there this evening and stay until the return of the regular incumbent."

"But the regular incumbent is dead," Don Camillo stammered.

"Exactly," said the Bishop, making a gesture which indicated that he had nothing more to say.

Don Camillo bowed his head and went to pack his bag.

Monterana was one of the most forsaken spots on the surface of the globe: half a dozen huts made of mud and stones, one of which was the church, but distinguishable from the others only because of the bell tower at its side. The road to Monterana was a stony ditch, called by courtesy a mule-track, but no mule would ever have ventured upon it. Don Camillo arrived at the top with his heart in his throat and gazed round. When he went into the presbytery the walls were so low that they seemed to crush him. A scrawny old woman came out of a hole and looked at him through half-open eyes.

"Who are you?" Don Camillo asked, but she threw out her arms as if to say that she had forgotten.

The main beam of the kitchen ceiling was supported by a tree trunk in the middle of the room, and Don Camillo was tempted to play the part of Samson and pull the whole place down around him. Then he realized that another priest, a man like himself, had spent a lifetime amid these same squalid surroundings, and this caused him to recover some of his calm. He went into the church, and the miserable condition of it brought tears to his eyes. He knelt on the step before the altar and raised his eyes to the cross.

"Lord . . ." he began, and then he stopped, because the cross was of crudely cut wood, black and peeling; it was completely bare. Don Camillo felt very nearly afraid. "Lord," he sorrowfully exclaimed, "You are everywhere in the universe, and I need no image of You to tell me that You are near, but here I feel as if You had abandoned me. . . . My faith must be a very poor thing, if I feel so terribly alone."

He went back to the presbytery, and there he found a cloth on the table, a loaf of bread and a piece of cheese. The old woman was just bringing in a jug of water.

"Where did these things come from?" Don Camillo asked.

She threw out her arms and looked up to Heaven. Plainly, she didn't know. With the old priest it had always been like this, and now the miracle was repeating itself. Don Camillo made the sign of the cross, and involuntarily thought of the bare, black wooden cross he had just seen on the altar. He shivered, and reproached himself for being afraid. But indeed he had a fever, sent to him by Divine Providence, like the bread and the cheese and the water. He stayed in bed for three days, and on the fourth day he received written orders from the Bishop.

"You are not to leave your new post, for any reason whatsoever. Don't show your face in the village, for the people there must forget that they ever had a priest so unworthy. May God strengthen and protect you. . . ."

Don Camillo got up, with his head still reeling. He went over to the window and found that it was chilly outside with a premonition of fog in the air.

"Winter will be here any minute," he said to himself with terror, "and I shall be snowbound and all alone . . ."

It was five o'clock in the afternoon, and he must not let night overtake him. He rolled rather than walked down the mule-track and reached the road just in time to catch a bus to the city. There he went to several garages, until he found someone who would take him by car to the crossroad at Gaggiola. From the crossroad, Don Camillo cut over the fields and at ten o'clock he was in Peppone's garden.

Peppone stared at him with a worried air.

"I must transport some things to Monterana," said Don Camillo. "Can I hire your truck?"

Peppone shrugged his shoulders.

"Did you have to wake me up for that?" he asked. "We can discuss that to-morrow morning."

"We're going to discuss it right away," the priest insisted. "I need your truck to-night."

"Are you mad?" Peppone asked him.

"Yes," Don Camillo answered.

Upon receiving such a logical reply, Peppone could only scratch his head.

"Let's hurry," said Don Camillo. "How much will it cost?"

Peppone took the stub of a pencil and made some calculations.

"Forty miles there and forty miles back, that makes eighty. Sixty-five hundred lire-worth of petrol and oil. Then there's the charge for my services, which are higher paid at night. But since it's to help you get out of this village, and I'm happy to see you go . . ."

"Come on," said Don Camillo. "How much is it?"

"Ten thousand for the whole job."

Don Camillo agreed, and Peppone stretched out his hand.

"Cash will do it," he muttered.

Ten thousand lire represented Don Camillo's savings of years.

"Get your truck going, and meet me halfway down the Boschetto road."

"What in Heaven's name can you be loading there?"

"That's none of your business, and not a word to a soul."

Peppone muttered something to the effect that in the woods at midnight he probably wouldn't find many people with whom to exchange conversation. Don Camillo's fever excited rather than tired him. He made a detour through the fields and approached the church from the orchard. Or rather he bumped straight into it, because there was a thick fog all around. He had his keys in his pocket and went in by the tower door. He had to go out by the main entrance, but no one saw him.

Peppone had a bright idea. When he saw the fog and thought of Don Camillo trying to make his way through it with all his bags and baggage, he decided to blow his horn to guide him. Led by the horn and the excitement of his fever, Don Camillo arrived panting at the meeting-place. Peppone started to get down from the truck to help him, but the priest said:

"I don't need any help. Start up your motor and be ready to go when I give the word."

When he had loaded everything on to the truck, Don Camillo went to sit beside Peppone, and off they went. The fog pursued them for the first twenty miles, but they made the second half of the trip as fast as if they were flying. At two o'clock in the morning Peppone brought his truck to a halt at the beginning of the famous mule-track leading to Monterana. Don Camillo once more refused Peppone's help in unloading. Peppone heard him scuffling about at the back of the truck and then, when he saw him in the glare of the headlights, his eyes opened wide.

"The Crucified Christ from the altar!"

Don Camillo started the painful ascent of the mule-track, and Peppone had pity and overtook him.

"Father, can I give you a hand?"

"Hands off!" shouted Don Camillo. "Go home, and think twice before you spread any gossip!"

"Here's wishing you a safe arrival!" said Peppone.

And so it was that Don Camillo's Stations of the Cross began.

The crucifix was large and heavy, made out of solid oak. And the figure of the Crucified Christ was carved out of equally heavy, hard wood. The mule-track was steep and its stony surface was bathed by the rain. Never had Don Camillo carried such a weight on his shoulders. His bones creaked, and after half an hour he had to drag the crucifix. The crucifix became heavier and heavier and Don Camillo was more and more tired, but still he did not give up. He slipped and fell on a sharp stone, and felt the blood trickling down from one knee, but still he did not stop. A branch carried away his hat and scratched his forehead, thorns ripped his cassock, but on he climbed, with his face bent low, near to that of the Crucified Christ. Even a gushing spring did not tempt him to linger. One, two, three hours went by.

It took him four hours to reach the village. The church was the building farthest away, and to reach it he had to climb up a path which was less rocky, but filled with mud. Everyone was still in bed and he toiled on quite alone, borne up by the hope that is born of despair. He entered the empty church, but his task was not yet over. He still had to dismount the bare, black cross and install his own crucifix on the altar. After one last struggle, his mission was accomplished. Then he collapsed on the floor. But when the bell rang he jumped up, went to wash his hands in the sacristy and said his first Mass. He lit the candles himself; there were only two of them, but they seemed to shed a very great light.

Only two people came to Mass, but Don Camillo had the sensation of a multitude, because one of the two was the old woman who had forgotten her name, and the other was Peppone. He had been too tired to drive his truck back and had followed Don Camillo step by step up the mountain. Although he did not have the cross on his shoulders, he had felt the priest's weariness as if it were his own. As he went by the poor-box in the church he slipped into it the ten-thousand lire note given him by Don Camillo.

"Lord," whispered Don Camillo raising his eyes to the Crucified Christ. "I hope you don't mind my having brought You to this wretched place."

"No, Don Camillo," said the Lord. "The place is wonderful." And He smiled.

WHEN THE RAINS CAME

EVERYONE WAS WAITING for the arrival of the new priest, but nobody came except old Don Anselmo, who for years had had the parish of Torretta, two miles away. Since the two villages were so close, he had obviously been asked to fill in until a replacement was found for Don Camillo.

Don Anselmo looked round during his first Mass, and saw that there were only two people in the church, himself and his acolyte. And the acolyte was there only because Don Anselmo had called for him at his own house. Things went on in this way for some time, until Don Anselmo went to talk to the Bishop.

"Monsignore," he concluded, "that's not all. It's a serious business. They behave as if neither church nor priest were there. No one comes to confession. 'I'll go when Don Camillo comes home,' they say. When babies are born, they don't bring them to be baptized. 'That can wait for Don Camillo,' is still the refrain. And they get married in the Town Hall and say they'll wait for Don Camillo to perform a church wedding. So far no one has died, and I suppose there'll be no necessity for a funeral until Don Camillo comes for it."

The Bishop threw out his arms in despair.

"That blessed Don Camillo is fated to be a thorn in my flesh even when he's not there!" he sighed. "But people must get it into their heads that he made a mistake and has to pay for it."

Don Anselmo shrugged his shoulders.

"It is my duty to report on everything I know," he said. "And I may as well tell you that many people don't think it was a mistake for Don Camillo to snatch the pitchfork away from someone who was trying to stick it into his stomach."

"Quite right," the Bishop agreed. "It wasn't a mistake to snatch it away; the mistake was to hit those two fellows over the head with the handle."

"Even then, some people think that Don Camillo had right on his side," Don Anselmo said in a respectful manner. "It is my further duty to inform you that under the circumstances I should have done the same thing myself."

The Bishop raised his eyes to Heaven.

"Lord, forgive this old madman!" he exclaimed. "He doesn't know what he is saying."

Don Anselmo was not just an impulsive boy; he was well on towards eighty, and now he hung his head in embarrassment but continued to be of the same opinion. The Bishop delivered a long and very wise sermon, and ended up by saying: "Now go on house-to-house visits, to explain to the people that Don Camillo made a mistake and must be punished for it. It's your plain duty to make them see reason."

Don Anselmo went from house to house, and everywhere he received the same answer:

"If he did make a mistake, then it's only right that he should pay. We're waiting for him to finish paying and come back, that's all."

Meanwhile the Reds were beside themselves with joy. They had got Don Camillo out of the way and no one was going to church. One evening Peppone accosted Don Anselmo.

"It's sad to see an old racket like the Vatican closing down," he sighed. "If we weren't excommunicated, we'd come to your Mass ourselves! Anyhow, if you decide to lease the premises, give me an option on them."

Don Anselmo did not let himself be perturbed.

"I can't even ask you to lease me your brain in return!" he retorted. "You leased that out a long time ago. I only hope you didn't let your soul go with it."

Then it began to rain. It rained on the mountains and in the valleys. Old oak trees were shattered by lightning, the sea foamed up in a storm, the rivers began to swell, and as the rain continued, they overflowed their banks and flooded whole towns with their muddy waters. Most dangerous of all, the mighty Po was rising, pressing harder and harder against its embankments. During the war, the embankment was bombed at a point called La Pioppa, and they had neglected to mend it until within the last two years. Everyone looked fearfully at La Pioppa, feeling sure that if the pressure became too great this was the point where the embankment would give way. The earth hadn't had time to pack solidly, and whereas the rest of the bank would hold just as it had always held before, La Pioppa would crumble.

Meanwhile it continued to rain, night and day, and after each momentary respite it came down harder than before. The papers were filled with news of squalls, floods and landslides, but the village people thought only of their own danger. Already a lot of old crones were saying:

"Ever since Don Camillo went away, taking the altar crucifix with him, there's been trouble brewing."

The crucifix had a long-standing association with the river. Every year the people of the village carried it in a procession to the banks, where the priest gave the waters his blessing. The old crones shook their heads.

"As long as he was here, we were protected. But now he's gone away."

As the river rose, they spoke more and more of the crucifix, and even the wisest among them lost their heads. One morning the Bishop found a village delegation waiting upon him.

"Give us back our crucifix," they implored. "We must form a procession at once and hold a blessing of the waters. Otherwise the village will be swept away."

The Bishop sighed.

"Brethren, have you so little faith?" he asked them. "God seems to be not within your souls but extraneous to them, if you pin all your trust to a wooden image, and without its help fall into despair."

Some of the men of the delegation hung their heads. And one of them, old Bonesti, stepped forward to say:

"We have faith in God, but we have lost faith in ourselves. All of us love our country, but when we go into battle, we need to see our regimental flag. The flag keeps us fighting for the country whose love is within us. That crucifix was our flag, and Don Camillo our flag-bearer. If we can have our flag back, we shall face our troubles more courageously."

Don Camillo came back during the night, when no one was expecting him. But he had no sooner walked from the presbytery to the church the next morning than the whole village knew it. They crowded to hear his first Mass, and afterwards they gathered round him to say:

"We want a procession!"

"The Lord has gone back to His altar, and there He stays," said Don Camillo severely. "He will not move until we hold the regular procession next year. This year, the waters have been blessed already."

"Yes, but the river is rising."

"He knows that," said Don Camillo. "No one needs to refresh His memory. All I can do is pray that the Lord will give us strength to bear our sufferings serenely."

The people were obsessed with fear, and when they insisted on a procession Don Camillo had to speak to them even more sternly than before.

"Have a procession, then, but rather than carry a wooden cross about the streets, carry Christ in your hearts! Let every one of you hold a private procession of this kind. Have faith in God, and not in graven images. And then God will help you."

But the people's fear continued to rise, along with the river. Engineers came to inspect La Pioppa and declared it would hold, but they advised the villagers to get their belongings together and be prepared for evacuation. The engineers went away at ten o'clock in the morning, and at eleven the water was still rising. Then fear turned into terror.

"There's no time to save anything," someone was saying. "The only thing to do is to cross the river and cut an opening in the embankment on the other side."

No one knew who was the first person to suggest this blasphemy, but very soon everyone was repeating it. Eighty people out of a hundred were trying to work out the best way to cross the river and make a cut that would channel the overflow to the opposite shore. Sooner or later someone might have actually done it. But all of a sudden the rain ceased, and hope returned to their hearts. The church bells called them to the square, and there Don Camillo addressed them.

"There's only one thing to do, and that is to carry our most important belongings to safety."

Just then the rain began to fall again.

"There's no time!" the people shouted. "La Pioppa won't hold."

"Yes, it will," said Don Camillo firmly.

"That's what you say!" they shouted.

"That's the word left by the engineers," said Don Camillo.

"It's only a word!" someone shouted.

"It's a fact, I say!" Don Camillo retorted. "I'm so sure it will hold that I'll go and stand on the weakest point of the embankment. If I'm mistaken, then I'll pay!"

Don Camillo raised his big umbrella and walked towards the river, with a crowd following after him. They followed him along the embankment until he came to the newly-built stretch at La Pioppa. There Don Camillo turned round.

"Let everyone go and pack up his things calmly," he called out. "I'll wait at La Pioppa for you to finish."

He walked on, and fifty yards farther he came to the exact point where everyone thought there would be a break. The crowd looked in bewilderment first at the priest and then at the raging water.

"I'm coming to keep you company," a voice shouted, and out of the crowd stepped Peppone, with his eyes upon him.

"The embankment will hold," Peppone shouted; "there's no danger. Don't do anything silly, but prepare to evacuate in good order, under the chief councillor's direction. To prove my confidence in the embankment, I'll stay here."

When they saw the priest and the Mayor at the point of what they thought was the greatest danger, the people hurried to get their livestock out of the stables and load their household goods on trucks and wagons. The rain continued to come down and the river to rise, and the village population made ready. Meanwhile, Don Camillo and Peppone sat on two big stones under the umbrella.

"You'd be better off if you were still exiled in the mountains, Father," said Peppone.

"Oh, I don't know about that," Don Camillo answered.

Peppone was silent for a few minutes and then clapped his hand to his hip.

"If this thing were to break while people are still loading their things and we're sitting here, that would be a pretty mess! We'd be done for and so would they."

"It would be a great deal worse if we'd saved ourselves by cutting the embankment, dealing out death and destruction on the other side. You must admit there's a difference between misfortune and crime."

Peppone shrugged his shoulders.

"I've got the better of you, in any case."

Towards evening the rain paused and the river fell. The village had been completely evacuated, and Don Camillo and Peppone left the embankment and went home. As they crossed the church square, Don Camillo said:

"You might thank God for saving your skin. You owe that good luck to Him."

"True enough," said Peppone. "But He saved your skin too, and that's enough bad luck to make us even!"

THE BELL

THE RIVER EMBANKMENT did not give way, even where everyone said it was sure to crack, and so the next morning many people went back to the village, which lay below the water-level, in order to fetch more of their belongings. But towards nine o'clock something unexpected happened. The water had risen higher, and although it did not penetrate the main embankment it found a weak spot elsewhere.

About a mile east of the village, the road running along the embankment went over a bridge across the Fossone, a tributary which poured at this point into the Po. The Fossone had solid banks of its own, but because the Po was so high, it had reversed its course and was running away from instead of into the river. Just below the bridge, where the banks of the Fossone joined those of the river, the water tunnelled underneath and then came up in a jet, making the hole larger and larger. There was no way of holding it, and the villagers soon returned with wagons and trucks to seek safety.

Don Camillo had worked all alone until three o'clock in the morning, carrying things to the second floor and attic of the presbytery. Then he was so tired that he fell into a dead sleep. At half-past nine in the morning he was awakened by the shouts of people running to take refuge on the embankment. Soon the noise died away, and he got up to look out of the window at the deserted church square. He went down to explore further and then climbed up into the bell tower. From this vantage point he could see that the water had already crept up on the lower part of the village and was slowly creeping higher. It had encircled the isolated hut of old Merola, and when it reached the ground-floor windows the whole thing crumbled. Don Camillo sighed. The old man had not wanted to leave, and it was by sheer force that they had taken him away. Now the pace of the advancing water was faster; the rain had left the earth so thoroughly soaked that it could not absorb a drop. It was up to the higher part of the village, which lay stretched out perfectly flat before it. Hearing a crash in the distance, he looked through his field-glasses and saw that a hundred and fifty feet of one bank of the Fossone had given way. Then, going over to another window, he noticed a crowd of people on the main embankment gazing in the direction of the village.

Those who had gone with their trucks and wagons for a second load of their belongings had been forced back. Now they stood with evacuees from other villages, who had brought their livestock and household goods with them, looking down at the newly flooded area, half a mile away. No one spoke, and old women shed silent tears. Their village seemed to be dying there before them, and they began to think of it as already dead.

"There is no God!" said an old man gloomily.

But just at that moment the church bell rang. There was no mistaking the sound, even if the tone was somewhat different from usual. All eyes were fixed on the church tower.

After Don Camillo had seen the crowd on the embankment he went back to the ground. The water had climbed the three steps leading to the church door and was running into the nave.

"Lord, forgive me for forgetting that it is Sunday," said Don Camillo, kneeling in front of the altar.

Before going to prepare himself in the sacristy, Don Camillo stepped into the little room at the base of the bell tower, whose floor was lower than that of the church and already covered with eight or ten inches of water. He tugged at a rope, hoping that it was the right one. It was, and when the crowd on the embankment heard it ring, they said:

"Eleven o'clock Mass!"

The women joined their hands in prayer and the men took off their hats.

Don Camillo lit the candles and began to say Mass. The water was climbing the altar steps and soon it touched his vestments. It was muddy and cold, but Don Camillo paid no attention. His congregation was dry and safe on the embankment. And when it was time for the sermon, he did not mind the fact that the church was empty, but preached to his parishioners just as if they were there before him. There were three feet of water in the nave, and pews and confessionals had overturned and were floating at random. The door was wide open, and beyond it he could see the submerged houses on the square and the lowering clouds on the horizon.

"Brethren," he said, "the waters have boiled up from the river bed and now are sweeping everything before them. But one day they will be calmed and return to their rightful place and the sun will shine again. Even if you lose everything you have, you can still be rich in your faith in God. Only those who doubt God's mercy and justice will be impoverished, even if their possessions are intact."

And he went on at considerable length in the flooded church, while from the embankment people continued to stare at the tower. When the bell sounded for the elevation, the women knelt down on the damp ground and the men bowed their heads. Then the bell rang again for the final blessing. The Mass was over, and people moved about freely and talked in a low tone of voice, hoping to hear the bell again. Soon afterwards it rang out gaily once more, and the men took out their watches and said:

"Noon! It's time to go for dinner."

They got into whatever vehicles they had with them and went to the improvised canteens and shelters. And looking back over their shoulders at the village, which seemed to be afloat in a sea of mud, they were obviously thinking:

"As long as Don Camillo's there, everything's all right."

Before Don Camillo went back to the presbytery he looked up at the Lord above the altar.

"Forgive me, Lord, for not kneeling. If I were to kneel, I'd be in water up to the neck."

His head was bent and he could not be sure that the Lord had smiled. But he was almost sure that He had, for there was a glow in his heart that made him forget the fact that he was soaked to the waist. He got over to the presbytery, seizing on the way a floating ladder, with whose help he managed to climb into a second-storey window. He changed his clothes, had something to eat and went to bed. Towards three in the afternoon there was a knock at the window.

"Come in," said Don Camillo, and there was Peppone.

"If you'll come down, there's a boat rowed by some of my boys waiting for you," Peppone mumbled.

When a man is lying in bed, or even sitting up in it, he is in no position to come out with a phrase that will go down in history. So Don Camillo leapt to his feet and shouted:

"The old guard dies, but it never surrenders!"

Although he was on his feet, he had nothing on but his drawers, and this detracted from the solemnity of the occasion. But Peppone was in no mood to notice.

"Then devil take you," he said angrily. "You may not get another chance to escape so soon!"

The rescue squad rowed on. When the boat passed in front of the open church door, Peppone shouted to the rowers to watch out on the left. While they were looking in the other direction, he had time to take off his cap and put it back without being observed. For the rest of the way he cudgelled his brain to know what Don Camillo had meant about the old guard that dies but never surrenders. Even if the water stood eight feet high, the flood seemed to him to have abated since he knew that Don Camillo was at his post.

EVERYONE AT HIS POST

MAROLI WAS AS OLD AS sin, and all skin and bones, but at times he could be as hard-headed as a young man of twenty-five. When the flood became really serious, his two sons loaded all their belongings on to wagons and prepared to take their families away, but the old man refused to budge. He said as much to his daughters-in-law when they came to carry him down from the bed to which he had been invalided for some time. And the two women told their husbands to do something about it themselves, because there was no use arguing with a madman. The sons and two grandsons went upstairs to try to persuade him, but they received the same answer:

"Here is my home, and here I stay."

His sons explained that the whole village was being evacuated because at any moment the river might overflow its banks, but Maroli only shook his head.

"I'm a sick man and I can't stand the exposure. I'm staying here."

The daughters-in-law came up again to tell their husbands to hurry. And one of them said:

"Don't be silly. No sick people are being left outside in the bad weather. They're all sheltered and taken care of."

Maroli sat up in bed and pointed a rheumatic finger at her.

"I see now. You want to get me away from here and into an institution. For a long time you've been looking for a way to get rid of me. But I don't want to go to the hospital and die there, alone, like a dog. I'll die here, among my own things, even if I am in your way. Here, in this bed where my wife died, I intend to breathe my last. And you must bury me beside her."

All of them together tried to persuade him, but he held fast. Finally his elder son came close to the bed.

"That's enough talking," he shouted. "You take his other shoulder, and you two women hold his feet. We'll carry him down on the mattress."

"Go away, the lot of you," the old man protested.

But they were all around him, holding on to the mattress. A minute more, and they would have lifted it up without the least difficulty, because the old man was light as a feather. He took hold of the shirt-front of his elder son and tried to push him away, but the son was beside himself with exasperation and tore himself loose. He threw the old man back on the bed and held him down.

"Stop this crazy stuff, or I'll bash your head in!" he shouted.

The old man tried to free himself, but it was as if a stone were bearing down on his chest and he could do nothing but suffer.

"Rosa! . . . Rosa! . . ." he called.

But what was a twelve-year-old girl to do?

She threw herself like an angry cat at the man who was pinning him to the bed, but a dozen hands caught hold of her, pushed her aside and slapped her.

"Keep out of this, you stupid girl! Are you crazy?"

The old man was breathless with rage.

"*You're* crazy!" he shouted. "And chicken-hearted too! If her father were alive, you wouldn't dare treat me this way."

But Rosa's father was dead and buried, and so was her mother. The father was Maroli's favourite and most promising son, and his death had broken the old man's heart.

"We're all you've got now," said his eldest, jeeringly, "and you'll have to do what we say. Let's hurry."

A dozen impatient arms raised up the mattress, while the heavy hands of the eldest son kept the old man still. Just then they heard Rosa's voice:

"Let him go, or I'll shoot!"

A shotgun in the hands of a young girl is more terrifying than a tommy-gun in those of a man. And Rosa was not only a young girl, but not quite right in the head as well, so that naturally enough the owners of the dozen hands (two men, two women and two boys) agreed to let the old man go. They put down the mattress and the eldest son withdrew his hands.

"Go away, or I'll fire!" said the girl.

They backed out of the door and when they were gone the girl chained it.

"I'll send the police and a male nurse after you," shouted the eldest son from the stairs.

The old man was undaunted.

"Better mind your own business, because if anyone comes near I'll burn the house down," he retorted.

As in all the peasant houses of the region, there was a direct connection between the living quarters and the stable. The old man's room was just above this, and next door to the hayloft. He had chosen this room, formerly used to store wheat, because he could look through a hole in the floor and see the animals in the stable below as well as the movements of the men who took care of them. The hayloft was full of hay, and with a piece of tow on the end of a stick he could easily have set it on fire. For this reason his threat threw the rest of the family into a cold perspiration. The old man had a shotgun, a kerosene lamp, a can of kerosene and a mad girl at his disposal.

"We'll leave you alone," they called back from the stair.

"You'd better!" he said mockingly.

When they got out into the yard one of the daughters-in-law had a bright idea and called up to the old man's window:

"If you choose to stay, that's your own business. But let the girl go. You have no right to expose her to danger. Let her come along with us."

The old man was momentarily taken aback.

"Rosa," he said, "the water's rising and there may be danger. If you want to be safe, go along."

The girl shook her head and closed the shutters.

"God blast the two of them!" said the bright daughter-in-law.

And the grandsons observed that if both the old man and the girl were to perish, it would be a gain to everybody, themselves included. Maroli's two sons maintained a gloomy silence. But when they and their possessions had reached safety they looked in the direction of the house and the elder one said angrily:

"This won't last forever. And when we go back, we'll have to put things in order. He must be sent to a hospital and she to an asylum."

"Yes," said his brother approvingly. "They can't get away with it any longer."

The old man and the girl remained alone in the house and no one knew that they were there. When she was sure that the last of the family had gone, she went downstairs, locked the doors and bolted the windows. There was plenty to eat in the kitchen and the old man told her what to bring upstairs. Finally he told her to put an empty barrel in his room and gradually fill it with buckets of water from the pump below. When evening came she was dead tired and lay down on a mattress on the floor.

"That blessed family may come back," the old man grumbled. "You go ahead and sleep and I'll watch out for them. If I hear anything I'll call you."

He sat on the edge of his bed, shotgun in hand, but nobody came. The next morning the river overflowed its banks and the water rose to within two feet of the downstairs ceiling.

"Now we can set our minds at rest," said the old man.

Toward eleven o'clock they heard a bell ringing and the old man sent the girl to look out of the attic window. She came down after some time and said:

"The church door is open and there's water everywhere. And there's a crowd of people up on the embankment."

At three o'clock she went up to look again and ran down to report:

"There's a boat going round from one house to another."

"Rosa, if you want to go, go," the old man sighed.

"If they come for us we'll set fire to the hayloft," she answered.

The boat came through their yard, and the girl looked out at it through a crack in the shutters.

"There's that big mechanic who always wears a red kerchief," she said to the old man.

And a minute later Peppone called out:

"Is there anyone here?"

The old man and the girl held their breath, and the boat went away.

"The family must have been scared to say anything about us," muttered the old man. "Now we can have some peace and quiet."

Don Camillo awakened suddenly and found himself in the dark. He was so tired that he had fallen asleep in the afternoon, and now evening had overtaken him. When he threw open the window he looked out over an expanse of water as wide as the sea, and saw on the horizon a red fringe left by the sunset. The silence was oppressive, and the memory of cheerfully lighted houses seemed very far away. Now the houses were all blacked out and the water came to within two feet of the ground-floor ceilings. The distant howl of a dog reminded him of his own Thunder. Where was Thunder now? Where had the flood surprised him? The howling continued, and now it seemed to come from directly below and filled him with a mixture of anxiety and fear. He lit the lamp, took a piece of iron and prised up a piece of the floor. There was Thunder, floating on a raft. And the raft was the downstairs table.

Thunder must have been caught by the flood away from home, and God only knows how he had been saved. When the first wave had subsided he must have swum back and in through the front door. Here he would have been a prisoner had not the table left downstairs by Don Camillo provided him with a perch and safety. The water had stopped rising and Thunder waited for help from above, until help actually did come from the ceiling. Don Camillo pulled him through the hole, and Thunder shook himself so joyfully that his master was splashed all over.

It was time to ring the Ave Maria bell. Don Camillo was of the school which believes that the old guard dies but never surrenders, and as a corollary to this he believed that the old guard should not resort to swimming for transportation. With four empty petrol tins and a big washing-board he had built himself a raft, upon which he now made his way to the church to talk on his knees to the Lord on the Cross above the submerged altar.

"Lord, forgive me for bringing Thunder to Your house, but he is the only living creature in the village and I couldn't leave him behind. As a matter of fact, You've seen many a church-goer that's more of a dog than Thunder. . . . And forgive me for attaching my old army field altar to the bell tower and saying Mass over there. A flood is something like a war, and I feel as if I had been called to combat duty."

The Lord sighed.

"Don Camillo, what are you doing here?" He asked. "Shouldn't you be with your people?"

"My people are here," Don Camillo answered. "Their bodies may be far away, but they are here in their hearts."

"But, Don Camillo, your strong arms are inactive and useless, instead of bringing help to those who are weaker than yourself."

"I can best help them by ringing the familiar bell to keep up their hope and faith while they are gone. And then, Lord, when Thunder was lost he came to look for me at home rather than among the evacuees. Which means that my post is here."

"It's a pretty poor fellow that looks to an animal for a rule of conduct rather than to his own powers of reason. God gave you a brain to think with, not a dog."

"But God gave me a heart, too. The heart may not reason, but sometimes it is more powerful than the brain. Forgive my heart and Thunder. . . ."

Don Camillo tied up the raft below his bedroom window and went to sleep. Because of the oppressive silence, he slept for a very long time. He was awakened by the barking of Thunder, who was jumping up at the window. Don Camillo took his shotgun and without lighting the lamp peered out between the closed shutters. Someone called him, and he played a flashlight over the water below. He saw a big vat with a bundle of rags stirring at the bottom.

"Who's there?" he called.

"Rosa Maroli," said the bundle of rags. "Grandfather wants to see you."

"Grandfather?"

"He's sick, and wants to die like a Christian."

Don Camillo put the girl on his raft and pushed off with a long pole in his hand.

"What in Heaven's name are you doing here?" he asked her.

"Grandfather wanted to stay and I want to keep him company."

"Haven't you been scared?"

"No. Grandfather was there. And we could see a light in the presbytery and hear the church bell."

Old Maroli had not much longer to live.

"They wanted to send me to the hospital to die like a dog," he said. "But I want to die a Christian death in my own house. . . . And they said I was crazy . . . yes, and that she was crazy too."

The girl stared at him dumbly.

"Rosa," he panted, "is it true that you're crazy?"

She shook her head.

"Sometimes my head aches and I can't seem to understand," she said timidly.

"Her head aches, do you hear?" said the old man. "She fell on a stone when she was little, and there's a bone pressing on her brain. The doctor told me that himself. He told me they could cure her with an operation. Then I fell ill, and the others wouldn't spend the money. . . . They want to send her to the asylum, because it hurts their conscience to see her."

"Calm yourself; I'm here," said Don Camillo, trying to check the old man's growing excitement.

"You must arrange for that operation . . ." said the old man. "Now, just pull my bed out a little. . . . There on the wall . . . Lift out that striped brick . . ."

Don Camillo moved the brick and found a heavy bag behind it.

"Gold!" panted the old man. "Gold coins . . . All mine, and all for her! Have her operated on, and send her to stay with someone who can give her an education.

We'll show them how crazy we are, Rosa, won't we?"

The girl nodded.

"I want to die like a Christian," panted the old man.

When Don Camillo rose from his knees, it was dawn. Old man Maroli had died like a Christian, and the girl was staring with wide-open eyes at his motionless body.

"Come with me," said Don Camillo gently. "No one will upset your grandfather any more. And no one will upset you, either."

He took hold of a chair and with his enormous hands broke a leg in two as easily as if it were a breadstick.

"That's what I'll do to anyone who touches you."

Thunder waited for them, barking, at Don Camillo's window. The priest poled up to it and told the girl to go through.

"Lie down on the first bed you find," he said, "and have a good sleep."

Then he went over to the church and stopped in front of the altar.

"Lord," he said, "now you see what I meant. She said herself that she wasn't afraid because she could see my light and hear the church bell ring. . . . And she isn't crazy. She had a bad fall as a child. The operation will cure that."

"You must have had a bad fall as a child, too," said the Lord gently. "But there's nothing can cure you. You'll always listen to your heart rather than your brain . . . may God keep that heart of yours whole!"

Thunder kept watch at the foot of the bed where Rosa lay sleeping. The bell tolled for old man Maroli's death, but no one heard it, because the wind carried the sound away.

At last the big river returned to its bed and the people were busy putting their land and homes in order. A thick autumn fog hung over the drenched valley, but everybody felt the danger had passed and that, above the mist, the sky was serene. Once more Don Camillo was able to celebrate Mass in his little church. The organ notes vibrated in thanksgiving, and from the towers of church and Town Hall the chimes echoed through the valley while the golden wings of the great angel seemed to spread over the little world.

DON CAMILLO'S DILEMMA

ELECTIONEERING IN THE HOME

PEPPONE HAD HARDLY gobbled down the last mouthful of his supper when, as usual, he started to jump up from the table and go out for the rest of the evening. But this time his wife didn't let him get away.

"I want to have a talk with you."

"I haven't time," said Peppone. "They're waiting for me at headquarters."

"Let them wait! After all, you're not married to them. For months we haven't been able to exchange a word."

"Don't harass me," said Peppone, breathing hard. "You know I'm not going out for fun. Elections are coming. Just a few days more, and then here's hoping we've seen the last of them for another five years."

"Good. But if we don't discuss it now, when election day does come around, I'll find myself with a ballot in my hand and not a thought in my head. What am I supposed to do? For whom should I vote?"

"That's the limit!" exclaimed Peppone. 'You want me to tell you how to vote!"

"Where should I go to ask? To the priest? You're supposed to tell me what's what."

"But things are exactly the way they were before."

"Then I vote again for you?"

"No, when you voted for me, it was a local election. This is a nation-wide affair, the way it was in 1948."

"I see. Then I should vote for the Garibaldi ticket."

"No, silly! The Garibaldi ticket's a thing of the past. Every party has a symbol of its own. Do you at least know the symbols?"

"Yes, I do."

"Then all you have to do is make an X over the symbol of the party you have chosen. I don't see what else there is to explain. Nothing has changed."

She shook her head in perplexity.

"Even now that he's dead, is the Party just the same?"

"Just the same, only more so!" shouted Peppone, bringing a fist down on the table. "Men may pass, but ideas are eternal!"

"But this Malenkov doesn't seem to me as powerful as Stalin. He lookes more like a compromiser."

"Don't listen to foolish gossip! Just give Malenkov a chance and you'll see! He employs different tactics, but the goal is still the same."

"Then you think we're still moving toward the proletarian revolution?"

"It's closer than every!" Peppone declared. "Present tactics are designed to allay the enemy's suspicions. Then, when the time comes, we'll put one over."

She did not appear to be altogether convinced.

"You say the situation's the same as it was in 1948 . . ."

"Where Communism's concerned, it's a hundred per cent. better. In 1948

Communism was terrific, and now it's tremendous. Stalin may be dead, but his spirit marches on, at the head of the victorious armies of liberation."

"So it isn't true that the Russians want peace, the way they say they do, is that it?"

"Of course it's true! They want peace, but as long as there are warmongers, peace is impossible. In order to obtain peace, the western warmongers must be eliminated. And that means America, the Vatican, big businessmen, priests, land-owners, reactionaries, fascists, royalists, liberals, social-democrats, imperialists, nationalists, militarists and intellectuals. It will take an enormous blood-path to cleanse the world of this medieval residue. We must destroy a rotten old world in order to build up one that's healthy and new. Don't listen to gossip, I tell you. The Garibaldi ticket has been replaced by one that bears our own symbol, but the situation is just what it was before. You can go right ahead, without any misgivings, and vote as you did in 1948."

"All right, Chief," she said, not mentioning the fact that in 1948 she voted for the Christian Democrats.

"Anyhow," Peppone said as he got up, "I'm not imposing my choice upon you. You're free to do as you please, and I shan't even ask what is your decision. Even as a husband, I'm genuinely democratic."

"Oh, I'm not changing my mind," she protested. "I chose, once and for all, last time."

"Good," said Peppone, starting toward the door. "And would you get my gun out of the drawer this evening so I can clean it when I come home? If we win, then we're to start shooting. That's orders."

After Peppone had gone, his wife stared for a long time at the door. Then she raised her eyes to heaven and prayed:

"Lord, make them lose!"

Meanwhile, as Peppone passed by the church on his way to the People's Palace, he mumbled to himself:

"Lord, please let us win. But without my wife's vote, if you don't mind!"

BACK TO 1922

IN THE VILLAGE and its surroundings there were quite a lot of people who started as early as February to lay aside money for the pre-Lenten Carnival. There were twelve rival clubs, five in the village and seven in the countryside, and every Saturday the members contributed part of their pay to the decoration of the floats which each one entered in the parade. In short, the brief Carnival season was a very important affair.

The floats came into being bit by bit in farmyards scattered over the plain. Each club chose the farmyard most suitable for the purpose and with poles, sticks, reed mats and blinds, strips of canvas and tarred paper built a shed which housed the construction. Only members of the club were allowed to look in until the great day came. Then the shed was joyfully torn down and the float emerged, for all the world like a chick newly hatched from the shell. There were sizable prizes to be won, and individual floats and costumed figures came from nearby townships and even from the city. For three whole days the village was crowded.

The Carnival was a serious affair, not only because it drew so many people in a spending mood to the village, but also because it brought with it a complete truce to all political activities. For this reason Don Camillo never made it the butt of any of his sermons.

"Lord," he explained to Christ over the main altar, "we've come to a point where men behave themselves only when they're silly. Let's allow them their fun: *Semel in anno licet insanire.*"

As for Mayor Peppone, he frowned upon the Carnival because it irritated him to see that men couldn't pull together for any cause other than a frivolous one.

"They'll all come across with the money to decorate one of those stupid floats," he protested. "But just try to put over something worthwhile, such as the People's Revolution, and every last of one of them is a skinflint."

Peppone spoke against the Carnival for six months of the year. For the other six months he worked overtime organizing the parade and helping to build his own club's float. Incidentally, he put up considerable money. And if a local float failed to win the first prize, he took it as a personal insult.

That year everything smiled upon the Carnival, because it came in a period of exceptionally fine weather and people came from far and wide to see it. Competing floats and wearers of fancy dress arrived from a widespread area, and no one had ever witnessed so long a parade, which as usual wound its way around the village three times. From his post in the grandstand Peppone looked down at the first round with general satisfaction, finding it worthy of the population gathered in such large numbers to acclaim it. As a result his deportment seemed to be modelled upon that of the Lord Mayor of London.

When the parade came around for the second time, he began to look more closely at the various entries in order to determine whether those of the village were likely to carry away the first prize, or at least the second, third, fourth and fifth prizes. In other words, he was transformed from Lord Mayor of London into mayor of his own town. And among the single competitors for a fancy-dress prize his eyes fell upon a Red Indian riding a motorcycle. After the fellow had gone by, he wondered exactly what had drawn his attention, for the costume had nothing extraordinary about it, being composed chiefly of a big cardboard nose and a band of chicken feathers around the head. He concluded that it must have reminded him of something from times gone by, and sure enough, it came to him in a flash that it was the poster figure that used to advertise "Indian Motorcycles."

During the third round Peppone ascertained that there was indeed a basis for his conclusion. This was the "Indian Motorcycle" figure, and no mistake about it. Only the figure wasn't riding an "Indian" at all; he was astride an old BSA model. Where motorcycles and their engines were concerned, Peppone was like one of those musical quiz experts, who no sooner hear a few notes from a piece than they can tell you its title and composer. And there was a further reason why he could make no mistake: this particular motorcycle had been in his hands for repairs at least a hundred times. Only one question remained in Peppone's mind: Who was riding in Indian costume on Dario Camoni's old BSA?

He left the grandstand, having momentarily lost all interest in the parade. This was a matter that had nothing to do with the mayoralty; it was of a strictly private character. He made his way with difficulty through the crowd, trying to keep up with the Indian, and during a brief pause, the latter turned his head and looked at him. Peppone's doubts vanished. The rider of Dario Camoni's old BSA was Dario Camoni. Even behind a cardboard mask, those were unmistakably his eyes.

Peppone continued to follow the parade, step by step, and nothing in the world could have stopped his implacable *Panzer* pursuit. When the parade had gone around for the third time it drew up in the open space between the village and the river and disbanded. There was such an array of floats, lorries and farm wagons that the Indian could not possibly escape. The only opening in the crowd was on to the street that had led them away from the central square. He was aware that Peppone had been following him and did not hesitate to turn around in this direction, even at the risk of running down a pedestrian. But after he had gone a few yards an enormous float blocked the street and he had to dart into an alley on the right, with Peppone practically panting down his neck from behind.

The smaller square in front of the church was deserted, and the redskin sped up the alley with this destination in view. A few seconds later, he braked his machine abruptly in order not to run down Don Camillo, who was smoking a cigar butt in front of the rectory. Once upon a time this alley had made a right-angle turn just in front of the rectory and gone into the road leading to the river, but for the last ten years it had been blocked off.

Don Camillo was stunned by the abruptness of the motorcycle's arrival. His impulse was to grab the fellow by the chest and knock his head against the wall for his reckless folly. But he was too late. The motorcyclist had dropped his machine on the street and dashed through the rectory's open door. A second later Peppone rushed upon the scene, and without so much as a glance at the priest, followed the fugitive's example. But Don Camillo's powerful body stood in the way.

"What the devil?" Don Camillo shouted. "What in the world are you doing? First an Indian nearly runs me down with a motorcycle and then a mayor bumps into me on foot. Is it all part of some symbolical charade?"

"Look, you've got to let me in," panted Peppone, reluctantly drawing back. "I have a score to settle with Dario Camoni."

"Camoni? How does he come into the picture?"

"That Indian is Camoni!" said Peppone between clenched teeth.

Don Camillo pushed Peppone back, went into the rectory and fastened the door behind him with a chain. The Indian was sitting in the study, and the first thing Don Camillo did was to pull off his cardboard nose.

"Well, it's me, all right," said the Indian, rising from his chair. "What are you going to do about it?"

Don Camillo sat down at his desk and relighted his cigar.

"Nothing at all," he answered, after he had blown several puffs of smoke into the air. "But you'd be better off if you really were an Indian."

Back in 1922 the river country of the little world was still in a state of political ferment, even although elsewhere the Fascists had consolidated their governmental position. The land had something to do with it, and so did the boiling-point of its people. Dario Camoni was seventeen years old, and he wanted to make up for the time when he was too young to take part in the Black-versus-Red battle. In 1919, when he was a mere fourteen years old, some Reds had beaten up his father for refusing to take part in a farm labour strike, right in front of his eyes. This explains, among other things, why three years later Dario was still in a combative mood, and ready to beat up any stray Red he could find for revenge.

Dario Camoni was a husky boy, and above all a hotheaded one. When he went into action his eyes blazed in a way that was more convincing than any amount of words. Peppone was several years older and stood head and shoulders above him, but those cursed eyes caused him to steer clear. One evening when Peppone was talking to his girl on the bridge in front of her house, Dario Camoni rode up on a motorcycle.

"Sorry to intrude," he said, "but I've been given a job to do."

He took a glass and a bottle out of his pocket and proceeded to empty the contents of the bottle into the glass.

"The doctor says you have indigestion and a little laxative will do you good," he continued, advancing with the full glass in one hand and his other hand grasping a hard object in his pocket. "My advice to you is to take your medicine, because some of this castor oil dripped on to my revolver and I don't want the trigger to slip in my fingers. If the dose is too strong for you, you can share it with your girl. I'm going to count to three. One . . . two . . ."

Peppone took the glass and drained it to the last drop.

"Good for you!" said Dario Camoni, mounting his motorcycle. "Be careful not to step on certain people's toes, or you may get something worse next time."

Although Peppone had managed to drink the castor oil, a form of punishment which the Fascists had brought into style, he could not swallow the insult, which was all the more grave because Dario had humiliated him in front of his girl. As it happened, he married the girl later on, but that made it worse rather than better. Every time that he raised his voice at home his wife taunted him:

"If the fellow who gave you the dose of castor oil that night were here, you wouldn't be up on such a high horse, would you?"

No, Peppone had never forgotten this dirty trick, and neither, for that matter, had Don Camillo. In that far-away 1922, Don Camillo was a greenhorn priest, just out of the seminary, but he was nobody's fool and preached a sermon against violence in general, and in particular against the bullies who were going around forcing unsavoury drinks upon other people. For this reason, one night he was called downstairs because someone was fatally ill and needed Extreme Unction. When he came down, there was Dario Camoni, with a Mauser in one hand and a glass of castor oil in the other.

"You're the one that needs the oil, Father, even if it's unholy. This will make your motor hum. And because I owe you particular respect as a member of the clergy, I'll count to four instead of to three."

And Don Camillo drank his ration down.

"There, Father," said Dario Camoni, "you'll see how much more clearly your brain will function tomorrow. And if you really want to be reduced to a condition where you'll need holy oil rather than unholy, just go on sticking your nose into our business."

"The Church's business extends to everything that concerns good Christian people," objected Don Camillo.

"If we'd used Christian behaviour toward the Reds, your church would be a Red headquarters and seat of the Consumers' Co-operative today! Anyhow, whenever you need to change the oil in your motor, just whistle!"

Like Peppone, Don Camillo had found it easier to swallow the oil than the insult.

"Lord," he said several times to Christ over the altar. "If he'd beaten me up, it would be different. But castor oil is too much. You can kill a priest, but you have no right to make him ridiculous with a dose of castor oil!"

Years went by, and Dario Camoni remained an active Fascist as long as there was strong-arm work to be done. Then he retired from politics altogether. But he had oiled and beaten up too many people in his time to be forgotten. When the régime was overturned, in 1945, he found things too hot for him and went away. And Peppone sent word after him to say that if he showed his face in the village it would be at the risk of his skin. More years passed, without news of Dario Camoni. And now he had returned, in the disguise of a Red Indian.

"I'd like to know what got into your head to think up something like this," Don Camillo said to Dario Camoni.

"I've been away from home for six years," murmured the Indian, "and I wanted like anything to come back. The only way I could do it was in disguise. Seems to me it wasn't such a bad idea."

"Poor Camoni!" Don Camillo said with a sigh. "You're so comical in your Indian dress that I'm inclined to be sorry for you. An Indian on a motorcycle, who takes refuge in the priest's house from a mayor who is chasing him on foot. It's almost as melodramatic as the comics. Well, you may as well take it easy. You're almost a hundred per cent safe. If there weren't that glass of castor oil between us, I'd say a hundred per cent with no reservations."

"Is that silly business still on your mind?" asked the Indian, who was still panting from the chase. "That was thirty years ago and childish."

Don Camillo was about to embark upon a long harangue when the study door swung open and Peppone appeared on the scene.

"Excuse me, Father, for coming through the window," he said, "but I had no other choice, since I couldn't come through the door."

The Indian had leaped to his feet, for the expression on Peppone's face wasn't exactly pretty. Moreover, Peppone had an iron bar in his hand and looked as if he intended to put it to use. Don Camillo stepped between them.

"Don't let's have a tragedy in the middle of the Carnival," he interposed. "We must all be calm."

"I'm perfectly calm," said Peppone, "and I have no intention of causing a tragedy. I have a job to do, that's all."

He took two glasses out of one pocket, then without taking his eyes off the Indian, a bottle out of the other and divided its contents between them.

"There," he said, standing back against the door. "The doctor says you have indigestion and a little laxative will do you good. Hurry up, because the oil has greased my iron bar and I'm afraid it may slip and fall on to your head. Drink down both glassfuls, one to my health and the other to the health of Don Camillo. I'm happy to pay my respects to him in this way."

The Indian turned pale as he backed up against the wall, and Peppone was truly fear-inspiring.

"Drink them down, I tell you!" he shouted, raising the iron bar.

"No, I won't," answered the Indian.

Peppone rushed forward and grabbed him by the neck.

"I'll make you drink!" he shouted.

But the Indian's neck and face were covered with grease-paint and he managed to free himself. He leaped behind the table, and as Peppone and Don Camillo noticed too late for their own good, he took down the shotgun hanging on the wall and pointed it straight at Peppone.

"Don't do anything crazy," shouted Don Camillo, drawing over to one side, "that thing is loaded."

The Indian advanced on his enemy.

"Throw down that bar," he said sternly, and his eyes were as blazing as they had been thirty years before. Peppone and Don Camillo both remembered them distinctly, and knew that Dario Camoni was quite capable of shooting. Peppone let the bar fall to the floor.

'Now *you* drink,' the Indian said between clenched teeth to Peppone. "I'll count to three. One . . . two . . ."

Yes, he had the same wild eyes and the same voice as long ago. Peppone gulped down the contents of one of the glasses.

"And now go back where you came from," the Indian commanded.

Peppone went away, and the Indian barred the study door.

"He can send his police if he wants to," he said, "but if I'm killed, I won't go to Hell alone."

Don Camillo relit his cigar.

"That's enough of your horseplay," he said quietly. "Put down that gun and go away."

"Go away yourself," said the Indian coldly. "I'm waiting for them here."

"Very unwise, Redskin," said the priest. "I don't believe the palefaces will come, but if they do, how can you defend yourself with an empty gun?"

"That's an old joke and poor one," laughed the Indian. "I wasn't born yesterday, for your information!"

Don Camillo went to sit down on the other side of the room.

"Just look and see," he suggested.

The suspicious Camoni peered into the gun and his face whitened. The gun was not loaded.

"Put the gun down," said Don Camillo quietly; "take off your costume, leave the rectory on the garden side and cut through the fields. If you hurry, you'll catch the bus at Fontanile. I'll put your motorcycle in safe-keeping, and you can either let me know where to send it or else come and fetch it in person."

The Indian laid the gun on the desk.

"No use looking for the cartridges," Don Camillo told him. He had put on his glasses and was reading the paper. "The cartridges are in the cupboard and the key to the cupboard is in my pocket. I warn you that unless you get out of here in double-quick time, I'll be reminded of that drink you pressed upon me long ago."

The Indian tore off the remains of his costume and wiped the grease-paint off his face. He took a cap out of his pocket and jammed it down over his head. Dario Camoni started to leave the room, but he lingered at the door and turned hesitantly around.

"Let's even the score," he said, and picking up the second glass of castor oil, he drained it.

"Quits?" he said interrogatively.

"Quits," answered Don Camillo, without even raising his head.

And the Indian disappeared.

Peppone came back later, looking green around the gills.

"I hope you won't sink so low as to go around telling what happened to me," he said gloomily.

"I should say not," Don Camillo answered with a sigh. "You had one glass, but that wretch made me drink the other."

"Has he gone away?" asked Peppone, sitting down.

"Gone with the wind."

Peppone stared at the floor and said nothing.

"Well, what can I say?" he finally mumbled. "It was a little like going back to the time when we were young, thirty years ago. . . ."

"True enough," said Don Camillo. "That Indian brought back a bit of our youth."

Peppone started to relapse into anger.

"Easy there, Peppone," Don Camillo advised him. "You don't want to endanger the dignity of your office."

Peppone went cautiously home, and Don Camillo made a report to the crucified Christ over the altar.

"Lord," he explained, "what else could I do? If I'd told Peppone the gun wasn't loaded he'd have killed the other fellow for sure. Those Camonis are too pig-headed to ever give in. As things are, there was no violence, and the Indian had a dose of oil, which You must chalk up to his credit. And by sacrificing my personal pride, I managed not to humiliate Peppone."

"Don Camillo," Christ answered, "when the Indian told Peppone to drink the oil, you knew the gun wasn't loaded and you could perfectly well have stepped in."

"Lord," said Don Camillo, throwing out his arms in resignation, "what if Peppone had found out that the gun wasn't loaded and failed to get that healthy drink?"

"Don Camillo," Christ said severely, "I ought to prescribe a drink of the same kind for you!"

It seems that as Don Camillo left the church he was muttering something to the effect that only Fascists could order any such prescription. But this is not altogether certain. In any case, when he hung the shotgun up on the wall, he placed the Indian bonnet as a trophy beside it, and every time he looked at it he reflected that there is perfectly good hunting to be found without benefit of a gun.

A SOUL FOR SALE

NERI, THE MASON, had been hammering away for three hours without accomplishing much of anything. The wall seemed to be an unbreakable solid mass, and he had to smash every brick before he could get it out. He stopped for a minute to wipe the sweat off his forehead, and cursed when he saw how small a hole he had made with so much effort.

"It's going to take patience," said the voice of old Molotti, who had engaged him to do the work, behind him.

"Patience, my eye!" Neri exclaimed ill-humouredly. "This is no wall, it's a block of steel. It'll take something more than patience to pierce a door."

He started pounding again, but a few minutes later he dropped his hammer and chisel and let out another oath. He had given his left thumb a tremendous crack and it was bleeding.

"I told you take it easy," said Molotti. "If you'd had a bit more patience you wouldn't have lost your temper and banged your own thumb."

Neri's only answer was another outburst of profanity.

Old Molotti shook his head.

"God Almighty has nothing to do with it," he said. "You can only blame the fellow who was wielding the hammer. And remember, you'll never get to Heaven without a lot of pain."

"It's painful enough to make a living," Neri retorted angrily. "I don't give a damn for your Heaven."

Neri was as Red as they make them, and one of Peppone's most excitable followers, but although Molotti was over ninety years old, he wasn't going to let that upset him.

"I'd forgotten that you don't give a damn for our Heaven," he said. "You're one of the Reds, aren't you, and they promise some sort of heaven on earth."

"That's a lot more honest than promising it somewhere up in the sky," countered Neri. "We promise things you can see and touch with your own hands."

"Never fear!" said Molotti, raising an admonitory finger. "Some day you'll see and touch things that are now hidden from you."

Neri burst into loud laughter.

"When I'm dead, I'm dead, and that's the end of everything for me. Anything else is just priest's chatter."

"May God save your soul!" sighed old Molotti.

Neri resumed his hammering.

"Who could have believed that people would still go around preaching all that stuff and nonsense!" he muttered. "My soul, eh? A soul flapping through the air with a brand-new pair of wings, and receiving a prize for its good behaviour! You must take me for a complete idiot!"

"If I didn't think you were talking tough just to enjoy the sound of your own voice, when all the time you know better deep down inside, then I'd say you were crazy."

"You priests and landowners are crazy, to imagine you can still hand us out all that nonsense!"

Old Molotti shook his head. "Do you really think the soul dies with the body?" he asked.

"Just as sure as I am to be alive. There isn't such a thing as a soul!"

"And what have you got inside you?"

"Lungs, liver, spleen, brains, heart, stomach and intestines. We're flesh-and-blood machines, which run just as long as these organs are working. When one of them breaks down, the machine stops, and if the doctor can't repair it, then it's good-bye, machine."

Old Molotti threw out his arms in indignation.

"But you've forgotten the soul!" he shouted. "The soul is the breath of life!"

"Bunk!" said Neri. "Try taking out a man's lungs and you'll see what happens. If the soul were the breath of life, he ought to be able to get along without them."

"That's blasphemy!"

"No, I'm just using my reason. Anyone can see that life is linked to the internal organs. I've never seen a man die because they've taken his soul away. And if you say the soul's the breath of life, then chickens must have souls just like the rest of us, and go to the same Heaven, Purgatory and Hell."

Old Molotti saw that it was no use to argue further and so he walked away. But he hadn't given up the struggle and at noon, when Neri had stopped to eat his lunch, he came over to the shady spot where he was sitting.

"Look here," said Neri, "if you want to fight some more, you're wasting your time, I can tell you."

"I have no intention of fighting," said the old man. "I want to make you a strictly business proposition. You're perfectly sure, are you, that you have no soul?"

Neri's face clouded over, but Molotti did not give him time to protest.

"In that case, you may as well sell it to me," he continued. "I'm offering you five hundred liras."

Neri looked at the banknote in the old man's hand and burst out laughing.

"That's a good one! How can I sell you something I haven't got?"

"That's not your worry," Molotti insisted. "You're selling me your soul. If you actually don't possess such a thing, then I lose my money. But if you do have it, then it's mine."

Neri began to enjoy himself thoroughly. He thought the old man must have softening of the brain.

"Five hundred liras isn't much," he said gaily, "you might at least offer me a thousand."

"No," said Molotti. "A soul like yours isn't worth it."

"But I won't take less!"

"Very well, then, a thousand. Before you go home we'll put it in writing."

Neri hammered away, more cheerfully, until evening. When it was time to knock off, the old man brought him a fountain pen and a sheet of legal paper.

"Are you still willing?" he asked.

"Of course."

"Then sit down and write: 'I, Francesco Neri, hereby legally bind myself, in return for the sum of one thousand liras, to sell my soul to Giuseppe Molotti. Having paid me this sum, Molotti enters from this day forth into possession and can dispose of my soul as he sees fit. Signed: Francesco Neri.' "

Molotti handed Neri a thousand-lira note, and Neri made his signature with an appropriate flourish.

"Good!" said the old man. "The business is done, and that's all there is to it."

Neri laughed as he went away. Yes, Molotti was in his dotage, that was the only explanation. He only wished he'd asked for more money. But this thousand-lira note was so much gravy.

As he pedalled off on his broken-down bicycle, he couldn't get the strange contract off his mind. "If Molotti isn't in his dotage, as he seems to be, why would he give me a thousand liras?" he wondered. The rich old man was notoriously stingy, and he wouldn't part with his money for no purpose. All of a sudden Neri saw the whole thing clearly. He let out a volley of oaths and pedalled back as fast as he could in order to make up for his stupidity. He found old Molotti in the yard and came out immediately with what was on his mind.

"Look here," he said gloomily. "I was a fool not to think of it before. But better late than never. I know your reactionary methods. You got that contract out of me for propaganda purposes. You're going to publish it in order to ridicule my Party. 'Here are the Communists,' you'll say, 'people that go around selling their souls for a thousand liras!' "

The old man shook his head.

"This is a strictly private affair," he answered. "But if you like, I'll add a guarantee to the contract: 'I swear never to show this document to anyone whatsoever.' Does that suit you?"

Molotti was an honourable man, and his solemn oath was to be respected. He went into his study, wrote down the codicil and signed it.

"You've nothing to worry about," he said. "But as far as that goes, you needn't have worried before. I didn't buy your soul for political purposes. I bought it for my own private use."

"That is, if you can lay hands on it!" said Neri, who was restored to his good humour.

"Naturally," said Molotti. "And as far as I'm concerned it's good business. I'm quite sure you have a soul, and besides, this would be the first time in my life I'd failed to strike a good bargain."

Neri went home feeling completely reassured. Molotti had softening of the brain. At his age, that wasn't surprising. He wanted to tell his cronies the story, but he was afraid that if it got around, the reactionaries would use it to shock their public of churchgoing old ladies.

The alterations of Molotti's house lasted for over a week and Neri met the old man every day. But Molotti made no mention of the contract and entered into no political discussion. It seemed as if he had forgotten the whole thing. After the job was done, Neri had no further occasion to see him, and a whole year went by before the matter returned to his mind.

One evening Peppone called him to lend a hand in the workshop. He had forged the parts of a wrought-iron gate, and now it was a question of putting them together.

"It's an order from old man Molotti," Peppone told him, "and he wants it finished by tomorrow morning. The gate's for his family tomb. He says he wants to have it made before he dies, because none of the rest of them has enough sense to do the proper thing."

"Is he sick?" Neri asked.

"He's been in bed for a week with a bad cold that's gone down into his lungs. And at ninety-three years of age, that's no joke."

Neri began to work the bellows.

"Then there's one more reactionary swine gone," he muttered. "Even the family ought to be glad, because he's in his dotage."

"I wouldn't say that," put in Peppone. "Only a month ago he made a deal with the Trespiano farm which netted him at least fifteen million liras."

"Just disgusting good luck," said Neri. "I happen to know that he's been dotty for some time. Chief, shall I tell you a story?"

And he proceeded to tell how he had sold his soul to Molotti. Peppone listened attentively.

"Don't you think a man must be soft in the head to buy another man's soul for a thousand liras?" Neri concluded.

"Yes, I do, but the man that sells it is even softer."

"Well, of course I should have got much more money than that out of him," said Neri, shrugging his shoulders.

"I'm not speaking of the price," said Peppone.

Neri took his hand off the bellows.

"Chief, are you joining the Children of Mary? What in the world do you mean? Never mind the attitude of the Party and the policy of not making a frontal attack upon organized religion, but just between ourselves, don't you agree that the soul, Heaven, Hell and all the rest of that stuff are just priestly inventions?"

Peppone continued to hammer out the red-hot iron.

"Neri," he said, after a long pause, "that's irrelevant. I say that for a man to sell his soul for a thousand liras is non-productive and counter-revolutionary."

"Now, I understand, Chief," said Neri with relief. "But you needn't worry. In order to prevent him from turning the thing to political use, I had a codicil added, which stipulates that Molotti will never speak about it to anyone."

"Well, with that codicil, it's different," said Peppone. "That makes it your own private business, which is of no concern to the Party. As far as the Party goes, you're in perfectly good standing."

Peppone proceeded to talk of other matters, and Neri went home at midnight in an excellent humour.

"The main thing is to be in good standing with the Party," he said to himself before falling asleep. "Then everything else is in line, too."

Molotti got worse and worse every day. One evening, when Don Camillo was coming back from his bedside, he ran into Neri.

"Good evening," said Neri, and Don Camillo was so bowled over that he was moved to get off his bicycle and go and look him in the face.

"Extraordinary!" he exclaimed. "You're Neri, sure enough, and you said good evening to me. Are you sure you weren't making a mistake? Did you take me for a tax collector instead of the parish priest?"

Neri shrugged his shoulders.

"With you, it's hard to know how to behave. If we don't speak to you, you say we're godless Reds, and if we do, then you think we're crazy."

"You've got something there," said Don Camillo, throwing out his arms. "But that's not the whole story. Anyhow, good evening to you."

Neri stared for a minute at the handlebars of Don Camillo's bicycle. Finally he said:

"How's old man Molotti?"

"He's dying by slow degrees."

"Has he lost consciouness?"

"No, he's perfectly clear-headed and has been all along."

"Has he said anything to you?" asked Neri aggressively.

Don Camillo opened his eyes wide in astonishment.

"I don't understand. What should he say?"

"Hasn't he said anything about me and about a contract between us?"

"No," said Don Camillo, convincingly. "We've talked about practically everything, but not about you. And besides, I don't go to talk to a dying man about business matters. My concern is with souls."

This last word caused Neri to start, and Don Camillo nodded and smiled.

"Neri, I have no intention of preaching at you. I told you what it was my duty to tell when you were a little boy and came to hear. Now all I do is answer your questions. I've had no talk about any business contract with Molotti and I have no intention of bringing up any such subject. If you need help of that kind, consult a lawyer. But hurry, because Molotti has one foot in the next world, already."

"If I stopped you, it's because I needed a priest's help, not a lawyer's," Neri insisted. "It's just a small matter but you must give Molotti a thousand liras and ask him to return a certain legal paper."

"A legal paper? A thousand liras? That sounds to me very much like a lawyer's affair."

By this time they had come to the rectory, and after casting a suspicious eye about him, Neri followed Don Camillo in. The priest sat down at his desk and motioned Neri to a chair.

"If you think I can really help you, go ahead and tell me what it's all about."

Neri twisted his hat in his hands and finally said:

"Father, the fact is this. A year ago, in return for a thousand liras, I sold Molotti my soul."

Don Camillo started. Then he said threateningly:

"Listen, if you think that's a good joke, you've come to the wrong place. Get out of here!"

"It's no joke," Neri protested. "I was working in his house and we had a discussion about the soul. I said there was no such thing and he said: 'If you don't believe the soul exists, then you may as well sell yours to me for a thousand liras.' I accepted his offer and signed a contract."

"A contract?"

"Yes, an agreement written and signed by my hand, on legal paper."

He knew the terms of the contract by heart and recited them to Don Camillo. The priest could not help being persuaded of his sincerity.

"I see," he said, "but why do you want the paper? If you don't believe you have a soul, then why do you care whether or not you sold it?"

"It's not on account of the soul," Neri explained. "I don't want his heirs to find that paper and make political capital out of it. That might damage the Party."

Don Camillo got up and stood in front of Neri with his hands on his hips and his legs far apart.

"Listen to me," he said between clenched teeth. "Am I supposed to help you for the sake of your party? You must take me for the stupidest priest that ever was! Get along with you!"

Neri went slowly toward the door. But after a few steps he turned back.

"Never mind about the Party!" he exclaimed. "I want my paper!"

Don Camillo was standing with his hands on his hips, defiantly.

"I want my paper!" Neri repeated. "For six months I haven't had a decent night's sleep."

Don Camillo looked at the man's distraught face and eyes and the perspiration on his forehead.

"My paper!" he panted. "If the swine insists upon making money, even on his deathbed, then I'll pay something extra, whatever he asks. But I can't go to his house. They wouldn't let me in, and besides, I wouldn't know how to put it."

"Take it easy!" interrupted Don Camillo. "If it's not for the Party, what does it matter? The soul and the next world and all that sort of thing are priestly, inventions——"

"The reason's not your affair," Neri shouted. "I want my paper, I tell you!"

"Very well, then," said Don Camillo resignedly, "I'll try to get it for you tomorrow morning."

"No, right now!" Neri insisted. "Tomorrow morning he may be dead. Take the thousand liras and go to him right away, while he's still alive. I'll wait for you outside. Hurry, Father, hurry!"

Don Camillo understood, but he still couldn't tolerate the miscreant's peremptory way of speaking. And so he continued to stand there with his hands on his hips, looking into Neri's distraught face.

"Father, go ahead and do your duty!" Neri shouted in exasperation.

All of a sudden Don Camillo was overtaken by the same impatience. He ran out, minus his hat, jumped on to his bicycle and rode away in the darkness.

An hour later Don Camillo returned and Neri once more followed him into the rectory.

"Here you are," said the priest, handing him a large sealed envelope. Inside were another envelope, closed with sealing-wax, and a short letter. The letter ran as follows: "The undersigned, Giuseppe Molotti, hereby declares null and void the contract he made with Francesco Neri and restores it to him." And there, in the smaller envelope, was the famous piece of legal paper.

"He didn't want the thousand liras," said Don Camillo. "Take them. He said to do with them whatever you liked."

Neri did not say a word, but went out with all his belongings in his hands. He thought of tearing up the contract, but on further reflection decided to burn it. The side door of the church was still open and he could see candles blazing. He went in and paused in front of the big candle behind the altar rail. Holding the paper in the flame, he watched it crumple, then squeezed it in his hand until it was reduced to ashes. Finally he opened his fingers and blew the ashes away. Just as he was about to leave, he remembered the thousand liras, took them out of the envelope and stuffed them in the poor-box. Then, quite unexpectedly, he took another thousand-lira note out of his pocket and put it in the same place. "For a blessing received," he thought to himself as he went home. His eyes were drowsy and he knew that this night he would sleep.

Shortly after this, Don Camillo went to lock up the church and bid good-night to the Christ over the altar.

"Lord," he asked, "who can possibly understand these people?"

"I can," the Crucified Christ answered, smiling.

BEAUTY AND THE BEAST

THEY HAD MET dozens of times in the People's Palace, marched side by side in parade, gone out as a team to collect signatures for the Peace Crusade and other devilries of the same kind, and so it was natural enough that things should come spontaneously to a head one summer evening.

"It seems to me we two work pretty smoothly together," Marco said to the girl as they came out of the People's Palace.

"I think so too," Giulietta admitted.

They didn't say anything more, but the next evening Marco went over to Brusco's house to call for Giulietta. Then they went to sit together on the bridge that spanned the Po River. That was how it all began, and everyone found it the most logical thing in the world. Marco and Brusco's daughter did indeed seem to be made for one another. They were of the same age and had the same wild ideas, and if Giulietta was the prettiest girl in the village, Marco was certainly an up-and-coming young man. Both of them were so bitten by the political bug that they thought of practically nothing else.

"Marco," said Giulietta, "I like you because you're different from other boys. You talk to me as if I weren't just a mere woman."

"Giulietta," he answered, "what difference does it make if we're of opposite sexes, as long as our ideals are the same?"

They continued way into the autumn to meet four evenings a week on the bridge. Finally, one time when it was pouring with rain, Giulietta's mother met Marco at the door and said he and Giulietta might as well come on to the porch for shelter. And when winter came, she suggested that they'd better come into the house. Brusco's wife was a truly old-fashioned woman. She was completely absorbed in her home and thought of everything beyond the bridge as a foreign land, whose goings-on were of no interest to her. As far as she knew, this foreign land was just the same as it had been twenty or thirty years before. And so, when Marco came into the kitchen she pointed to a chair near the cupboard and said:

"Sit down."

After that she motioned her daughter into a matching chair on the other side of the cupboard and returned to the seat where she had been knitting, in front of the fire. Giulietta and Marco went quietly on with the conversation they had begun on the porch. Two hours later Marco went away and Giulietta took herself off to bed. Her mother didn't say a word, but she thought plenty, and when Brusco came home, she let off steam.

"That young man came to the house," she told him.

"Did he?" asked Brusco. "And what do you think of him?"

"He's a poor wretch, that's what I think."

"He's a good boy, a boy with his head on his shoulders," said Brusco. "I know him well."

"I say he's a wretched creature," his wife repeated. "For two whole hours they talked of nothing but politics: political parties, party papers, Russia, America and other such ridiculous things. And she lapped it up! Poor wretches, both of them, that's what I say."

"What do you expect them to talk about?" said Brusco. "That's what interests the youth of today."

"Chattering about politics doesn't lead anyone to get married. Marriage means starting a family, not a political party. No, I don't like the fellow at all."

"Well, you don't have to marry him," said Brusco, starting upstairs. "The main thing is that he's a thoroughly good boy."

"No one that belongs to your godless party can be a good boy!"

"Well, your daughter belongs to my godless party, too," Brusco countered. "And isn't she a good girl?"

"She's not my daughter, she's yours!" answered his wife, throwing out her arms in despair.

As she thrashed about in her bed, trying vainly to sleep, a suspicion came into her mind. Perhaps they had talked about those ridiculous things simply because she was there. When they were alone, they might talk of something completely different.

She decided to put this suspicion to the test, and when Marco came to call she said she was dead tired and supposedly went up to bed. Once upstairs, she lifted up a board which she had previously loosened from the floor, and was able to hear everything they were saying below. Marco and Giulietta talked quietly for some ten minutes or so, and then Marco raised his voice to say:

"Now that your mother's gone to bed, we can talk more freely. I say that if we go on with the halfway methods of Peppone and your father, we'll never get anywhere. We've got to get tough with the landowners if we want results."

"I agree with you a hundred per cent.," said Giulietta gravely. "Next time there's a meeting, we'll have to let Peppone know what's what. As for my father, I've been trying to put it over for some time, but it's no use. They're getting old, and you can't expect them to have any flexibility in their thinking."

Upstairs, the woman held her breath. This was even looser talk than that of the night before. But it was so boring that she couldn't keep her eyes open, and when Brusco came up he found her asleep, with her ear glued to the floor.

"Fine ideas they have, those two!" she exclaimed, pulling herself together. "If you want to know, your daughter told that wretched boy that you and Peppone are old fuddy-duddies and the landowners twist you around their fingers."

"These young people are full of enthusiasm," said Brusco, shaking his head, "but of course they carry everything to extremes. And as far as Peppone and myself are concerned, we're in perfect harmony with the Party."

Things went on in very much the same way, but Brusco's wife had lost all interest in Giulietta and her young man. Whenever he appeared upon the scene, she simply said:

"Here comes the committee!"

Finally something different did happen, and it was brought about by Giulietta. One evening she came late to supper, waving a magazine in her hand.

"Look at this!" she shouted, opening it up before them, "I'm in the finals!"

Brusco looked at the magazine and passed it over to his wife.

"Do you know who this is?" he asked, pointing to a photograph.

"It looks like her," his wife answered.

"It looks like me so much that it *is* me," said the girl, laughing. "And there's my name underneath to prove it."

Still her mother didn't understand.

"What's it all about?"

"It's the contest for 'Miss New Life.' I'm in the final round."

Her mother looked again at the magazine and shook her head uncomprehendingly.

"Anyone can see," said Giulietta. "*New Life* is our Party magazine and it runs a contest every year. Girls from all over the country send in their pictures and a jury decides among them. Those that last as far as the finals are called to Rome to be looked over in person, and then the winner is proclaimed 'Miss New Life.' Now I'm one of the eight called to Rome for the final selection."

There was still something her mother didn't understand.

"But what's the basis of the selection? What sort of a contest is it?"

"A beauty contest, of course!" Giulietta exclaimed. "The prettiest girl wins the title and a whole lot of prizes. It's a serious business, I tell you. The jury is made up of artists, moving-picture directors, newspapermen, and so on. And you can be sure it's conducted the way it should be, since it's sponsored by the Party."

The woman turned to her husband. "Are you letting your daughter get her picture into print and then show herself off in Rome?"

"Don't turn it into a tragedy," said Brusco, shrugging his shoulders. "There are plenty of contests of this kind, and I don't see anything the matter with them. Haven't there been beauty queens as long as we can remember?"

"There've been no-good girls as long as we can remember, too," she said, "but that doesn't mean we have to encourage ours to be one."

"Don't be stupid, Mother!" cried Giulietta angrily.

The woman looked at her husband, but he went right on eating. Finally she got up and went over to the stairs. Brusco wolfed down the rest of his supper and hurried out, mumbling something about a meeting. Giulietta cleared the table, washed the dishes and sat down to wait for Marco. This was his regular evening, and he arrived promptly.

"Have you seen this?" she said at once, showing him the magazine.

"Yes, I have," he answered. "Your picture came out very well. I didn't know you'd sent it in."

Giulietta was still in a state of excitement. She leafed through the magazine pages.

"Look at the other girls in the finals," she said, "and tell me what you think."

"It's hard to judge from a print on cheap paper," he said, after a thorough examination.

"That's why they call us to Rome," said Giulietta. "There they'll look us over from head to toe. And all modesty aside, it seems to me I have a chance."

"When do you go to Rome?" he asked.

"On the twentieth, it says here. That's just four days away."

"It's a long trip," Marco observed.

"Four hundred miles! And all expenses paid. It's the opportunity of a lifetime to see the city."

Marco agreed that it was an opportunity.

"But this whole idea of a beauty contest has something terribly bourgeois about it," he added.

"Beauty isn't a bourgeois monopoly," laughed Giulietta. "Beauty's universal."

"Right," Marco admitted, "but you don't catch them holding beauty contests in Russia."

"Russia's different," she protested. "They don't have strikes or seizures of factories there, either. In Russia everything's done for the People. There's not a beastly bourgeoisie whose propaganda paints all Communists as monsters, as creatures with three nostrils and the like. *New Life*'s contest will prove there are plenty of pretty girls in the Party, much prettier than your bourgeois young ladies. If the contest didn't have a serious purpose, the Party wouldn't permit it. The Party knows its business, after all."

Marco agreed that the Party was always right.

"But, personally, I'm a little sorry that you sent in your picture."

"Marco," she said severely, "what sort of silly talk is this? Are you giving in to ordinary masculine conventions?"

"You misunderstood me," answered Marco. "I've always admired you because you weren't like other women. You didn't seem to have their vanity and petty ambition . . . now . . . your idea of going into this contest makes me wonder . . ."

Giulietta drew herself up proudly.

"If the Party's sponsoring it, that means it's beneficial to the Party. And if I can benefit a cause that benefits the Party, it's my obligation to do so."

"Forgive me, Giulietta," Marco said, blushing. "To tell the truth, I have feelings I've never had before. It bothers me to see your picture on display and it bothers me to think of your going to Rome."

Giulietta gave a sarcastic laugh.

"Control yourself, Comrade, or you'll turn into one of those idiots that lose their head every time they see a pretty girl. And I don't want you to disappoint me. After you've led me to believe you were different from other men and capable of a platonic friendship, please don't show yourself up as the kind that thinks only of putting over a fast one."

"Giulietta!" cried Marco, turning very pale. "Now you've hurt my feelings."

"No, Marco, you've hurt mine. And besides that, you've insulted my father. Because, remember, my father hasn't breathed a word of opposition."

"Don't take it so hard, Giulietta," said Marco throwing out his arms in despair. "I don't want to hurt or insult a soul. I'm only asking whether, for my sake, you're not willing to give up the trip to Rome. Why do you care about being the *New Life* beauty queen, when you're the queen of my heart?"

He spoke in a most unusually gentle voice, which caused Giulietta to stare at him in disgust.

"You fool!" she shouted.

Marco turned even more pale, and came toward her, attempting to grasp her hand.

"Go away, and don't hurry back!" shouted Giulietta, pushing him back roughly and pointing to the door.

Marco lowered his head and started to go. But he wasn't really such a fool; in fact, he was a young man of considerable character. So it was that he wheeled around and said sternly:

"Giulietta, I forbid you to go to Rome. I won't have you take part in a beauty contest or anything of the kind. Your father may be an idiot, but I'm not."

Giulietta planted herself in front of him with her hands on her hips.

"Forbid me?" she shouted. "What right have you to do that? Who do you think you are?"

"I'm somebody that loves you," said Marco, losing his usual self-possession. "I'm not the kind that puts his wife on public display."

Giulietta giggled, and after a minute or so Marco clenched his fists and said:

"You're not going to Rome, I tell you!"

Giulietta stopped giggling and looked him straight in the eye.

"Instead of waiting four days, I'm going tomorrow," she said defiantly, "and I'll appear before the jury in a bathing-suit. I have a new one right here in the drawer, if you want to see it, in two pieces . . ."

She could not finish because Marco tore the package out of her hands, threw the contents on the floor and stepped on them.

"There are plenty more where that came from," said Giulietta angrily. "You'll see my picture in a bathing-suit in all the papers. And now get out of my house! I'll send you a postcard from Rome."

Marco was beside himself with rage and despair, but there was nothing he could do. He look around without knowing exactly what for, and saw a shotgun, with a hunting bag and cartridge belt hanging up on the wall beside it. And on the mantelpiece another sinister object was gleaming. Giulietta didn't have time to escape because Marco had reached out with one hand while with the other he grabbed Giulietta by the neck. His fingers were like iron bands, and Giulietta could barely breathe. Marco raised the weapon and brought it down on her head. The girl couldn't even cry out, because fright had caused her to faint away.

When Giulietta came to, she was sitting on the floor and Marco was watching over her. She didn't yet know what had happened, because her head felt quite empty. No wonder, for the object that Marco had taken from the mantelpiece was a pair of shears and with it he had shorn all the long, silky hair from her head. Now he threw the scissors at her feet and Giulietta began to realize what he had done.

"Go to Rome, if you like," said Marco fiercely. And he disappeared through the door.

Lying on the floor of their upstairs room, Brusco's wife had through the aperture left by the removed board followed every detail of the scene.

"I told you he was a good boy, didn't I?" murmured Brusco, who had sneaked home through the garden and in by the back door and was now on watch beside his wife.

The next day the whole village had heard about the shearing. There was no way of knowing who told the tale but in the river country of the little world everyone knows everyone else's business. And, of course, a girl friend came to see Giulietta in the afternoon and told her that the whole village was buzzing.

"Listen, Giulietta," her friend said through a crack in the door; "nobody's actually seen you. If I were you, I'd clear out and go to your uncle's up in the mountains for a couple of months. While you're there you can wear a little wig and tie a scarf around it. And meanwhile your hair will grow back."

"Thanks for the good advice," said Giulietta coldly.

She stayed at home all day, but after supper she went to sit on the side of the bridge. It was a magnificent August evening, with an enormous moon in the sky, and the first passer-by could see Giulietta's condition quite clearly. He ran to spread the news, and soon a whole procession of people came by. And at the end of the crowd came Marco. He stood there hesitatingly until Giulietta said:

"Well, aren't you coming to see the show?"

Marco swallowed hard and then said: "Giulietta, if you want your revenge, take it right away. But don't throw vitriol in my face. I'd rather you shot me."

"Shoot you?" said Giulietta in amazement. "If I shoot you while I'm in this condition, where can I find another fool ready to marry me right away?"

Giulietta wore a Party-approved grey tailored suit and a blouse with a black bow to the wedding, and when Don Camillo found this strange pair standing before him he looked in perplexity from one to the other, with his eyes coming to a pause on Giulietta's shorn head.

"Which one of you is the groom?" he asked.

"He is," sighed Giulietta, covering her baldness with a veil.

A COUNTRY PRIEST'S DIARY

BRUSCO LOOKED AT the wall and shrugged his shoulders.

"Well, what do you say?" asked Don Camillo.

"I don't know," Brusco answered.

"If a mason doesn't know whether or not he can make a door through a wall, then he'd better change trades!" exclaimed Don Camillo. "Perhaps I should call Neri."

"This wall is as old as the hills," Brusco explained, "and an old wall can be very tricky. Unless you let me knock off a bit of plaster and explore underneath, I can't give you any definite reply."

And so Don Camillo authorized him to make an exploration.

"Just remember you're in a sacristy," he admonished him; "try to do a neat job and not cover the place with litter."

Brusco took a hammer and chisel out of his bag and began to knock plaster off the wall.

"It looks bad," he said after two or three strokes of the hammer. "The wall's filled with clay and stones. If it were made of bricks, we could put a reinforced cement architrave in just at the point of the first break-through and then carry the break down to the floor. But this way, it looks like trouble."

Don Camillo borrowed the hammer and knocked some plaster off another part of the wall. But here, too, he came upon a conglomeration of stones and clay.

"Queer," he observed. "The outside walls of the church are all brick. Why should they have put stones inside?"

Brusco threw out his arms with a baffled air.

"They may have made the supporting columns and an outer layer of bricks," he said, "and then stuffed the rest with stones. But let's take it easy and explore a little deeper."

By means of a big nail he loosened the clay around an uncovered stone and pulled it out. Then he hammered at the clay behind it and came to another stone. While he was trying to dig this out too, it disappeared.

"There must be an empty space behind the stones, and I don't understand it. You'd expect the stones to go all the way to the brick outer wall."

Don Camillo widened the hole and soon they found an enormous wardrobe which the secondary wall had been built to conceal. Of course the priest was feverishly anxious to open it, and when they had come back down into the sacristy he said to Brusco:

"Thanks. I don't need you any more."

"I'm afraid you do," said Brusco calmly. "A wall fifteen feet long, nine feet high and eighteen inches thick makes a considerable mass of stones and clay. And if you want to open the wardrobe, the whole thing will have to come down."

"And what makes you think I'll tackle that wall?" Don Camillo asked. "I'm not totally mad."

"You're worse than that; you're Don Camillo!" Brusco retorted.

But when Don Camillo had thought twice about the dimensions of the wall he had to acknowledge that it was too much for him.

"Very well," he said. "Go and get enough men to tear it down and wagons to carry the debris away. But once the work is done, I want it understood that you will all go home. I want to open the wardrobe myself."

Ten minutes later most of the people of the village were on the church square and all of them for this reason:

"Don Camillo has discovered a hidden treasure in the sacristy."

They imagined pots and pans filled with gold ducats, paintings and all sorts of other objects of art, and so great was the excitement that everyone wanted to see. Brusco's eight helpers soon turned into eighty, and a long line of volunteers passed buckets full of debris from one hand to another. The wall came down very fast and the majestic wardrobe began to stand out in all its mystery. Darkness fell, but no one thought of going away, and soon after the last bucketful of clay and stones was carried away. Don Camillo took up his stand right in front of the wardrobe and said to the crowd in the sacristy:

"Thanks for your help, and good night to you!"

"Open it up! Open it up! We want to see!" they shouted at him.

"It's not your personal property," said an angry woman. "A hidden treasure belongs to all of us together."

"You're not out in the public square," Don Camillo replied. "You're in the church. And I'm responsible for everything in the church to the ecclesiastical authorities."

The carabinieri and their sergeant lined up beside Don Camillo, but the people were so frenzied that no one could keep them from pushing forward.

"Very well," said Don Camillo; "step back and I'll open it up."

They stepped back, and Don Camillo opened the first door. The compartment was filled with books, every one of which bore a number. And there were more and more books in all the other compartments. Don Camillo pulled out a book at random and leafed through it.

"It *is* a treasure," he explained, "but not of the kind you imagined. These are birth, death and marriage registers of the two hundred and fifty years ending in 1753. I don't know what happened in that year, but apparently the priest was afraid they might be destroyed and walled them up here for safe-keeping."

Things had to be arranged in such a way that everyone could see with their own eyes the truth of what Don Camillo was saying, and only when they had all marched by the wardrobe could Don Camillo call it a day.

"Lord," he said when he was left alone in the church, "forgive me if through my fault Your house was turned into an encampment of sacrilegious gold-diggers. I repeat that the blame is not theirs but mine; I was the first one to be in an indecent hurry. When the shepherd acts like a madman, what can you expect of his flock?"

In the course of the following days Don Camillo was stricken with another madness: his impatience to examine all the registers at once. He looked at them quite at random, one after another, and this turned out to be a good idea, for along with the registers of 1650 he found a notebook in which the priest had written up all the events worthy of remark every day.

He threw himself eagerly upon this diary and discovered all sorts of curious things. But among the notes of May 6, 1650 he found two really remarkable items, the first one of which was concerned with Giosue Scozza, whose marble statue stood in the main square of the neighbouring village of Torricella on a pedestal marked with the following inscription:

Giosue Scozza
Creator of Divine harmonies
Beloved son of Torricella
Who wrote its name and his
own on the rolls of Glory
1650–1746

Torricella had dedicated to this favourite son not only this monument but also its main square, the theatre, the widest street, the primary school, the public orphanage and the local band. His name inevitably came out in every piece of writing or speech-making in these parts and even big-city newspapers and magazines always referred to Giosue Scozza as "the swan of Torricella."

For centuries there had been a feud between the two villages, and the compatriots of Don Camillo and Peppone could not bear to see or hear this name. Now, in the old diary, Don Camillo found a passage which, translated into contemporary language, ran:

"Today Geremia Scozza, blacksmith, moved away to enter the service of Count Sanvito of Torricella. With him went his wife, Geltrude, and his son, Giosue, born in this parish on June 8, 1647."

The records of 1647 confirmed the fact that the great man had indeed been born in this parish, and those of preceding years made it clear that the same was true of his family. In short, Torricella had acquired its "swan" when he was three years old.

This item in the diary was preceded by another equally extraordinary:

"Today, May 6, 1647, Giuseppe Bottazzi, blacksmith, 48 years old, was decapitated in the public square, having on April 8 made an armed attack and inflicted wounds upon Don Patini, rector of Vigolenzo for the purpose of stealing a bag of gold. Giuseppe Bottazzi, a skilled worker but a man of sacrilegious ideas, was not born here but came twenty years ago and married a local girl, Maria Gambazzi, who bore him a son baptized Antonio, now fifteen years old. Giuseppe Bottazzi has turned out to be the chief of a band of brigands who have committed thefts and murders in the land of Count Sanvito. Last December they surprised and murdered the men-at-arms of the Castello della Piana where Count Sanvito himself was in residence and managed to save his life only by fleeing through the secret underground passage.''

Don Camillo took a look at the records of later years and clearly established the fact that the present-day Giuseppe Bottazzi, known as Peppone, mayor and Red leader, was a direct descendant of this blacksmith of the same name.

"When elections come around, I'll cook his goose," muttered Don Camillo. "I'll have this page of the diary photographed and plaster it up at every street corner, and under it the phrase: 'Blood will tell.' History repeats itself !"

This project was one that could not be carried out until the time was ripe, but its appeal was tremendous, for it meant killing two birds with one stone. Don Camillo planned to stake an indisputable claim to "the swan of Torricella" and strike a fatal blow at Peppone.

But the news about Giosue Scozza was so exciting that Don Camillo couldn't help dropping hints about it, and one day Peppone came to the rectory to see him.

"Father," he said, "there's a lot of talk about some of the things you've discovered in the famous books. Since it's no political mattèr, but one concerning the honour of the village, may I ask you to tell me the whole story?"

"What's this?" muttered Don Camillo, throwing out his arms. "It's just a bit of history, that's all."

"What do you mean by history?"

"I mean something in the nature of geography—geography is what makes history, you know."

"I don't get it," said Peppone, scratching his head. "Will you kindly explain?"

"I don't know whether it's really proper."

"I see. You're cooking up some of your usual reactionary propaganda and planning to destroy somebody's reputation."

Don Camillo turned bright red.

"If I go in for propaganda, there's nothing false about it. I have documents to show that 'the swan of Torricella' was born not in Torricella, but right here, three years earlier than it's always been stated."

Peppone leaned forward.

"Either you're telling tall tales or else you're a man completely without honour. Because if you can demonstrate in private that Scozza came from here rather than from Torricella and refuse to do so openly, then you're depriving the village of a God-given right."

Don Camillo pulled out the diary and shoved it in front of Peppone's nose.

"Here's the whole truth for you; and there's other proof, besides."

"Then why don't you release it?"

Don Camillo lit his cigar butt and blew several mouthfuls of smoke up to the ceiling.

"The only way to release the news is to print a photograph of a whole page of the diary, or at least to be ready to show it to anyone who asks to see."

"Well, what's the matter with that?"

"I can't make up my mind to do anything so drastic. The note about Scozza is preceded by another one corroborating the date, which happens to bear *your* family name. So, in the last analysis, it's up to you."

"*My* family?" exclaimed Peppone, dumbfounded.

"Yes, the Giuseppe Bottazzi who fills the entry for May 6, 1647 is the unfortunate ancestor of the tribe of Peppone. I've checked the whole thing, and it's indubitably correct."

Don Camillo pointed out the entry to Peppone and the latter proceeded to read it.

"Well," he said afterwards, "what have I got to do with a Bottazzi of 1647?"

"You know how people are. The original Giuseppe Bottazzi revealed to be a blacksmith, a priest-baiter and gang-leader, just like you! Your enemies would be able to put that to good use in their campaign. Just think it over."

Peppone read the two items several times and then gave the diary back to Don Camillo.

"I don't care what the reactionary swine may say. The important thing is to add Giosue Scozza to our village's glory. I put the village's reputation before my own. So go ahead and make the whole thing public."

Peppone started to go, then wheeled about and went over to the desk where Don Camillo was sitting.

"And do you know what?" he added. "I'm proud to have that Bottazzi for an ancestor. It means that Bottazzis had the right idea even in 1647; they knew that they must get rid of priests and land-owners, even at the cost of their own lives. And it's no use your smiling, Father. Your turn is coming!"

"Remember that my name's Don Camillo, not Don Patini!" said the priest in reply.

"Politics may divide us, but for the good of the village, we are as one," Peppone shot over his shoulder. "We'll talk of that later; meanwhile, let's get after Giosue Scozza!"

Don Camillo threw himself like a lion into the chase for "the swan of Torricella." Without dragging Peppone's ancestor into the picture, he placed devastating articles in the provincial paper. Eventually the big-city papers chimed in. The romantic discovery of the archives sealed into the church wall made a good story, and they spread it so widely that Torricella had to surrender. And when people of Torricella were convinced that Giosue Scozza belonged to their enemies, they turned against him. A "public safety committee" was formed, for the purpose of wiping out all traces of the interloper, beginning with the statue in the public square, which was to be replaced by a fountain. Thus the blot would be washed away.

At this point Peppone appealed to the Reds on the other side. He proposed to give Torricella a marble fountain in exchange for the marble statue of the great man. It was settled that the exchange of gifts should be made into a solemn occasion. A wagon drawn by white oxen would carry the fountain to the boundary-line of the village, and meet there a similar wagon, bearing the statue. The money for the fountain was quickly raised, and a month later the wagons set forth. Giosue Scozza arrived in the village nailed to his pedestal and tied with ropes to the sides of the wagon, but looking very proud indeed. And Peppone, who was waiting to receive him, with the rest of the persons in authority and the local band, pronounced a speech written for the occasion, which began:

"Greetings, illustrious brother, upon your return, after centuries of absence, to your native place. . . ."

It was all very moving. When the wagon from Torricella had taken over the fountain and gone away, Peppone took a hammer and chisel out of his pocket and knocked off the tablet which described Giosue Scozza as the "beloved son of Torricella." The smashed tablet was thrown outside the boundary line, and the little procession wound its way happily into the central square. There everything was ready: masons, marble-workers, a crane and a stone for the base. Soon the statue stood erect on its new foundation and a new tablet was fastened to the pedestal. A canvas had been thrown around it, and this was removed at just the right moment. Don Camillo pronounced a blessing and made a short speech on the theme of the return of the prodigal son. The welcoming committee, which was non-political in nature, had done things proud, and the festivities did not end until evening, when Peppone rose to explain the significance of the occasion.

"We have seen your face, dear long-lost brother," he said, "but we have not heard your voice, that divine voice which you raised to the heights of immortal glory. And so a string orchestra is to play a programme which will acquaint all of us with the greatest melodies of our own celebrated Giosue Scozza."

The square was crowded with people, and after Peppone had finished speaking there was a burst of applause, followed by a religious silence. The string orchestra, which had been brought from the city, was really first-class, and the first of the twelve pieces on the programme, *The Andantino Number Six*, turned out to be a musical jewel. After this came the *Air in C sharp Minor* and the *Sonata in D*, which met with equal success. But when the fourth piece, *Ballet in F*, began, there was a chorus of voices shouting:

"Verdi, Verdi!"

Peppone and Don Camillo were sitting in the front seats, and the conductor looked beseechingly at Peppone. Peppone looked at Don Camillo and Don Camillo nodded. Then Peppone called peremptorily:

"Verdi!"

Everyone was wild with joy. The conductor held a whispered consultation with his musicians, tapped the music stand with his baton, and the crowd was silent. At the first notes of the prelude to *La Traviata*, people had difficulty restraining their applause and after it was finished it was almost overpowering.

"This is real music!" shouted Peppone.

"You can't beat Verdi," answered Don Camillo.

Verdi supplied all the rest of the programme, and at the end the orchestra conductor was carried off in triumph. As Smilzo passed in front of the statue of Giosue Scozza, "creator of divine harmonies," he observed:

"The climate of Torricella didn't do him any good."

"Exactly," said Bigio. "If he'd stayed here, he'd have written much better music."

"Historical things are beautiful even when they're ugly," put in Peppone severely. "Giosue Scozza belongs to history, and he'll go down as a very great man, don't you agree, Don Camillo?"

"Of course," Don Camillo answered. "You must always look at an artist against the background of his times."

"But Verdi . . ." objected Smilzo.

"What's Verdi got to do with it?" Peppone interrupted. "Verdi's no artist; he's just a man with a heart as big as this——"

And he threw out his arms so eloquently that they cut a wide swathe all around him. Don Camillo wasn't agile enough to get out of the way, and received a blow in the stomach. But out of respect for Verdi he said nothing.

REVENGE IS SWEET

THE PEOPLE OF TORRICELLA were furious over having lost their musical supremacy and were dead set on winning a championship in some other field. So one fine morning our villagers found posters stuck up all over the place, which read as follows:

> If you have eleven young men
> who know the difference
> between a soccer ball
> and a tin of tomato sauce,
> Send them to the sports field at
> Torricella
> to see what's going on.

As soon as Peppone had read this challenge he turned to his lieutenant, Smilzo, and said:

"Tell the Dynamo team to start training immediately and then go to Torricella to decide on a day for the match."

Smilzo got on his bicycle, rode off at full speed and came back an hour later. Peppone was waiting impatiently in his office, and before him were proofs of the poster to be plastered, by way of a reply, on the walls of Torricella.

"Well, is it all set?" he shot at Smilzo.

"Set, my eye!" Smilzo growled. "We missed the boat."

"What do you mean?"

"I mean that the priest's team got there ahead of us."

Without hesitation Peppone pulled his cap down over his eyes and marched on the rectory. He found Don Camillo in the square in front of the church and plunged right into the subject which was on his mind.

"If there's any team that has a right to defend the village honour, it's the Dynamos," he stated emphatically.

"Ditto for the Diehards," answered Don Camillo.

"The Diehards aren't a team, they're a deformation."

"The Dynamos aren't a team, they're a collection of chickens."

On these premises, there seemed to be no likely agreement, and the argument continued in such an excited key that it attracted nearly a hundred listeners. Finally, after Peppone and Don Camillo had reached so high a pitch that it seemed as if they could never climb down from it, the voice of reason intervened. The voice was that of the local chemist.

"There can be no real discussion here," he said. "The teams are neck and neck, and we must choose between two solutions. Either we toss a coin to see which one is to represent the village, or else we take the best men of both and weld them together."

"The Diehards have eleven best men," maintained Don Camillo.

"And the Dynamos twelve," retorted Peppone, "because I'm including the masseur, who may be lame but rates as high as any Diehard you care to mention."

But the idea of welding the best men of both teams into one was obviously sensible and eventually both Peppone and Don Camillo had to admit it.

"We'll talk about it another day," said Don Camillo, retiring to the rectory.

"Yes, another day," echoed Peppone, withdrawing to the People's Palace.

The next day the two men met on neutral ground, each of them accompanied by a group of backers.

"I don't want to be mixed up in this business," said Don Camillo. "My job is to be a priest, and so I've turned it over to this committee of experts."

"My job is to be mayor," echoed Peppone, "and so I've put it up to a committee too."

"Then let the two committees get together," concluded Don Camillo.

"Exactly," said Peppone, "I shall stay on merely as an observer, and whatever the committees decide suits me. It should be easy enough to reach a decision, because after having made a dispassionate analysis of the Diehards, it's obvious that we should take their centre man and leave the rest of the places to the Dynamos."

"That's just what we thought after we had taken the Dynamos under careful consideration. Give us Smilzo, and we'll supply the other ten."

Peppone gritted his teeth.

"I don't want to influence the committees' decision, but one thing is sure: if you like it, then it's just as I say, and if you don't, then it's just as I say too. And you can thank God for the honour of having one of your men play with a team like ours."

"Smilzo will be a decided handicap to the Diehards," said Don Camillo, "but we want to show that on our side there's a real spirit of conciliation."

"Then you and your dummies can go to hell," Peppone shouted.

"If the committee have no more to say," said Don Camillo, "we may as well adjourn."

The head of the committee chosen by Don Camillo threw out his arms in despair. And so did the head of Peppone's committee. Then both parties went home.

Three days later a new challenge arrived from Torricella.

NOTICE
In order to give a chance to the two teams
which we have challenged
Instead of beating them one after the other,
Our Torricella team has decided to take
them both on together.
Hence the Torricella Eleven will play the
Diehard-Dynamo twenty-two.

The necessity of forming a single team was now more urgent than ever, and the chemist, together with the doctor, managed to form a committee to effect a liaison between the two already existing committees. This was a very complicated affair, but finally the two committees met for the purpose of making a final decision.

"I bow to the will of the joint committee," said Don Camillo, who was the first to take the floor. "But since it's inevitable that the committee make up a half-and-half team, I say that the Diehards will furnish six players and the Dynamos five."

"I agree," said Peppone, "Diehards five and Dynamos six."

For a moment Don Camillo respected the silence which followed upon this declaration. Then he said:

"Since this point is bound to hold up the committee's deliberations, why don't we settle it by drawing cards?"

A pack of cards was produced, and Don Camillo and Peppone drew a card each. Peppone won by a single point, and it was decided that the Dynamos should contribute six men to the team and the Diehards five.

"In that case," said Don Camillo, "it's only fair that a Diehard be the captain."

"Democracy has very definite regulations," retorted Peppone. "You may not know it, Father, but there you are. In a democratic system the majority rules. So we shall choose our own captain."

Don Camillo shook his head.

"That's Communism for you!" he exclaimed. "Once they've seized power, they install a dictatorship under a democratic label."

"Sport has nothing to do with politics," Peppone protested. "But in order to give the lie to your reactionary slander, let's settle it with another draw."

This time Don Camillo won, and the Diehards chose a captain for the team. The next day the mixed team met for a first practice. The game lasted exactly eight minutes, after which the two factions had a free-for-all-fight. The next day brought considerable improvement, because the Dynamos and Diehards began roughhousing in the dressing-room long before the game. On the third day the players didn't fight either in the dressing-room or on the field. They fought outside the field, before they ever got there. On the fourth day, after they had exhausted all other possible dodges, they actually played a game, but with the saddest results imaginable. And the following day things went even worse. They couldn't muster any teamwork whatsoever, but seemed to be eleven savages who were making their first acquaintance with a ball and kicking it around at random.

Meanwhile, time was going by. The day of the match was drawing near, and still no progress had been made. Finally the last day came. After the final, eminently unsuccessful practice game, Don Camillo and Peppone found themselves going back to the village together.

"So," said Peppone, "we're going to reap the result of your stubbornness tomorrow. If you'd given in to me and let the Dynamos defend the honour of the village, we shouldn't be having any of this trouble."

"Peppone," said Don Camillo, "I know my boys, and I say that all our trouble is your fault. You used your usual obstructionist tactics to make us hand you over the controls. I said 'make us' because anyone with fine feelings and conscience will always yield a point, and that is exactly what we are going to do. Your bullying has met with success. The Diehards are withdrawing and your Dynamos will play. Don't pretend to make a fuss, because I know that the Dynamos have been holding a practice of their own every day, on the sly, and your pretence of training with us hasn't hurt your form."

Peppone did not bother to make a denial. He slipped away, and two hours later the village was plastered with big red posters.

> The Diehards have withdrawn their men
> because of admitted technical failings
> and so tomorrow's match will be
> played by an all-Dynamo team,
> sole defender of the village's honour.

Before going to bed Don Camillo went to kneel before the Crucified Christ.

"Lord," he prayed, "don't let them lose the match tomorrow. Not for their sake, because they don't deserve to win, but for mine. Don't let them lose, that is, unless you want to lead me into the temptation of rejoicing over their defeat."

"Don Camillo," Christ answered, "you know that I have no dealings with sport!"

Peppone's men made a miserable showing and Torricella scored a large number of goals against them. Don Camillo was unable to resist temptation and inwardly rejoiced over their discomfiture. He rejoiced outwardly as well, and with the devil hot upon his trail challenged the Torricella team to a match with the Diehards the following Sunday. The Diehards won. This victory seemed to call for a celebration and he called the Diehards together.

"Boys," he said, "I have three magnificent capons in my chicken coop. On Sunday evening we'll eat them and drink to the health of the Dynamos. This isn't top secret, so if you happen to say something about it, no harm is done."

Obviously several people did, quite accidentally, spread the good word, because almost immediately the whole village knew that on Sunday evening the rectory would be the scene of what was dubbed "the revenge supper."

In order to make the occasion more festive, the Diehards needed a song, and Don Camillo sat up most of one night in order to write the words and most of the next in order to set them to music on the church organ. On Thursday night, he emerged from the sacristy with words and music complete and plenty of time to teach his boys the song so that they could come out with it at the supper. The tune was simple, and if necessary they could always read the words. He was quite pleased with himself as he returned to the rectory for the night, and before going to bed, he decided to take a look at the three capons in his chicken coop. Alas, the capons were gone, and so were three hens. All that was left were one bedraggled chick and a scrawny rooster. To take the place of the missing capons, a sign was hung on the wall which said in dog-Latin: *Crescete et moltiplicorum.*

Increase and multiply, indeed! Don Camillo was breathless with indignation, and seizing the sign, he went to tell his troubles to the Christ over the main altar.

"Lord," he panted, "they've stolen my chickens!"

"I'm sorry to hear it," Christ answered with a smile. "But before making any such categorical statement you'd better make sure they didn't just run away."

Don Camillo held up the sign.

"I know what I'm talking about, Lord," he said. "Look what the thieves left behind! Isn't it disgusting?"

"You don't expect a petty thief to write good Latin, do you, Don Camillo?"

"I'm not talking about the Latin. I'm concerned with the impudence of his adding insult to injury. Lord, who in the world could it be?"

These words reminded Don Camillo of the real delinquent, his dog Thunder. Why hadn't Thunder barked and given the alarm? He went to look for the dog and found him lying peacefully in his kennel.

"You traitor!" the priest shouted. "You're in enemy pay!"

What angered him even more than the loss of the chickens were the disturbances of the festive supper. He was pacing up and down the church square, when a voice roused him from his ire.

"Have you insomnia, Father? What keeps you up so late?"

The speaker was the carabinieri sergeant, who was coming back from his evening rounds, together with one of his men.

"I've been robbed of my chickens!" Don Camillo exclaimed. "At ten o'clock, when I went into the sacristy, they were there, and when I came out at eleven, they had disappeared. I was playing the organ, and someone crept up, under cover of the music . . ."

"Didn't your dog bark?"

"That's just what I mean. Perhaps he did bark, but I couldn't hear him."

"And do you suspect anyone in particular?"

Don Camillo threw out his arms.

Don Camillo shut himself up in the rectory and refused to see a soul. The whole village knew what had happened, and the Reds were rubbing their hands and laughing.

"It seems that the Sunday-night supper will be a paltry affair. Well, if they haven't the capons they can feed on their new song!"

The supper was cancelled, and that evening Don Camillo was in the depths of despair. At eight o'clock he whistled for Thunder to come and get a bowl of soup, but Thunder failed to respond. Don Camillo resolved to find him, and went out on the road leading away from the village. Ten minutes later he walked through Peppone's vegetable garden and into the dark hall of his house. From the kitchen there came echoes of loud laughter, and Don Camillo turned the doorknob and went in. Peppone was sitting at the table, together with Smilzo, Brusco, Bigio and the rest of the gang, over a dish of roast chicken, and at the sight of Don Camillo they were positively petrified in their chairs.

"Excuse me, Peppone," said Don Camillo, "but I'm looking for my dog. Do you happen to have seen him?"

Peppone shook his head, but Don Camillo had keen eyes and knew better. He lifted up the edge of the table-cloth and saw Thunder crouching under the table with a heaping dish of chicken bones before him.

"He just dropped in," Peppone exclaimed lamely.

"I see," said Don Camillo.

Thunder flattened himself out on the floor in shame.

"If you'd care to join us, Father, please sit down," said Peppone.

"I've had my supper, thank you. Good evening."

Don Camillo walked out, and Thunder, after a questioning look at Peppone, followed the priest at a distance, dragging his tail. When they reached the rectory, the priest turned on him and said indignantly:

"You thief !"

And since this word seemed to make very little impression the priest added with utter scorn:

"You've sold out to the Russians!"

The next day the carabinieri sergeant received several anonymous letters, and the affair assumed a sudden importance. Six chickens don't amount to much, but when there is reason to think that the theft has been committed by the mayor, then there is a political angle to it. Peppone received an unexpected visit from the law.

"Sorry, Mr. Mayor, but I must do my duty. Can you tell me where you were between ten and eleven o'clock of last Thursday evening? You weren't at home, we know that. At five minutes past ten you were seen climbing over the fence around the rectory garden. There are three witnesses to that. And others saw you climb over your own fence three quarters of an hour later."

Peppone was as confused as a child.

"That's my business," he finally sputtered.

"And where did you get the five chickens you ate at your house Sunday night?"

"That's my business, too."

The sergeant received equally unsatisfactory replies to his other questions, and finally went away saying:

"You'll have to tell the court."

Now the affair took on really colossal proportions. Mayor Giuseppe Bottazzi was accused of being a vulgar chicken thief and summoned to appear before the magistrates' court in the nearest city. How had the mighty fallen, when the tamer of lions was laid low by a church mouse.

Don Camillo found himself in court, without knowing exactly why. But there he was, and there in the dock was Peppone. It looked very much like the end of his career.

"The accused has steadily refused to say where he spent the hour between ten and eleven o'clock, that is between the time when he was seen climbing the rectory fence and the time when he was seen sneaking back over his own. Has he, even at this late date, anything to say?"

The magistrate looked at Peppone and everyone in the courtroom turned their eyes in his direction. But Peppone helplessly threw out his arms.

"I can't say where I was," he answered in a low voice.

"Do you refuse, absolutely?"

"It isn't that I refuse, Judge. I simply can't do it."

At this point Don Camillo asked if he might be allowed to say a word.

"From ten o'clock, Mayor Bottazzi was with me in the sacristy," he stated.

"Why didn't you say so before?"

"Nobody asked me. And besides, before testifying, I had to secure my superiors' permission."

The magistrate shot him a questioning look.

"Excuse me, Father, but what brought him to the church at that hour, when you were playing the organ? Was it for a singing lesson?"

"The sound of the organ doesn't prevent one of the faithful from saying his prayers."

"I don't deny that, Father, but I don't see why the accused didn't give the law this explanation. No one need hesitate to use church-going as an alibi. If I'd spent my time in church I'd be glad to say so."

"But you're not a Communist Party leader and a mayor of a village in a region where the Party is so strong," Don Camillo replied. "He comes to church at an hour when his Party comrades can't see him. If your Honour requires any further explanation . . ."

"No, nothing more," the magistrate interrupted, smiling broadly.

"Then just let me say this: Giuseppe Bottazzi is a good-hearted, hard-working, God-fearing fellow," concluded Don Camillo.

Don Camillo made the trip home on Peppone's motorcycle, but Peppone did not open his mouth the whole way. When they came to the rectory he gave a deep sigh.

"You made a laughing stock of me," he said plaintively. "The reactionary press will have a field-day with this story."

"They'd have treated you a good deal more roughly if you'd been convicted of being a chicken thief," said Don Camillo.

"But you've got me in hot water with the Party. If I tell the truth they'll bawl me out for being so stupid as to steal chickens. And if I stick to your version of events, then they'll brand me as even more of a fool."

"Never mind about the Party," grumbled Don Camillo. "I'm in hot water with Almighty God. Here I am, a priest, and I've given false testimony before a court of law! How shall I ever get up my nerve to go into church?"

Peppone jumped off his motorcycle and marched into the church and straight up to the main altar. He remained standing there for several minutes and then went back outside.

"You can go in now," he said. "I've fixed things up for you. I'd like to see you straighten things out for me with the Party in the same way!"

Don Camillo threw out his arms.

"Of course it's easier to deal with God than one of your Party bosses. They never forgive anything."

Exactly in what terms Peppone had "fixed things" up no one ever knew. But when, late that night, Don Camillo summoned up the nerve to go into church and kneel in front of the main altar, the Crucified Christ said:

"What in the world have you been up to now, Don Camillo?"

"I had the bishop's permission," said Don Camillo in justification of his perjury.

"He's quite a fellow, too!" Christ sighed, half smiling.

THE MAN WITHOUT A HEAD

DON CAMILLO LEAPED to his feet and very nearly shouted, because the discovery was so sensational. Just then the sound of the clock in the church tower ringing three o'clock in the morning brought him around to the thought that the only sensible thing to do at that hour was to go to sleep. But before dozing off he read over the extraordinary bit of news he had just found in his predecessor's diary. "On November 8, 1752," the passage began, "something quite terrible happened . . ."

The eighteenth-century parish priest had explained the mystery of the black stone and at the same time provided Don Camillo with an excellent subject for his Sunday sermon. Now he closed the book and hurried to bed, because three hours of Sunday morning had already gone by.

"Brethren," Don Camillo began his sermon, "today I want to talk to you about the black stone, the one you have all seen in one corner of the cemetery with the mysterious inscription: *November 8, 1752. Here lies a man without face or name.* For years this stone has been the subject of research and discussion. Now at last the mystery has been made clear."

A murmur of amazement greeted these words. And Don Camillo continued:

"Every evening for the last few months I've been looking over the old books and registers which turned up in a forgotten wardrobe some time ago, and as you know I've found all sorts of interesting information. But just last night I came across the most extraordinary item of all, which I shall now translate into contemporary language for your benefit.

" 'On November 8, 1752, something quite terrible happened. For a whole year some marauders, known as the "hole-in-the-wall gang" because of the method they used to break into respectable houses, had been wreaking havoc all over the countryside. None of them had ever been caught red-handed. But on the night of November 8, Giuseppe Folini, from Crocilone, a merchant by profession, was awakened by a suspicious noise and after he had got out of bed to go down to his cellar storeroom, he realized that the noise came from that part of the wall which bordered on the open fields and had no door or window of any kind. Obviously someone was boring his way into the cellar and such an enterprise could only be conducted by the "hole-in-the-wall" gang.

" 'A few minutes later, while Folini was still standing there, indecisively, a piece of plaster fell from a spot about six inches above the floor and the moonlight streaming in from a window across the way allowed him to see a brick moving. Soon the brick was lifted out and a gaunt white hand came through the hole and removed another brick beside it. Now that the hole was sufficiently widened, an arm came through, all the way up to the elbow, and began feeling the surface of the surrounding wall in order to ascertain whether anything hung there which might fall and spread the alarm.

" 'Folini, who is a big, strapping fellow, took hold of the wrist, determined not to let it go, and at the same time he shouted for help. Various members of the family arrived upon the scene and one of his sons tied a rope around the intruder's arm, thus making him a prisoner.

" 'Because Folini's house is in a lonely and isolated spot, they could not hope to arouse the village by giving the alarm. And for fear of falling into a trap set by the prisoner's accomplices, they did not dare set foot outside until morning. They had captured one member of the gang and when he was turned over to the police he would probably supply the names of the others.

" 'They ventured out at dawn and made their way cautiously toward the back of the house. But all they found was a headless body. The bandits had feared that the captured man might be compelled by torture to reveal their names, or that the knowledge of his name might lead to the discovery of the rest. And so, in order to cheat the law of any clue whatsoever they had chopped off his head and carried it away.

" 'Since nothing on the body permitted identification, I buried it by night in one corner of the cemetery and raised a stone over the grave with the inscription: *November 8, 1752. Here lies a man without face or name.' "

Don Camillo closed the old diary, looked down for a moment at the confusion written upon his hearers' faces and concluded:

"And so, brethren, this terrible tale has cleared up a mystery. Under the black stone there sleeps a man without face or name. A terrible tale, indeed. But there is something far more terrible rampant among us at this very hour: the presence of a hundred headless men in this village of ours who are working night and day to bore a hole through the unguarded wall of our houses, steal the householders' brains away and leave in their place the propagandistic stuffing of an extreme left-wing party, which for obvious reasons I shall not call by name. . . ."

The story of the headless man made a great impression upon the village, and everyone felt an urge to go and look at the black stone. The old Folini house at Crocilone was still standing, but it served only as a barn and the foot of the wall on the side of the open fields was overgrown with weeds. Now these weeds were cut down and the hole mentioned in the story was exposed to view. All those who passed this way after dark pedalled their bicycles extra fast or accelerated their motorcycles because of the shiver that ran up and down their spines.

Then came the November mists, and the river took on a dark and mysterious air. One evening, as she walked along the embankment road, on her way back from Castellina, old Signora Gabini met a man without a head. She ran all the rest of the way home and arrived in such a state of collapse that she had to be put to bed. She asked for the priest, and the fellow who went to the village after Don Camillo stopped for a drink in the arcade café and told the whole story. It spread like wildfire through the village, and when Don Camillo returned from his visit to Signora Gabini he found a small crowd of people waiting in the church square to hear what sort of devilry was in the air.

"Sheer nonsense!" said Don Camillo. "If the old woman weren't in such a bad way, it would be laughable."

As a matter of fact, she had told a tale that made very little sense.

"Father! I saw him!"

"Saw whom?"

"The headless man, the one buried under the black stone. I came face to face with him, all of a sudden."

"Face to face? But if he didn't have any head? . . ."

"He didn't have any head, that's just it. He was riding slowly along on a bicycle . . ."

Here Don Camillo couldn't help smiling.

"That's a good one! How could he ride a bicycle if he died in 1752, before bicycles were invented?"

"I don't know," she stuttered. "He must have learned how in the meantime. But I know it was him for sure, the man without a head."

Don Camillo's retelling of this account proved to be highly amusing and the notion of the headless man's having learned to ride a bicycle after his death was repeated from one house to another. For a couple of weeks, nothing out of the way happened, and then suddenly the man without a head reappeared. Giacomone, the boatman, met him shortly after dusk, on the path leading through the acacia grove. This time he was not on a bicycle, but on foot, a means of locomotion much more suitable to an eighteenth-century ghost. Giacomone himself told the story to Don Camillo.

"You've been drinking too much, Giacomone," was the priest's comment.

"I've sworn off for the last three years," Giacomone replied. "And I'm not the sort to be easily scared. I'm just telling you what I saw with my own eyes: a man minus a head."

"Don't you think he might have been a man with his jacket pulled up over his head in order to protect himself from the rain?"

"I saw the stump of his neck, I tell you."

"You didn't really see any such thing; you just fancy you did. Go back tomorrow to the exact place where you thought you saw him and you'll find the branch or bush that gave you the illusion."

The next day Giacomone did go back, and some twenty other villagers with him. They located the exact spot of the encounter, but they saw no feature of the landscape which might have seemed to be a man without a head. But the headless man appeared a week later to a young man, and at this point people stopped wondering whether or not the apparitions were genuine. They asked, rather: "Why is the headless man among us? What is he after?" And they did not have to look far for an answer. The headless man was looking for his head. He wanted it to lie with the rest of his body, in consecrated ground. Only Don Camillo refused to offer any guess as to the motive which caused the headless man to wander about the river roads and embankment. "I don't want to hear such foolishness," he said to anyone who questioned him. But one day he was deeply disturbed and confided his trouble to the Christ above the altar.

"Lord, since I've had this parish, I've never seen so many people come to church. Except for Peppone and his henchmen, the whole village has turned up, old and young, infirm and healthy."

"Well, aren't you glad, Don Camillo?"

"No, because they're driven only by fear. And I don't mean the fear of God, either. And it bothers me to see them in distress. I wish the nightmare could have an end."

Christ sighed.

"Don Camillo, aren't you one of these fear-stricken people yourself?"

Don Camillo threw out his arms in protest.

"Don Camillo doesn't know what fear is!" he said proudly.

"That's very important, Don Camillo. Your fearlessness is sufficient to liberate the others from their fear."

Don Camillo felt better, but the apparitions of the headless man continued, and they were further complicated by the intervention of Peppone, who came up to him one day in the square and said in a voice loud enough to be heard on the other side of the river:

"Father, I hear strange talk of a man without a head. Do you know anything about him?"

"Not I," said Don Camillo, feigning astonishment. "What's it all about?"

"It seems that a man without a head has been seen at night around the village."

"A man without a head? It must be someone looking for the People's Palace in order to sign up with your party."

Peppone did not bat an eyelash.

"Perhaps it's a ghost cooked up in the rectory and sent out to scare people into hiding behind the skirts of the priest."

"No ghosts are cooked up in the rectory, either with or without a head," retorted Don Camillo.

"Oh, do you import them from America?"

"Why should we import them, when your party manufactures the best headless ghosts to be found?"

Peppone gave a mocking laugh.

"It's a known fact that the ghost is of your fabrication."

"It's fabricated by diseased minds. It's true that I told the story of the headless man, but that's history. Anyone can see the document for himself."

Don Camillo led the way to the rectory, with Peppone, Smilzo, Brusco, Bigio and the other Red big shots following after. The book was still on the priest's desk, and now he pointed it out to Peppone.

"Look up November 8, 1752, and read what you can find there."

Peppone leafed through the diary until he came to the passage in question. He read it twice through and then handed the book to the others.

"If you have any doubts as to the authenticity of the document, you're free to submit it to any expert you please for study. My only fault is not to have foreseen that a two-hundred year old story would work so dangerously upon people's imaginations."

Bigio nodded.

"So there's some truth to the story of the headless man, after all," he mumbled.

"The truth is just what's set down in that diary," said Don Camillo. "All the rest is reckless imagination."

Peppone and his henchmen went thoughtfully away. That same evening two more villagers ran into the headless man, and the next day a delegation of mothers came to Don Camillo.

"Father, you must do something," they told him. "You must bless the grave marked by the black stone or say a Mass for the repose of the occupant's tormented soul."

"There's no tormented soul," said Don Camillo firmly. "There are only your benighted imaginings, and I don't want to bolster them by appearing to take them seriously."

"We'll go to the bishop!" the women shouted.

"Go where you please. But no one can compel me to believe in ghosts!"

The nightmare became more and more of a menace. Dozens of people had seen the headless man and even the most hard-headed of the villagers were tainted with the contagion of fear. Don Camillo finally resolved to do something about it. Late one night, after everyone had gone to bed he knocked at Peppone's door.

"I've been called to the bedside of a dying man. It's too far for me to go by bicycle. Will you take me in your car?"

It was pouring rain, and this request seemed logical enough. Peppone took out the car which served by day as a public bus.

"Just drive me by the rectory first," said Don Camillo.

Once they were there he got out and insisted that Peppone come inside.

"I've got to talk with you," he explained once they were in his study.

"And was it necessary to put up such a show?"

"Yes, and this isn't the end of it, either. The whole village is going mad and those of us with our wits still about us must do something to dissipate this terror. What I am about to propose isn't honest, but I assume full responsibility for it before God and man. We must pretend to have found a skull. We'll decide together on the most appropriate place, and I'll bury it there, together with half of an eighteenth-century coin. The other half, of course, will go under the black stone. Then you, as mayor, will order some digging in the place where we have left the skull. Is that clear?"

"It seems rather gruesome to me," Peppone stammered, with perspiration breaking out on his forehead.

"It's more terrible to see the growth of a collective frenzy among our people. We must drive out one fear with another. Now, let's get down to details."

It was two o'clock in the morning when Peppone went out to his car. Almost immediately he began cursing.

"What's the matter?" called Don Camillo from the door.

"The battery must be run down; it won't start."

"Leave it here and come back tomorrow morning," said Don Camillo. "I'll walk home with you. Getting wet doesn't bother me."

They had walked some distance along the road skirting the village when all of a sudden Peppone halted and gripped Don Camillo's arm. There walking ahead of them was the headless man. A flash of lightning allowed them to make him out quite clearly. He walked slowly on, and Peppone and Don Camillo followed. At a certain point he took a narrow road leading toward the river, and stopped under an old oak tree. Don Camillo and Peppone stopped too, and once more they saw his figure in a flash of lightning. A third flash followed, and almost simultaneously a blast of thunder. The lightning had struck the hollow oak and levelled it to the ground. And the headless man had disappeared.

Don Camillo found himself curled up in bed without the slightest idea of how he had got there. They awakened him early the next morning and dragged him outside. Half the village was gathered around the fallen oak and amid the uptorn roots there shone a white skull. No one had any doubt whatsoever. The skull belonged to the man without a head, and the way it had appeared proved it. That same morning they buried it under the black stone, and everyone knew for certain that the nightmare was over. Don Camillo went home in a daze and stopped to kneel before the altar.

"Lord", he stammered, "thank you for having punished my presumption. Now I know what it is to be afraid."

"Have you taken up a belief in headless ghosts, Don Camillo?"

"No", the priest replied. "But for a brief moment last night, my mind was invaded by the collective fear."

"That's practically a scientific explanation," Christ murmured.

"It's just a way of covering up my shame," Don Camillo said humbly.

Anyhow, the headless man acquired a head. Was it rightly his, or no? The main thing is that it pacified him and he no longer inflamed the popular imagination. And the great rolling river quietly carried one more story, like a dead leaf, down to the sea.

THE STRANGER

THE DILAPIDATED LITTLE CAR drove slowly around the village square, skirting the arcades, and came to a stop in front of the draper's. A thin, almost distinguished looking man about forty-five years old, got out. His left arm seemed to be glued to his side, all the way down to the elbow, and this detail contributed to the definite picture his appearance left in the mind of an onlooker. He took a big leather case out of the car and strode decisively into the draper's shop. The draper didn't need to look at the calling-card held out by the visitor to know what he was after.

"I'm overstocked," he explained. "Business has been slow for some time, and the floods gave it a knockout blow."

The stranger opened his case and showed his samples. The material was very fine, and the draper couldn't help eyeing it with interest.

"I can't buy a thing just now," he said finally. "Try coming back in the spring. I can't make any promises, but I hope we can do some business together."

The salesman thanked him politely, asked if he might jot down the name and address, put his samples back in the case and returned to the car, which sputtered some twenty yards down the street and then stopped, obviously because there was something drastically wrong with the engine. Luckily for the stranger, Peppone's workshop was only fifty yards farther on, and he was able to cover this distance fairly fast in spite of the fact that he had to get out and push the car. When Peppone heard the blast of a horn, he came promptly to the door.

"Hello there," said the stranger. "I'm having a little trouble. Can you see what it's all about?"

Peppone had shuddered when he heard the stranger's voice, and now he said rudely:

"Not now. I'm too busy."

"Well, I can't get it started, so I'll just leave it here. Have a look at it as soon as you can, will you?" And he walked away, while Peppone stared after him from the door.

"As soon as I can, eh? No, as soon as I feel like it!"

He went back to his lathe in the workshop, but try as he would to put the matter behind him, he couldn't get the stranger off his mind. No matter how often he told himself that the similarity was a matter of pure coincidence, the more he was persuaded that it wasn't coincidence at all. Finally he interrupted his work, threw open the wide glass-paned door of the workshop and pushed in the car. Shutting the door behind him, he searched the car's dashboard compartment for its registration papers. He took a quick look at them and quickly put them back where he had found them. No, it wasn't a coincidence at all. He had a wild impulse to kick the car to pieces, but on second thought he decided to repair it. The roar that burst from the engine when he pulled out the self-starter caused him to chortle with joy.

"I'd like to see his face when he finds out what a mess it's in!" he said to himself. He lifted off the bonnet and started to work. When he had taken out the cylinder block, he called his boy and sent him to find Smilzo. A few minutes later he was giving Smilzo some very definite instructions.

"I'm your man, Chief," said Smilzo. "I'll stand out there under the arcade and as soon as I see the fellow coming, I'll run to call the police. Then, when a policeman arrives, I'll follow."

Ten minutes later the stranger returned and immediately scrutinized the engine of the car.

"I thought so," he said after a while.

"It's a serious business," Peppone explained, enumerating all the minor bits of business connected with it. But he was interrupted by the arrival of the village policeman, in full uniform.

"Good morning, Mr. Mayor," said the policeman, lifting his fingers to his cap in a salute. "There's a paper here which you must sign."

Peppone looked at him with annoyance.

"Tell the clerk that this isn't my time for signing papers. I'll sign it when I come to the Town Hall this afternoon."

The policeman saluted again and about-turned. Peppone continued to list the deficiencies he had found in the engine until for the second time he was interrupted. Smilzo drew himself to attention before him, raising his left arm and a clenched fist.

"Chief," he said, "the proofs of our poster are here. We've got to decide whether the speech will be at nine o'clock or ten."

"Ten," Peppone answered decisively.

"Very good, Chief," said Smilzo, raising his fist again and swinging about on his heels.

This time Peppone managed to finish his description of the engine's woes. And at the end the stranger said:

"Now tell me whether you can make the repairs, and if so how long you will take and what you will charge me."

Peppone shrugged his shoulders.

"If we telephone to the bus station in the city, we may be able to get the necessary parts out by the evening bus. The work will take two and a half days and the cost will be, in round figures, between twenty and twenty-five thousand liras."

The stranger did not blench.

"I'll put in a telephone call to Milan and an hour from now I can give you an answer."

Peppone went back to his lathe.

"Nuts to you!" he whispered to himself as the door closed behind the stranger.

Early in 1943, when Peppone had received his call-up papers, he went to the nearest recruiting station to say:

"I'm forty-four years old and I went all through the last war. Why do you have to pick on me?"

"If you hadn't been called up and were left at home, what would you do?"

"I'd keep up my usual trade, which is that of a mechanic."

"Then just pretend you're still at home. It's because you're a mechanic that the army needs you."

Peppone was sent to some old barracks, which had been turned into a repair depot for army vehicles, and there, in the uniform of a corporal, he went on with his old trade. For a month this job was quite a soft one, because in spite of the grey-green uniform and insignia, Peppone and his fellows enjoyed considerable liberty. Until one day a cursed captain came into the picture, and then their troubles began.

The cursed captain had been on active service all over the map. On his chest he wore a complete assortment of decorations and in his buttonhole a German ribbon. During the retreat from Russia a shell fragment had put his left arm out of commission, and because he didn't want to be invalided home, they had sent him to create some order in the depot where Corporal Giuseppe Bottazzi was working. At first the boys thought that within a week they could make mincemeat of the captain with the withered arm. But instead, after a week had gone by, they found that their soft job had turned into a very tough one, for the captain was a martinet who had army regulations on the brain.

Corporal Peppone, the top mechanic, simply couldn't believe it when he was confined to the guardhouse for ten consecutive days. One morning, in the courtyard, when the captain with the withered arm passed by, he presented arms with a shaft of cement which the strength of three ordinary men would not have sufficed to lift off the ground. But the captain was not impressed. He looked at Peppone and said coldly:

"An ordinary crane, without even the rank of corporal, can lift heavier weights than that with less waste of energy. Perhaps that's because the crane is more intelligent than you are. Ten more days of confinement will give you time to think it over."

Two days later Peppone's wife and child came to the nearby town for a visit, but Peppone wasn't allowed to see them. When the captain looked in at his cell he found him a raging tiger.

"Take it easy, Corporal," he said, "or you may get into really hot water."

"I want to see my wife and son!" howled Peppone.

"Thousands of better men than you would like to see their mothers and wives and children, but they've given their lives for their country. You're a very poor soldier and you're only getting what you deserve."

Peppone could have knocked the captain down with a single blow, but all he did was grit his teeth and protest:

"I went all through the last war and brought home a silver medal!"

"The fact that you were of age when the last war came around isn't any particular virtue. And it isn't enough to win a medal; you've got to live up to it."

Every last man at the depot had it in for the captain with the withered arm. He stood over them from reveille to taps, and because he knew a thing or two about motors, he wouldn't let them get away with any work that wasn't absolutely first class.

One the evening of July 26, 1943, Mussolini suffered his well-known eclipse from the political scene. The next morning the captain was in the sleeping quarters when the men got up. Before they could go to breakfast he addressed them as follows:

"There's to be no change here. The same repair jobs are waiting for us, and it's still our duty to carry them out as best we can."

During the heavy air-raids of that August, the captain arrived at the men's quarters along with the first signal of alarm and stayed until the all-clear had sounded. On September 8, the Germans' liberation of Mussolini complicated the political situation further. There were panic and disorganization everywhere. The captain gave each of his men a gun and a round of ammunition and said simply:

"You'll sleep fully dressed, in order to be prepared for any emergency."

He slept on a table in the quartermaster's office and the next morning, after inspecting his men, he told them:

"The colonel has assigned us to the defence of the west side of the barracks and the vehicle entrance. Our orders are to let nobody in."

The west side of the barracks, including the repair depot, was located in the former stables, adjacent to the open fields, and when Peppone and the others heard the word "defence," they thought of the single round of ammunition each one of them had upon him, and stared nervously at one another. At ten o'clock the place was surrounded by German tanks and a German officer came to ask the colonel to surrender. Upon the colonel's refusal, the heavy *Panzer* in front of the main gate shattered it with a single shot and rolled in. Meanwhile, the *Panzer* at the vehicle entrance didn't even bother to fire. It just bumped the rusty gate, and with the first bit of pressure put upon the hinges, the whole thing collapsed, as if it had been attached to the walls with thread.

Some of the mechanics were drawn up along the wall, while Peppone and four others were stationed in the sentry-box which guarded the gate. Now, where the gate had been, there stood the cursed captain with the withered arm, his legs spread far apart and a pistol in his hand, pointing at the *Panzer*. It was a ridiculous thing, if you like, but the captain wore a German ribbon in his buttonhole and this brought the German tank to a stop. These professional military types have a special way of looking at things and you can't take it away from them. One of the tank turret popped a German officer, who proceeded to give a salute. The captain put his pistol into its holster and answered in kind. The German jumped down from the *Panzer*, drew himself up with puppet-like stiffness in front of the Italian and saluted him again, receiving the same salute in return.

"I'm sorry to say, I must ask you to surrender," said the German type in hesitant Italian.

The Italian type took the decoration out of his buttonhole and handed it to the German. Then he stepped out of the way. The German made a slight bow, climbed back into the tank, stood up to his waist in the turret and shouted an order, which caused the vehicle to move forward. As he passed before the Italian, the German raised his hand to his cap in a salute, which the Italian duly returned. After that, the Italian calmly lit a cigarette and when two German soldiers approached, he preceded them to the centre of the courtyard, where the colonel, along with the other officers and men who had been made prisoners, had been standing waiting.

The mechanics made for the open fields. Peppone was the last of them to run for freedom, because he wanted to see the business of those two military types through to the end. Two hours later he was in civilian clothes, and the next day, from the attic in which he was hiding, he saw a little group of Italian soldiers marched off under German Tommy-guns to the train that was to take them to a prison camp far away. At the end of the group were the officers, and among them the cursed captain with the withered arm.

"I hope you don't come back until I call for you in person," Peppone mumbled to himself.

But he did not forget the captain. The final insult still rankled in his mind. When the *Panzer* was still outside the gate and the captain was on his way to meet it, he had called out to Peppone, who was trembling in the sentry box with his four companions:

"Now we'll see if Corporal Battazzi is a real weight lifter!"

Peppone had sworn that one day he would make the captain with the withered arm eat these words, and now by some miracle he had the fellow at his mercy. It gave him no little satisfaction to see the cocky "active service" officer reduced to the status of travelling salesman.

The stranger didn't go to make a telephone call. He went to sit down in the church, where he could quietly count his resources. Turning his pockets inside out and squeezing the last penny from them, he figured that he had twenty-two thousand three hundred liras. And he would have to spend two or three days in the village.

"If it comes to the worst, I can always pawn my watch," he concluded, and he went back to Peppone's workshop.

"All right, you can go ahead with the work," he said. "And when you've finished, send word to me at the tavern, where I expect to rent a room. Try to get it done as fast as you can."

Without looking up Peppone muttered:

"*As fast as I can,* eh? We're not in the army now, good-looking! Here I work as I please."

That evening, before he laid off, he cast a scornful glance at the dilapidated car.

"His good times are over, all right!" he sneered.

At the tavern he saw the stranger sitting in a corner over a plate of bread and sausage, with a bottle of water in front of him.

"If all your customers are so lavish, you'll soon be a rich man!" he whispered to the proprietor.

The proprietor grimaced.

"They're just as proud as they're poor," he grumbled.

Peppone went home early. Sleepy as he was, he went into the workshop first. The bus had brought the parts necessary for the repair of the car. Peppone looked at the package and then swung it against his bench.

"*As fast as you can,* eh?" he exclaimed angrily. "Half starving, and he thinks he can still give out orders in the old way! I'll take three or four days, or a whole week, if I want to! And if that doesn't suit you, push your rattle-trap straight to hell. If you start kicking, I'll give you a couple of punches to go with it!" And as he passed in front of the midget car, he spat into the engine. "There's for you and your driver, you little fool!" he exclaimed.

After he had gone to bed he thought with irritation of the stranger, sitting there in the tavern.

"Stony broke, and yet he eats his salami with a fork!" he said disgustedly.

"Who's that?" asked his wife, waking up with a start.

"A pretty rascal, I can tell you! If he has the nerve to open his mouth, I'll murder him!"

"Don't get yourself in trouble, Peppone," murmured his wife, going back to sleep.

His anger at the rascal with the withered arm so upset Peppone's stomach that he got up after half an hour and went down to the kitchen for some bicarbonate of soda. He fancied he heard a noise from the workshop and took a look inside. Everything was in good order, and the dilapidated midget car was waiting peacefully, with its guts exposed to the air.

"*As fast as you can*, eh?" he exclaimed ironically. "Go and give orders in your own house, jackass! The days of the puppets in uniform are over, you beastly reactionary warmonger!"

A moment later he turned back from the door.

"I want to look at those parts that came down by bus," he said to himself. "Here's hoping there are a few mistakes, such as to cause further delay. And you'll have to grin and bear it, that is unless you want to push your car away."

The parts seemed to be quite satisfactory. In order to be quite sure, Peppone took the worn parts out of the engine and compared them. One piece had to be fitted more closely, and he started to adjust it.

At six o'clock in the morning, Peppone was still working frantically, sweating and swearing all the while.

"I want to get this thing out of the way," he shouted between clenched teeth. "Otherwise I'll find myself in trouble."

At noon Peppone got into the car, slammed the door and tested the engine.

"It moves, and that ought to be enough to suit you," he grumbled. "If once you're out on the highway it breaks down, that's just too bad."

The important thing was to be sure it really would reach the highway. With this end in view, it was natural enough for Peppone to regulate the engine again, change the oil, test the clutch, brakes, points, carburettor and tyres, tighten some screws on the chassis, fill the battery with distilled water, grease all the points that needed greasing and finally take a hose and wash the body. There is a limit to everything, and logically enough Peppone did not feel like doing any more. So Peppone's wife was the one to brush the upholstery, and not knowing anything about the rascal of an owner she did the job with impartiality and care.

When everything was done, Peppone sent his boy to tell the proprietor of the tavern to pass on the word that the car was ready. Meanwhile Peppone went upstairs. He wanted to impress the stranger with his physical appearance as well as his accomplishment, and so he washed, shaved and put on a clean shirt.

"Now is the time for the real fun!" he said, inwardly rejoicing. From the living-room he took a big sheet of paper with the heading: *Giuseppe Bottazzi. Repairs. Welding. Brakes. Ignition. Grease and oil.* He had always been proud of this paper, and now if ever was the time to use it. "*Bill no . . .*" And he proceeded to add the date and the debtor. He knew the stranger's first and last name perfectly well, but it seemed to him more impressive to leave them out. Let him appear to be someone totally unknown. Then he began to itemize the charges.

New Parts (detailed)	11,000	liras
3 quarts of oil	1,200	
Greasing and washing	800	
Telephone call and bus delivery	500	
Total expenses	13,500	
Labour	7,000	
Overtime	4,500	
Grand total	25,000	

Twenty-five thousand liras, and he could cough up every last one of them, if he wanted his car back. "*As fast as you can*, eh?" But it costs more to get something in a hurry. It used to be different, but that was in the army!

Peppone came downstairs upon the stranger's arrival.

"Your car's ready," he said coldly.

"All fixed?"

"All fixed."

"And how much do I owe you?"

Peppone was inwardly jeering. This was the big moment. He took the bill out of his pocket, looked at it and then put it back.

"Everything included, parts and labour, 13,100 liras."

The stranger took three five-thousand lira notes from his wallet.

"Keep the difference," he said, getting into the car.

At the door he leaned out to ask:

"Do I make a left turn for the highway?"

"Yessir!" said Peppone, clicking his heels.

"Good-bye, Sergeant Bottazzi," said the stranger.

A quarter of a mile along the road, the stranger wondered why the devil he had dubbed the fellow a sergeant when he knew perfectly well that he was only the most pestiferous of corporals? Then he listened to the hum of the engine, which was acting as if it had only three instead of thirty thousand miles behind it.

Peppone stood at the door to the workshop, looking after the car.

"Devil take you and whoever brought you this way!" he exclaimed angrily as he went back inside. But he felt as puffed up as if he really were a sergeant.

THE WHISTLE

As USUAL, WHENEVER he went shooting, Don Camillo started out from the orchard, and this time, in the farther field, behind the church, he saw a boy sitting on the stump of a tree and apparently waiting for him.

"Can I go over with you?" the boy asked, as he got up and started to walk over.

Don Camillo looked hard and saw at a glance who the boy was.

"Go along with you," he answered brusquely. "You don't think I want one of you little devils for company, do you?"

The boy stood stock-still and watched the priest and his dog Thunder go on their way. Pino dei Bassi was not even thirteen years old, but he had already been enlisted by the Reds. They had signed him up in their youth organization and sent him out to distribute propaganda leaflets or to dirty the walls with diatribes against this, that and the other. He was the most active of the lot, because while the other boys had chores to do at home, he hung about the streets all day long. His mother, the widow of Cino dei Bassi, carried on her husband's trade. Every morning she hitched the horse to the wagon and went around the countryside selling pots and pans and cotton goods of every description. The boy had weak lungs and could not help her, so he was left in charge of his grandmother, who had a mere glimpse of him at noon, when he came home for something to eat. One day Don Camillo stopped the widow and told her she'd better keep an eye on the boy or else the company he was keeping would get him into trouble. But she answered tartly:

"If he goes with them, it's because it's more fun than going to church."

Don Camillo saw that there wasn't any use insisting. And he knew it was useless to preach at a good woman who wore herself out with hard work every day in order to keep body and soul together. Every time he saw the house and wagon go by he thought of Cino dei Bassi, one of his very best friends, whom he had seen die before his eyes. And he thought of Cino again whenever he went shooting. If Cino had known Thunder, he would have been wild about him. Cino had shooting in his blood and was one of the best shots in the countryside. He had an unerring nose for game and an unerring eye for shooting, and his expeditions carried him to places no one had visited before. Whenever Cino went to a duck shoot or target competition, half the village tagged along behind, as if he were a one-man football team. He was Don Camillo's boon companion, and it was while they were out shooting together that Cino had stumbled into a ditch and by some mischance fallen on the trigger of his shotgun. He had sent a volley into his own chest and died in Don Camillo's arms.

This kind of death seemed to be written into the fate of the Bassi family. Cino's grandfather, who was a mighty nimrod in his time, had accidentally killed himself with a gun, and Cino's father had been shot in the course of a shoot. Then death came to Cino the same way. And he had left his gun to Don Camillo.

"You keep it," were his dying words, "and put it to good use."

Now the sight of Cino's son sharpened Don Camillo's memory of his old friend, and when the boy asked if he could come along, he wished violently that he could knock some sense into his head and wipe out the disgrace he was bringing upon his father's good name.

"Thunder," he said, relieving himself of his feelings to his dog, "the next time we meet the little rascal, we'll practically shave the hair off him. It's plain as day that they're training him to make trouble and sent him to pester me."

Thunder did not swerve from the path, but growled lightly in reply.

Four or five days later, Don Camillo found Pino waiting for him in the same place.

"I've quit," said the boy. "Can I go with you this time?"

"Quit? What do you mean?" asked Don Camillo.

"I'm not with them any longer. I resigned."

Don Camillo looked him over with a feeling of perplexity. The boy had a welt under his left eye and a slightly battered air.

"What did you do?" he asked.

"They beat me up. But I'm not with them any longer. Today, will you take me?"

"Why do you want to go?"

"I'd like to see some shooting."

Don Camillo walked on and the boy trailed him as silently as a shadow. He did not get in the way and his footsteps made no echo upon the ground. His pockets were stuffed with bread and he did not ask for a thing during all the hours they were walking. Don Camillo did a good bit of shooting, and although he made no sensational hits he gave a very creditable performance and Thunder wasn't vexed with him too often. For when it came to his profession, Thunder was a strict taskmaster. He operated by the book and when Don Camillo made a whopping error he growled at him. On one occasion, early in their acquaintance, when the priest missed a hare almost the size of a calf, Thunder stood in front of him and bared his teeth.

Now Don Camillo had made a better-than-average record. He was ready to call it a day and go home, when suddenly Thunder showed signs of excitement.

"Can I have a shot?" whispered Pino, pointing to the shotgun.

"Of course not. You don't even know how to hold a gun to your shoulder."

Thunder took a few cautious steps forward and then froze into a pointing position.

"Give it here!" said the boy.

Don Camillo put the gun into his hands, but it was too late. A bird rose up out of the field, and only the kind of sportsman that likes to hear the sound of his own weapon would have taken a shot at it. That is, only a perfect fool, or else a marksman of the calibre of the late Cino dei Bassi. The boy raised the gun to his shoulder and fired. And the bird fell like a stone, because this was Cino's son, wielding his father's gun.

Don Camillo broke out into perspiration and there was a tight feeling about his heart as he remembered that this gun was responsible for the death of Cino. Impulsively he snatched it. Meanwhile Thunder had streaked away and come back to deposit a quail at the boy's feet. The boy leaned over to pat his head, and a second later the dog raced off to the far end of the field to show off the power of his lungs and legs together. There he stopped and waited. At this point the boy gave out a whistle that Don Camillo hadn't heard since the days when Cino was his hunting companion, and the dog responded instantly. A shiver ran down Don Camillo's spine. Meanwhile the boy handed the quail over to him.

"You shot it, so it's yours," said the priest roughly.

"Mother doesn't want me to shoot," the boy mumbled, and two minutes later he had gone away.

Don Camillo stuffed the quail into his bag and walked homeward, with Thunder frollicking before him. All of a sudden the dog stopped in his tracks, bringing Don Camillo to a halt just behind. In the distance sounded Cino's special whistle, and Thunder was off like a shot in reply.

"Thunder!" Don Camillo shouted, causing the dog to pause and look around. "Thunder, come here!"

But the whistle sounded again, and after a brief whinny of explanation, Thunder ran on, leaving Don Camillo in the middle of the narrow road. The priest did not continue straight on his way. Instead of crossing the ditch, he walked along it for at least a quarter of a mile. The evening mist was descending, filling up the rents left in the sky by the dried branches of the bare trees. Beside the ditch, at a spot marked by a wooden cross, Cino had fallen, releasing the trigger of his gun. Don Camillo bowed his head, took the quail out of the bag and laid it at the foot of the cross.

"I see you're still in good form, Cino," he whispered, "but please don't do it again."

Don Camillo had no more taste for shooting. The episode of Pino had given him such a chill that merely to look at the shot-gun hanging on the wall sent a tingle down his spine. And Thunder kept him company. The dog had received a major whacking and his demeanour was so humble that it seemed as if he must have understood every word, from the first to the last, of the little speech that had gone with it. If his master went out on the church square for a breath of air, he followed, but with his tail hanging. Then one afternoon, while the dog lay on the ground looking up at Don Camillo, who was pacing up and down with the usual cigar butt between his lips, the famous whistle sounded again. Don Camillo stopped and looked down at Thunder. Thunder did not budge. The whistle sounded again, and this time, although Thunder did not move, he traitorously wagged his tail and kept on wagging it until Don Camillo shouted at him. The confounded whistle sounded for a third time, and just as Don Camillo was about to grab his collar and pull him indoors, Thunder slipped away, jumped over the hedge and disappeared.

When he came to the field behind the church Thunder stopped to wait for further orders. Sure enough, he heard another whistle, which led him farther. The boy was waiting for him behind an elm, and they walked on together in the direction of an old mill which for the last fifty years had been nothing but a pile of stones beside a dried-up canal. When a dike had been thrown up to prevent floods, the course of the river had been changed, and the mill served no longer.

Now the boy climbed among the ruins, with Thunder at his heels. When they came to a half-collapsed arcade, he took away a few stones, revealing a long, narrow box behind them. Out of this he took an object wrapped in oily rags. Thunder looked on with a puzzled air, but in a minute he saw what it was all about. Enveloped in the rags was an old musket, as highly polished as if it had just come from the maker.

"I found it in the attic," the boy explained. "It belonged to my great-grandfather, who was a keen shot in his day. It takes a while to load it, but it shoots perfectly well." With which, he proceeded to load it. Then he put the powder-horn in his pocket, hid the musket under his coat and led the dog away.

Thunder had very little confidence in this strange contraption. And when he heard a bird stir in the grass, he pointed without any particular enthusiasm. But when he saw the bird drop to the ground he put his heart into his work, because he knew that it was worthwhile. This boy shot as Thunder had never seen anyone shoot before, and when they came to tuck the musket away in its hiding-place at the old mill the boy's pockets were bulging with quail.

"I can't take them home, because if my mother and grandmother were to find out that I had been shooting, they would raise the roof," Pino explained. "I give my catch to a fellow from Castelletto who deals in poultry, and he lets me have powder, tow, buckshot and cartridges in exchange."

Thunder's reaction to the announcement of this trade was not expressed very clearly. But then boy and dog alike were true artists. They didn't shoot for the sake of garnishing spits or frying pans, or just because they had a barbaric taste for bloodshed.

From this time on Thunder led a double life. He stayed quietly at home for days on end, but whenever he heard Pino's whistle he threw off all restraint and made for the field behind the church. Eventually Don Camillo took offence and put Thunder out of the front door.

"You're not to set foot in my house until you've given up this shameful behaviour," he said aiming a swift kick to underline his meaning.

And Thunder rejoiced, because his newly won independence favoured the enterprise on which he had set his heart.

Pino got it into his head that he must bring down a pheasant.

"I'm tired of these small pickings," he explained to the dog. "Now I want to do some real shooting. We've got to find a pheasant. To have bagged a pheasant is the badge of a true shot."

Thunder did the best he could, but even a blue-ribbon shooting dog can't find a pheasant where none is to be found. And yet there were some pheasants not too far away. They had only to go to the game preserve and worm their way through the wire fence. There thousands of pheasants awaited them.

But three wardens reigned over the preserve, and they were no joking matter.

However the prospect of bringing down a pheasant was overwhelmingly attractive. And so one day Pino and Thunder found themselves up against the fence. They had chosen just the right sort of weather, for there was a mist in the air just thick enough to afford vision combined with invisibility and to muffle the sound of gunshot. Pino had a pair of pincers and he lay down on the ground to loosen just enough of the wire to allow himself and the dog to squeeze under. They stalked silently through the tall grass, and before they had gone very far Pino found a pheasant to shoot at. The bird came down like a ton of bricks, but once it hit the ground it recovered sufficient strength to make a last flight which ended in a thicket. Thunder was just about to go for it when the boy called him back. Someone was running after them and calling upon them to halt or else. Pino ran like a demon, holding his head low, and Thunder followed after. The thickness of the mist and the general excitement caused the boy to strike the fence at a point slightly to the right of where he had made the hole. He realized this too late and lost time finding the right place. Just as he was bending down to slip through he was felled by the warden's gun.

He sank noiselessly to the ground and in spite of his ebbing strength tried to squeeze himself under. Just then the warden overtook him. Thunder stood in front of the boy, barking and baring his teeth. The man stopped short and when he saw the boy's bloodstained body on the ground he turned pale and did not know what to do. Pino was still trying to propel himself with his hands across the ground and Thunder, without taking his eyes off the warden, took the lapel of his jacket between his teeth and pulled him along. The warden stood there in a daze until at last he ran away. Pino had reached the other side of the fence, but he lay still and was apparently no longer breathing.

Thunder ran up and down, howling like one of the damned, but no one came by and finally he ran straight as an arrow to the village. Don Camillo was in the process of baptizing a baby when the dog rushed into the church, caught hold of his cassock and dragged him to the door. There Thunder let go, ran ahead, paused to bark, came back to take the priest's cassock between his teeth again, pull him forward and then dash on ahead to show the way. Now Don Camillo followed of his own free will, wearing his vestments and with his book in hand. And as he ran along the road, people from the village came after him.

Don Camillo brought the boy back in his arms, accompanied by a silent procession. He laid him down on his bed, while the old grandmother stared at him and murmured:

"There's fate for you! All of them died the same way."

The doctor said there was nothing to do but let him die in peace, and the onlookers lined up against the wall like so many statues. Thunder had disappeared, but he came back all of a sudden and took up his place in the middle of the room. In his mouth was the pheasant, which he had fetched from the thicket where it had fallen inside the preserve. He went over to the bed and put up his front legs and laid it on the boy's right hand which lay motionless on the bedcover. Pino opened his eyes, saw the bird, moved his fingers to stroke it and died with a smile on his face.

Thunder made no fuss but remained lying on the floor. When they came the next day to put Pino into his coffin they had to call upon Don Camillo to take the dog away, because he would not let anyone come near. Don Camillo put the body into the coffin himself and Thunder realized that if his master did it then it must be done. The whole village came to the funeral, and Don Camillo walked before the coffin, saying the office of the dead. At a certain moment his eyes fell upon the ground, and there was Thunder with the pheasant between his teeth. When they threw the first handful of earth over the coffin, Thunder let the pheasant drop among them. Everyone was scared by the dog's uncanny behaviour and left the cemetery in a hurry. Don Camillo was the last to go, and Thunder followed him, with his head hanging low. Once they were outside he disappeared.

The three wardens of the game preserve were grilled for forty-eight hours by the carabinieri, but every one of them made the same reply: "I know nothing about it. There was a heavy mist, and I saw and heard nothing in the course of my rounds. Some other poacher must have shot him." Finally they were all dismissed for lack of proof.

Thunder lay all day in the rectory, but when night came he ran away and did not come back until dawn. For twenty nights in succession he did the same thing, and for twenty nights a dog howled under the window of one of the three wardens. He howled uninterruptedly and yet no one could find the place where he was hiding. On the twenty-first morning the warden gave himself up to the sergeant of the carabinieri.

"You may as well lock me up," he said. "I didn't mean to kill him, but the shot was mine. Do what you like with me, because I can't stand that confounded dog's howling."

After this everything returned to normal, and Don Camillo resumed his shooting. But every now and then, in the middle of some remote, deserted meadow, Thunder came to a sudden stop. And in the silence there rang out the whistle that was peculiar to Cino dei Bassi.

THE EXCOMMUNICATED MADONNA

ONE MORNING A YOUNG man rode up on a bicycle to the square in front of the church and began to look inquiringly around him. Having apparently found what he wanted, he leaned his bicycle up against a pillar of the arcade and unpacked the bundle on the carrier behind the saddle. He took out a folding stool, an easel, a paint box and a palette, and a few minutes later he was hard at work. Fortunately the village children were all at school and he had a good half hour of peace and quiet. But gradually people crowded around and a hundred pairs of curious eyes followed his every brush-stroke. Just then Don Camillo came along, walking as casually as if he just happened to be passing that way. Someone asked him what he thought of the painting.

"It's too early to say," the priest answered.

"I don't see why he chose the arcade for a subject," said a member of the would-be intelligentsia. "There are far more picturesque scenes along the river."

The painter heard this remark and said without turning around:

"Picturesque scenes are for penny postcards. I came here to paint just because it isn't picturesque."

This statement left the villagers puzzled, and they continued to stare somewhat mistrustfully at the artist's work for the rest of the morning. At noon they went away and he was able to put in two solid hours without interruption. When the villagers returned they were so agreeably surprised that they ran to the rectory.

"Father, you must come and see. His picture's a beauty."

The painter was, indeed, a talented fellow, and Peppone, who happened to be among the onlookers, summed it up aptly by saying:

"There's art for you. I've been looking at that arcade for almost fifty years and I never realized that it was so beautiful!"

The painter was tired and packed his painting things away.

"Have you finished?" someone asked.

"No, I'll finish tomorrow. The light's changed and I can't get the same effects at this hour."

"If you'd like to leave your things at the rectory, there's plenty of room and I can answer for their safety," said Don Camillo, who saw that the young man didn't know what to do with his wet canvas.

"I knew the clergy would try to take him over," said Peppone disgustedly, as the artist gratefully accepted Don Camillo's offer.

After the young man had put his things in the hall closet he asked Don Camillo to recommend some simple lodgings.

"You can stay here," said Don Camillo. "I'm happy to have an artist under my roof."

A fire was lit in the rectory and supper was on the table. The young man was cold and hungry, but after he had eaten the colour came back into his cheeks.

"I don't know how to thank you," he said.

"You mustn't even try," said Don Camillo. "Will you be staying in these parts for long?"

"Tomorrow afternoon I must go back to the city."

"Has your enthusiasm for the river country suddenly left you?"

"No, it's a question of money," sighed the young man.

"Have you work waiting for you?" the priest asked him.

"Oh, I just scrape along from one day to the next," the artist told him.

"Well, I have no money," said Don Camillo, "but I can give you board and lodging for a month if you do some work in the church for me. Think it over."

"That's quickly done," said the young man. "It's a bargain. That is, if you let me have some time to paint for myself."

"Of course," said Don Camillo. "I need you for only a couple of hours a day. There's not so much to be done."

The church had undergone some repairs a month before and where the workmen had replaced some fallen plaster there was a gap in the decoration.

"Is that all?" asked the painter. "I can do that in a single day. You're offering me too much in return and it would be dishonest to accept it. You'll have to find something more for me to do."

"There is something more," said Don Camillo, "but it's such a big job, I haven't the courage to mention it."

"Let's hear."

Don Camillo went over to the rail of a side-chapel and threw on the light. A great spot filled the space above the altar.

"There was a leak," Don Camillo explained. "We caught on to it too late, and even though we mended the roof, the seepage had loosened the plaster. And so the painting of the Madonna was completely destroyed. The first thing to do, of course, is to replace the plaster. But I'm much more concerned over the repainting of the Madonna."

"You can leave that to me," said the artist. "Go ahead and get the plaster put in order, and meanwhile I'll make a sketch and have it ready to transfer to the wall when the mason gives me the word. I've had some experience in frescoes already.

But I'll have to insist upon some privacy. You can see the job when it's done, but I can't bear to work with people staring at me."

Don Camillo was so pleased that he didn't have breath enough even to answer: "Yes, sir!"

The young man had a genuine passion for painting, and the agreeable surroundings plus three square meals a day fired him to tremendous enthusiasm. When he had finished his widely admired picture of the arcade on the church square, he set off to explore the surrounding country and to find a model for the Madonna. He didn't want to paint a conventional figure, but to spiritualize a genuine face, which he hoped to discover in the vicinity of the village. During the first week he patched up the decorations in the main body of the church and restored an oil painting over the choir stalls. But he was restless and dissatisfied because he had not yet found his model. By the end of the second week the replastered chapel wall was ready for him to work on, but he was unable to begin. He had looked at hundreds of women in and around the village without finding a single face that interested him. Don Camillo became aware that something was wrong. The young man seemed listless and often came back in the evening without a single sketch in his notebook.

"Don't you care for this country any longer?" he asked. "There are all sorts of beauty you haven't yet discovered."

"Only one kind of beauty interests me just now," the artist complained. "And that I can't seem to find."

The next day the young man mounted his bicycle, making this resolution: "If I don't find what I'm after today, then I'm going home." He rode at random, stopping in farmyards to ask for a glass of water or some other trifle and looking into the face of every woman he saw along the way. But he was only confirmed in his disappointment. At noon he found himself in the settlement of La Rocca, a small place not far from the village, and rather than communicate his chagrin to Don Camillo he stopped for a bite to eat at the Pheasant Tavern. The big, low-ceilinged room with prints of characters from Verdi's *Othello* on the walls was completely deserted. An old woman appeared and he asked her for bread, sausage and a bottle of wine. A few moments later, when a hand deposited this simple fare on the dark table before him he raised his eyes and was startled almost out of his skin. Here was the inspiration for which he had been searching. The inspiration was about twenty-five years old and carried herself with the nonchalance of eighteen. But what captured the artist's fancy was the girl's face, and he stared at it, hardly daring to believe it was true.

"What's the matter?" the girl asked. "Have I done something to annoy you?"

"Please forgive me . . ." he stammered.

She went away but returned a little later to sit down over some sewing at the door. At once the young man took a pad and pencil and began to sketch her. She felt his eyes upon her and broke in upon his work with a question:

"May I ask what you're doing?"

"If you don't mind, I'm drawing you."

"What for?"

"Because I'm a painter and take an interest in everything beautiful."

She gave him a pitying smile, shrugged her shoulders and went on with her work. After an hour she got up and went to look over the young man's shoulder.

"Do I really look like that?" she asked him, laughing.

"This is just a preliminary sketch. If you'll allow me, I'll come back to finish tomorrow. Meanwhile, how much do I owe you for lunch?"

"You can pay when you come back."

As soon as the artist got back to the rectory he shut himself up in his room to work. The next day he worked until noon, when he went out, locking the door behind him.

"I've got it, Father!" he exclaimed as he rode away.

When he reached the Pheasant he found things just as they had been the day before: bread, sausage, wine and his inspiration sitting at the door. This time, after he had worked for a couple of hours, the girl showed more satisfaction with what he had accomplished.

"It will be better yet if I can come back tomorrow," he sighed.

He came back for the two next afternoons and then no more, for he had reached another stage of his work. For three whole days he remained in his room and then, in agreement with the mason, started in on the chapel. No one could see what he was doing, because a broad partition had been thrown up to protect him from the public view and he alone had the key to the door leading through it. Don Camillo was consumed with curiosity, but he contained himself and did no more than ask every evening:

"How's it going?"

"You'll soon see," said the young man excitedly.

Finally the great day came. The young man put a cloth over the fresco and tore down the boarding. Don Camillo rushed to the rail and waited, with his heart pounding. Then the young man took a pole and lifted the cloth off his "Madonna of the River." It was a most impressive painting, and Don Camillo stared at it with his mouth hanging open. Then all of a sudden something caught at his heart and perspiration broke out on his forehead.

"Celestina!" he shouted.

"Who's Celestina?" the young man asked.

"The daughter of the tavern-keeper at La Rocca."

"Yes," said the young man calmly. "She's a girl I found at the Pheasant Tavern."

Don Camillo took hold of a ladder, carried it over to the far end of the chapel, climbed up and draped the cloth over the fresco. The young man couldn't imagine what was wrong.

"Father, are you out of your head?" he asked him, but Don Camillo only ran back to the rectory, with the young man at his heels.

"Sacrilege!" he panted, once he had reached his own study. "Celestina from the Pheasant Tavern! You mean you don't know about Celestina? She's the most ardent Communist anywhere around and to present her face as that of the Madonna is like painting Jesus Christ in the likeness of Stalin."

"Father," said the artist, recovering some of his calm. "I was inspired not by her political beliefs but by her beauty. She has a lovely face, and that was given her by God, not by the Party."

"But the black soul behind it came straight from the Devil!" shouted Don Camillo. "You don't appreciate the gravity of the sacrilege you've committed. If I didn't realize that you were completely innocent about it, I'd send you packing."

"I have nothing on my conscience," said the artist. "I gave the Madonna the most beautiful face I could find."

"But the portrait doesn't reflect your good intentions, it represents a damned soul! Can't you see the sacrilege involved? The only fitting title to the fresco is 'The Excommunicated Madonna!' "

The young man was in terrible distress.

"I put everything I had in me into bringing out the spiritual qualities of that face. . . ."

"How do you expect to spiritualize the face of such a wanton creature? Why, when she opens her mouth, teamsters blush at the words that come out of it! No one can wish a face like that upon the Madonna."

The artist went to throw himself on his bed and did not come down to supper. About ten o'clock Don Camillo went up to see him.

"Well, are you awake now to the sacrilege you have committed? I hope that a second look at your sketches has revealed to you the essential vulgarity of that face. You're a young man and she's a provocative girl. She spoke to your senses, and your artistic discrimination went by the board."

"Father, you're misjudging and insulting me."

"Just let's look at your sketches together!"

"I've torn them all up."

"Then let's have another look at the chapel."

They went down to the empty church and Don Camillo took the pole to pull down the cloth covering the fresco.

"Look at it calmly and tell me if I'm not right."

The artist turned two powerful lights on the painting and shook his head.

"I'm sorry, Father," he said, "but there's nothing wanton or vulgar in that face."

Don Camillo stared at it again, scowling. The expression of the Madonna of the River was calm and serene and her eyes were pure and clear.

"Incredible!" exclaimed the priest angrily. "I don't know how you managed to get anything spiritual out of that creature."

"Then you admit that my picture has a spiritual and not a vulgar quality about it!"

"Yes. But Celestina hasn't. And anyone looking at it can't help saying: 'There's Celestina playing the part of the Madonna.' "

"Well, don't take it so tragically, Father. Tomorrow I can destroy it and start all over."

"We'll decide that tomorrow," said Don Camillo. "As a painting it's stupendous, and it's a crime to wipe it off the wall. . . ."

Indeed, this Madonna of the River was one of the most stunning things Don Camillo had ever seen. But how could he tolerate Celestina in the guise of Our

Lady? The next day he called five or six of his most trusted parishioners together, unveiled the fresco before them and asked for their honest opinion. Without exception they exclaimed:

"Marvellous!" and then a second later: "But's that's Celestina from the Pheasant Tavern!"

Don Camillo told them of the painter's misadventure and concluded:

"There's only one thing to do: wipe the whole thing out!"

"Too bad, because it's a masterpiece. Of course, it wouldn't do for our Madonna to have an excommunicated Communist's face. . . ."

Don Camillo begged the members of this little group not to say a word, and as a result the story spread like wildfire. People began to pour into the church, but the fresco was draped with a cloth and the entrance to the chapel barred. The news travelled outside the village and that evening, when Don Camillo was closing up the church he detected in the shadows the malicious face of Celestina in person.

"What do you want?" he asked gruffly.

"I want to see that idiot of a painter," she told him, and just then the idiot came upon the scene.

"Aside from the fact that you ate four meals at the Tavern without paying for them," Celestina said to him threateningly, "I'd like to know who gave you permission to misuse my face!"

The young man looked at her in amazement: here indeed was the face of which Don Camillo had spoken. He wondered how in the world he had seen anything spiritual in it. He started to make a hesitant reply, but she overrode him:

"You fool!" she exclaimed.

"Let's have less noise, my girl," Don Camillo interrupted. "We're in church, not in your father's tavern."

"You have no right to exploit my face and pin it on to a Madonna," the girl insisted.

"No one's exploited you," said Don Camillo. "What are you driving at, anyhow?"

"People have seen a Madonna with my face!" Celestina shouted. "Deny it if you can!"

"Impossible!" said Don Camillo. "But since it's true that some people see a slight resemblance, the fresco is going to be scraped away and done over."

"I want to see it!" Celestina shouted. "And I want to be present when you take my face out of it!"

Don Camillo looked at her ugly expression and thought of the gentle countenance of the Madonna of the River.

"It isn't your face," he said. "Come and see for yourself."

The girl walked quickly to the chapel and came to a halt in front of the rail. Don Camillo took the pole and removed the cloth cover. Then he looked at Celestina. As she stood motionless, staring up at the picture, something extraordinary happened. Her faced relaxed while her eyes lost their malice and became gentler and more serene. The vulgarity disappeared, and gradually she seemed to take on the expression of the painting. The artist gripped Don Camillo's arm.

"That's how I saw her!" he exclaimed.

Don Camillo motioned to him to be silent. A few moments later Celestina said in a low voice:

"How beautiful!" She could not take her eyes off the picture, and finally she turned to say to Don Camillo: "Please don't destroy it! Or at least, not too soon." And to his surprise she knelt down in front of the Madonna of the River and made the sign of the cross.

When Don Camillo was left alone in the church, he covered the fresco and then went to talk to the Crucified Christ over the main altar.

"Lord, what's going on?" he asked anxiously.

"Painting's not my business," answered Christ with a smile.

The next morning the young artist rode off on his bicycle to La Rocca. The tavern was empty, as usual, and Celestina sat, leaning over her sewing, at the door.

"I came to pay what I owe you," said the young man.

She raised her head, and he felt better because she had the gentle and serene expression of the painting on her face.

"You're a real artist!" she sighed. "That Madonna is a beauty. It would be a shame to take her away."

"I quite agree. I put my heart and soul into her, but people say an excommunicated Madonna won't do."

"I'm not excommunicated any longer," said Celestina with a smile. "I fixed that up this morning." And she proceeded to explain what steps she had taken.

Then she took advantage of the young man's surprise to ask whether it was his wife that kept his clothes so well mended and in such good order. He said that it wasn't, because he lived all alone and had no one to look after him. She observed with a sigh, that after a certain age, living alone was a tedious affair, even when a girl had any number of suitors. The time came when the thing to do was to settle down and have a family. He agreed on this point, but said that he had barely enough money to support himself. That, said Celestina, was because he lived in the city, where things were twice as expensive. If he were to move to the country, life would be much simpler, especially if he found a girl with a little house of her own and a parcel of land that only needed further development. He started to say something else, but just then the clock rang out noon. The hours have a way of flying when one engages in a conversation of this kind. Celestina went to fetch the usual bread, sausage and wine, and when he had finished eating he asked her:

"How much do I owe you?"

"You can pay tomorrow," she answered.

The Madonna of the River remained concealed for about a month longer. But on the day when the artist and Celestina were married, with all possible splendour, including organ music, Don Camillo drew the curtain and threw on the lights in the chapel. He was slightly worried about what people might say about the Madonna's resemblance to Celestina. But their only comment was:

"Celestina must wish she were equally beautiful! But she doesn't really look like Her at all!"

THE PROCESSION

DON CAMILLO WAITED patiently for things to come to a head, and although he waited a long time, it was not in vain. One morning the man he was expecting turned up at the rectory.

"Is there any change in the programme, Father," he asked, "or is it just the same as other years?"

"Just the same," said Don Camillo, "except for one detail: no music in the procession."

This "one detail" made Tofini, leader of the local band, suffer considerable distress.

"No music?" he stammered. "Why not?"

"Orders from higher up," said Don Camillo, throwing out his arms helplessly. Still Tofini couldn't believe it.

"Do you mean there's to be no more band-playing in any parades?"

"No," said Don Camillo, with icy calm. "It means that there's no more room in *my* procession for *your* band."

Tofini's collection of brasses was known as the "Verdi Band," but it was no great shakes from a musical point of view. However, it was no worse than other bands in that part of the country and no one had ever dreamed of looking elsewhere for the musical accompaniment to a religious or patriotic display.

"If we suited you in previous years and now you don't want us any more, what's the matter?" asked the dismayed Tofini. "Have we lost our art?"

"That's something you never had. But you know the reason perfectly well."

"Father, I don't know a thing!"

"Then ask around until you find out who played the *International* in the village square two months ago!"

"We did," answered Tofini, "but I don't see anything wrong in that."

"I do, though."

"But you know us, Father. You know we don't go in for politics. We play for anyone that hires us. Two months ago the mayor asked us to play in the square and we put on a programme of marches and operatic airs. Then people called for the *International*, the mayor said to play it, and we obliged."

"And if you'd been asked for the Fascist anthem, *Giovinezza*, or the *Royal March*, would you have played them too?"

"No. They're forbidden by law. But the *International* isn't forbidden."

"It's forbidden by the Church," said Don Camillo. "If you respect the laws of the State and not those of the Church, you may be a good citizen, but you're a very bad Christian. As a good citizen, you can go on playing in the square. But as a bad Christian, you can't play in a Church procession."

"Father, that's no way to reason. Everyone has his own way of making a living. And if everyone that works for the Communists were a bad Christian, where would we be now? Printers couldn't put out Communist papers, chemists couldn't sell medicine to Party members. . . . When a man pursues his regular trade, politics and religion don't come into it. A doctor takes care of anyone that's sick, regardless of his party. And when we make music for money, we're simply dealing in the only commodity we have to sell. The *Overture to William Tell* and the *International* are all the same to us. The notes may be in different order, but they're still the same old A B C."

"Quite so," said Don Camillo, warming up to the debate. "One piece is as good as another, within the law. So if I'd come to the square on that occasion and asked for the anthem of the Christian Democrat Party, you'd have played that too?"

"Certainly, if I wanted a beating," said Tofini with a shrug of his shoulders.

"It's not forbidden by law," said Don Camillo, "so why wouldn't you have played it?"

"If the Reds pay me, I can't very well play their opponents' song."

"When you say that, you're talking politics, after all. You appreciate the propaganda value of the *International* and you're a bad Christian to play it."

"Theory's one thing and practice is another," said Tofini. "A man's got to live."

"What matters more is that he's got to die. And our accounts with God are more important than those with any shopkeeper."

"God can wait," laughed Tofini, "the shopkeeper won't give me anything to eat until I pay."

Don Camillo threw out his arms.

"Are you reasoning like a good Christian?" he asked.

"No; like a poor devil that has to live as best he can."

"Very well, but there are other poor devils who manage to be very good Christians just the same. So why should I give you the preference? From now on the bands from Torricella, Gaggiolo and Rocchetta will play at funerals and all other religious processions. They're just as much out of tune, but at least they have more sense."

Tofini was so perturbed that he went to Peppone and a few hours later Peppone went to Don Camillo.

"Are fellows to be thrown out of work just because they played the anthem of a legally constituted party?" he shouted.

"Orders from higher up, Mr. Mayor," said Don Camillo regretfully. "Like you, I have to do what my superiors say."

"Even if their orders are stupid?"

"That's never been the case, where my superiors are concerned," said Don Camillo, calmly.

"Don't try to be funny," said Peppone, clenching his fists. "It hurts my conscience to see this man harmed through a fault of mine."

"There's no fault of yours. You didn't play the *International*. Tofini's band did, and that's why I must look for another."

"All right, then. You'll see," said Peppone, as he took his leave.

Don Camillo waited until the last minute to engage another band. And when he got around to it, he found that all three nearby bands had previous commitments.

He searched farther afield, only to meet everywhere the same answer. Don Camillo smelled a rat, and sure enough he finally came upon a band leader willing to tell him the truth.

"Father, we're willing to play but not to take a beating."

"Did someone threaten you?"

"No, but we were given some friendly advice."

Don Camillo went home feeling considerably depressed. The procession of the Madonna was scheduled for the next evening and no band was to be found. He spent a night haunted by musical nightmares and woke up feeling even worse than when he had gone to bed. Around ten o'clock Tofini dropped by.

"I heard you were looking for me, Father," he said.

"You're wrong, Tofini. You were looking for me, but I wasn't in."

"Very well," said Tofini. "At your service, in case of need."

"You may serve the mayor," said Don Camillo, "but you won't serve me."

After noon the village was in a ferment. That was always the way during the hours preceding the night-time procession of the Madonna. Every window was decorated with paper lanterns, luminous stars, candles and tapers, and out of every windowsill hung a rug, a piece of crimson damask, a garland of paper flowers, a bedspread, a linen sheet or a strip of lace or embroidery. The poorest houses were often the most artistically decorated, because ingeniousness took the place of money.

The village was in a ferment, then, during the afternoon, but toward evening, when the decoration was done, it grew calm. This year, however, the calm was only skin-deep, for everyone was curious. Would Don Camillo call upon Tofini or would he give up the idea of a band? And what about the People's Palace? The year before, the People's Palace was the only building which displayed no light. But at the last minute, just as the procession was getting under way, a red, white and green star appeared at a second-storey window, only to disappear after the marchers had gone by. No one ever knew quite how that came about but everyone was speculating upon what would happen this year. Either there would be a star or there wouldn't. Or else the star would be all red, instead of a patriotic red, white and green. Don Camillo threatened a fourth hypothesis:

"If they show a red star with a portrait of Malenkov in the centre, and they make me furious over the absence of music, I'll hold up the procession. . . ."

But his hypothesis did not go any further. He knew that if the Reds deliberately provoked him, he would come to a halt. But he didn't know what he would do next. And this unknown worried him intensely.

Night fell, and when the bells rang, every window was illuminated, that is, all except those of the People's Palace. The procession began to move, and the voices of women and children sang out the hymn *Behold this Thy people*. But the song was a melancholy one without the re-enforcement of Tofini's band. Everyone felt uneasy, and as they approached the People's Palace, the uneasiness grew. It looked as if, this time, there would be nothing but grim darkness. The head of the procession was within twenty-five feet of the People's Palace when Don Camillo began to pray:

"Lord, let there be a star, no matter what the colour! That dark, hermetically closed building gives me the impression of a world deprived of Your Divine Grace. Let some light be lit behind those dark windows in order to demonstrate Your presence. To tell the truth, I am afraid. . . ."

Now the head of the procession was passing right in front of the People's Palace, and still there was no sign of life or light. All hope was gone, and the procession wound slowly on. The picture of the Madonna was about to pass by, but it was too late now to hope for a miracle. And no miracle happened. What happened was that all the windows were suddenly thrown open, flooding the street with light. A volley of fireworks went off in the sports field, and in the courtyard Tofini's band, flanked by the bands from Torricella, Gaggiolo and Rocchetta, burst into *Behold this Thy people*.

An atomic bomb could not have made any more of an impression. With their eyes glued to the fireworks and their ears deafened by the din of the music, the marchers were completely at a loss. Don Camillo was the first to recover his aplomb. When he realized that the procession had come to a stop and the Madonna was stalled in front of the People's Palace, he shouted:

"Forward!"

The procession went on, and a thousand voices rose as a single voice, because they had four rival bands to sustain them.

"Lord," said Don Camillo, raising his eyes to heaven, "they did it all just to spite me!"

"But if in spiting you they've honoured the Holy Mother of God, why should you worry?"

"They don't mean to honour anyone, Lord. It's all a trick played upon poor, innocent people."

"They can't trick me, Don Camillo."

"I see, Lord. I was wrong, then, not to take the band that had played the *International* in the public square."

"No, you weren't wrong, Don Camillo. The proof is that four bands, instead of one, have gathered to give thanks to the Mother of God."

"Lord, this is just a deceitful game," Don Camillo insisted. "It's all because Russia's putting out peace feelers!"

"No, Don Camillo; I say it's all because Peppone isn't Russia."

Deep down in his heart, Don Camillo thought so too, and was thankful for geography.

HOLIDAY JOYS

IN RETALIATION FOR excommunication, the Reds decided to abolish Christmas.

And so on Christmas Eve Peppone came out of the People's Palace without so much as a glance at Bigio, who was waiting for him at the door, and hurried home, avoiding the main square in order not to run into the crowd returning from Midnight Mass. Smilzo trailed after him in disciplined style, but got no reward for his pains, because Peppone slammed the door of his own house behind him without so much as a good-night. He was dead tired and lost no time in falling into bed.

"Is that you?" asked his wife.

"Yes," mumbled Peppone. "Who do you expect it to be?"

"There's no telling," she retorted. "With the new principles you've just announced, it might just as well be some other official of your Party."

"Don't be silly," said Peppone. "I'm not in a joking mood."

"Neither am I, after this very uninspiring Christmas Eve. You wouldn't even look at the letter your son had left under your plate. And when he stood up on a chair to recite the Christmas poem he learned in school you ran away. What have children to do with politics, anyhow?"

"Let me sleep, will you?" shouted Peppone, rolling over and over.

She stopped talking, but it took Peppone a long time to fall asleep. Even after he finally dozed off, he found no peace, for nightmares assailed him, the kind of nightmares that go with indigestion or worry. He woke up while it was still dark, jumped out of bed and got dressed without putting on the light.

He went down to the kitchen to heat some milk and found the table set just the way it was the evening before. The soup bowl was still there and he lifted it up to look for the little boy's letter, but it was gone. He looked at the spotted tablecloth and the scraps of food upon it, remembering how his wife once decorated the table on past Christmas Eves. This led him to think of other Christmases, when he was a boy, and of his father and mother.

Suddenly he had a vivid memory of Christmas 1944, which he had spent in the mountains, crouching in a cave in danger of being machine-gunned from one moment to the next. That was a terrible Christmas, indeed, and yet it wasn't so bad as this one because he had thought all day of the good things that went with a peacetime celebration, and the mere thought had warmed the cockles of his heart.

Now there was no danger, and everything was going smoothly. His wife and children were there right in the next room, and he had only to open the door in order to hear their quiet breathing. But his heart was icy cold at the thought that the festive table would be just as melancholy on Christmas Day as it had been the evening before.

"And yet that's all there is to Christmas," he said to himself. "It's just a matter of shiny glasses, snow-white napkins, roast capons and rich desserts."

Then he thought again of Lungo's little boy, who had built a clandestine Manger in the attic of the People's Palace. And of the letter and poem of his own little boy, which had no connection with all the foodstuffs he had insisted were the only true symbols of the season.

It was starting to grow light as Peppone walked in his long black cape from his own house to the People's Palace. Lungo was already up and busy sweeping the assembly room. Peppone was amazed to find him at the door.

"Are you at work this early?"

"It's seven o'clock," Lungo explained. "On ordinary days, I start at eight, but today isn't ordinary."

Peppone went to his desk and started looking over the mail. There were only a dozen routine letters, and within a few minutes his job was done.

"Nothing important, Chief?" asked Lungo, sticking his head around the door.

"Nothing at all," said Peppone. "You can take care of them yourself."

Lungo picked up the letters and went away, but he came back soon after with a sheet of paper in his hands.

"This is important, Chief," he said. "It must have escaped your notice."

Peppone took the letter, looked at it and handed it back.

"Oh, I saw that," he said; "there's nothing unusual about it."

"But it's a matter of Party membership and you really ought to make an immediate reply."

"Some other day," mumbled Peppone. "This is Christmas."

Lungo gave him a stare which Peppone didn't like. He got up and stood squarely in front of his subordinate.

"I said it's Christmas, did you understand?"

"No, I didn't," said Lungo, shaking his head.

"Then I'll explain," said Peppone, giving him a monumental slap in the face.

Lungo made the mistake of continuing to play dumb, and because he was a strapping fellow, even bigger than Peppone, he gave him back a dose of the same medicine. With which Peppone charged like an armoured division, knocked him on to the floor and proceeded to change the complexion of his hindquarters with a series of swift kicks. When he had done a thorough job, he grabbed Lungo by the lapels and asked him:

"Did you understand what I was saying?"

"I get it; today's Christmas," said Lungo darkly.

Peppone stared at the little Manger Lungo's son had built.

"What does it matter if some people choose to believe that a carpenter's son, born two thousand years ago, went out to preach the equality of all men and to defend the poor against the rich, only to be crucified by the age-old enemies of justice and liberty?"

"That doesn't matter at all," said Lungo, shaking his big head. "The trouble is that some people insist he was the son of God. That's the ugly part of it."

"Ugly?" exclaimed Peppone. "I think it's beautiful, if you want to know. The fact that God chose a carpenter and not a rich man for a father shows that He is deeply democratic."

Lungo sighed. "Too bad the priests are mixed up in it," he said. "Otherwise we could take it over."

"Exactly! Now you've hit the real point. We must keep our heads and not mix up things that have no real connection. God is one thing and priests are another. And the danger comes not from God but from the priests. They're what we must seek to eliminate. It's the same thing with rich people's money. We must eliminate them and distribute their money among the poor."

Lungo's political education had not gone so far, and once more he shook his head uncomprehendingly.

"That isn't the essential question. The fact is that God doesn't exist; he's merely a priests' invention. The only things that really exist are those that we can see and touch for ourselves. All the rest is sheer fancy."

Peppone didn't seem to put much stock in Lungo's cerebrations, for he answered:

"If a man's born blind, how is he to know that red, green and the other colours exist, since he can't see them? Suppose all of us were to be born blind; then within a hundred years all belief in the existence of colour would be lost. And yet you and I can vouch for it. Isn't it possible that God exists and we are blind men who on the basis of reason or experience alone can't understand His existence?"

Lungo was completely baffled.

"Never mind," said Peppone abruptly. "This isn't a problem that requires immediate solution. Forget about it."

Peppone was on his way home when he ran into Don Camillo.

"What can I do for Your Grey Eminence?" he asked gloomily.

"I wanted to offer you my best wishes for Christmas and the New Year," said Don Camillo blandly.

"You forget that we Reds have been excommunicated," said Peppone. "That makes your good wishes somewhat illogical."

"No more illogical than the care which a doctor gives a sick man. He may quarantine him in order to protect others from his contagious disease, but he continues to look after him. We abhor not the sinner but his sin."

"That's a good one!" said Peppone. "You talk of love, but you'd kill us off without hesitation."

"No, we'd be very poor doctors of men's souls if we killed them in order to obtain a cure. Our love is directed at their healing."

"And what about the violent cure you spoke of at the political rally the other day?"

"That had nothing to do with you and your friends," Don Camillo answered calmly. "Take typhus for instance. There are three elements involved. The typhus itself, the lice that carry it and the suffering patient. In order to overcome the disease we must care for the patient and kill the lice. It would be idiotic to care for the lice and insane to imagine that they could be transformed into something other than a vehicle of contagion. And in this case, Peppone, you are the sick man, not the louse."

"I'm perfectly well, thank you, Father. You're the sick one, sick in the head."

"Anyhow, my Christmas wishes come not from the head but from the heart; you can accept them without reservation."

"No," said Peppone, "head, heart or liver, it's all the same. That's like saying: 'Here's a nice little bullet for you; it's a gift not from the percussion cap but from the barrel.'"

Don Camillo threw out his arms in discouragement.

"God will take pity on you," he murmured.

"That may be, but I doubt that He'll take pity on you. Come the revolution, He won't prevent your hanging from that pole. Do you see it?"

Of course Don Camillo saw the flagpole. The People's Palace was on the right side of the square and from his study window he couldn't help seeing the pole sticking insolently up into the free air, with a shiny metal hammer and sickle at its summit. This was quite enough to ruin the view.

"Don't you think I may be a bit too heavy for your pole?" he asked Peppone. "Hadn't you better import some gallows from Prague? Or are those reserved for Party comrades?"

Peppone turned his back and went away. When he reached his own house he called his wife outside.

"I'll be back about one o'clock," he told her. "Try to fix everything in the usual Christmas way."

"That's already attended to," she mumbled. "You'd better be back by noon."

Shortly after noon, when he came into the big kitchen, Peppone rediscovered the atmosphere of Christmases gone by and felt as if he were emerging from a nightmare. The little boy's Christmas letter was under his plate and seemed to him unusually well written. He was ready and eager to hear the Christmas poem, but this did not seem to be forthcoming. He imagined it would come at the end of the meal and went on eating. Even when they had finished dinner, however, the child showed no intention of standing up in his chair to recite, in the customary manner. Peppone looked questioningly at his wife, but she only shrugged her shoulders in reply. She whispered something in the little boy's ear and then reported to her husband:

"Nothing doing. He won't say it."

Peppone had a secret weapon: a box of chocolates which he extracted from his pocket with the announcement:

"If someone recites a poem, this is his reward!"

The child looked anxiously at the chocolates but continued to shake his head. His mother parleyed with him again but brought back the same negative reply. At this point Peppone lost patience.

"If you won't recite the poem, it means you don't know it!" he said angrily.

"I know it, all right," the child answered, "but it can't be recited now."

"Why not?" Peppone shouted.

"Because it's too late. The Baby Jesus is born now, and the poem is about the time just before."

Peppone called for the notebook and found that, sure enough, the poem was all in the future tense. At midnight the stall at Bethlehem would be lit up, the Infant would be born and the shepherds would come to greet Him.

"But a poem's not like an advertisement in the paper," said Peppone. "Even if it's a day old it's just as good as it was to start with."

"No," the child insisted, "if Baby Jesus was born last night, we can't talk about him as going to be born tomorrow."

His mother urged him again, but he would not give in.

In the afternoon Peppone took the little boy for a walk and when they were far from home he made one more attempt to bring him around.

"Now that we're all alone, can't you recite the poem?"

"No."

"No one will hear you."

"But Baby Jesus will know."

This sentence was a poem itself, and Peppone appreciated it.

The allotted number of days went by and then New Year's Eve arrived in the village. In the little world as everywhere else it was the custom to welcome the New Year with lots of noise. The irrepressible high spirits of the villagers found this an excellent excuse for letting go with every available firearm at midnight. So the New Year was started off right and the dying year killed off for good and all. Don Camillo had a hundred good reasons for disliking this custom, but this year he felt a perverse desire to kill the old year and have done with it. A few minutes before midnight he opened his study window and stood there, gun in hand, waiting for the bell in the church tower to ring. The lights were out but there was a fire in the fireplace and when Thunder, his dog, caught the gleam of the gun in Don Camillo's hand he was highly excited.

"Quiet there," Don Camillo explained. "This isn't my shooting gun. It's the old firing-piece I keep in the attic. It's a matter of shooting the old year out, and a shotgun won't answer the purpose."

The square was empty and the lamp in front of the People's Palace lit up the flagpole.

"It's almost as conspicuous by night as it is by day," muttered Don Camillo. "Seems as if they put it there just to annoy me."

The first of the twelve peals of midnight sounded, and at once the shooting began. Don Camillo leaned on the window-sill calmly and fired a single shot. Just one, because the gesture was a symbolic one and this was quite sufficient to give it meaning. It was very cold. Don Camillo carefully shut the window, leaned the gun against a chest and stirred the fire. All of a sudden he realized that Thunder wasn't there. Obviously he was so excited over the shooting that he had run out to join the fun. The priest was not particularly worried. The dog would slip back in just as easily as he had slipped out a few minutes before. Soon after this the door creaked and he looked up expectantly. The cause was not Thunder but Peppone.

"Excuse me," he said, "but the door was ajar and I came to pay you a call."

"Thank you, my son. It's always pleasant to be remembered."

"Father," said Peppone, sitting down beside him. "There's no doubt about it, truth is stranger than fiction."

"Has something unfortunate happened?" asked Don Camillo.

"No, just a curious coincidence. Someone shooting into the air hit our flagpole just at the top, where the metal emblem is joined on to the wood. Don't you find that extraordinary?"

"Extraordinary indeed," Don Camillo agreed, throwing out his arms.

"And that's not all," Peppone continued. "In its fall the emblem very nearly hit Lungo on the head. He thought someone had thrown something at him on purpose and gave the alarm. We all went out to look, and although there was nothing on the ground we noticed when we looked up that the emblem was missing from the flagpole and that, as I told you, it had been clipped off very neatly. Now who do you think can have taken it away as a trophy from the deserted square?"

"To be quite frank," said Don Camillo, "I can't imagine who would be interested in a piece of junk of that kind."

Meanwhile Thunder had come back in and sat motionless between the two men. The hammer-and-sickle emblem was between his teeth and at a certain point he dropped it on to the floor. Don Camillo picked it up and turned it around in his hand.

"A poor quality of metal," he said. "From a distance it didn't look so frail. Take it home if it interests you."

Peppone looked at the emblem which Don Camillo was holding out to him and then looked into the fire. Since no hand was extended to take it, the priest threw it into the flames. Peppone gritted his teeth but said nothing. The emblem grew red hot, its joints melted and the various parts curled up like so many snakes.

"If Hell weren't just an invention of us priests . . ." Don Camillo murmured.

"It's the other way around," muttered Peppone. "Priests are an invention of Hell!"

While the priest poked at the fire Peppone went to look out the window. Through the glass he could see the decapitated flagpole.

"How many shots did it take you?" he asked without turning around.

"One."

"American model with telescope attachment?"

"No, a regular old ninety-one."

Peppone came to sit down again by the fire.

"That's still a good gun," he mumbled.

"Guns are ugly things at best," murmured Don Camillo.

"Happy New Year!" muttered Peppone as he went out the door.

"Thanks, and the same to you," Don Camillo answered.

"I was speaking to Thunder," said Peppone roughly.

And Thunder, who was stretched out in front of the fire, responded to the mention of his name by wagging his tail.

A LESSON IN TACTICS

A MASSIVE PIECE OF machinery distinctly resembling a car, with a "U.S.A." licence plate at the rear, drew up in front of the rectory, and a thin man, no longer young, but of erect and energetic bearing, got out and walked over to the door.

"Are you the parish priest?" he asked Don Camillo, who was sitting on a bench just outside, smoking his cigar.

"At your service," said Don Camillo.

"I must talk to you," said the stranger excitedly, stalking into the hall for all the world like a conqueror. Don Camillo was momentarily taken aback, but when he saw that the stranger had reached a dead end and was about to descend into the cellar he moved to restrain him.

"This way!" he interjected.

"Everything's changed!" said the stranger. "I don't get it."

"Have you been here before, when things were differently arranged?" Don Camillo asked, leading him into the parlour, near the front door.

"No, I've never set foot in this house," said the stranger, who was still in a state of agitation. "But I still don't get it! Sermons won't cure the situation, Father. Nothing but a beating-up will teach those Reds a lesson."

Don Camillo maintained an attitude of cautious reserve. The fellow might be an escaped lunatic, for all he knew. But when a lunatic travels in a car with a "U.S.A." licence and a liveried chauffeur, it is best to handle him with kid gloves. Meanwhile the stranger wiped his perspiring forehead and caught his breath. The priest scrutinized the somewhat hard lines of his face and tried to connect them with something in his memory, but to no avail.

"May I offer you some sort of refreshment?" he asked.

The stranger accepted a glass of water, and after he had gulped this down, apparently he felt a little calmer.

"You have no reason to know me," he said. "I come from Casalino."

The priest scrutinized him again, this time mistrustfully. Now Don Camillo was a civilized man and one ready to acknowledge his own mistakes; he had plenty of common sense and a heart as big as a house. Nevertheless he divided mankind into three categories: good people who must be encouraged to stay good; sinners who must be persuaded to abandon their sin and, last of all, people from Casalino, a village which from time immemorial had feuded with his.

In ancient times the struggle between the two villages had been violent and men had lost their lives in it. For some years past it had degenerated into a cold war, but the substance of it was still the same. Politicians from Casalino had wormed their way into the provincial administrations and the national governmment, particularly the departments of public works and engineering. As a result, whenever there was plan to do something for Don Camillo's village, these politicians blocked it or turned it to their own advantage.

So it was that although Don Camillo worked hard to keep good people good and to persuade sinners to abandon their sin, he left Casalino in God's care. When things got especially tense he would say to Christ, "Lord, if You created these people, there must be some reason for it. We must accept them like death and taxes, with Christian resignation. May Your infinite wisdom rule over them and Your infinite kindness deliver us from their presence!"

"Yes, I'm from Casalino," the stranger repeated. "And if I have humiliated myself to the point of coming here, you can imagine that I must be very angry."

This was easy enough to understand, but Don Camillo could not see the connection with the big American car.

"I was born in Casalino," the stranger explained, "and my name is Del Cantone. Until 1908, when I was twenty-five years old, I lived on a farm with my father and mother. We worked like dogs, because we had no peasants to help us. Then all of a sudden, those damned souls . . ."

He turned red in the face again and perspired profusely.

"What damned souls do you mean?" asked Don Camillo.

"If you, a priest, don't know that the Reds are damned souls, then you must be blind as a bat!'' the stranger shouted.

"Excuse me," said Don Camillo, "but aren't you speaking of events of some forty years ago?"

"The Reds have been damned souls from the beginning, ever since Garibaldi invented that infernal red shirt. . . ."

"I don't see much connection with Garibaldi," demurred Don Camillo.

"You don't? Wasn't the doctor who introduced socialism to this part of the world a follower of Garibaldi?" the stranger retorted. "Didn't he put all sorts of ideas into people's heads and start subversive organizations?"

Don Camillo urged him to tell the rest of his own story.

"Well, in 1908 those damned souls made a big splash, with a farm-workers' strike and nonsense of that kind. They came to our place and insulted my father, and I took a shotgun and shot a couple of them down. No one was killed, but I had to run away to America. There I worked like a dog, too, but it took me a number of years to make any money. Meanwhile my father and mother died, in extreme poverty. All because of those damned souls. . . ."

Don Camillo gently remarked that after all the shotgun was to blame. But the other paid no attention.

"When I heard about how Mussolini was taking care of the Red menace, I thought of coming back to settle my private account with them. But by that time, I was thoroughly tied up with a growing business. I did send someone to raise a gravestone to my parents in the cemetery. After that, more time went by, and now I'm in my seventies. . . . Anyhow, here I am, after four decades of absence. And I haven't much time. I came back to do something more to commemorate my father and mother. A gravestone is something as lifeless as those that lie beneath it. What I wanted to do was to give their name to some charitable institution, a fine, modern building with plenty of grounds around it. And my idea was to have the building divided in two parts: one a children's home and the other a home for old people. Old people and children could share the grounds and come to know one another. The end of life would be drawn close to the beginning. Don't you think it's a good idea?"

"Very good," said Don Camillo. "But the building and grounds aren't all that's necessary——"

"I didn't come all the way from America to learn anything so elementary. You don't think I imagine that an institution can live on air, do you? I meant to endow it with a thousand-acre, self-supporting farm. In fact, for the whole project I have put aside a million dollars. I haven't much longer to live and there are no children to inherit from me. Taxes and lawyers' fees will eat up most of what I leave behind. And so I transferred the million dollars to this, my native land. But now I've decided to take them back to America."

Don Camillo forgot that the loss of this sum would be a loss to Casalino. In fact, with the notion of a million dollars earmarked for charity coursing through his mind he was willing to take the inhabitants of Casalino out of the category of untouchables and consider them in the same light as the rest of mankind.

"Impossible!" he exclaimed. "God inspired you with a truly noble idea. You mustn't go back on His inspiration."

"I'm taking the money home, I tell you," the stranger shouted. "Casalino shan't have a penny of it. I went there straight from Genoa, and what did I find? Red flags all over the village and on every haystack around! Red flags, posters bearing the hammer and sickle and threatening death to this one and that. There was a rally in the public square and the loudspeakers brought me every word of it. 'Now let us hear from our comrade the Mayor,' they were saying. And when they saw my licence plate, they shouted at me: 'Go back to Eisenhower! Go back to America!' One of them even damaged the top of my car. You can see for yourself if you don't believe me."

Don Camillo looked out the window and saw that this was indeed true.

"Well, I'm going back, never fear," concluded the stranger, "and taking my money with me. I'll give it to the Society for the Prevention of Cruelty to Animals, rather than to the damned souls of Casalino!"

"But not all of them are Reds," protested Don Camillo.

"They're all swine, though. The Reds because they're Reds, and the others because they're too weak to kick them out. Yes, I'm going back to America."

Don Camillo thought it was pointless to argue. But he wondered why the old man had come to him with this story.

"I understand your disappointment," he said. "And I'm ready to do anything I can to help you."

"Of course . . . I had forgotten the most important thing of all," said the stranger. "I came to you for a very good reason. I've money to burn and expenses don't matter. I'm willing to make this my legal residence or do whatever else is necessary, to organize a secret raid and enlist the devil himself to carry it out. But my parents can't be at rest in the cemetery of Casalino, and I want to bring their bodies here. I'll erect a new gravestone in your cemetery, a monument of colossal proportions. All I ask is that you take care of the whole thing, I'm content to pay."

And he deposited a pile of banknotes upon the table.

"Here's for your preliminary expenses," he added.

"Very well," said Don Camillo. "I'll do whatever's possible."

"You may be called upon to do the impossible," said the stranger.

Now that he had got all this off his chest, he seemed to be in a more reasonable frame of mind. He consented to drink a glass of sparkling Lambrusco wine, which brought back memories of his youth and restored his serenity.

"How are things here, with you, Father?" he asked. "Terrible, I suppose. I have an idea that the whole area is pretty much like Casalino."

"No," answered Don Camillo. "Things are quite different here. There are Reds, of course, but they aren't on top of the heap."

"Isn't your local government in Red hands?"

"No," Don Camillo said shamelessly. "They're on the village council, but not in the majority."

"Wonderful!" exclaimed his visitor. "How do you do it? You can't tell me that sermons have turned the tide."

"There you're wrong," said Don Camillo. "My sermons aren't without effect. The rest is a matter of tactics."

"What do you mean?"

"Well, it's hard to put into words, so I'll give you a concrete example." And out of a drawer he took a pack of cards. "Say each of these cards is a Communist. Even a tiny child can tear them up one by one, whereas if they're all together it's almost impossible."

"I see," said the stranger. "Your tactics are to divide your enemies and overcome them one by one."

"No," said Don Camillo; "that's not it at all. My tactics are to let the enemy get into a solid block in order to size up their strength correctly. Then when they're all together, I go into action."

So saying, he tore the pack of cards in two in his big, bare hands.

"Hooray!" the old man shouted enthusiastically. "That's terrific! Will you give me that pack of cards with your autograph on one of them? The only trouble with such tactics is that they require unusually strong hands!"

"Strong hands aren't lacking," said Don Camillo calmly. "We can handle a pack easily enough. But what shall we do when there are sixty or more? We're still on top, but they're working day and night to put us down. And they have powerful weapons."

"Weapons? And you haven't any? I'll send you plenty of those!"

"That's not the sort of weapons I mean. The Reds' chief weapon is other people's selfishness. People who are well off think only of holding on to their possessions; they show no concern for their neighbours. The richest people are often the more stingy; they fail to see that by clinging to their individual piles the whole lot of them will lose everything. But don't let's worry over that, Signor Del Cantone. Have another glass of wine."

"There's the Old World for you!" sighed the stranger, turning down the offer of a second drink. "I want to speak with the mayor right away. I see a way of killing three birds with one stone. I'll raise an enduring monument to my father and mother, save Western civilization and madden those damned souls of Casalino by making this village the seat of my institution."

Don Camillo saw stars. Then he hastily pulled himself together.

"The mayor's not here today. But I'll have him on deck here at the rectory tomorrow morning."

"Good. I'll be here. Remember I have very little time, and be ready to present your choice of location. I have the building plans in my pocket. And my agent has rounded up several big farms for raising all the produce the institution can consume."

"No," said Peppone, "I won't take part in any such dirty comedy. I am what I am and I'm proud of it."

"There's nothing dirty about it," said Don Camillo. "All you have to do is pretend to be a decent sort of person."

"And there's no use your trying to be funny, either. I'm no puppet! I'll turn up at the rectory tomorrow morning, if you like, but with my red kerchief around my neck and three Party membership pins."

"Then you may as well save yourself the trouble. I'll tell him to hang on to his million, because the mayor has no use for it. Our mayor intends to build a children's and old people's home with the funds they send him from Russia. In fact, I'll have the whole story put into print so that everyone can know."

"That's blackmail!" said Peppone angrily.

"I'm only asking you to be quiet and let me do the talking. Politics shouldn't come into it. Here's a chance to do something for the poor, and we must make the best of it."

"But it's a fraud!" said Peppone. "Among other things, I have no intention of tricking that poor old man."

"All right," said Don Camillo, throwing out his arms. "Instead of tricking a millionaire, let's trick the poor! To think that you claim to be fighting for a fairer distribution of rich people's money! Come, come! Is there any trickery in persuading a madman that you're not a Communist, in order to obtain funds for the needy? I see nothing wrong. Anyhow, I leave it up to the Last Judgment, and if I am found guilty I shall pay. Meanwhile our old people and children will have shelter and a crust of bread. This madman wants to build something to commemorate his parents. Why shouldn't we help him?"

"No! I say it's dishonest and I won't have any part of it!"

"Very well," said Don Camillo. "You're sacrificing a cool million to Party pride. Perhaps tomorrow, when you're polishing up the weapons you've stowed away for the Revolution, a bomb will explode in your hands, leaving your son an orphan."

"I hope you explode first," retorted Peppone. "And my son will never beg for your reactionary charity!"

"That's true. He'll have your pension from Malenkov. But what if you live long enough to achieve second childhood and there's no old people's home to take you in?"

"By that time Malenkov will have fixed things so that every old person has a home of his own."

"What if Malenkov disappoints you?"

"I'm not worried about that. Meanwhile, I'll have nothing to do with this plan."

"All right, Peppone. I have to admit that you're right. I was so carried away by the idea of doing something for the poor that I lost my head completely, and it took a hardened unbeliever like yourself to remind me of God's law against lying. It's never permissible to sacrifice principle to profit. Come along tomorrow morning, and we'll tell that madman the truth. I have sinned and it's up to me to atone."

Don Camillo did not have the courage to speak to the Crucified Christ over the altar that evening. He slept uncomfortably and waited for the next morning to restore his peace of mind. Sure enough, the big American car pulled up in front of the rectory and the stranger walked in. Peppone, who was waiting outside with Brusco, Smilzo and Bigio, followed after.

"Here are the mayor and three members of the village council," said Don Camillo.

"Good!" said the old man, shaking hands all around. "I suppose that Don Camillo has already told you my story. . . ."

"Yes," said Peppone.

"Splendid. I presume you belong to the clerical party."

"No," said Peppone.

"We're independents," put in Smilzo.

"So much the better!" said the old man. "I don't hold particularly with the priests. If you're free and independent, then of course you're against the Reds. Castor oil and a beating, those are the only treatments for them. Don't you agree?"

His slightly wide eyes were fastened upon Peppone.

"Yessir," Peppone answered.

"Yessir," echoed Bigio, Brusco and Smilzo.

"These cursed Reds . . ." the old man continued, but Don Camillo broke in.

"No more!" he said firmly. "This comedy has gone far enough."

"Comedy? What comedy do you mean?" the old man asked in amazement.

"You were so excited when I saw you yesterday, that in order to calm you down I said some things that are not exactly true," explained Don Camillo. "Things are just the same here as they are at Casalino. The mayor and most of the members of the Village Council are Reds."

"Did you want to make a fool of me?" the stranger asked with a grim laugh.

"No," answered Peppone calmly. "We simply wanted to help the poor. For their sake we were willing to stoop to almost anything."

"And what about those famous tactics of yours?" the stranger said ironically to Don Camillo.

"They're still valid," the priest answered determinedly.

"Then why don't you explain them to the mayor?" the old man asked vindictively.

Don Camillo gritted his teeth and took a pack of cards from a desk drawer.

"Look," he said. "Even a tiny child can tear them up one by one, whereas if they're all together it's almost impossible . . ."

"Just a minute," said Peppone. And taking the pack out of Don Camillo's hands he tore it in two with his own.

"Amazing!" exclaimed the old man. "Record-breaking!" And he insisted that Peppone gave him a split card with an autograph upon it.

"I'll display them both in the window of my shop in America," he said, putting the whole pack in his pocket. "On one side the priest's and on the other the mayor's. And in between their story. The fact that both of you can split a pack of cards is important," he added. "Likewise the fact that you can league together for the good of the village against an outsider. I still have the same low opinion of you cursed Reds. But I don't care if they burst with envy at Casalino; this is the place where I want to build my institution. Draw up a charter for it tomorrow and choose a board of directors with no politicians among them. All decisions made by this board must be approved by two presidents, who have a lifelong term and the power to choose their successors. The first two men to hold this office shall be Don Camillo and (if I have the name right) Giuseppe Bottazzi. Before we American businessmen embark upon any enterprise we obtain a thorough report on the people and places with which we expect to be concerned. Yesterday, when your priest told me that the local government was not predominantly Communist in character, I had a good laugh. Today I didn't find it quite so funny. But I have learned something I didn't know before and I shall go home happy. Push this thing through fast, because I want to settle it tomorrow. I'm buying the farm today."

Don Camillo went to kneel before the Crucified Christ over the main altar.

"I'm not especially pleased with you, Don Camillo," Christ said. "The old man and Peppone and his friends behaved themselves more creditably than you did."

"But if I hadn't stirred up the situation a bit, nothing would have come out of it," protested Don Camillo weakly.

"That doesn't matter. Even if some good comes out of your evil-doing, you're responsible to God for what you did. Unless you understand this, you've misunderstood God's word completely."

"God will forgive me," murmured Don Camillo, lowering his head.

"No, Don Camillo, because when you think of all the good which your sin has done for the poor you won't ever honestly repent."

Don Camillo threw out his arms and felt very sad, because he knew that Christ was quite right.

PEPPONE HAS A DIPLOMATIC ILLNESS

"THIS IS AN OUTRAGEOUS hour," grumbled Don Camillo when Peppone's wife came to the rectory.

"I thought priests and doctors were available twenty-four hours a day," she answered.

"All right, all right, but say what you have to say without sitting down. That way you won't stay too long. What is it you want?"

"It's about the new house. I want you to bless it."

Don Camillo clenched his fists.

"You've come to the wrong counter," he said sternly. "Good-night."

The woman shrugged her shoulders.

"You must forgive him, Father. He had something on his mind."

Don Camillo shook his head. The matter was too serious to be forgotten, even after six months had gone by. Peppone had had an irresistible impulse to make a change; he had sold his shabby, run-down workshop, borrowed money until he was in debt up to his ears and built himself a new house just outside the village, on the main road running parallel to the river. The workshop was as well equipped for making repairs as that of any big city garage, and there were living quarters on the second floor. He had acquired the franchise for a well-known brand of petrol, and this promised to bring him many customers from the heavy traffic on the highway.

Of course Don Camillo couldn't resist his curiosity, and one fine morning he went to see. Peppone was deep in a disembowelled engine and decidedly not in talkative mood.

"Fine place you've got here," said Don Camillo, looking around.

"Yes it is, isn't it."

"A big courtyard, a flat on the second floor, a petrol pump and everything," Don Camillo continued. "There's only one thing missing."

"What's that?"

"Once upon a time, when a man moved into a new house he called upon the priest to bless it. . . ."

Peppone drew himself up, wiping the sweat off his forehead.

"Here's the holy water of our day and age," he said aggressively, "consecrated by good hard work instead of by one of your priestlings."

Don Camillo went away without saying a word. There was something alarming in Peppone's words, something he had never heard before. Now this request from Peppone's wife carried him back to the feeling of disgust he had suffered six months before.

"No," he told her.

"You've simply got to come," she said, no whit discouraged. "My husband's not the only one in the house. There's myself, and my children. It's not our fault if Peppone was rude to you. If Christ were to . . ."

"Christ doesn't come into it at all," interrupted Don Camillo.

"He does, though," she insisted.

And so, after pacing for several minutes around the room, Don Camillo answered:

"All right, then. I'll come tomorrow."

"No, not tomorrow," she said, shaking her head. "You must come right now, while Peppone's out. I don't want him to know, or the neighbours to see and report to him, either."

This was too much for Don Camillo.

"So I'm to be an underground priest, am I? Perhaps in order to bless a house I should disguise myself as a plumber. As if it were something shameful that had to be hidden! You're more of a heathen than your wretched husband!"

"Just try to understand, Don Camillo. People would say that we were having the house blessed because we're in trouble."

"Because you're in trouble, eh? And actually you want it blessed for some totally different reason. Out with it, woman!"

"Because we *are* in trouble, to tell the truth," she explained. "We've had bad luck ever since we moved into the new house."

"So because you don't know where to turn, you thought you might try God, is that it?"

"Well, why shouldn't I? When things go well, we can look out for ourselves, without bothering God Almighty."

Don Camillo took a stick out of the pile beside the fireplace. "If you aren't at least as far away as the square in the next two seconds, I'll break this over your head!" he told her.

She went away without a word, but a second later she stuck her head through the door.

"I'm not afraid of your stick," she shot at him. "I'm afraid of your unkindness and bad temper."

Don Camillo threw the stick on to the fire and watched it go up in flames. Then brusquely he threw his overcoat over his shoulders and went out. He walked through the darkness until he came to Peppone's house and there he knocked on the door.

"I knew you'd come," said the wife of Peppone.

Don Camillo took the breviary out of his pocket, but before he could open it, Peppone came like a whirlwind into the hall.

"What are you doing here at this hour?"

Don Camillo hesitated, and Peppone's wife spoke up: "I aksed him to come and bless the house."

Peppone looked at her darkly. "I'll settle accounts with you later. As for you, Don Camillo, you can go at once. I don't need you or your God either."

This time Peppone's voice was hardly recognizable. To tell the truth, Peppone was not the man he had been before. He had bitten off more than he could chew, and in throwing himself into this new venture he had borrowed on everything he had and some things he hadn't. Now he was in really hot water and didn't see how he was ever going to get out of it. That evening, for the first time in his life, he had surrendered and asked for help.

After Don Camillo had left, Peppone exploded. "So you'd betray me too, would you?"

"I wouldn't betray you. There's a curse on this house and I wanted to break it. I didn't do anything wrong."

Peppone went into the large kitchen and sat down at the table.

"Bless the house, indeed!" he shouted. "He didn't come to bless the house; he came to spy on us, don't you understand? To see how things are going and dig up some proof of our desperate situation. If he'd got into the workshop, he'd have noticed that my new lathe is gone . . ."

"Tell me, what happened?" his wife broke in.

"Well, the lathe's taken care of, and no one saw me carrying it away."

"Someone will notice tomorrow," his wife sighed. "The first man to come in will see that it's not there."

"No one will see a thing," Peppone reassured her. "With the money I got for the lathe, I paid off our two most pressing creditors, and tomorrow I won't open the shop for business. I've taken care of that too."

His wife looked at him questioningly.

"I called the village council together and told them that I was ill and needed a long rest. I'm going to shut myself up in the house and not let anyone see me."

"That won't do any good," she answered. "Notes will fall due, no matter how tightly you shut yourself up."

"The notes will fall due in another month. Meanwhile, the lathe is gone, and that's a fact we must cover up. There are all too many people who'd be happy to know that I'm in trouble."

Then Peppone asked his wife for a big sheet of paper and printed on it in big letters:

WORKSHOP TEMPORARILY CLOSED
DUE TO ILLNESS OF OWNER

"Go and stick that on the door," he ordered.

His wife took a bottle of glue and started out, but Peppone stopped her.

"That won't do," he said sadly. "*Owner* is far too bourgeois a word."

He sought in vain for some less reactionary term and finally had to content himself with a vague:

CLOSED, DUE TO ILLNESS

As a matter of fact, the whole business was sick, and not just Peppone.

Peppone did not stick his nose outside, and his wife explained to everyone that he was in a state of exhaustion and mustn't be disturbed until he got better. Ten days went by in this way, but on the eleventh day there was bad news. In the local column of the farm paper there was an item that ran:

LOCAL CITIZEN IN THE LIMELIGHT

We are happy to say that the popularity of our mayor, Giuseppe Bottazzi, is always on the increase. Today's list of called-in promissory notes carries three mentions of his name. Congratulations on the well-deserved publicity.

Peppone ran a genuine temperature and went to bed, asking his wife to leave him completely alone.

"I don't want to see any letters or newspapers. Just let me sleep."

But three days later she came sobbing into the room and woke him up.

"I've got to tell you something," she said. "They've seized all the new tools in your workshop."

Peppone buried his head in the pillow, but he heard what she was saying. He sweated all the fever he could out of himself and then suddenly decided to jump out of bed.

"There's only one thing to do," he exclaimed. "I'll have to go away."

"Just forget about the whole thing," his wife begged him, in an attempt to bring him back to reason. "Let them seize and sell whatever they like. There's a curse on the whole business. We still have the old house and the old workshop. Let's start all over again."

"No!" Peppone shouted wildly. "I can't go back to the old place. That would be too humiliating. I must go away, that's all. You can say that I've gone to the mountains on account of my health, and meanwhile I'll try to think up a solution. I can't concentrate in these surroundings, and there's no one to advise me. I'm not breaking off for good; I'll leave everything as it is. If things continue to go badly, they'll blame it on my poor health. But I can't bear to take a step backward and give satisfaction to my enemies."

"Whatever you say," his wife conceded.

"I still have my lorry," said Peppone. "That's something. I don't know where I'll go, but you'll be hearing from me. Don't breathe a word to a soul, even if they kill you."

At two o'clock in the morning, Peppone started up the lorry and drove away. No one actually saw him, but he was the subject, even at this late hour, of many conversations.

"His creditors have jumped on him just because he's sick," some people were saying.

"That illness of his is just an excuse to cover up his crimes," said others.

"He's a coward."

"Serves him right!"

"The main thing is for him to get well and come back to his job as mayor."

"If he has any decency, he ought to resign."

Peppone's name was on hundreds of mouths, and all the while he was hurrying away in his old lorry, pursued by the "complex of bourgeois respectability," whose influence is felt in every class, including the proletariat.

The days went by and after the news of the seizure came an announcement of a public auction of Peppone's new tools and machinery.

"Lord," said Don Camillo, pointing to the newspaper, "here's proof that God does exist!"

"You're telling Me!" Christ answered.

Don Camillo lowered his head. "Forgive my stupidity," he murmured.

"The stupid things you say are entirely forgivable. I know how that tongue of yours is always getting you in trouble. But what worries Me is your way of thinking. God doesn't care about seizures and auctions. Peppone's bad luck has nothing to do with his demerits, any more than a rascal's rapid rise to riches has anything righteous about it."

"Lord, he has blasphemed Your Name, and ought to be punished. All the decent people of the village are sure that it's because he refused to have the house blessed that he ran into difficulty."

Christ sighed. "And what would these decent people say if Peppone had prospered? That it was because he turned down the blessing?"

Don Camillo threw out his arms impatiently.

"Lord, I'm only telling you what I hear. People——"

" 'People?' What does that mean? 'People' as a whole are never going to get into Heaven. God judges 'people' individually and not in the mass. There are no 'group' sins, but only personal ones, and there is no collective soul. Every man's birth and death is a personal affair, and God gives each one of us separate consideration. It's all wrong for a man to let his personal conscience be swallowed up by collective responsibility."

Don Camillo lowered his head. "But, Lord, public opinion has some value. . . ."

"I know that, Don Camillo. Public opinion nailed Me to the Cross."

On the day of the public auction, a flock of vultures arrived from the city. They were so efficiently organized that for a mere pittance they divided up and carried away the worldly goods of Peppone. Don Camillo was somewhat depressed when he came back from the sale.

"What are people saying, Don Camillo?" Christ asked him. "Are they happy?"

"No," Don Camillo answered; "they say it's too bad that a man should be ruined because he's ill and far away and can't defend himself."

"Be honest with me, Don Camillo, and tell me what people are actually saying."

Don Camillo threw out his arms. "They're saying that if God really existed, such things wouldn't happen."

Christ smiled.

"From the 'Hosannas!' of the acclaiming crowd to the same crowd's cry of: 'Crucify him!' there isn't so very far to go. Do you see that, now, Don Camillo?"

That same evening there was a stormy meeting of the village council. Spiletti, the only councillor belonging to the Opposition, raised the subject of the mayor.

"For two months we've had no news of him. He's lost all interest in the village and even in his own private affairs. Where is he, and what's he doing? On behalf of a large number of my fellow-citizens, I demand a definite answer."

Brusco, who was serving as deputy mayor, got up to reply.

"I shall give you a detailed answer tomorrow."

"I'm not inquiring into any top secret, am I?" objected Spiletti. "I demand an answer right away. Where is the mayor?"

Brusco shrugged his shoulders.

"We don't know," he admitted.

There was a grumbling protest from all those present. The thing was simply incredible.

"Nobody knows the whereabouts of the mayor!" Spiletti shouted. "Then let's put an ad in the paper: *Reward to anyone who can find one Red mayor, two months missing.*"

"It's not so funny as all that," said Brusco. "Not even his wife knows where he is."

Just then a voice boomed out from the back of the room.

"I know," said Don Camillo.

Everyone was silent, until Brusco spoke out: "If you know, tell us."

"No," said Don Camillo. "But I can bring him here tomorrow morning."

In a gloomy section of the suburbs of Milan, Peppone was shovelling scrap iron and plaster from a recently demolished building into his lorry. When the noon whistle sounded, he threw down his shovel, took a sandwich and a copy of the Communist paper, *Unity*, out of the pocket of his jacket and went to sit down with his back against a fence, alongside his fellow-workers.

"Mr. Mayor!"

The shrill voice of Spiletti brought him to his feet with a single bound.

"There aren't any mayors around here," he answered.

"And the trouble is we have no mayor in our village, either," said Spiletti. "Can you tell me where to find one?"

"That's none of my business," said Peppone, sitting down on the ground.

"You look to me as if you'd recovered your health," Spiletti insisted. "You must be well enough to send us a postcard."

"You don't catch me sending a postcard to you, you tool of the clergy! How happy I am not to have you on my mind!"

"That's no way for a mayor to talk!" Spiletti protested.

"I'm speaking as a free man."

"Well said!" said the other workers, who had left their lunch to gather around Peppone.

"If you want to be free, then resign from your position!" Spiletti shouted.

"Just to please you, eh?" grumbled the workers. "Hold on to it, Comrade!"

"Well, if you're not resigning, we'd like at least to know your intentions."

Peppone shrugged his shoulders.

"If you'd rather have fun in Milan than do the job to which you've been appointed, then you've simply got to give up the job."

"We'll take *your* job away, that's what," threatened the workers. But Peppone turned around.

"Easy, boys," he said authoritatively. "This is a democratic country, and threats don't go."

Meanwhile Brusco, Bigio and the rest of Peppone's henchmen had appeared upon the scene and sat silently down around him.

"Chief," said Brusco sadly, "why did you desert us?"

"I'm not deserting anybody."

"What are we to do about the new road? Here's a letter from the Ministry of Public Works."

And Brusco held out a sheet of paper, which Peppone proceeded to read.

"As long as there's a certain crowd in the government, we'll never get anywhere," he observed.

"Never mind about the national administration!" Spiletti shouted. "It's up to you to make a concrete proposal."

"We made one, long ago," Bigio put in.

"That was just propaganda!" Spiletti shouted. "There was nothing concrete about it."

Smilzo had a word to put in at this point, and so did Peppone. Soon they were in the middle of a heated discussion. Amid the refuse from a demolished building in Milan, they held one of the most unusual village council meetings ever to be seen. When five o'clock came and they were still debating, the night watchman said he must close the gate and send them away. The whole council, including the Opposition, transferred the debate to Peppone's lorry.

"Let's go and find a quieter place," said Peppone, starting up the motor.

There was no telling how it happened, perhaps because none of them knew the layout of the city too well, but soon the lorry was rolling down the highway. Peppone bent with clenched teeth and tense muscles over the wheel. There was something on his mind, which for a long time he had been unable to say. All at once he threw on the brakes. One of those cursed hitch-hikers was standing practically in front of the truck and signalling that he wanted a lift in the same direction. He had a cake and a toy balloon in one hand and a priest's hat on his head. Smilzo got down from the seat beside Peppone and went to sit in the back of the truck, along with the rest of the village council. Don Camillo climbed up to take his place, and Peppone started off with a jolt like that of a tank.

"Do certain people always have to be hanging around?" he grumbled.

The lorry was travelling like a racing car, and the roar coming out of the engine was like the orchestra of Toscanini. All of a sudden, over the crest of the river embankment, they saw the church tower.

"Ah!" Peppone exclaimed ruefully.

" 'Ah' doesn't make the first two letters of 'happy,' " observed Don Camillo.

"Yes, it does, even if the letters aren't in the right order," said a voice that only Don Camillo could hear.

A BALL BOUNCES BACK

WHEN WOMEN GO IN FOR politics they're worse than the most rabid of the men. The men throw their weight around for the sake of "the cause," whereas the women direct all their wiles toward the discomfiture of the enemy. The same difference as there is between defending one's country and going to war in order to kill as many people as possible on the other side.

Jo del Magro was up to her ears in politics, and because of her fiery temperament she did not only her share but that of her husband as well. He died, poor fellow, leaving her with a three-year-old son, but her grief for his loss must have been to some degree compensated by the fact that she ignored the priest and carried him to the grave to the muted notes of the Red anthem.

Jo was good-looking enough, in her way, and could perfectly well have found a second husband to look after her. But she clung obstinately to her hard lot, feeding upon it the embitterment which held the place of faith in her heart. She supported herself by heavy farm work—sowing, reaping, threshing and wine-pressing—in the summer, and in the winter by making reed baskets which she peddled about the country. She worked fiercely, as if weariness were an end in itself and her only satisfaction. And even the boldest men took care not to bother her, because she was not only strong-armed, but had a vocabulary coarse enough to put theirs to shame.

The little boy grew like a weed. When he wasn't left alone in their isolated shack but was allowed to trail after his mother, she set him down in the farmyard where she was working and told him to shut up and "keep out of her hair." When he was five years old he could throw stones as well as a boy of ten and destroy a laden fruit-tree in less than half an hour. He nosed about like a hunting-dog among the chicken coops, leaving a mess of broken eggs behind him; he strewed bits of glass on the roads and perpetrated other tricks of the same kind. His only distinction lay in the fact that he was a lone wolf and preferred to operate on his own rather than to run with the pack. When two gangs of boys were engaged in battle he hid behind a bush or tree and threw stones indiscriminately at both factions. He was anti-social by nature and had an extraordinary ability to disappear from the scene of his misdemeanours. The evening of the grape-gathering festival he let the air out of the tyres of some fifty bicycles and threw the valve caps away. No one could lay hands on him, but everyone was saying:

"It must be that confounded little Magrino!"

A few days later some well-meaning ladies went to call on his mother and tactfully intimated that instead of letting him run wild she should turn him over, during her working hours, to the day nursery. Jo grew red in the face and shouted that rather than give her son over to a priestly institution she'd leave him with certain women whose reputation they knew all too well.

"Tell Don Gumshoe Camillo to look after his own business!" she said, adding a volley of oaths which caused the well-meaning ladies to pull up their skirts and run. Their leader reported the upshot of their visit to Don Camillo, concluding:

"Father, I can't repeat the name that unfortunate creature fastened upon you!"

"I know it already," he answered gloomily.

The weather was fine and the children of Don Camillo's day nursery were out on the playing field most of the afternoon. The swings and see-saws had been restored to good order and even the grumpiest children were all smiles. Don Camillo lay in a deck chair, smoking his cigar and enjoying the warm sun, when he had a sudden feeling that something was wrong.

The playing field bordered, on the river side, on a field of alfalfa, from which it was separated by a galvanized wire fence. Now Don Camillo was struck by an unaccustomed ripple in the alfalfa, and his sportsman's instinct told him that it was neither a dog nor a chicken. He did not move, but half closed his eyes in order to observe without being detected. Slowly something rose out of the grass and Don Camillo felt Magrino's eyes converging upon him. He held his breath while Magrino, feeling sure that he was not watched, transferred his gaze to another objective. He was following the children's game and such was his curiosity that at one point he forgot himself and raised his whole head above the alfalfa. No one noticed, and of this Don Camillo was glad. All of a sudden his head disappeared. A big ball, with which some of the bigger boys were playing, had been kicked over the fence and they called out to ask Don Camillo if they could go and get it. The priest pretended to wake up with a start.

"Is the ball out of bounds again?" he shouted. "I've told you to be more careful. That grass can't be trodden down. No more ball-playing today. You can go and get the ball tomorrow, and meanwhile let me sleep!"

The boys grumbled a bit; then they found another ball and played with that, while Don Camillo pretended to be sleeping. Actually, he was more alert than ever. Ten minutes later the alfalfa stirred again, but this time the line of rippling moved farther and farther away. Magrino was leaving, but he was following an odd course, which for the moment led him to the centre of the alfalfa field.

"He must be cutting across diagonally," thought Don Camillo, "in order to emerge along the hedge parallel to the canal."

Instead, Magrino stopped short and made an abrupt turn to the left. Obviously he had found the ball, picked it up and now was carrying it away.

"Rascal!" muttered Don Camillo. "You've pulled off the trick handsomely. But when you reach the row of trees at the end of the alfalfa you'll have to show yourself!"

But Magrino knew better. When he was out of the tall grass he slid on his stomach until he came to a ditch which ran at right angles to the trees and afforded him perfect cover.

"Lord," Don Camillo murmured, "how can a five-year-old boy have learned to be so tricky?"

"Don Camillo," the Lord answered, "how do fish learn to swim? By instinct, of course."

"Instinct?" Don Camillo exclaimed gloomily. "Are men instinctively evil?"

Don Camillo bought the boys another ball and made no mention of the escapade of Magrino. He hoped that the stolen ball would act like bait and bring Magrino back later. Every day he scanned the field of alfalfa, but there was no ripple. Then someone told him that Magrino was ill and confined to the house. As a matter of fact, Magrino had come down with a fever the night after he had taken the ball. The ditch was full of water, and in crawling through it he was chilled to the bone. Then, before going into the shack he had buried the ball in a hole. His mother came home late, and found him shivering all over. At first it seemed like nothing at all, at least nothing that couldn't be cured with a few pills and a hot-water bottle. Then things took a turn for the worse and one evening he became half delirious. He muttered something over and over, and finally Jo understood him to mention a big rubber ball.

"Don't worry," she said. "Hurry up and get well, and I'll buy a ball for you."

Magrino quieted down, but the next night, when his fever rose again, he resumed his insistence upon the ball.

"Take it easy!" said Jo. "I told you I'd get it as soon as you're well."

"No . . . no . . ."

"Do you want me to get one right away?"

"No . . . no . . . The ball . . ."

Evidently he couldn't take his mind off it. But the doctor said there was no use looking for a meaning in the ravings of a delirious child. And so, on the third night, Jo simply answered:

"All right. . . . Whatever you say. . . ."

He raved until one o'clock when the fever went down sufficiently for him to sleep. Then, at last, the exhausted Jo was able to go to bed.

The next morning at five o'clock Don Camillo stood shaving in front of the mirror hanging from the sash bolt of his window. It was a clear, cool day, and he took his time, looking out over the fields to the row of poplars along the river bank and beyond them the gleaming river. Directly below him lay the playing field, empty and silent at this hour, but soon to be overrun by the day nursery. He smiled to himself at the thought of all the freshly washed little faces.

As his glance fell upon the field of alfalfa and the wire fence, he murmured to himself: "The little rascal! . . ." Then he started as a moving white object caught his attention. Only when it was within a few yards of the fence did he recognize it. It was little Magrino, bundled up in a long white night-shirt, which his father had formerly worn by day, weaving in and out of the tall grass, like a drunkard or a sleepwalker. He stumbled and fell, but stood up again and went on, clutching all the while a big rubber ball. When he reached the fence he threw it up in the air, but the fence was too high and it fell back on the same side. He threw it again and it hit the wire. Don Camillo's forehead was covered with perspiration.

"Lord," he prayed, "give him the strength to throw it over!"

Magrino was tired out and the tiny arms sticking out of the shirtsleeves seemed to have lost all their former skill. He staggered in order to remain erect and paused for several minutes before making another try. Don Camillo shut his eyes, and when he opened them the ball was in the playing field, while Magrino lay motionless among the alfalfa. The priest went like an avalanche down the stairs. When he picked up the little boy the lightness of his burden struck terror into his heart. Magrino's eyes flickered open, and finding himself in the enemy's grasp he whispered:

"Don Gumshoe . . . the ball's inside. . . ."

"Good fellow!" said Don Camillo.

The bell-ringer, who went to tell Jo, found her beside herself over the disappearance of her son. When she saw him lying on a couch before the fire in Don Camillo's study her amazement knew no bounds.

"I found him in a dead faint among the alfalfa, just twenty minutes ago," Don Camillo told her.

"And what in the world was he doing there? My head is completely woozy."

"Always has been, hasn't it?" asked Don Camillo.

The doctor told Jo not to dream of taking the boy away but gave him an injection and left precise instructions for his care. Meanwhile Don Camillo was in the sacristy, preparing for Mass.

"Lord," he said to the Crucified Christ as he stood before the altar, "how did it all happen? After the upbringing that boy's had, how could he know the difference between good and evil?"

"Don Camillo," said Christ, "how do fish learn to swim? By instinct. And conscience is instinctive in the same way; it's not something that can be transmitted from one person to another. It's not like taking a light into a dark room. The light is burning all the time, covered by a thick veil. When you take the veil away, the room is lit."

"Very well, Lord, but who unveiled the light in that boy's soul?"

"Don Camillo, when the darkness of death is impending, everyone instinctively searches within himself for a ray of light. And now, don't you bother your head about how it came about; just rejoice in it and thank God."

Magrino stayed for a fortnight in the rectory and Jo came morning and evening to see him; that is, she knocked at the window and when Don Camillo opened it, she said:

"I've come to see the prisoner."

Don Camillo made no reply but let the two of them talk together. After a fortnight had gone by he came home one day to find Magrino letting the air out of his bicycle tyres. He gathered together the boy's few clothes and took him to the door saying:

"You're cured. Go along home!"

That evening Jo came boldly to the door.

"How much do I owe you?" she asked.

"Nothing. The most that you can do for me is to stay out of my sight for ever, *per omnia saecula saeculorum.*"

"Amen," mumbled Jo.

But out of sheer spite she appeared at eleven o'clock Mass the following Sunday, sitting in the front pew, with Magrino beside her. Don Camillo shot her a terrifying glance, but from the bold way in which she stared back at him he knew perfectly well that she was saying to herself:

"Don Gumshoe, don't make those ferocious eyes at me. I'm not the least bit afraid!"

THE CARD SHARPERS

SMILZO HAD THE POST office job of taking around special delivery letters, and now he braked his bicycle in breakneck Mao Tse-tung style right in front of the sunny bench where Don Camillo was quietly reading his paper.

The method of stopping a bicycle by sliding off the saddle toward the rear and at the same time jerking up the handlebars in such a way as to lift the front wheel off the ground and produce the effect of a bucking bronco had been known until recent years as "Texas Cowboy" style. Now, for obvious political reasons, this reactionary Western name had given way to an appellation from the proletarian and revolutionary East.

Don Camillo raised his eyes and viewed Smilzo's cyclonic arrival distrustfully.

"Does a certain Jesus Christ live here?" Smilzo asked, pulling a letter out of the bag hanging over his shoulder.

"Someone lives here that may give you a swift kick," Don Camillo answered tersely.

"Due respect must be paid to all officials engaged in the public service," said Smilzo. "The address on this Special Delivery letter is: *Jesus Christ, Parish House.* If no such person resides here, then I write: *Unknown at the above address,* and that's all there is to it."

Don Camillo took hold of the letter, and sure enough, the address was just what Smilzo had represented it to be.

"I'll take it," he said. "It will give me grounds for a complaint to the postal authorities. They have no right to encourage such a piece of sacrilegious imbecility."

"The postal authorities are only doing their duty," said Smilzo. "The parish house exists, and they don't have to know who's inside. A man can have anyone in his house he wants to. And the name doesn't matter; it may be an alias for all we care."

Don Camillo bent over with studied indifference and the intention of taking off his shoe to serve as a missile, but Smilzo rode off like a flash, before he could reach it.

The joker who had written the sacrilegious address had added the word *Personal,* and underlined it, and Don Camillo went to give vent to his indignation before the Crucified Christ over the altar.

"Lord," he exclaimed, "won't You tell me who pulled off this disgraceful trick? Won't You enable me to go and wring his neck and force him to eat the letter?"

"Don Camillo," Christ answered with a smile, "we must respect the privacy of the mails. We can't go against the principles of the Constitution."

"Then, Lord, are we to allow these fellows to blaspheme You with the written word as well as the spoken one?"

"How do you know that the author of the letter is a blasphemer?" Christ asked. "Mightn't he be a simple-minded man or a mad one? You'd better read it before you condemn him."

Don Camillo threw out his arms in resignation, tore open the envelope and took out a sheet of paper with words printed in capital letters upon it, which he read slowly to himself.

"Well, Don Camillo? Is it as dreadful as you imagined?"

"No, Lord; it's the work of a madman, who deserves only compassion."

Don Camillo stuffed the letter into his pocket and started to go away, but Christ called him back.

"What does this madman ask of Me, Don Camillo?"

"Nothing in particular. His letter's a mass of chaotic sentences, with no order or meaning."

"All well and good, but you mustn't pass such a quick judgment upon the expression of a troubled mind. Madness has a logic all its own, and the understanding of this leads to a discovery of the cause of the trouble."

"Oh, the trouble is a vague sort of affair," said Don Camillo hurriedly. "It's impossible to understand it."

"Read it to Me, Don Camillo."

Don Camillo shrugged his shoulders in resignation, drew the letter out of his pocket and read it aloud.

"Lord, I beg you to illuminate the mind of a certain priest and convey to him that he is carrying his political activity too far. In fact, if he carries it much farther, he may find his hind quarters in contact with a hickory stick. To exercise the priesthood by vocation is one thing, and by provocation is another. Signed—A friend of democracy."

"What priest do you suppose he means?" Christ asked at the end of the letter.

"I haven't the slightest idea," said Don Camillo.

"Do you know any priest who carries his political activity too far?"

"Lord, I get around so very little. . . . All the priests in this part of the country are quiet, well-balanced fellows. . . ."

"What about yourself, Don Camillo?"

"Lord, we were speaking of priests in this part of the country. If the letter had referred to me, it would have said 'the local priest,' or 'the priest of this parish,' instead of 'a certain priest.' As You so rightly remarked, madness has a logic all its own, and I am trying to reason along the lines of this logic."

"Don Camillo," Christ sighed, "why are you trying to keep the truth from Me? Why don't you admit that you are the priest in question?"

"Lord, do You pin Your faith on poison-pen letters and anonymous accusations?"

"No, Don Camillo, but I'd pin My faith on any accusation you care to make against yourself."

"Lord, the election is very near, and we're waging an important battle. I must be loyal to the parish priest. I can tell him to be careful, but I can't bring any accusation against him."

"You mean you'll advise him to keep his hind quarters out of contact with a stick, is that it?"

"No, Lord, I'm concerned not with my body but with my soul."

With which Don Camillo went to meditate in his study, and as a result the next day Smilzo brought a Special Delivery letter to Peppone.

"What are we to do with this, Chief?" he asked.

Peppone saw that the address on the envelope was: *Mr. Malenkov, People's Palace*. Undaunted, he took out the letter and read the printed text:

"Mr. Malenkov, please inform your follower known as 'a friend of democracy' that his interesting letter will be photographed for reproduction in the local reactionary press. Gratefully yours. A Certain Priest."

Peppone turned purple with anger, but Smilzo calmed him down.

"Chief, you'll just have to take it and let the whole thing blow over. He's manoeuvred himself into a favourable position."

"He's got himself out of range of a hickory stick," roared Peppone, bringing his massive fist down on the desk. "But if I beat him up with a branch of elm or acacia, then no one will suspect me."

"Naturally, Chief. There are dozens of ways you can get the better of him, without giving yourself away by the use of hickory. All nature is on the People's side!"

The publication of the letter aroused considerable talk and everyone accused the Reds of its authorship. In self-defence Peppone decided to relax the general tension by organizing a "Poker Tournament for the Peace Crusade." In this part of the world, which is cut off by the winter fog from the rest of humanity, poker is not so much a game as it is a vital necessity and a tournament of this kind, even if it was organized under the shadow of the wings of Stalin's Peace Dove, was bound to be a success.

Tournament headquarters was set up at the Molinetto tavern, which was filled every evening with people of every class and condition. The match grew more and more exciting as poor players were eliminated and undisputed experts held the field. At last it came to a final showdown, which brought two champions face to face. Don Camillo informed Christ of the latest developments.

"Lord, this evening brings the last round. Everyone's excited, because as always happens in these parts, politics has entered the situation. I shouldn't be surprised if fists were to fly before the evening's over."

"How does that happen, Don Camillo?"

"Lord, politics has a way of changing the aspect of everything it touches, and so the last round of the tournament has turned into a duel between the People's champion and the champion of Reaction. The finalists are Farmer Filotti and Peppone. If Filotti wins, then it is a victory for Reaction, and if, instead, Peppone manages to beat him, then the proletariat will rejoice."

"This is all very silly," said Christ. "What interests are tied up in this game?"

"It's just a matter of prestige. Foolish, if you like, but in politics it makes a big difference. Anyhow, we're certain to be defeated. I say 'we' because the Reds are our natural enemies. But it had to end this way. Peppone isn't coming up against our best player. Filotti may be good, but he's not our top man. And Peppone's such a schemer that he's not above pulling off some funny business with the cards. Now, it may be blasphemous to speak of 'Justice' in something so frivolous as a game of poker. But, if I may be allowed to say so, it's unjust that victory should go to someone who doesn't deserve it. . . ."

"Don't take it too hard, Don Camillo," Christ interrupted. "You said yourself that it's a frivolous matter. As a matter of fact, all such games are bad for a man, even if they are playing for nothing more than fun. Card-playing is a vice, just like everything else that serves merely to kill time."

"Of course," said Don Camillo, with a bow. "But if it's legitimate to draw up a scale of values among all these vicious games, I should say that poker was the least harmful of the lot, because it's based on reason and provides mental gymnastics as well as wholesome reaction."

"Don Camillo, you talk like a real fan."

"No, just like someone that knows the game. Like a very mediocre player, but one that could beat three Peppones to a frazzle. . . . But of course it's unthinkable for a priest to mingle with card-players in a tavern, even if he is motivated by a noble desire to prevent a leader of godlessness from carrying off an undeserved victory."

"Quite right," Christ answered. "A priest must never set foot in a tavern simply in order to take part in some petty game. Priests serve the King of Heaven, not the kings of clubs and diamonds."

It was late by now, and Don Camillo started off to bed. Meanwhile the crowded Molinetto tavern was the scene of the final battle. Peppone was in good form; indeed, he seemed to have a calculating machine in place of his brain. The last game won him deafening applause. Filotti threw his cards down on the table and called for a glass of white wine.

"Let's have a drink on it," he said. "There's nothing else I can do."

Peppone was the winner and the Reds were so wild with joy that they began to shout for a speech. Amid general silence Peppone took the floor.

"Comrades! In the battle of sport as well as the battle of labour, the working man must win. This victorious tournament, played under the auspices of . . ."

But at this point he stopped short, because someone was knocking at the window which gave on to the street. Smilzo prudently opened it, and there behind the grating was the face of Don Camillo. There was a dramatic silence.

"What do you want?" Peppone asked threateningly.

"I want to play," answered Don Camillo.

"To play? Play with whom?"

"Anyone that's not afraid to play with me."

Peppone shot him a pitying glance.

"I'm not afraid of anybody. But the tournament is over. If you wanted to play, you should have signed up for it."

"I did sign up," Don Camillo explained. "If you look at the list, you'll find a registration under the name of *Il Calmo*, or 'The Calm Man.' "

"That doesn't mean anything," retorted Peppone. "Anyone can come along and claim to have signed up under that name."

"No, because *Il Calmo* is an anagram for 'Camillo.' "

"This isn't an anagram contest or a Latin lesson; it's a serious card game."

Don Camillo explained the nature of an anagram, and after Peppone had counted the letters he had to admit that Camillo and *Il Calmo* came to the same thing.

"Of course if His Honour the Mayor is afraid of coming a cropper, then I'll go away."

"Come on in," shouted Peppone.

"I can't do that," said Don Camillo; "it wouldn't be proper. I'll stay here and we'll play on the windowsill."

"That may be a good idea," said Peppone. "You'll feel safer that way."

Don Camillo grasped two bars of the grating in his hands and twisted them back.

"That makes it more convenient," he explained, "but if the fresh air bothers you, you can fix it the way it was before."

"It does bother me," said Peppone, grasping the bars and pulling them back into their original position.

The crowd had never seen a more formidable sight. People held their breath the way they do at the circus when two tightrope walkers advance to the roll of drums. Peppone took a pack of cards and laid it on the windowsill; Don Camillo picked it up and shook his head.

"These are too thin and frail for a temperament like mine," he objected. And taking the pack in his big hands, he tore it in two. Peppone paled, and Smilzo came up with another pack of cards.

"Will this do?" asked Peppone.

"No," said Don Camillo.

"I don't like it myself," said Peppone, picking up the pack and mangling it in exactly the same way.

Someone offered them a third pack.

"It has to be brand new and in its original wrapping," Don Camillo insisted. "Trust is all very well, but mistrust is better."

Smilzo brought out a pack of cards still wrapped and sealed in cellophane paper, which Peppone examined carefully and then handed to Don Camillo.

"I'm satisfied," he said. "What about you?"

"It's all right with me," said Don Camillo, turning the cards over in his hands and giving them back to Peppone. "Go ahead and shuffle, but keep your hands out of mischief."

Peppone gritted his teeth, shuffled the cards and laid them on the windowsill.

"The tournament's over, and I won it," he said. "The Cup goes to the Party, and no one can take it away. But in order to make this a good game and lend it some social significance, I'll put up my shotgun as stakes. What about you?"

A murmur went through the room. Peppone's gun was the finest for miles around and everyone knew how he prized it. He would have cut off a leg rather than give up that precious gun. Everyone waited for Don Camillo to make a fitting reply. And it did not disappoint them.

"I'll put up my dog!" he said boldly. And everyone knew that the dog was the apple of Don Camillo's eye.

The game that followed was of an epic character. If Homer's heroes had played poker they would have played it in just the same way. The two men fought with all their wits until the bitter end, and Don Camillo won. No one dared applaud him. Finally Don Camillo tipped his hat.

"Thanks for the good game, and good-night. Gambling debts are due within twenty-four hours."

Don Camillo went straight to the rectory, without passing through the church, but Christ's voice overtook him.

"At this late hour, Don Camillo!"

"I went to look in at the last round of the tournament. But I didn't set foot in the tavern; I stayed just outside the window. And just as I thought, Peppone was the winner."

"Did that cause any trouble?"

"No, everything went smoothly, and there was general agreement that the best man won."

"Don Camillo, this game of poker interests me. I gather from what you say, that is must be played with a pack of brand-new cards, in their original wrapping."

"That's a wise precaution, especially if you're playing with nimble-fingered fellows who may connive with the tavern-keeper to use marked cards."

"I see. So a pack of new cards is brought out; the first player examines it and passes it to the second, who then slips it into his pocket and puts in its place another identical pack, inconspicuously marked with his thumb-nail and rewrapped in the original paper. Isn't that the system?"

"Oh, I wouldn't put it that way," said Don Camillo.

"Then what have you got in your pocket?"

"I can't imagine how in the world it got there," stammered Don Camillo, pulling out a pack of new cards and laying it on the table.

"Peppone gave it to you and you slipped his pack into your pocket and gave him another pack which you had brought with you."

"Obviously there was a mix-up of some kind," said Don Camillo.

"Yes, you mixed up right and wrong, and added to the immorality of a gambling game. But you're the real loser, Don Camillo."

Don Camillo was wiping the perspiration off his forehead when Peppone came into the room. He took his famous shotgun out from under his coat and handed it over.

"Gambling debts are paid promptly," he said, "but if you're an honest man, you'll give me a chance for revenge."

Then he noticed the pack of cards on the table.

"This is luck," he added. "Here's a brand-new pack, which guarantees a fair game. Open it and shuffle the cards."

They sat down at the table and Don Camillo opened the pack and shuffled. The game was just as Homeric in character as the one that had gone before, but this time Peppone won.

"Shall we play a third game to break the tie?" he suggested.

Don Camillo did not answer, because he was fingering the cards.

"Aha!" he said all of a sudden. "So you mark the ace like this, do you?"

Peppone did not blench. He pulled another pack of cards out of his pocket and searched for the seven.

"And your mark is these two fine lines, isn't it?" he countered.

Don Camillo picked up Peppone's pack and threw it on to the fire. And Peppone did the same thing with Don Camillo's.

"Well, we're even," said Peppone as he got up to leave.

"No," said Don Camillo; "I'm the loser."

And he said it so sorrowfully that Peppone was touched.

"Father, don't take it too hard. In a game of poker the prospect of winning addles a man's brain and he can't help himself. I'll lend you my gun to go hunting, and you can lend me your dog in return. How about it?"

After Peppone had gone, Don Camillo stared into the fire.

"Don Camillo, I said that you were in the service of the King of Heaven, not of the kings of clubs and diamonds. You ought to be ashamed!"

Don Camillo threw out his arms, raised his eyes to heaven and exclaimed:

"Lord, I know I'm in the wrong. But you heard what he said about the game and how it addles a man's brain."

Then something caught Don Camillo's eye. It was Peppone's pack and the flames of the fire were just beginning to curl round it. In a moment it would be too late to find out how an expert like Peppone marked the kings and queens.

Christ sighed.

"Don Camillo, who's going to save you from burning in Hell?"

Don Camillo did not answer, but he sat quite still and did not go up to bed until the glowing coals had turned to ashes.

HUNGER STRIKE

SMILZO'S MOTHER HAD paralysed legs, but she also had a head on her shoulders, and even though she had been confined to a chair for five or six years, she knew exactly what was going on. When she was present Smilzo and his wife didn't dare talk politics, but she had a keen ear and heard much of what they didn't even say. They thought they had everything under control but a few days after their son was born the old woman came out and said:

"It's time to baptize him."

Smilzo was taken by surprise and stood there gaping, but his wife jumped into the breach.

"There's no hurry," she said. "Let's wait at least until this cold spell is over."

The old woman said nothing, but two days later she attacked again.

"Well, is he going to be baptized or isn't he?"

With the passage of time she became more and more insistent, and finally Smilzo screwed up his courage to say: "Don't let's hear any more talk about this business of baptism. Times have changed in a great many ways that you don't know."

The old woman shook her head. "From the day when Jesus Christ started his business of baptism, times have changed over and over and any number of things have happened, but newborn babies have always been baptized."

Smilzo muttered something about political parties and excommunications but the old woman knew what she was talking about and stuck to it.

"Newborn babies aren't party members. And so they've got to be baptized."

Smilzo repeated that she didn't understand, but she went on shaking her head.

"I understand perfectly well. Your father was worse than you are when it comes to political notions, but you were baptized shortly after you were born."

"Things were different in those days," Smilzo's wife exclaimed.

"And wives were different too!" retorted the old woman.

"Wives were different? What do you mean? What have you got against me?"

"The fact that you're a silly girl!"

"All right, then," the wife shouted. "I won't have my baby baptized for certain. If when he's older he feels like being baptized, then he can do something about it."

The old woman looked at her son, but he failed to agree with her.

"It's putting something over on children to baptize them when they don't know what it's all about," he mumbled.

"Very well," said the old woman. "From now on, I'm not eating. I shan't eat until the baby's been baptized."

"You'll starve for years, then," said her daughter-in-law with a mocking laugh.

Smilzo said nothing, but brought his fist down on the table and went out of the house.

The next day the old woman did not drink her usual cup of milk for breakfast and at noon she sat quietly in her chair, watching the others eat their lunch. It was the same thing at supper, and finally Smilzo lost his patience.

"You've behaved quite long enough like a spoiled child," he said. "Go ahead and eat, instead of trying to upset me."

"She'll eat when she's hungry," his wife reassured him. But another day went by in the same way, and the daughter-in-law began to be worried.

"We must call the doctor," she said, "tell him what's happened and have her taken away. Otherwise, if she dies of starvation, we'll be blamed for it. Can't you see her little game? She wants to ruin our reputation."

At this point the old woman spoke up.

"Give me pen and paper and I'll write down that I'm dying of my own free will. I'm not trying to ruin your reputation; I simply want to save my grandson's soul."

Smilzo's wife had an attack of nerves and began sobbing: "She hates me! I won't have any milk for the baby if she goes on this way."

"What of it?" said the old woman. "Snake's milk won't do him any good."

Smilzo ran out of the house in despair. But he could just as well have stayed at home, because the old woman did not open her mouth to speak again. The third day she chose to stay in bed.

"I'd rather die in this position," she explained. "Please call the priest."

"No!" shouted her daughter-in-law. "No!"

"It doesn't really matter," said the old woman. "God will listen to me just the same."

"You'll die with a curse upon you!" shouted her daughter-in-law. "It's a clear-cut case of suicide, because you won't eat."

"No, you've prevented me from eating by refusing to have the baby baptized."

She closed her eyes and sank back on the pillows, while her daughter-in-law withdrew uneasily. Smilzo had been listening just outside the door.

"Something must be done in a hurry," he said.

"Are you going to give in to the priests?" his wife panted. "They've thrown you out of the Church and you ask them to baptize your son? That doesn't go very well with the beliefs you profess in public."

"Take it easy!" said Smilzo. "We've got to find a way to kill two birds with one stone. I'm going to see Peppone."

Peppone was in his workshop when Smilzo burst in upon him.

"Chief, you've got to help me. I'm in hot water." He proceeded to tell his thorny story and concluded: "Chief, I don't want to betray my political principles, but I can't let my mother die. Suppose I get a fancy, lace-trimmed baptismal dress; you put on your best clothes and come for us in your car. We'll have the baby all rigged out in white and show him to his grandmother, with you in a godfather's role. We'll drive to the People's Palace, sneak in through the courtyard, drink a bottle of wine and then go back and say to my mother: 'Here he is, fresh from the font, just as you wanted!' Then she'll start eating again and my conscience will be clear."

"I see," said Peppone. "But what if she ever finds out?"

"She won't," said Smilzo curtly. "And the main thing just now is to get her to eat."

Peppone shrugged but agreed to co-operate and while Smilzo went to buy a robe he put on his best clothes. Half an hour later they were at Smilzo's house. The house was in a lonely spot and there was a heavy fog in the air, both of them favourable circumstances. Smilzo's wife ran to wake up the old woman.

"If you really don't want to ruin our reputation, then get up for a minute. The baby's godfather is here."

"His godfather?" exclaimed the old woman, opening her eyes wide.

"Yes, the mayor himself, who's honoured us by consenting to present him for baptism."

Voices rang out downstairs, and the old woman pulled herself into an upright position and threw a shawl around her shoulders.

"Where's the baby?" she asked.

"They're dressing him now."

"Is he fitted out properly?"

"You'll soon see."

There was a knock at the door, and Smilzo came in, carrying the baby wrapped in the most elaborate outfit that can be imagined. Behind this dazzling white vision was the massive figure of Peppone. But the old woman had eyes only for the baby.

"What a little beauty!" she sobbed, raising her gaunt hands as if before some miraculous apparition.

Even the mother was amazed to see her child in such festive array. She snatched him out of Smilzo's arms in order to smooth out the pleats and straighten the bows of the baptismal robe and put the cap at the proper angle on the tiny pink head.

"How are you?" Peppone asked the old woman.

At last she managed to take her eyes off the baby and look at Peppone.

"What an honour you are paying us, Mr. Mayor!" she exclaimed, grasping one of his big paws. "God bless you! I know it's thanks to you that my son came around to reason. But never mind about that; it's all over. . . ."

Peppone tried to free his hand, but she held it in an iron grasp.

"Don't say that!" he replied. "Your son doesn't need advice from anybody. He's a fine man. And the honour of being his child's godfather is all mine. . . . But tell me how you are feeling."

"Splendid, thank you," she answered. "I had a touch of flu, just like everyone else this winter, but I'm quite well now."

"Take good care of yourself!" Peppone admonished her in an authoritative tone. And after this he could find nothing else to say.

"We must hurry along," put in Smilzo. "The priest is waiting."

The old woman insisted on looking at the baby again and laid a finger on his forehead.

"He's smiling!" said Peppone. "Seems as if he knew you already."

The baby had clutched the old woman's hand and for a moment he would not let go.

"He wants me to come along," she sighed, "but I'm in no condition to go. When I hear the church bells ring I'll be happy."

"You may not hear them at all," mumbled her daughter-in-law nervously. "There's fog outside so thick you could cut it with a knife."

"I've a keen ear, and besides, I'll open the window," the old woman answered, smiling.

In the bar of the People's Palace, there was no one but Bigio, who was engaged in going over some accounts. He was startled to see Peppone and Smilzo come in, bearing the decked-out baby.

"Pull down the blinds," said Peppone, "and bring us a bottle of dry white wine."

Bigio brought the bottle of wine and three glasses.

"Aren't you having a drink too?" asked Smilzo.

"Well, there are three of us, aren't there? And I've brought three glasses."

"What about the fourth?" asked Smilzo, pointing with a laugh at the white bundle on the table.

"I don't get it," Bigio said.

"A proletarian baptism!" explained Smilzo, raising his glass. "To the health of a new comrade!"

Bigio and Peppone drained their glasses. Then, while Peppone told Bigio what it was all about, Smilzo dipped his finger into the wine and held it up to the baby's lips.

"Look how he sucks it!" he said proudly. "It's plain he'll grow up to be a very fine fellow!"

The others made no answer, and Smilzo drank down another glass of wine. For several minutes he was absorbed in his thoughts, but finally he said:

"The church bells! She wanted to hear them ringing!"

Just then the church bells actually rang, and the three men jumped as if in the presence of something supernatural.

"Oh yes," said Bigio. "Today they were going to baptize the chemist's baby." Smilzo gave a roar of joy.

"She wanted to hear the church bells, did she? Well, there they are! What luck!"

The bundle on the table began to wriggle and Peppone touched the baby's warm, rosy forehead with his enormous hand. The baby took hold of his middle finger and would not let it go. Peppone reflected that a short time before the baby had held his grandmother's old hand in the same way. Now the baby held fast again. Meanwhile Smilzo drank a third glass of wine.

"We can go home now," he said, slamming the empty glass down on the table.

Peppone and Bigio did not move.

"Ring down the curtain!" said Smilzo. "The play is over, and I'm a perfect swine."

Peppone and Bigio had never heard what the Party calls confession couched in such very honest and appropriate terms.

"Go to it, Bigio," said Peppone, "and make it snappy."

And Bigio was off like a shot.

"What's this?" asked Don Camillo, going over to the baptismal font.

"My son!" said Smilzo, straightening the ribbons which stuck out of the bundle on Peppone's arm.

"Poor boy!" sighed Don Camillo. "Couldn't he have chosen a better father?"

The baby was in good form by now and proceeded to grasp Don Camillo's middle finger. "Brat!" Don Camillo said severely. "Are you trying to take other people's belongings away from them so soon?"

Smilzo wanted to say something, but Don Camillo drowned out his voice.

"Silence! As you know, no convinced Communist can serve as a godfather. Are you a convinced Communist, Peppone?"

"No sir!" said Peppone.

"God only knows whether you are telling the truth, and He'll call you to account for it on Judgment Day."

After the ceremony was over and Peppone had gone out to the car, in which

Bigio was waiting before the church, Smilzo went up to Don Camillo.

"How much do I owe you for your trouble?" he asked.

"Nothing. You too can settle your accounts with God Almighty."

Smilzo looked at him with mistrust.

"You won't get my next baby, though!" he said defiantly.

"The future is in God's hands, my son!" said Don Camillo, throwing out his arms. "But get out of here in a hurry, because the present might be in my feet!"

This was a theory just like any other. But Smilzo knew the size and strength of Don Camillo's feet and so he took it into due consideration.

PEPPONE GOES BACK TO SCHOOL

PEPPONE DECIDED TO GO all out against clerical interference in the primary schools, and an announcement to this effect came out in the bulletin nailed to the wall of the People's Palace. In it was the proposal that a supervisory committee be set up and empowered to visit the schools at any time to make sure that the teaching was in accord with democratic principles.

Of course, the next day, the bulletin of the Opposition printed a reply:

"We don't for a moment criticize our Mayor for the fact that he never finished school. We believe that ideas are much more important than good grammar. But for purposes of the present discussion we must note that it seems singularly inappropriate for primary instruction to be in the hands of someone who never finished his own. Let the Mayor hand over this job to Smilzo, who stayed two years in first grade and three years in both second and third, thus acquiring considerably more experience in the field of education."

This piece caused considerable talk in the village, and Don Camillo made a copy of it which he took to read to the Christ over the altar.

"I am still of the same opinion," Christ told him. "This was written by a man just as stupid as the one who pencilled the word 'Donkey!' on the margin of some other declaration by Peppone."

"But, Lord," Don Camillo objected, "this is an entirely different matter. Isn't it stupid of a man with one leg to insist on entering a race?"

"Don Camillo, you're not playing fair! A man with only one leg can't acquire another in its place, but a man who doesn't know grammar can always learn it. If you know the person who wrote these words, tell him that they are very stupid."

"I'll try to explain," said Don Camillo, throwing out his arms, "but it's going to be uphill work, because he honestly believes he's in the right."

"He can't honestly believe that, when he's out of harmony with God's law. You know that perfectly well, because I've told you."

"Don Camillo is always in hot water," the priest sighed.

Peppone couldn't take the counter-attack lying down, and so he brought out another broadside:

"We can confidantly state that if our unknown adversary were to look after his priestly affairs instead of the affairs of other people, it would be a very good thing. There are two kinds of ignorance: the ignorance of those who for obvious reasons have not been able to continue their schooling and that of persons like the ignorant priest in question, who has studied a great deal but learned nothing. He reminds us of a shiny copper pot, with a hole in the bottom, looking down at a tarnished old pot, which is obviously much more serviceable for cooking."

This was only the beginning, and the rest was couched in much grosser terms. When Don Camillo went to kneel in front of the altar, Christ asked him if he had read Peppone's new innuendo.

"Yes, Lord."

"And have you resisted the temptation to reply?"

"Yes, Lord."

"Will you be able to keep up your resistance?"

Don Camillo threw out his arms.

"The future is in God's hands," he answered.

"But the draft of your reply is in your right hand pocket, and so in this case the future is in the hands of Don Camillo."

Don Camillo took the sheet of paper out of his pocket and burned it in the flame of a candle.

"The election is just around the corner," he observed, "and to my mind these are mistaken tactics, from a political point of view."

"That may be, Don Camillo. But don't worry about the election. I'm not for or against any ticket. I won my battle a long time ago."

When Peppone was beside himself with political passion, he proceeded with about as much delicacy as a Sherman tank, and so, naturally enough, this piece of prose which began with the famous "confidantly" was full of errors. People laughed immoderately at it, even without any instigation on the part of Don Camillo, and Peppone's pride was deeply injured. He tried throwing a few punches around and received a few from persons upon whom he had not inflicted any, but he was aware that this did not alter the situation and that his grammar was just as stumbling as ever. And so he dropped the fight for a supervisory committee and fastened his energies upon the fulfilment of a very ambitious dream. No one except his wife knew anything about it. Every evening, when he set off on his motorcycle, she gave an anxious sigh, and toward midnight, when he returned she immediately asked:

"How did you do?"

"It's hard going, but I'll make it."

This went on for three and a half months, until one night, upon his return from the mysterious trip, Peppone announced:

"This is it! I'm taking the plunge!"

"What if you don't succeed?"

"I must, that's all."

"Think how those wretched people will laugh if you fail. Couldn't you do it in the city, where nobody knows you and if you don't make the grade, it doesn't matter?"

"No, if I did it anywhere else, they'd say there was something tricky or dishonest about it. It's got to be done in the light of day, with everything legal. I'm putting in an application tomorrow."

"Well, be sure not to make any mistakes in the application!"

"You don't need to worry about that," Peppone reassured her. "I've got the application all ready. They typed it up for me in the city!"

"I, Giuseppe Bottazzi, etc., etc., respectfully ask permission of the Board of Education to take the eighth-grade examinations . . ."

The bomb burst with a noise almost atomic in intensity, and Smilzo ran to Peppone's house with his eyes popping out of his head.

"Chief, people are saying that you want to take the eighth-grade examinations!"

"Well, what's so remarkable about it?"

"Chief, the eighth grade is tough!"

"Good! 'Live dangerously!' must be our motto."

"Chief, if you fail, you're a goner!"

"Verdi failed at the Conservatory, and then did pretty well."

In the face of such confidence, Smilzo could find nothing to say. With all the nonchalance of a gentleman flicking an ash off the end of his cigarette, Peppone added:

"If I haven't got an inferiority complex, why should you have one?"

This was the last straw. If Peppone knew the meaning of an inferiority complex, then he must be up to his ears in culture.

"Chief," Smilzo stammered, "have you been studying all these months? It must have cost you an awful lot of money?"

"Why? I took a cramming course at a night school in the city, for adults and children together. At the desk next to mine there was a twelve-year-old boy called Mario Bibelli, a little fellow that didn't come up to my shoulder. He'll pay me a visit here some Sunday."

"Amazing!" exclaimed Smilzo. "It sounds like an old-fashioned, romantic novel."

"Reality is the true romanticism of both yesterday and today," said Peppone didactically. "Both De Amicis and De Sica are neo-realists, even if the former did his writing a century ago."

Smilzo went away completely convinced of one thing: Peppone had turned into an intellectual.

"It wouldn't surprise me if he were to write for some literary magazine," he said to Brusco, Bigio and the rest of Peppone's henchmen. "This is going to be a bitter pill for some people to swallow."

It was a bitter pill for Don Camillo, who was burning up with eagerness to talk to Peppone and size up his new education. Peppone seemed to be avoiding him, and this exasperated his curiosity all the further. Finally he did get hold of him, by means of a personal visit to the workshop. Peppone greeted him with gentlemanly indifference.

"What can I do for you?" he asked.

"I was just passing by," said Don Camillo, "and wanted to inquire about the health of our mayor."

"There's no mayor here. Here you have only Giuseppe Bottazzi, the blacksmith, descendant of the blacksmith of the same name who brought the family to this village several centuries ago and was beheaded because he stripped a priest of his ill-gotten gains. There's the nemesis of history for you!"

"The nemesis of history? How do you mean?" asked Don Camillo in utter astonishment.

"I mean that maybe this time there'll be a different ending and Giuseppe Bottazzi will not only strip the priest of his ill-gotten gains, but kill him!"

"Ill-gotten gains? But I have no more money than a jumping jack-rabbit!"

"I'm not speaking of money. You've captured the confidence of a great many ignorant people, and we shall take it away!"

The conversation was taking an unpleasant turn, but Don Camillo swallowed his pride for the sake of acquiring further information.

"What will be, will be," he said. "How about the examinations?"

"Trifles!" answered Peppone. "The important examination is the one I take every day with this hammer and anvil. And I pass it, time after time."

As Don Camillo was going away he saw Peppone's wife at the door.

"Did you come to rag him?" she said aggressively. "It's eating you up, isn't it, that you can't brand him as someone that never got through school?"

"No," said Don Camillo. "But it's still too early to say. We'll see what happens when he's put to the test."

Don Camillo went home in a gloomy state of mind.

"Lord," he said to the Christ over the altar, "that poor fellow is so swollen with pride that he deserves to fail every single subject."

"I don't know about that, Don Camillo. I'm not on the examination committee. That's for them to decide."

"God is everywhere," objected Don Camillo, "and He'll be in the schoolroom where that country bumpkin comes to make a fool of himself."

"Certainly, Don Camillo, God is everywhere. Right now He's here listening to the stupid things you are saying."

Don Camillo threw out his arms in discouragement.

"For some time now, I haven't been able to say the right thing!"

The matter of examining Mayor Peppone was a headache to the Board of Education. Things had to be conducted with such scrupulous care that no one could find an excuse for saying that either success or failure was due to the candidate's political office or party affiliation. A special commission was made up of the board's director and two teachers from another township, one a stiff, elderly woman and the other, a middle-aged man. Peppone was in a radiant mood, with no doubts at all as to his ability to get through. When he received notice that the examinations would be held the next day he burst out with:

"It's about time! I was beginning to be thoroughly bored."

He went to bed in a good humour and got up in one that was even better. Immediately he put on his best suit, filled his fountain-pen, tested it on a piece of paper and started to leave the house.

"I'll go with you as far as the school," his wife suggested.

"Don't let's be silly about it!" said Peppone.

"Your son insists on going," she told him.

"Don't make me look ridiculous; I'd seem like a schoolboy, and all those wretched people will be staring out their windows at me."

And so Peppone went off alone, but when he reached the school, his wife and son were already there, lurking behind a hedge, all red in the face from having run across the fields to beat him. As he started up the steps into the schoolhouse, they waved to him and he waved back at them with his hand hidden halfway down his back. The commission welcomed him with icy politeness.

"Sit down," said the director. "You will have written examinations in arithmetic and composition. Remember that the allotted time is four hours."

Then they set before him four sheets of officially stamped examination paper, two for a rough copy and two for the finished product.

"Shall we begin?" asked the director, after Peppone had sat down and taken out his pen.

"By all means," said Peppone.

"Then take this down: 'Problem: A cement basin of parallelepiped form has a base 40 by 60 centimetres in size and is fed by two taps. The first tap pours in 8 litres of water a minute and the second tap 5 litres of water every other minute. In thirty minutes the flow from the second tap alone fills two-fifths of the basin. How long will it take to fill the whole basin if both taps are open? How high is the basin?' "

As Peppone diligently wrote down the problem, he noticed that his hand had begun to tremble. "I shouldn't have done so much hammering last night," he said to himself. "It has tired my hand." Meanwhile the director told him to shift to another sheet of paper and take down the composition theme set for him by the woman teacher.

"Theme: Narrate some event, either recent or long ago, which made a strong impression upon you."

Peppone took this down with some difficulty, for his hand continued to tremble. Then he ran a handkerchief over his perspiring forehead. He looked over the two sheets, and reread the arithmetic problem. A parallelepiped—what the devil was that? Two minutes earlier, he had known perfectly well, but now it had gone out of his head completely. The tap whose flow sufficed to fill two-thirds of the basin filled him with confusion. What could be meant by two-fifths of a parallelepiped? And what about the other tap, which poured in water continuously?

His head was empty, as he looked again at the theme for a composition. What was an event? What events had he witnessed, and how could he tell the story of any one of them? He thought back to his night school classes and tried to fish out of his memory some of all that he had heard there in the last three and a half months. But not a single word could he recapture. Then he thought of his wife and son waiting for him outside, and there was an ache in his heart.

The three examiners sat around a table at the far end of the room, as stiff as statues. Peppone wiped the perspiration off his brow. The clock in the church tower rang ten. How perfectly terrible! He looked out the window to make sure he had heard correctly. Yes, the hands were pointing to ten, and so were those of the clock in the schoolroom. He had barely written down the questions, and it was ten o'clock already. And those damned taps were still pouring water into the damned parallelepiped!

The old charwoman brought the news to the rectory.

"Father, I saw him with my own eyes. He's been staring for a whole hour and a half at the paper, and perspiring as if he had a high fever. Not a single word has he written!"

Don Camillo listened to her with satisfaction.

"That's what he gets for being so stuck-up," he exclaimed.

"He looked just like a schoolboy," the old gossip continued. "He came up the road alone, but he got his wife and son to walk along parallel to him, behind the hedge. They met him at the schoolhouse door and waved good-bye."

With that the charwoman went away, promising to come back later. She came at eleven o'clock, even more excited than before.

"Things are still exactly the same," she reported. "He's still perspiring, and still staring at the paper. In two more hours, time will be up. His wife and child are still hiding behind the hedge. She's chewed up half a handkerchief, she's so nervous. Father, I only wish you could see the state that big bully is in now!"

And Don Camillo thought he had every right to see the big bully brought so low.

The two strokes of half-past eleven rang out, and Peppone was thinking that he had only an hour and a half more. Just then the charwoman came to call the director. The director went out into the hall and met Don Camillo.

"Excuse me," said the priest, "but even if the mayor is playing schoolboy he can't neglect his municipal duties. There's a poor woman who may die if he doesn't sign the papers authorizing her immediate removal to a city hospital." And he held out a sheet of paper, adding: "Will you give it to him?"

"That's not regular," the director stammered.

"I know, but it would be still more irregular for a poor woman to die simply in order not to disturb an examination. I don't think this will upset your examinee."

The director shrugged his shoulders.

"Father," he said in a low voice, "it's positively nerve-wracking: all he's done is perspire!"

Don Camillo smiled.

"All these boys are the same way. Outside school they go in for a lot of big talk, but in class . . ."

The director took the sheet of paper and started to go back into the classroom. Then he changed his mind.

"Father, I'll send him out here and let you give it to him in person. I'll leave the door open."

Don Camillo glimpsed the sad state of Peppone and calmly waited for him. Meanwhile after Peppone had heard what the director had to say, he slowly got up and came out into the hall.

"Forgive me, Mr. Mayor," said Don Camillo, "but it's an urgent matter."

Peppone took the sheet of paper and read: "I, Angiolina Pateri, widow, without means of support, state as follows . . ."

"I've already told you that I can't do anything for her," he said, handing the paper back to Don Camillo. "I had this same statement in my hands two weeks ago."

"Two weeks ago, things were different," Don Camillo shot back at him. "Please read on. Here you have the notarized signature of the doctor."

Just then the director came out into the hall again.

"Mr. Mayor," he said, "since you're called upon to decide an important matter, this time won't be counted. The commission has noted the exact hour at which you left the room."

"Thank you," said Don Camillo. "I shouldn't want to have on my conscience the theft of time from a mathematics exercise or a literary masterpiece."

Peppone gritted his teeth and shot a bitter glance at Don Camillo.

"Come, Mr. Mayor, hurry!"

Peppone reopened the paper and scrutinized the declaration: "The undersigned certifies that Angiolina Pateri is in a desperate condition and must be sent away for a surgical intervention; *meanwhile, ten minutes from now, you ask for permission to go to the toilet.*"

He reread the last two lines, fearing that he had misunderstood them. Then he looked at Don Camillo and asked:

"Why?"

"If the doctor says so, then it's got to be done," answered Don Camillo. "Just sign here."

Peppone signed the paper and handed it back. When he returned to the classroom the commission took note of the hour. Don Camillo thanked the director and then said to him in a whisper: "He may not seem to be so very bright, but you'll see. He's a slow starter."

"Very slow indeed, Father," said the director with a low laugh.

Ten minutes went by, and then suddenly Peppone raised the thumb and forefinger of his right hand.

"Go right ahead," said the director. "And smoke a cigarette while you're there, if you want to. We'll subtract the time."

Peppone walked unsteadily to the toilet, which was at the end of the long hall. A window looked out over some empty fields.

"Psss!"

Peppone nailed his face to the grating over the window. Just below there was a pile of dried grass and sticks, and this was the source of the whistle.

"Hurry up, you jackass! Light a cigar and pretend to take it easy. Quick, tell me the problem!"

Peppone told him the problem between one puff of smoke and another.

"Parallelepiped. . . . Basin . . . 40 by 60 centimetres . . ."

"What's 40 by 60 centimetres!" came the voice from the outside.

"The base . . . two taps . . . one 8 litres a minute . . . other 5 litres every two minutes, but in 30 minutes fills two-fifths of the basin . . ."

"And what do they want to know?"

"How long it would take to fill the basin with both taps running. And the height of the parallelepiped."

"Jackass! That's child's play."

Don Camillo proceeded to explain it to him.

"Do you get it?" he said in conclusion.

"No, but now that you've given me a hint, I'll try to think it out."

"Beat it, then!"

Peppone jumped.

"How about the composition?"

"What's the theme?"

"An event which made a strong impression upon me."

"Well, you'll have to work that out yourself. What do I know of your affairs?"

"But I can't remember a single thing! What shall I tell?"

From the pile of grass came a suggestion, and Peppone took it back with him to the classroom. He thought hard over what Don Camillo had told him about the arithmetic problem, and having caught on to the general idea he was able to work it out on paper. He was still perspiring, but in a different way. And the trembling of his hand was not the same, either. The director's voice aroused him:

"It's one o'clock and allowing you ten minutes for each of the two interruptions, you've only twenty minutes left."

Peppone fell once more into a panic. Twenty minutes to make clean copies of both the problem and the composition! He looked around in search of help and his eye fell on the clock in the church tower.

"It isn't yet one o'clock," he exclaimed. "It's twenty minutes to."

The examiners remarked that the hands of the classroom clock pointed to one.

"But I came with the tower clock and it's only fair that I leave with it too."

"Very good," said the director, who wanted above all to have everything proceed smoothly.

Peppone copied first the problem and then the composition, and when the tower clock pointed to one-eighteen he handed in both papers. Don Camillo was watching with a spyglass from the bell tower, and when he saw Peppone coming down the steps he adjusted the mechanism of the clock.

"Now try to catch up on those twenty minutes I set you back!" he murmured.

Looking out again through his spyglass, he saw Peppone jump over the hedge and start home with his wife and son.

"Wretched creature!" the priest murmured. "I wonder if at the oral examinations tomorrow, you'll find another shady character to help you the way I did today!"

But the next day Peppone did very well without any help whatsoever and the old woman teacher felt impelled to say:

"Allow me to congratulate you not only on your thorough preparation but on your good manners and sensitivity as well."

Her fellow-examiner and the director both agreed, and Peppone went trium-phantly home, not across the fields, this time, but down the street, with his head held high. Don Camillo sat in the church square, smoking his usual cigar butt, and Peppone marched decisively over to him.

"Did you get your diploma?" Don Camillo asked.

"Yes," said Peppone gloomily. "But you were your usual perfidious self to suggest 'The Day of my First Communion' as subject for a composition. I was down and out, and you took advantage of me."

"I can see that it puts you in real danger," admitted Don Camillo. "If Malenkov comes this way and this composition gets into his files, then you're done for! That's what you get for your pursuit of culture!"

As Don Camillo was passing in front of the main altar, Christ's voice stopped him.

"Where were you yesterday morning, Don Camillo?" Christ asked. "You were away from here for some time."

"Lord, please let it go by for the moment, will You? Later on we'll draw up accounts, and I'll pay up what I have to pay."

"You're shamefully lucky, Don Camillo," Christ said with a sigh. "Even when that time comes you'll find Someone to overlook what you owe Him and give you more credit."

"Forgive us our debts as we forgive our debtors," said Don Camillo, throwing out his arms. Then he remembered how Peppone's wife and child had waited for him behind the hedge.

"I did it for the sake of those two, Lord," he said.

"For the sake of those three," Christ corrected him.

"Oh well, one more or less doesn't matter," concluded Don Camillo.

A BABY CONQUERS

PEPPONE WOKE UP AT four o'clock that morning. He had gone to bed the night before with something on his mind, and hence there was no need of any alarm clock to arouse him. A little before midnight, when he was just about to retire, he had received news that the clerical group was holding a meeting at the house of Filotti. His informant, who was on watch in the vicinity, had overheard one of the big shots say in a loud voice as he came away from the meeting: "We'll have a good laugh tomorrow."

What could be going to happen? Peppone had no idea, and after cudgelling his brain in vain he had decided that the wisest thing was to go to bed and get up early the next morning in order to meet trouble wherever he found it.

Now, at a quarter past four, he left the house and made an inspection of the sleeping village. Apparently there was nothing new. The posters on the wall were the same as the day before, and so were the electoral pennants and banners. This was in a way reassuring, but in another it wasn't. If his rivals' latest trick were not connected with propaganda, what could it be? Perhaps it would come out in the newspaper, and in this case there was nothing to do but await the paper's arrival.

Peppone crossed the square in the direction of the People's Palace. His head hung low, heavy with thought, and when he raised it to fit the key into the lock he leaped back with surprise. On the step at the foot of the door was a suspicious looking bundle, which made him think immediately of a time-bomb. But this hypothesis proved false a few seconds later, when the bundle emitted a cry and waved a tiny hand.

Peppone moved cautiously nearer, and having lifted up a corner of the black cloth covering, discovered that the tiny hand was attached to a tiny arm and the tiny arm to a tiny baby. Never had he seen such a beautiful specimen. It couldn't have been more than three or four months old, and lacked only a pair of wings to be mistaken for an angel. On the clothes there was pinned a piece of paper with a scrawled message which read: "If yours is the poor people's party, then this is the poorest creature in the world, being possessed of absolutely nothing, not even a name. It is brought to you by an unhappy mother."

He read this incredible message several times over, remained no longer than necessary with his mouth hanging open and let forth a piercing cry. People ran out from everywhere, with sleepy eyes and nothing on but their nightclothes. And when they had read the note they were equally taken aback.

"Is it really possible that in our atomic age something of this sort can happen?" Peppone shouted. "It seems to come straight out of the Middle Ages."

"Except that in the Middle Ages, children were left on the steps of the church," put in Smilzo, who had just arrived upon the scene.

Peppone turned around and looked at him with perplexity.

"Just what do you mean by that?" he mumbled.

"I mean that times have changed," Smilzo explained unctuously. "Nowadays an unmarried mother no longer puts her baby into the hands of the priest, but . . ."

Peppone grabbed the lapels of his jacket and pulled him toward the door without waiting for the end of the sentence.

"Pick up the baby and come on in!" he ordered.

Smilzo bent over to pick up the bundle and followed him.

"Chief," he said when they had reached Peppone's private office, "why did you treat me so roughly? Have I said something wrong?"

"Smilzo," said Peppone excitedly, without stopping to answer his question, "take pencil and paper and get that idea down in writing without a single second's delay. We'll be the ones to laugh last today."

The wife of Lungo was called in to look after the baby, and Smilzo hastened to develop his idea. He worked over it for a whole hour, and then read the result to Peppone:

"Fellow-citizens! Very early this morning, under the cover of darkness, an unknown woman abandoned her baby on the steps of the People's Palace, where Comrade Giuseppe Bottazzi found it. Pinned to its clothes was a note reading: 'If yours is the poor people's party, then this is the poorest creature in the world, being possessed of absolutely nothing, not even a name. It is brought to you by an unhappy mother.'

"Although we condemn this reckless gesture on the part of the mother, we cannot help calling attention to the social injustice by virtue of which the rich have more money than they can use and the poor have not enough to feed their helpless young.

"The mother forced to abandon her child was a commonplace of the feudal society of the Middle Ages. But today the poor no longer think in medieval terms. In those days babies were left at the church door, but now they are brought to the People's Palace. This signifies that people have lost confidence in the priests and now pin their hopes on the Communist Party, which looks upon all men as equal and entitled to an equal place in the sun.

"And so, fellow-citizens, while we take charge of the abandoned baby, we urge you to vote all together for our candidates in the coming election.

"Local Group of the Italian Communist Party."

Peppone had him read the statement again, discussed a few commas and then sent him to order Barchini, the printer, to make five hundred copies. That same afternoon the posters were ready and the paste-pot squad plastered them all over.

Almost at once there was trouble. That is, Peppone received a visit from the sergeant of the carabinieri.

"Mr. Mayor, is this Communist story true?"

"Why, Sergeant, you don't suppose I'd make it up, do you? I found the baby myself."

"And why didn't you report your discovery?"

"Well, five hundred posters are reporting it!"

"Yes, but you should have come to the police in person to make a signed statement, which we must, in turn, amplify and send on. A woman who abandons her child is guilty of a crime. And how can you be sure that the baby really belongs to the woman who wrote the note? You don't even know that the writer is a woman. What if the baby was kidnapped and then disposed of in this way?"

As a result, Peppone made the required statement, the sergeant questioned other witnesses and drew up his own official account of the story.

"Where is the baby now?" he asked when this was completed.

"In his new home, the People's Palace."

"And who has charge of him?"

"The Communist Party. We've adopted him."

"But a political group can't legally adopt a baby or even hold one in temporary care. The baby has to be turned over to the proper institution. We'll get in touch with a place in the city and you can take the baby there tomorrow."

Peppone looked at the sergeant with exasperation.

"I'll not take that baby anywhere. I'm adopting him myself, personally."

The sergeant shook his head.

"Mr. Mayor, I take my hat off to your generosity. But you can't do that until we have made the necessary investigation."

"Well, while you're investigating, the baby may as well stay with my wife and myself. We're experienced parents. It isn't as if you were putting him into the hands of the first-comer. After all, I am the village's number one man."

The sergeant could find no more objections. "Let's go and take a look at the creature," he suggested.

"Don't inconvenience yourself. I'll have him brought here and you can turn him over to me officially."

Shortly after this, Lungo's wife came with the baby in her arms. And when the sergeant saw him, he exclaimed, "What do you know about that! What a handsome little fellow! I don't see how anyone could abandon him."

Peppone sighed.

"No matter how handsome a baby may be, he can't live on thin air."

The sergeant's investigation didn't have to go too far. That very evening he was called to Torricella, a couple of miles away, where a woman's dead body had been found on the railroad track. In her bag was a note saying: "Mine is just the same old story of a girl left all alone in the world and then jilted by her lover. . . ." There were also identification papers, which made it possible to write to the police of the city whence she had come for further information. A reply was soon forthcoming and brought news that this girl was, as she claimed, quite alone in the world and had registered the birth of a baby without the father's name.

"Now the way is clear," the sergeant said to Peppone. "If you want to proceed with the formalities for adoption, you can go and do so. Of course, if you've changed your mind . . ."

"Of course I haven't changed my mind," said Peppone.

The baby was a very handsome one indeed, and everyone admired him. A wealthy couple by the name of Bicci, whose only misfortune was that they had no child, took a special fancy to him and went to Don Camillo about it.

"He'd be a godsend to us," they told him. "And you're the only one that can wangle it. Peppone wouldn't listen to anyone else."

So Don Camillo went to knock at Peppone's door. Peppone gave him an unpromising welcome.

"Politics?" he asked ill-humouredly.

"No, something much more serious than that. I came to see you about the baby."

"I'd like even politics better. The baby doesn't need a thing. If you must know, he's already been baptized. His mother gave him the name of Paolo."

"I know all that. But it's not true that he doesn't need a thing. First of all, he needs a father and mother. And you don't really need another child."

That's none of your business, Father. I'm quite capable of looking after my own family affairs. I've come to love that baby as much as if he were my own."

"I know that, too. That's why I've come. If you really love him, then you ought to give him all the advantages you can. The Biccis have neither child nor relatives. They're anxious to adopt the child and leave him everything they have."

'Is that all you came to say?" asked Peppone.

"Yes."

"Then the door's down there to the right."

But Don Camillo had a parting shot ready.

"I see. The baby is useful to you as political propaganda. You don't really care about his future."

Peppone left his anvil and came to stand squarely in front of Don Camillo.

"Look, I'd be justified in knocking you over the head with a hammer. But that wouldn't serve any purpose other than that of throwing me into a criminal role. And that's a role I prefer to save for you. Let's go and see the carabinieri together."

Peppone went out of the door and Don Camillo, with his curiosity aroused, followed after. They found the sergeant at his desk.

"Sergeant," said Peppone, "is it true what they said in the papers, that the poor girl left a note in her handbag?"

"Of course," said the sergeant cautiously. "It was addressed to the judicial authorities and I transmitted it to them."

"So nobody else knows what is in it, is that right?"

"Nobody."

"Well, I do."

"What's that?" exclaimed the sergeant. "Will you kindly explain?"

"Before the girl threw herself under the train she posted from Toricella a letter identical to the one found in her bag. And that letter was addressed to me.'

"To you? Did you know her, then?"

"No. The letter was addressed: 'Director of the People's Palace,' and it was delivered to me in person."

The sergeant smiled incredulously. "It does seem likely enough, since that's where she left her baby, that she should have written to you about it. But how can you be sure that letter is an exact copy of the note found in her bag?"

"Because she wrote on it: 'I have sent an exact copy of this letter to the judicial authorities.' I have the original letter of hers in safekeeping. But I've brought with me a typed copy, which I shall now read to you. 'Mine is just the same old story of a girl left all alone in the world and then jilted by her lover. My betrayer is a rich but egotistical and dishonest man. Before dying I wish to leave my son in the hands of people who are against the dishonesty and egotism of the rich. I want him to be educated to combat them. My desire is not for revenge but for justice.' Now tell me, isn't that the exact text?"

"Don't ask me," said the sergeant. "I passed the note on to the proper persons, and only they can answer."

"Very well, Sergeant. Meanwhile, I have a signed letter addressed 'Director of the People's Palace.' I could have had this letter reproduced and used it for campaign purposes. . . ." Peppone turned and gave Don Camillo a withering look. "Now, do you see what material I had there for propaganda? . . . And you, Sergeant, don't you agree?"

"Mr. Mayor, that's not up my alley. I have said all I have to say."

Don Camillo and Peppone walked away in silence, until Peppone said:

"Now, wasn't I justified in wanting to knock you over the head with a hammer?"

"No, only God has a right to take away human life."

"All right. But isn't it God's duty to take away the life of the priest of this parish?"

"God has rights, not duties. Duties are what men have in relation to God."

"Perfect!" shouted Peppone. "And before God, what is my present duty? To give the baby to the Biccis and let them bring him up to be a little egotist like themselves?"

"Or to bring him up in the school of hate to which you belong?" retorted Don Camillo.

They had reached Peppone's house and now they walked in. There was a cradle in the kitchen, and in it the baby lay sleeping. When the two men drew near he opened his eyes and smiled.

"What a beautiful child!" exclaimed Don Camillo.

Peppone wiped the perspiration off his forehead and then went to fetch a paper.

"Here's the original letter from the mother," he said. "You can see for yourself that I was telling the truth."

"Don't give it to me!" said Don Camillo, "or else I'll destroy it."

"Never mind!" Peppone answered. "Go ahead and look!"

As he handed it across the cradle, a tiny had stretched out and grabbed it.

"Lord help us!" said Don Camillo, with his eyes wide open in astonishment. Just then Peppone's wife came in.

"Who let the baby have that paper?" she shouted. "It was written with an indelible pencil, and if he puts it in his mouth he'll be poisoned!"

She snatched the paper away and threw it into the fire. Then she picked up the baby and raised him into the air.

Turning to Don Camillo she said, "Isn't he a handsome fellow? I'd like to see if your De Gasperi could produce his equal!"

And she spoke as if the baby were her very own. Don Camillo did not let this remark upset him, but took his leave with a polite farewell greeting.

"Good-bye, Mr. Mayor; good-bye, Signora Bottazzi; good-bye, Baby Bottazzi!"

And Baby Bottazzi answered with a gurgle which filled Don Camillo's heart with comfort and hope.

THE ELEPHANT NEVER FORGETS

THUNDER, OF COURSE, WAS Don Camillo's dog. And Antenore Cabazza, known as "Thunderer," was a follower of Peppone. The dog was the brainier of the two, which fact is noted simply in order to give some picture of his two-legged namesake, with whom we are concerned in this story.

Thunderer was an enormous fellow, who, once he got into motion, proceeded with all the grace and implacability of an elephant. He was the ideal man to carry out orders but for some reason Peppone took especial care not to entrust him with their execution. And so most of Thunderer's Communist activities took place at the Molinetto tavern, where he went to play cards whenever he wasn't working. He was an enthusiastic poker player, and his phenomenal memory made him a formidable opponent. Of course memory isn't always the deciding factor in a card game, and every now and then Thunderer took a trouncing. But the experience he had one Saturday with Cino Biolchi was worse than anything that had ever happened to him before. He sat down to play with five thousand liras, and five hours later he was left without a penny. Now Thunderer couldn't stomach the idea of going home in this condition.

"Give me my revenge!" he panted, grasping the cards with shaking hands.

"I've given you I don't know how many thousand chances for a revenge game," said Cino Biolchi. "But now I've had enough."

"Let's have just one game, for all or nothing," said Thunderer. "That way, if I win, I get back my five thousand liras."

"And what if you lose?" asked Cino Biolchi.

"Well, you can see I haven't got any more money," stammered Thunderer, wiping the perspiration off his forehead, "but I'll stake anything you say."

"Don't be a donkey," said Biolchi. "Go off to bed and forget about it."

"I want my revenge!" Thunderer roared. "I'll put up anything . . . anything at all. You name it!"

Biolchi was an original fellow. And now, after a moment of thought, he said:

"All right; I'm with you. Five thousand liras against your vote."

"My vote? What do you mean?"

"I mean that if you lose, you promise to vote for whatever party I say in the next election."

Gradually Thunderer was convinced that the other meant just what he was saying. And he had accepted the terms in advance. So it was that Biolchi put a five-thousand lira bill upon the table and gave Thunderer a pen and paper.

"Just write: 'The undersigned Antenore Cabazza solemnly swears to vote on June 7 for such-and-such a party. . . .' You can leave the name of the party blank, and I'll put it in when I feel like it."

Thunderer wrote it duly down and then shot Biolchi look of resentment.

"It's strictly between ourselves," he said. "And sometime between now and election day, on June 7, you have to play off the game."

"That's a bargain," Biolchi replied.

Peppone was just leaving the People's Palace when Thunderer loomed up before him.

"Chief, I've just lost everything I have to Biolchi in a card game."

"Too bad. But that's none of my business."

"Yes, it is, too. Because I lost something else; I lost my vote."

Peppone laughed after Thunderer had told him the story.

"You don't have to worry," he said reassuringly. "After all, we have a secret ballot, and once you're in the booth you can vote for whom you please."

"No I can't," said Thunderer ruefully. "I signed a paper."

"Devil take the paper! That doesn't bind you."

"I gave my word of honour, and we shook hands on it. And I'm not the kind of a fellow that breaks his word."

Yes, Thunderer had the character of an elephant rather than a jack-rabbit. He had a motor in place of a brain, and the motor ran with a logic of its own, which no one could stop without causing breakage. Peppone realized that the matter was more serious than he had thought, and that Thunderer was adamant on the subject of his honour.

"Keep your shirt on," he said. "We'll talk it over tomorrow."

"At what time, Chief?"

"At ten thirty-five," muttered Peppone, meaning: "Devil take you for your stupidity!"

But at exactly ten thirty-five the next morning Thunderer turned up at the workshop, saying:

"It's ten thirty-five."

It was obvious that he hadn't slept a wink, and he stood there with bewildered, drooping eyes. Peppone's first impulse was to hit him over the head with a hammer. And when you come down to it, that impulse was a healthy one. But he felt sorry for the fellow and threw his hammer down on the floor instead.

"You ass!" he shouted. "I ought to expel you from the Party. But elections are coming up and we can't let our opponents use this story. Here are five thousand liras; now go tell Biolchi to release you from your word. If he won't do it, let me know."

Thunderer pocketed the banknote and disappeared, but he came back no more than a quarter of an hour later.

"He won't do it."

Peppone put on his jacket and cap and hurriedly went out.

"Wait for me here!" he tossed over his shoulder.

Biolchi greeted him politely.

"What can I do for you, Mr. Mayor?"

"Never mind about the mayor part of it. I've come about that stupid Thunderer. He must have been drunk last night. Anyhow, take the money and release him from his word."

"He wasn't drunk at all. In fact, he was in full possession of his mental faculties. And he was the one to insist on my choice of a stake. Our agreement is crystal-clear. And I'm ready anytime between now and June 7 for the return game."

"Biolchi, if I were to go to the police about this, they'd lock you up. But since I don't want to make a public scandal, I'm here to tell you that unless you give me back the paper I'll flatten you out against the wall like an electoral poster!"

"And who'd go to the police, then? That would be very unwise, Peppone!"

Peppone clenched his fists, but he knew that Biolchi had him cornered.

"All right, then. But if you have any decency, you'll play the return game with me instead of with that idiot, Thunderer."

Biolchi shut the door, took a pack of cards from a drawer and sat down at the table, with Peppone across from him. It was a desperately hard-fought game, but at the end, Peppone went away minus his five thousand liras. That evening he met with his henchmen in the People's Palace and told them the story.

"That rascal doesn't belong to any particular party, but he's against us, for sure. We must settle this business quietly, or else he'll turn it into a tremendous joke. Has anybody a suggestion?"

"Well, we can't settle it at cards, that's certain," said Smilzo. "Biolchi can play all of us under the table. Let's try offering him ten thousand liras instead of five."

Although it was late at night, they went in a group to Biolchi's door. He was still up and in a restless mood, as if something out of the way had happened. In answer to Peppone's proposition, he regretfully threw out his arms.

"Too late! I just played cards with Spiletti, and he won fifteen thousand liras off me, plus Thunderer's paper."

"Shame on you!" said Peppone. "It was agreed that the matter was strictly between you."

"Quite right," said Biolchi. "But Thunderer was the first to spill the beans, when he went to you about it. This simply makes us even. Anyhow, I got Spiletti to promise that he wouldn't tell the story and that before June 7, he'd give Thunderer a chance for revenge."

A pretty kettle of fish! The paper was in the hands of the head of the clerical party and there was no telling what use he would make of it. Peppone and his gang went back to headquarters, where Thunderer was anxiously waiting.

"This is no time for talking," said Peppone. "We've got to act, and act fast. Tomorrow morning we'll post news of Thunderer's expulsion from the Party."

"What's that?" said Thunderer, pitiably.

"I said that the Party is purging you for undignified behaviour. And I'll date the expulsion three months back."

Peppone braced himself for an explosion of anger. But there was nothing of the sort.

"You're quite right, Chief," said Thunderer in a voice that was anything but thunderous. "I deserve to be kicked out like a dog." And he laid his Party membership card meekly on the table.

"We're not kicking you out like a dog!" exclaimed Peppone. "The expulsion is just a pretence, to stave off an attack from the opposition. After the elections, you can make your little act of confession and we'll take you back into the fold."

"I can confess right now," Thunderer said mournfully. "I'm a donkey, and after the elections I'll still be a donkey. There's no use hoping I can change."

Thunderer went dejectedly away, and the spectacle was such that for several minutes Peppone and his henchmen could not settle down to business.

"We'll prepare the announcement," said Smilzo, "but don't let's post it tomorrow. Perhaps Spiletti will keep his word."

"You can't know him very well!" said Peppone. "But just as you say."

For the next two days nothing unusual happened, and it seemed as if the silence would remain, for a while at least, unbroken. But toward evening Thunderer's wife came in a state of agitation to the People's Palace.

"He's stark mad!" she burst out. "For forty-eight hours he hasn't eaten. He lies flat on the bed and won't look at a soul."

Peppone went to survey the situation, and sure enough he found Thunderer in bed immobile. He shook the fellow and even insulted him, but could not get him to say a single word or to abandon for even a second his pose of absolute indifference to the world around him. After a while Peppone lost patience.

"If you're really mad, I'll call the asylum, and they'll take care of you, all right."

With his right arm Thunderer deliberately fished for an object between the bed and the wall. And his eyes seemed to be saying: "If they come from the asylum, I'll give them a proper welcome."

Inasmuch as the object in his right hand was an axe, there was no need of words. Finally Peppone sent everyone else out of the room and said sternly:

"Surely you can tell me confidentially what's got into you to make you behave this way."

Thunderer shook his head, but he put down the axe, opened a drawer of the bedside-table and took out a pad on which he wrote with considerable effort: "I've made a vow to the Madonna not to speak, eat, move or get up for any purpose whatever until I recover that paper, Signed: Antenore Cabazza."

Peppone put this note in his pocket and went to call Thunderer's wife and daughters.

"Don't let anyone into the room unless he calls. Leave him strictly alone. It's nothing serious, just an attack of simple psychosis, a sort of spiritual influenza, which requires rest and a severe diet."

But he came back the next evening to inquire after the patient.

"Exactly the same," said his wife.

"Good," said Peppone. "That's the normal course of the affliction."

Things were still stationary on the fourth day, and so Peppone went from Thunderer's bedside to the rectory. Don Camillo sat at his desk, reading a type-written paper.

"Look," said Peppone, "do you know the story of this fellow who lost his vote over a game of cards and . . ."

"Yes, I happen to be reading it this minute," answered Don Camillo. "Someone wants to make it into a poster."

"Oh, it's that rascal Spiletti, is it? He gave his word of honour that he'd make no use of it before election day, and that he'd give the loser a revenge game."

"I don't know anything about that. All I know is that we have here an interesting document signed by the loser's own hand."

Peppone took out the sheet of paper he had torn off Thunderer's pad.

"Then read this authentic document as well. That will give you the whole story, and it may be even more interesting if the signer starves himself to death, as seems quite likely." And he went away, leaving the paper in Don Camillo's hands.

Spiletti came to the rectory a quarter of an hour later.

"Father, was there anything you didn't like in my draft?"

"No, but the trouble is that Thunderer came around here to demand his return game."

"His return game? Nonsense! I'm giving him nothing of the sort. This document is entirely too precious, and I have no intention of relinquishing it."

"What about your promise?"

"Why should we have to keep a promise made to one of that mob which deals exclusively in lies?"

"I see your point. But Thunderer is quite a menace when he's well, and now he's half crazy. If you deprive him of his revenge, he's capable of bumping you off like a fly. And although propaganda is important, it's more important for you to stay alive."

"Let's play the game, then. But what if I lose?"

"You mustn't lose, Spiletti. If you beat Cino Biolchi, then you ought to make mincemeat out of Thunderer."

"The truth is that I didn't beat Cino Biolchi, Father. I didn't win the paper away from him; he gave it to me so as to get rid of Peppone. . . . Look here, Father, why don't you play in my place? I'll say that now the document is yours, and I doubt if Thunderer will come anywhere near you."

Don Camillo was a shark at cards, and so he said laughing:

"If he plays with me, I'll demolish him! And he won't dare say a word. Never fear, Spiletti, we shall win!"

The next day Don Camillo went to see Peppone.

"The document is now in my hands. If your fasting friend wants it back, then I'm his opponent. If he refuses, then it will go on public display."

"What?" said Peppone indignantly. "How can a poor wretch who's had nothing to eat for almost a week stand up to you at a game of cards?"

"You're just as much of a wretch as he is, although you eat a large meal every day. If you like, I'll play with you."

"Good enough!"

"Then it's five thousand liras against the famous paper."

Peppone put a banknote on the table and Don Camillo covered it with the incriminating document. It was an exceedingly fierce game, and Peppone lost it. Don Camillo put the money into his pocket.

"Are you satisfied?" he asked. "Or do you want a return game?"

Peppone put up another five-thousand lira bill. He fought hard but played a miserable game. However, Don Camillo's game was even more miserable, and Peppone won.

"Here's Thunderer's paper, Comrade," said Don Camillo. "I'm satisfied with the money."

Peppone had been present for a whole hour at Thunderer's "Liberation dinner," when Don Camillo appeared upon the scene.

"Thunderer," said the priest, "you lost five thousand liras to Biolchi, didn't you?"

"Yes," the elephant stammered.

"Well, thanks to Divine Providence, here they are. Remember that when the elections come around, and don't vote for God's enemies."

"Yes, of course, that was understood in my vow," sighed the unhappy Thunderer.

Peppone waited for Don Camillo outside the door.

"You're a snake in the grass! You build up the reputation of Divine Providence with my money!"

"Comrade, infinite are the ways of Divine Providence!" sighed Don Camillo, raising his eyes to heaven.

THE BEST MEDICINE

PEOPLE COULDN'T GET OVER the fact that Don Camillo was in such a state over Thunder.

"After all," they said, "a dog's only a dog."

But it's the last straw that breaks the camel's back. And at this time, that was Don Camillo's situation.

The day before the official opening of the shooting season, Thunder went out of the house around noon and failed to return in the evening. He didn't turn up the next day, either, and Don Camillo searched wildly for him until night. When he came home empty-handed he was too miserable to eat supper. "Somebody's stolen him," he thought to himself, "and by this time he's probably in Piedmont or Tuscany." Then all of a sudden he heard the door creak, and there was Thunder. It was obvious from his humble look that he was aware of having done something very bad. He didn't have the nerve to come all the way in, but stood half outside, with only his nose sticking around beyond the door.

"Come in!" shouted Don Camillo, but the dog did not budge. "Thunder, come here!" the priest shouted again.

The order was so definite that Thunder obeyed, coming forward very slowly, with his head hanging low. When he reached Don Camillo's feet, he stopped and waited. This was the last straw. For it was then that Don Camillo discovered that someone had painted Thunder's hindquarters bright red.

Love me, love my dog; if you insult my dog, I am insulted.

This is especially true of a sportsman. And in this case, nothing could have been more cowardly. Don Camillo felt a grinding pain deep down inside and had to go and take a breath of fresh air at the open window. There his anger passed away, giving place to melancholy. He leaned over to touch the dog's back and found the paint already dry. Evidently it had been applied the day before and Thunder had been afraid to come home.

"Poor fellow," said Don Camillo. "You were caught just like an innocent puppy."

Then he stopped to think that Thunder wasn't the kind of dog to let strangers get too near him or to fall for the offer of a chunk of meat. Thunder was a thoroughbred, and didn't take to all-comers. He trusted only two people, and one of these was Don Camillo.

This shed more light on the situation, and Don Camillo impulsively decided to clear it up completely. He went out, calling Thunder, and Thunder followed somewhat shamefully after. Peppone was still in his workshop when Don Camillo appeared, like a ghost, before him. He went right on hammering, while Don Camillo went to stand on the far side of the anvil to ask him a question.

"Peppone, have you any idea how Thunder got into this condition?"

Peppone looked over at the dog and shrugged his shoulders.

"How should I know?" he said. "Perhaps he sat down on some bench that was freshly painted."

"That could be," said Don Camillo calmly. "But I have a notion you're mixed up in it, somehow. That's why I came straight here."

Peppone grinned at him.

"I'm a blacksmith and mechanic," he said. "The dry cleaner is on the other side of the square."

"But the fellow who asked me to lend him my dog to go hunting and then painted the dog red because I refused him is right here before me!"

Peppone dropped his hammer and stood up to Don Camillo with his hands on his hips, defiantly:

"Now, exactly what do you mean?"

"That your revenge was abject and unworthy!"

Don Camillo was panting with indignation. He heard Peppone shout something at him but could not catch the words. His head was whirling strangely and he groped for the anvil in order to keep his balance. Peppone eyed him coldly.

"If you've been drinking, you'd better go and sleep it off in the rectory, where it's cooler."

Don Camillo managed to grasp this last sentence and started reeling home, where he arrived without knowing how he had done so. Half an hour later Thunder's incessant barking drew the attention of the sacristan. He noticed that the rectory door was open and an electric light burning inside. And a moment later he cried out in astonishment. Don Camillo lay stretched out on the floor and Thunder was howling beside him. The priest was bundled into an ambulance and taken to a hospital in the city. And the villagers did not go to bed before the ambulance came back and they had some news.

"Nobody knows what's wrong," said the driver. "It seems as if his heart and liver and nervous system were all involved. Then he must have given his head a nasty crack when he fell. All the way to the city he was delirious, raving about how someone had painted his dog red."

"Poor Don Camillo!" the villagers murmured as they went to bed. The next day they found out that the dog really had been touched up and that Don Camillo's raving was by no means as delirious as it had seemed. And although they were still just as sorry that he had been stricken, they found his concern over Thunder exaggerated. "A dog's only a dog," they were saying.

This was because they didn't realize that the last straw can break the camel's back.

Every evening someone brought back the latest news from the city. "He's not at all well. They won't allow anyone to see him." And early every morning Thunder came to Peppone's workshop, lay down in the doorway and fixed his melancholy eyes upon Peppone. He stayed there until eight o'clock, when the square began to fill up with people going about their daily occupations. Peppone paid him very little attention, but after this performance had been repeated for twenty-five days in succession, he lost patience and shouted:

"Can't you let me alone? Your master's ill, that's all. If you want to know more than that, you'll have to go and see him."

The dog did not budge an inch and Peppone still felt those melancholy eyes upon him. At seven o'clock he could not stand it any longer. He washed, put on his best suit, got on his motorcycle and rode away. After he had gone a mile he stopped to see how he was off for petrol. He found the tank full, and proceeded to check the oil and the pressure of the tyres. After this, he scribbled something in a notebook. A few seconds later Thunder caught up with him, his tongue hanging out with exhaustion, and jumped into the side car.

"Devil take you and your master!" grumbled Peppone as he started the engine.

At eight o'clock he arrived in front of the hospital and left Thunder to watch over the machine. But at the door they told him that it was entirely too early for a visit. And when they heard which patient he wanted to see, they told him it was no use waiting. Don Camillo's case was so serious that no visitor could be admitted to his room. Peppone did not insist. He remounted his motorcycle and rode off to the Bishop's Palace. Here, too, he was refused admittance, but finally his persistence and his big hands caused the secretary to relent.

The bishop, older and tinier and whiter-haired than ever, was walking about his garden, admiring the bright hues of the flowers.

"There's some sort of ruffian outside who says he's Your Grace's personal friend," the secretary explained breathlessly. "Shall I call the police?"

"What's that?" said the bishop. "Do you hold your bishop in such low esteem as to think that his personal friends are wanted by the police? Let the fellow in."

A few seconds later, Peppone torpedoed his way into the garden, and from behind a rose bush the old man held him off with the end of his cane.

"Forgive me, Your Grace," stammered Peppone, "but it's a serious matter."

"Speak up, Mr. Mayor. What's wrong?"

"Nothing's wrong with me, Your Grace. It's Don Camillo. For over three weeks . . ."

"I know all about it," the bishop interrupted. "I've been to see him already. Poor Don Camillo!" He sighed.

Peppone twisted his hat between his hands.

"Something's got to be done, Your Grace."

"Only God Almighty can do it," said the bishop, throwing out his arms in resignation.

But Peppone had an idea of his own.

"There's something you can do, Your Grace. You can say a Mass for his recovery, for instance."

The bishop looked at Peppone incredulously.

"Your Grace, please try to understand. I'm the one that painted his dog red."

The bishop did not answer, but walked down the garden path. Just then his secretary came to tell him that lunch was ready.

"No," said the bishop. "Not just yet. Leave us here alone."

At the far end of the path was the bishop's private chapel.

"Go down there and ask them for a altar boy," said the bishop.

Peppone shrugged his shoulders.

"I can serve at the altar. I did it often enough as a boy. . . ."

"A very special Mass, with a very special altar boy," said the bishop. "Go on in and lock the door behind us. This is something that must remain strictly between ourselves. Or rather, between ourselves and God."

When Peppone left the Bishop's Palace, he found Thunder on guard in the side car. He jumped on to the saddle and rode back to the hospital. Again they were unwilling to let him in, but Peppone bullied his way through.

"We can't be responsible for what happens," the nurses told him. "If he takes a turn for the worse, then you're to blame."

They led him to the second floor of one of the pavilions and left him in front of a closed door.

"Remember, as far as our records are concerned, you made your way in by sheer force."

The room was flooded with light, and as he opened the door, Peppone drew back in alarm at the sight of Don Camillo. Never had he imagined that twenty-five days of illness could lay a man so low. He tiptoed over to the bed. Don Camillo's eyes were closed, and he seemed to be dead but when he opened them he was very much alive.

"Have you come to claim an inheritance?" he said in a thin voice. "I have nothing to leave you but Thunder. . . . Every time you see that red behind of his, you can think of me. . . ."

"The red's almost all gone now," said Peppone, in a low voice with his head hanging. "I've scrubbed him with turpentine every day."

"Well, then, you see I was right to bring him to you rather than to the dry cleaner," said Don Camillo with a wan smile.

"Forget about that. . . . Thunder's downstairs. He wanted to come and see you, but they won't let him in. . . ."

"Funny people they are," sighed Don Camillo. "They let you in, and you're much more of a dog than he."

Peppone nodded assent.

"Sounds to me as if you were getting better. You're in high spirits, that much is certain."

"Soon they'll be so high that they'll carry me up into the blue beyond. I'm done for; my strength is all gone. I'm not even strong enough to be angry at you."

Just then a nurse came in with a cup of tea.

"Thank you," said Don Camillo, "but I'm not hungry."

"This is something to drink."

"I'm not thirsty, either."

"You really must make an effort to get something down."

Don Camillo sipped at the cup of tea. Once the nurse was out of the room he made a face.

"Soups and slops, for twenty-five days, without interruption. I'm beginning to feel as if I were a bird. . . ." And he looked down at his gaunt, white hands. "It's no use offering to match fists with you now."

"Don't let yourself worry," said Peppone, lowering his head.

Don Camillo slowly closed his eyes and seemed to fall asleep. Peppone waited for a few seconds and then started to go away, but Don Camillo reached out a hand to touch his arm.

"Peppone," he whispered, "are you a dastardly coward or an honest man?"

"I'm an honest man," Peppone replied.

Don Camillo motioned to him to lower his head and whispered something into his ear. He must have said something very terrible, because Peppone drew himself up abruptly, exclaiming:

"Father! That would be a crime!"

Don Camillo looked into his eyes.

"Are you going to let me down?" he panted.

"I'm not letting anybody down," said Peppone. "Is it a request or an order?"

"An order!" murmured Don Camillo.

"Let your will be done!" Peppone whispered as he left the room.

The maximum speed of Peppone's motorcycle was fifty-five miles an hour, but on this occasion it made seventy. And on the way back it didn't roll over the ground, it positively flew. At three o'clock in the afternoon, Peppone was back at the hospital. Smilzo was with him, and the attendants made an attempt to block the two of them at the door.

"It's a serious matter," explained Peppone. "It's concerned with an inheritance. That's why I brought a notary along."

When they came to Don Camillo's door, Peppone said, "You stay out here and don't let anyone in. You can say that he's making his confession."

Don Camillo seemed to be asleep but he was only dozing and quickly opened his eyes.

"Well then?" he asked anxiously.

"Everything's just as you wanted it," answered Peppone, "but I still say it's a crime."

"Are you afraid?"

"No."

Peppone proceeded to take a parcel out from under his jacket and unwrap it. He put the contents on the bedside table and then pulled Don Camillo into a sitting position, with the pillows at his back. He spread a napkin over the priest's lap and moved the contents of the parcel on to it: a loaf of fresh bread and a plate of sliced salame. Then he uncorked the bottle of red Lambrusco wine. The sick man ate and drank deliberately, not in order to prolong any gluttonous enjoyment but simply to get the full savour of his native earth. For you must realize that Lambrusco is no ordinary wine but something unique and particular to that section of the river valley. Every mouthful made him homesick for the river and the misty sky above it, the mooing of the cattle in their stalls, the distant thumping of tractors and the wail of threshing machines in the poplar-bordered fields. All these seemed now to belong to another world, from which he had been taken away by a succession of malevolent medicines and insipid soups. When he had finished his meal he said to Peppone:

"Half a cigar!"

Peppone looked fearfully at Don Camillo, as if he might stiffen and die before him.

"No, not a cigar!"

Eventually he had to give in, but after a few puffs Don Camillo let the cigar drop to the floor and fell into a deep sleep.

Three days later Don Camillo left the hospital, but he did not return to the village for three months, because he wanted to be in perfect health for his arrival.

Thunder gave him a wildly enthusiastic welcome, turning around in circles and chasing his tail in order that Don Camillo might see that his hindquarters were in perfect condition. Peppone, who happened to be passing in front of the rectory, was attracted by Thunder's barking and asked Don Camillo to note that there was not a trace of red left upon him.

"Quite so," said Don Camillo. "He's all right. Now to get the red off the rest of you dogs."

"You're yourself again, all right," mumbled Peppone. "Almost too much so, in my opinion."

ONE MEETING AFTER ANOTHER

"LORD," DON CAMILLO SAID to the Christ over the altar, "this is our great day!"

Christ was obviously surprised.

"What do you mean, Don Camillo?"

"Lord, it's written in letters three inches high on posters plastered all over the countryside. The Honourable Betio is making a speech in the village square this afternoon."

"And who might the Honourable Betio be?"

"Lord, he's one of the big shots of our party."

Christ seemed even more surprised than before. "Are we enrolled in a party? Since when, may I ask?"

Don Camillo smiled and shook his head.

"Lord, I didn't express myself clearly. By 'our party,' I meant the party which supports us."

Christ sighed.

"It's all very sad, Don Camillo. To think that we have a party to help us keep the universe in order, and we didn't even know it! We're not as omniscient as we used to be. God Almighty is slipping. . . ."

Don Camillo lowered his head in humiliation.

"Lord, I failed utterly to put across what was in my mind. When I said 'our party' I meant the party of all those good Christians that rally around the Church and seek to defend it against the forces of the anti-Christ. Of course, these good Christians aren't so presumptuous as to claim that they help God run the universe."

Christ smiled.

"Don't worry, Don Camillo. I can read your heart like an open book, and I shan't judge you merely by what you say. Just tell Me this: is this party of good

352 THE WORLD OF DON CAMILLO

Christians a large one? How many people belong?"

Don Camillo replied that the party was quite strong and gave the approximate number of its members.

"Ah!" Christ sighed. "Unfortunately there aren't nearly as many good Christians as there are bad ones!"

Don Camillo told Him that beside the enrolled party members there were a lot of sympathizers. He mentioned more figures.

"But there aren't so many of them, either," Christ exclaimed. "Good, honest people are a minority compared to the number of bad, dishonest people that belong to other parties or sympathize with them. Don Camillo, you've given Me very sad news! I thought there were a great many more good people than that. But let's make the best of it. The idea of gathering all good people into one group makes our job a comparatively simple one. Those who are actually enrolled in the good party will go straight to Heaven, the sympathizers to Purgatory and all the rest can be bundled off to Hell. Please oblige Me with the exact figures."

Don Camillo threw out his arms helplessly.

"Lord, punish me! I've said too many stupid things."

"No," Christ answered. "I'm concerned not with your words but with your intentions. Your heart's in the right place, even if your tongue does trick you. Watch that tongue of yours, Don Camillo; it has a way of getting you into trouble."

Don Camillo thanked Christ for his indulgence, and feeling somewhat reassured he went out into the village. Everything was going the way it should. Busloads of people were arriving to hear the speech and their numbers were rapidly filling the square.

"Efficiency, that's what did it," someone said behind Don Camillo.

Don Camillo turned around and found just the person he was expecting, that is, Peppone, flanked by Smilzo, Brusco and three or four other members of his general staff.

"Were you speaking to me, Mr. Mayor?" asked Don Camillo.

"No sir," Peppone said with a smile. "I was speaking to Smilzo. I was saying that the success of the meeting is due to the efficiency of the postal system. If it weren't for that the pink notification cards wouldn't produce such a remarkable result."

Don Camillo took the cigar butt out of his mouth and flicked the ashes away with his little finger.

"Take if from me, Mr. Mayor," he said heartily, "an efficient postal service isn't the whole story. Sometimes an organization can send out thousands of cards and yet get no more than two hundred and twenty-seven people together."

Peppone gritted his teeth. The last meeting he had summoned, the "Peace Assembly," had been a complete flop, with no more than two hundred and twenty-seven people present.

"I don't agree with you," he retorted, "on the matter of the relationship between the number of notices sent out and the number of people actually in attendance. You can count those that turn up for the meeting, but how can you know how many notices were distributed?"

"That's easy," said Don Camillo, pulling a notebook out of his cassock: "two thousand nine hundred and fifty-seven!"

Peppone turned indignantly to his henchmen.

"There you are!" he shouted. "See what's become of the privacy of the mails!"

"Thanks for bearing out the exactness of my calculations!" said Don Camillo slyly.

"Exactness, my eye!" shouted Peppone. "We send out exactly two hundred and thirty!"

Don Camillo put the notebook back in his cassock.

"Good! That shows the privacy of the mails is inviolate and the anonymous information given me was all wrong. As far as we're concerned, there's nothing to hide. We sent out two thousand four hundred and seven postcards, exactly!"

"Six thousand nine hundred and forty-three!" shouted Peppone.

Don Camillo looked at him with a preoccupied air.

"I can draw only one of two conclusions: either the privacy of the mails has been violated or else you're telling a lie."

Peppone paled. He had fallen into the trap like a perfect simpleton.

"I heard mention of some such figure," he muttered. "I'm only telling you what people say."

"Just as I thought," said Don Camillo triumphantly. "The number of notices sent out is two thousand four hundred and seven, as I was saying a short time ago. I'm very happy to see that about three times as many people have chosen to come. And they're not all here yet."

Peppone turned around to go away, but Don Camillo called him back to look at a mimeographed sheet.

"Here's something that just happened to fall into my hands," he explained. "This is a copy of the notice of today's meeting. Since your notice wasn't very effective, I'll let you copy this one. I have an idea that the secret of success is in the letterhead. If you put 'Christian Democrat' in the place of 'Communist Party,' you might have better luck."

Peppone let Don Camillo speak without opening his mouth to reply, but his general staff had to lay hold of him and drag him away.

The square was crowded to capacity, and when the Honourable Betio appeared in the grandstand, he was greeted by a thunderous ovation. He began by speaking of the general political situation and the platforms of the various parties. When it came to the royalists, he pulled out all the stops:

"Speaking of the royalists, who want to overturn our democratic republic and restore a monarchy which in its time betrayed us, let them take note that the sovereign people . . ."

But here he was interrupted by the loud notes of the 'Royal March.' He tried to protest against this seditious act, but the music rang out from somewhere overhead, all the louder. Meanwhile the vastly annoyed public was aroused to commotion. Some people started to sing the republican song, "Brothers of Italy," while others embarked upon the Christian Democrat party anthem. The resulting confusion made it difficult to identify the place from which the disturbance had come. Actually it came from the fourth-storey window of the very house against which the grandstand was erected, and therefore was a real stab in the back of the republic. At least, so the Honourable Betio defined it.

Once the window was identified, a carabinieri sergeant ran up to locate the door of the apartment to which it belonged. He found it easily enough, but it was so strong and securely locked that he could not smoke out the offender and decided to call upon the blacksmith to help him. He turned around and found the blacksmith at his elbow. Peppone had availed himself of his office of mayor to come through the barrier which the sergeant had hastily thrown up at the downstairs door in order to prevent mob justice from taking over a governmental function. Now he stood on the landing, with Smilzo at his side.

"For heaven's sake, open that door!" the sergeant exclaimed excitedly.

"In my capacity as mayor or in my capacity as blacksmith?" asked Peppone.

"As blacksmith," the sergeant answered promptly.

While the criminal behind the armoured door went merrily on playing a record of the "Royal March," Smilzo dashed off to fetch the proper tools from Peppone's workshop. Because of the crowd in the square, it took him some time to get there, but he finally made it. When he came back, Peppone peeled off his jacket and hesitantly fingered the tools.

"Why don't you get to work?" the sergeant asked him.

"The blacksmith in me is arguing a point with the mayor," said Peppone, "and they can't seem to reach an agreement."

"Mr. Mayor," the sergeant muttered, "tell the blacksmith that if he doesn't hurry he'll find himself in trouble with the police."

Peppone set to work at taking the door off its hinges, while the record went right on playing the provocative tune. At last, when the door was unhinged, the sergeant made his way in. But in the presence of the disturber his anger faded to irritation. For Colonel Mavelli, an eighty-year-old retired army officer, had nothing of a dangerous rebel about him.

"Stop that gramophone, and come along with me," the sergeant ordered.

The old man obeyed, but when he had removed the record he broke it over one knee, as if it were a sword, and consigned it to his captor.

"Sergeant," he said, in a voice that seemed to come straight from the front lines, "do your duty!"

Before this unexpected demonstration of nineteenth-century heroics, the sergeant was so embarrassed that he thought it was his duty to draw himself to attention. And he was not altogether mistaken. Finally, however, he remembered the circumstances and recovered his aplomb sufficiently to tell the colonel to hold himself at the disposal of the law. And Peppone, before going downstairs, managed to whisper into the rebel's ear:

"As mayor, I told the blacksmith he'd better open your door if he didn't want to get in trouble with the police. Now, as an ordinary citizen, I shall request the mayor to order the blacksmith to repair it."

Don Camillo was thoroughly indignant.

"Lord," he said to the Christ over the altar, "that fool of a Monarchist ruined a magnificent meeting. I can't see where he got the idea of debating a point by means of a gramophone record."

"I'm sure I don't know," Christ answered. "Unless he got it from someone I know who once rang the church bells when the Red commissar was speaking and thereby wrecked the rally."

Don Camillo bowed his head and walked back through the sacristy.

"*For they have sown the wind, and they shall reap the whirlwind,*" Christ called after him.

Naturally enough, Peppone wanted his revenge, and he tried to work it out so as to kill two birds with one stone. He organized a mammoth meeting, to be addressed by an important speaker who had previously come to celebrate the Red victory in the last local election. It was upon this occasion that Don Camillo had interrupted the speech by ringing the church bells.

"I want the meeting to be of historical proportions," Peppone told his henchmen. "I want to crush the enemy to a pulp."

He worked over it for a month, until finally the great day came. The speech was scheduled for four o'clock in the afternoon, but the square was teeming by three. At half-past three Don Camillo was striding nervously up and down the empty church. Finally he stopped and looked up at the altar.

"Lord," he said, "don't You think I might go and look out of the window?"

"Of course," Christ answered, "but as far as I know, the rose window above the main door of the church is the only one with a view over the square."

"There is one other," said Don Camillo, "but it's up in the bell tower."

"I wouldn't go up there," said Christ. "For one thing, it's very draughty."

"Oh, I've plenty of warm clothes on," said Don Camillo reassuringly.

"I appreciate the fact, Don Camillo, but I'd be sorry to see you repeat what you did last time and ring the bells in the middle of the speech."

Don Camillo spread out his arms in rueful assent.

"*Errare humanum est, diabolicum perseverare,*" he admitted.

"Let's hope you don't forget that on your way up the stairs."

"My memory's good enough," said Don Camillo.

He was panting when he arrived at the top of the tower and it was only natural that he should fan himself with his big white handkerchief. And it was equally natural that when Peppone saw the handkerchief from the grandstand below he should be stricken with apprehension.

"He's up there again, just as he was the time before," the speaker from the city whispered into his ear. "I trust you've taken measures to prevent a repetition of the bell-ringing."

"Don't worry, Comrade," said Peppone. "Two husky boys are hiding on the next-to-last landing, just below the bells. If he tries to start anything, I don't think he'll get very far."

Everyone in the square was aware of Don Camillo's presence, and nervousness spread through the crowd. When it was time to begin, Peppone made a welcoming speech, but the proximity of Don Camillo caused him to stutter, and when he passed the microphone to his guest, he was swimming in perspiration.

"Comrades!" said the speaker. "This is the second time I have addressed you here, and once more I see the black buzzards of Reaction perched in their nests, ready to swoop down and cloud the blue sky, with the beating of their lugubrious wings."

Peppone looked upward, but the black buzzard was perfectly quiet, and only his huge white handkerchief was stirring.

"Comrades!" went on the speaker, emboldened by the calm of his adversary, "today skies everywhere are darkened by black buzzards, and the dove of peace has a hard time surviving . . ."

The crowd looked upward, too, but neither buzzards nor doves were to be seen. Instead, an aeroplane flew over the scene, spiralling lower and lower and releasing tiny parachutes, which fluttered down among the crowd. The crowd became restless, because everyone wanted to grab one of them. And the restlessness grew when it was discovered that attached to every parachute were smoked sausages, tins of fruit and meat, cigarettes and chocolate bars. Except for the sausages and cigarettes, these things were all from America. The speaker proceeded at once to decry such provocatory and offensive propaganda, but he was interrupted by another visit from the aeroplane, whose second batch of parachutes met with even more acclaim than the first. A moment later the aeroplane came back a third time, but failed to calculate distances correctly, with the result that three quarters of the parachutes fell on to the street leading from the square into the country. People started to rush down this street, and on the fourth and fifth round (it turned out that two planes were involved), the parachutes were dropped even farther from the centre of the village. Now it was plain that the purpose of the whole manoeuvre was to draw the crowd away from the meeting. And the manoeuvre was eminently successful, for at a certain point no one remained in the square except Peppone and the visiting speaker. The surrounding houses, too, were left empty, while their occupants joined the wild chase into the surrounding fields. Peppone was foaming at the mouth with rage; he shook his fist and when he was able to speak he shouted through the microphone at the placid Don Camillo:

"This is political banditry! Come on down, if you dare, you big black buzzard!"

Don Camillo came as fast as if he had flown rather than walked down the stairs and stood defiantly in front of the grandstand.

"Come down, yourself!" he shouted at Peppone.

But the visiting speaker tugged at Peppone's shoulder.

"Don't do it, Comrade. He's only trying to make trouble. I order you not to go down."

Peppone gritted his teeth.

"Come up here, if you're so brave!" he shouted, while the Party satrap tried to shut his mouth.

Don Camillo rolled up his sleeves and mounted the grandstand. By now, both men were beside themselves, and they leaped at one another, in spite of the efforts of the visitor, who was caught between them. Peppone got in the first blow, which landed on the left side of the speaker's head. And Don Camillo countered with a swat which hit it on the right. The poor man collapsed like a rag doll on the grandstand floor. Peppone and Don Camillo stared at one another. Then Don Camillo threw out his arms and said:

"There you are! Every time this fellow comes out here from the city, he seems to suffer a ringing defeat!"

He walked slowly back to his base of operations and then tried to slip noiselessly by the main altar. But Christ called him back.

"Where are you going, Don Camillo?"

"Lord," Don Camillo replied. "I didn't have any lunch, and now I'm going to bed without any supper. That way, I shan't be able to sleep a wink, and I'll have plenty of time to think over my mistakes!"

HAMMERING IT IN

AFTER THE INCIDENT ON the grandstand, the atmosphere grew increasingly heated. The political truce was over and the Reds were on the warpath again. But Don Camillo seemed serene.

Only when he read in the bulletin nailed to the wall of the People's Palace Peppone's comment on the Pope's last speech did he lose patience and set forth in plain terms from the pulpit exactly what he thought of Peppone and his irresponsible band.

He must have thought and said plenty, because as soon as Peppone was told of the contents of the sermon he marched upon the rectory with the avowed intent of "bumping off that cursed priest," so as to settle once and for all the question between them.

But he found no priest to be "bumped off" in the rectory, for the simple reason that Don Camillo was in the church, in fact standing in the pulpit from whence he had thundered at Peppone a short time before. He was equipped with a hammer and chisel and intent on boring a hole in the stone column which supported the pulpit. In the course of his vehement sermon he had heard the old wood of the pulpit creak ominously, and now he was making place for a solid iron rod which was to run from the supporting column to the upper edge of the pulpit and eliminate any chance of a collapse.

Peppone, having received no answer to his knock at the rectory door, was just about to return to his home base, when the sound of hammering from inside the church caused him to change his mind. The main door of the church was closed and so was the smaller one leading through the tower, but the window of the Chapel of Saint Anthony was open. Peppone made a small pile of bricks and stones below it and stood on top of this to look through. The pulpit was directly across the nave from where he was standing and at once he recognized the nocturnal worker. His anger redoubled in intensity.

"Father, are you pulling the church down?"

Don Camillo looked up with a start and in the light of the candle burning before the statue of Saint Anthony he saw the face of Peppone.

"Not I," he answered. "Other people make that their business, as well you know. But it's no use. The foundation is solid."

"I wouldn't be so sure of that," said Peppone. "Solid as it may be, it isn't strong enough to protect the deceivers who hide behind it in order to insult honest men."

"Quite right," Don Camillo replied. "There's no salvation for the deceivers who insult honest men. Only here there's no such deceiver."

"You're here, aren't you?" Peppone shouted. "And you're a hundred deceivers rolled into one."

Don Camillo clenched his teeth and kept his self-control. But once Peppone had started, there was no limit to what he would say.

"You're a coward and a liar!" he shouted.

Don Camillo could contain himself no longer, and hurled the hammer at the chapel window. His aim was terrifyingly exact, but God willed that a gust of wind should cause a hanging lamp to swing in such a way as to deflect the hammer from its course and send it into the wall, a foot from its destination. Peppone disappeared, leaving Don Camillo in the pulpit, with his nerves strained to the breaking-point. Finally he shook himself and went to confide in the crucified Christ over the main altar.

"Lord," he said breathlessly, "did You see that? He provoked and insulted me. It wasn't my fault."

Christ made no answer.

"Lord," Don Camillo continued. "He insulted me right here in the church."

Still Christ was silent.

Don Camillo got up and paced anxiously to and fro. Every now and then he turned around in discomfort, because he felt two eyes staring at him. He went to make sure that both doors to the church were locked fast; then he looked among the pillars and in the confessionals. No one was to be found, and yet Don Camillo felt sure that someone in the church was watching. He wiped the perspiration off his cheeks.

"Lord, help me," he murmured. "Someone's staring at me. I can't see him, but someone's here; I can feel his eyes. . . ."

He wheeled around, because he thought he could feel the stranger breathing down his neck. There was nothing but empty semi-darkness around him, but he did not feel the least bit reassured. He opened the gate of the chancel and went beyond the rail to the steps of the altar.

"Lord!" he cried out. "I am afraid. Protect me!"

Then, turning his back on the altar, he looked slowly around. All at once he jumped.

"The eyes!"

The stranger's eyes lurked in the Chapel of Saint Anthony Abbot. It was from there that they were staring at him. Never in his life had he seen two eyes like these. The blood froze in his veins and then rushed hot and tumultuous through them again as he clenched his fists and swept forward. When he came to the chapel, his fists were thrust out ready to grab the intruder. He went one, two, three steps farther, and when he thought the stranger must be within his grasp he rushed at him. But his nails only scratched the walls, and the eyes were still staring.

Don Camillo took the lighted candle from the altar and held it near to the staring eyes. Really, there was nothing so mysterious about it. The hammer which Divine

Providence had mercifully deflected against the wall had knocked down a big piece of plaster. And underneath this there was a fresco, which some priest of times gone by had covered over when he decided to pierce a window.

Don Camillo proceeded to scrape off more pieces of plaster and thus to enlarge his vision of the past. Finally he uncovered the brown face and mocking smile of a devil. Was it an ingenuous figure from Hell or a symbol of temptation? This was no time for research; Don Camillo was interested above all in the staring eyes. His foot brushed against an object on the floor, and stooping down he found at the devil's feet the ill-starred hammer. Just then the clock in the tower struck ten.

"It's late," Don Camillo reflected. And he added: "But it's never too soon for an act of humility."

He walked rapidly through the darkness. Most of the village houses had gone to sleep but there was still a light in the workshop of Peppone. Don Camillo groped for the catch of the iron grille. The shutters were open and he could hear Peppone breathe heavily as he hammered out a red-hot iron bar.

"I'm sorry," said Don Camillo.

Peppone stared, but quickly took hold of himself and continued to hammer without lifting his head.

"You took me by surprise," Don Camillo went on. "I was nervous. . . . When I realized what I had done, the hammer was already out of my hands."

"You must be slow-witted, Father, if you don't wake up to your misdeeds until after you've committed them."

"There's some merit in admitting a mistake," said Don Camillo cautiously. "That's the sign of an honest man. When a man won't admit that he was wrong, then he's dishonest."

Peppone was still angry and went on pounding the iron, which had by now lost its red glow.

"Are we going to begin all over?" he roared.

"No," said Don Camillo. "I came to put an end to it. That's why I began by asking you to excuse the unforgivable gesture I made against you."

"You're still a coward and a liar. And I'll put all those hypocritical excuses of yours right here!" And Peppone slapped the base of his spine.

"Quite right!" said Don Camillo. "That's where stupid fellows like you keep everything sacred."

Peppone couldn't stomach it, and the hammer flew out of his hand. It was aimed with diabolical accuracy at Don Camillo's head, but God willed that it strike one of the narrow bars of the grille. The bar was bent, and the hammer fell on to the workshop floor. Don Camillo stared in amazement at the bent bar and as soon as he could move, he set off at full speed for home and arrived, all choked up, at the foot of the altar.

"Lord," he said, kneeling before the crucified Christ, "now we're even; a hammer for a hammer."

"One stupidity plus another stupidity makes two stupidities," Christ answered.

But this simple addition was too much for Don Camillo, who by now had a raging fever.

"Lord," he stammered, "I'm just a poor, lone priest, and I can't take it!"

After this Don Camillo spent one of the worst nights of his life, pursued by a nightmare of hammers whistling out of his hand and then whistling back at him. The devil with the fearful eyes had emerged from the chapel wall, with a whole crowd of other devils in his train, and one of these rode astride the handle of every ricocheting hammer. He dodged them as well as he could, until weariness overcame him and they pounded his head with a monotonous "bang . . . bang . . . bang . . ." that finally sent him off to sleep.

Only at six o'clock in the morning did the banging cease, simply because at that hour Don Camillo woke up. His head was still so fuzzy that he hardly knew what he was doing and did not recover his self-possession until he stood saying Mass at the altar. The celebration of this Mass required truly epical courage, and God seemed to appreciate his effort, for he rewarded him by giving him the strength to stand on his two feet. When he had taken off his vestments, after Mass, Don Camillo went to look at the Chapel of Saint Anthony. The maleficent eyes were still there and the cursed hammer lay in a pile of plaster on the floor below.

"Aha!" said a voice behind him. "The criminal is drawn back to the scene of his crime!"

Don Camillo wheeled around and of course found himself looking into the eyes of Peppone.

"Are we beginning again?" asked the priest wearily.

Peppone shook his head and slumped on to a bench. His eyes were bleary and his hair glued to his forehead, and he was breathing heavily.

"I can't stand it any longer," he said. "Fix things whatever way you like."

Don Camillo suddenly realized that Peppone was laboriously handing him something wrapped up in a newspaper. When he took the object into his hands, it seemed to weigh a ton. He unwrapped it and discovered an elaborate wrought-iron frame which enclosed, instead of a commonplace picture, a copper sheet, and attached to it with brass wire an ordinary hammer. On the copper sheet were engraved the words:

To Saint Anthony for making me miss

"Lord," Don Camillo said the next day, when he was feeling stronger and more hopeful. "Thank You for Your Help."

"Thank Saint Anthony," Christ answered; "he's the protector of dumb animals."

Don Camillo looked up anxiously.

"Is that how you judge me, Lord, at this moment?" he asked.

"At this moment, no. But it was the unreasonable animal in you that threw the hammer. And Saint Anthony protected that animal."

Don Camillo bowed his head.

"But I wasn't the only one, Lord," he stammered. "Peppone . . ."

"That doesn't matter, Don Camillo. One horse plus one horse makes two horses."

Don Camillo checked the count with his fingers.

"Lord, that's not correct, because I'm a jackass."

And he said it so very earnestly that the Lord was moved to forgive him.

DON CAMILLO RETURNS

IN SPITE OF HELP FROM Saint Anthony, Don Camillo found himself increasingly provoked by the Reds as the pre-election campaigns got under way. Peppone managed to create a number of incidents in the centre of which a certain party found himself with fists flying. These incidents were deemed "unfortunate" by the bishop who sent Don Camillo (and it was not the first time) for a period to an isolated village in the mountains. There the air was cooler. Don Camillo's days were so monotonous that it was hardly worthwhile tearing the leaves off the calendar, for they were perfect blanks, bare of any event worth recording.

"Lord," Don Camillo complained to the Crucufied Christ from the altar, "this will drive me mad! Nothing ever happens!"

"I don't understand you, Don Camillo," Christ answered. "Every day the sun rises and sets, every night you see billions of stars wheeling their way overhead, and all the while grass grows and one season succeeds another. Aren't these the most important of all happenings?"

"Forgive my stupidity, Lord," said Don Camillo, hanging his head, "I'm only a poor priest from the plains."

But the next day he repeated the same complaint. There was an ache deep down inside him, which grew every day, and was indeed the only thing to impinge upon his attention. Meanwhile, down in the little world of the river valley, nothing very remarkable happened either. Except for a multitude of petty things, which would have distressed Don Camillo had he known anything about them.

The young priest sent to hold the fort during Don Camillo's political convalescence was a splendid fellow. In spite of his theoretical outlook and his polished big-city vocabulary, he did wonders in adapting himself to circumstances and made a mighty effort not to rub the villagers the wrong way. People of every political colour responded to his courtesy and goodwill and flocked to church in large numbers, but with this gesture they drew the line. No one, for instance, went to confession. "Don't worry, Father," they explained. "It's just that we're so used to Don Camillo. We'll catch up when he returns." And weddings were put off in the same way. It seemed as if even birth and death were engaged in a conspiracy, for since Don Camillo's departure no one had either come into the little world or gone out of it. Things went on like this for months, until finally a woman came to the rectory one day to say that old man Tirelli was dying. The young priest mounted his bicycle and hastened to the bedside.

Old Tirelli had lived so many years that even a bank teller would have tired of counting them and he himself had lost track of them long ago. He had always been hale and hearty, that is until the atomic blast upset climatic conditions and a mammoth attack of pneumonia laid him low. Before entering his bedroom, the young priest questioned the doctor, who was just coming away.

"Is it serious?" he asked.

"Technically speaking he should be dead. It's an affront to medical science that he should still be breathing."

The priest went in, sat down by the bed and began to pray. Just then the old man opened his eyes and gave him a long stare.

"Thanks," he sighed, "but I'll wait."

The priest felt perspiration break out on his forehead.

"While God gives you time, you'd better put your conscience in order," he advised.

"I know," said the old man, "but I'll wait for his return."

The priest couldn't bear to argue with a dying man, so he went to talk to the members of his family, in the next room. They knew the seriousness of his condition and how miraculous it was that he should still be alive. It was up to them to persuade him to make his confession. They went to the bedside and informed the old man of the doctor's verdict, but although he respected the doctor and was in full possession of his usual common sense, he only answered:

"Yes, I know it's a serious matter. There's not a moment to be lost. Go and call Don Camillo, because I want to leave this world with my conscience clear."

They told him that, first of all, Don Camillo could not abandon his new parish in order to give one sick man his blessing, and second, it would be a matter of hours to fetch him from so far away. And this was a question of minutes. The old man saw the point of these objections.

"Quite right," he said: "we must cut down the time. Put me in a car and take me to him."

"Look here, Tirelli," said the doctor, who had overheard the parley from the next room, "if you hold my opinion in any esteem, listen to me. This is utter madness. You wouldn't last more than a mile. And surely you don't want to die like a dog, on the road. Stay in your bed and take advantage of this borrowed time to set your conscience at rest. God is the same down here in the plains as up there in the mountains and this young man is just as much of a priest as Don Camillo."

"I know," murmured Tirelli, "but I can't be unfair to Don Camillo. Surely the young priest understands. Let him come along, and if I give way during the trip, I'll make my confession to him. Let's hurry."

The old man was still alive and hence in his own house he was the master. They called an ambulance and loaded him into it, with the priest at his side. His son and the youngest of his grandchildren followed after on a motorcycle. The ambulance went as speedily as the power of its four cylinders would allow, and every now and then the old man exclaimed:

"Faster! Faster! I'm racing against time."

When the car reached the mule track leading up to Monterana, the old man was still alive. His son and grandson pulled out the stretcher and proceeded to carry it up the mountain. The old man was only a sack of bones, some nerve and an inordinate amount of obstinacy, and so the weight was not too much for their shoulders. The priest followed after, and in this way they walked for two hours, until the village and its church were no more than two hundred yards away. The old man's eyes were shut, but he saw them just the same.

"Thank you, Father," he whispered to his escort. "You'll receive some compensation for all the trouble I've caused you."

The young priest blushed, and leaped like a goat back down the mountain.

Don Camillo sat smoking his usual cigar butt in front of the hut which bore the name of rectory. At the sight of the stretcher borne on the two Tirellis' shoulders, his mouth dropped open.

"He insisted that we bring him here," explained the son, "in order that you might hear his confession."

Don Camillo lifted up the old man and all his covers, carried him into the house and laid him gently on the bed.

"What shall we do?" asked the old man's son, peering through the window. Don Camillo motioned to him to go away and then sat down beside his father. The old man seemed to be in a stupor, but he was aroused by Don Camillo's prayers.

"I couldn't be unfair to you," he murmured.

"Now you're being unfair to God," Don Camillo protested. "Priests are ministers of God, not shopkeepers. The confession is what matters, not the confessor; that's why the priest stays behind a grating which serves to hide his face. When you make your confession you don't tell your life-story to one priest or another; you speak to God. . . . What if you had died on the way?"

"I had your substitute along with me," murmured old Tirelli, "and I shouldn't really have minded unburdening my conscience to him. When a man's spent his life at hard labour, he hasn't much time left for sin. . . . The fact is that I wanted to say good-bye and ask you to accompany my body to the grave, wherever you may be. When you have a send-off from Don Camillo, you're sure of a safe arrival."

After this, he confessed his sins, and as might have been expected they were so trivial that he received an immediate absolution and blessing.

"Don Camillo," the old man said at the end, "do you mind if I don't die right away?" And he was quite serious about it.

"Suit yourself," said Don Camillo, "if you live two thousand years longer, you won't disturb me."

"Thank you," the old man sighed.

It was a fine day, with a warm sun and a blue, blue sky. Don Camillo threw open the window and went out, leaving the old man asleep with a smile on his face.

"Lord," Don Camillo said to Christ, "something happened today that I can't understand."

"Don't torment yourself about it," Christ answered. "There are things which don't require understanding. And don't go forgetting that old man. He may need you."

"He needs You rather than me!" exclaimed Don Camillo.

"Aren't you content with the fact that he came so far in safety?"

"I'm always content with what God gives me. If He holds out His finger, I don't grab His hand. . . . And yet often I wish I could."

Don Camillo remembered that the old man's son and grandson were waiting outside and went to speak to them.

"He's made his peace with God and is sleeping," he explained. "Do whatever you think best."

"The miracle's done now," said the grandson; "there's no use expecting another. I'll go down the mountain and tell the ambulance to wait. We'll carry him back and bury him at home." Before Don Camillo could say that the old man had expressed a wish to be buried in this his new parish, the boy's father put in:

"Go down, if you like, but tell the ambulance to go away. I'll come after you and we'll go home together."

The grandson ran off, and the son turned to Don Camillo:

"We'll leave everything up to you," he said.

Don Camillo spent the night near old Tirelli. When he had to go and say Mass the next morning he called the old woman that took care of the house to replace him. After Mass he rested for a while and then, having assured himself that the old man was still alive, he went to a house near the public fountain, where he had to take something to a boy that had broken his leg. On the way back he heard someone calling him from a second-storey window. Looking up he saw a face which he was so unwilling to see that at first he actually didn't recognize it. But finally he called up to its smiling owner:

"What on earth are you doing here?"

Beside the girl's face popped up that of a sullen youth.

"We're here for a holiday," he said. "Must we have your permission?"

"Watch your tongue, young man," said Don Camillo. "If you've come here to spread propaganda, I'm warning you that the place isn't healthy."

The young man cursed and withdrew his head, but the girl went on smiling.

"We'll be coming to see you," she said.

"All right, but don't come without an invitation," said Don Camillo as he went on. And he added, under his breath: "What can those two savages be up to? Who knows what trouble they're in now?"

The trouble was a sizable one, and the direct consequence of an episode in which this same pair—Mariolino della Bruciata and Gina Filotti—had already involved Don Camillo. Their courtship had been a stormy one, their families disagreed violently on political matters and it had taken all Don Camillo's persuasiveness to get them to agree to the wedding. After some months of marriage it was Gina and Mariolino who disagreed violently.

"In my opinion it's going to be a boy, and I'm glad of it, because I know you want a girl," said Gina.

"I'm positive it will be a girl, in spite of the fact that you and that family of yours all want a boy," he retorted.

"Of course. Girls take after their fathers and boys after their mothers," she exclaimed, "and I'd hate to see a girl with a character like that of the men of your family. You Bolshevik criminal! I'm going home to my mother!"

"Then good-bye for good; I'm going back to my father. Living with a reactionary's daughter is too much for me."

The logical corollary of these violent propositions was that, in the absence of both of them, their baby would be left quite alone. And they made up over this discovery.

A few weeks later they were faced by another grave problem.

"We've got to think of a name," Gina declared. "Boy or girl, we must have a name ready."

The names suggested by Mariolino were all tendentious because they started with Lenina and ended with La Pasionaria. While Gina's choice ranged from Pius to Alcide. Finally they came together on Alberto and Albertina.

"And how's it to be baptized?" groaned Gina.

"It's not to be baptized at all," answered Mariolino. "But if it is, the way to do it is to take it to church and get it over with."

"To church? But Don Camillo's not there any longer!"

"That's like saying you'd rather be eaten by a lion called Leo than a lion called Cleo," Mariolino said sarcastically. "One priest's as bad as another!"

Gina started to take up the cudgels on behalf of the clergy, but all of a sudden she grew pale and sank into a chair.

"Take it easy, Gina," said her husband gently. "You keep calm and so will I."

"When I think that I married a godless individual like yourself, it's almost more than I can bear. Poor little baby boy, I'll defend you from your father's intemperance!"

"Poor baby girl!" sighed Mariolino. "If I weren't here to save you from your mother's clutches . . ."

They went on this way until late that night, when Gina interposed:

"After all that Don Camillo's done for us, we can't let anyone else baptize our baby. But babies have to be baptized immediately after they're born. We can't wait six or seven months for Don Camillo's return."

"That's easy enough to solve," said Mariolino. "We'll register the baby's birth at the Town Hall, because, after all, Peppone did just as much for us as Don Camillo, and then we'll take it up in the mountains to that one and only priest!"

"Impossible," said Gina. "Babies have to be baptized in the parish where they're born. And the time's getting short. I'm going to pack a suitcase tomorrow."

Six days went by without anything happening. Old Tirelli hung between life and death and Don Camillo stayed home partly in order to look after him and partly because the girl he hadn't wanted to recognize had called out: "We'll be coming to see you." Early in the afternoon of the seventh day, his housekeeper came excitedly into the room:

"Come quickly, Father. There's something very unusual downstairs."

Don Camillo hurried down and saw an extraordinary sight: Mariolino and Gina, with the village midwife between them, bearing a beribboned baby in her arms.

"Well, what's this?" asked Don Camillo.

"The lady came here for a holiday, and proceeded to bear this very fine baby," the midwife announced.

Don Camillo wrinkled up his nose.

"Did you come all this way for that reason?" he asked the young couple.

"I'd never have come," said Mariolino, "but she insisted that you baptize the baby. As if all priests didn't come out of the same pudding. . . . Well, if you don't want to baptize him, so much the better."

Don Camillo pondered the complications of the matter and made an indistinct noise. He went into the church, but the young couple did not immediately follow. Apparently, they were waiting for something. And indeed, while Don Camillo was preparing the baptismal font two groups of strangers invaded the village. One came from the mule track and was composed of members of the land-owning Filotti family; the other came up a parallel path and was, naturally enough, the Red band of della Bruciata. From opposite sides of the square they converged upon the church door, and the young parents led them in.

"Who is the godfather?" asked Don Camillo.

Old Filotti and old della Bruciata both stepped forward, gritting their teeth and reaching out for the lacy robe of their reactionary-revolutionary descendant.

"Hands off!" said Don Camillo threateningly. And he signalled to a newcomer at the church door.

"Step forward, godfather!" he commanded.

And Peppone—for it was he—obeyed, although it was plain that the honour had been forced upon him. When the ceremony was over Don Camillo was called away by his housekeeper.

"The old man is asking for you," she panted.

Don Camillo burst impetuously into the dying man's room.

"No, Tirelli," he said, most uncharitably; "you simply can't throw cold water over the celebration by choosing this moment to die!"

"Father, I called you to say that I've decided to go on living. This mountain air has healed me. Send word to my daughter to come and move me into other quarters."

Don Camillo was breathless over the succession of events. When he went downstairs he found waiting for him the young substitute priest and Peppone.

"I'm here merely as the driver of a public conveyance," Peppone told him. "The priest asked me to bring him here, and after I'd left the car at the bottom of the mule track I came to see how things were going along. Unfortunately I find you bursting with good health!"

The priest, in his turn, gave Don Camillo an envelope.

"It's a letter from the bishop," he explained. "I've come to announce a change of the guard. You can go back in Peppone's car."

"I contracted only for a one-way trip," Peppone objected. "I have no wish to take certain people back with me."

"I'll pay extra," said Don Camillo.

"It's a question of principle, not of money," Peppone replied. "The later you come back the better. Don't get big ideas from the visit of a soft-headed old man and two young rascals. We're getting on famously without you."

"All the more reason for me to hurry back!" said Don Camillo.

Two hours later, Don Camillo emerged from the church with the crucifix over his shoulder.

"Driver, take my suitcase!" he called out to Peppone.

He proceeded down the mule track, and this time the cross was as light as a feather. At the end of the trail stood the jeep which Peppone called a taxi. Don Camillo climbed in, holding the crucifix before him like a banner.

The della Bruciata band had come in a lorry, and now they started off after Peppone. Nearby stood the two big, shiny cars of the Filotti family, and in the first of these sat Gina with the baby in her arms and Mariolino at the wheel. Mariolino skilfully steered his car in between the jeep and the lorry, while the second one, with his father-in-law driving, brought up the rear.

At this point Smilzo rode up like a demon on his motorcycle, having been worried over his chief's delay. When he saw the little procession, he turned around and rode ahead of it, in order to clear the way. When they were within two miles of their destination he responded to a nod from Peppone by stepping on the gas and leaving the others behind him.

So it was that at the entrance to the village Don Camillo found the local band ready to greet him. And the Crucified Christ came home to the strains of the "International."

"Under the rope and to victory!" rejoiced Peppone, bringing the jeep to an abrupt stop in front of the church door.

DON CAMILLO
AND
THE DEVIL

OPERATION SAINT BABILA

SAINT BABILA WAS perpetually in Don Camillo's way, but Don Camillo didn't know how in the world to get rid of him. On that far-away day when he first came to take over the parish he found Saint Babila in the sacristy, and there he left him. Every now and then he moved him from one corner to another, but Saint Babila continued to be cumbersome, because he was in the form of a lifesize terracotta statue, six feet tall and heavy as lead.

In the beginning the statue must have been properly robed and vested, with artistically painted face and hands, but the passage of time had caused all the ornamentation to fall to pieces, leaving the terracotta crude and bare. If it hadn't been for the worn inscription "Saint Babila, B——" (for Bishop) on the base, no one would have thought there was anything holy about it. Several generations of acolytes had chosen to use it as a coat-rack, and as a result the head and shoulders looked as if they had been thoroughly sandpapered. From the waist down it might have been modelled with a shovel, and from the waist up brushed with a chicken feather.

For years, then, Saint Babila had been a nuisance to Don Camillo. Any number of times he had thought of getting rid of him, but even though it is made of identical material, a saint's statue is not the same thing as a chipped kitchen pot. You can't take a hammer and smash it, or simply toss it into the dustbin. And even if banished to the cellar or woodshed it remains just as cumbersome as before. Don Camillo had in mind at one point to haul it all the way to the barn, but he was afraid that the loft floor would collapse under its weight. If only it had been made out of bronze, he could have melted it down and recast it as a bell. But how can a sacred image, sculptured in terracotta, be destroyed without profanity? One day, however, Don Camillo did find the answer, and he hurried at once to the sacristy to talk it over with Saint Babila.

The saint stood in one corner, his worn head and shoulders emerging from a crude vestment whose folds, moulded by some rustic potter, made it look as if it were a piece of corrugated sheet-iron.

"I have it!" said Don Camillo. "And it's for your good as well as mine." Then, removing the incense-pot censer which an irreverent acolyte had hung round the saint's neck, he continued:

"This is no place for you. Here there's no telling who may lay dirty hands upon you and fail to show the respect that is your due. I'm going to take you to a refuge where no one can touch you and you can abide in safety for ever and for ever. No, I'm not going to bury you underground, either. Underground means death, and running water is life-giving. . . ."

Don Camillo fancied he detected a grimace on the saint's worn face, and he protested impatiently:

"What about the 'Christ of the Deep Sea' near Portofino? Wasn't his statue purposely lowered into the ocean bottom? You've no reason to make trouble! . . ."

Saint Babila made no trouble, and that very night Don Camillo proceeded to carry out his plan. It required an immense physical effort, because the statue weighed over three hundred pounds. Finally, however, without being seen by a single soul, he succeeded in removing it from the sacristy and loading it on to a wagon. A few minutes later, with his overcoat pulled up to his hat-brim, he got into the driver's seat and drove towards the river. The night seemed particularly propitious to an Operation Saint Babila. It was freezing cold and the countryside was deserted.

When they reached the river, Don Camillo persuaded the horse to go all the way down to the water's edge, where with the help of two long boards he pushed the statue on to a rowing-boat. Then, having loosened the rope by which the boat was tied up, he took the oar and rowed towards midstream. He had a very clear idea of where he was going. The river, at this point, was so wide that it seemed like the sea and had a particularly deep bottom. This was to be the resting-place of Saint Babila.

At the last minute the saint abandoned his docile behaviour and made so much trouble that Don Camillo nearly fell overboard. But eventually the statue resigned itself to making the plunge and disappeared into the river.

When he got back home Don Camillo put the horse in the stable and before going to bed went to pay his respects to the Christ over the main altar.

"Lord," he said, "thank you for not letting Saint Babila drag me into the water. I have reason to be happy tonight, because Saint Babila is settled *per omnia saecula saeculorum,* and that means for ever and ever."

"*Amen,*" murmured Christ with a smile. "But remember, Don Camillo, that in human events there are no absolutes."

Operation Saint Babila had taken place between eleven-thirty and one-forty-five of a freezing November night, without a single soul to see. Don Camillo had conducted it with extreme prudence and had no cause for worry. But since in human events there are no absolutes, it happened that at one-forty-seven of the same night Comrade Peppone, the Communist mayor of the village, was awakened by a pole knocking against the shutters of his bedroom window. He got up and cautiously opened the shutters, to find that one of his Party henchmen, Smilzo, was standing below, at the far end of the pole, trembling with cold and excitement.

"Chief," he shouted, "something very serious has happened."

Peppone went downstairs to open the door. As soon as Smilzo was in the house he exclaimed:

"A sacrilege!"

"A sacrilege?" echoed Peppone. "Who's guilty of a sacrilege?"

"The priest!" shouted Smilzo.

Peppone took hold of Smilzo's ragged jacket and shook him violently.

"Smilzo, you must have been drinking."

"Not I, chief. The priest has committed a sacrilege, I tell you. I saw him with my own eyes and followed him the whole way. Do you remember the dusty statue of Saint Babila that stood in one corner of the sacristy?"

Peppone did remember. "Saint Babila, B——" (for Blessed Virgin, he imagined), he must have read those words a thousand times on the base of the statue, which had most often been seen serving as a rack for coats and vestments.

"Well, I saw that statue, I tell you. He put it on a wagon and took it down to the river, then he transferred it to a boat and threw it into the water. I didn't see him exactly throw it but I heard the splash, and when the boat came back there was no more statue. That's a sacrilege, Chief!"

This was quite obviously true. Otherwise Don Camillo would not have feared the light of day. If he had done it all alone, in the dead of night, then there must have been something reprehensible about it.

This was the period of "peaceful co-existence", when the Reds changed their line and passed themselves off as quiet folk, with a genuine respect for other people and especially for other people's religion. Peppone wasted no time. He got dressed and went with Smilzo to check up on what had taken place. Peeping through the sacristy window he saw that the statue had disappeared. Then he found the imprint of the horseshoes and the track left by the wagon-wheels, all leading down to the river. On the shore there was a still more important piece of evidence. While Don Camillo was transferring the statue to the boat, a fragment had been chipped off and now lay there, bearing witness to the truth of Smilzo's story. With all these elements in hand, Peppone sent Smilzo to gather his henchmen together. At eleven o'clock the next morning the village was plastered with posters carrying the following message:

"Citizens:

"Under cover of darkness a sacrilegious hand profaned the Lord's House and stole the sacred image of the Virgin Saint Babila. In order to abolish its veneration and to uproot even its memory from the hearts of the faithful, this same sacred image was then, most nefariously, thrown into the river.

"Before this ignoble deed the local section of the Communist Party cannot but lay aside its political enmity towards the clerical intriguers. Along with all good Christians we deplore this loss and intend to organize a searching party, whose mission is to restore Saint Babila to the place of honour which she held before.

—GIUSEPPE BOTTAZZI."

Everyone that read these words hastened to the church, and since the whole village read them the church was soon overcrowded and Don Camillo was in serious trouble. People wanted to know how, when and why, and he couldn't very well answer: "There was no theft and no sacrilege. I am the one that threw the statue into the river." Suddenly now that the statue was gone, all the villagers, including those who were completely unaware of its existence, declared that it was the church's most treasured possession. Words could not express the resentment they harboured against the thief.

When Don Camillo could stand no more, he threw out his arms in a gesture of despair and fled to the rectory, where he took to his bed with a raging fever.

"Poor Don Camillo!" said his parishioners. "He's overcome by sorrow."

Meanwhile the proponents of the "peaceful co-existence" line had gone into action, and the next morning they were hot on the trail, down by the river. From a motor-boat, where he cut the figure of an admiral, Peppone directed dredging operations. In the area pointed out by Smilzo not a single inch of the river bottom was left untouched. And when the workers came back to the shore for lunch, Peppone announced:

"If we're unsuccessful we'll call upon the union of deep-sea divers. Saint Babila shall be found; we have sworn it before God and the people!"

This fine phrase made the round of the entire village. Meanwhile, after lunch, the dredging was resumed, and soon the search centred about the deepest part of the river. All of a sudden a cry passed from mouth to mouth on the shore:

"They're getting hot!"

And half an hour later there was a loud explosion of joy:

"Saint Babila is found!"

Don Camillo was still nursing his fever and trying to keep his mind off his troubles when they were quite forcibly called to his attention. A crowd of excited men and women burst into his room shouting:

"Father, they've fished up the statue!"

"Father, they're forming a procession on the bank of the river!"

"Father, the procession is on its way, bringing the statue home!"

"The whole village is marching, and a lot more people from the country around!"

"Father, you'll simply have to get up and receive them!"

The procession was indeed drawing near. When Don Camillo sat up in bed and looked out of the window he could see a multitude of people winding their way along and singing: "Look down on the people, Thou Blessed One", to the music of the local brass band. There was nothing to do but get dressed and go downstairs. He threw open the church door and stood there, waiting for Saint Babila.

They had put the statue on a litter, borne on the shoulders of the eight liveliest devils of Peppone's gang, with Peppone himself and his closest cronies preceding it. Behind the litter came the brass band, followed by some two or three thousand people. Those of the villagers who had stayed at home scattered flowers from their windows.

When the head of the procession reached the church square and the litter-bearers were in front of the door, Peppone signalled to them to lay their burden gently down. The winding line broke up and rushed forward. When the crowd had gathered round him Peppone turned to Don Camillo and said in a thundering voice:

"Father, the people's calloused but honest hands have brought you back the venerable image of their protectress, Saint Babila, stolen by some sacrilegious criminal but washed and purified in the waters of our country's mightiest river!"

Don Camillo wished for his eyes to be transformed into loaded machine-guns, but all he could do was bow his head as if to say: "Thank you, Mr. Mayor. May the heavens open and strike you dead!"

After this a group of true believers took the place of Peppone's henchmen and

Saint Babila was carried triumphantly into the church. Naturally the statue could not be banished to the sacristy. The image of Saint Lucius, patron of dairy-farmers, was moved out of one of the chapels in order to give it an honoured place.

An hour later, when peace and quiet were restored, the wife of Bigio came to the church to have her latest offspring baptized. The baby was a girl, and if she hadn't been the offspring of a rascally infidel, she might have been called pretty.

"What do you want to call her?" asked Don Camillo between clenched teeth.

"Babila," the mother answered defiantly.

"That won't do," said Don Camillo.

"And why not?" said the mother with a sarcastic laugh. "Just because our Party fished the saint out of the river?"

"No," said Don Camillo glumly. "Because Babila is a man's name."

The woman shook her head and turned to look at the saint. On the base was printed: "Saint Babila, B——."

"Saint Babila, Blessed, I suppose," she said, laughing again.

"No," said Don Camillo, "that B is for 'Bishop'."

The mother, the godparents and their friends looked at one another dis-appointedly.

"A bishop!" the mother muttered ill-humouredly. "We might as well have left him at the bottom of the river!"

"Very well, then," said Don Camillo, grinding his teeth; "what's to be the name?"

The little group wore a puzzled air.

"Palmira, like our leader, Palmiro Togliatti," one suggested.

"Marilyn," said the godmother, who was a passionate reader of film magazines. And Marilyn it was.

PEPPONE'S PILGRIMAGE

SELDOM HAD THERE been such a miserable autumn; when it didn't rain cats and dogs, it drizzled. If, by virtue of some miracle, the sun peeped out in the morning, by afternoon there was a fog thick enough to be cut with a knife and even wetter than water. The ground was damp and rotted, and the peasants were at their wit's end because they saw no prospect of sowing the wheat. Mules and oxen sank up to their bellies in the lush grass, and tractor wheels could only spin idly, becoming more and more heavily weighed down with mud. No one but a madman would have ventured out if he didn't have to, that is, no one but a madman or a hunter, because a hunter is only a madman who hasn't been shut up in an institution.

On this mid-November afternoon a hunter was walking, or rather ploughing his way, along the Canal. He wore high rubber boots, and every now and then he had to stop and wipe them, because the mud stuck to them and pulled him down. He hadn't yet fired a single shot and it seemed unlikely that he would fire one, but he continued to trudge along, accompanied by a totally unenthusiastic dog. At a certain point the dog was so disgusted that he turned round and started for home.

"Thunder!"

The dog stopped, looked round at his master and trotted further away.

"Thunder! Come here!"

The hunter's voice was charged with anger, and the dog finally went to him, growling.

"As long as I'm here, you've got to stick by me," he said, as the dog came near.

And if the dog could have spoken he would doubtless have said:

"Just because you're a jackass, Reverend, doesn't mean that I have to be one too!"

Don Camillo continued to mutter under his breath for a while, and then, when the fog began to close in around him, he decided that Thunder's idea wasn't such a bad one after all. After a decent silence, he said:

"If you want to go home, run along. I'm tired of having you underfoot."

He shot the last round from his shotgun and hung it, with the barrel pointing down, under his heavy coat, from the right shoulder. Just then Thunder pricked up his ears, moved a few feet forward and stiffened all over.

"Why did it have to be just now?" grumbled Don Camillo, reaching under his coat for the gun.

But hardly had he extricated it than he realized that Thunder was pointing to no ordinary game, for he was barking, in deep, gloomy tones, in the direction of a clump of acacias. Don Camillo attempted to quiet him and then took up his stand behind a mulberry tree. He saw the acacia branches move, and a moment later there appeared a shadowy, tall human figure, without a head, advancing slowly upon him. All of a sudden Thunder leaped forward, barking joyfully now, as if in recognition. Don Camillo saw that this was no headless ghost, but a big man, holding a coat over his head. Actually, the coat was over the head of the child he was carrying on his shoulders.

"For a minute I thought you were a man without a head," said Don Camillo, when the giant stopped in front of him. "And considering the little use that head of yours is to you, I wasn't so very far wrong."

The man stuck his head out from the folds of the coat.

"Father," he said, "if it weren't for the respect I bear your dog, I'd give you the answer you deserve."

"Take it easy, Peppone," Don Camillo said with a laugh. "I didn't mean to insult you."

"I shall insult you, though, Father, if you don't remove yourself and let an honest man go his way."

"Strictly speaking, you're not going your way; you're poaching on someone else's property. But, be that as it may, no one is stopping you."

"Then, Father, don't block the whole path; I don't want to wet my feet in the grass. Instead of wasting your dog's time, you'd do better to go and pray to your Boss to send us a bit of sun!"

"My Boss needs no advice from me," said Don Camillo, stepping aside. "He knows when to make the sun shine or the rain fall."

"It doesn't seem that way to me," said Peppone, starting to walk along. "Your Boss goes in for politics instead of attending to business."

Don Camillo did not bother to reply, but slung his gun over his shoulder and walked along, behind Peppone. Once they had left the Canal, Peppone said, without turning round:

"How much longer are you going to trail me?"

"I'm going my own way," Don Camillo replied. "A hunter's way is through the open fields. But, if I may ask, where are *you* going?"

"Where I please," shouted back Peppone. "Hasn't anyone a right to find the fields open but you?"

"Yes," said Don Camillo. "But I have a right to find it very odd indeed that a man should go walking in the mud with a five-year-old child on his shoulders who would be much better off at home."

"My son is my own concern," roared Peppone. "Kindly keep your mind on your own affairs!"

"That's just the point. I baptized him and entered him in my books. That's why I have a right to say that your head must be full of cotton-wool if you carry him around on a day like this."

Peppone did not answer, because just then he slipped in the mud and would have fallen to the ground had not Don Camillo bolstered him up from behind.

"Do you see what I mean?" the priest asked him. "You might have knocked his brains out."

"It's all your fault!" shouted Peppone, stamping his feet in order to shake off some of the mud that had stuck to them. "You needle me until I can't see where I'm going."

Don Camillo opened his coat, took off his shotgun and set it up against another mulberry tree.

"Give the child to me, while you wipe your big horseshoes," he said, lifting the burden from Peppone's shoulders.

Peppone cursed to himself as he plucked a branch and angrily scraped the mud off his boots. It was a tedious job, and the little boy whispered restlessly into Don Camillo's ear:

"Piggy-back, please!"

"Be quiet!" said Don Camillo gruffly.

The little boy pouted and made as if to cry. In order to avoid a scene, Don Camillo lifted him up to his shoulders. As he raised his arms his coat started to slip off, and he stopped it only by leaning against a tree.

"Catch it, will you?" he shouted to Peppone.

"Catch what?" asked Peppone aggressively.

"My coat. It's about to fall into the mud."

Peppone stopped scraping and went to pick up the coat. From the priest's shoulders the little boy signalled to his father, pointing repeatedly at his own head.

"No," said Peppone. "Wait till I take you back. He wouldn't like it."

"What wouldn't I like?" roared Don Camillo.

"For him to put your coat over his head."

"Go on, throw it over his head, and hurry up with what you're doing," said Don Camillo, holding fast to the little legs that swung down over his chest.

Peppone threw the coat over the child's head, and for a minute the priest's eyes were covered. When he had parted the folds and looked out he saw Peppone balancing unsteadily on one foot and then falling backwards into a puddle.

"Neat work!" the priest exclaimed. "If the 'cells' of your Party are as solid as the cornerstone, then the revolution will be here soon!"

"If your hind quarters were as wet as mine," Peppone grumbled, "you'd display a little more Christian charity!"

He struggled to his feet and came over to take back his son, but Don Camillo stepped away.

"Leave him with me," he said; "with my rubber boots I'm not so likely to stumble. Take my gun, and when we reach the road I'll turn over this little monkey to you."

"I'm not going to the road," said Peppone glumly.

"Then where are you going?"

"I'm going where I see fit. Give me back my boy and let me alone."

Don Camillo peered out from among the folds of his coat at Peppone.

"Look here, wild man, this child has a raging fever. If you don't take him straight home . . ."

"Taking him home wouldn't help," muttered Peppone. "For two months now it's come on him every evening, and the doctor can't find a cure. Give him back and stop bothering me!"

"*Quo vadis,* Peppone?" asked Don Camillo, shaking his head.

"*Quo vadis* wherever I please, and *quo venisti,* too, in spite of all the cursed clergy in the world put together! I'm going where I have to go."

"Can't you go by the road?"

"No, I tell you! I have to cross the fields. I don't mind humbling myself before Almighty God, but I won't be a laughing-stock of priests and priest's pets."

Don Camillo looked hard at Peppone's agonized face.

"Very well, I won't say another word. Let's get going."

"I'll carry the child."

"No; he's safer on my shoulders. And no use carrying the shotgun. We may as well leave it here and Thunder will keep watch over it."

The fog had closed in on them and it was wetter and wetter underfoot, but they kept on walking. For part of the way they moved in a direction parallel to that of the road, but neither of them mentioned it. The distance of seven miles seemed interminable. Finally, just before the fog made everything invisible they arrived at their destination. It was a big brick building, darkened by age, which rose at one side of a little-travelled road, with barren fields, where once upon a time rice had grown, all round it. Three hundred years earlier it had been a mere chapel, but later it had become the sanctuary of the Madonna of the Fields. Peppone, with a rough gesture, took his son into his arms.

"You stay outside," he said brusquely to Don Camillo. "I don't want you spying on me."

Don Camillo waited at the door, while Peppone hoisted the little boy on to his shoulders and went in. The church was cold and half-dark, and not a soul was there. The Madonna of the Fields was the only living thing, with her eyes gleaming from above the altar. Don Camillo kept watch at the door. For several minutes he knelt down on a stone and told the Madonna all the things that Peppone probably didn't know how to tell her. When he heard the door creak he got up.

"If you have anything to say, you can go in now," said Peppone.

"I've had my say already," said Don Camillo.

And they started back across the fields, with the child under the coat, on Don Camillo's shoulders. The fog was so thick that towards the end they nearly lost their way. Don Camillo whistled, and Thunder came to guide them. It was dark when they reached the rectory, and Peppone said:

"I'll take back my load."

He slipped off Don Camillo's coat and saw that the child's head was reclining on his.

"The little fellow's asleep," he murmured.

"Not as fast asleep as you might think," said Don Camillo.

"What do you mean?"

"If your neck were as wet as mine, you wouldn't have to ask," said Don Camillo, handing the child over.

Peppone stood for a moment as if he had something important to say, but could not find the words.

"I hope you won't go around telling how we tough Reds go back in an emergency to . . . our childhood," said Peppone hopefully.

"I'm no tell-tale," said Don Camillo. "But if only you weren't such a silly fellow . . ."

"Don't ask the impossible,"said Peppone firmly.

Don Camillo ran to kneel down in front of the main altar.

"Forgive me, Lord," he said, "if I wasn't here for vespers."

"Absence excused!" Christ said with a smile.

THE NEW LOOK

WHEN THE OFFICIAL news came through, along with the first directives, Peppone was staggered. In the good old days he had fought like a lion to have one of the village streets called after Joseph Stalin and had even given his name to the Consumer's Co-operative. As if this were not enough, the great hall of his emporium and meeting-place was decorated with a bigger-than-life-size portrait of the great man.

Such was Peppone's discomfiture that when he had called his henchmen together he found himself for the first time with nothing to say. All he did was toss the sheet of paper containing the directives on to the table and throw out his arms in a helpless and disconsolate manner. The others read the paper through and looked at one another. Then Smilzo summed up the situation.

"What fault have we, Chief, if we believed what the higher-ups told us? Anyhow, it's all perfectly simple. We take down the street sign, change the Co-operative's name and splash a bucket of white-wash over that wall. Stalinism has gone down the drain."

They had met in the Co-operative, and on the wall in front of them was the gigantic portrait of the moustachioed, posthumously purged Leader. Peppone looked at it very sadly. He suffered not only from the blow to his faith, but from a vivid memory of the amount of money the portrait had cost. He himself had insisted that it be a fresco, because, as he had declared at the unveiling, "it must endure as long as the glory of the father of all peoples, that is, forever and ever".

In the great hall were gathered only Peppone and his general staff; the hoi polloi were playing cards and listening to the radio in two other rooms. Thus they were spared the sight of the discredited leader, while Peppone and his intimates could discuss the situation more freely. Naturally enough, when Don Camillo's voice suddenly boomed forth in their midst they started as if a cannon had sounded.

"Good evening," he said heartily, and went to sit down at a small table.

"This hall is reserved for private deliberations," Smilzo told him.

Don Camillo settled back in his chair, stuck a cigar butt between his lips and calmly lit it.

"Is there some celebration?" he asked, after he had blown a smoke-ring up at the ceiling.

"When a visitor sees that he's not wanted," put in Peppone, "the least he can do is go away without stopping to argue."

"Certainly," said Don Camillo. "But when a visitor is taking advantage of his last chance to admire a masterpiece of art which is about to be destroyed, then, wanted or not wanted, it's his duty to remain."

He scrutinized the painting on the wall with a connoisseur's eye and then ended:

"Because it's a fresco, you'll have to scrape and replaster the wall. Twelve square yards of plastering are no joke."

There was no reply. Peppone clenched his fists but held his tongue.

"Oh well, politics is politics. I don't run the same risk, thank heaven. My Leader's held his own for nearly two thousand years."

Peppone jumped to his feet.

"Father," he said, "if you want to pick a fight, you've come to the right place."

Don Camillo shook his head.

"Never again, Mr. Mayor, never again! We've fought quite often enough over that fellow with the bushy moustache. I came simply to indulge in the legitimate satisfaction of seeing you destroy the image of your former god."

Peppone brought his fist down on the table and shouted:

"You shan't have that satisfaction!"

Again Don Camillo shook his head.

"Mr. Mayor, you've misunderstood me. I don't say that you must take a hammer and start to knock off the plaster in my sight. I just want to know that you've given orders for the demolition. Farewell, Face! . . ."

Peppone brought down his other fist on the table.

"I'm giving no such orders. As long as I live, that face won't be touched."

"Then you're disobeying the higher-ups. You're running foul of Party discipline."

"No, I'm not," shouted Peppone. "The Party doesn't order me to give satisfaction to a rascally priest or other such garbage."

When Don Camillo had left home it wasn't with the intention of getting Peppone into so much trouble, but now that things had taken this turn he let him stew in his own juice.

"Well, do as you see fit," he retorted blandly. "But at least I'll have the satisfaction of seeing Stalin's name obliterated from the façade of the Co-operative and the street sign."

"You shan't see anything at all!" shouted Peppone.

Peppone got into really hot water because the reactionary papers took up the story and carried pieces about "deviations", "Stalinist factions" and "possible splits". Very soon a bright young man was sent from national headquarters. He called a meeting of Peppone's chief henchmen and addressed them as follows:

"The reactionary papers are printing the usual absurd stories, but there's no use contradicting them. The only answer is to go ahead and get rid of the painting and the street sign and the name on the façade of the building, as originally intended."

The man from headquarters was a stickler for discipline, the sort of young Party worker that wears spectacles and a double-breasted suit. But he made no impression on Peppone.

"My personal prestige is at stake," Peppone told him. "We're not getting rid of anything. I won't hear of giving that miserable priest such satisfaction."

The man from headquarters tried to explain that where the dignity of the Party is involved, that of the individual must take second place. He brought in the dangers of the "personality cult" and its terrible consequences. Then, when he saw that Peppone was still looking askance at him, he thought up a compromise solution.

"Comrade, I know how to reconcile our points of view. We'll send you off on a mission, and while you're away, your men will obey our orders to wipe everything out."

Bigio was a man of few words, and those he did speak tumbled out of his mouth like bricks falling from the top of a scaffolding.

"It will have to be *your* men that carry out *your* orders. We're not wiping out a thing. You got us into all this trouble. Why couldn't you tell us before he died just how things stood?"

The man from headquarters looked round and then explained that he was only a link in the chain of command.

"Very well, then," he concluded. "I'll make a report on your objections."

He did exactly this, and as a result Peppone received an ultimatum; either to knuckle under or else to be expelled from the Party for indiscipline and other damaging reasons.

It was a peremptory letter, and having read it several times Peppone went to the rectory and threw it down in front of Don Camillo. Don Camillo read it over and over in his turn and then came out with the single word:

"Garibaldi."

"Garibaldi?" muttered Peppone suspiciously. "Where does he come in?"

"Because he has the same first name as Stalin, and you can leave the first half of the inscription on the façade of the Co-operative the way it is. As for the painting, you don't need to deface it. You can just pierce a hole and put in a glass door connecting the great hall with the pergola and the bowling-alley. As for the street sign, never mind about that. One day it will fall, all by itself."

Peppone pounded his fists on the table and thrust his chin out in the direction of Don Camillo.

"I said I wasn't going to give you any satisfaction!"

"I don't want any. You've won, and this is my surrender. You're the stronger of the two."

"Father, I can't trust you. There's something here that doesn't meet the eye."

"Only a little common sense," said Don Camillo, shaking his head. "I'd rather have a live Peppone than a dead Stalin. It's better to thumb a nose at Stalin than at you. Just think it over and see if you don't agree."

Peppone thought for a moment, and then said:

"From my point of view, you're quite right."

"From mine too . . . Lambrusco wine or Fontanella?"

"Lambrusco," said Peppone without hesitation.

It was an unusually fine bottle and so were the two that followed. At a certain point Peppone raised his glass and shouted:

"Hurrah for Garibaldi!"

"Hurrah!" said Don Camillo, clinking his glass against the other.

Then they had to drink a toast to the conscripts born in 1899, iron men, one and all.

"We ninety-niners! . . ." exclaimed Peppone.

And he said these three words in such a way that they were as meaningful as a long oration.

THE CASE OF THE DISAPPEARING DOG

DON CAMILLO'S DOG, Thunder, had fallen from grace, and was punished by being tied up, for several weeks, on a chain. Just when it seemed as if he had mended his ways he made for the garden gate, returned to the gay life and for several days on end failed to put in an appearance.

"The fact that the hunting season is over doesn't dispense you from the every-day duties of a well-bred dog," said Don Camillo. "You're not a mutt or a stray, you have a pedigree. *Noblesse oblige,* and although you're quite free to go out by yourself, you must come home at night."

Thunder cocked his head and listened with a penitent air, but these high-sounding words went in one ear and out the other. Don Camillo was genuinely fearful of losing his beloved pet. Even the loss of his indispensable motor-cycle would have been less difficult to bear. But fate willed, perversely, that Don Camillo should lose his dog. Thunder disappeared on Saturday morning while Don Camillo was saying his first Mass. For a couple of days the priest hoped for his return, then he betrayed his worry by making inquiries of his neighbours. No one in the village had seen him, and gradually Don Camillo extended his search to the outlying farms.

Actually, his first thought had been to question Peppone, for Peppone was the only other person for whom Thunder felt affection. One day Peppone had even gone so far as to say: "Politics may divide us, but Thunder makes us one. Nevertheless, come the revolution, Thunder won't save you from the fate you so richly deserve!" Now Peppone was just the man to whom Don Camillo wanted to turn, but the political situation was unusually tense, and if he had made any contact with the Red leader, an earthquake might have ensued. In the long run, however, after he had exhausted all other possibilities, Don Camillo did have to knock at Peppone's door, that is he wrote him a letter.

"Dear Mr. Giuseppe Bottazzi:

My dog, Thunder, has been missing for two weeks past. If you can give me any news of him, I shall be most grateful. Yours very truly . . ."

The answer came by return of post:

"Dear Mr. Priest:

If your dog has run away, it means that he, too, has got wise to you. Very truly yours . . ."

Don Camillo did not abandon his quest, and after a month had gone by he asked Barchini to print fifty notices, which he proceeded to post in the surrounding district: *"Lost: Hunting dog. Reward to anyone bringing information which leads to his return."*

After three days Don Camillo received a missive with crudely printed letters and no signature at the bottom:

"Reverend: If you want to find your dog, without having to give any reward, go to the acacia grove at Pragrande and look in the vicinity of the sewer."

Without losing a single minute, Don Camillo set out across the fields in the direction of Pragrande. He didn't have to look far, because near the sewer entrance there was a pole sticking out of the ground, with a dog-collar wired to it, and a crudely printed sign saying: *Here lies one of the two dogs of the rectory. He was run over by a truck: too bad, because the other one is more of a dog than he."*

With his stick Don Camillo dug up the loose earth round the pole. After he had gone down a couple of feet he replaced the dirt and went away. Back in the rectory he shut himself up in his bedroom in order to quiet the sorrow and indignation that welled up in his breast. Turning the collar over and over in his hands he repeated to himself: "They killed him . . . they killed him. . . ." There was no doubt in his mind: out of sheer spite, someone had murdered the dog. But who could it be? In spite of his resentment, Don Camillo could not bear to think that the murderer was someone he knew. No one in the village could have been so vile. There were people who might have killed a man, but never a dog, just in order to hurt the master. All day long he was in the dumps, and when evening came he was as exhausted as if he had unloaded a transatlantic steamer. He had no wish to talk, and when he went to close the church and found the old Desolina Fiorini waiting to see him he started to dismiss her roughly.

"Father," she said mysteriously, "I have a secret to tell you."

"What is it?" asked Don Camillo curtly.

"I read the notice about the dog. . . ."

"Well . . ." said Don Camillo, taken by surprise.

"It's no use your offering a reward. Someone knows where the dog is, but he's not talking."

"Well, you can talk, can't you?" panted Don Camillo. "Don't you trust me?"

"I trust you, Father, but I don't want to get in trouble with those people. . . ."

"What people?"

"The usual people, Father. Didn't the dog disappear on the twenty-fourth of last month?"

"Yes."

"Well, I saw him with one of them on that day."

Don Camillo could contain himself no longer. The old woman's caution was driving him crazy. Still, it would have been unwise to put too much pressure upon her.

"Speak up, Desolina," he said. "After all, you know me."

"I know them, too. . . . This wasn't the first time your dog had gone out with them, either. First he took up with the ringleader; he was always underfoot in the workshop. After that he shifted his attentions to the ringleader's right-hand man. I must admit I was shocked to see the company your dog was keeping."

"They made the overtures," protested Don Camillo. "And what does he know of politics?"

"Nothing, of course, Father. But I know that it could only come to a bad end. Anyone that takes up with the Reds . . ."

"Desolina," said Don Camillo prudently, "when you speak of 'the ringleader's right-hand man', do you mean Smilzo?"

"Yes," she said unwillingly, after a fearful look around her. "That was his special friend. I saw them go off more than once together, on Peppone's truck. . . . On the twenty-fourth of last month, which was a Saturday, that's exactly what happened. Only that time Smilzo came back alone."

Don Camillo had heard all too much. After reassuring the old woman, he went back to the rectory and brooded over his wrong in bed. He slept very little, rose at dawn and as soon as he had said Mass made straight for the workshop of Peppone. It looked suspiciously like a coincidence that Smilzo should be on the scene as well. But Peppone was obviously unprepared to see Don Camillo turn up at this early hour and with such an angry look on his face.

"Did you have a bad night, Father?" he asked.

"I did. But I slept better than someone with a dungheap where a conscience should be."

"For instance?. . ." asked Peppone threateningly.

"For instance the fellow who murdered my dog simply in order to spite me."

Peppone shook his head.

"The loss of the dog has affected his mind," he muttered. "There's nothing to do but let him have his say. He's dreamed that somebody killed the dog and come to tell us about it instead of going to a soothsayer who might have interpreted the dream in terms of a winning lottery number."

"I didn't dream it at all," said Don Camillo, pulling Thunder's collar out of his pocket, along with the letter and sign. "I found him dead over at Pragrande, with this sign for a tombstone."

Peppone read both documents.

"Too bad," he said. "But you're barking up the wrong tree. Here there are people that would have been glad to kill you in order to please the dog, but none that would have killed the dog just to spite you."

"This isn't the wrong tree at all," Don Camillo insisted. "I'm looking for a fellow who on the twenty-fourth of last month rode off on the truck belonging to a certain Giuseppe Bottazzi, who rode off with my dog and rode back without him."

Peppone took a step forward.

"You're barking up the wrong tree, Father, I tell you!"

"The police sergeant won't bark up the wrong tree, though, after I've told him my story and given him the names of witnesses."

"I'm not afraid of you or the police, either. If somebody killed your dog, we can't do anything about it. The sins of priests who have sold their souls to America are visited upon innocent dogs!"

"We'll see who has the last laugh!" shouted Don Camillo, moving towards the door. "Ten minutes from now there's going to be an H-bomb explosion, and then the fun will begin."

Smilzo had turned as pale as the lady of the camellias. He grasped Peppone's arm and pleaded:

"Chief, don't let him go!"

But Peppone stared at him in amazement and shook him off.

"What's the matter, you fool?" he asked.

Don Camillo had stopped to look around.

"I'll expose you and your whole miserable gang," he shouted towards Smilzo. "No use your putting on an act like that with me."

"Father, I didn't kill your dog, I swear it!" Smilzo exclaimed.

"Good for you! Then swear that you didn't write this sign and this letter. And while you're at it, swear that you didn't take Thunder away with you on Peppone's truck on the twenty-fourth of last month!"

"I'm not swearing indiscriminately," Smilzo objected. "I simply swore that I didn't kill your dog."

"And what dog is buried at Pragrande, then?"

"I can't tell you," said Smilzo. "I found him dead on the road a week ago and buried him there. He looked a lot like Thunder, that's all. Afterwards I wrote you an anonymous letter in order to make you stop whining about your lost dog."

Peppone took Smilzo by the lapels of his jacket and shook him as if he meant to make a single hash out of brains and belly.

"Come out with the whole story," he shouted, "or I'll kill you like a dog."

After Smilzo had caught his breath, he told everything he knew.

"Thunder and I were great friends. He's a good dog; you'd never suspect he belonged to a priest."

Don Camillo picked up a hammer.

"Be calm, Father," said Peppone. "There's no use scaring an innocent witness like me. . . . Go ahead, Smilzo."

"We were friends, as I say. Every Saturday, when I went round to the markets with Peppone's truck, he came along. Once we stopped in a tavern at Peschetto and a fellow asked me if I'd sell the dog. I said that he wasn't mine, that I'd found him on the road. He said he had to have the dog to go hunting and put a thousand-lira note into my hand. I had had a good bit to drink, so I took it and went away. A mile farther on, I realized what a fool I'd been and started to go back for Thunder. While I was turning round Thunder himself ran up and made a flying leap on to the truck. We stopped at the next tavern along the way and drank up the thousand liras."

"You lout!" said Don Camillo disgustedly. "Did you teach him to drink, as well?"

"That was just a manner of speaking. I drank red wine and he ate a dish of red meat, such as I wager he never enjoyed when he was with the clergy."

"Never mind about the clergy," said Peppone. "Tell what you have to tell."

"There isn't much more," said Smilzo. "The following Saturday I thought over what had happened. Before stopping to eat lunch in Fornella I took off the dog's collar, smeared him with mud and took him in with me on the end of a piece of rope. Of course the rope was tied around his neck in clerical style, so that it could be slipped off, and I had showed him how to get free. I went to a tavern frequented by hunters and there I found a man who wanted to buy him for two thousand liras. And so on, and so on."

"What do you mean, 'and so on'?"

"I mean that I drove a mile or so down the road, stopped and waited for Thunder to catch up with me. When he came we had another bout of eating and drinking, just as before. In short, I'd found a first-class racket. I sold him, he ran away, and then we split the profits."

"And did he enjoy this game?"

"Of course he enjoyed it. He hasn't sold his soul to America, like you. He understands the economic situation and the necessity of sharing the wealth."

Once more Don Camillo picked up the hammer.

"And where is Thunder now?" he demanded.

"Last time I saw him was at Castelmonti, where I sold him for three thousand liras, but he never came back. I suppose he never managed to get away. That's the whole story. I didn't kill him; I only pretended he was dead in order to stop your whining about him."

"Good enough," said Don Camillo, waving the card in the air. "Theft, embezzlement, libel . . ."

Peppone felt he had to step in.

"To say that you're more of a dog than Thunder isn't libel; it's no more than the simple truth."

"We'll see what the court has to say," said Don Camillo. "I for one shan't let you off so easily."

"For once it's not a matter of politics," said Peppone. "Smilzo may have done wrong, but he did it entirely on his own, and with the complicity of your dog, who didn't hesitate to second him. Your legal action is directed at a private individual. If you want to send him to jail, go right ahead."

Don Camillo brought the hammer down on the anvil.

"I don't want to send anyone to jail. I want my dog! Between a thief who sells another man's dog for three thousand liras and a brute who cheats him by paying only a twentieth of the real value, there's not much to choose. But the dog is mine, and I want him back."

Peppone took his jacket off the hook and slipped it on.

"Shut your holy mouth," he said. "You shall have your dog." And followed by Smilzo he went out and climbed into his truck.

"I'm coming along," said Don Camillo.

"To Castelmonti," said Peppone, as Smilzo took the wheel. "We'll inquire in the tavern who bought the dog and then ransom him, by fair means or foul."

The truck speeded over the dusty roads of the lower Po valley in the direction of the distant hills. But after seven or eight miles Smilzo abruptly threw on the brakes.

"What's the matter?" Peppone asked impatiently.

Smilzo opened the door and a dog leaped into the cab. The dog was Thunder. Nobody said a word, and Smilzo turned round and made for home. After a mile the silence was broken by an angry growl and again Smilzo came to a sudden stop.

"What's the matter now?" asked Don Camillo.

"Our understanding is that at the first tavern we stop and divide the spoils," Smilzo explained. "I still owe him his share from the last time."

With Thunder at his heels he got out and went into the tavern in front of which he had stopped the truck. Peppone followed suit, leaving Don Camillo alone. It was as hot as summer, and under the metal top of the cab Don Camillo soon began to perspire. Finally he got out, went into the tavern and asked for a glass of water.

"Come in, Father," said the host, going by with a huge bowl of spaghetti in his arms. "Your friends are waiting for you in the next room."

The room was shady and quiet, and the spaghetti emanated an ambrosial odour. Don Camillo sat in front of a heaping plateful, and only then did Thunder abandon his reserved air and show his adoration. But Don Camillo was not to be corrupted.

"I'm paying for what I eat," he said stoutly. "No dishonestly gained bread for me!"

"Nor for me," said Peppone. "Every man must pay for himself, and the devil take the hindmost. But Smilzo's paying for both himself and Thunder."

"Then I'll pay for you, Peppone," said Don Camillo. "That way Smilzo and I shall both have dog guests!"

And he proceeded to enjoy his meal, because having the last word made it worthwhile to pay for an entire regiment.

VICTIMS OF WAR

MILCO DIDN'T KNOW how to begin, but finally he managed to say:

"It's about that German woman. Today is the twenty-sixth, and she'll be here the day after tomorrow."

He seemed to be intensely worried, and Don Camillo couldn't see why.

"Every twenty-eighth of March since 1946 she's descended upon you. She may just as well come this year, too."

Milco shook his head.

"You don't know the whole story, Father," muttered Milco; "that's why you can't understand."

True enough, Don Camillo knew no more than did the rest of the village. The story went back to the end of September 1943, when a small detachment of Germans had occupied the village. Among them was Sergeant Fritz, who functioned as quartermaster. He himself was lodged in Milco's house at La Torretta, not very far from the village, between the highway and the Stivone River.

At this time Milco was thirty years old, but he had stayed at home because of a lame leg and also because, in spite of this disability, he was the only man able to run the farm. Milco's wife was not strong, and his extremely healthy son was only eleven years old. There were no other members of the family, and in time of war, when agriculture is just as important as heavy industry, there can be no question of leaving the land deserted and unproductive.

Sergeant Fritz was a good-natured fellow, the same age as Milco, who went about making war as another man might have gone about store-keeping or accounting. Good German that he was, he had a weakness for Italian wine, and when he had drunk a bit more than necessary he would pull out of his wallet the photograph of a handsome, blonde young woman and a ten-month-old blond baby boy, which invariably moved him to tears.

Sergeant Fritz was happy in Milco's house, and both Milco and his wife treated him like one of the family. He had a happy-go-lucky temperament, and since he was in charge of the commissary department he never came back to the farm empty-handed. The sergeant stayed in Milco's house until 28 March, 1945. On the evening of that day he did not come back, and the next day he was fished out of the Stivone River, near Brugello. But it was plain that he had not drowned, for three bullets from a P-38 had gone clean through his head. In those days the Partisans were very active, and Sergeant Fritz had run into one of their bands.

The twenty-eighth of March after the war was over, a blonde young German woman and her blond baby came to La Torretta. The woman knew about four words of Italian and Milco knew about four words of German, so that they were able to understand one another.

"I am the widow of Sergeant Fritz," she told him, "and I have come to lay flowers on his tomb."

Milco took her to the cemetery, and she laid her flowers at the foot of the crude wooden cross on which was written the Sergeant's life story:

Fritz Hauser
2 March 1925 – 28 March 1945

Milco and his wife asked the woman and her child to stay with them for a whole week. The woman talked about the dreadful conditions in Germany and the difficulties she had encountered on her trip. But above all she talked about Fritz. She said that Fritz had written her a very moving account of Milco and his family, and that she had come not only to visit his tomb but also to pay a tribute of gratitude to them, in short, to thank them for all they had done for her husband.

"I had to sell every last bit of gold I possessed in order to make the journey," she told them. "Now I have nothing. But I hope to find a job, so that next year I shall have another money to come see you again."

She kept her word, and turned up promptly the next year and the one that followed. Punctually, on every twenty-eighth of March, she came with her child to stay for a week at La Torretta. By now everyone in the village knew her and her story. Whenever they met her in the street, they greeted her profusely because, among other things, she was "a fine figure of a girl". She had the generously proportioned sort of beauty which is especially appreciated in the fertile Po valley.

Don Camillo was still perplexed.

"I don't see what it is that requires such special understanding," he muttered. "No one can criticize you for letting her stay in your house, even if you're a widower. After all, you don't live there alone; you have your son and his policewoman of a wife with you. And your wife—God rest her soul!—was already dead when this German woman came last year. What has happened since then to change the situation?"

Milco hesitated for a moment and then said abruptly: "I simply don't want to see her again!"

Don Camillo shrugged his shoulders.

"Well, then, why have you come to me? That's none of my business. If you don't like her face, just write her a letter and tell her to stay away."

But Milco had something more on his mind, as was plain to see from the way he twisted his hat in his hands.

"As long as my wife was alive, I could talk things out with her. But now, who is there for me to talk to?"

By now the channel of communication was opened, and Don Camillo had only to let Milco have his say.

"Father, you remember how it was. I was tied up with the Resistance movement, and they had put me in charge of transmitting their radio messages. I had the radio hidden under a barrel in my barn. On that evening of 28 March 1945 Fritz caught me red-handed. . . ."

"Fritz caught you?" stammered Don Camillo.

"Yes. As usual, after we'd finished supper, I said: 'I'm going to have a game of cards with Ronchini.' And as usual, he said: 'Good luck to you!' I went out and started to walk across the fields, but when I reached the beech-tree I stayed there for a quarter of an hour and then retraced my steps. There was a little door at the rear of the barn which I was the only one ever to use. I slipped through it and took out the transmitting apparatus, just as I had done a hundred times before. But this time the worst possible thing happened: Fritz burst in and caught me at it. . . ."

He paused and wiped the perspiration off his forehead.

"A light went on, and there was Fritz standing before me, quite beside himself with rage. 'Traitor!' he shouted, with his hand on the butt of his pistol. I had my own finger on the trigger of a loaded P-38, which was always in my pocket, and I beat him to the draw. . . . Cursed war! . . ."

And he stopped again to wipe his forehead.

"If he hadn't called me 'Traitor', perhaps I wouldn't have shot him, but the word sounded like a death sentence. . . . It was dark and rainy outside. I loaded his body on to my shoulders, carried it down to the river and threw it in. The Stivone was running high and the body was swept a couple of miles downstream, to the place where it was later found. No one had the slightest suspicion. My wife was the only one ever to know, and now she's dead."

Don Camillo pondered for several minutes over this story. Finally he muttered:

"What can I say? Am I to call you a patriot or an assassin? Your own conscience must be your guide."

"That's why I'm here," Milco exclaimed. "I can't look at it from the patriotic angle. Even if I were to get a medal, I'd still consider myself guilty of murdering Fritz. I can't sleep at night. . . . The first time that German woman came and started to thank me for all I'd done for her dead husband, I thought I'd go through the floor with shame. . . . I killed him and she thanks me! And the fatherless child calls me uncle! No, I can't stand it any longer. I can't live through fifty-one weeks of the year dreading the fifty-second. I don't want ever to see her again; I don't want my stomach to turn over. Father, you can't imagine what I've gone through in the last ten years."

"Yes, I can imagine," said Don Camillo. "And I'm glad that you suffered. It shows that your conscience is working."

"Yes, it is," said Milco excitedly. "That's why I came here. I'm not looking for comfort. You can say what you please, but the fact remains that I murdered Fritz. You'll have to help me shake off that woman. I haven't the heart to do it, but surely you can tell her the whole story."

"I?" exclaimed Don Camillo, with wide-open eyes.

"Yes. She's arriving the day after tomorrow. You must talk to her. . . . It isn't right that she should thank me for my kindness and treat me like a friend. I'm taking something that isn't due. She must be told that I killed her husband, and then she must tell her son. That way she'll never come back, and my sufferings will be at an end."

Don Camillo shook his head.

"No, Milco, if you really have a conscience, then you mustn't seek to evade further suffering. It's not enough to repent; you must make amends as well. If the sight of this woman makes you suffer, then you must thank God for letting you see her. And why should you wish to hurt her still more? Aren't you satisfied with having killed her husband?"

Milco waved his arms wildly.

"Of course I don't want to hurt her!"

"Well, that's just what you're going to do. She trusts you and thinks of you as one of the family, and you'd rob her of this last illusion. If her presence gives you pain, so much the better. I'll say a prayer for you."

After Milco had gone away, Don Camillo went into the church to pray for him. But it was a very strange prayer.

"Lord," Don Camillo said to the Christ on the altar, "in this filthy land, there are tens of thousands of persons who killed tens of thousands of others. And they're not sorry; in fact, they brag about it. They want medals and positions; they want to be deputies to parliament, senators and publishers; they want their pictures in the school-books of the nation! . . . Now here's a poor devil who has suffered ten years just because he killed a man, and we are powerless to help him. We can't say: 'Look here, Milco. . . . When Fritz caught you with the radio, he called you a traitor, didn't he? Well, you could have called him the same thing! While you were in the barn working for the Resistance Movement, your wife, abetted by Sergeant Fritz, was working for Germany. . .without thought of resistance!'. . . No, Lord, we can't tell this to Milco, because his wife revealed it on her death-bed, and a priest can't violate the secret of the confessional. Lord, You know best, but is it right, I ask You?"

"Yes, it is, Don Camillo," Christ answered. "The sin of the wife doesn't cancel the sin of the husband. Each one has to pay. . . ."

March 28 rolled round, and with it came the Germans. As soon as Don Camillo heard of their arrival he hurried out to La Torretta, where Milco greeted him like a long-lost friend. It was a fine, sunny day and while the little boy played in the yard with the dog, his mother, Milco and Don Camillo went to look at the fields, which were just stirring from their long hibernation.

"You haven't much colour in your cheeks," said Don Camillo to the German woman.

"I work at a factory in a big city, where there's lots of smoke," she explained.

"That's no good," said Don Camillo gravely. "And don't you have to pinch and scrape all year in order to make this visit?"

"I don't mind pinching and scraping," she answered with a smile.

"Why don't you come and live here, near Fritz?" said Don Camillo. "That would make Fritz happy, I'm sure."

She stared at him in amazement.

"Don't you like it here?" Don Camillo asked her.

"Oh, very much! Italy is the most wonderful place! But I have a home and a job. . . ."

Don Camillo waved in the direction of Milco's house.

"Why not have a home and a job here?"

Don Camillo had no gift for parlour games, and so he came straight to the point:

"You marry him . . . he marries you . . . I perform the ceremony . . . that way everyone will be happy!"

The woman was thirty-seven years old, but she still knew how to blush and proceeded to do so. Milco was forty-two and too old for blushing, but he turned pale. Don Camillo was no matchmaker, and now embarrassment overcame him.

"Very well," he said. "Think it over. When you're ready you'll find me in my office. *Guten Abend.*"

And with that he went away.

Apparently they did think it over, for three days later Milco came to see him.

"Well, Father, you shall have your way, and we'll get married."

"Exactly. It's your way, too, I trust."

Milco heaved a sigh.

"Here's hoping that to have her around all the time won't give me more pain than ever. If my conscience still hurts me. . ."

"Let's get this straight, Milco," said Don Camillo. "Where Fritz is concerned, things are just the same. You took away his life, and you can't restore it. That will have to stay on your conscience. But when it comes to the woman and child, it's a different matter. You deprived her of her husband, but you're giving her another. . .and there'll no longer be a fatherless boy. Don't mix your accounts!"

"God help me, that's all I can say!" exclaimed Milco.

"He's helped you already!" retorted Don Camillo.

STRANDED IN THE STRATOSPHERE

WHEN THE CARNIVAL came for the mid-May holiday that year, the tents had to be pitched on the grounds that usually served as a livestock market. The whole region was in a political ferment and the Left-wingers planned to hold a series of meetings in the village square.

The carnival's improvised pitch was out of the way, on the outskirts of the village, along the road to Molinetto. But there were two startling new attractions: a big autodrome and a stratospheric merry-go-round. The stratospheric merry-go-round was a cornucopia of steel rods resembling the skeleton of an inverted umbrella. At the top end of every rod, there was a miniature aeroplane, and when the merry-go-round revolved, every rider could raise or lower his vehicle by simply pressing a lever.

The rectory was no more than three or four hundred yards away, and every evening, when Don Camillo retired to his room, on the second floor, he looked for half an hour or so out of the window at the revolving merry-go-round before drawing the curtain and going to bed. There is nothing in the least sinful about riding on a merry-go-round, either on the ground or in the air, but it is an amusement in which a priest cannot indulge. People have eyes to see and not much grey matter for thinking, and the sight of a priest on a merry-go-round would surely rouse them to derision. All this Don Camillo ruefully understood.

The autodrome and the stratospheric merry-go-round were the carnival's two great money-makers, and late in the evening, when the other attractions had closed down, they continued to draw the crowd. And the merry-go-round stayed open longest of all. Don Camillo did not fail to notice this fact, and one fine evening, after the autodrome had stopped running, he went downstairs and out of the house and walked, in a studiedly indifferent manner, across the alfalfa field behind the rectory. When he had reached the hedge bordering the Molinetto road he stood behind it and bided his time. Across the way, the carnival booths lay in darkness, with only the merry-go-round, in the centre of a small island of light, still turning.

Don Camillo's plan was eminently simple. As soon as the last load of riders had dismounted and started home to bed, he would come out from behind the hedge and ask the proprietor to let him enjoy a ride. He did not have long to wait before the merry-go-round came to a halt and a group of young fellows got down, leaped on to their motor-scooters and rode noisily away into the night. Don Camillo stepped across the ditch and walked straight towards his goal. The proprietor of the merry-go-round, who had stepped into the cabin to count his receipts, jumped when the great dark mass appeared before him.

"First priest you've ever seen?" asked Don Camillo.

"No, Father, but the first one I've ever seen out at this late hour. What can I do for you?"

"I sleep over there," said Don Camillo, pointing to the rectory, "and you've no idea of how your cursed music disturbs me."

"I'm truly sorry," said the man, throwing out his arms to signify that there was nothing he could do about it. "But a merry-go-round without music would be a funereal affair. Late in the evening, I turn the volume very low, but after dark the slightest sound seems to be booming."

"I quite agree," said Don Camillo. "But after you've upset so many of my evenings you ought to be ready to do me a favour."

"Certainly, Father; anything you say."

"Then give me a ride on your machine. And I mean right away."

The proprietor assumed a sincerely regretful air.

"Father, I'll have to ask you to be patient. I'm waiting for a group that arranged to have a couple of rides all together. There they are now."

Don Camillo wheeled round with the intention of making his escape, but it was too late. The group was directly behind him, and at its head stood Peppone.

"Our beloved parish priest!" he exclaimed. "Were you expounding the view that it's a mortal sin to ride on the merry-go-round?"

"No, I was simply saying that the music keeps honest folks from sleeping."

"Oh, is that it? I thought for a minute that *you* were the one that couldn't sleep."

Smilzo, Bigio, Brusco, Lungo and Fulmine, in short all the rest of the gang, had paid no attention to the encounter but were gaily clambering into their seats in the planes.

"And what has brought you here, Mr. Mayor?" asked Don Camillo in his turn. "Did you come to give your bad boys some wholesome recreation?"

"Come on, Chief!" called out Smilzo from the merry-go-round.

"Go along, Mr. Mayor," said the smiling Don Camillo. "The bad boys are calling. What fun to see such a great hulk of a mayor flying a miniature plane!"

"Not half as much fun as to see a great hulk of a priest like yourself at the same occupation!" Peppone retorted.

"The fact is, however, that I shall see a flying mayor, but you're not going to see a flying priest."

"Well, enjoy the sight while you can," roared Peppone, striding towards the merry-go-round." And don't fail to write a sensational article about it in the scandal sheet with which you plaster the village walls."

Peppone hoisted himself into a plane while the proprietor prepared to start up the motor, which was inside the cabin.

"Have fun, Father!" repeated Peppone. "Tell all your good little boys and girls that the Communist administration is spending the taxpayers' money on nocturnal orgies!"

The motor began to run, and out of a loudspeaker came the muted notes of a sprightly march.

"Give her gas, boss!" shouted Peppone, as his plane swung in front of the cabin. "That way the good Father will have a lullaby to put him to sleep."

"Shut your big trap!" sounded a voice directly behind him, and when Peppone turned round he saw that Don Camillo was in the plane following his.

By now the merry-go-round was turning at full speed and everyone was having a good time. But soon the damp night air got the better of Don Camillo.

"Tell that fellow down there to go a little more slowly," he shouted to Peppone.

Peppone pressed the lever and his plane dipped down. As it swung past the cabin he started to call out, but the words stuck in his throat.

"What about it?" shouted Don Camillo.

Peppone muttered something unintelligible and pointed to the cabin. Then Don Camillo went down in his turn and caught sight of what had startled Peppone. What he caught sight of was this: three men with handkerchiefs over their faces, all the way up to the eyes, and revolvers in their hands. The proprietor stood facing the wall and the three men were pushing the barrels of their revolvers into his back, while a fourth one of them dipped into the cash-register drawer and transferred handfuls of paper money to a brief-case. Meanwhile the merry-go-round was whirling at full speed, to the customary musical accompaniment.

The robbers were not satisfied with what they had taken, and two of them went with the proprietor to the trailer where he had his sleeping quarters in order to dig out something more. When they came out they were more dissatisfied than ever and began to manhandle their victim.

"It's no use insisting," he protested. "I took the rest of the money to the bank this morning. Look in my wallet and you'll find a receipt for it."

They found it and tore it angrily into a thousand pieces. And the merry-go-round kept on turning.

"Stop this thing, blast you!" shouted Smilzo as he passed by.

One of the bandits aimed a revolver threateningly in his direction and all the members of Peppone's flying squad pressed their levers simultaneously until the little planes were every one high flying. At this point the merry-go-round really looked like an umbrella turned inside out by the wind. The bandits were furious that their haul was so meagre, but their leader had an abundance of bright ideas.

"We'll separate those fools up there from their money," he suggested, and raised his face to shout in their direction:

"Empty your pockets, or else we'll shoot the brains out of you."

"Go to hell!" answered Peppone.

The leader gave an order to his second-in-command, who went into the cabin and turned a handle which caused the planes to whirl faster. Peppone's men cried out, but the bandits' third-in-command turned up the music until it drowned their cries. After half a dozen rounds, the leader jerked his head and the second-in-command brought the velocity to a little less than it had been before.

"Put your money in your handkerchiefs, knot them and then, when you pass in front of the cabin, throw them in. I'm giving you exactly half a minute to do what I say."

When the half-minute was up, he went on:

"Beginning with that fellow all in black, start throwing them in!"

Don Camillo, who was obviously the one answering this description, took what little money he had in his pocket and threw his knotted handkerchief into the cabin, and the others followed his example. The bandit leader picked them up and counted the money.

"Too little!" he shouted. "Throw your wallets with all the rest in them, or else I'll step up the speed. . . . I give you exactly five seconds. Beginning with that fellow all in black, start throwing them in!" Don Camillo, knowing he had practically nothing in his wallet and feeling that this was certainly one time that the poverty of the clergy paid off, threw his wallet. The others followed somewhat more reluctantly but soon seven wallets landed at the leader's feet; they were duly emptied and tossed into a corner. Then the leader turned to the proprietor.

"Don't stop that merry-go-round until a quarter of an hour after we've gone. And you'd better not try to double-cross us, because we'll know how to find you again. We'll set your whole outfit on fire and roast you alive."

Then the four of them ran for the car they had left on the road and drove away at top speed.

"Stop us, damn you!" shouted the high flyers to the proprietor below. But he was shaking with fear and let the merry-go-round run for the full quarter of an hour which had been enjoined upon him. Then the motor came slowly to a stop and the umbrella gradually closed. The seven took twenty minutes to collect sufficient strength to get out of their planes. Finally they joined the proprietor in the cabin and picked up the empty wallets from the floor. So far, no one had said a word, and now Peppone was the first to speak, grasping the lapels of the proprietor as he did so.

"If you breathe a word of what went on here tonight, I'll not only smash your head, but I'll see to it that you can't hold your carnival in any of the villages in our control."

"And those in *our* control won't have you either," added Don Camillo.

Then all seven of them trudged across the field together. Behind the rectory they said goodbye.

"When all is said and done, we had a very pleasant if somewhat expensive evening, did we not, Mr. Mayor?" said Don Camillo.

Peppone answered him with a roar which shattered the velvety stillness of the night and roused echoes miles and miles away.

Don Camillo slept well that night, dreaming of a heavenly merry-go-round which transformed even the most black-hearted customer into little children roaring with delight.

THE RAINS CAME

THE WEATHER CONTINUED to be wretchedly unseasonable. After a few sunny days, just enough for the ground to begin to dry, there came another downpour. It had started raining early in July of the preceding year, just when the wheat most needed sun. Then, when the wheat crop was practically ruined, the implacable rain went on to kill off the grapes. There was no opportunity to do the regular autumnal sowing, and immediately after Christmas, when the rain finally stopped, it was followed by an unprecedented fall of snow. And as soon as this melted there came more rain. The peasants were beside themselves, because the sprouting wheat was yellow instead of green, and many of them had to give back the seeds distributed by the beet-sugar manufacturers. Both oxen and tractors risked bogging down if they were taken out, for the irrigation canals were filled to overflowing and the fields were one vast sea of mud.

That Tuesday was a market-day, and the arcades around the square were crowded with peasants and tenant farmers, condemned to idleness by the bad weather. Their talk was all of the farm chores which the rain had prevented them from accomplishing, and some of them went so far as to involve the Deity in their tribulations.

"I don't see why Almighty God has it in for us poor farmers!"

As Peppone and Smilzo came out of a café together they caught this exclamation on the wing, and Peppone was quick to turn it to his advantage.

"Almighty God has nothing to do with it, my friends. He's attending to His own business, and there's no use dragging Him in. The fault lies with those people who are exploding the universe."

Peppone was a natural rabble-rouser. He knew just when to put in a word and had an infallible eye for spotting the one man in the crowd that would make a perfect foil. This time it was Girola, one of the oldest peasants for miles around, who was standing in the front row of the little assembly.

"You there, Girola," said Peppone "in all the ninety-seven years of your life, have you ever seen anything like this crazy weather?"

"No," said Girola, slowly shaking his head. "I've seen a bit of everything, storms and floods, and hurricanes that lasted for days or even weeks at a time. But an upset like this, going from one year over to another, is something I've never seen."

"And what do you say is the cause?" asked Peppone.

"Who knows?" muttered Girola, shrugging his shoulders.

"Don't say that, Girola," Peppone shouted, warming up to his subject. "You know, and you've been heard more than once to voice your opinion. There's no reason for you to keep mum about it now. No one's going to claim that it's a fairy-tale, that the rain comes only when God wills it."

So saying Peppone pulled a newspaper out of his pocket.

"Girola's not the only one to have seen clearly; now scientists have reached the same conclusion."

And Peppone held up the headlines for all to see. No one could say that this was a Party publication; it was an independent newspaper with a Rightist slant.

"Here is the voice of world science," Peppone continued, "and it says that we are quite right to be disturbed in our minds over the explosion of the Americans' hydrogen bomb. Their atomic energy has got out of control, and there's no telling what may happen. If you want to read about the damage caused in a three-hundred-mile radius by this last explosion, you can buy the paper. Just to bolster up Girola's opinion, I can tell you this much: a group of Swiss scientists has studied the matter thoroughly and concluded that the earth's balance is threatened by the atomic bomb. Here it is:

" 'Atomic explosions have created powerful currents in the upper atmosphere, moving in the direction of the North Pole. When the resulting centres of condensation reach the Pole, they are precipitated in the form of snow and ice. Such artificial precipitations may affect the balance of our planet: already the North Pole is eighteen per cent heavier than the South.' "

Peppone lifted his head from the paper and looked triumphantly about him. But his satisfaction was marred by the sight of a newcomer to the group, whose presence was anything but welcome. Nevertheless he asked a rhetorical question:

"What is the meaning, then, of this lack of balance between the poles? I never went further than the fifth grade and don't know a word of Latin, so I turn the problem over to an eminent Dutch scientist.

" 'Dr. Schneider, director of the Legerkusen Laboratories in Holland, says that the radio-active particles launched into the atmosphere by atomic explosions act as nuclei of condensation and determine the precipitation of rain and snow.'

"So why hold it against Almighty God if we have three feet of snow or a whole year of rain? The Americans are to blame."

Don Camillo had made his way up to the front row of Peppone's interlocutors, and when Peppone once more lifted his head from the paper, he immediately encountered the priest's eyes. They angered him to the point where he became aggressive.

"Yes," he repeated. "Don't hold it against God, hold it against the Americans.

Unless the Reverend Father, here present, has such regard for America that he'd rather you took it out on God!"

"No indeed!" exclaimed Don Camillo. "God has nothing to do with human folly. And He meant men to use their brains to think clearly. We've no business to hold anything against God; let us rather examine ourselves."

"Father, let's stick to the point," said Peppone. "The criminal stupidity of which we are talking is not ours, it's the Americans'. We're speaking of the hydrogen bomb, you know."

Don Camillo nodded assent.

"Right, Mr. Mayor. These things are too serious to be mixed with political propaganda. We must truthfully say that all the disasters, present and future, inherent in experimenting with the atomic bomb are to be laid at the Americans' door. Because, as the mayor has just told us, only the Americans have the bomb."

Without stopping to think, Peppone retorted:

"Nonsense! The Russians have the bomb too, and in a form a hundred times more powerful. It's no use your trying to twist the facts."

Don Camillo shook his head mournfully.

"Things are even worse than I thought, Mr. Mayor. If it goes on raining, these people will have to be told that the Russians, as well as the Americans, are to blame."

The little crowd laughed, and Peppone gritted his teeth.

"The Russians are not in the least at fault," he protested. "The Americans had the bomb first, and the Russians were forced to develop it for the sake of self-protection."

Don Camillo threw out his arms in mock despair.

"Mr. Mayor, if I were to shoot off my gun, whom would you blame? Me?——or the inventor of gunpowder?"

"And if I were to shoot off a gun at you," shouted Peppone, "whose fault would that be? Mine——or that of the bell-ringer at Torricella?"

"Neither one," said Don Camillo calmly. "I'd say it was the fault of those who taught you to deny God and shoot at the defenceless clergy."

"No one has taught me to deny God or shoot at the clergy!" shouted Peppone.

"Then your masters' teaching programme isn't up-to-date. But they'll catch up in time. That's what they've taught everywhere else."

At this point Smilzo stepped forward.

"Chief, there's one thing we have been taught, and that's not to let an adversary who's in patent bad faith bait us. Don't waste time arguing with him."

But Peppone was like a dog with a bone, and wouldn't let go. "We're not to be trapped by professional baiters," he said, "but this is an amateur. He deserves a lesson, and we shall see that he gets it."

Peppone had recovered his aplomb and now he turned to Don Camillo with a smile.

"Father, you say that atomic disasters are due to Americans and Russians alike, because both of them have the bomb. But can you tell me this? Why has public opinion been aroused only now, after the explosion of the American hydrogen bomb? Why is it that committees of scientists and statesmen have chosen to protest at this particular time? Because we've had ten months of rain and can't sow our beets? Is that it?"

"That I can't say, Mr. Mayor."

"Then I'll tell you. Public opinion and world science have been mobilized for a very good reason. The explosion of the last bomb has proved that atomic energy has escaped the Americans' control. When they set off bombs, nowadays, they don't know what may happen. That's the scientists' opinion, not mine. And who, may I ask, has been clamouring for years for mutual control of atomic energy? Russia or the United States? Russia, Father! America is to blame for having lost control of the atom, while Russia has kept it."

Don Camillo looked as if he were hard hit by the logic of Peppone. After a pause he said:

"Mr. Mayor, I can't say you're altogether wrong. You admit, then, that the American bomb is more powerful than the Russian?"

"I admit nothing of the sort!" shouted Peppone. "The Russians have the most powerful bomb by far. Only they haven't lost control of it, like the Americans. An effect obtained by calculation and one due to mere chance are two different things altogether."

Don Camillo nodded his head.

"Mr. Mayor, what do you say to continuing the argument with your hands?"

"Hands, feet, machine-guns, cannons, anything you say. . . ."

"Don't misunderstand me; I don't want to get you into a boxing-match. The rain has let up, and we can play a game that may prove to be amusing."

In the middle of the square there were still some remnants of the carnival: a shooting-gallery, a merry-go-round and an instrument for measuring a fellow's strength by means of a hammer. The test was to swing a hammer and bring it down on an iron base to which there was attached a measuring-rod and a mobile block which rose, under the blow, to a point numbered between zero and one thousand. If the block went all the way to the top it rang a bell and won a prize. When the two men stood in front of the instrument Don Camillo said:

"I'm the United States, and you're Russia; does that suit you, Mr. Mayor?"

The crowd ringed them round and listened in silence.

"The iron block is atomic energy. Is that clear?"

"Yes."

"I'm America, and since I've lost control of atomic energy I strike at random, not knowing how far I'll go. You're Russia and in full control; you strike a calculated blow."

Don Camillo took an enormous handkerchief out of his pocket and put it over his eyes.

"I'll just take one last peek in order to see where I'm to place the blow."

Then Peppone and he each took a hammer.

"Ready?" said Don Camillo.

"Ready," said Peppone.

Don Camillo spread his legs apart, raised the hammer and brought it down. The block went up to six hundred.

Peppone struck the next blow and sent it up to seven hundred.

With his second blow Don Camillo sent it up to eight hundred and ten. Peppone nine hundred.

Don Camillo nine hundred.

Peppone struck wildly and went back to eight hundred and fifty.

"Russia's weakening," jeered a reactionary at Peppone's shoulder.

And Don Camillo proceeded to score nine hundred and ten. Peppone summoned all his strength, clenched his teeth and struck a blow that would have shattered an anvil. The iron block went up like a V-2; it passed the thousand mark and hit the electric bell. When he heard the bell ring Don Camillo laid down his hammer and took the handkerchief away from his eyes.

"It happened to you," he said, "but it might just as easily have happened to me. Anyhow, now that we've hit the ceiling and made the world go up in flames we may as well go and have a glass of wine together."

Peppone was perplexed for a moment and then exclaimed:

"No, Father, the comparison doesn't hold water. The fault is yours. If we were to make an agreement to control atomic energy, neither of us would hit the ceiling."

"Exactly," said Don Camillo, "if we knew what the ceiling was. What if it were seven hundred and fifteen or six hundred and three? Do either American or Russian scientists know the limit of Divine Patience?"

It was raining again, and after witnessing the contest, the little crowd had once more taken refuge under the arcades. Don Camillo and Peppone were left alone beside the atomic machine.

"Devil take all bombs!" muttered Don Camillo.

"It's Almighty God's fault for having created Americans and Russians," said Peppone ill-humouredly.

"Don't be blasphemous, Comrade," said Don Camillo severely. "The human race has a big bill to pay, and the present generation has to make up for the deficiencies of the one that preceded it. We're late in coming upon the scene."

"Then the late-comers are fools," observed Peppone.

"No, Comrade; the only fools are those that haven't won a good place for themselves in the eternal life to come."

Peppone pulled the lapels of his coat together and said wryly:

"And while we're waiting for the life to come, it just goes on raining."

MADE IN USSR

"DON CAMILLO," said the old Bishop, "your letter grieved me, not so much for what it said as for what I read between the lines. What is the meaning of your discouragement? Have you lost the faith that has been your bulwark for so long?"

"My faith is unaltered, Your Grace," said Don Camillo sadly; "it's a question of technique, of mechanics."

And when the Bishop looked at him in astonishment he went on to say:

"The young people are getting away from me. It's as if they were racing off on motor-cycles and I were panting after them on foot. It's not faith that's lacking, but a motor-cycle."

"That's not good reasoning, Don Camillo; it's a play on words."

"Nevertheless, Your Grace, it reflects the true situation. I don't want to compete with the devil on his own ground; just because young people would rather dance than listen to my sermons, I shan't hold wild parties in the rectory. But because they are so dead set on the films, I want to show some that are a cut above the average. That's the point of what I'm trying to say."

"How can that be the point, Don Camillo?" said the Bishop, throwing out his arms in bewilderment. "Haven't you been putting on educational pictures for the last five or six years? What's so new about that?"

"The practice isn't new, Your Grace. And neither is the projector. It's an obsolete model, practically falling to pieces, and . . ."

"That's quite enough, Don Camillo," the Bishop interrupted. "If the Good Lord lets obsolete models—such as myself—endure so long, it must be because they're still use in one way or another. No, Don Camillo, you're trying to trick me. It's not true that you *need* a motor-cycle, you just wish you had one!"

But Don Camillo wasn't really trying to trick him. His 16-mm. projector was no longer a machine, it was the ghost of a machine that might have been. And a motor-cycle without a front wheel and saddle is a far less serviceable vehicle than shank's pony. Even the best film, when it came out of Don Camillo's projector, was a cinematographic omelette, and the sound-track was a cacophonic zigzag.

"The only thing I can suggest doing," said the big-city repair-man to whom Don Camillo had taken it, "is adding it to the rubbish, that is, if the Department of Sanitation will consent to take it!"

When he went back to the village Don Camillo was strongly tempted to throw the thing in the river, but he could not give himself this satisfaction until he was sure of obtaining a replacement, or at least of obtaining the money with which to buy one.

In spite of his remonstrances, the old Bishop did not send Don Camillo away empty-handed. He gave him all the money he could, and although it wasn't very much, Don Camillo went home feeling happy. The first step was taken. There were thousands more steps to go before he reached his goal, but they did not weigh upon him. No landslide ever starts until the first pebble has fallen from the top of the mountain.

And so, after due time, came the promised day, and the arrival of the projector, a brand-new model with a sound-track as smooth as velvet. Don Camillo white-washed the walls of the room and varnished the chairs. He rented a superlative film and posted announcements at every street corner. The afternoon before the great event he ran up and down the streets so often that inevitably he ran into Peppone.

"Is the mayor going to honour us with his presence tonight?" he asked. "It's such a big occasion that our first citizen should really be on deck."

"What big occasion do you mean?" asked Peppone in astonishment.

"The opening of the new picture palace."

"I've never heard of any picture palace, old or new," answered Peppone. "All I know is that for some years past you've shown magic-lantern slides for the benefit of choir-boys."

Don Camillo let this sarcasm go by.

"Let the dead bury their dead," he suggested. "We have a real hall and a fabulous new projector."

"Fabulous as it may be, you're probably coming in on the last guard's van, as usual."

"After you've been to one of our new shows, you'll see that this guard's van is up at the head of the train and moving faster than even a diesel engine."

"Fast or slow, the film is a superannuated medium," said Peppone. "It's dead as a door-nail, and there's no place for it outside a church hall."

"What medium is in step with the times, then?" asked Don Camillo. "The evening class in everyday revolution?"

"Leave politics out of it," said Peppone. "Progress has left the film behind. The coming thing is television."

Just then Smilzo arrived upon the scene and threw out the question:

"Chief, what do you say? The expert is here and wants to know where to put the aerial."

"Wherever he thinks best. I deal in combustion-engines, and television's not up my street."

Smilzo hurried away, and after swallowing a lump in his throat, Don Camillo asked:

"Is our mayor a pioneer television owner?"

"Not myself personally, but the workers' Party, whose place is in the vanguard of progress. The TV set is for the People's Palace, and tonight is the first showing. But we shan't offer you any competition, Father. The set is a product of the State Radio Plant of Moscow, and only Party members are invited. I can't ask you to come, Father, much as I regret it, that is, unless you take out a membership card."

"I admit that I'd like to see what this thing called television is all about," said Don Camillo between clenched teeth, "but I can wait a little bit longer."

"*Fate vobis*," said Peppone, throwing out his arms.

Don Camillo went home with a queasy feeling in his stomach and took his troubles to the Christ on the main altar.

"Lord," he panted, "Peppone and his gang have a TV set!"

"They're not the only ones in the world, are they?" Christ answered. "And it's not a death-dealing machine, is it?"

"They're not the only ones in the world, but they're the only ones in the village."

"But why do you worry? Are you afraid that the appeal of something so new may lure some of your followers into the bear's lair?"

"No, only Party members can enjoy it. But I had hoped that my film hall would attract some of Peppone's hangers-on, and I could save them from the bear's embraces."

Christ sighed.

"Are these your weapons, Don Camillo?" he asked. "I didn't have any machines with which to seize men from the devil's grasp and put them on the path of righteousness."

"Lord, forgive me," said Don Camillo, humbly bowing his head. "But the devil didn't have any machines then, either. If the devil rides a motor-cycle, why should I pursue him on foot?"

"Don Camillo, I can't follow your cycling metaphor. But the vehicles that carry men to heaven or hell are just the same now as they were then."

The television set poisoned Don Camillo's entire evening, and in spite of the success of the film show, he was unable to sleep. Something about the affair was not clear in his mind, and the thought of this elusive, shadowy zone would not let him rest. The next morning, when he looked out of the window that gave on to the church square and saw the television aerial rising above the People's Palace, he was suddenly enlightened. That afternoon he managed to run into Peppone again and said to him brusquely:

"In this television business, are you following a directive from the higher echelons, or did you think it up yourself?"

"What do directives have to do with television?" asked Peppone. "I do what I please."

"Then you're a jackass, Peppone. Only a jackass could imagine that anyone in this village would take out membership in the Communist Party for the sake of seeing the idiocies projected by your teletrap, 'made in USSR'. Who believes that they have television sets in Russia?"

"Oh, I forgot that in Russia they don't have either watches or bicycles!" said Peppone, throwing out his arms. "According to you, this set of ours, which has 'made in USSR' on every single part, is really a 'product of USA', is that it? As you like! Those that have television can enjoy it, and the have-nots will just have to swallow their bile!"

Don Camillo's anger was plain to see, and he did well to go away without answering this last sally. When he reached the rectory he had to hear some first-hand reports on the village reaction to the new TV.

"It seems to be positively wonderful."

"And it was really made in Russia, so they say."

"The Reds who went to the first showing are wild with joy. They say the Americans had better go and bury their heads in the sand."

That night Don Camillo turned over and over in his bed, and his long quest for sleep was thwarted by the chatter of several noise-makers who wagged their tongues immediately under his window, on the church square.

"Too bad, though, that when they have colour TV we'll need a new set."

"A new set? Not a bit of it! They haven't got colour at all in America, but in Russia they've had it for the last two years. And the sets made for export are geared to both black-and-white and colour. Did you see that red lever on the right side? You just pull it down, and there's the whole rainbow."

"If I were Peppone, I'd put it on display at the Party's retail store, so that everybody could see. That way they'd stop saying that we keep it to ourselves because it's either home-grown or made in America."

"Not on your life! They can say what they like, but if they want to see, they'll have to join the Party!"

Don Camillo was a captive audience. And when they stopped talking so loudly and began to laugh and whisper, he jumped out of bed and glued his ear to the aperture of the shutters.

". . . a hall just as dismal as the other . . ."

". . . films more idiotic than ever . . ."

". . . and they say the sound is ear-splitting . . ."

". . . but what should he know about machines? They saw him coming . . ."

". . . you know what it is, when a man has a wad of money, whether it's a few liras more or less . . ."

In order not to burst with rage, Don Camillo dived back into bed, where he didn't shut an eye before morning. But by the time morning came he had swallowed his anger and his brain was functioning in a normal manner. "A canny player plays his cards close to the chest, and no one can guess what he has up his sleeve. If you're not showing your Soviet TV set, it's because the whole thing's a big story. You'll puncture your own balloon, if I give you time, Comrade Peppone!"

And so Don Camillo inaugurated a policy of complete indifference. When anyone spoke of the famous Russian TV set, he answered with a smile:

"If the Russians have the atomic bomb, why shouldn't they have TV sets and send them to their friends abroad?"

"What about the colour TV?"

"They've always been colourful! Why shouldn't they apply this quality to television?"

And so one, two, three months went by. Every evening there was a change of the guard at the People's Palace, and a different group went to see the show, gathering afterwards below Don Camillo's window, on the church square, for an exchange of extravagantly laudatory impressions. Don Camillo was rudely awakened, and had to listen in grim silence. He held out for some time, but on perhaps the ninetieth occurrence it was too much for him to endure. "Enough is enough!" he muttered to himself. "I've taken all I can, God forgive me!"

This was ten days after the snowstorm which had caused the collapse of the roof of the People's Palace and the attic below. The roof and the attic ceiling had been promptly repaired, but the night watchman's quarters were still uninhabitable, because the walls had been soaked with water and the cement was not yet dry enough to permit removal of the scaffolding. The watchman, Lungo, and his wife and child were temporarily quartered elsewhere, and from midnight to four o'clock in the morning the People's Palace was empty.

One foggy evening a man went through the open door leading to the courtyard and climbed resolutely to the attic, where he lay for several hours in ambush. At midnight Lungo let down the iron curtain at the front of the retail store, gathered up the day's receipts and accounts, inspected the premises, locked the doors and went to his mother-in-law's house. The intruder had such self-control that he waited two hours more before going into action. Slowly he made his way to the ground floor and the assembly hall. All the shutters were closed, and he was assured of complete privacy. With the aid of a torch he surveyed the scene. What he was looking for seemed to be veiled by a piece of cloth at the opposite end of the room. He walked over, removed the cloth and gazed upon a shiny, new TV set, surmounted by a metal plate bearing the inscription "Made in USSR". It wouldn't have been very hard to nail a plate of this kind on to a case containing an American or British or Italian machine, and so the investigator detached the back cover. At this point his emotion was so great that he dropped the torch on to the floor.

"Lord," panted Don Camillo, throwing himself on to his knees before the altar, "something utterly astounding has happened. A fellow who accidentally got into the People's Palace last night took a look at the famous Russian TV set. And what do you think was inside the case? Nothing! Did you hear me? N-o-t-h-i-n-g! The case was empty!" And after wiping the perspiration from his brow he went on: "Yes, Lord, empty! For ninety consecutive evenings those poor fools have taken turns going in groups to the People's Palace and then coming out to tell of the miraculous things they've seen. What colossal nerve, Lord! For three months no one has let the cat out of the bag. Just imagine the fun there'll be tomorrow, when the secret is known! The Russian TV! And yet I'll wager that if the discoverer doesn't tell his story they're quite capable of keeping up the farce indefinitely. Isn't it utterly ridiculous? Are they stark mad, to play a part like this, without ever giving themselves away? Self-discipline, they call it, but I have another name . . . Lord, you aren't even listening. . . ."

"I was thinking of the sorrows of the world, Don Camillo, not of the tall tales you've been telling. What is it, then, that the visitor to the People's Palace saw?"

"Lord, a fellow accidentally got in there last night and saw the famous TV set," said Don Camillo, hanging his head. "It's authentically 'made in USSR'."

Don Camillo didn't breathe a word to a soul, but a week later when he ran into Peppone he couldn't resist remarking:

"Comrade, when will your faithful give up the game of the empty box?"

"When the time is ripe, Rev.!"

"Isn't it all very silly?"

"Just try getting up something equally silly among your highly respectable people!"

To this Don Camillo found no reply.

The next morning the village was startled by an amazing piece of news. A short circuit had caused the famous TV set to go up in flames.

"*But the enemies of the People have no cause to rejoice,*" said the poster which Peppone put up on the façade of the People's Palace. "*The working class, no matter how ground down it may be, will have another TV!*"

They took up a collection, and ten days later the People's Palace no longer had an empty box; it had a box full of TV.

"It's not nearly as good as the Russian set we had before," proclaimed Peppone's henchmen, "but it's better than nothing."

And from their point of view, they weren't so very wrong.

INFLATION IN THE PO VALLEY

THE QUESTION OF television continued to be a sore point with Don Camillo, and smart salesmen have a way of sensing such things. The young man with the handsome tan briefcase was all smiles when he came to the rectory, insisting that all he wanted was to make the acquaintance of the most famous priest of the lower Po valley. Don Camillo still had some hundred jars of "Atomic Floor Wax" in the basement, and he wasn't going to fall for sales talk, no matter how many blandishments went with it.

"Thanks for your kind words, but I really don't need a thing."

"Father, you misunderstand me," the young man protested. "I'm no salesman, I work for Guardian . . ."

"I see, it's life insurance . . ."

"No, Father, you must be thinking of some other organization. 'Guardian Purchases' is an entirely different matter, as you can see for yourself."

These last words meant that he had managed to open his briefcase and put a dazzlingly illustrated catalogue into Don Camillo's hands.

"Motor-cycles, bicycles, cameras, typewriters, refrigerators, radio and television sets . . . 'Guardian' buys all these things direct from the makers at such a discount that it can make house-to-house sales on the instalment plan, with no increase over the list prices."

Don Camillo tried to give back the catalogue, but the young man would have none of it.

"Don't worry, Father, I'm not here to sell. I only mean to give you an idea of all the lines we carry. If ever you want to buy any of these things, I'm sure you'll come to us. For instance, some day you'll surely get a television set, and it'll be worth your while to look over our large assortment. . . ."

The smiling salesman must have been Satan in disguise, or else how could he have known that Don Camillo was crazy to have a television set? But so far nothing serious had happened. Just to look at photographs of television sets didn't mean promising to buy one. The young man made this very clear.

"You have here an enormous range of models, from the cheapest to the most luxurious, all of them well-known makes. You can see for yourself that we charge the normal retail price, and the payments are extraordinarily easy. We call ourselves 'Guardian Purchases' because our system actually guards and protects you. The debt you contract with us practically pays itself."

Don Camillo was so taken with the television sets that he forgot about the store of useless wax in the basement. But he did not forget that his personal finances were disastrously low. And so, after feasting his eyes on the catalogue, he insisted on returning it.

"I'll keep what you told me in mind," he said by way of farewell.

"Thank you," said the salesman, tucking it away in his briefcase. "Just let me repeat that you needn't worry about the money. The day you decide to make your purchase just let me know and I'll come to write out the contract and pick up the initial payment. Of course, if here and now you happen to have as little as five thousand liras, it would be even simpler. . . ."

He must indeed have been Satan in disguise, or else how could he have known that, besides the burning desire for a television set, Don Camillo had exactly five thousand liras in his wallet? In any case, when he walked out of the rectory he had them in his pocket, together with a signed contract and a sheaf of signed promissory notes. Of course, he said that these notes were a mere formality and Don Camillo mustn't worry about meeting them. Don Camillo didn't worry. For some time he had warm feelings about the smiling young man, because the television set was a beauty and worked very well. But one day he found himself in trouble.

At the end of the fourth month Don Camillo couldn't meet the payment. The television set was his own personal luxury and he had to pay for it out of his own personal funds, which at this point were not merely low but virtually non-existent. Eighteen thousand liras aren't so very much, but if a poor country priest hasn't got them, what is he to do? He can't work overtime or give private instruction in the catechism. There was no excuse for appealing to his wealthier parishioners, for no object or institution of charity was involved. And no matter how poor he was, Don Camillo had his dignity. He couldn't borrow money to meet the payment due for a television set; after all, it was an extravagance and he ought never to have taken it if he didn't have extra means.

Finally he wrote to "Guardian Purchases", but they wrote back that although they appreciated the unusual circumstances in which he found himself and were truly sorry, there was nothing they could do. The note had been sent to the bank and he must either pay up or submit to the bank's demand for payment. Complications increased, because Don Camillo was unable to pay the next instalment either. This time he did not have the nerve to write; he simply said a prayer and waited for pandemonium to break loose. The situation was particularly delicate for this reason. Although with time Don Camillo would doubtless have been able to restore his affairs to good order, a local election was at hand, and this was not the moment to have the bank publish his name. Don Camillo was not a candidate for office; he was not even enrolled in any political party. But the Christian Democrats' opponents were sure to seize any pretext for attacking a priest. Furthermore, to tell the truth, Don Camillo had been active in the last national election and the Christian Democrats had discussed their tactics with him. He broke out into cold perspiration at the thought of what Peppone and his gang would do if they had the bank's list of bad accounts in their hands.

After a number of sleepless nights and tormented days, the time for the bank bulletin's publication came round, and Don Camillo went all the way to the city to get a copy. Sure enough, the first thing he saw was his own name. He went back to the village in a state of great dismay and shut himself up in the rectory where nobody could see him. For he imagined that everyone must be in the know. That evening he ate no supper and could not even make up his mind to go to bed, but paced up and down the hall, with black thoughts crowding his mind. Peppone and his gang had acquired a formidable weapon against him, and he could just hear the accusations they would make in political meetings. His horror was all the more intense because he seemed to hear the crowd laughing. He must do something—anything—about it. And so, abruptly, he did.

Peppone was still hammering away in his workshop, and the sight of Don Camillo caused him to start.

"You must have something on your conscience," said Don Camillo.

"A priest flitting about by night is bound to startle even an honest man," said Peppone dryly. "What do you want?"

There was no use making a short story long.

"I want to talk with you, man to man."

"What about?"

"The promissory notes."

Peppone threw his hammer into one corner.

"I have something to say, man to man, too," he said. "And I'd like to point out that, in spite of our enmity, I've never made political capital out of your personal misfortunes."

"I can say the same thing," said Don Camillo.

"I'm not so sure about that," Peppone grumbled. "But there's one thing that *is* sure: if you dare to be funny about my overdue note, I'll wring your neck."

Don Camillo thought he must have misunderstood.

"What's your note got to do with it?" he asked.

Out of his pocket Peppone pulled a crumpled paper, which he thrust roughly at the priest.

"If you haven't seen or heard about it, you'll be sure to see or hear tomorrow. On the list of notes that have not been honoured there's one signed by your humble servant, Giuseppe Bottazzi."

And there, under the letter *B*, was listed a note for twenty thousand liras in Peppone's name. Don Camillo had never noticed it simply because he was so intent upon looking for his own.

"Is that the only thing of interest you found?" he asked, shaking the bulletin in front of Peppone's nose.

"I confine myself to my own business," said Peppone. "I wanted to know if I was there, and there I was."

Don Camillo put the bulletin into his hand, pointing to a certain line. Peppone read and re-read it, and then stared hard at Don Camillo.

"No!"

"Yes!" Don Camillo exclaimed. "Devil take 'Guardian Purchases'!"

Peppone started.

" 'Guardian Purchases'? A most agreeable young fellow with a big tan brief-case?"

"Exactly."

"And did you get a refrigerator, too?"

"No, a television set."

Peppone launched into a tirade against instalment buying, an institution worse than the atomic bomb. Just a spot of cash and a trifle to pay every month, a debt that pays itself. . . . Then when you're unable to pay, you see that you were the trifler, and two hundred thousand liras of debt are . . . two hundred thousand liras. Finally he calmed down.

"Well, since my refrigerator is working perfectly well, and you're in the same boat, there'll be no political consequences. Why worry? Don't you agree?"

"That's what I say," said Don Camillo. Then a sudden thought caused him to turn pale.

"What about the third ticket?" he shouted.

The third ticket was a group of candidates put up by the Rightists, who were opposing both Peppone's Reds and the Christian Democrats' Shield and Cross. These candidates would have a cogent argument against both their adversaries, and the village would enjoy no end of laughter. Pietro Follini, the Rightist leader, was a fast thinker and an eloquent speaker. Peppone too turned pale.

"The idea that because of these filthy notes they may bracket me with the wearer of a clerical collar makes me see red!" he shouted.

"And the idea of being dragged down to the level of a godless fool makes me see black!" retorted Don Camillo.

They mulled it over for a quarter of an hour, and then Peppone pulled on his jacket and said:

"I'll go through the fields, and you go along the river. We'll have a showdown with that miserable Pietro Follini. First, you try to make him see reason. If he doesn't respond, I'll make him see stars."

Follini had gone to bed, but he came downstairs when he heard Don Camillo calling. Great was his amazement when he saw Peppone beside him.

"Have you set up a common front?" he asked. "I'm not surprised. Reds and clericals have the same end in view: dictatorship!"

"Follini, keep your wit for political meetings," said Peppone. "See if you can grasp what Don Camillo is going to tell you."

They went to sit down in the parlour, and Don Camillo at once showed Follini the bank bulletin.

"Have you seen that?" he asked.

"Yes, I've seen it. I went to the city this morning for the express purpose of buying it. When I saw my name, I took it hard. But when I saw the names of the priest and the mayor, I felt better."

Don Camillo took back the bulletin and thumbed nervously through it. Under the *F*'s there was Pietro Follini, listed as owing forty thousand liras. The three men looked at one another in silence, until Don Camillo said:

"I owe 'Guardian Purchases' twenty thousand liras for a television set; he owes them the same for a refrigerator. How about you?"

"I owe them forty thousand for a television set *and* a refrigerator. Both of them are working very well."

"Same here!" said Peppone.

"Same here!" echoed Don Camillo.

Follini opened a bottle of wine. They drank together and before Don Camillo went back along the river he muttered:

"I'm glad there's not a fourth ticket!"

And before Peppone went back through the fields he mumbled:

"We're neatly matched. Television against television, refrigerator against refrigerator, and promissory note against promissory note! It's democracy in action!"

THE DEVIL SWISHES HIS TAIL

MICHAELMAS WAS CLOSE at hand, and festive preparations were under way, when the bombshell burst. It burst in the form of a notice posted by Don Camillo.

> "*For too many years the coming holiday has been celebrated with indecent public dancing in the square. It is time for all good Christians to join in outlawing this immoral spectacle. If foolish folk of both sexes and all ages must cavort like monkeys to the accompaniment of jungle cacophony, let them find a place more appropriate to their carnival than the square in front of God's house.*
>
> "*It is prohibited by law to organize public dancing or other offensive activities in the neighbourhood of a church, and I call upon the duly constituted authorities to enforce this prohibition.*"

Of course, the notice sent Peppone into a paroxysm of anger, for he and his gang were the sponsors of the "indecent public dancing" in question. The "Public Welfare Committee" was called into immediate session at the People's Palace, and proceeded to discuss counter-measures to this act of clerical aggression. When Brusco was called upon to speak, he declared:

"We have all the time in the world to counter-attack. Just now we must concentrate on obtaining a permit for the dancing. After that is cleared, the priest can protest till he's blue in the face."

The majority seconded him, and Peppone went by bicycle to police headquarters.

"I was just about to bring you the permit," the sergeant told him.

"So we can go ahead with our dancing, just as in previous years?" asked Peppone with relief.

"Yes, you have the all-clear of the provincial police. Only you mustn't dance in the square. The carnival ground isn't the legal distance from the church."

"But, Sergeant," Peppone exclaimed, turning purple with rage, "the distance was legal enough for the past seven years! What's the matter with it now?"

"The distance was never legal, Mr. Mayor. But as long as the priest didn't kick, the police winked at it. Now that there's been a protest, we've had to open our eyes."

It's a matter of only a few yards, and it's up to the priest's discretion."

"But if we can't dance in the square, where *can* we dance?" asked Peppone in dismay.

"Anywhere you like, just as long as the carnival is set up at a legal distance from the church. The permit is issued under that condition."

Peppone called the committee together again and explained the situation.

"This cursed village seems to be laid out in a way designed to benefit the clergy and poison honest working people! If you take away the square, there's no space large enough to hold a carnival. It's either the square, or the outskirts; there's no other alternative. And if you stage it in the outskirts, what happens? First, you miss the crowd from the cafés and taverns on the square; second, you have to pay rent for the use of the land; and third, you are humiliated by having to operate in the middle of a sea of mud, littered with fallen apples."

Brusco had a word to put in.

"Chief," he said, "since the sergeant told you it was up to the priest's discretion, why don't we go and talk reason to Don Camillo?"

Peppone pounded the table with his fist.

"I'll never lower myself to the level of a priest! Never!"

"I didn't say you should be the one to go parley with him. There are twelve of us, all able to speak up and hold our own. Let's write our names on slips of paper and then draw one out of a hat. Tell the barman's son to bring us something to write on."

And so, after each one had written his name, folded his sheet of paper and thrown it into Brusco's hat, the barman's son proceeded to the drawing.

"Peppone!" he announced.

"Did it have to be me?" Peppone groaned.

Brusco threw out his arms.

"Never mind; I'll go," muttered Peppone. "Brusco, you stay here, and the rest of you can go on home."

When Brusco and he were alone togther, Peppone picked up the hat and took out the eleven remaining ballots. He unfolded them, one by one, and spread them out in a row on the table.

"Look at those, Brusco, and then tell me whether or not you're a bunch of rascals!"

Brusco examined the ballots and saw that every one bore the name of Peppone.

"Brusco," Peppone shouted again, seizing his companion by the shoulder; "is this the way the comrades rat on their leader?"

"No, Chief, it only goes to show what confidence they have in him!"

"Father," said Peppone, sitting down on the chair which Don Camillo pointed out to him, "have we come to the point where we have to argue over a matter of inches?"

"I'm not arguing over inches," Don Camillo replied. "I'm raising a moral question, which defies all measurement."

"But in past years you didn't raise any moral question. There wasn't anything wrong then, so what can there be now?"

"There was always a moral question involved, Mr. Mayor. But I was hoping you would see it for yourself."

"It's much simpler than that," jeered Peppone. "The fact is that you were more afraid of us in past years."

"I was never afraid of a living soul, and you know it," said Don Camillo, shaking his head. "If I didn't step in before, it's just because I knew people were incapable of seeing the light. It's no use arguing with madmen. Now the atmosphere is calmer, and the question can be raised. When people have lost all sense of proportion there's no point in talking about inches. Everything has its proper time."

"I see, Father," assented Peppone. "According to you, the Communists have lost strength and so you can speak your mind. You may think as you please, but I consider you're making a mistake. One day you'll find out that the Communists still count."

"I don't doubt it, Comrade; otherwise I should have ceased to combat them. Wolves stay wolves, and sheep can't be anything but sheep. When the wolves are prowling around the sheepfold, the sheep daren't stick out their noses, but when the wolves go back to the woods, the sheep may come out and nibble a few blades of grass."

"So I'm a wolf, am I?" muttered Peppone.

"Yes."

"And you're an innocent lamb, is that it?"

"Exactly."

"A fine lamb you are!" shouted Peppone, leaping to his feet. "You're a Bengal tiger!"

As he went towards the door, Don Camillo called out: "See you soon, baboon!"

Peppone, still fuming, informed the committee of the upshot of this conversation.

"Curse that priest! Devil take him and his legal distance! We'll dance in the outskirts, but with two orchestras playing so loudly that they'll be heard on the square. It's only a matter of finding the right location."

While Peppone, was holding a meeting in the People's Palace, Don Camillo addressed a group of landowners whose property lay in the outskirts of the village.

"I called you together," he said, "because you are good Christians and hence lovers of law and order. Once more the day sacred to Saint Michael is going to be defiled by the Reds' public ball. I have managed to prevent its being held, quite shamelessly, on the square. But the Reds won't give up so easily; they'll simply transfer it to the outskirts. Even there, they'll be checkmated, because you'll refuse them the use of your land. I trust you are all in agreement."

His eight hearers were all ferociously anti-Red, but Don Camillo's words were not greeted with the enthusiasm which he had expected. They said nothing, and stared at the mat on the oval table before them.

"Well, then?" said Don Camillo in amazement. "If you don't see things in the same light, just say so."

They stared at one another, until finally Cerelli said what was on all their minds.

"Father, you're quite right. But to tell the truth, I don't see the necessity for a clash with the Communists on this particular occasion. If they ask me for the use of a piece of land and are willing to pay for it, why should I say no?"

The other seven admitted that they felt the same way. Don Camillo crossed his arms over his capacious chest.

"Very well. Your priest calls for your help and you refuse to give it."

"No," said Cerelli. "We'd do anything for you, Father. But you mustn't ask us to do more than we feel like doing."

"And what if I were to ask you to do something involving no risk and giving you a chance to make some money?" asked Don Camillo, bringing his fist down on the table. "How would you feel about that?"

"It sounds good, Father."

"Splendid! How much do you think Peppone may offer you for your land?"

They said somewhere between fifteen and twenty thousand liras.

"Excellent," said Don Camillo. "Then the eight of you must agree that anyone who wants your land must put down a sixty-thousand lira deposit. Just think, some one of you may actually pocket that much money!"

This idea won his listeners' favour.

"Good," said Don Camillo. "But we'll have to be sure that no one puts anything over on his neighbours by accepting less. Are you willing to give me your word of honour that nothing less than a deposit of sixty thousand liras will induce you to do business?"

They all swore, and shook hands on it. It's not that way in the city, but in the Po valley, when a man gives his word it is considered binding. And so Don Camillo went to bed with his mind at rest. To spend sixty thousand liras for a couple of days would be utter folly, and Peppone's plans were doomed from the start. It wasn't really the season for a carnival, anyhow; the bulk of the dancers would come from other villages near by. Without the usual contributions from the storekeepers on the square and faced with the prospect of digging up sixty thousand liras in cash, Peppone would have to surrender.

Peppone knew nothing of the trouble which Don Camillo was brewing for him, and the next day he sent Smilzo out on a reconnoitring mission.

"Go and see about renting some land. Remember that you are fortunate enough to be dealing with eight separate owners. If any one of them asks too much money, you can afford to pass him by in favour of one of the seven others. Don't worry about their doing you in. Rich people don't know how to organize such a thing as joint action. Their only wish is to rub up against one another. So remember that I don't want to spend more than twelve thousand liras, to be paid when the carnival is over."

Smilzo went bravely off, and when the first landowner he approached asked for sixty thousand liras cash, he laughed in his face. He laughed again when the second made the same demand. But the third aroused no more than a faint smile, and the fourth wiped that off his face. When he had finished making the rounds, Smilzo came gloomily back to where he had started.

"Chief," he began, "two hours ago you said that rich people were too stupid to organize a joint action."

414   THE WORLD OF DON CAMILLO

"Well, what of it?" asked Peppone.

"You're dead wrong, Chief. This time they've all banded together and none of them will rent his land for less than sixty thousand liras, paid in advance."

Peppone began to describe in a loud voice that sink of iniquity which was the soul of Don Camillo. He concluded his tirade by saying:

"Comrades, there are two alternatives before us: either to concede the clericals' victory, or to squeeze out sixty thousand liras. Choose! But think first which course is the more expensive in the long run."

"Chief, we haven't really an idea of the market prices," Brusco observed.

"But you have an Ideal, for which you are willing to die, haven't you?" Peppone shouted.

Brusco wanted to answer that pledging one's life to an Ideal and promising to pay sixty thousand liras are two quite different things. Especially when the liras have to be put down on the spot, for a man who pledges his life to an Ideal isn't compelled to die in advance for it. But he did not say any of these things, and so it was decided that a clerical victory would cost more grief than the outlay of sixty thousand liras. Because none of the Committee had brought any money, Peppone was the one to fork out.

Don Camillo took it hard when he learned that Peppone had put down sixty thousand liras in cash for the rent of a field to the left of the Molinetto road, just outside the village. He hadn't anticipated any such blow. And when he read posted announcements of the carnival, he took it even harder. The posters made extravagant promises: prizes for the best single dancers, the best-matched and most ill-assorted couples and the presence of two orchestras, together with well-known popular singers.

"They're getting up something tremendous," his informants told Don Camillo. "It's advertised in the villages for miles around, with a special appeal to their Party groups. Yes, it's become a political football, an act of resistance to clerical interference."

Don Camillo lost his head. Wasn't the whole fault his? Hadn't he asked for trouble? If he hadn't intervened, the carnival tents would have been pitched on the square; Peppone and his gang would have organized the usual uninspired celebration.

Yes, Don Camillo lost his head. Whenever this happened the consequences were disastrous, for the devil's tail began to swish with anticipation. After having foamed impotently at the mouth with anger, one whole day long, Don Camillo called his most reliable follower, Gigi Lollini.

"Gigi," Don Camillo said to the young man, "have you seen what those damned souls are up to now?"

"Yes, Father, I have."

"Gigi, we've got to make it fail. You must form a committee and set up another carnival, just across the way. If the Reds have two orchestras, then hire three; if they have three contests, stage half a dozen. You have a head start, because while Peppone's had to advance sixty thousand liras, you'll get the land for next to nothing. Go to Cerelli, whose place is just opposite the one rented by Peppone.

Only don't let on that I'm in any way concerned. A parish priest can't sponsor a forty-eight-hour dance marathon."

Lollini was a violent anti-Red and undertook the assignment with enthusiasm. He scuttled away and went first to rent some of Cerelli's land. Soon he came back to the rectory.

"Father, that old skinflint wants sixty thousand liras. I asked the other six, and they told me that they had all promised to accept no less. After imposing these terms on Peppone, they feel they must stick to their guns. The main thing is that they don't want trouble. . . . I found some fellows to go into partnership with me, but they refuse to spend more than fifteen thousand liras, and I haven't any cash to advance myself."

Yes, the devil's tail was swishing ominously. Don Camillo paced up and down the rectory hall and then said:

"I can get my motor-cycle later on. Here are the sixty-five thousand liras I've been saving up; I'll give you all but five of them."

"Don't worry, Father, you'll get them all back. We have a programme that will put the Reds to shame, and we'll give it plenty of publicity. . . ."

The next day the village was filled with posters announcing "the carnival of the century", put on by the "Good Fun Company". Afternoon and evening dancing were to appropriately honour the feast of Saint Michael.

The morning of the last day before the celebration Smilzo and Lollini came to blows over trifles. Soon after noon a truck arrived with material for the Reds' carnival, and two hours later, while it was still being erected, came the material for Don Camillo's, just across the way. At two-thirty, the rival gangs met in the middle of the road and beat each other up enthusiastically. By evening, both carnivals were nearly ready, but it looked as if the next day were going to be the saddest Michaelmas the village had ever known.

"Lord," said Don Camillo to the crucified Christ on the main altar, "if You don't step in, tomorrow is going to be ugly for all of us. Everything in this crazy village revolves round politics, even an immoral but non-political ball. Because of the rivalry between the two groups which have organized the dances, it's likely that the celebration will end in a free-for-all fight. Unfortunately, a minister of your church is mixed up in it, because he ill-advisedly supported one group against the other. He had good intentions, Lord. . . ."

"Don Camillo!" the Lord interrupted, "you know what's paved with good intentions! And since when does the end justify the means?"

"Lord," whispered Don Camillo, "unless it's a lie circulated by God's enemies, You Yourself once drove the money-changers from the temple. Of course, I don't say that beating people up is a sin, but after all . . ."

"Don Camillo, how do you dare criticize your own God?"

"I'm not sacrilegious, Lord, but I do say that when one of God's creatures has an ailing tooth, then even if the dentist hurts him by pulling it out . . ."

"Don Camillo," Christ said gravely: "why do you walk in the tortuous path of sophistry?"

"Because I've got off the right track, Lord, and I wish someone would put me straight, with a swift kick, if need be."

Slowly Don Camillo raised his head to look at Christ's face, but his eyes remained on the feet, nailed to the Cross.

It was a terrible night for Don Camillo. He woke up at four o'clock and ran to the window. It was raining, raining buckets and torrents. And as the hours went by, it continued to rain. It rained all day, and by midnight the floor boards of the two carnivals were floating in mud. It rained all of three days more, and amid the downpour both carnivals were dismantled and shipped away. Then, when God willed it, out came the sun, and Don Camillo ran into Peppone.

"Father," Peppone said bitterly, "your manoeuvres cost me sixty thousand liras out of my own pocket."

"They cost me the same," sighed Don Camillo.

"That makes me feel better," said Peppone.

"Then we're even," put in the priest.

"But on Michaelmas of next year . . ." Peppone began, threateningly.

"You mean, if it isn't raining . . ."

"I forgot that you clericals are in on God's little secrets," Peppone shouted angrily. "But it won't go on like this forever. There'll be a day of reckoning!"

"That is, if it doesn't rain, Mr. Mayor!"

"We'll fight with umbrellas," Peppone said solemnly, as if he were speaking for history.

And in order not to spoil the effect, Don Camillo said nothing more.

RING OUT THE OLD, RING IN THE NEW

DON CAMILLO WAS called to the Bishopric, but since the old Bishop was ill Monsignor Contini received him.

"Tell me all about the 'Bridge' church."

This was the last question Don Camillo had expected and for a moment he was so taken aback that he could not open his mouth.

"The 'Bridge' church? Forgive me, Monsignore, but I don't know what you mean."

"It's not so hard to grasp. There's a building within the boundaries of your parish known as the 'Bridge' church, isn't there?"

"Yes, Monsignore."

"Well then, tell me all about it."

Don Camillo gathered his thoughts together and then told the brief story.

"The so-called 'Bridge' church was until fifty years ago in an independent parish in the Pioppetta section. Then, as the village grew, the Pioppetta parish was integrated with ours. But the 'Bridge' church remained officially open, by virtue of a yearly Mass celebrated on St. Michael's day."

Monsignor Contini shook his head.

"According to what I'm told, there's something more to say. The faithful who live out that way would be happy if Mass were said there every Sunday. Isn't it so?"

"Undoubtedly, Monsignore. The Pioppetta section is quite far out, and the road leading to the centre of the village is in miserable condition. To come in every Sunday is a real hardship, especially for the old people."

"Then everything we have been told is true. We are distressed only that you shouldn't have been the one to inform us."

"But, Monsignore, no one from the Pioppetta section has ever said anything to me."

"Very well. But when you've noticed a number of people from there failing to turn up at Sunday Mass, especially during the winter, you might have thought to report the situation. In any case, now that it has been reported, we shall see that something is done about it. Every Sunday and holy day of obligation Mass shall be said at the 'Bridge' church."

Don Camillo bowed his head.

"With God's help, I shall carry out the Bishop's orders."

"With God's help and the help of the young priest we are going to send to assist you. We aren't asking you to make an unreasonable effort."

Don Camillo's mouth fell open.

"But, I really don't need . . ." he stammered.

"Don Camillo," Monsignor Contini interrupted him, "we know your good will. But for all of us the years are going by. You're getting to be, well, shall we say, a mature man. . . ."

"I?" exclaimed Don Camillo, throwing out his chest. "I can still carry a three-hundredweight sack of wheat up to a second storey!"

"I don't doubt it! But your job is not weight-lifting, and muscles are not the prime requisites."

"Monsignore, I've always carried out my priestly mission. . . ."

"I'm sure of that, Don Camillo. But we can't expect you to go beyond the call of duty. We shall send you a bright, enthusiastic young fellow, who'll relieve you of some of the drudgery of parish work. The rectory is big enough to lodge him, and the generosity of Divine Providence is unfailing, so that you'll have no trouble in putting him up."

"I shall obey orders, as faithfully as ever."

"As *almost* ever," his superior corrected him. "We know Don Camillo and esteem him at his just worth, but in all truth we can't say that he is an example of perfect discipline. Don Camillo is an honest, diligent priest, but he has a bit of temperament . . . or am I mistaken?"

"No, Monsignore. I admit to my weaknesses."

"Let's forget about them," said Monsignor Contini. "When you go back to the village, put the "Bridge' church in order, so that it can be turned to full-time use as soon as possible."

"Monsignore," said Don Camillo, throwing out his arms. "When it was a matter of saying only one Mass a year, I brought the necessary supplies with me. But what are we to do now? The church is an empty shell."

"There are people in your village who are not only well off, but who have means far beyond their needs. You must make the rounds of all those who are in a position to give. Tell them that by contributing to this little church they will warm their ailing Bishop's heart."

These words particularly caught Don Camillo's attention.

"Is he so very ill, Monsignore?"

"Yes, but there's no reason to be alarmed or to spread the alarm. It's nothing you can put your finger on, but simply the effect of old age. What His Grace needs above all is complete rest and peace of mind. We must not allow him to worry."

"He needn't worry about the little church under my jurisdiction!" exclaimed Don Camillo. "All that he wishes shall be done. Even if I have to use brute force . . ."

"Come, come, Don Camillo! . . ."

"That's just a manner of speaking."

The "Bridge" church was in a sorry state. The walls were sturdy enough, but the ceiling looked like a sieve; the plaster was in tatters, the floor uneven and the pews cracked or cracking. Even a minimum amount of repairs called for a considerable sum of money, and the collection of such a sum called, in turn, for what seemed like an infinity of patient endeavour. When Don Camillo had drawn up an estimate of the costs, he drew a deep breath as well. "I'll do everything I can, and Divine Providence will look after the rest," he concluded.

His campaign got off to a lame start, when he knocked first at the door of Filotti, the richest landowner in the vicinity. Don Camillo spoke of the old Bishop and of the pleasure it would give him to hear that the little "Bridge" church was back in use. But Filotti shook his head.

"Father, when you've asked for money for the poor or for the Orphan Asylum, I've always been happy to contribute. But this time I don't feel like giving. The village church is quite sufficient. And, frankly, I don't see why, at this point, I should help to finance propaganda directed against my own class."

"Come now!" exclaimed Don Camillo. "Have I ever supported propaganda against landowners?"

"Father, I'm not speaking of you personally. I refer simply to what I read in your newspapers and the speeches made by your senators and deputies to parliament."

"The Church has neither senators nor deputies!" Don Camillo protested.

"That isn't the way you sounded around election time," said Filotti calmly.

Don Camillo's second stop was at the house of Valerti, who listened quietly to all he had to say and then likewise shook his head.

"Why should I give you money?" he asked. "It would mean that those of us whom you call 'neo-Fascists' would be blasted from two pulpits instead of one."

Without seeking to defend himself, Don Camillo continued his rounds, but his third visit was no more fortunate than the other two, for Signora Meghini hardly waited for him to end his plea before she started violently shaking her head.

"Father, if you're looking for money with which to open a second church, go to the Republicans. Don't forget that you refused Absolution to all of us who voted for the Monarchist Party."

Don Camillo went next to Moretti, a landowner of pronounced clerical tendencies. Moretti listened piously to all he had to say, and answered with a sigh:

"Since you speak of the Bishop, I can't say no. But mind you, it's only for his sake."

"Very good," said Don Camillo, "but why must you tell me that only the good Bishop inspires you? Have I failed to please you in some way?"

"Not you personally," said Moretti, shaking his head. "But generally speaking, I can't approve of combating Communism by attacking the upper class."

Don Camillo pocketed Moretti's contribution and went to knock at still another door. Perini opened it in person and gave him ill-humoured attention.

"There's not much I can do, Father," he said. "My family just manages to get along, from day to day. Here's my mite, but let's hope that the new priest is up-to-date."

"Up-to-date?" exclaimed Don Camillo. "What *do* you mean?"

"It's time people got it into their heads that the world is turning definitely to the Left. We militant Catholics insist upon a social programme, and until the clergy catches up with us, Communism will continue to gain ground. And Communism's no joke, Don Camillo. Don't go imagining that all Communists are like Peppone!"

Don Camillo said that he imagined nothing of the sort, and went to knock at the next door. He made a hundred or more visits, and everywhere he received a reply like one of those quoted above. After several days of going from place to place he unburdened himself to the crucified Christ on the main altar.

"Lord," he said, "the rich reproach me for championing the poor, the poor accuse me of conniving with the rich; the whites call me black, the blacks call me white; to the reactionaries I'm a subversive, and to the radicals I'm an obstacle to progress; and as for the Reds, they won't listen to me at all. Am I truly the most ineffective of God's ministers?"

Christ sighed and then answered:

"Don Camillo, you're a skilled hunter and fisherman, aren't you?"

"Yes, Lord."

"You hunt with a gun and fish with a hook and line, don't you?"

"Yes, Lord."

"Then if one day you were to see fish flying through the sky and birds slithering under water, would you still fish with a hook and line and hunt with a gun?"

"No, Lord, I'd fish with a gun and hunt with a hook and line."

"That's where you're wrong, Don Camillo! Because you'd fail completely in both endeavours."

"Lord, I don't understand."

"Many do not understand, Don Camillo, because they look at mere words instead of realities."

Don Camillo collected only enough money to repair the roof of the abandoned church, and it was with a heavy heart that he reported to the Bishopric.

"Never mind, Don Camillo," said Monsignor Contini. "Divine Providence will take care of the rest."

And indeed, after Don Camillo had finished patching the roof, money came from the city for the rest of the repairs. As soon as the work was all done he went to give the good news to Monsignor Contini.

"Then next Sunday you can celebrate the first regular Mass at the renovated church," the Monsignor told him.

Don Camillo's face lit up with joy.

"Monsignore, does that mean you're going to leave me in charge?"

"No, Don Camillo, that would make too heavy a load for you to handle. The new curate is to join you tomorrow. But for a while you'll officiate at the 'Bridge' church, while he takes your place in the village. After that, you'll take turns for a while, before settling upon a definitive division of labour."

"I don't see the reason for so many changes, Monsignore."

"That's not hard to understand. I know the mentality of your village people. They have a mistrustful and hostile attitude towards anything new. The faithful from the outskirts would be quite capable of making the arduous trip to the centre of the village rather than go to a Mass celebrated by a *new* priest. But if you are there for the first few Sundays, they'll surely come. Then, when they've fallen into the habit of going to the renovated church, they'll continue to do so after your assistant has taken it over. The Bishop wants you to follow this procedure."

"May I speak to His Grace?" asked Don Camillo, humbly bowing his head.

"His Grace is very ill. He must have complete rest."

"I'd only like to wish him well."

"He can't talk to anyone. Even listening tires him. The doctor's orders are that he is not to talk or listen or read. Yes, the good man is seriously ill."

Don Camillo sighed.

"Where is the Bishop's room?" asked Don Camillo. "As I go out, I'd like to look up at his window."

"It's on the third floor, but the window gives on to the courtyard, so that no noise can disturb him. I'll try to find a propitious moment for conveying your good wishes to him."

"Thank you, Monsignore," said Don Camillo, bowing his head.

"When the new curate arrives, I trust you'll give him a hearty welcome and tell him about the local political situation. He's an extremely capable young man, and up-to-the-minute on social problems."

"Yes, Monsignore."

Don Camillo went slowly down the majestic stairs. When he reached the empty front hall he paused for a moment to look into the courtyard, surrounded by arcades, like those of a convent or monastery. The entrance to the courtyard was just across from the front door, and Don Camillo pushed it open and went in. The courtyard garden was untidy, filled with snow and surrounded by high walls. Don Camillo raised his eyes to look at the long row of windows on the third floor. Which one, he wondered, belonged to the old Bishop? Behind the blackened trunk of a withered tree, he waited for some sign of life from the third floor. But nothing moved, and after lingering for some time, he went away, with his feet soaked from the snow and a chill in his heart.

THE NEW CURATE

AT NINE O'CLOCK the sky abandoned its ambiguous and threatening air; the clouds were brushed away and the sun's honest face started beaming. After the unseasonably stormy weather which had prevailed all through the Spring, Don Camillo at last found cause to rejoice as he hoed his garden. But his joy was short-lived, for the bell-ringer's mother came to disturb him.

"Father, the young curate has come," she announced.

Don Camillo was prepared for the shock and took it with apparent nonchalance.

"Bring him along, then," he said, still intent upon his hoeing.

The old woman looked perplexed.

"I just showed him into the hall," she muttered.

"Well, since I'm not in the hall, but out in the garden, show him out here."

The old woman went away and a few minutes later the young priest was standing at Don Camillo's side.

"Good-day, Father," he said.

Don Camillo straightened up, and the young priest added:

"I'm Don Gildo."

"Very happy to see you, I'm sure," said Don Camillo, giving him a handshake powerful enough to strangle a boa constrictor.

The young priest paled, but he had been instructed in sports and sportsmanship, and so he managed to smile.

"I have a letter from the Bishop's secretary," he said, holding out a large envelope.

"If you don't mind, I'll look at it right away," said Don Camillo, taking the letter out of the envelope. After he had finished reading it, he added: "I told the Bishop's secretary that I was still able to carry on. But since it is the Bishop's will to relieve me of part of my burden, then there's nothing I can do but bid you a hearty welcome."

Don Gildo bowed politely.

"Thank you, Don Camillo. I am at your service."

"Those are kind words; I have something for you to do at once."

He went over to the cherry-tree, took down a hoe that was hanging from one of the branches and put it into the young priest's hands.

"Two of us can finish the job more than twice as quickly as one," he observed.

The young priest stared first at the hoe and then at Don Camillo.

"To tell the truth," he stammered, "I've no experience of instruments of this kind."

"That doesn't matter. Stand beside me and do exactly what I do."

The young priest flushed with annoyance. He was sensitive, and besides, he had his dignity.

"Father," he said, "I have come to look after souls, not gardens."

"Of course," said Don Camillo calmly. "But if we are to have fresh fruit and vegetables on our humble table, then the garden must receive some looking after."

He went on hoeing, while the young man continued to stand helplessly beside him.

"Well," said Don Camillo at last, "you mean you really won't help this poor, feeble old man?"

"It's not that I don't want to help you," the other protested. "But the fact is that I came here as a priest."

"The first requisite of the priesthood is humility," said Don Camillo.

The young priest clenched his teeth and started, somewhat ferociously, to lay about him with the hoe.

"Don Gildo," observed Don Camillo mildly, "if I have offended you, take out your resentment on me rather than on this innocent ground."

The young man made an effort to wield the hoe more gently. It took two hours to finish the work. When the two priests, splattered with mud up to their knees, came back to the rectory, it was eleven o'clock.

"We've just time to do another little job," said Don Camillo, leading the way to the shed, where there were some elm logs to be sawed.

Not before noon did Don Camillo call a halt. The young man had stored up so much bile in the last three hours that he had no inclination to touch his food. After a single spoonful of soup, he pushed the bowl away.

"Don't worry if you seem to have lost your appetite," Don Camillo told him. "It's the change of air."

Don Camillo had a tremendous appetite himself, and after he had cleaned up two big bowls of vegetable soup with salt pork, he resumed the conversation.

"How do you like the place?" he asked.

"I've hardly had a glimpse of it," the young man replied.

"It's a village just like any other," Don Camillo told him, "with good people and bad. The only difficulty is in telling which is which. As far as politics goes, the Reds are very strong. And the trouble is they seem to be getting stronger. I've tried everything possible, but things continue to worsen."

"It's all a question of method," the young man assured him.

"Have you a new method better than the old?" Don Camillo asked curiously.

"I don't mean to make any comparison, and I don't pretend to have found a sure cure. But I do say that we must approach the question from a fresh point of view, or at least without the blinkers which have prevented us from seeing social realities. Why are the Communists so successful among the lower classes? Because they say to them: 'Come with us if you want to be better off; we take away from the rich and give to the poor. The priests promise you pie in the sky, but we invite you to cut yourselves a slice here on earth'."

Don Camillo threw out his arms.

"Quite so, Don Gildo, but we can't embrace the materialistic point of view."

"That isn't necessary. We must cease creating the impression that we defend the status quo. We must speak of rights as well as duties. Of course, if everyone did his duty, he would automatically respect his neighbour's rights. But we have to assert the rights of the poor in order to compel the rich to do their duty. That way, Communism will cease to have any meaning."

Don Camillo nodded gravely.

"Very true. In other words, we should compete with the Communists on their own ground, even to the point of breaking the law of the land."

"Exactly. When the law of the land upholds privilege and permits poverty, then it is contrary to justice and hence to divine law."

Don Camillo threw open his arms.

"My dear Don Gildo, I can follow your train of thought, but I'm too old to adapt myself to it. I haven't the mental agility any longer. You'll have to forgive me."

Because the curate's mental agility was youthfully intact he poured out a stream of big words, expressive of concepts that were startlingly new. He was aware, moreover, of having a definite mission.

"Father, we know where we're going, and we shall surely attain our goal. You've done a remarkable job, under truly difficult circumstances, and it's high time you had someone to help you. And I don't mean only to help you hoe your garden or saw wood."

"Forgive me," said Don Camillo humbly. "I had no idea how widely read and excellently trained you were."

The curate had scored a conspicuous triumph. That very afternoon he began making his own contacts in the village and laying plans for future action.

Three days later Don Camillo said to his new assistant:

"You came at just the right moment. I need a complete rest. If it isn't too much for you, I wish you'd take my place entirely for a while. The weather has got me down. I need warmth and dry air, and for months it's done nothing but rain."

This suited the curate perfectly. He answered enthusiastically that Don Camillo should have no worry at all, for he would shoulder everything, gladly. And so Don Camillo went into retirement. He went no further than the second floor of the rectory, whose two large rooms looked out, one over the garden and the other over the sports field. The bell-ringer's old mother brought him his food, and he stayed there, in complete seclusion. In one room he had his bed and in the other a small field altar where he said Mass every day, all alone, but very close to God. He had brought up a box of books and spent a great part of the time reading. After two weeks had gone by the old woman broke her habitual silence and said:

"Don Camillo, as soon as you feel up to it, come back downstairs. The new curate is making plenty of trouble."

"Trouble? He seems like a very quiet young man."

"Quiet? He's not a priest, he's a permanent political rally. Lots of people are staying away from church."

"Don't let yourself be disturbed. New days, new ways. They'll get used to him in the long run."

But the new ways really weren't going over, and a few days later the bell-ringer's mother made a new report, which epitomized the whole situation.

"Father, do you know what Peppone said yesterday? He said that as soon as

Don Gildo succeeded in emptying the church completely, he'd take him on as group chaplain."

After another interval of a few days, she informed Don Camillo of the answer Filotti had given to somebody who asked why he hadn't been seen at Mass lately. "I'd rather go and listen to the harangues Peppone gives in the People's Palace. He's not nearly so insulting."

Don Camillo held his counsel as long as he could. But after forty days he knelt down impatiently in front of the crucifix on the camp altar and said:

"Lord, I bowed humbly to the Bishop's will. I withdrew in order to give Don Gildo complete freedom. You know, Lord, how much I've suffered all this time. Forgive me if I go downstairs, take Don Gildo by the scruff of his neck and dispatch him back to the city."

It was eight o'clock in the morning, and because Don Camillo wanted to look his best when he finally put in an appearance, he decided to shave. Throwing open the shutters, he discovered that it was a radiantly beautiful day. He paused to take in the peace of the sunlit scene. But a minute later he heard a loud noise. He drew back, but continued to look out at the boys of the "Invincible" soccer team as they ran nimbly on to the field and started at once on a practice game. Forgetting his beard, he watched them play, but to his sorrow they were far below standard and continually fumbled the ball.

"If they play that way against Peppone's team, they'll take a terrible beating," he reflected.

Just then Don Gildo ran out on to the field and stopped the game in order to confabulate with the players.

"So he's going to ruin my team as well as everything else," roared Don Camillo. "If he doesn't decamp, I'll smash him into small pieces!"

But the curate seemed to have no intention of vacating the centre of the field. At a certain point he took over the captain's place and with the ball between his feet, embarked upon a breathtaking display. Don Camillo cast prudence to the winds and flew, rather than walked, down the stairs. When he reached the field he took Don Gildo by the collar and hauled him into the rectory.

"Take off your cassock, put on a jersey and a pair of heavy shoes and go on with your coaching!"

"How can I?" the curate stammered.

"Wear long trousers, a mask and a fake moustache, if you insist, but go ahead and play! You've got to lick that team into shape."

"But my mission, Father . . ."

"Your mission is to secure a victory of our team over the Reds. That will be a knock-out blow."

The "Invincibles" shattered the Red "Dynamos" and made mincemeat out of them. They celebrated madly, while Peppone and his team were in the dumps. That evening Don Camillo gave a banquet in honour of the curate. After it was over he said:

"From now on, forget about your social programme and concentrate on the soccer team. I'll look after the Communist menace!"

THE CHAMPION

RENZO WAS THE sort of fellow that for twenty-five years had jumped on to his racing cycle every morning and ridden all the way to the city to buy the daily *Sport Gazzette*. Of course, he could have bought it on the village square a little later in the day, but that wouldn't have given him the same joy. To pedal fifteen miles to the city and back was his only regular occupation. The rest of the time he was ready to accept any odd job he could get, as long as it allowed him time to buy his paper and read the section concerned with cycling.

Renzo wasn't touched in the head and he wasn't a loafer or a drinker. Cycling was his only interest, and he knew everything there was to know about it. Because he devoured not only the cycling section of the *Sport Gazzette*, but every single piece of printed matter on the subject of bicycles and bicycle races that he could lay his hands on. Renzo was forty years old, and during all the twenty-five years that he had been under the sway of this ruling passion people considered him of no account whatsoever.

Then, all of a sudden, thanks to the Marshall Plan for aid to western intellectuals, the television quiz game was imported from the U.S.A. and Renzo's life took a new turn. When he heard that one of the programmes was to feature a cycling expert, he hurried to glue his eyes on the screen at the Molinetto tavern. And when the master of ceremonies opened the sealed envelope and began to read out the cycling questions, Renzo came up with every one of the answers. The first evening, the tavern habitués took a mild interest in what he was saying; the second week, when he continued to say the right thing, their interest grew. Then, the third week, when the questions got really tough and the expert was shut into a cabin, Renzo's quick thinking caused quite a sensation. The final week, the expert fell down badly on the three decisive questions, but Renzo knew better than he, and the tavern habitués were visibly impressed.

"Why, he could be in the big money!" they exclaimed.

This wasn't the end of the story. Another amateur expert was called on to the programme and walked away with the maximum prize. And the Communist mayor of Reggello, where he came from, organized a big reception, with a brass band and speeches, and hailed him as a man who had brought honour and distinction to his native town.

At this point Peppone called his henchmen together.

"Any political party that manages to enrol Renzo will have a big attraction for the masses. Local elections are just round the corner and we need all the votes he can bring in. Renzo has got to join up, cost what it may!"

They discussed the problem far into the night and the next morning, when Renzo was mounting his bicycle to ride to the city, he found Brusco, Bigio and Smilzo in his way.

"Renzo," they said, "why don't you join the Communist Party? We can get you a road-worker's job and give you a new suit into the bargain."

"I don't want to be mixed up with political parties," said Renzo, and pedalled away.

The comrades saw that there was no point in pressing him too hard, and so Renzo was able to go and buy the *Gazzette* as usual. But at the Pioppaccia intersection a group of Christian Democrats was lying in wait.

"Renzo," they said; "you're a God-fearing man, and you owe it to yourself to join God's party. If you sign up, we'll get you a job at a garage and a new suit of clothes."

But Renzo shook his head.

"I joined God's Party when I was baptized," he retorted.

The stakes were high, and there were hard-headed men on both sides. When the Reds made their second attack they had more to offer: the post of road-work inspector, a suit, an overcoat and a dozen handkerchiefs.

The Christian Democrats were not slow to match them, holding out not only the job at a garage and the suit of clothes, but an overcoat, a raincoat, a dozen handkerchiefs and six pairs of stockings as well. This moved Peppone to come forward with a desperate last-minute bid: a brand-new racing cycle. After which, their rivals could propose no less than a motor-scooter.

"Choose any make you like," they said to Renzo, "and we'll foot the bill."

"No," was Renzo's reply.

At this point they lost patience and their leader said shrilly:

"What the devil *do* you want, then? A car?"

"I don't want anything," explained Renzo. "I don't give a hang about political parties. I get round very well on my bicycle and I don't need either an overcoat or a raincoat."

By this time the espionage and counter-espionage departments had had ample time to function. The Reds were acquainted with the Christian Democrats' tactics, and vice-versa. Since Renzo showed no signs of giving in, and all the while television quizzes were becoming more and more popular, Peppone disregarded his position in the Party and fell back on that of mayor. He called representatives of all the democratic parties to a meeting in the town-hall and addressed them as follows:

"My fellow-citizens! When the spiritual and material interests of the community are at stake, partisan politics must take a back seat. We have gathered together out of concern for the general welfare, and I am speaking as one of you. The achievements of the champion from Reggello and the praise given him by his mayor point to the necessity of forming a non-partisan committee to present our candidate for television honours and win for ourselves the same glory."

These stirring words met with loud applause, and the committee turned out to have five Communist and five Christian Democrat members. They went to work at once and closed their first session with a highly satisfactory order of the day. The next morning they went in a body to Renzo's house and set forth the situation.

"Renzo, this is no question of politics or political parties. It involves the interests of the whole village, not to mention your own. You must get on the next television quiz. We'll start the ball rolling, somehow or other, and put you over. Because the good name of the village is at stake, we'll get you a whole outfit of new clothes, send you to Milan by car and give you some cash besides. That way you can win the prize money and our village will be in the headlines. Besides, the *Sport Gazzette* is published in Milan and you'll be able to get it hot off the press."

But Renzo only shook his head.

"The *Gazzette* I buy in the nearest city is quite good enough for me. I don't have to go all the way to Milan."

"And what about the money? You're not too high-and-mighty for that, are you?"

"I said I didn't want to get mixed up in politics, didn't I?" said Renzo.

"But this isn't a matter of politics. No one's asking you to join any party."

Renzo continued to shake his head.

"Five of you offered me a road-work job, and the other five a job in a garage. I simply don't trust you."

The next step was logical enough. Peppone with his five Reds and Piletti with his five Blacks converged upon the rectory. Don Camillo greeted them with considerable perplexity.

"Father," said Peppone, "I am speaking as first citizen of the village and representative of all the rest. You're the only man who can convince Renzo that it's not politics, but a matter concerning the village reputation. He has a good chance of winning the jackpot of the television quiz programme and so he simply *must* compete for it."

Don Camillo stared at him with amazement.

"Do you mean to say that you want to put the village idiot on the air?"

"Who else is there?" said Peppone. "You, Father? Do you know when and in what race Girardengo had cramps in his right leg?"

"No, I don't," admitted Don Camillo.

"Well, we need a fellow that knows just this kind of thing. And that means Renzo. He may very well win the big prize."

"What? Renzo win five million liras?"

At this point Piletti, the leader of the Christian Democrats, intervened:

"Father," he said with some annoyance, "I'm afraid I'll have to remind you of something you surely know, since it isn't among the rules of the quiz contest: 'Blessed are the poor in spirit, for theirs is the kingdom of heaven.' "

"Come, come," Don Camillo retorted; "I have a distinction to make there. The Gospel doesn't tell us that the 'poor in spirit' are village idiots."

"This is no time to bicker about trifles," put in Peppone. "You know perfectly well how things stand, and it's your job to tell Renzo that politics don't enter into them."

Don Camillo threw out his arms and exclaimed:

"May the people's will be done!"

★

"Renzo," the priest said. "If I guarantee that politics has no part in this affair of the television quiz, will you believe me?"

"Yes, Father."

"And if I give you my word of honour that they want to help you only in order that you may win the big money and put our village in the public eye, will you believe me?"

"Yes, Father."

"Then accept their offer, and sign up for the quiz."

"No, Father."

Don Camillo was frankly puzzled.

"Renzo, you simply don't want to be quizzed. Tell me why."

"Because I have my dignity, Father."

Don Camillo did not insist. He paced up and down the room and then came to stand with outspread legs right in front of his interlocutor.

"Renzo, if you're giving up all that money, you deserve some recompense. I'll hire you as bell-ringer."

Renzo was taken with this idea. What more suitable occupation could he hope to find? He thought it over for five whole minutes and then shook his head.

"I can't do it, Father. The bells have to be rung in the morning, and that's when I go to the city to buy the *Sport Gazzette*."

"But exactly the same paper is sold here!" shouted Don Camillo.

Renzo laughed.

"No, Father; the city paper is an entirely different thing. . . ."

In matters of stubbornness Don Camillo was something of an expert but in this case all he could do was mutter some semi-biblical phrases about the stiff-necked race of sport fans.

THE CARBURETTOR

THE NEWSPAPERS WERE still full of the story of the child whose life had been saved by the miracle drugs sent by plane from America. Even after the child had recovered they continued to feature the story. According to the Hammer-and-Sickle crowd, it was nothing but a propaganda stunt cooked up by the United States ambassadress.

It all happened in a village on the big river, some twenty miles from the parish of Don Camillo, and so when the dispute was at its hottest Peppone felt he must step in, in order, as he said, "to protect the good reputation of the lower Po valley". His version of the tale was embroidered with so much fancy that Don Camillo found it necessary to run into him—by sheer chance, of course—under the arcade in front of the café, just as he was holding forth on the whys and wherefores of the miraculous cure. As soon as Peppone saw the priest's bulky form looming on the horizon he raised his voice to announce:

"Of course, where political propaganda is concerned, anything goes. But there is a limit to everything, and when it comes to exploiting a helpless child, I draw the line. Any family man will understand what I mean, but naturally one that wears a long black skirt and has no hope of having any children can't be expected to realize . . ."

The bystanders turned to look at Don Camillo, and feeling their eyes upon him, he nonchalantly shrugged his shoulders.

"Mr. Mayor," he said blandly, "if the patient was a child, there was no way of saving an adult, was there?"

"What do you mean by 'save'?" retorted Peppone. "There was never any real danger."

"Well, if you're a medical authority, I've nothing more to say."

"I never claimed to be a medical authority," said Peppone. "But specialists stated that there was no need to bring the medicine from overseas when it was available in Holland."

"I'm quite willing to bow to the specialists' opinion. But there's one detail which you and the rest of the comrades seem to have overlooked. The baby didn't need the milk of a contented Dutch cow or the air flailed by a Dutch windmill. He had to have a certain gamma globule which is the exclusive property of the state of Michigan, so why shouldn't the United States ambassadress send there for it?"

Peppone shook his head and laughed loudly.

"*Latinorum latinorum!* When they're at their wit's end they come out with their *latinorum*, their *alpha* and *gamma* and *omega* and all the rest, and if you're not a Latin scholar, you can't reply."

"Mr. Mayor, *gamma* is a Greek letter and not a Latin one. And anyhow, scientists rather than priests gave this haemoglobin its name."

"Very well," said Peppone, pulling another Soviet propaganda card out of his sleeve, "but what about the Madonna that appeared to the child in a dream? Didn't the priests think up that one?"

"Mr. Mayor," said Don Camillo, with an expression of astonishment on his face, "the clergy does not interfere with children's dreams, or with those of adults, either. They dream when and what they please."

"Listen to this, though," shouted Peppone. "While the plane commandeered by that platinum fox of an ambassadress was flying over the Atlantic, the sick child did dream. And what did he dream about? The Madonna! In his dream the Madonna carried him to Paradise and introduced Jesus Christ, who said that thanks to the United States and Clare Booth Luce, the story would be crowned by a happy ending."

"What was the child to dream, Mr. Mayor?" asked Don Camillo, throwing out his arms in resignation. "Was Lenin to carry him off to the Kremlin and Stalin to explain the Five-year Plan?"

Someone in the group laughed and Peppone grew angrier than ever.

"Let's keep politics out of it!" he exclaimed. "We'd never saddle a child with a dream of this kind. First, because we don't make propaganda out of children, and second, because we don't have to resort to fairy stories. . . ."

". . . And third, because no one would believe them if you did," Don Camillo concluded.

"And who believes *your* fairy stories, may I ask?"

"There are people, quite a few of them, who not only believe in Paradise, but are willing to behave in such a way as to go there, people that live good, quiet lives and trust in Divine Providence."

Peppone pushed his hat back on his head and placed his hands on his hips.

"Divine Providence, eh? When the medicine came from the U.S.A.! If it had come from Russia, the Reverend here would have said it was a work of the devil!"

"No, Mr. Mayor. The Reverend, as you call him, uses his God-given faculty of reason. He'd never say anything quite so stupid, because he knows that Divine Providence knows neither nation nor party."

"Amen," muttered Smilzo.

"In any case," Don Camillo continued, "this time Divine Providence came from the West rather than the East."

"Then hurrah for America, and down with Russia!" shouted Peppone.

"Hurrah for America, if you insist. But why down with Russia? Russia did no harm in this affair; Russia didn't prevent the child from getting well. I am quite capable of cool detachment, Mr. Mayor, and I'm not afraid to say that this is one instance—perhaps the only one—in which Russia did no damage whatsoever. But, Mr. Mayor, instead of yelling Hurrah for America, why not yell Hurrah for Divine Providence, since Divine Providence cured the child?"

Peppone was as red in the face as the October Revolution.

"Why didn't Divine Providence stop the child from getting sick, in the first place?" he asked.

"Divine Providence didn't bring about the sickness," Don Camillo explained. "Sickness is a product of Nature, and Nature is governed, fortunately, by very rigid laws. If we fail to observe them, then trouble is bound to ensue. As a skilled mechanic, you know, Mr. Mayor, that a motor runs smoothly just as long as its single parts are in good order. If a carburettor is out of order, is it the fault of Divine Providence or of the dirt that got into it? Everything connected with Matter is in the providence of Nature. There is sickness even in Russia, which was created not by God but by Lenin."

Peppone had gradually relaxed and at the end of Don Camillo's little harangue he turned to Smilzo and said with a smile, pronouncing every word slowly:

"Smilzo, apropos of the carburettor, would you ask the Reverend whether when this mechanic gets the dirt out of the carburettor he represents Divine Providence?"

Smilzo looked over at Don Camillo, and asked:

"Has the defendant heard the plaintiff's demand?"

"Yes," Don Camillo replied. "The plaintiff's complaint is a weakness of the brain, but at any rate the defendant has heard it. The mechanic doesn't represent Divine Providence; all he represents is a screwdriver, with a man attached to the handle. All this lies in the realm of the very lowliest kind of matter. Everything happens in accord with natural rather than divine law."

This reply seemed to give Peppone further satisfaction.

"Let's put it differently, Father," he said. "Let's say that the carburettor isn't working for lack of a screw. Unfortunately, it's an American carburettor, and we haven't the right screw to replace it. What are we to do? Scrap the car? Fortunately the United States ambassadress sends a plane to Washington to get it; the screw is put in and the car moves. We're still in the realm of matter, because a humble carburettor is the protagonist of our story. But since the new screw comes from the U.S.A. we must shout Hurrah for Divine Providence. If the carburettor comes from the East you reason one way, and if it comes from the West another."

Peppone's gang hooted their approval, and Don Camillo let them hoot to their hearts' content. Then he said:

"My reason works the same way in both directions."

"Bunk!" shouted Peppone. "If the child's sickness is the result of natural law, just as the carburettor is broken for lack of a screw, then why is Divine Providence responsible for the American ambassadress's offer of the missing part, or, in this case, the missing medicine?"

"Because a child isn't a carburettor, that's all," said Don Camillo calmly. "A carburettor can't have a child's faith in God. And this child gave proof of his faith in a spectacular way. The human machine, its disturbances and remedies are material and natural affairs. Faith in God is something quite different, which you, Comrade Carburettor, seem unable to understand. Instead of seeing Divine Providence, you see only the United States ambassadress and the Atlantic Pact. A man without hearing can't hope to understand music, and one without faith in God can't fathom the workings of Divine Providence."

"Well then, this Divine Providence is something for the privileged rather than the needy. If a hundred persons are starving and only seven of them have faith, then God is unjust to send a tin of Spam only to these seven."

"No, Comrade Mayor, God sends the Spam to the whole lot of them, but only seven possess a tin-opener, with which the rest will have nothing to do."

Peppone had once more lost his self-possession and was sweating under the collar.

"Father, let's drop the parable and look at reality. In our country only seven people out of a hundred and seven eat meat, because they believe in Divine Providence and have the tin-openers with which to get at it. Whereas in Russia, where nobody believes in Divine Providence, there are tin-openers for all."

"But no tins of Spam," said Don Camillo.

The bystanders laughed at Don Camillo's thrust and Peppone was beside himself with fury.

"You're clever at playing with words, Father, and you reduce every argument to a word game. But we have concrete facts for our premises. This whole thing is a political trick, an American propaganda stunt built round an innocent child. None of your big words have proved the contrary."

"I know," said Don Camillo, with a shrug of his shoulders. "I'll never be able to prove a thing to you, not even that two and two make four, because you've been taught that they make five. I can tell you this, though. If political propaganda saved a child's life, then I say Hurrah for political propaganda. If I had a child and his life depended on some Russian medicine, I can assure you that I . . ."

"Not I," Peppone interrupted. "I have children, but if their lives depended on medicine flown in by the United States ambassadress, I'd let them die!"

Don Camillo only opened his eyes wide in horror.

At three o'clock in the morning Peppone was still unable to sleep. He got up and dressed, then with his shoes in his hand went to peer into his young son's room. He switched on the light and scrutinized the child's face. After some time he put out the light and tiptoed away. A few minutes later, with his coat collar raised all the way to his eyes, he walked through the icy streets to the church square. Under the rectory windows he stooped to look for a stone, but the hardened snow had stuck them all to the ground. He scratched at the frozen ground and with every passing minute his anxiety grew. Finally he loosened a stone and threw it at the shutters of the second window from the left of the second floor. The sound that it made when it struck the shutters was somehow reassuring. The shutters were thrown open and a rough voice called down:

"What do you want?"

"Come downstairs."

Don Camillo draped the bedspread over his shoulders and came to open the door.

"What can you want at this hour? What's the matter?"

"Nothing's the matter," said Peppone glumly.

"Good. When I first saw you I was afraid."

"Afraid of what? I'm not a burglar."

"I'm always afraid when someone rouses me at night. People don't come to see a priest at an hour like this just in order to tell him a funny story."

Peppone stood with lowered head for a minute and then mumbled:

"When a fellow holds a public discussion, he often says more than he means."

"I know," said Don Camillo. "There's no use taking such things too seriously."

"But other people take them seriously."

"Nonsense! They know what kind of reasoning to expect from a carburettor."

Peppone clenched his fists.

"Father, you're the one that's talking stupidly."

"You may be right. But then a carburettor has no right to wake up a priest at three o'clock in the morning."

Peppone stood his ground until the priest asked him:

"Is there something you want, Comrade Peppone? Do you need a tin-opener?"

"I have a tin-opener," said Peppone gloomily.

"Good! See that you don't lose it. And may God shed a little more light upon you next time you talk in public!"

Peppone went away, and before Don Camillo got back into bed he knelt down before the crucifix in his room.

"Lord," he said, "he hasn't become a carburettor, or anything else soulless and purely mechanical. He's just the same poor fellow that he was before. May Divine Providence be praised!"

And then he, too, was at last able to go to sleep.

THE CLOSED GATE

THE HIGHWAY UNROLLS its asphalt ribbon along the bank, matching the peaceful flow of the river. But the tributary roads which run into it, although they come from an area as flat as a billiard-table, are tortuous and winding. A city driver, bitten by the mania for speed, would find them unutterably irritating, but they exactly suit a man who works his own land and is jealous of its boundaries.

The Quarta road, doubtless a former cow-path, is such a one. Just a few hundred yards beyond the village it leaves the northbound highway and winds its way for five miles or so before rejoining it, only one mile farther on. The last section of it runs parallel to both highway and river, then, just half a mile away from the junction, it makes a right-angle turn and climbs straight up the bank. The farm known as the *Cantone* is there at the turn, with the road bounding it on two sides and the farm buildings right at the corner.

The curve is a dangerously blind one, and because the Quarta road runs by a number of properties and is the only line of communication between the village and the outlying community of Torricella, it is heavily travelled. The farmhouse is at the side of the road just before the right-angle turn to the east, and the barns, which are joined to it, just after. Between them lies the bare, rectangular barnyard, open towards the south and towards the river. The main entrance to the farm was originally at the south-east corner of the house.

All these topographical details serve only to explain something very simple: if some luckless fellow were to come carelessly out of the barnyard and another, equally luckless, were to drive at top speed towards the curve, it was obvious that they might run straight into each other. Something of the sort did happen, and as a result the gate was closed and creeper allowed to grow over it.

Marco Stocci had inherited the farm from his father, after many years of working at his side. Now he continued to work, with his wife and one hired man to help him. He was forty years old, but he had married late and Gisa, the eldest of his three children, was only just over twelve years old. With this family to bring up and a large amount of land to till, it is not surprising that Marco was a difficult and sometimes intractable man. He had an exceedingly quick temper and if his children annoyed him, he struck out at them with a violence which might have caused pain even to a grown person. The two little boys, eight and ten years old, took all this in a sporting spirit and were careful only to stay out of his reach. But twelve-year-old Gisa had a more sentimental nature and was mortally afraid of her father. Being a delicate and sensitive child she suffered most when he struck her in the presence of strangers, and in this he seemed to take particular joy. The last time that Marco mistreated his daughter was when the barnyard was full of men who had come for the threshing.

★

The threshing was a meagre affair that year; after an unusually severe winter, the wheat yielded very little grain. Marco Stocci was boiling over with resentment. Every now and then he plunged his hand into the sack hanging under the threshing-machine, pulled out a fistful of grain and then put it back, cursing. There was another major worry on his mind: his best cow was mortally ill and the vet showed no signs of coming. His two sons, aware of the oppressive atmosphere, had taken to the bush, but Gisa had been given the job of carrying water to the men on the machine and could not get away. The vet arrived around noon, when the men had just come in from the fields and were sitting down to lunch, amid considerable confusion. He went to look at the ailing cow, wrote out a prescription and said to Stocci:

"The pharmacy's closed at this hour. At three o'clock, when it reopens, send someone there to pick up this medicine. I'll be back at four to give the injection."

While the men lingered over their lunch in the cool hall, Stocci went into the parlour. He remembered that the pharmacist had sent him a bill the month before and it seemed like a good time to pay it. The bill was in a yellow envelope; it came to 4500 liras, which meant that 10,000 liras would easily cover the present prescription as well as those that had gone before. He put the prescription into a pink envelope, lying on his desk, together with a 10,000-lira note. Then he thought it would be simpler to have everything together, and put it all in the pharmacist's yellow envelope.

It was a hot day, and the men were anxious to finish the threshing early and go on to another job. Stocci had barely enough time to eat a few mouthfuls of lunch and gulp down half a bottle of wine before they were ready to return to work. At half-past two, when the machine was just about to swallow up the last bale of wheat, Stocci remembered the vet and the sick cow and called to his daughter:

"Take the yellow envelope from the parlour table and run to the pharmacy. Hand him the envelope and then wait for what he gives you. Hurry!"

Gisa took the envelope and started off, walking alongside her bicycle, as her parents had always told her she should do until she was on the open road. She went through the gate and continued to walk until she was round the dangerous curve. Then she mounted the bicycle and rode to the village by the shortest road, which was that along the bank of the river. When she came back the threshing was over, and while some of the men were making the machine ready to go, the others were cooling off with glasses of wine. Stocci was in the loft, over the sealed door between the house and the barn, and when he saw Gisa arrive with a small parcel attached to the handlebars of her bicycle, he called down from the window:

"Have you got everything?"

"Yes, father."

"How much change did he give you?"

"What change?" she stammered.

"Change from the 10,000 liras that were in the envelope!"

"There were two sheets of paper in the envelope, and nothing more," she said, shaking her head.

Money is a sore subject where a peasant is concerned, because it is so very hard for him to come by. It's safer to cut off his ear than to touch his money. And so Stocci let out a loud cry.

"Nothing more! I put the money in with my own hand! And now you've gone and lost it, you little good-for-nothing! If you don't find it, I'll kill you!"

Blind anger made the veins stand out on his forehead and muddled his brain. Not content with shouting, he started to climb down the wooden ladder up which he was later to carry sacks of wheat. And Gisa, instead of waiting for him, fled in terror. She jumped on to the bicycle and pedalled furiously in the direction of the gate. Her father ran after her, but she had a head start, and had already reached the road. The road was covered with gravel, and as she turned to the right, she lost control and went off to the extreme left, at the edge of the ditch. Just then a truck roared down the road at full speed, and as it cleared the curve Gisa was directly in its way. She was killed on the spot, in plain sight of her father.

This was why Stocci closed the gate to his farm. He fastened it with a heavy chain and lock, and put the key in his pocket so that no one could ever go through the gate again. The portion of the highway which ran parallel to the country road, some hundred and fifty feet away, was connected with it at another place, where there was no blind corner. The creeper, which formerly had covered only the gate-posts, now ran over all the iron grating. After a month had gone by, Stocci recovered a measure of calm. He was not very different from what he had been before, but he no longer shouted, and he let his wife look after the little boys.

One of the gate-posts was up against the corner of the house, while the other marked the beginning of the hedge which separated the barnyard from the road. Beside the latter post grew a tall poplar tree, and in the summer Stocci sat in its shade looking out through the over-grown bars of the closed gate at the dusty, white road, with the sun beating upon it.

It was an August afternoon, and the air was particularly heavy. Almost everyone was asleep in the river valley, and silence and solitude reigned. Stocci sat under the tree, staring at the gate. Suddenly someone rode up the road on a bicycle and stopped directly in front of it. The leaves had grown so thick that Stocci could not make out who it was. He got up and went nearer. It was Gisa, staring at him out of her deep blue eyes. Stocci searched his best pocket for the key. The lock was so rusty that the key was hard to turn, and it was no easy job to tear away the vine, but there was a feverish strength in Stocci's hands and soon he had the gate open.

"Come in," he said to his daughter, but she only shook her head, remounted the bicycle and rode off towards the fatal curve.

For a minute Stocci could not move. But when she was out of sight he ran back to his own bicycle, which was leaning against the wall of the house. He leaped on to the saddle and pedalled out through the open gate, just as fast as Gisa had pedalled to her death before him. He skidded on the gravel and veered to the left just in time for the luckless driver coming round the curve to find him in his way and run him down.

It was two o'clock in the afternoon, and old Antonietta, whose insomnia made her the only person left awake in the heat, swore that she saw Stocci and Gisa riding their bicycles along the road in front of her house. They rode side by side, in true cyclists' fashion, and every now and then they looked at each other and smiled.

Sheer imagination, of course. But in the secret compartment of Stocci's wallet they found a pink envelope containing the 10,000-lira note which Gisa had never lost because her father, in the confusion, had never put it in with the bill and the prescription. This part of the story is absolutely true, and Stocci's widow gave the 10,000-lira note to Don Camillo.

"Say some Masses," she told him.

"For whose soul?" he asked her.

"For both of them, Father."

So spake Stocci's widow, and she closed the gate again, this time with the aid of a blow-lamp. After which the creeper resumed its temporarily interrupted process of growing.

LULLABY

PEPPONE SAT IN front of the fireplace, while his wife and children set the supper-table, at the same time watching the pot and frying-pan on the stove. Just then Smilzo burst into the house with a large rolled-up paper in one hand.

"Here's the corrected proof, Chief," he said. "If it's O.K., we're ready to print it."

"Stand away," ordered Peppone. "I want to get the general effect."

Smilzo stepped several steps back, unrolling the paper. At this distance the poster was most effective. It stated very clearly that a Very Important Party Person would come to the village at three o'clock Saturday afternoon and explain to the citizenry "the true story of the Hungarian counter-revolution".

"All right," said Peppone. "The posters have got to be up by tomorrow morning."

After Smilzo had gone away, Peppone's wife said:

"Haven't you killed those poor devils enough by now?"

"What nonsense are you saying?" asked Peppone, wheeling brusquely around.

"It's no nonsense. If you were an honest man, you'd get out in a hurry."

Peppone was in no mood for an argument and so he turned back to the fire, with one parting shot over his shoulder.

"I'm an honest man. But a soldier can't abandon his post just because the general has changed his tactics. Ours is a just struggle, because we're fighting for the good of the working-class."

"You don't do much good to the working-class by killing it off," said his wife severely. "They weren't capitalists, they were peasants and workers, and students, peasants' and workers' sons."

"That's all propaganda," jeered Peppone; "just the usual line."

"Propaganda isn't what goes over with me," said his wife. "I listen to my conscience, and I'm getting out of the Women's League, I can tell you."

Peppone wasn't prepared for such a drastic decision, and for a few minutes he was left speechless.

"Keep your mind on the supper," he said in a surly voice. "I don't feel like joking."

"It's no joke," she retorted, and taking a card out of the top bureau drawer she tore it into tiny pieces and threw them on the table. "There is my membership," she said, "and tomorrow morning I'll go and tell Gisella to take my name off the list."

Peppone jumped to his feet in a towering rage and shook a fist in his wife's face.

"You'll do no such thing," he shouted. "You'll stay right here. I wear the trousers in this house."

Peppone's wife wasn't a woman to be easily buffaloed. Taking advantage of the fact that she was on the other side of the table from Peppone, she seized the pot and frying-pan off the stove and threw their contents down the sink.

"If you wear the trousers, then eat the supper."

Such a bit of rebellion would have indisposed the most peaceful of men, and Peppone was anything but peaceful. Because of his bulk and masculine dignity he couldn't very well jump over the table, but he did move with astonishing swiftness to lay hands on his wife. He had counted without her bodyguards, however, and his impetus was checked by four little children crawling around his legs and shattering his eardrums with their cries. A second later his wife had disappeared up the stairs and his pursuit was blocked by the attic door.

"Open up, or I'll break through!" he roared, hammering at it with his fists.

When he received no answer, he threw the full weight of his shoulder against the door and erupted into the attic, which, to his discomfiture, was empty. His wife had climbed through the skylight on to the roof, and there, in spite of the darkness, Peppone finally detected her, hanging on to a chimney. His rage was transformed into worry and he drew back, with cold sweat breaking out on his forehead. Meanwhile the children too had reached the attic, weeping and calling for their mother.

"Shut up and get out of here!" said Peppone irritatedly.

Fearfully they retreated towards the door, until the oldest suddenly broke away from the rest, scuttled up the ladder standing under the skylight and joined his mother on the roof. With this Peppone turned tail and fled.

When Peppone came home, after midnight, he found things just as he had left them: the table still set and the scraps of the membership card scattered all over it. The big double bed in the bedroom was empty and so were the beds of the children. The rebels, all five of them, had taken refuge in the room which had formerly belonged to his wife's parents. Peppone made a feeble attempt to force the door but soon realized that it was barricaded. Back in the empty, disorderly kitchen, where the fire in the stove was dead and cold, he attempted to stay his appetite with bread and cheese, but they only made his stomach turn over. Before going out again he knocked once more at the rebels' door.

"Tomorrow noon, if I don't find lunch, I'll smash everything in sight."

"Smash what you please," his wife answered calmly. "Either you let me go and see Gisella, or else tomorrow you'll find the house empty."

Peppone start to kick at the door, but the children's weeping and wailing caused him to desist.

"I said noon, mind you!" he shouted. "That's the deadline for putting everything in order. I'll go and see Gisella myself. If you resign, we'll have to publish an announcement to the effect that you've been kicked out for deviationism. I've got to settle things in such a way that I won't be a laughing-stock."

"Go ahead," said his wife, "but just don't try to put over anything on me like what they pulled in Budapest!"

Peppone roared for an answer.

Gisella, the fiery head of the Women's League, had, with Don Camillo's accidental assistance, been tinged in red of the deepest hue by the most ferocious of her former adversaries, now her husband. She had turned into a professional politician, which meant that her husband, after working hours, had to do the housekeeping, to cook his meals if he wanted to eat, to make his bed if he wanted to sleep, and to sweep up if he didn't want the place to be a pigsty. Ever since Gisella had become a big wheel of the Party, the poor fellow had lost all his revolutionary spirit. He confined himself to being a good proletarian husband and let politics strictly alone. Indeed, to talk politics in his presence was like referring to rope in the house of a man who has died on the gallows.

At ten o'clock in the morning Peppone went to the People's Palace to hold a private meeting with Gisella upon the subject of his wife's rebellion. But Gisella was at home, ill. In view of the fact that the big rally was to take place at three that afternoon and Gisella was in charge of the women's participation, she must have been very ill indeed or else nothing in the world would have kept her away from the job. And so Peppone went to the forsaken shack where she and her husband lived and found her in bed, looking anything but well.

"What's the matter, Comrade?" he asked her.

Gisella only shook her head sadly, for she had not strength enough to speak.

"Arthritis," said her husband, who had stayed at home to look after her. "The poor girl's bones are broken."

To tell the truth, if Gisella had a bad case of broken bones, arthritis wasn't the reason. It had all happened the previous evening, after supper, a sketchy sort of supper prepared by Gisella's husband while she worked for the second consecutive day on the speech she was scheduled to deliver at the rally. When the comrade from the city had finished telling the true story of the Hungarian counter-revolution, Gisella was to voice the village women's acclaim of the peaceful settlement effected by the glorious Soviet army. Naturally, so important a speech couldn't be improvised from one moment to the next, and by the time Gisella had said everything she had to say, her crude handwriting covered some twenty long pages. At the end of the meagre meal, Gisella's husband sat down by the fire while she put the finishing touches. When it was all done she had an urge to rehearse it.

"Even if you don't care a fig for politics," she said to her husband, "you can tell me whether or not my speech makes sense. Just listen. . . ."

The poor fellow threw out his arms helplessly, and Gisella launched into her oration. When she got to the end she asked him:

"Well, what do you say?"

He tapped his pipe on one of the bricks of the fireplace, then put it back in his mouth and jerking his chair round said brusquely:

"Eat it."

"What do you mean?" she asked in amazement.

"I said to eat it," he repeated, pointing to the pad on which the speech was written. Gisella stood with arms akimbo and looked at him with disgust, as if she were about to put him in his place. But before she could open her mouth she received a stunning blow across the face. The blow was painful, but Gisella was even more pained by the fact that the browbeaten little man should have found the nerve to administer it. The worm had turned at last.

"Eat it," he said again, following up the first blow with a second.

Gisella didn't understand for some time, but at last it got into her head that if she wanted the blows to let up she would have to eat all twenty pages of her speech and her card of membership in the Women's League as well. That evening Gisella couldn't get up the stairs by herself. Alone, she had received enough blows to fell the entire women's group of the local party. Her rebellious spouse carried her upstairs, as if she had been a sack of potatoes. And that is just about what she was.

Now Peppone told Gisella not to worry. "While you're recuperating I'll put a substitute in your place. We'll wait for you to get well."

"She's not going to get well," said her husband darkly. "It's a chronic disturbance, isn't it, Gisella?"

Gisella nodded assent.

"It's not really a substitute that I'm putting in," said Peppone. "No one can take your place. The best thing is to disband the group and build it up again on a new foundation."

"I agree," said the husband.

"Take good care of yourself, Comrade," said Peppone, moving towards the door. "The Party needs you."

"I'll take care of her, don't worry," said the husband. "I need her too."

When Peppone came home at noon, he found everything in good order. He sat down cheerfully at the table, with a whale of an appetite, as his wife knew very well. But she stood skittishly near the sink, holding the bowl of spaghetti in her hand and ready to repeat the gesture of the day before.

"Well?" she queried at last.

"Everything's all right. Gisella is ill and I've had to disband the group."

He exhibited a copy of the announcement, and in return was served his portion of hot food.

The rally was scheduled for three o'clock in the afternoon, and by two the square and the road leading to the highway were patrolled by a detachment of police sent from the city. It wasn't clear what had drawn out so large and aggressive a crowd. The windows of all the houses were shut and the storekeepers had closed their stores, making the village seem quite dead. At a quarter to three Smilzo arrived breathlessly at the house of Peppone.

"Everything's ready, Chief. The comrades have gathered in the auditorium, and outside all is quiet. The enemy doesn't dare let himself be seen."

At that very moment, however, the enemy let himself be heard, for from the church tower the death-knell sounded. Deeply and gloomily it tolled against a background of perfect silence. Peppone listened for a few minutes and then said:

"Go back to your place. I'm going to do something about this."

"Be careful, Chief," said Smilzo; "it's a critical moment."

"In moments like this we must show that we are not afraid."

He put on his coat, pulled his hat down over his eyes and hurried off towards the church.

Up in the bell-tower, Don Camillo was pulling intently at the rope when Peppone's head appeared at the trap-door, followed by his body.

"Father," he said, "there's got to be an end to this provocation."

"There's an end to everything," said Don Camillo. "In human affairs, nothing is eternal."

"I can't answer for what may happen."

"Never mind, Comrade Mayor; I'll answer for it."

Peppone looked cautiously out of the window. From this height he had a clear view of the empty square, the police car and the forces of law and order. It was a grey day, and even without the tolling bell there would have been something infinitely lugubrious and funereal about it. Punctually at three o'clock, the Party speaker's car, with its police escort, drew up in front of the cinema.

"Comrade, aren't you going to the rally?" asked Don Camillo, between one sound of the bell and another.

"I want to see for myself exactly how long you'll go on with this music," said Peppone, sitting down on the floor.

"For a very long time," said Don Camillo. "This is no ordinary death; it's the death of a whole people."

Peppone sat hunched up in one corner with his hat over his eyes. He was dead tired and soon this gloomy lullaby sent him off to sleep. So it was that he never heard the true story of the Hungarian counter-revolution.

TOGO THE BULL

IT WAS ONE of those things that usually come out in the tabloid papers. If it didn't, the reason was that certain ramifications of the affair induced the village people to pretend to have seen and heard nothing.

It was the afternoon of December 31, and everywhere people were preparing to celebrate the arrival of the New Year. Those who weren't at home were out going from shop to shop or else just loitering in the square. Children had been dashing madly about all day long, whiling away the hours before the climactic noise-making, with the explosion of an occasional firework.

In the Rotti farmyard there was a big band of boys, letting off crackers in this way, in spite of their elders' admonitions. But when it was time to lead the animals out of the stable to water, old man Rotti came into the yard and said that if he heard as much as a squeak, he'd give the whole lot of them a beating. The boys quieted down, and the animals enjoyed their drink. But just when Togo reached the trough, an unfortunate cracker rose up from behind the fence, whistled across the yard and landed on his nose.

Togo was a Carnation-type bull, a Sherman tank of such massive proportions that the very sight of him was intimidating. With a single leap he broke away from the cowherd, smashed the bars of the gate and rushed out on to the road. The Rotti farm was hardly outside the village; fifty yards away the road became a village street, leading in a few hundred feet to the square. And by the time the Rottis had recovered from their surprise and started to pursue him, this was where Togo had arrived, or rather erupted. It was a confused scene, and one of only a few minutes' duration. Togo started to vent his wrath on a group of hysterical women, who squeezed themselves into the narrow space between a wall and two big trucks, while the sergeant of the Carabinieri appeared from nowhere and stood in the way with a pistol in his hand.

The sergeant's shot grazed the bull's side and only intensified his anger. It looked as if both the sergeant and the little group of shrieking women were in danger of being trampled down. Only a volley of machine-gun bullets into Togo's brain could have stopped him in his mad course. And, just in the nick of time, there was just such a volley. No one knew where it came from, but it hit the target, and the bull collapsed at the sergeant's feet. He put his pistol back in the holster, took off his cap and wiped the cold sweat from his forehead, looking down all the while at the great carcass of the bull.

People all around him were making a racket, and the women were shrieking just as loudly as if the bull were still charging upon them, but in the sergeant's ears there rang only the rattle of the machine-gun. The gun was silent now, but he felt sure that he had only to turn round and look up in order to pick out the window from which it had been fired. This was the real reason for his sweating. He knew that he ought to turn and look, but he didn't have the courage to do so.

The sergeant's paralysis was broken by a heavy hand on his shoulder.

"Good for you, Sergeant!" said Don Camillo. "These people owe you their lives."

"He's a very brave fellow," wheezed an old crone who was standing near by, "but if it hadn't been for . . ."

She meant to say "for the fellow who fired the machine-gun", but she never finished the sentence because someone stepped on her foot so hard that she almost fainted away, and a moment later the gathering crowd absorbed her.

"Good for you, Sergeant!" everyone was shouting.

Don Camillo went back to the rectory and waited for the sergeant to turn up. After an hour he did free himself and turn up, as expected.

"Father," he said, "you're the only person to whom I can say what's on my mind. Will you listen to me?"

"That's why I'm here," said Don Camillo, seating him in front of the fire.

"Father, did you see exactly what happened?" the sergeant asked him after a few seconds had gone by.

"Yes, I was just coming out of the tobacconist's, where I had gone to buy some stamps, and I saw the whole thing. I saw you throw yourself in front of the bull and shoot him down."

The sergeant smiled and shook his head.

"Did see me shoot *at* him with a pistol and *bring him down* with a machine-gun?"

Don Camillo threw out his arms.

"Sergeant, I'm not an arms expert. I know you had a firearm of some sort in your hand, but I couldn't swear to what it was."

"Do you mean that you can't tell the difference between a pistol-shot and the crackle of a machine-gun?"

"It's not taught in the seminary, Sergeant."

"But it's taught at the public schools, I can tell you. And so I can't help knowing that the animal at which I shot my pistol was killed by a volley from a machine-gun."

"Sergeant, if you say so, I can't contradict you. I repeat, that's not my speciality. The main thing is that the bull was killed before it could gore the life out of you and those poor women who were huddling behind you. I don't see any point in a discussion of ballistics."

"Yes, the machine-gun volley did save the lives of quite a few people. The only trouble is that it had to come from a machine-gun."

Don Camillo shrugged his shoulders.

"I'm no expert, as I've said twice before," he insisted. "But I may say that what you call a 'machine-gun volley' might just as easily have come from a shotgun. I don't see how your higher-ups could find anything wrong with that."

"If it were just a matter of explaining to the higher-ups, that's a plausible story," said the sergeant. "But how am I to justify it to myself? You see, Father, a Carabiniere is never alone; there is always another Carabiniere on watch inside him."

The Carabiniere touched his breast, and Don Camillo smiled.

"If you were dead, would he be dead too?"

"Exactly. But I'm not dead, and the Carabiniere inside me says: 'Someone in the village has a machine-gun, in perfect working order. This is against the law, so you must proceed against him.' "

Don Camillo lit and puffed at the butt of his cigar.

"There's no use talking in riddles," he said. "Say what you have on your mind. If you suspect me, I am at your disposal. You and your double can proceed against me."

"Father, let's drop the joking. I know who shot the machine-gun, and so do you, because you saw it."

"You've come to the wrong place," said Don Camillo harshly, looking him straight in the eyes. "I'm the last person in the world to give out such information. And, if you like, you can summon me for failing to co-operate with the law. I haven't another Carabiniere inside me, but I have my conscience, and there is a lot that the both of you could learn from that."

"There's one thing it couldn't teach us! A private citizen, who is the local leader of a movement in favour of revolution and mob rule, has no right to own a machine-gun!"

"I don't care about revolutions and their local leaders," said Don Camillo. "I only want to tell you that I'm neither a spy nor an informer."

"You've misunderstood me," said the sergeant, shaking his head. "I only came to ask you how an honest man can report and turn in someone who has just saved a number of lives, including his own. And how can an honest man *not* report and turn in the owner of a weapon which is a menace to the community?"

Don Camillo was somewhat pacified.

"Sergeant," he said, "as you've just put it, the weapon is the menace, not its owner. There's been entirely too much melodrama for strictly political reasons, over machine-guns. They're certainly lethal arms, but not everyone that has one in his possession is a criminal. The owner of a hammer or a kitchen knife may be just as much of a threat to society. When a man has been through the war, his machine-gun may be a sentimental reminder of an honourable past, of days of faith, hope and self-sacrifice. . . ."

"I see," the sergeant interrupted. "Just a well-oiled little souvenir that can fell the biggest bull for miles around!"

"And save the lives of several citizens, including a sergeant of the Carabinieri!"

"Father," said the sergeant, rising from his chair, "I can look, successfully or unsuccessfully, for the machine-gun's owner. But I simply *must* find the gun."

"You'll find it," said Don Camillo, rising in his turn to bid his guest good-bye. "I'll bring it to you myself."

Once the sergeant had gone, Don Camillo hurried over to the house of Peppone.

"You did a good job, killing the bull," he told him. "Now hand over that machine-gun."

"Are you trying to make me laugh?" asked Peppone.

"Peppone, the sergeant knows that you fired the gun. Even if you saved his life, it's his duty to report you for the possession of a concealed weapon. . . ."

"The sergeant must be mad. He can't know anything of the kind. I don't own a machine-gun, and I never, even in my wildest dreams, killed a bull."

"Peppone, stop joking. You shot the bull; I saw you with my own eyes."

"Then go and tell the sergeant. Why come to me?"

"I'm not a spy, I'm a minister of God, and God doesn't need me to tell *Him* anything."

"You're a minister of the Vatican and the U.S.A.," Peppone retorted; "that's why you want to make trouble for honest men."

Don Camillo had resolved not to let himself be drawn into an argument, and so did not answer, but merely sought to convince Peppone of the gravity of the sergeant's dilemma. But Peppone jeered at all his supplications.

"I don't know what you're taking about," he said. "All these machine-guns, bulls and sergeants have nothing to do with me. You'd better knock at some other door. Better luck next time! You might try the parish priest. See if he doesn't come up with a machine-gun!"

Don Camillo was disconsolate as he left Peppone's house. From the door he fired his parting shot:

"I shan't mind if you're called up by the police. It's no more than you deserve. But I *am* sorry for the sergeant because he'd never choose to repay you in this fashion for saving his life and the daily bread of his children."

"Don't worry about me," sneered Peppone. "If I'd had this machine-gun you're talking about, I'd have shot the sergeant, not the bull!"

When he got back to the rectory Don Camillo paced restlessly up and down the hall. At last he came to a decision and went precipitately upstairs. The dusty attic was pitch-black, but he needed no light to find what he was looking for. Immediately he located the brick which had only to be pushed at one end to open out at the other. He removed this from the wall and stuck his arm into the opening until his fingers caught hold of a nail with a wire wrapped around it. He unhooked the wire and pulled until a long, narrow box came out of the wall. Then he took out the contents of the box and went to his second-floor bedroom in order to see if it was in good condition. After that he put on his coat and left the house, making his way first through the hedge and then across the open fields. When he came to the area of underbrush near the Canal he waited for midnight to arrive. As the bells rang and fireworks and guns began to pop, he contributed a salvo of his own. Then he made straight for the headquarters of the Carabinieri. The sergeant was still there and Don Camillo said at once:

"Here's what you called a machine-gun. Don't ask me where it came from or who gave it to me."

"I'm not asking anything," answered the sergeant. "I'm simply thanking you for your co-operation, and wishing you a Happy New Year."

"Happy New Year to you, and to the other Carabiniere inside you!" muttered Don Camillo, wrapping his coat about him and hurrying away.

Ten minutes later the sergeant's doorbell rang again, and when he went to open the door a heavy object which had been leaning up against it fell on to the floor.

Attached to it by a wire was a piece of cardboard, on which someone had pasted letters cut out from newspaper headlines. These bore the message: "A machine-gun guilty of having saved the life of a police *sargint*."

"By their spelling, ye shall know them," the sergeant said, laughing to himself.

Then, having laid the object beside the one brought in a few minutes before by Don Camillo, he threw out his arms and exclaimed (contrary, perhaps, to the feelings of Togo, the bull):

"Thanks, all too many thanks, to Saint Anthony Abbot, patron saint of the lost-and-found!"

A POACHER'S PENANCE

DON CAMILLO HAD planned an epoch-making celebration of the New Year, based on the simple slogan: "A Chicken in Every Poor Man's Pot". He started, a fortnight in advance, to take a collection, visiting every landowner and tenant-farmer in his parish and receiving their unanimous approval. Unfortunately, in many barnyards he was told that there had been a round of diseases; in some all the poultry had been sold and those that were left after a penurious autumn were noticeably scrawny. In short, Don Camillo found himself on December 30th with only half a dozen chickens, the fattest among them looking like Smilzo in disguise. Six chickens, when he needed at least thirty! In his distress he went to the crucified Christ on the altar.

"Lord," he said, "is it possible for people to be so niggardly? What's one chicken, to a man that has a hundred?"

"It's one chicken, after all," Christ answered.

Don Camillo threw out his arms in protest.

"Lord," he went on indignantly, "how can people fail to make a small sacrifice which would yield them so much joy?"

"Don Camillo, too many people regard any sacrifice as a great one and are entirely wrapped up in seeking their own happiness. To them happiness may mean *not* giving something they don't need."

"Lord," said Don Camillo impatiently, between clenched teeth, "if You know these people so well, why don't You treat them the way they deserve? Why don't You send a frost to freeze the wheat in their fields?"

"Bread belongs to everyone, not merely to the man that sowed the wheat. The land does not bear its fruits only for the benefit of those that own it. It is blasphemy, Don Camillo, to ask the Lord to freeze the wheat in the ground. Don't we all say: 'Give us this day our daily bread'?"

"Forgive me," said Don Camillo, bowing his head. "I only meant that certain selfish people aren't fit to own land."

"If they had sown stones instead of wheat, then they wouldn't be entitled to any reward. But if they raise what it is proper for the land to bear, then they are entitled to own and run it their own way."

Don Camillo lost patience altogether.

"Lord," he said, "You're on the side of the landowners!"

"No," said Christ with a smile: "My interest is in the land itself. . . . Once upon a time there was an island, inhabited by very poor people. There were two doctors on the island, one generous, the other grasping. The first doctor asked very small fees, but unfortunately he was less skilled in his art than the other. And all the sick flocked to the more competent man. Was this fair?"

Don Camillo shrugged his shoulders.

"It was only normal that they should go to a doctor who could cure them. But I can't accept the fact that a good man should be in need, while a bad one should be making money. That isn't just."

"It isn't just, Don Camillo, but it's human. It's human that sick people should pay heavy fees to the abler of the two. On the other hand, it's just that God should punish him for abusing his God-given talents."

"Lord," insisted Don Camillo, "I . . ."

"If you lived on the island in question, would you ask God to destroy the competent doctor and preserve the inept one?"

"No," said Don Camillo, "I'd ask Him to teach the competent man to be generous and the generous man to improve his skill."

"Well, isn't a farmer a kind of doctor responsible for the health and prosperity of the land?"

"Lord," Don Camillo explained, "I understand now, and beg God to forgive my foolish words. But I can't help worrying about the fact that I need thirty chickens and have no more than six in hand."

"Eight," Christ corrected him.

"Yes, eight," said Don Camillo, who had forgotten the fact that there were two capons in his own yard.

It's no easy job to find twenty-two chickens from one day to the next. Don Camillo knew this perfectly well, because he had searched a fortnight for half a dozen. But he had no intention of falling down on his slogan, "A Chicken in Every Poor Man's Pot".

He was eating out his soul for an answer, when suddenly another question rose before him.

"Yes, a chicken's just a chicken. But what is a pheasant?"

To be logical, a pheasant is a pheasant. But is it necessary to be so precise? Couldn't a pheasant be called a "flying chicken"? He concluded that the celebration would be the same with the slogan of A Pheasant in Every Poor Man's Frying-pan. There were only two drawbacks to this variant. First, the question of finding twenty-two pheasants, and second, the lack of time for them to season. Don Camillo walked for miles up and down the rectory hall, debating these problems. Finally he resolved them by a further modification of the original slogan. Now it was A Pheasant in Every Poor Man's Shopping Bag. All the essentials were there.

Don Camillo's dog, Thunder, agreed that the main thing was to find twenty-two pheasants to replace the missing chickens. He found it quite natural that his master should don a pair of trousers, a corduroy jacket and a cyclist's cap. It wasn't the first time that Don Camillo had gone hunting in places where a cassock would have been in the way. What was unnatural was that Don Camillo should go out of the house without his shotgun over his shoulder. The dog felt sure that it was a lapse of memory, and just as the priest was about to step through the garden he barked at him to return to the house. When they were back in the dining-room, Thunder looked up at the gun and cartridge-belt and game-bag that were hanging on the wall.

"Come on, Thunder!" ordered Don Camillo.

"Take your gun, and then I'll come," Thunder answered, without moving. He said all this by barking, but it was perfectly understandable to Don Camillo.

"Stop that noise, and come along," the priest answered. "The shotgun's staying there. We can't possibly take such a noisy weapon."

Then, when Thunder remained obstinately still, Don Camillo dug into the left leg of his trousers and came up with a single-barrelled gun. Thunder looked at it in a puzzled fashion and compared it with the gun hanging on the wall.

"That isn't a shotgun," he said at last. "The shotgun's up there."

Don Camillo knew that Thunder's pedigree lent him a certain dignity and entitled him to be treated with respect.

"This is a shotgun, too," he explained. "A small, old-fashioned model, with the charger on the barrel. It's not very powerful, of course, but if you shoot at a distance of two or three yards at a silly pheasant it will bring him down."

He gave a demonstration of how to load it and then, opening the window over the garden he aimed at a tin can which someone had mounted on the end of a pole. The gun gave a faint click, and the can hit the dust. Thunder ran downstairs to follow up the prey. Soon he called back:

"Let's go hunting for tin cans, then, if you insist!"

The pheasants perched lethargically on the lowest branches of the trees. For three years the Finetti family had lived abroad, and in all that time no one had fired a shot on their preserve. The pheasants were so fat and self-confident that it was hardly necessary to shoot them; they could have just as easily been swept up in the crown of a hat. Nevertheless, Don Camillo chose to use his gun. Every time the gun clicked a pheasant fell to the ground. Although he had to waste considerable time searching for the bodies, Don Camillo bagged twenty-one pheasants without the least trouble. But the twenty-second was appointed by fate to give him trouble.

Thunder was showing signs of restlessness, and this signified the presence of something other than pheasants and rabbits. But Don Camillo was so intent on bagging the twenty-second "flying chicken" that he told the dog to be quiet and let him get on with the job. Thunder unwillingly obeyed until, just as Don Camillo was shooting his intended victim, he really barked an alarm. It was too late, because the game warden was already near. Don Camillo threw his gun into the bushes, and picking up the bag that contained the twenty-one pheasants, he ran off on the double. Evening was starting to fall and a thick fog mercifully interposed itself between Don Camillo and his pursuer. Thunder masterfully led the strategic withdrawal, and having found a hole in the high wire fence around the preserve he stood by it until Don Camillo had passed through.

Don Camillo was of elephantine proportions and the bagful of pheasants was quite bulky, but he dived into the fence with all the ardour of a goalkeeper in a soccer game. The warden arrived only in time to see Don Camillo's hindquarters disappearing through the fence. He shot at them, without much hope of hitting the mark. A few minutes later Don Camillo emerged on to the road. He couldn't cut across the fields because just opposite the fence there was the eight-feet wide canal, swollen with water. The road was the only way he could go, and here the warden would surely have found him, because it ran parallel to the fence for half a mile in either direction.

"Home, Thunder!" he shouted to the dog, who set out immediately in the right direction, while he himself continued to run. "He's not going to identify me, even if I have to throw myself into the canal," he muttered to himself.

At the curve of the Wayside Shrine, Don Camillo saw a big truck coming down the road. He stood on the ridge along the Canal and waved his cap. Then, without waiting for the truck to stop, he jumped on to the running-board. The driver wore a concerned expression as he jammed on the brakes. Within a second Don Camillo had opened the door and installed himself in the cab.

"Keep going, man, for the love of God!" he shouted.

The driver depressed the clutch, and the truck regained speed as if someone had kicked it in the rear. After half a mile or so, the driver mumbled:

"I took you for a gunman. Why, in heaven's name, are you in such a hurry?"

"I've got to make the six-twenty-two train."

"Oh, you are a wild-fowl fancier, are you?"

"No, I sell detergents for washing black souls."

"I was a fool," said the driver. "I should never have picked you up, and then the game warden would have seen your typically Vatican-agent face. Well, I must admit that you've done things in a big way. Are you expecting a lot of people to dinner?"

"Yes, thirty. I had two chickens and people gave me six more. After that, I had to find twenty-two birds of some other kind, in order that there should be one for every neighbour of ours that couldn't afford it. I had just taken aim at the twenty-second when the game warden saw me. That's the whole story. Do you need any more data to report to your Party?"

"All I need is some idea as to what is your moral code."

"That of a good Christian and an honest citizen."

"Then, Mister Priest, let's take a look at the past," said Peppone, slowing the truck down. "Last month, when I suggested that we make common cause to pro-cure firewood for the unemployed, you wouldn't hear of it; in fact you fought me all along the line. Why was that?"

"Because I couldn't encourage people to break the law," said Don Camillo, lighting the butt of his cigar.

"What law?"

"The law for the protection of private property. The poor have a right to fire-wood, there I agree. But one can't say to them: 'Let's go and take it from the rich landowners!' 'Thou shalt not steal' is the law of both God and man."

" 'Thou shalt not steal,' is that it?" shouted Peppone. "If workers can't touch the property of the rich, what right have the rich to rob the workers of a decent wage and thus make it impossible for them to go on living?"

"It's no use your haranguing me as if I were at a political rally," expostulated Don Camillo. "I can't help anyone to break the law."

"Very well," said Peppone. "Then let's look at the chapter you've just written. The poor have a right to a good New Year's Day dinner, but the rich won't give it to them. So what does the priest do? He breaks the law of God and man by stealing pheasants from a private hunting preserve. Do priests have a moral code all their own, or have they a right to violate the so-called public law with impunity?"

"Comrade, I claim no such right. I took off my priestly garb and disguised myself in order to break the law without attracting attention to my person. But last month I couldn't parade through the streets, arm in arm with our comrade mayor, shouting: 'The law is unjust! Down with the law! We're taking the law into our own hands! . . .' If I am a soldier parading before a general, I have to salute him; if I don't want to do it, then I must get out of the parade. The one thing I can't do is parade in front of him with my hands in my pockets, shouting: 'I'm not saluting any such no-good general as you! . . .' Yes, I did steal the pheasants. But I didn't call out: 'Come on, Comrades; the pheasants are ours!' "

Peppone shook his head and pounded with one fist on the steering-wheel.

"You preach against stealing, and then you steal!" he objected. "Your preaching is one thing, and your practice another."

"According to your standards, Peppone, I preach what's wrong and practise what's right. But I still maintain that the opposite is true. If I tell people the right thing, then I am doing them good. And if then I go and do something wrong, quite off my own bat, I'm wronging only myself. Of course, I must answer for my wrongdoing and be punished for it. I may elude human justice, but God's justice will catch up with me, sooner or later."

"That's a convenient way to look at it," sneered Peppone. "You allow yourself to get away with practically anything in this world, by saying that you'll pay for it in the next. I say that you ought to pay up on the spot!"

"Don't worry; I'll pay soon enough, because my conscience will prick me. As a good Christian and an honest citizen, I'm aware of having violated the law of both God and man."

"Hmmm . . ." said Peppone. "I tell you where that Christian and civic conscience of yours is—it's at the . . . base of your spine!"

"Very well, Peppone," said Don Camillo, with a sigh. "Granted that my conscience is located where you say, does that have any effect on what I have just told you?"

"What are you driving at now, Father?" asked Peppone disgustedly.

"Nothing so very deep. I'd just like to know, Comrade, whether you've ever had a bullet in the base of your spine?"

Don Camillo's voice seemed to come from very far away, and when Peppone switched on the light on the dashboard he saw that the priest was deathly pale.

"Father! . . ." he gasped.

"Put out that light, and don't worry," said Don Camillo. "It's just a little prick of my conscience, and I'll get over it. Take me to the old doctor at Torricella; he'll take the lead out of my pants without asking any questions."

Peppone drove as if he were jet propelled over the bumpy road and put Don Camillo down at the doctor's door. While he was waiting for him to come out he wiped the blood off the seat. Then he hid the bag of pheasants below it and went for a stroll in the course of which he had ample time for meditation. An hour later Don Camillo emerged from the doctor's house.

"How goes it?" asked Peppone.

"Well, my conscience is at rest, in a manner of speaking, but for spiny or spinal reasons I must admit that I'm better off in a standing than in a sitting position. If you don't object, I'll stand in the rear of the truck, and mind you don't go too fast!"

Fortunately the rear of the truck had a canvas cover, so that Don Camillo did not suffer too much from the wind. The fog was thicker than ever and so he was able to slip into the rectory unnoticed, followed by Peppone, carrying the bag of birds, which he deposited in the cellar. When Peppone came upstairs he found Don Camillo back in his priestly uniform. The black cassock made his face look all the whiter.

"Father," he muttered, "if there's anything I can do for you, don't hesitate to call on me."

"I'm quite all right," said Don Camillo, "but I'm worried about Thunder. See if you can find him."

There came a whimper from under the table, which was Thunder's way of answering "Present!" to the mention of his name. Peppone bent over to look at him more closely.

"It seems as if his . . . conscience were bothering him too," said Peppone. "Shall I take him to the same discreet doctor?"

"No," said Don Camillo. "This is a strictly family affair. Carry him up to my bedroom and I'll operate on him myself."

Thunder allowed Peppone to carry him up to the second floor. When Peppone came down he stood at the door, with one finger pointing to heaven, and looked severely at Don Camillo.

"The sins of the priests are visited upon the innocent dogs," he observed sententiously.

"Not fair!" retorted Don Camillo. "The priest in question is half-dead!" He was still standing on his two feet and still looking very pale.

When Peppone had gone he barred the front door and went down to the cellar to look at the twenty-one "flying chickens". There turned out to be twenty-two of them, because while he was waiting for Don Camillo to come out of the doctor's Peppone had bought a magnificent capon. Before Don Camillo went to throw himself (face down) on his bed, he went to kneel before the crucified Christ on the altar.

"Lord," he said, "I can't thank You for having protected me, because I was doing a dishonest deed and one that deserved to be punished. Perhaps the game warden's shotgun ought to have dispatched me to the next world."

"Even the worst of priests is worth more than twenty-two pheasants," answered Christ severely.

"Twenty-one, to be exact," whispered Don Camillo, "I'm not responsible for the twenty-second."

"You meant to shoot him down, however."

"Lord, my heart is very sore, because I know that I have done wrong."

"You're lying, Don Camillo. Your heart is full of joy, because you're thinking of the happiness coming to thirty needy families tomorrow."

Don Camillo rose, stepped back and sat heavily down in the first pew. Perspiration trickled down his increasingly pale face.

"Rise!" said the crucified Christ. "*Ego te absolvo.* Your sins are forgiven."

AN EXCHANGE OF COURTESIES

"THE ONLY WAY to have a genuine exchange of courtesies with the Catholic workers is to belabour them with a stick. But directives are directives, and so we'll simply tickle them with a feather."

These were Peppone's words to his lieutenants, and he accompanied them with the observation that talk is all very well, but that to get anything concrete accomplished by workers—Catholic or non-Catholic—you must begin by subtracting something from their wallets.

"When the priest is in the pulpit, he's unbeatable," Peppone went on. "If he has nothing better to say, he can always fall back on dogma, the Ten Commandments, Heaven, Hell and all the rest. But when he stands behind the counter of the Co-operative Store, then his authority is not the same. There's where we must attack him."

For a long time the "People's Co-operative" had been a thorn in Don Camillo's side, a thorn whose sting even the "White Co-operative" of his own creation could not remove, because the Reds dealt not only in food and other articles but they had also a bar, a tobacco shelf, a television set and petrol pump. Altogether it was big business and functioned very smoothly; he knew that he would never be able to transform his frail enterprise into one equally powerful. He ate his heart out continuously, and every time he was told something new about the Red Co-operative he felt as if he had taken a beating.

As soon as the plan for "an exchange of courtesies" was put into action, Don Camillo's beating was worse than ever. For one day the Reds lowered the price of bacon, another the price of cheese, the next oil and so on. Soon Camillo could not compete with these crazy reductions and so he simply tried to stop up as many holes as he could and stay afloat. He was hardened by now to adversity and when he felt especially low in his mind and sought the succour of the Christ on the main altar, he simply threw out his arms disconsolately and said:

"Lord, You see how things are. I don't ask You to take an interest in my paltry shop, but I do beg You to help me keep my temper."

God did help him and he achieved considerable self-control, but when he heard about the new department in their Co-operative store his temper boiled up within him. He was not satisfied with other people's description and went to see for himself. The window which had formerly served to show groceries was now given over to the new merchandise, and a big sign explained that in order to meet its customers' every want the Co-operative had undertaken to sell materials and patterns for making baptismal, First Communion and wedding outfits, not to mention handsomely decorated candles. "Compare prices," said the sign, "and see who is exploiting the religious feelings of good Catholic workers." This sign was set up in the middle of the display, at the feet of a big statue of Saint Joseph the Worker, while another sign, nearby, explained that the "People's Co-operative" also furnished printed invitations to any of the above functions, with a wide variety of conventional texts.

As if by chance, Smilzo appeared at the Co-operative door and whispered into Don Camillo's ear:

"Father, you'd better get some of those candles. We give a fifteen-percent discount to active clergy. That means we lose money, but what does it matter? We want to help the Church."

There was a small crowd in front of the window, and Don Camillo could not afford to lose his temper. All he could do was seize the peak of Smilzo's cap between the thumb and forefinger of his left hand and pull it down all the way to the chin. But Smilzo managed to have the last word.

"Nothing doing, Father!" he exclaimed from under his cap. "The Dark Ages are over!"

The next morning Don Camillo found three handsomely decorated votive candles burning in the Lady Chapel. The day after there were six, and it was quite obvious that the Reds had put them there, simply to annoy him. In order to be certain he hid in a confessional, and sure enough, that very afternoon an elderly man came into the church, crossed himself and made resolutely for Saint Anthony's chapel. From underneath his coat he extracted one of the famous candles, which he proceeded to light and then to fit into a holder. It was just at this moment that Don Camillo appeared at his side. To the priest's amazement, the fellow was not a Red but one of his own faithful, Matteo Frossi by name.

"Matteo," exclaimed Don Camillo; "I'd never have expected *you* to play a filthy trick like that!"

"Is it a filthy trick to light a candle to Saint Anthony?" asked the astonished old man.

"It's a filthy trick to light one of *those* candles, and you know it!"

"Father, if I can give thanks to Saint Anthony and save thirty liras at the same time, why should you object? The wax of this candle and the wax of yours come from the same place!"

After Frossi had gone away, Don Camillo gave vent to his feelings before the crucified Christ on the main altar.

"The human race is growing cheaper and cheaper, Lord," he told Him. "Judas sold You for thirty pieces of silver, but this fellow sells You for thirty miserable liras!"

"Who are you talking about, Don Camillo?"

"This fellow, Frossi, who just lit a candle to Saint Anthony."

"Don Camillo, didn't you promise never to drag me into the affairs of your paltry shop? Have you lost your memory?"

"No, Lord; I've lost my temper." And Don Camillo humbly bowed his head.

Eventually, although it cost him a considerable effort, Don Camillo regained his composure. In the pulpit and out of it he said what he thought he should about the ridiculous tactics with which certain people tried to deceive the faithful. He explained that Satan employs the most devious means to win men's souls, and that, like the Greeks, he is most to be feared when he brings gifts. For every apparent gift, Satan extracts a hundredfold return; he exploits our sloth and our avarice together.

Certainly Don Camillo himself didn't play Satan's game. Rather than buy it at the "People's Co-operative", he ate a whole meal one day without salt, and one rainy night he rode eight miles on his bicycle in order to purchase a cigar at Torricella. This was the least of what he was willing to do for the sake of boycotting Peppone. He was called upon to make the supreme sacrifice the day when he went to collect donations for the Orphan Asylum. As usual, he borrowed a truck from Filotti and with the aid of a husky boy picked up produce from all the neighbouring farms. When the truck was filled with wheat, maize, potatoes, apples and wood he drove happily back to the village. The motor had worked like a dream, the farmers had given cheerfully and it was a mild, sunny day. He turned down the main street of the village, which went by the "People's Co-operative" and then, two hundred yards farther on, to the square in front of the church. Just thirty yards from the "People's Co-operative" the engine began to sputter. It seemed as if Satan himself must have had a hand in the matter, for it came to a stop in front of the petrol pump. Don Camillo got out, opened the hood and then went round to take the cap off the tank.

"We're out of fuel," he told his helper.

"Well, we're pretty lucky," said the boy gaily. "There's the pump, right beside us."

A roar from Don Camillo compelled him to silence. But the enemy was already in the know. The enemy was standing at the door of the Co-operative, enjoying the autumn sun. And he had not only keen hearing but also knew a lot about engines.

"Good evening, Father," he said amiably.

"Good evening, Mr. Mayor," Don Camillo answered between clenched teeth, and turned to talk to the boy.

A minute later the entire group of Peppone's lieutenants and a large number of his followers poured out of the door and stood round their leader.

"What's up, Chief?" asked Smilzo.

"He's out of fuel," answered Peppone.

"Too bad it didn't happen out in the country," said Smilzo. "Here, for just over a hundred liras, he can get enough to take him home."

"You mean to say he'd have the nerve to buy no more than a quart?" muttered Bigio.

"He's just as likely to ask for a pint," Smilzo answered, with a mocking laugh.

"You don't know how tough and stingy these priests can be."

They talked among themselves, turning their backs to Don Camillo, but in such loud voices that they could be heard all the way to the edge of the village. It was only natural that Don Camillo's temper should rise to boiling-point, but he held it in and continued to confer, from the place where he was standing, with the boy in the seat of the truck. At this point Peppone entered his henchmen's discussion.

"A pint, did you say? He can't use a single drop of it. This is the devil's own petrol, and if he were to take so much as a teaspoonful the Standard Oil Company would excommunicate him."

"Then what's he going to do, Chief?" Smilzo asked.

"That's easy," said Peppone to the small crowd which had gathered about him. "Priests' cars have two fuelling systems: one of them runs on petrol and the other on prayers. He'll fill the tank with Our Fathers, press the starter and the Holy Ghost will ignite the motor."

They all laughed. At this Don Camillo couldn't resist looking them in the face and saying what was on his mind. Swelling up his chest and shaking his fist in the direction of Peppone, he said:

"You can leave the Holy Ghost out of it. I'll manage alone."

"That's what you think," Smilzo retorted. "But a Don Camillo won't do; it will take a Don Caterpillar!"

Don Camillo lost control of himself altogether.

"Hold the wheel!" he shouted to the boy, leaping to the rear of the truck and pushing on it.

Something creaked: either Don Camillo's bones, or the rear of the truck, perhaps both of them together. Don Camillo was no longer a man, he was a living jack. Peppone's gang was breathless, for one of two things was bound to happen: either the truck would move or Don Camillo would break into small pieces. With God's help, the truck moved slowly ahead. Peppone's gang paraded after it, in horror and fascination. After fifty yards Don Camillo had to catch his breath. He stood up straight and turned around:

"If four of you big oafs are capable of doing what I did alone, let them step forward," he said.

Naturally no four of them moved; only the massive Peppone solemnly answered the challenge. He signalled to Don Camillo to get out of the way and applied his shoulder to the rear of the truck. Once more there was a creaking sound; once more nothing broke and the truck moved slowly ahead. Ten, twenty, thirty, forty, fifty yards, but Peppone did not stop even when he had reached a hundred. As the truck rolled down the street the Reds exulted; they broke into loud shouts and soon the street was filled with people. Peppone was like a powerful traction-belt; he went on to a hundred and ten, a hundred and twenty yards, and finally all the way to the church square, where the crowd thunderously applauded him. Don Camillo did not bat an eye-lash; he waited until Peppone had stopped panting and the applause had subsided. Then he raised his arms to ask for silence.

"Good enough," he observed. "I was looking for some sucker to push the truck all the way home for nothing."

"I'm not so much of a sucker as you may think," shouted Peppone.

His henchmen caught the idea. Smilzo edged the boy out of the seat and took the wheel; the others hurled themselves at the front of the car and pushed it all the way back to the petrol pump. There they stopped, and when Don Camillo re-joined them Peppone had his say.

"He who laughs last laughs best. The rectory is still two hundred yards away. Go to it, Father!"

Don Camillo kept cool and lit the butt of his cigar.

"Will you have some petrol, Father?" asked Smilzo, going over to the pump.

"Thanks, I've got some," said Don Camillo, climbing on to the seat, opening the emergency valve and pressing the starter. Under its own power the truck went triumphantly back to the church square. Peppone's gang looked on with their mouths hanging wide open, until their leader threw his cap on the ground and began to protest:

"That's the second time he's fooled me with his emergency valve!"

But Smilzo had something more to say:

"Chief, you did a hundred and fifty yards to his fifty. You lost one to three, and saved your honour."

Thus they sought to find what consolation they could in writing an end to the story. But people still talk about it and bid fair to go on talking.

A SPEECH TO GO DOWN IN HISTORY

"FOR THAT MEETING on the twenty-sixth, we've got to think up something special," Peppone said gravely.

Bigio, Brusco and Smilzo all looked puzzled, and Peppone hastened to enlighten them.

"We're lucky enough to have our rally scheduled as the last one before the election, which means that no matter what we say no one can contradict it. But we're called upon for some substantial oratory, not just the usual hot air. There's no question of bringing in a speaker from the outside, because this is a local election, and we're on our own. We've got to produce something smashing, something that will go down in history."

His three aides relaxed. If this was all he had on his mind, there was no need to worry.

"Chief, we're riding the crest of the wave," Smilzo answered gaily. "All you have to do is drive the last nail in their coffin!"

Peppone shook his head.

"A concluding speech is no joke. Election eve is not the time for a political harangue. It's got to be something factual: a record of past accomplishments and a pledge of others to come. It's one thing to promise social justice, and another to date the opening of a public laundry. Big ideas are all very well for a national election, but on the local level it's better to stick to the concrete. The question is how to make parish-pump politics sound epoch-making."

Smilzo continued to dissent.

"If a fellow knows what he wants to say, it's simple enough to say it."

"Simple, indeed!" retorted Peppone. "But one point I grant you. It's a question not of just the appropriate thing, but of what you *want* to say. An historical speech can't be improvised; it must be thought out in advance, with every word weighed and every effect calculated. Words aren't enough; you've got to know their meanings. It takes spade-work with the dictionary."

"You have a big enough vocabulary, Chief," Smilzo assured him. "Why work so hard over it?"

"A big vocabulary isn't enough, I tell you," shouted Peppone. "I need peace and quiet, for purposes of meditation. That's why I've called you together. Even if the People's Palace goes up in smoke, or Togliatti himself makes a tour of inspection, yes, even come the revolution, I'm not to be disturbed. No one must break the continuity of my speech. Have I made myself clear?"

They understood him perfectly.

"Chief," said Smilzo, "even if we have to guard your house with machine-guns, no one shall come near you. Just leave it to us!"

This is why, at a certain point, Peppone disappeared from circulation.

Just as election day was drawing close and the atmosphere was growing hotter and hotter, when his enemies were showing their claws and a strong hand was needed to put them in their place, Peppone vanished from sight. Had he been taken ill? Purged? Gone underground? Sent on a secret mission? His workshop was silent and the sign hanging on the door carried the simple word "Closed". The windows and doors of his own house were barred and his children were staying at their grandmother's, with not a word to be got out of them. Even his wife was gone.

Don Camillo sent out spies and alerted all the gossipy old women of the village. He himself walked by Peppone's house, but found no clue to the mystery. But in a village so small that everyone knew everything about his neighbour, such a situation could not long endure. News leaked through to the rectory that Peppone's house was not deserted, that his wife had been seen at the window and every night Smilzo delivered a parcel there and then came home empty-handed. Smilzo was tailed and found to be going every day to buy food at Castelletto, food sufficient to fill two hungry mouths. When it was discovered that Smilzo also bought cigars, then it was obvious that although one of the mouths might belong to Peppone's wife, the other indubitably belonged to Peppone. Decoys dogged Smilzo's footsteps, and one evening he let them treat him to too many glasses of sparkling red *lambrusco* wine. They brought up the subject of politics and remarked how strange it was that Peppone should be absent from the scene. One of the decoys said argumentatively:

"There's nothing so strange about it. It's a bad case of yellow liver. He knows the game is up and doesn't dare show his face."

"Just wait till you hear his historical speech, after all the work he's putting into it!" said Smilzo, falling like a ton of bricks for their little game.

Five minutes later Don Camillo was informed, but the news did not disturb him.

"Is that all?" he puffed. "Not worth talking about!"

And indeed he did not bring up the subject again. But that very night an unknown hand wrote on Peppone's door:

"Here lies Comrade Giuseppe Bottazzi,
Who has sought solitude
In order to write an historical election-eve oration.
The question is whether, when it's written,
He'll know how to read it."

Although Don Camillo had dismissed the matter as unworthy of mention, this epigraph caused all malicious tongues to wag about it. Such tongues are not too numerous in the Po valley, or at least there is no more than one to every inhabitant, and not the six or seven which seem to be the sources of so vast a volume of gossip.

Meanwhile the blissfully ignorant Peppone continued to toil over his epoch-making speech. His faithful and discreet wife moved about the house in bedroom slippers in order not to break its continuity. Peppone had never worked so hard in all his life. He worked as hard as if he were forging a hundred-foot iron fence, complete with an ornate gate. The stakes were high. His enemies were dead set on getting into power, whereas Peppone and his gang sought their third consecutive re-election. What with weighing every word and polishing every sentence, Peppone expended far more time than he had imagined, and the final touches were added no earlier than the Friday morning before the historical Saturday night. Then, oddly enough, the scribbler's prophecy was fulfilled, and Peppone was unable to read what he had written. Fortunately, this possibility had been taken into consideration. Smilzo had been standing by for two days, and now he took over the precious manuscript, jumped on to his motor-cycle and rode madly to the city, where a loyal typist proceeded to tap out two copies, one for Peppone and the other for . . . history.

It was late at night and Don Camillo was about to go to bed when Caroline, a poor old creature that went about collecting wood and stale bread, brought him a cardboard folder.

"I found it on the edge of a ditch down near *La Pioppaccia*," she told him. "It's full of papers and they may be important to someone. Can you say something about it in church and see if there are any claimants?"

After she had gone away Don Camillo examined the papers. Soon he realized, to his amazement, that he had Peppone's historical speech in hand, the original and two copies.

Meanwhile Smilzo was sitting under a poplar on the river bank, with death in his heart. He had lost the folder containing the speech. It had slipped out of his pocket while he was riding home, full speed, from the city. Twice he had retraced a portion of the route, vainly searching, and then he had sat down to nurse his despair.

"If I come back empty-handed, the chief will kill me," he said to himself over and over.

And he was not far from right.

*

Peppone spent an agonizing night. After waiting and waiting for Smilzo to come, he put in a long-distance telephone call. The typist told him that Smilzo had left four hours before, with the masterpiece under his arm. Then he called his general staff, and they sent out search-parties. At four o'clock in the morning, there was still no news of Smilzo, and Peppone, who had been angrily pacing up and down the hall, suddenly collapsed.

"Traitor!" he exclaimed, and let himself be carried off to bed, where he fell into a leaden sleep, accompanied by a high fever.

Smilzo turned up at Bigio's house at nine o'clock. When Bigio heard that the speech was lost he was speechless with dismay. He stared hard at Smilzo and said:

"You may as well emigrate to Venezuela."

New orders were sent out to the search-parties. They were to stop looking for Smilzo and watch out for a yellow folder which the miserable fellow had lost on the road. A large-scale manoeuvre of this kind could not escape attention. People took note, asked questions, gossiped, put two and two together and came, by afternoon, to this conclusion: the text of Peppone's famous speech was lost and that evening he would find himself in exceedingly hot water. Which meant that a large crowd would gather to see him squirm.

The meeting was to start at nine o'clock, and by half-past eight the square was full. At this last minute Peppone's henchmen collected their courage and went to wake him. They had quite a job to get him even to open his eyes. He was still feverish and his eyelids were leaden. They explained that a huge crowd had gathered in the square and he must make up his mind what to do.

"How about Smilzo?" Peppone asked in a dim far-away voice.

"He's found," said Bigio.

"And the speech?" Peppone panted.

"It's lost," said Bigio, prudently retreating three steps.

But he need not have been so cautious. Peppone was too far gone to be a menace. He simply closed his eyes and sighed.

"Chief, what are we going to do?" asked Bigio anxiously.

"Go to the devil, the lot of you," murmured Peppone, as if in a dream.

"What about the crowd? And the Party?"

"Devil take the crowd and the Party too," said Peppone pacifically.

His henchmen stared at one another. This was the end.

"There's nothing we can do," said Bigio. "We'll have to tell the crowd that the meeting is adjourned because the speaker is ill."

Just then Don Camillo appeared upon the scene. Obviously he did not expect to find Peppone so stricken, and he looked down in bewilderment at the inert form on the bed. He did not say a word or make his presence felt in any way, but in a few moments Peppone opened first one eye and then the other.

"I'm not ready yet for Extreme Unction," he muttered.

"Too bad," said Don Camillo.

"You can go; I don't need you."

"You always need me, Comrade!" said Don Camillo, taking a big yellow folder out of his pocket and throwing it on to the bed. Peppone reached out, opened it and stared at the contents.

"Check it, now, Comrade," said Don Camillo, with a laugh. "Everything's there: the original manuscript and two copies. Remember that 'incontrovertible' takes only one *b* and be thankful to your parish priest."

Peppone slowly slipped the papers back into the folder and hoisted himself into a sitting position. Then he clenched his teeth, looked into Don Camillo's eyes and said brusquely:

"I'd rather not thank him."

Peppone's hands were as big as shovels. With a single gesture he ripped the folder and its contents in two, then, as if he were prey to some uncontrollable madness, he tore both pieces into shreds, rolled them up in a ball and threw them out of the window. Next, he leaped out of bed.

It was nine o'clock, and the crowd in the square was beginning to murmur, when suddenly Peppone walked on to the platform. His fever had fallen, or rather it was not the same sort of fever. This was clear at once from the way he said: "Fellow-citizens! . . ." The crowd was silent and Peppone spoke. He improvised; a dozen times he said "ain't" and "don't" for "isn't" and "doesn't"; he referred to the "Nemesis of history" and the "Nemesis of geography", but the most awkward phrases quite plainly came from a full heart, so that even his severest critics had to admit that he was a good fellow.

So it was that Smilzo didn't emigrate to Venezuela and Peppone was re-elected mayor, without having to thank Don Camillo, but indebted, none the less, to Divine Providence for preventing him from pronouncing a speech that would have gone down in history as abysmally stupid. And Don Camillo was not too perturbed by the outcome of the election, for he knew that in politics we can often obtain more from our enemies than from our friends.

THE WAR OF THE CARNATIONS

THIS IS A commonplace sort of love-story, which had an unexpected ending on the main square of the village, to be exact, near one of the low stone columns which divide this square from the smaller one in front of the church. There were a large number of witnesses, because the main square was occupied by the May-Day celebration of Peppone and his gang, wearing red carnations in their buttonholes, and the church square by the white-carnationed followers of Don Camillo.

In some broken-down shacks in the Po River valley there are still to be found cheap prints of an old religious painting which shows Jesus and Saint Joseph, clad in unmistakably red garments, working at a carpenter's bench. This was quite a find, from a political point of view, and it was taken up, at one time, by the old-line socialists. Long after they had abandoned it, the representation of Christ and Saint Joseph as workers and craftsmen was re-introduced as the theme of a May the 1st Catholic Labour Day.

The final episode of our little love-story took place on the first of these new-style holidays, celebrated on adjacent squares by the conflicting Red and White parties. It was a cool Spring morning, but the political temperature was boiling over.

Among the most active members of the White team was Gilda Marossi, an exceedingly pretty young girl, whose political ardour was as great as that of two men put together. And among Peppone's most active henchmen was Angiolino Grisotti, nicknamed Gioli, a heavy-handed sort, who if he hadn't been such a violent Red might have passed for a normal, handsome fellow. The story wouldn't be so commonplace if the two had never met. But they did meet, when they were mere school-children and politics was a complete mystery to them. They met several times after that, too, upon various festive occasions, when they had some notion of what politics was about, but cared more for dancing. Then, when they were in politics up to the ears and discovered that they were sworn enemies, they began to avoid such meetings. One day, however, they found themselves face to face on a bus. For a time they tried to outstare each other, but finally Gilda could hold her peace no longer and said brusquely:

"If some people had the least bit of self-respect they wouldn't stare at their betters."

"Just what I was thinking, myself," said Gioli.

Having said all they had to say, they continued to exchange lowering glances all the way to their destination. In spite of their mutual disdain, it was obvious that she was prettier than ever and that in spite of his association with the Reds he was a strikingly handsome fellow. When the bus reached the city, they went their own ways, but a few minutes later Gioli could have kicked himself for his stupidity. He had taken courses in propaganda technique, sponsored by the Party, and now he realized that he had muffed the chance to use an old friendship either to make a convert or to gain insight into the tactics of the enemy. In order to wipe out this error he hatched a new plan.

"A good Communist," he said to himself, "must be a psychologist as well. And what does psychology say? It says that a girl who takes a bus to the city must be going shopping. She won't go into the first shop she sees, no, not she; she'll look into a dozen windows and compare qualities and prices before she buys a single thing. After wasting so much time window-shopping, she'll be dead tired and just manage to catch the last bus home. That's where I come in. . . ."

And so Angiolino Grisotti, nicknamed Gioli, was one of the first to arrive at the last bus, where he put down a parcel on the seat facing him and patiently waited. According to the dictates of psychology, Gilda should have been the last to arrive and have found every seat except the one which he had reserved for her taken. Unfortunately, she arrived shortly after Gioli, and when he saw her coming he turned pale. When Gilda got on the bus, she could have sat anywhere she pleased, but psychological considerations made her set her mind upon the seat occupied by Gioli's parcel.

"Is this place taken?" she asked firmly, tossing her head in the parcel's direction.

He picked up the parcel and she sat down. They sat stiffly, face to face, for several minutes, until Gioli was inspired to take out a packet of cigarettes and offer one to the silent figure across the way.

"*We* don't smoke in public places," said Gilda coldly. "*Your* girls do practically anything, either in public or in private, but *we*'ve been taught better."

"Let's leave politics out of it," said Gioli, putting the cigarettes back in his pocket. "Why not talk about you and me?"

"What do you mean by 'talk'?" queried Gilda aggressively.

"I mean the way we used to talk when we went dancing together."

"Only a godless Communist would have the nerve to throw a woman's past weaknesses in her face," said Gilda stiffly. "Why don't you print on one of your posters that for a while I lent an ear to your foolishness?"

"Why should I?" asked Gioli. "This is a personal matter, not a Party one. Of course, if you can't talk to me for fear of offending the fiancé whom the parish priest has forced upon you, that's a different story."

"I have no fiancé," Gilda retorted. "You're the one that had better step softly if you don't want to arouse the jealousy of Comrade Gisela Cibatti."

Gioli protested, Gilda answered him back, and so they went on for the rest of the journey. Even then the argument wasn't over, and they continued it all the way to Gilda's house. It was dark, and after more discussion Gilda started to say good-bye and go in.

"Too bad," she said on the threshold, "that politics should divide us!"

A silly comment, if ever there was one, because a few minutes before, when she and Comrade Gioli had embraced each other, politics hadn't entered into it at all. Love-stories are all exactly the same, and it's absurd that after so many hundreds of thousands of years the human race should take an interest in them. Be that as it may, two evenings later Gilda looked out of her window and saw Gioli sitting on the parapet of the bridge nearby. She gazed at him for a while, until sheer annoyance impelled her to go down and ask what he was doing. She was ready for anything and prepared to repay it in kind, but when he said quite simply that he had come in the hope of seeing her, she was so taken aback that he was able to kiss her. Instead of taking offence she decided to reap full advantage from the situation.

"Since this jackass is so crazy about me," she said to herself, "I may as well give him some encouragement. I'll get him to the point where he leaves the Party and then drop him like a hot potato!"

For several evenings Gilda proceeded to encourage him. Then, at the psychological moment, she brought up her heavy artillery.

"Gioli, you swear you love me. Are you willing to prove it?"

"I'm ready for anything."

"Then get out of that cursed Party! I can't marry a man who's been excommunicated."

Gioli drew back.

"Gilda, you swear you love me, don't you? Then the burden of the proof is on you. Get out from under those Christian Democrats! I have no intention of marrying a priestess!"

Gilda's tone of voice altered.

"Then you and your filthy Russia can go straight to hell!"

"All right! And while I'm on my merry way, I only hope a fate worse than death overtakes you, and your Vatican and your America!"

Proudly they turned their backs on one another. But the God of lovers had other designs. No sooner had they parted than both their families joined the fray. According to Gioli's relatives and friends, the young man owed it to his own dignity never to look at that pious and pretentious little fraud again. And Gilda's people were equally vociferous in arguing that Gilda ought to give up seeing that dirty Bolshevik for good and all. Both sides hammered away for a whole week, at the end of which time, the mulish Gioli wrote Gilda a special-delivery letter: "If I look for you tomorrow evening on the bridge in front of your house, will you be there?" To which Gilda made answer: "I'll meet you at eight o'clock on the Molinetto bridge, where more people will see us!'

They met, then, at eight o'clock, and practically everybody in the village saw them. And those that didn't see them heard about it from those that did. The opposition became more violent than ever. Both Gilda and Gioli found all their friends and acquaintances, including of course their fellow party-members, against them. But the more all these well-intentioned people sought to separate them, the closer they were drawn together.

The subversive Gioli was fundamentally a good boy, and the virtuous Gilda had a strongly rebellious, perhaps even revolutionary nature. Because they were both very proud, they did not speak of the battles they were waging inside their own camps; they relieved their tension by loving each other more and more every day. But when Gilda's people came out with ugly threats, she lost patience.

Peppone was flabbergasted to receive her visit at such a late hour. He wondered what could be the ulterior motive of this girl who had made a fool of one of his most stalwart followers.

"Can you keep a secret until tomorrow morning?" Gilda asked him.

"If it's an honest secret, I can."

Gilda took out of her pocket-book a card with the party emblem of shield and cross, tore it into pieces and threw it on to the table.

"Give me one of your cards, now," she said, "and keep quiet about it until tomorrow morning. I want to surprise Gioli and also those wretched people who've been trying to get me away from him."

Peppone remained for several minutes with his mouth hanging open, and then objected:

"But you've come here out of sheer spite. It's not true faith that makes you want to join our party."

"What does that matter? Since when have you Communists been such senti-mental souls that you wouldn't delight in thumbing your noses at the parish priest?"

Peppone had been eating his heart out over the rival May-Day celebration, and these last words roused a definite reaction.

"I'll make you a member thirty times over, if it will make the priest suffer!"

With card in hand, Gilda went away. And when Peppone had time to think it over, he concluded that Comrade Gioli had scored a personal and party triumph.

"Love is on the Communist side," he observed sententiously.

The next dawn was that of the First of May and the main square was filled with red, the church square with white carnations. Peppone was overcome by excitement. While on the one hand he hoped to avoid Don Camillo, on the other he would have given almost anything to run into him. Finally they did meet, near the row of low stone columns which separated the two squares.

"Hurrah for Christ the Worker!" exclaimed Peppone, smiling broadly.

"Exactly! He may not have belonged to the union, but He worked as a carpenter, at the side of His father, Joseph."

"I seem to remember hearing that God was his Father," Peppone retorted.

"Just so, Mr. Mayor. His Father is the greatest Worker of all. He created the universe before there was any such thing as raw materials!"

Peppone swallowed hard and then said between clenched teeth:

"And all the rest of you clerics that are taking part in this labour celebration, just what work do you do?"

"I pray for your sin-stained soul," said Don Camillo, "and that's hard work, I can tell you!"

Peppone looked around, and seeing that everything was in good order, he came out with his sensational news:

"There's another soul you can pray for," he said, pointing to a certain segment of the Red throng.

Don Camillo's eyes popped with astonishment. There in a red dress, with a red carnation in her hair, standing close to the red flag, stood Gilda Marossi. What could he say? But before Peppone could enjoy his triumph to the full, a horrible sight met his eye. In the church square, with a white carnation in his buttonhole, practically wrapped in the folds of the Christian-Democrat banner, stood ex-Comrade Angiolino Grisotti. After a moment, Gilda and Gioli caught sight of each other, too, for both of them had been scanning the rival assembly. After standing thunderstruck with amazement they moved instinctively towards the columns dividing the two squares, by which Don Camillo and Peppone still lingered. They exchanged curious glances and then Gilda said:

"I wanted to surprise you!"

"Same here!" said Gioli.

Some of the bystanders burst into laughter. Gilda and Gioli looked into each other's eyes and reached a speechless understanding. As if by preconceived accord they stripped themselves of their carnations, and laid them on one of the low stone columns; then arm in arm they walked away from the centre of the village and out of political life for ever and ever. Don Camillo and Peppone stared raptly at the two carnations.

"Well! . . ." muttered Peppone, shrugging his shoulders.

"Well! . . ." echoed Don Camillo, characteristically throwing out his arms.

And these were the most eloquent speeches that either of them made during this May-Day celebration.

COMRADE
DON CAMILLO

GOLD FEVER

THE NEWS EXPLODED like a bomb around Monday noon, upon the arrival of the newspapers. Someone in the village had won ten million liras in the national soccer sweepstakes. The papers gave the name of the winner as Pepito Sbezzeguti, but no one in the town was known under such an exotic name. The bet collector, besieged by a curious mob, threw out his arms hopelessly.

"I sold any number of tickets to fellows from out of town at the market on Saturday," he said. "It must be one of them. Ten million liras! He's bound to show up."

But no one showed up, and the village continued to fret, because they felt sure there was something fishy about the name. Sbezzeguti was plausible, someone of that name might have come to the market. But Pepito was going a little too far. Nobody who dealt in wheat, corn, hay, livestock and Parmesan cheese would be called Pepito.

"It's a phony name, if you ask me," said the proprietor of the Molinetto. "And someone using a false name isn't likely to be a stranger. It must be a villager who doesn't want it known that he played the sweeps. Maybe he doesn't want his debtors to know, or his wife."

The argument was logical enough. The villagers dropped the theory of the winner being an outsider and concentrated upon their fellow townsmen. They concentrated as intently as if they were trying to identify a common thief rather than the winner of a legitimate pool.

Don Camillo followed the affair less passionately but with a certain amount of interest. And because he felt that Christ did not altogether approve of his leanings towards the trade of a detective he offered Him an explanation.

"Lord, it's not a matter of idle curiosity; I'm doing my duty. A man who has received such a favour from Divine Providence has no right to hide it."

"Don Camillo," replied Christ, "Divine Providence may take an interest in the soccer sweepstakes, although personally I doubt it, but surely not in all the publicity about the winnings. The fact of the matter is all that counts and it's quite adequately known. Someone has won a considerable sum of money, but why must you beat out your brains to discover his identity? Your business is to look after those who are less fortunate."

But Don Camillo couldn't rid himself of his curiosity. The mystery of Pepito continued to occupy his mind until finally a great light dawned upon him. It was all he could do not to ring the church bells in exultation, and quite beyond his powers to resist putting on his cloak and going for a walk in the village. In time he arrived at the workshop of Peppone, mayor and blacksmith. Don Camillo stuck his head through the door and greeted his enemy.

"Good morning, Comrade Pepito!"

Peppone stopped hammering and stared at the priest in dismay.

"What do you mean, Father?"

"Nothing at all. Pepito's a diminutive of Peppone, after all, and by some strange chance Sbezzeguti is an imperfect anagram of Giuseppe Bottazzi."

Peppone resumed his hammering.

Don Camillo shook his head.

"What a shame that you're not the Pepito who won the ten millions."

"A shame, yes. In that case I'd be able to offer you two or three millions to go back home."

"Don't worry, Peppone. I do favours for nothing," said Don Camillo, going away.

Two hours later the whole village knew what is meant by an anagram, and in every house Pepito Sbezzeguti was vivisected to find out if Comrade Giuseppe Bottazzi was lurking inside. That same evening the Reds' general staff held a special meeting at the People's Palace.

"Chief," said Smilzo, "the reactionaries have gone back to their old tactics of smearing a good name. The whole village is in an uproar. They say you won the ten millions. There's no time to be lost; you must nail down their slander."

Peppone threw out his arms.

"To say a fellow has won ten millions in the soccer sweepstake isn't slander. Slander means accusing someone of having done something dishonest, and the sweepstakes are quite on the level."

"Chief, in politics to accuse someone of a good deed is a smear. And an accusation that hurts the Party is definitely slanderous."

"People are laughing behind our backs," put in Brusco. "We've got to shut them up."

"We must print a poster!" Bigio exclaimed. "We must come up with a statement that makes everything clear."

Peppone shrugged his shoulders.

"We'll put our minds to it tomorrow," he said.

Whereupon Smilzo pulled a sheet of paper out of his pocket.

"We've something ready, Chief, in order to save you the trouble. If you approve we'll print it right away and paste up the posters tomorrow morning."

And he proceeded to read aloud:

> The undersigned, Giuseppe Bottazzi, declares that he has no connection with the Pepito Sbezzeguti who won ten million liras in the soccer sweepstakes. It is useless for the reactionaries to accuse him of being a millionaire. All it proves is that they are a gang of neo-Fascists.
>
> —Giuseppe Bottazzi.

Peppone shook his head.

"It's all right," he said, "but until I see something in print I'm not going to rush into print myself with an answer."

But Smilzo stuck to his argument.

"Why wait to shoot until someone has shot at you? Good strategy calls for beating the opponent to the draw."

"Good strategy calls for a kick in the pants to anyone who sticks his nose into my private affairs. I can defend myself without help."

Smilzo shrugged his shoulders.

"If you take it like that, there's nothing more to say."

"That's how I do take it!" shouted Peppone, bringing his fist down on the table. "Every man for himself, and the Party for the lot of us!"

The general staff went away grumbling.

"To let himself be accused of having won ten million is a sign of weakness," observed Smilzo. "And besides, there's the complication of the anagram."

"Let's hope for the best," sighed Bigio.

Soon enough the rumour appeared in print. The landowners' paper published an insert that said: "*Scratch a Peppone and you'll find a Pepito*", and everyone in the village found this exceedingly clever and funny. The general staff held another meeting in the People's Palace and declared unanimously that something had to be done.

"Very good," said Peppone. "Go ahead and print the poster and paste it up."

Smilzo made a bee-line for the printer's. Little more than an hour later the printer, Barchini, brought Don Camillo a copy of the proofs.

"This is bad business for the newspaper," said Don Camillo sadly. "If Peppone really did win the money I don't think he would put out such a statement. That is, unless he's already gone to the city to collect it or sent someone else to collect it for him."

"He hasn't made a move," Barchini assured him. "Everyone in the village is on the alert."

It was late, and Don Camillo went to bed. But at three o'clock in the morning he was awakened by the news of a visit from Peppone. Peppone sneaked in from the garden, and when he was in the hall he peered out anxiously through the half-closed door.

"Here's hoping no one has seen me," he said. "I feel as if I were being followed."

Don Camillo glanced at him anxiously.

"You haven't gone crazy, have you?" he asked.

"No, no fear of that."

Peppone sat down and wiped the perspiration from his brow.

"Am I talking to the parish priest or to the village gossip?"

"That depends on what you came to say."

"I came to see the priest."

"The priest is listening," said Don Camillo gravely.

Peppone twirled his hat between his fingers and then confessed:

"Father, I told a big lie. I *am* Pepito Sbezzeguti."

For a moment Don Camillo was speechless.

"So you did win the millions, did you?" he said when he had recovered his aplomb. "Why didn't you say so?"

"I'm not saying so. I was speaking to you as a priest, and you should have no concern with anything but the fact that I told a lie."

But Don Camillo was concerned with the ten millions. He shot a withering look at Peppone and moved to the attack.

"Shame on you! A proletarian, a Party member winning ten million liras in a soccer sweepstake! Leave such shenanigans to the bourgeoisie! Communists earn their living by the sweat of their brow."

"I'm in no mood for joking." gasped Peppone. "Is it a crime to place a bet in the soccer sweepstake?"

"It's no joke," said Don Camillo. "I didn't say it was a crime. I said that a good Communist wouldn't do it."

"Nonsense! Everyone does."

"That's very bad. And all the worse for you because you're a leader of the class struggle. The soccer sweepstake is a diabolical capitalist weapon turned against the People. Very effective, and it costs the capitalists nothing. In fact, they stand to make money. No good Communist can fail to combat it."

Peppone shrugged his shoulders in annoyance.

"Don't get excited, Comrade! It's all part of a vast conspiracy to persuade the proletariat to seek riches by other means than revolution. Of course that's pure fraud, and by abetting it you're betraying the cause of the People!"

Peppone waved his arms wildly.

"Father, let's leave politics out of it!"

"What's that, Comrade? Are you forgetful of the Revolution?"

Peppone stamped his feet, and Don Camillo smiled indulgently.

"I understand, Comrade," he said, "and I don't blame you. Better ten million liras today than the Revolution tomorrow!"

He went to poke up the fire and then turned around to look at Peppone.

"Did you come here just to tell me you'd won the money?"

Peppone was in a cold sweat.

"How can I get the cash without anyone's knowing?" he asked.

"Go for it, that's all."

"I can't. They're watching me like hawks. And besides my denial is coming out tomorrow."

"Then send a trusted comrade."

"There's no one I can trust."

"I don't know what to say," said Don Camillo, shaking his head.

Peppone held out an envelope.

"You go for me, Father."

He got up and went away, leaving Don Camillo to stare at the envelope.

The next morning Don Camillo set out for the city. Three days later he made his return. He arrived late in the evening, and before going to the rectory went to talk to the Christ over the altar. Opening up his suitcase he said sternly:

"Jesus, here are ten bundles, each one of them containing a hundred ten-thousand-lira notes. In other words, the ten million liras that belong to Peppone. All I have to say is this: he doesn't deserve them."

"Tell that to the sweepstake operators," Christ replied.

Don Camillo took the suitcase away. When he reached the second floor of the rectory he switched the light on and off three times in succession as a signal to Peppone. Peppone replied by means of the light in his bedroom. Two hours later he arrived at the rectory, with his coat collar turned up to hide his face. He came in from the garden, through the door with the heavy padlock hanging from it.

"Well, then?" he said to Don Camillo, who was waiting in the pantry.

Don Camillo pointed at the suitcase, which was lying on the table, and Peppone approached it with trembling hands. When he saw the bundles of banknotes he broke into perspiration.

"Ten million?" he whispered questioningly.

"Ten million cold. Count them for yourself."

"Oh no," demurred Peppone, staring fascinatedly at the money.

"A pretty pile," commented Don Camillo, "at least for today. Who knows what it may be worth tomorrow? A single piece of bad news is enough to bring on inflation and turn it into worthless paper."

"I ought to invest it right away," said Peppone. "With ten millions I could buy a farm, and land always has value."

"It's the peasants that have a right to the land," said Don Camillo. "At least that's what the Communists say. They don't mention blacksmiths. They'll take it away from you, you'll see. Communism is the wave of the future, Comrade. . . ."

Peppone was still staring at the banknotes.

"I have it!" he exclaimed. "Gold! I'll buy gold and hide it away."

"What good will it do you? If the Communists take over, everything will come under the control of the State and your gold will lose its purchasing power."

"I could always deposit it abroad."

"Tut, tut! Like a regular capitalist! You'd deposit it in America, I suppose, because Europe is going Communist for sure. But when America is left out on a limb it will have to surrender to the Soviet Union."

"America's got real power," said Peppone. "The Soviet will never take it over."

"I wouldn't be so sure, Comrade."

Peppone took a deep breath and sat down.

"My head's whirling, Father. Ten million liras."

"Please oblige me by taking them home. But don't forget to send back my suitcase. That's my private property."

"No, Father," said Peppone. "Keep the money for me, will you? I'd rather talk about it when I can think straight, perhaps tomorrow."

After Peppone had gone away Don Camillo carried the suitcase up to his bedroom and went to bed. He was dead tired, but his sleep was interrupted at two o'clock in the morning by the reappearance of Peppone, together with his wife, both of them swathed in heavy coats.

"Forgive me, Father," said Peppone. "My wife just had to take a squint at the money."

Don Camillo brought down the suitcase and deposited it on the pantry table. At the sight of the banknotes Peppone's wife turned deathly pale. Don Camillo waited patiently, then he closed the suitcase and escorted the two of them to the door.

"Try to get some sleep," he said as they went away.

He tried to do the same thing himself, but an hour later he was once more awakened by Peppone.

"What's this?" he protested. "Isn't the pilgrimage over?"

"I came to take the suitcase," explained Peppone.

"Nothing doing! I've stowed it away in the attic and I have no intention of bringing it down. You can come back tomorrow. I'm cold and tired and entitled to my rest. Don't you trust me?"

"It's not a question of trust. What if something were to happen to you during the night? How could I prove that the money is mine?"

"Don't worry about that. The suitcase is locked and there's a tag with your name on it. I've thought of every contingency."

"I appreciate that, Father. But the money's safer in my house."

Don Camillo didn't like his tone of voice. And he changed his own to match it.

'What money are you talking about?"

"My own! The money you went to get for me in Rome."

"You must be crazy, Peppone. I never got any of your money."

"The ticket's in my name," shouted Peppone. "I'm Pepito Sbezzeguti."

It's plastered all over the walls that you're *not* Pepito Sbezzeguti. You signed the statement yourself."

"I am, though! Pepito Sbezzeguti is an anagram of Giuseppe Bottazzi."

"No it isn't. It's an anagram of Giuseppe Bott*e*zzi. I have an uncle of that name and it's for him that I cashed in the ticket."

With a trembling hand Peppone wrote *Pepito Sbezzeguti* on the margin of the newspaper lying on the table, and after it his real name.

"Damnation!" he exclaimed. "I put an *e* for an *a*. But the money's mine."

Don Camillo started up the stairs to his bedroom, with Peppone following after.

"Don't take it so hard, Comrade," he called out as he climbed into bed. "I won't steal your money. I'll use it for your own cause, for the cause of the downtrodden people."

"Devil take the people!" Peppone shouted.

"You benighted reactionary!" said Don Camillo, pulling the sheet up over his head. "Go away and let me sleep!"

"Give me my money, or I'll kill you like a dog!"

"Take the filthy stuff and go away!"

The suitcase was on the chest of drawers. Peppone seized it, hid it under his coat and ran down the stairs.

When Don Camillo heard the front door slam he gave a deep sigh.

"Lord," he said sternly, "why did you let him ruin his life by winning that money? He doesn't deserve such punishment."

"First you scold me because he didn't deserve such a prize and now you call it a punishment! I can't seem to please you, Don Camillo!"

"I wasn't talking to you, Lord; I was talking to the sweepstake operators," Don Camillo murmured as he finally fell asleep.

DON CAMILLO'S REVENGE

"LORD," SAID DON CAMILLO, "he's gone a bit too far, and I shall destroy him!"

"Don Camillo," said the crucified Christ over the altar, "they went a bit too far when they hung me up on this Cross, but I managed to forgive them."

"But they didn't know what they were doing! Peppone had his eyes wide open and deserves no pity."

"Look here, Don Camillo," Christ retorted; "ever since Peppone became a senator haven't you been particularly hard on him?"

These words hit home, and Don Camillo resented them.

"You wouldn't say that, Lord," he protested, "if you knew me a little better."

"Oh, I know you well enough," Christ sighed in reply.

Don Camillo knew when to stop. He hastily bent one knee, crossed himself and glided away. But outside the church his resentment was reawakened. Just beside the rectory door some unfortunate fellow had just pasted up a copy of the poster which had aroused his original anger. It was a story that dated back to two years before.

One gloomy winter evening, when Don Camillo was just about to go to bed, someone had knocked at the rectory door. Don Camillo saw that of course it was Peppone. He motioned him to a chair and handed him a glass of wine, which Peppone drained with a single gulp. It took two more glasses to loosen his tongue, and then he came out with:

"I can't stand it!"

From under his heavy black cape he pulled out a bundle.

"Ever since I've had this in the house I haven't been able to sleep."

It was the famous ten million liras, of course, and Don Camillo replied:

"Then put it in the bank."

Peppone gave a wry laugh.

"That's a very poor joke! How can a Communist mayor deposit ten million liras in the bank without saying where he got them?"

"Convert them into gold and bury it in the ground!"

"That way I wouldn't get any interest on my capital."

Don Camillo was sleepy, but his patience was not yet exhausted.

"Come along, Comrade," he said pacifically; "let's get to the point."

"Well then, Father, you know that businessman who takes such good care of other people's money. . . ."

"No, I don't know him."

"Surely you do. He belongs to your camp. A fellow that gets a lot of business from Church people and then eases his conscience with big donations to religious charities. . . ."

"Oh yes, I have an idea whom you mean. But I've never had any dealings with him."

"But you can get in touch with him very easily. The priest at Torricella is one of his agents."

Don Camillo wearily shook his head.

"Comrade," he said, "just because God gave you an inch, do you have to take a mile?"

"God has nothing to do with it, Father. I had a stroke of good luck and now I want to take advantage of it."

"Then it's perfectly simple. Go to the priest at Torricella and ask him for an introduction."

"No, I can't do that. People know my face too well. If they were to see me hanging around the rectory at Torricella or the businessman's office, I'd lose my reputation. Imagine a Communist getting mixed up with the Church and high finance! If I can keep my name out of it, then it's strictly a matter of money. I can't let it become a political football."

Don Camillo had always taken a dim view of the businessman who earned sky-high interest rates for his clients and then contributed to the building of new churches. But the Torricella priest was a thoroughly decent fellow and, if he had acquired a sports field, a swimming pool, a moving-picture projector and other attractions to compete with those offered by the Reds, it was all thanks to the generosity of this wealthy parishioner. And so Don Camillo suspended his judgment.

"I don't want to get myself involved in any more complications," he said. "Tomorrow evening at this time, I'll arrange to have the priest come over from Torricella. I'll go to bed and leave you to talk with him."

Twenty-four hours later Peppone and the other priest met in Don Camillo's study. They seemed to have reached some agreement, for Don Camillo heard no more of the affair. A year later Peppone was elected to the Senate, and from then on Don Camillo was besieged by some devil.

"Peppone is an ingrate," the devil whispered in his ear. "You were a good friend to him when you went to collect the sweepstakes money, and what has he done for you in return? No sooner was he elected than he made an inflammatory speech in the public square."

Portions of the inflammatory speech had been brought to Don Camillo's attention. In boasting of his electoral triumph Peppone had made scathing references to "*a certain priest who used all sorts of pious platitudes to prevent a victory of the People, a priest who would better be employed as a bellringer if only he knew how to ring a bell.*" Quite obviously Don Camillo was tempted to retaliate by telling the story of Peppone's clandestine sweepstakes winnings.

For two whole years the priest staved off this temptation. He had just about banished it from his mind when he saw the new Communist poster. Just at that time the famous businessman had got his name into the headlines as the central figure of a financial scandal. When the scandal was at its height, Peppone launched this attack against him, in which he included "*certain conniving priests who, for love of money, did not hesitate to join hands with a notorious swindler in order to rob the faithful of their hard-earned savings."*

This shameless accusation was more than Don Camillo could take, and he made up his mind to explode a little bomb of his own.

Peppone came back quite often to the village. He was now a very different man, carrying a brief-case full of state papers and wearing a self-important and pre-occupied air, as if the affairs of the whole world weighed upon his shoulders. He greeted the local people distractedly and inspired fear even among his Party comrades. Whenever anyone brought him a problem he said solemnly: "I'll take it up in Rome." He went in for dark, double-breasted suits and conventional felt hats and never appeared without a tie. The poster contained glaring grammatical errors, but since his personality was quite strong enough to overshadow his style, no one dared make fun of them. Don Camillo laid his plans and accosted him at eleven o'clock one night at the door of his house.

"Excuse me," he said, while Peppone was turning the key in the lock, "but do you happen to be one of the poor innocents fleeced by conniving priests who joined hands with a notorious swindler?"

Peppone had succeeded in opening the door and now he had no choice but to let Don Camillo in. At once Don Camillo drove his point home.

"Comrade Senator," he went on, "the next trick is mine. When I tell the whole truth, you'll be the laughing-stock of the whole country. Just wait until your electors find out that you cheated both the tax collector and the Communist Party of your sweepstakes winnings! And how you cheated them again by turning over your ten million liras to a criminal speculator, one of those whom you define as the Enemies of the People!"

Peppone threw out his chest defiantly.

"I'll sue you for libel," he retorted. "You can't prove a thing."

"I'll prove the whole story. Your name is in that man's files. He sent your interest payments by cheque, and I have the cheque numbers."

Peppone wiped a sudden access of perspiration from his brow.

"You'd never play me a dirty trick like that!"

Don Camillo sat down and lighted his cigar butt.

"It's no dirty trick," he said. "It's just a reply to your poster."

Peppone let himself go. He tore off his jacket and threw it on to a sofa and loosened his tie. Then he sat down directly across from Don Camillo.

"You don't need to take revenge," he groaned. "I lost every penny."

"But you'd been getting such exorbitant interest for the past two years that you pretty nearly came out even."

Peppone felt trapped, and in desperation he blurted out:

"Father, will you settle for three million?"

"Comrade, you have no right to insult me with such an offer. That will cost you something extra."

He pulled out a newspaper, unfolded it and pointed out an article on one of the back pages.

"You see, Senator, we know what's going on. We see that you have been given the important job of picking ten deserving comrades whom you're to escort on a free tour of Soviet Russia. We shan't interfere with this project. But as soon as you've left the country we'll let the cat out of the bag. The embarrassment of your Party leaders will add to the fun."

Peppone was speechless. Knowing Don Camillo as he did, he realized that there was no chance of stopping him. His crumpled air moved the priest to compassion.

"Comrade," he said, "you can consider yourself liquidated. That is, unless . . ."

"Unless what?" groaned Peppone, raising his head.

Quite calmly Don Camillo set forth the only means of escaping disgrace. Peppone listened with his jaw sagging.

"Father, you're joking," he said when the priest had finished.

"It's no joke. It's do or die."

"You're mad, Father," said Peppone, leaping to his feet. "Stark, raving mad!"

"Exactly, Comrade. That's why you'd better think twice before you say no. Madmen can be dangerous. I give you until tomorrow night."

Two days later Don Camillo went to the old Bishop, who heard him out patiently to the end of his story.

"Is that all?" he inquired. "I think that with a rest cure in the mountains you may get over it."

Don Camillo shook his head.

"I meant every word," he insisted. "It's the opportunity of a lifetime. Two whole weeks of direct contact with a group of our most ardent Communists and also with the Russians! . . ."

The Bishop looked at him with dismay.

"My son, who put this idea into your head?"

"Nobody. It just came upon me. Who knows? Perhaps it was inspired by the Lord."

"I can't believe it," muttered the Bishop. "Anyhow, you're dead set upon it, and you expect me to let you go without breathing a word to a soul. What if they discover who you are?"

"They won't discover that, I promise you. I'll take pains to disguise myself. I don't mean so much by the clothes I wear as by my frame of mind. That's what really counts. A normal mind has to take on Communist processes of thought, if facial expression and tone of voice are to fit in with the Communist pattern."

The Bishop tapped his cane against the stool where he was resting his feet.

"It's sheer madness, my son," he concluded.

"Yes, Your Grace," agreed Don Camillo.

"But you may go," the Bishop added.

Don Camillo knelt down, and the Bishop laid a wasted hand on his bowed head.

"God be with you, Comrade Don Camillo," he said, raising his eyes to heaven.

He spoke in such a low voice that Don Camillo barely heard what he was saying. But God had no difficulty hearing.

DON CAMILLO IN DISGUISE

"Good morning, Senator," said the sharp-tongued cleaning woman who was scrubbing the boarding-house floor.

"Good morning, Comrade," cautiously murmured the milkman, who was just making his morning delivery.

"Good morning, you poor fool," said a stout-bodied man who was standing square in the middle of the pavement, waiting for him to come by.

Peppone did not deign to answer; he pushed him aside and went on his way. The scene was Rome, at nine o'clock in the morning. The vast machinery of the capital was slowly getting under way and a remnant of sleepiness still dulled the crisp freshness of the autumn air.

"Good morning, you poor fool," repeated the stout-bodied man, this time in a cordial, almost affectionate manner. "Up in the country this is the beginning of a wonderful day. Mist is rolling off the ploughed fields, the clover is shiny with dew and the vines are heavy with clusters of ripe, honey-sweet grapes, half-hidden by russet leaves. . . ."

Peppone grunted in reply. Did his enemy have to lie in ambush every morning in front of the boarding-house and then buzz about him with the latest village news? To quiet his nerves he lit a cigarette.

"Of course," the other jeered. "A cigar would never do. City people don't like strong smells, and if your landlady were to see you with a cigar butt hanging out of one corner of your mouth, senators would go down in her esteem. A very nice old lady she is, by the way, and you did well to tell her you were an 'independent'. It would be quite a shock to her to find out that you're a Communist."

Peppone threw away his cigarette and loosened his tie.

"Yes, I know that you used to feel more comfortable with your shirt open and a handkerchief knotted around your neck. But a senator can't go around looking like a hayseed. You're a big shot now, with a telephone on your desk and marble tiles on your office floor."

Peppone glanced at his watch.

"Don't worry," said the voice beside him. "You're doing a very good job. You displayed excellent judgment in the choice of candidates for your Russian tour. Only one name is missing from the list."

Peppone took off his hat and wiped the perspiration from his forehead.

"It's all the fault of that speculator! I wish I'd never met him."

"Look here, my boy," said his interlocutor with genuine feeling, "you don't have to let yourself in for any of this. Why go looking for trouble? You can kick off the traces and come on home."

"No, I can't," groaned Peppone.

"Then good-bye until tomorrow, and God help you!"

They had come to the bus stop, and Peppone watched his friendly enemy walk away and lose himself in the crowd. Did the fellow have to haunt him every morning with memories of the past, of days when he had been a simpler but happier man, to tease him with the siren call of "Home, Sweet Home"?

On the bus Peppone sat down across from a man who was reading the Communist daily, *L'Unità del Popolo*, which he held wide open before him, as stiffly as if it were mounted on a wooden frame. Peppone could not see his fellow passenger's face, but this dramatically provocative pose convinced him that he must be a jackass. *"Every Party member should wear a Party emblem in his buttonhole, but to display it ostentatiously is contrary to common sense."* So Peppone himself had decreed in the good old days, when someone had played a miserable, low-down trick on his dog, Thunder. Don Camillo had scolded Peppone for failing to take off his hat when the Blessed Sacrament went by, and Peppone had answered with insulting remarks. Shortly after this, Thunder had come home with all his hair shaved off, except on his rump, where it had been trimmed in the pattern of a hammer and sickle. And every time that Don Camillo met the dog, he tipped his hat in mock respect for the Party emblem.

"Those were the days," Peppone thought to himself, "before people were really bitten by the political bug and a good laugh straightened out their relationship better than any amount of bitter discussion."

The conventionally dressed man across the way lowered his paper and Peppone had to admit that he didn't look like a jackass. His eyes were expressionless, but this was doubtless because the thick lenses of his glasses concealed them from view. He was wearing a commonplace light suit and an even more commonplace grey hat. Somehow or other he was unpleasant, and Peppone was annoyed to see him get off at the same bus stop as himself.

"Sir," the man asked him, "can you show me the way to . . . ?"

Peppone lost all control.

"I can show you the way to go to hell," he shouted.

"Exactly what I wanted to know," said the man calmly.

Peppone strode rapidly away, and the other followed after. Five minutes later he sat down at the same isolated table in a small, empty café. After Peppone had cooled himself off with a heaping dish of ice cream he regained sufficient self-control to speak.

"Your bad joke has gone far enough," he decreed.

"Not a bit of it. This is only the beginning."

"You don't expect me to take you seriously, do you?"

"I not only expect it; I demand it."

"Now, Don Camillo—"

"Call me Comrade Tarocci. . . ." And he took a passport out of his pocket. "There it is, in black and white: 'Camillo Tarocci, linotypist'."

Peppone turned the passport over and over in his hands, looking at it disgustedly.

"A false name, a false passport, false colours."

"No, Comrade, the passport is genuine. It was issued to Camillo Tarocci, linotypist, and I'm practically his spitting image. If you don't believe me, just look at this." And holding out a piece of paper, he explained: "Here you have a membership card of the Communist Party, issued to Camillo Tarocci. Everything's authentic and in good order." And before Peppone could interrupt him he went on: "There's nothing to be surprised about. Some of the comrades aren't what they seem. But since Tarocci is one of the star members of his cell, you have only to write and ask him for the names of half a dozen fellows particularly deserving to be taken along on your tour and then choose him instead. Then while he takes a fortnight's country vacation I'll tag along with you. I'll have a good look at Russia, and when I come back I'll tell him all about it."

It was all Peppone could do to keep his temper.

"I don't know or care whether there really is a hell," he spluttered. "But if there is one, that's where you're going."

"Then we shall meet again in the next life, Comrade."

At this point Peppone's defences broke down.

"Father," he said wearily, "why are you dead set on destroying me?"

"Nobody's dead set on destroying you, Comrade. My presence on your Russian tour isn't going to affect the state of things in Russia. The good things will be good and the bad things will be bad whether I'm there or not. Why are you so nervous? Are you afraid it isn't the workers' paradise that your newspapers make it out to be?"

Peppone shrugged his shoulders.

"As far as I'm concerned," Don Camillo went on, "I'm hoping it isn't as bad as our papers paint it."

"Very fine feelings!" exclaimed Peppone sarcastically. "How objective and disinterested you are!"

"I'm not disinterested at all," Don Camillo retorted. "It's to my interest that the Russians should be happy. That way they'll stay quietly at home and not go bothering other people."

A week later Comrade Camillo Tarocci received the news that he had been chosen to go on the Russian tour. Carrying a cheap suitcase he reported at the Communist Party headquarters, along with the nine other tour members. A young Party official received the little group introduced to him by the Senator and issued terse parting instructions.

"Comrades, you have a definite mission to perform. You are to keep your eyes and ears open, not only on your own behalf but also on behalf of your comrades at home. When you come back you must tell friends and foes alike about the technical accomplishments and peaceful spirit of the glorious Soviet Union."

While Peppone visibly paled with apprehension, Don Camillo asked permission to make a statement.

"Comrade," he said, "it's hardly worthwhile to travel so far merely in order to come back and tell our friends something they already know and our foes something they refuse to admit. My idea is that our mission should be to convey to our Russian hosts the joyous and grateful greetings of the Italian people for their liberation from the threat of war."

"Of course, Comrade," muttered the Party official; "that goes without saying."

He went away, sticking out his chest and looking slightly annoyed, and Peppone turned ferociously on Don Camillo.

"When something goes without saying then it needn't be said. Besides, you must speak in a way that shows some respect for the person to whom you are speaking. Obviously you don't know who that was."

"Oh yes, I do," Don Camillo imperturbably replied. "He's a twenty-five-year-old young man, who was about ten when the war began. He never fought with us up in the mountains against the Germans and so he can't possibly know what a terrible thing war is or how psychologically important is Comrade Khrushchev's trip to America to forward the cause of peace and disarmament."

"Well spoken," said Comrade Nanni Scamoggia, a hulking fellow from the proletarian Trastevere section of Rome, with a tough and devil-may-care air about him. "When there's fighting to be done, you'll never see one of these Party big shots on the scene."

"And when these bureaucrats start setting up a bureaucracy—" added Comrade Walter Rondella, a working-man from Milan. But before he could say any more Peppone interrupted.

"We're not here to hold a meeting. If we don't step fast we'll miss the train."

He walked briskly towards the door, shooting Don Camillo an atomic glance loaded with enough power to topple a skyscraper. But Don Camillo preserved the stony expression of a comrade who, whatever the cost, will not deviate a single inch from the Party line.

On the train Peppone's chief preoccupation was not to let the diabolical Comrade Camillo Tarocci out of his sight. He sat directly in front of him in order to block his way. But Don Camillo did not seem to be in a mood for making trouble. He took out of his pocket a book with a red jacket and a gold hammer and sickle stamped upon it and with an impenetrable expression on his face immersed himself in its perusal. At rare intervals he raised his eyes and looked out at the fields and villages gliding by the train. As he closed the book and started to put it back in his pocket, Peppone remarked:

"Must be good reading."

"The very best," said Don Camillo. "It's a collection of excerpts from Lenin." And he added, handing it over for inspection: "Too bad it's in French. But I can translate any part you'd like to hear."

"No thanks, Comrade," said Peppone, closing the book and returning it to its owner.

He looked cautiously around him and breathed a sigh of relief when he saw that all his other travelling companions were either dozing or turning the pages of illustrated magazines. No one had noticed that in spite of the red jacket and the French title, *Pensées de Lénine,* the book was actually a Latin breviary.

At the first stop several of the men got off the train. Comrade Scamoggia came back with a bottle of wine and Comrade Rondella with an extra of an evening newspaper, over which he was shaking his head disgustedly. On the front page there were pictures of Khrushchev's last day in America and the usual crowd of smiling faces around him.

"I don't know what it is, but to see him smile in the company of those grinning mugs is more than I can stomach."

"Politics is a question of brains, not of feeling," said Don Camillo. "The Soviet Union has been struggling all along to achieve peaceful co-existence. The capitalists who fostered the Cold War are the ones who have very little to smile about. The end of the cold war is a capitalist disaster."

But Rondella had all the obstinacy of the typical organized Milanese worker.

"That's all very well. But I have a perfect right to say that I hate capitalists and I'd rather be seen dead than caught smiling with them."

"You have a perfect right to say what you please. But don't say it to us; say it to Khrushchev. By the time we get to Moscow he'll be there. You can ask to see him and then say to his face: 'Comrade Khrushchev, you're on the wrong track'."

Don Camillo was as sly as the slyest Communist secret agent. Comrade Rondella turned pale.

"Either you can't or you won't understand me," he protested. "If I have to handle manure in order to fertilize a field, then I'll handle it. But no one can force me to say that it has a good smell."

"Comrade," said Don Camillo quietly, "you fought with the Partisans, I know. When you were ordered into danger, what did you do?"

"I went."

"And did you tell your comrades that you couldn't stomach the idea of risking your life?"

"Of course not. But what's the connection?"

"War is war, Comrade, whether it's hot or cold. And the man who's fighting for a just cause can't afford to have opinions of his own."

"Drop it, Comrade Rondella," intervened Peppone. "We're going to a country where you won't run into any capitalists, that's one thing sure."

"And it makes me feel considerably better," admitted Rondella.

"The thing I'm happiest about," said Comrade Scamoggia, "is that for a whole fortnight we shan't run into any priests."

Don Camillo shook his head.

"I wouldn't be too certain about that, Comrade. In the Soviet Union there's freedom of religion."

"Freedom of religion? Ha! ha!" jeered Scamoggia.

"Don't laugh! The Soviet Union takes its freedom seriously."

"You mean there are priests there too? Does that filthy breed really defy extermination?"

"It will die out of its own accord, when poverty and ignorance are gone," put in Peppone. "Poverty and ignorance are meat and drink to those black crows."

But Don Camillo was colder and more severe than ever.

"Comrade Senator, you know better than I that in the Soviet Union poverty and ignorance have been done away with already. If there are still priests, it can only be because they have some power which there is as yet no way to overcome."

"What *have* they got?" Scamoggia shouted. "Aren't they made of flesh and blood, like ourselves?"

"No!" shouted back Peppone. "They're the dregs of the earth! They're a band of cowards, hypocrites, blackmailers, thieves and assassins! Even a poisonous snake will go out of his way to avoid a priest, for fear of being bitten.''

"You're going overboard, Comrade Senator," said Don Camillo. "Your violence must be based on something personal. Tell me, did some priest do you dirt?"

"The priest's yet to be born that can do me dirt!" protested Peppone.

"What about the priest that baptized you?"

"I was only one day old!"

"And the priest that married you?" Don Camillo insisted.

"Don't argue with him, Chief," laughed Scamoggia. "This comrade is the dialectical, hair-splitting type; he'll always have the last word."

And he added, turning to Don Camillo:

"Comrade, you're a man after my own heart! You know what you're talking about and you hate the priests just as much as I do."

He poured wine into the paper cups and proposed a toast:

"To the Soviet Union!"

"Down with capitalists!" said Comrade Rondella.

"Death to priests!" roared Peppone, looking Don Camillo straight in the eye.

As Don Camillo raised his cup he gave Peppone an eloquent kick in the shins.

It was midnight when the train reached the frontier. The moon was full, bathing in its light the villages perched among the mountains. Every now and then the travellers caught a glimpse of the plains below, with rivers running like ribbons across them and cities that were clusters of sparkling lights. Don Camillo stood at one of the corridor windows, puffing at his cigar butt and enjoying the sight. Peppone came to stand beside him, and after gazing at length out of the window heaved a deep sigh.

"You can say what you like, but when a man is about to leave his country he suddenly appreciates it."

"Comrade, you're indulging in outworn rhetoric and nationalism. Don't forget that our country is the world."

"Well then, why do so many poor fools want to go to the moon?" Peppone asked without thinking.

"Comrade, something distracted my attention, and I didn't hear your question."

"It's just as well you didn't," mumbled Peppone.

OPERATION RONDELLA

THE TRI-MOTOR PLANE on which the little group embarked at an airport in East Germany was so noisy that no one could make his voice heard above the din. Comrade Don Camillo was forced to hold his tongue and Peppone enjoyed relative peace of mind. Nevertheless he remained alert, for Don Camillo was a dangerous character even when he was silent. For the moment he was confining his anti-Communist activities to reading the supposed excerpts from the works of Lenin, and Peppone had no cause for worry until the priest closed the book and smote his forehead with one hand, as if he had just had a bright idea. But he quickly neutralized the effect of this alarming gesture by stroking his hair and then dusting off the lapels of his jacket.

"Amen," muttered Peppone with a deep sigh, which cleared his sputtering carburettor. The plane was gradually losing altitude and soon put down its wheels on Soviet soil.

"Lord, my little church seems very far away!" Don Camillo thought as he went down the waiting steps.

"But Heaven is very near," the Lord reassured him.

Don Camillo pulled himself together and resumed the role of Comrade Tarocci.

"Comrade," he said gravely to Peppone, "don't you feel an urge to pick up a clod of this sacred earth and kiss it?"

"Yes, and after that to ram it down your throat," Peppone muttered between clenched teeth.

Notice had been received of the visitors' arrival, and a girl stepped forward to meet them, followed by a man in a flapping, faded raincoat.

"Greetings, Comrades!" she said brightly. "I am Nadia Petrovna, your interpreter, and this is Yenka Oregov from the Government tourist bureau."

She spoke excellent Italian, and if it hadn't been for her fixed stare and the severity of her tailored suit, she might have been a girl from our own part of the world.

Peppone introduced himself and his companions, and after an orgy of hand-shaking the tourist-bureau official made a little speech welcoming them in the name of their Soviet brothers, co-fighters for the cause of freedom, social justice and peace. He was a stocky fellow, some forty years old, with a shaven head, a square jaw, thin lips, darting eyes and a bull neck. Standing there in the raincoat that came almost down to his ankles, he had the unmistakable air of a policeman. He spoke without moving the muscles of his face and with such wooden gestures that if his speech had not been translated to them they might have taken it for a prosecutor's harangue rather than a welcome. Comrade Nadia Petrovna affected the same official stiffness, but there was something definitely softer about her.

Comrade Nanni Scamoggia was struck dumb, although she was by no means the first pretty girl he had seen in the course of his heartbreaker's career. He was twenty-eight years old and every inch a Roman, with shiny, black, wavy hair, eyes that had a slightly perverse expression and long lashes, an ironical twist to his lips, broad shoulders, narrow hips and feet as small as a ballet dancer's. He wore tight-fitting trousers, a red shirt and a black leather jacket, and a cigarette drooped out of one corner of his mouth. He was half tough, half dandy, quick to use his fists and accustomed to having his way with women.

As the little group crossed the airfield, with Peppone, Comrade Oregov and Comrade Nadia Petrovna leading the way, Scamoggia regained his power of speech.

"Comrade," he said to Don Camillo, "how's *she* for an atom bomb? Do you find her as easy on the eyes as I do?"

"I do," answered Don Camillo, mentally asking the Lord's indulgence. "They don't make girls any prettier than that one."

He spoke loudly, for the benefit of Comrade Rondella, who promptly rose to the bait.

"She's pretty enough," he admitted, "but we've got just as pretty girls at home."

"At home they know how to dress," said Don Camillo. "But put one of them into the clothes Comrade Petrovna is wearing and she'd cut a very poor figure. This girl has real classical beauty; she's not just one of those dolls you see in our cities. Especially in Milan, where they're born knowing all the answers."

"Nonsense, Comrade!" protested Rondella. "There are girls in Milan as pretty as you could hope to see."

"Cool off, Comrade," intervened Scamoggia. "We've got pretty girls, all right, but this one has something special. I can't put my finger on it, but it's there."

"It depends on the environment in which she was brought up. It's environment that shapes the man, and also the woman. This is an elementary truth, but plenty of people don't seem to understand it."

Comrade Rondella had another two cents' worth to put in, but a sudden halt interrupted him.

"Customs inspection," announced Peppone, threading his way back among them. And he added, in Don Camillo's ear: "I hope you aren't carrying anything that will get us into hot water."

"Comrade," said Don Camillo reassuringly, "I know the ways of the world."

The inspection was quickly over, because Peppone had made efficient preparations for it. Every member of the group had the same type of cheap suitcase and all the contents had identical weight. The only thing that gave any trouble was a bottle in the possession of Scamoggia. The customs inspector unscrewed the top, sniffed at the liquid inside and then handed it over to be sniffed by Comrade Petrovna.

"He wants to know why you're carrying a woman's perfume," she explained.

"It isn't a woman's perfume," Scamoggia told her. "It's eau-de-Cologne for after shaving. What sort of lotion do they have around here? Gasoline?"

She started to reply, but she could see that a fellow as tough-looking as this one wasn't to be put in his place so easily. And so she contented herself with translating only the first part of his statement. The inspector muttered something unintelligible and put the bottle back in the suitcase.

"Here they have pure alcohol," she informed Scamoggia. "He says you can keep it for your own personal use, but you're not to sell it."

After they had left the field Scamoggia stopped and reopened his suitcase.

"Wait a minute," he said. "If it's the custom here for men to use pure alcohol, then I'll follow their example. Since this is considered a woman's perfume, then a woman should have it."

He started to give her the bottle, but she drew her hand away.

"Aren't you a woman?" asked Scamoggia.

"Of course," she stammered.

"Then take it. I'm not putting it up for sale; it's a present."

She seemed perplexed, but finally she took the bottle and stowed it away in the bag swinging from her shoulder.

"Thank you, Comrade," she managed to say.

"You're welcome, good-looking!"

Comrade Petrovna tried to give him a haughty bureaucratic stare but succeeded only in blushing like a little capitalist. She ran to catch up with the rest of the party, while Scamoggia closed his suitcase, lit a cigarette and let it dangle from one corner of his mouth, with an air of obvious satisfaction.

A bus was waiting for them, and they climbed in. As Peppone was hoisting his suitcase on to a shelf above the seats Don Camillo tapped him on the shoulder.

"Chief," he said, "there must be some sort of mix-up. I seem to have your suitcase."

Peppone examined the tag and saw that it was indeed his. He took the other one down from the shelf and sure enough it was tagged with the name of Camillo Tarocci.

"Nothing serious," said Don Camillo. "Just as I said, it's a mix-up."

Peppone sat down, across from Don Camillo. After the bus had started a second thought crossed his mind.

"So when we went through the customs I was carrying your suitcase," he said.

"Accidentally, you were."

"And accidentally did your suitcase have something contraband in it?"

"Oh, nothing much. A few holy cards, a picture of the Pope and some communion wafers."

Peppone shuddered all over.

The bus was travelling through an endless expanse of flat country, where scrawny cows were grazing on the meagre autumnal grass. Comrade Petrovna announced that they were going to visit a tractor factory, after which they would be taken to a hotel for dinner and a night's rest.

The factory was on the outskirts of the city of R. It was an agglomeration of dismal grey cement buildings rising abruptly out of the plains to the north.

"This ugliness is the product of what's called an 'industrial civilization', and it's the same the world over," Don Camillo thought mournfully to himself, feeling acutely homesick for his faraway village, where every brick had been put in place by a man's hand and men and things were bound by invisible ties together.

The workers wore the indifferent, bored air common to their kind. Some parts of the factory were staffed exclusively by women, stocky little creatures who did not in the least resemble Comrade Petrovna. At a certain point Comrade Rondella could not help edging up to Don Camillo and saying:

"Comrade, these women don't look as if they'd grown up in the same favourable environment as our charming interpreter!"

Don Camillo made a shattering reply.

"Comrade, you can't look at women factory workers as if they were contestants in a beauty parade! Every self-respecting Communist knows that."

It was no time for an argument, especially as Peppone was shooting dagger looks in their direction.

The visit was prolonged beyond all measure, because a zealous young manager explained in detail even things that required no explanation, with volleys of statistics that Comrade Petrovna had to translate without omitting a single one. Finally they came to the end of the assembly line. Don Camillo seemed to be thunderstruck with admiration at the sight of a finished tractor and said, turning to Peppone:

"Comrade Senator, this tractor is just like the one which the Soviet government presented to your agricultural co-operative at home!"

Peppone would gladly have committed mayhem. The tractor in question had stubbornly refused to work, and the whole province had laughed about it. Now he was forced to smile and say what a boon it was to his peasant constituents. But when he had finished his little speech the mechanic in him won the upper hand. He took aside one of the engineers and pointed out a certain part of the fuel injection pump, which he explained did not function for such and such a reason. The engineer listened attentively and then shrugged his shoulders since he could make no better reply. Fortunately Comrade Petrovna came over and offered to interpret for him.

"He gets the point," she said to Peppone. "They're waiting for authorization to make the necessary changes."

The engineer laughed and said something more, causing the girl to knit her brow and hesitate for a moment. Finally, without looking Peppone in the face, she added:

"He says the authorization may arrive from one year to the next." She started to rejoin the group, but Scamoggia came to meet her.

"Comrade," he said, displaying a set of teeth as white as those of a Hollywood moving-picture idol, "I didn't hear those last figures about the replacement parts. Could you get the manager to repeat them?"

The manager obliged with a fresh volley of statistics, enough of them to choke an adding-machine. Scamoggia nodded approvingly and shook the manager's hand.

"Thank you," he said to Comrade Petrovna. "You don't know what pleasure you've given me."

"Are you particularly interested in agricultural machinery?" she inquired ingenuously.

"No, but I like to hear you talk."

This was a sacrilegious offence to a temple of labour and Comrade Petrovna paled and stiffened in proper bureaucratic style.

"Comrade . . ." she started to say in a harsh, metallic voice.

She had never been in the Trastevere section of Rome or looked into a pair of eyes like those of Scamoggia. They swallowed her up, and all her rigidity melted away.

R. was a typical Russian city of about a hundred and fifty thousand people, with few automobiles and little traffic of any kind on the streets. The hotel was small and ill kept and Don Camillo found himself in a thoroughly uncomfortable room. He wondered with whom he was to share it, but his doubts were soon put to an end by the arrival of Peppone.

"Look here, Father—I mean Comrade—," said Peppone, "you've got to stop pulling Rondella's leg. Let him alone, even if you don't like him."

"But I do like him," replied Don Camillo. "Where the Party's interests are at stake, I hew to the line. The fellow is sadly muddled; there are remnants of bourgeois ideology in his mind and it's up to us to clear them away."

Peppone threw his hat against the wall. "One of these days I'm going to strangle you," he hissed into the priest's ear.

The group gathered in the dingy dining-room. Comrade Oregov sat at the head of the table, with Peppone on his right and Comrade Nadia at his left. Don Camillo manoeuvred himself into a place opposite Rondella, thus causing Peppone's temperature to boil over. It boiled over again when he saw Don Camillo raise his hand to his forehead to make the sign of the cross as he sat down.

"Comrades," he exploded, "what wouldn't I give if some of those stupid reactionaries who are always talking down the Soviet Union could be with us? If only they could see it with their own eyes!"

"It wouldn't be any use, Comrade," Don Camillo said dismally. What with pretending to smooth his hair and brush the lapels of his jacket, he had successfully made his sign of the cross. "Their own eyes wouldn't convince them. They go around with blinkers."

Comrade Petrovna translated these words, and the tourist-bureau official nodded his shaven head in approval as he murmured a reply.

"Comrade Oregov says that you have hit the nail on the head," she said to Don Camillo, who acknowledged the compliment with a slight bow.

Scamoggia, who was always ready to second what Comrade Tarocci said, added an observation of his own.

"Our country is a century behind. Our stinking industrialists think they know it all, just because they produce a few miserable machines. But if they were to see a factory like the one we visited today, they'd have heart failure. And it isn't one of your biggest and best, is it, Comrade Petrovna?"

"Oh no, it's just a second-rate plant," she responded. "It's the last word in modern technology, but the production is relatively small."

Don Camillo shook his head sadly.

"We Italians ought to feel humiliated to see that a second-rate Soviet factory is so far ahead of the Fiat Company, which is our greatest producer of cars."

Comrade Peratto, from Turin, who so far had had very little to say, was wounded in his local pride.

"That may go for the tractor department, but when it comes to cars, the Fiat's not to be sneezed at. We have no right to belittle the Italian workers who made it what it is today."

"Truth above everything!" exclaimed Don Camillo. "Truth is more important than the pride of the Fiat Company. As long as national pride leads us to condone the backwardness of our social and economic system we shall never learn the lesson of efficiency which the Soviet Union can teach us. A man whose fiancée had only one leg insisted that two-legged women were inferior to her. That's exactly the attitude we have towards our half-baked accomplishments. Here in Russia industry has two strong legs to stand on."

"And what legs!" echoed Scamoggia, looking boldly at Comrade Petrovna.

"I don't see what you're driving at," Comrade Rondella said to Don Camillo.

"A Communist must face up to the truth, even when it is painful," Don Camillo explained. "We've come here to search for the truth, not to indulge in sentimentality."

The tourist-bureau official had followed the conversation carefully, asking Comrade Petrovna to translate every word. Peppone was sitting nervously on the edge of his chair, but fortunately just at this moment the food was brought to the table and the hungry group fell eagerly upon it.

The cabbage soup was not to their liking, but its taste was eclipsed by a savoury roast of mutton. Their hosts had even thought to provide them with wine, which relaxed the tension and loosened their tongues. The subject of the tractor was brought up again and Comrade Peratto, in order to wipe out the bad impression he had made by boasting of Fiat cars, called Don Camillo's attention to the ingenuity of a certain device in the Russian tractor factory's assembly line.

"Of course," said Don Camillo; "the Russian people are ingenious and inventive above all others. They have demonstrated their talent not only in the invention of the radio and the sputnik but also in the perfection of all sorts of lesser gadgets. Take the washbasins in our bedrooms, for instance. Instead of having one tap for hot water and another for cold, they join them together in a single outlet which allows you to run water of whatever temperature you choose. This may seem like a small thing, but where else are you to find it?"

Rondella happened to be a plumber and he could not let this go by.

"Comrade, don't be silly. My grandfather knew how to put two taps together. Where do you come from?"

"From the part of Italy that has more Communists than any other; in other words, from the most progressive part of the country. Besides, if I'm silly, I'm in good company. In Churchill's memoirs you can find the very same thing, and nobody can say that Churchill's a Communist."

Rondella's ideas were not muddled; they were crystal clear and he insisted upon expressing them.

"I don't give a damn about Churchill! I say that by exaggerating these things you play right into the enemy's hands. If truth comes above everything, then we must show it some respect."

Don Camillo took off his misted glasses, wiped them and put them back on his nose. Then he broke the silence with these solemn words:

"Truth? Truth is whatever coincides with the interests of the working class. Comrade, you trust your eyes rather than your reason. And your reason is weak, because there are too many capitalistic cobwebs in your brain."

"And you have a brain like a sieve," Rondella retorted angrily. "Besides that, you've gone out of your way to step on my toes ever since we met. When we get back home, I'll take care of you!"

I'm not as patient as you are," said Don Camillo, "and I'll take care of you here and now!"

It all happened in a flash. Rondella stood up and punched Don Camillo in the jaw and Don Camillo shot him a return blow which toppled him back into his seat. The tourist-bureau official conferred with the interpreter and she passed on what he had to say to Peppone. Peppone got up, took Rondella by the scruff of his neck and hustled him outside.

"Comrade," he said when Rondella had recovered some degree of composure, "the commissar noticed that you were out of sorts. Apparently this climate doesn't agree with you. An hour from now an aeroplanes leaves for Berlin, and he can arrange for your finding a place on it. From there you can go straight home."

"With pleasure!" shouted Rondella. "You can't imagine how glad I'll be to see the last of the whole bunch of you."

"Don't take it so hard. We'll see you when we return."

Rondella opened his wallet, took out his Party membership card and tore it to pieces.

"We may meet," he said, "but I'll be on the other side of the street."

Peppone had to give him a kick in the pants, but he did so with sincere regret. When he came back into the dining-room he put on a brave smile.

"It's all settled. He's most grateful for Comrade Oregov's thoughtfulness."

Then he raised his glass and proposed a toast to the victorious Soviet Union, to which Comrade Oregov responded with a toast to peace and the forthcoming liberation of the Italian working-class from capitalist tyranny.

"How about drinking to Nadia?" Scamoggia whispered in Don Camillo's ear.

"Take it easy, Comrade!" was Don Camillo's reply.

The dinner ended on a gay note. An hour later, while Comrade Rondella was flying towards Berlin, with a befuddled head and an aching behind, Peppone and Don Camillo retired to their room.

"Put out the light, Comrade," said Don Camillo. "You can put it on again as soon as we're in bed."

"Ridiculous!" exclaimed Peppone.

"Ridiculous, my eye! A priest can't be seen in his underwear by a Communist senator!"

When the light went back on Don Camillo took a notebook and wrote in it: *"Return to the fold of Comrade Walter Rondella."* Out loud he said:

"Another redskin bites the dust!"

"Only a priest could play so filthy a trick! But you're not putting over anything else on me!"

Don Camillo sighed.

"You'll have to consult the inhabitant of my pen about that."

Peppone stared at it with fascination, while Don Camillo unscrewed the top and extracted a slender object which turned out to be a crucifix.

"Lord," said Don Camillo, raising his eyes to heaven, "forgive me for putting hinges on Your arms and on those of the Cross. But there was no other way I could bring You with me."

"Amen!" roared Peppone, burying his head under the sheet.

A FORCED REST

"In illo tempore: Missus est Angelus Gabriel a Deo in civitatem Galilaeae cui nomen Nazareth, ad Virginem desponsatam viro, cui nomen erat Joseph, de domo David, et nomen Virginis Maria. Et ingressus Angelus ad eam dixit: Ave gratia plena; Dominus tecum . . . ."

The aeroplane on which he was travelling, together with the druggist, swooped so abruptly that Peppone was left gasping. He wondered confusedly what the Latin was doing way up there in the air and how that hatefully reactionary druggist had come to be with him on the trip to Russia. Before he could settle these questions in his mind the droning Latin broke in on his consciousness again.

"Quae cum audisset, turbata est in sermone eius, et cogitabat qualis esset ista salutatio. At ait Angelus ei: Ne timeas Maria, invenisti enim gratiam apud Deum . . . ."

With enormous difficulty Peppone raised an eyelid which seemed to weigh half a ton. Gradually his eye fell upon a faded tapestry hanging on the wall with Russian characters on it.

". . . et vocabis nomen eius Jesum. Hic erit magnus, et Filius Altissimi vocabitur . . . ."

Peppone opened his other eye and turned completely over. He was aghast to see that at the table which the Soviet hotel administration had allotted to this room Comrade Camillo Tarocci was celebrating Mass. Out of the red-jacketed volume of excerpts from Lenin he was reading the Gospel according to St. Luke.

Peppone leaped out of bed and ran to hold his eye to the keyhole of the door. His heart was pounding and for a moment he thought the only thing to do was to throw a sheet over Don Camillo's head. He thought better of this and began to shuffle around the room, making as much noise as possible in order to cover up the Latin sounds. He would have continued this indefinitely, had not the tinkle of a damned little bell rung in his buzzing ears. He didn't want to listen, but he was forced to acknowledge its reality, and when Don Camillo raised the tin cup which was serving as a chalice, he came to a halt and bowed his head. Steps rang out in the corridor, but Peppone did not budge.

"God help us!" he muttered to himself.

The steps stopped in front of the door; someone knocked and said in almost unrecognizable Italian:

"Time to get up, Comrade!"

Peppone grunted an answer, and the steps moved on to the next door.

"*Ite, Missa est . . . .*" said Don Camillo at last.

"It's about time," gasped Peppone. "You can keep the blessing for yourself."

"Lord, forgive him," whispered Don Camillo, bowing before the tiny crucifix which he had set up on the upturned bottom of an empty water carafe. "He's so jittery he can't think straight."

"I'd like to know if you weren't jittery when they knocked at the door," roared Peppone.

"Did somebody knock? I didn't hear."

Peppone didn't press the point because he knew that Don Camillo was telling the truth. Besides, he was dead tired and only wished he could go back to bed, even if it meant resuming his dream trip with the reactionary druggist.

"You're all ready, and the least you can do is get your trappings out of the way so that I can have room to dress," he said roughly.

"Comrade, you seem to be upset," said Don Camillo with a deadpan face. "Perhaps the climate of the Soviet Union doesn't agree with you."

"You're what upsets me!" shouted Peppone, shoving him through the door.

Then he saw something that upset him still more. The door wasn't locked, and whoever had come to call them could have simply turned the handle and walked in.

Comrade Nadia Petrovna was waiting at the breakfast table. As soon as they were all gathered together she said:

"We may as well start. Comrade Oregov won't be down for some time."

She was wearing her most forbidding bureaucratic manner and she spoke in a cold, impersonal voice, without looking anyone in the eye. Without a single unnecessary movement she lowered herself into a chair. She breakfasted on just a cup of tea, which she sipped distractedly, as if it were an unpleasant duty. It seemed as if she were enveloped in a sheath of ice, but, fortunately or unfortunately, there were cracks in the sheath and from them there issued an agreeable fragrance, which spoiled the effect of frigidity. Forgetful of the fact that she was a servant of the State, Nadia Petrovna had sprayed herself with the eau-de-Cologne given to her by Comrade Nanni Scamoggia. Comrade Scamoggia was sitting at some distance from her, but he had a keen sense of smell and was quite aware of the transformation.

Comrade Yenka Oregov arrived just as breakfast was over. He had a preoccupied air, and after a hasty good morning he took Comrade Petrovna aside. They held a long discussion, making frequent reference to a piece of officially stamped paper which Comrade Oregov had taken out of his brief case. After they had apparently established a course of procedure, Comrade Petrovna addressed herself to Peppone.

"Comrade Yenka Oregov has received from the tourist bureau a definite programme for the whole period of your stay. At nine o'clock this morning you are to visit the Red Star tractor factory."

Peppone stared at her in amazement.

"Comrade, if I'm not mistaken, that is the factory we visited yesterday afternoon."

Comrade Petrovna went back to confer with Comrade Oregov.

"The programme which we have just received states unequivocally that after resting from your trip yesterday afternoon, you are to visit the factory today. The original programme has been cancelled and therefore yesterday's visit must be considered as not having taken place."

Peppone threw out his arms in bewilderment and she conferred again with her superior.

"The programme is not subject to change, and this afternoon you are scheduled to take a sight-seeing trip around the city. Comrade Oregov does not insist that you pay another visit to the factory and so he suggests that you dedicate this morning to further rest, here in the hotel."

The travellers had not yet fully recovered from the weariness of their journey and so they jumped eagerly at this solution.

"Comrade Oregov is going to the factory to change the record of the date of your visit," said Comrade Petrovna. "I shall be at your service in the lobby."

And she went to sit on a broken-down sofa in the room through which it was necessary to pass going either in or out of the hotel. Her bearing was stiff and proud, but she left a train of fragrant eau-de-Cologne behind her.

Don Camillo went back up to his room, took off his shoes and threw himself down on his bed. But just as he was about to doze off, Peppone began to mutter to himself and pace the floor. After making his ablutions on the plane he had left his safety razor behind him.

"Take my razor and stop making such a racket," said Don Camillo.

"I never use any razor but my own," said Peppone. "And besides, I'm not used to that old-fashioned straight kind."

"Then go downstairs, change some of the liras you've taken from the taxpayers into roubles and buy yourself a new one. The General Store is nearby. Only be careful of the traffic and don't get yourself run over."

From the window there was not a car to be seen except for the bus which had brought them to the hotel, and Peppone was needled.

"The traffic will come in due time," he snorted. "We're not in a hurry. We are satisfied for the moment with the traffic with which we've peopled outer space."

"Buy me some wool socks," Don Camillo shouted after him. "In the forty years since the Revolution they must have made at least one pair."

Peppone slammed the door in reply.

Comrade Petrovna treated him with the utmost consideration and got the hotel

COMRADE DON CAMILLO   493

manager to exchange his bank note for a package of roubles. Then she wrote in Russian on a slip of paper: "*One safety razor and a dozen blades; one pair of men's wool socks, medium size.*"

The General Store was just across the street and the transaction was speedily effected. As soon as the salesgirl had read the request she handed the items to Peppone and wrote down the price. But when Peppone returned to his hotel room he did not look as happy as might have been expected. He tossed the socks to Don Camillo, who caught them in mid-air and looked at them with evident satisfaction.

"Beauties!" he exclaimed. "We couldn't make anything half so good. The idea of having one longer than another is particularly clever. No man's feet are exactly the same. How much did they cost?"

"Ten roubles," said Peppone, who was unwrapping his razor.

"And what was the exchange?"

"I don't know. All I can tell you is that for a ten-thousand-lira bill they gave me seventy roubles."

"Then they gave you a hundred and fifty liras to a rouble. It's just about the same as the Swiss franc. What did you pay for the razor?"

"Nine roubles."

Don Camillo made some mental calculations.

"The razor was one thousand three hundred liras and the socks one thousand four hundred and fifty."

Peppone was busily lathering his face and did not reply.

"How much would you pay for a razor like this at home?" Don Camillo insisted.

"Two hundred liras for an American brand," admitted Peppone. "I can't believe there's such a difference. It must be a mistake."

"I don't think so, Comrade. You probably got your old razor at a sale and you can't expect them to have such things here. Under the Communist régime both factories and retail shops belong to the State and they don't have to meet any competition. Besides your razor was American and this one is Russian; obviously there's no comparison between them. Then although the rouble's worth only forty liras on the free market, the tourist rate is a hundred and fifty. Communism hasn't been fighting its way for forty years just to give favourable exchange to visitors from abroad. Your razor would cost a Russian only three hundred and fifty liras."

Peppone had begun to shave. Suddenly he stopped, lathered his face again, changed the blade and started all over. Don Camillo stared at him quite pitilessly, but Peppone went grimly ahead. Then all of a sudden he swore and threw the razor at the wall.

"Comrade, where's your faith?" said Don Camillo gravely. Peppone, his face still covered with lather, shot him a bitter glance. Don Camillo relented; he searched his own suitcase and found an object which he handed over to Peppone.

"Is this that disgusting American razor of yours?" he asked. "I found it on the floor."

Peppone snatched it from him.

"Every day I live I'm more sure that to murder a priest is no crime!"

★

Meanwhile, as Comrade Petrovna kept watch at the front door, Comrade Scamoggia appeared before her. Before he could open his mouth she said brusquely:

"Comrade Oregov asked you to dedicate this morning to resting up in the hotel. It's not right for you to try to go out."

"I'm not trying to go out," said Scamoggia. "I want to rest up here beside you."

Comrade Petrovna gave him a puzzled stare.

"With so much room in the hotel I can't understand why you choose to rest in this particular spot."

"Must you treat your comrades so very formally?"

"No, only capitalists go in for formality."

"But I'm not a capitalist!" Scamoggia protested.

"You have certain capitalist ways."

"I may have made a mistake, Comrade. If you're willing to help me I'll conduct a self-examination."

Comrade Petrovna was softened by the earnestness of these words.

"Sit down, Comrade," she said, without altogether abandoning her severity. "Tell me about yourself."

"My name is Nanni Scamoggia. I'm twenty-eight years old and I've been a member of the Communist Party ever since I attained the age of reason. I sell and repair scooters."

"What are scooters?"

He pulled out of his pocket a photograph of himself, a muscular figure in white overalls astride a Vespa.

"There you are," he said. "Practically everybody has one."

"Very interesting. And do the other members of your family belong to the Party?"

"My father's a member of the Leghorn section. My mother's dead. My sister is a cell leader in the Dressmakers' Union."

"And your wife?"

"Comrade, do I look like a married man?"

She stared at him severely.

"At your age you need a woman."

"But why should I tie myself down to one woman, when there are so many available?"

Instinctively she drew away.

"There's another instance of bourgeois mentality. Only capitalists exploit women by treating them like playthings. In a socialist society a woman has the same station and dignity as a man."

"Comrade, I didn't express myself correctly. I was speaking of that category of women who hate work and have no political or social principles. They have no dignity and therefore no rights . . . ."

"I understand," she interrupted. "But when a comrade reaches a certain age, he ought to have a family and raise up new members of the Party."

"Comrade, I agree. But we live in a world very diffferent from yours, full of selfishness and hypocrisy. In our country priests have the upper hand and a large number of women are obedient to them. Many of them are secret agents of the clergy, and a man has to watch his step."

"Don't you know any good Communist girls?"

"Yes, quite a few," he said with a weary gesture. "Perhaps it's all my fault, but I don't really care for any one of them."

"I can't believe it, Comrade. Not a single one?"

"Oh, one or two, perhaps. But they're already married."

Comrade Petrovna thought for a moment and then said:

"It's a serious situation, Comrade, I can see. But you're not facing up to it the way you should."

"Comrade," said Scamoggia, letting down his defences, "the years go by, I know, but with our blue sky and bright sun, all the flowers growing around us, the music in the air and the good wine we have to drink, a man has the illusion of being for ever young. Our country has been blessed by God . . . ."

"*Comrade!*" she interrupted. "That's heresy! No country is either blessed or cursed by God. God doesn't exist!"

"I know. Perhaps it's on account of those miserable priests, and all the churches and shrines . . . but somehow we have the illusion that He is really there."

"You're mentally confused, Comrade!"

"Perhaps you're right. But can't you look me in the eye when you tell me so?"

'I mustn't fall into the same error as Stalin," she thought to herself. "You can't expect Russians and Italians to speak the same language. Every country has its own climate and customs. A single key won't open every lock."

But Comrade Scamoggia broke in on her reflections.

"Let's talk about you," he suggested.

"I'm a Soviet woman," she answered proudly. "A Party member and an employee of the Government tourist office. I'm twenty-six years old and I live in Moscow."

"Do you live alone?"

"No, unfortunately I don't," she answered, lowering her head. "I share my room with two other girls. But I have no reason to complain."

"I'm not complaining either!" exclaimed Scamoggia.

Comrade Petrovna raised her eyes and looked at him with surprise.

"What do you mean?"

"I thought you might live with a masculine comrade. Naturally I'm glad to hear you live with two other girls."

She continued to stare at him.

"I don't follow your reasoning," she said.

But this was a shameless lie. It was quite clear from the fact that she turned his photograph over and over in her hands and instead of giving it back to him slipped it into her bag. Even a dyed-in-the-wool Communist bureaucrat is subject to human frailty.

THE SPACE CELL

EXCEPT FOR DON CAMILLO, every member of the carefully chosen group was a Party militant of long standing—even the ill-fated Rondella, whom Don Camillo had perfidiously broken down and eliminated. Of the eight remaining stalwarts, Comrade Bacciga was perhaps the most solidly grounded in Communist doctrine, which he quoted at length on all appropriate occasions.

But Bacciga came from Genoa, and he was Genoese to the bone. Which means that he was above all a practical man, with a highly developed sense of business. Once Don Camillo had picked him for his next target this very sense of business was his undoing.

It happened on the afternoon of the first officially scheduled day, when the visitors were escorted on a sight-seeing tour of the city. The government-managed General Store, which Peppone had visited in the morning, was the first stop. Comrade Yenka Oregov instructed Comrade Nadia Petrovna to inform the visitors that by 1965 the Soviet Union would be producing eight billion yards of woollen materials a year and five hundred and fifteen million pairs of socks. Then, having assured them that everyone was free to buy what he chose, he stationed himself at the door to assure order.

Comrade Scamoggia wanted to know every detail of the store's operations and managed to draw Comrade Petrovna aside, into the housewares department. Peppone attached himself like a watchdog to Don Camillo and the others scattered in different directions.

The store was full of women, many of whom wore a worker's smock or the uniform of a mail-carrier or a trolley conductor. After making some purchases of food or household goods they went, for the most part, to admire the displays of women's dresses, shoes, underwear and beauty products.

"*Your true Communist woman,*" Don Camillo said to Peppone, "*is remarkable for her lack of vanity and her scorn for everything superfluous.* On this premise there are only two possible explanations of the sight we have before us. Either these women are not good Communists, or else, thanks to the high living standards attained by the Soviet Union, the things they are gaping at with such obvious envy are not to be considered superfluous."

"I don't see what you're driving at," muttered Peppone suspiciously.

"I mean that consumer goods are now so abundant that a woman may allow herself to feel like exchanging her trousers for a pretty dress."

And when Peppone did not rise to this bait, he continued:

"After all the roubles you got for your ten thousand liras, why don't you buy a petticoat for your wife? Of course, a State petticoat, made out of State material by State dressmakers, can't be expected to have the trimmings and fine points of a privately manufactured product."

At this point Peppone could no longer withhold a withering reply.

"It's better for a woman to wear a plain petticoat and to be free, than to shop at Christian Dior's and be a slave."

"Well spoken, Comrade," said Don Camillo, who meanwhile had caught sight of the member of the group he was looking for.

Comrade Bacciga had managed to get away from the others and to engage in conversation with the clerk in the fur department. Their conversation was in sign language and in quotations of bid and asked, which they jotted down in turn on slips of paper. After they had come to an agreement Comrade Bacciga pulled some shiny cellophane envelopes out of his pocket which she nimbly stowed under the counter. Then she wrapped up a mink stole for him to take away and the transaction was completed. Peppone had not noticed what was going on, but Don Camillo had followed every stage of the proceedings and now he was in a hurry to return to the hotel.

But they did not return until evening, for after the General Store they visited a hospital and a ball-bearing factory. Don Camillo went straight to his room, and Peppone, worried by his disappearance, hastened to rejoin him. He found Don Camillo sitting on the floor, studying some pamphlets and papers he had taken out of his suitcase.

'Couldn't you be satisfied with the excerpts from Lenin?" roared Peppone. "What other rubbish did you bring with you?"

Don Camillo did not so much as raise his head, but continued his scrutiny.

"Take this," he said, handing him a loose page, "and learn by heart the passages underlined with a blue pencil."

Peppone took one look at the page and started.

"This is something from the *Militant's Manual*!" he exclaimed.

"Well, what of it? Did you expect me to bring clippings from the *Osservatore Romano*?"

Peppone turned as violently red as the October Revolution.

"I say that this has been taken out of my own personal copy which belongs on the shelves of the local Party library!" he protested. "There's the library mark in it, right there. I'd like to know how . . ."

"Don't be excited, Comrade. You don't suppose I could have acquired my Communist culture in the library of the Archbishop's Palace, do you?"

Peppone leaned over to examine the material on the floor.

"Every bit of it's mine!" he exclaimed in horror. "You've ruined the whole collection! I'll . . ."

"Come now, Comrade!" interrupted Don Camillo. "It's disgraceful to rake up our petty personal differences here in a foreign land. Hurry up and memorize the passages underlined in blue. Those underlined in red are for me."

Peppone stared at him suspiciously.

"You're cooking up some mischief, for sure."

"Nothing of the sort. If you don't want to play the fool, go ahead and learn what I told you. You've got only half an hour."

"Very well. I'll have more to say to you later."

He sat down at the table, fixed his attention on the text and proceeded to learn his lesson. There were only two passages of a few lines each, but he was so indignant that he could have memorized a whole page.

"Now, let's hear you," said Don Camillo, putting the other papers back in the suitcase.

"Comrades!" said Peppone, "Lenin has said: '*Extremes are never advisable. But if we have to choose, we prefer absolute clarity, even if it is narrow and intolerant, to elusive and intangible haziness . . . .*' "

"Good! When I pretend that I can't remember a certain quotation from Lenin, then you are to come out with that. As for the other passage, your cue is when I ask you for the official opinion of the Party."

"For God's sake, what Party do you mean?"

"The one and only Communist Party, of course," said Don Camillo. "Which, as it says in the *Manual*, '*demands of all its members that they . . .*' "

" '*That they should, in their personal conduct . . .*' " broke in Peppone. And angrily he recited the whole piece, without omitting a single word or even a comma. Don Camillo listened with a somewhat sanctimonious air and said at the end:

"Good work, Comrade! I'm proud to be your pastor!"

Dinner was abundant and also educational, because Comrade Oregov illustrated with numerous statistics the progress which the Soviet Union would achieve in 1965. At the end, after the customary toasts to peace, the easing of international tension and the inevitable victory of Communism, Don Camillo rose from his chair.

"Comrades," he said. "Party membership obliges every one of us to follow certain principles, to exercise self-examination and constructive criticism of our fellows . . . ."

He talked very slowly, emphasizing every word and looking proudly at Comrade Oregov, to whom Comrade Petrovna conscientiously interpreted him.

"Before his Party conscience, a Communist must scrutinize his every action and question himself as to whether he could have performed it better. He must not hesitate to speak the truth, no matter how disagreeable it may be. Comrade, I can't remember the exact words of Lenin on this subject. Lenin said . . ."

He fumbled agonizingly for the words and Peppone put in:

"Don't fret, Comrade. Lenin said: '*Extremes are never advisable. But if we have to choose, we prefer absolute clarity, even if it is narrow and intolerant, to elusive and intangible haziness.*' "

Comrade Yenka Oregov nodded his head and smiled complacently.

"Thank you, Comrade," said Don Camillo, keeping his eyes on Comrade Oregov. "On this basis I feel myself authorized to speak clearly. The little unpleasantness of yesterday, concerning Comrade Rondella, recalled to me the fifth paragraph of the Party Constitution, which says: '*In case of an infraction of Party discipline every member has a right to be judged by a regular Party organization and to appeal to the assembly of his fellow members and also to higher authorities.*' Now I have this to say: If one member of the group led by Comrade Senator Bottazzi is guilty of an infraction of Party discipline, what Party organization is to judge him? Of course, the Comrade Senator represents the Party and can call his case to the attention of the federation, the regional section or the cell to which he belongs. But if the infraction is committed on Soviet soil and involves a local situation, who is to judge it? I maintain that it is to be judged here and now. Since we are not presently connected with any Party organization, such as those described in paragraph ten of the Party Constitution, I believe we can and should organize our own cell."

When Comrade Petrovna had translated these words, Comrade Oregov voiced no reaction and waited imperturbably for Don Camillo to go on.

"Comrades," he continued, "you look at me as if you were wondering what kind of cell I mean. Not a labour-union cell, since we are not engaged in labour; not a regional section, since this is not where we live. Of course it's true that we didn't come to the Soviet Union to amuse ourselves, but rather to learn and teach, and this is work of a very important kind. And even if we do not live here, the Soviet Union is our spiritual home. Let me tell you, then, what I have in mind."

Don Camillo was obviously sincere, and the others listened to him attentively.

"Comrades, we are a group of travellers who have removed themselves from an outworn, decrepit civilization and journeyed to a civilization which is in the pride of its youth. We are the crew of a flying machine which has left behind it the decaying world of capitalism and is making a voyage of exploration over the fascinating world of socialism. Our little crew is composed not of isolated individuals but of a group of men united by a single faith and a single will: to spread Communism throughout the globe. No, we are not a labour-union cell, or a regional cell, we are an interplanetary cell, a space cell. For the world from which we came is more distant from the socialist world than this planet of ours from the moon. And so I propose that our group organize itself into a cell named after the one man who embodies the Soviet people's desire for peace and progress: Nikita Khrushchev!"

Comrade Oregov was so overcome with emotion that he stood up, amid ringing applause, and pumped Don Camillo's hand for at least ten minutes. Don Camillo conferred with him, through the interpreter, and then said:

"In the name of the Italian Communist Party and in agreement with the representative of the Communist Party of Russia, I announce the constitution of the 'Nikita Khrushchev Cell!' "

The nine cell members held an immediate meeting, a very simple matter since they were all seated around the table, and pursuant to paragraph twenty-eight of the Constitution they voted for officers to represent them. Comrade Camillo Tarocci was elected leader; Comrade Nanni Scamoggia secretary and Comrade Vittorio Peratto treasurer. Peppone did not vote and it was not until he was raising his glass in a toast to the officers that he realized that the leader was to be Don Camillo. It was all he could do to choke down his glass of wine.

"Comrades," Don Camillo announced gravely, "I want first of all to thank you for this expression of confidence and to promise that I shall do everything I can to deserve it. I propose we start functioning without delay. Is there a suggestion of any business to be brought before the meeting?"

When no one spoke up, he jumped into the breach himself, to the accompaniment of an anguished glance from Peppone.

"Then, Comrades, I have something to suggest. No real Communist is afraid of the truth. The Party teaches us to be intolerant of failings, dissatisfied with anything that falls short of perfection. A Party member who is incapable of criticism, who does not demand a maximum of effort both of himself and his comrades cannot hope to be a leader or to win outsiders to the cause. Among the obligations listed in paragraph nine of the Constitution is that of 'leading a private life of exemplary integrity'. Comrade Bacciga, do you admit that this afternoon, in the course of our visit to the General Store, you bought a mink stole?"

"I do," replied Comrade Bacciga, turning deathly pale. "Comrade Oregov authorized us to buy anything we wanted."

"Correct. Do you further admit that you paid for the stole not with money but with nylon stockings which you brought from Italy? If you don't admit it, then you're a liar. And if you do, then you're admitting at the same time that you are party to one of those black-market transactions which are notoriously damaging to the Soviet economy, in short, that you're a saboteur. In either case your private life is not an example of integrity. With this I rest my accusation. Now the comrades will listen to your defence."

While Comrade Bacciga struggled to collect his thoughts Comrade Petrovna translated Don Camillo's words for the benefit of Comrade Oregov. When Comrade Bacciga did stammer a few lame excuses, they were unanimously judged to be insufficient. First, he had defrauded the Soviet customs; second, he had sabotaged the Soviet economy; third, he had betrayed the trust of his Soviet comrades. Comrade Oregov looked like a Robespierre come to judgment, and Comrade Bacciga had to conduct his self-examination before him.

"The frank admission of your fault is in your favour," Don Camillo concluded. "But that is not enough. On this matter I shall ask the opinion of Comrade Senator Bottazzi."

Striking up as authoritative a pose as the circumstances would allow him, Peppone replied:

"The Party does indeed demand that every comrade's personal conduct should be an example to others. It cannot be indifferent towards behaviour which lowers it in the public esteem. According to Marxist-Leninist philosophy, a Communist's private and Party life are one. The Party organization exercises a disciplinary function; it corrects such members as subordinate social responsibility to personal well-being and thereby tar themselves with the capitalist brush."

He delivered this harangue with such conviction that for the second time Comrade Oregov favoured him with an approving smile.

"But self-examination and condemnation do not atone for a crime," Don Camillo added. "Even priests, who are the embodiment of hypocrisy and dishonour, tell a penitent that he must make amends for his sin, and in the case of theft he must return the stolen goods to their rightful owner."

"Comrade, you don't know priests!" Peppone interjected angrily. "They're much more likely to connive with the thief than to condemn him."

"I was speaking of what they *should* do rather than of their actual practice," Don Camillo explained. "Certainly Comrade Bacciga's barter must be considered a theft."

After some further talk Comrade Scamoggia entered a resolution:

"I move that the stolen object be restored to the Soviet Union. Let Comrade Bacciga give it to Comrade Nadia Petrovna."

There was a chorus of murmurs, interrupted by Comrade Petrovna in person.

"I am grateful for your kind thought," she said, "although it is to some extent 'tarred by the capitalist brush', as the Comrade Senator was saying. But I have already told Comrade Oregov that you would like to give the stole to his wife, Comrade Sonia Oregovna."

This ingenious solution won a round of applause. Comrade Bacciga had to hand over the stolen stole to Peppone, who then presented it to Comrade Oregov, on behalf of the newly formed "Nikita Khrushchev Space Cell". As for the nylon stockings, they were entirely forgotten, that is except by Comrade Bacciga. When Don Camillo closed the meeting by sentencing Comrade Bacciga to six months of suspension from all Party activity, the latter shot him a look of fierce resentment. As they were going upstairs he caught up with his persecutor and hissed:

"Comrade, the Communist Party isn't big enough to hold the two of us!"

"Then surely the dishonest member should be the one to drop out," said Don Camillo.

Before putting out the light Don Camillo opened his famous notebook and wrote down: "*No. 2—Comrade Bacciga, morally liquidated.*"

Peppone stretched his arm out of bed, snatched the notebook and read the annotation. Then tossing it back to Don Camillo he said:

"Your next entry will be: '*No. 3—Liquidated: the undersigned, by Comrade Peppone.*' "

Don Camillo looked down his nose.

"Comrade," he replied, "you forget that you're talking to a leader. And a Communist leader isn't so easily liquidated."

"You don't know your Communist Party!" retorted Peppone.

POLITICS ON THE ROAD

"Comrade, have you the Party files of the members of our group with you?"

Peppone, who was busy shaving, wheeled angrily around.

"That's strictly my affair."

"Our affair, you mean. Now that I'm a cell leader I'm entitled to know my men."

"You're entitled to go straight to hell, and take your cell with you."

Don Camillo raised his eyes to heaven.

"Lord, did You hear him? Of all the Communist cells in the world this is the only one to have an accredited chaplain, and he says it can go to hell!"

Everything has its limits, and when a safety razor is used like a hoe it can be a very dangerous weapon. Peppone was hacking away at his chin, and his chin began to bleed. But how can a Communist senator have any peace of mind when he has brought with him to Russia a priest disguised as a Party militant of long standing and this diabolical Vatican emissary has set himself up as the leader of a cell? While Peppone was swabbing his nicked chin Don Camillo managed to replace in his room-mate's suitcase the files which he had deftly taken out of it for study.

"Comrade, if those files are so very private," he said, "let's forget them. But don't be surprised if I make some embarrassing errors."

Just then Scamoggia came to tell them that the bus was waiting in front of the hotel.

It was a grey autumn morning. Women in men's overalls were washing and sweeping the streets, running the trolley cars, tarring a paved square and doing construction work on a new building. In front of a *Gastronom* a long line of women, in simple but more feminine clothes, was patiently waiting. Don Camillo leaned towards Peppone and whispered in his ear:

"These women not only have men's rights; they have women's rights as well!"

Peppone did not even look up. He and Don Camillo were sitting on the back seats of the bus. Comrade Oregov and Comrade Petrovna sat in front, directly behind the driver, and the eight other comrades occupied the seats between. Whenever Comrade Petrovna stood up to translate some remark of Comrade Oregov she faced the entire group. This seating arrangement also allowed Don Camillo to talk in a low voice either to Peppone, who was sitting just across the aisle, or to Comrades Tavan and Scamoggia, who were sitting in the two seats directly ahead. Now that Don Camillo had liquidated Comrade Rondella of Milan and shaken the faith of Comrade Bacciga of Genoa, he was gunning for Comrade Tavan.

"Tavan, Antonio, forty-two years old, a native of Pranovo in the province of Veneto. Party member since 1943. Tenant farmer. Active, loyal, trustworthy. To be used only in peasant circles, on account of his limited acquaintance with social and economic problems. Socialist father. His family has worked the same land for 120 years. A skilful and hard-working farmer."

This was the desciption which Don Camillo had pilfered from Peppone's files, and now the peasant Tavan was a marked man.

They had left the city behind them and were travelling across the desolate countryside.

"We are now going through the 'Red Flag' *sovkos,*" Comrade Petrovna was explaining, "one of the first of its kind to be established after the Revolution. It has a total area of 30,000 acres, of which 10,000 are under cultivation, and is equipped with fifty-four tractors, fifteen reaping machines and fifteen trucks. There are three hundred and eighty agricultural workers. At the present time there are six thousand *sovkos* in the Soviet Union, with a total of four million head of cattle, six million hogs and twelve million sheep . . . ."

Rising up out of the wide, flat land they suddenly saw signs of human habitation, small houses clustered around large buildings with corrugated iron roofs, silos, barns and warehouses. As the bus bumped over a narrow dirt road, they noticed dozens of huge tractors abandoned hither and yon over the ploughed fields and covered with rust and mud. In the inhabited area other tractors, trucks and agricultural instruments stood about on the ground, exposed to the weather, in front of the farm buildings.

"Four million head of cattle!" exclaimed Don Camillo with a deep sigh.

"That's quite a number!" agreed Peppone.

"When you add those to the twenty-seven million of the *kolkhos*, they come to thirty-one million."

'Colossal!"

"By the end of 1960 there are supposed to be forty million," Don Camillo went on. "But for the time being there are still two million two hundred thousand head less than there were in 1928, before collectivization."

Peppone could not see what Don Camillo was after.

"Comrade," Don Camillo explained, "the Soviet Union is the only country in the world where everything is out in the open, where there is a public statement of whether or not things are going well. These are official statistics and from them we must conclude that whereas there has been enormous progress in science and industry, agriculture is still lagging. Volunteers have had to be sent from Moscow, Kiev and other cities to break ground in Siberia."

He threw out his arms in mock sympathy, then aiming his words at the ears of the peasant Tavan he added, ostensibly to Peppone:

"Comrade, you've seen the condition of those tractors and you can judge for yourself the validity of my conclusions. I tell you that the trouble is this: peasants are peasants the world over. Just look at the way things are at home. Who are our most backward people? Peasants! Yes, I know that the day labourers are struggling to improve their situation, but they are workers. Just try to change the ways of a peasant or a tenant farmer! See if you can make him class-conscious or involve him in the proletarian movement!"

Comrade Tavan had pricked up his ears and was not losing a single word of the conversation going on behind him.

"And now consider the state of things here in Russia," continued Don Camillo. "What people are holding the country back? The hard-headed *kolkhos* holders, who don't give a hang for the collectivized land and insist upon cultivating the few acres which the government has generously given them for their own private use. There are eighty thousand *kolkhos* and six thousand *sovkos*, but the *kolkhos* peasants have seventeen million head of privately owned cattle, as compared to fourteen million collectively owned between *kolkhos* and *sovkos* together. Those peasants don't deserve to own any land at all. And, mark my words, it will be taken away from them."

Comrade Tavan's ears had turned bright red.

"Look again at own country," said Don Camillo. "Who promoted the black market during the war? The peasants! And who promotes it here? The peasants of the *kolkhos*! With us, where is it that the priests still have most power? Among the peasants! And in the Soviet Union how do the surviving priests continue to retard the general progress? Thanks to the roubles they collect from the *kolkhos*!"

Comrade Tavan's ears were no redder than the cheeks of Peppone.

"Comrade," said Don Camillo, by way of winding up his peroration, "here we have a country that has beaten world records in every domain and won first place in the race to the moon. But among the *kolkhos* you still find selfish obstruction to progress. Beware of peasants! They're an ugly lot, I tell you!"

"Well spoken, Comrade!" said Scamoggia, from his seat in front of Peppone. "People make me laugh when they talk about giving the peasants land. Give it to them, and see what they'll do! They'll starve us! The land should be publicly owned, cultivated by the State. And peasants should be treated like workers. Just because the peasants work the land, are they to have its produce? Then why shouldn't a worker in an automobile factory be given a car? Who gave us our Fascist régime? The peasants! Wasn't a black shirt their everyday working garment in Emilia and Romagna, where you and the Comrade Senator come from . . .? Just look at the way that stupid fool out there is assassinating that tractor . . .!"

The careering tractor in the immediate vicinity of the bus seemed dangerously out of control. As a matter of fact the driver was not a peasant; he was a Government farm-bureau agent. But although his ineptitude was not forwarding the sixth Five-Year Plan it fitted in most opportunely with the purposes of Don Camillo.

"Lout!" called out Scamoggia as the tractor passed alarmingly close by.

But the lout took this imprecation for a friendly greeting and raised a clenched fist in reply. Comrade Tavan's ears had grown deadly pale. Peppone scribbled something on a scrap of paper and handed it to Don Camillo. For the benefit of their companions he said:

"Make a note on what we are seeing for the report we are to take back home."

But on the paper he had written:

"Keep your mouth shut, or I'll fracture your shin!"

Don Camillo nodded gravely. Meanwhile Scamoggia was distracted from his diatribe against the peasants by an explanatory harangue from Comrade Nadia Petrovna.

"We are not stopping at the 'Red Flag' *sovkos,* because it is concerned only with the cultivation of grain. The grain has already been harvested and there is nothing for us to see. We are proceeding now to the *kolkhos* at Grevinec, a co-operative enterprise covering four thousand acres of land which goes in for truck gardening and for raising cattle and hogs as well. It is completely autonomous and receives no Government aid, although the Government farm-bureau supplied its mechanical equipment. . . . Just now, Comrades, we have crossed the *kolkhos* boundary line . . . ."

This last bit of information was quite superfluous, because, although the terrain was the same as before, the general picture was entirely different. Here everything was the way it should be; the fields were tidily ploughed and the grazing livestock well fed. The village houses were the usual wooden shacks, but each one had its own neatly trimmed orchard and vegetable garden, a chicken yard, a hog run and a stall for the cow. Two solidly constructed buildings housed the administrative offices and the community school. Comrade Petrovna explained that ninety-seven per cent of the *kolkhos* were electrified, but unfortunately this one belonged to the more primitive minority.

In order to reach the heart of the village the bus had to go over a typically rutted road, and so while it was still half a mile away the "Space Cell" group requested permission to get out, stretch their legs and cover the remaining distance on foot. The mud had dried and hardened, and by taking care not to stumble into the ruts the visitors were able to walk without too much difficulty. Along the way they were overtaken by a horse and cart. In the cart sat a chubby man wearing high boots, an oilskin raincoat with a fur collar and a fur cap. Don Camillo scrutinized him attentively and hastened to catch up with Comrade Petrovna.

"Who is that fine gentleman, Comrade?" he asked her.

Comrade Petrovna laughed. She passed the question on to Comrade Oregov, who seemed to share her amusement.

"Comrade, you have eagle eyes," she said to Don Camillo. "That 'fine gentleman' is a priest."

"What? A priest?" exclaimed Comrade Scamoggia, who was of course walking at Comrade Petrovna's side. "What business has he here?"

She looked at him severely.

"Comrade, do you remember Paragraph 128 of the Constitution: '*In order to assure freedom of conscience, the Church is separate from the State and the Schools from the Church. Every citizen has a right to observe religious practices or to conduct antireligious propaganda, as he chooses.*' "

"But that fellow's not a citizen, he's a priest!" said Scamoggia indignantly.

Comrade Petrovna laughed again and when she had explained the reason for her hilarity to Comrade Oregov he once more chimed in.

"Comrade," she said, "in the Soviet Union priests have the same rights as anyone else. As long as they do not go in for obnoxious proselytizing, no one disturbs them. If someone wants a priest, he is free to pay for his services."

Scamoggia turned to Don Camillo.

"Comrade, you were right. And to think that one of my reasons for wanting to come here was to get the priests out of my hair!"

"Priests are the lowest order of creatures on earth!" roared Peppone. "When Noah got into the ark, he didn't want to take any snakes along, but God Almighty shouted to him: 'Noah, without priests how am I to survive?' "

When Comrade Oregov was informed of this witticism he laughed louder than ever and took it down in his notebook. Don Camillo laughed too, unenthusiastically, and fell back to the end of the line, where Peppone was walking.

"Comrade, that's cheating!" he protested. "I didn't tell you the story that way. Noah didn't want to take *donkeys*, and God said: 'Without Communist senators I wouldn't have any fun!' "

"My version is better," retorted Peppone. "Only I owe an apology to the snakes."

"You fraud!" hissed Don Camillo. "You're taking advantage of the fact that I'm a cell leader!"

They walked along in silence for a moment and then Peppone returned to the attack.

"I saw that fellow myself," he muttered; "all of us saw him. But you were the only one to detect the smell of a priest. The call of the blood, no doubt! But don't fool yourself. When we come to power you won't go about in a cart, or a car or even on your own two feet. Dead men don't stir."

"That's all right with me," said Don Camillo, calmly lighting the butt of his cigar. "Under a Communist régime anyone who stirs is dead, and one dead man's as good as another."

As they entered the village Scamoggia turned around and shouted back to Don Camillo:

"Comrade, you were right again when you said priests live off the ignorance of the peasants. Just look at that fellow now!"

In one of the vegetable gardens the priest was busily talking to an old couple. Don Camillo saw him plainly and so did Comrade Tavan. Once more the latter's flapping ears turned crimson. Comrade Petrovna shook her head.

"Don't get excited, Comrade," she said to Scamoggia. "He's in contact only with a few old people. That's the way it is all over. When they die off, then God will die, too. Even now He lives only in the minds of those who were brought up in an era of superstition. And when God is dead, the priests will follow. The Soviet Union has plenty of time ahead of it; we can afford to wait."

She spoke in a loud voice and even Don Camillo, at the end of the line, heard her.

"God can afford to wait too," he mumbled in the direction of the silent Peppone.

Comrade Salvatore Capece, a thirty-year-old Neapolitan, with an expressive face and flashing eyes, was standing nearby, and Don Camillo said to him provocatively:

"Comrade Petrovna has really got something, don't you agree?"

"She's got plenty," Capece eagerly responded. "I don't mind telling you that she's right up my alley."

Don Camillo smiled.

"From the way she keeps looking at you I think you've taken her fancy," he remarked.

Comrade Petrovna hadn't intentionally looked at him at all, but Capece was more than ready to swallow Don Camillo's flattery.

"Comrade, you know what's what," he agreed. "A woman can't be anything else but a woman."

And he quickened his step in order to rejoin her.

"You'll go to any lengths to stir up trouble, won't you?" said Peppone.

"Comrade, I've got to get busy while God is still alive. Tomorrow may be too late," said Don Camillo.

CHRIST'S SECRET AGENT

GREVINEC WAS PREPARED for the Italian visitors' arrival; the propaganda and publicity director was waiting for them at the entrance to the village and led them to the administrative headquarters of the local soviet, where the district Party leader and the head of the *kolkhos* gave welcoming speeches, translated by Comrade Nadia Petrovna. Peppone made a carefully rehearsed speech in reply and followed the local custom of joining in the applause.

Besides the bigwigs there were several minor dignitaries whom Comrade Petrovna introduced as the directors of the various departments: cattle and hog breeding, fruit, vegetable and grain production, machinery repairs and so on. The room in which the reception was held was barnlike in structure, furnished with a rough wooden table, rows of chairs and a portrait of Lenin on the wall. The reception committee had adorned the gilt-framed portrait with green branches, but this decoration attracted less attention from the guests than did the presence of numerous bottles of vodka on the table.

A glass of vodka, downed as rapidly as if it were red wine, is stimulating to both heart and body, and Peppone responded promptly and intensely to it. After Comrade Petrovna had explained that this particular *kolkhos* was a recognized champion in the production of pork, milk and cereals, he asked for the floor. Standing squarely in front of Comrade Oregov, he began to speak, quite extemporaneously, pausing after every sentence to give Comrade Petrovna time to translate it.

"Comrade," he said, "I come from the province of Emilia, where, exactly fifty years ago, some of the first and most successful people's co-operatives were established. In this region agriculture is highly mechanized, and the pork, dairy and cereal products are tops in quantity and quality alike. In my village my comrades and I have founded a co-operative of farm workers which was honoured, not long ago, by a magnificent gift from the Soviet Union!"

Here Peppone pulled out of his brief case a sheaf of photographs, which he handed over to Comrade Oregov. The photographs showed the triumphant arrival in the village of "Nikita", the gift tractor, and its operation on the co-operative's land. They were passed around to all those present and received unanimous approval.

"In our country the undermining of capitalism is under way," Peppone continued. "It is not yet in the final stage, but it is making progress, as Comrade Tarocci, who comes from the same region, can testify. Inevitably the privileges of the landowners and clergy will be wiped out, and a new era of liberty will begin. Soon agricultural co-operatives modelled on the *kolkhos* and the government projects modelled on the *sovkos* will replace the slave-labour conditions which form such a shameful hangover from the past. You can understand how deeply interested I am in the Russian *kolkhos*. I should like to ask Comrade Oregov and your leaders to show me every detail of the Grevinec operation."

Comrade Oregov replied that he did indeed understand the importance of the Italian comrade's request and would do everything in his power to satisfy it. He parleyed with the *kolkhos* leaders, and Comrade Petrovna transmitted the gist of their deliberations to Peppone.

"Comrade, everyone appreciates your interest in the technical and organizational aspects of our undertaking. But if I were to act as an intermediary between you and the *kolkhos* leaders for the whole time of your visit, your comrades would not be able to make the complete tour of the area which the programme provides for them. Fortunately, among the technicians here present there is one who can give you complete information in your own language."

She paused to beckon to one of the Russian group, and a thin, dark man between thirty-five and forty years old, in mechanic's garb, stepped forward.

"Here we have a man whose job is concerned with farm-machinery supplies and repairs, Stephan Bordonny, an Italian . . ."

"Stephan Bordonny, citizen of the Soviet Union," the thin man interrupted, holding out his hand to Peppone, but looking reproachfully at Comrade Petrovna. "Yes, I am a Soviet citizen, and so are my children."

Comrade Petrovna smiled to cover up her embarrassment.

"I stand corrected, Citizen," she said. "I should have specified that you are of Italian origin. While the rest of us make a general tour, you will be a private guide to Comrade Senator Bottazzi."

She went to join the group and Don Camillo started to go after her, but Peppone blocked the way.

"You are to stay with me, Comrade Tarocci," he said firmly, "and to take notes on everything we see."

"At your orders, Comrade," said Don Camillo wryly.

"Are you a Party member, Comrade?" Peppone asked their guide.

"No, I haven't yet been accorded the honour," the other replied with an impersonal and detached air.

Citizen Bordonny gave definite answers, which Don Camillo transcribed in his notebook, to every question asked by Peppone, but it was plain that he did so in the least possible number of words. He knew every detail of the *kolkhos*' operation and cited exact dates and figures, but without any comment of his own. He courteously refused the cigar and the cigarette which Peppone and Don Camillo in turn offered him. Because they were smoking he finally took out of his pocket a piece of newspaper and a pinch of *makorta* and deftly rolled a cigarette. They visited the wheat silos and then the warehouse used to store fertilizers, sprays and small agricultural tools. Everything was listed and in perfect order.

In one corner of the warehouse was an odd-shaped, brand-new machine and Peppone asked what it was used for.

"It's for carding cotton," Bordonny replied.

"Cotton?" exclaimed Don Camillo. "Do you mean to tell me that in this climate you can grow cotton?"

"No," said Bordonny laconically.

"Then what are you doing with this machine?"

"It came here by mistake. We had asked for a threshing machine for our wheat."

Peppone shot Don Camillo an atomic glance, but Don Camillo had caught on to a good thing and had no intention of letting it go.

"So are you going to adapt it to threshing?" asked Don Camillo.

"No," their guide said icily. "We've put together a machine of our own."

"And how do you suppose the other fellows who ordered the carding machine are managing to handle their cotton?"

"That's not our affair."

"Mix-ups of this kind shouldn't be allowed," said Don Camillo with a curtness which equalled Bordonny's.

"The area of your country is a hundred and fifty thousand square miles, and ours is eleven million," answered the other.

At this point Peppone intervened, at the same time stepping with an utter lack of delicacy on Don Camillo's foot.

"Citizen Bordonny, are you in personal charge of this operation?" he inquired.

"No. I have only a limited share of the responsibility."

"I'd like to see some of the larger machines," said Peppone.

The warehouse for the larger machines was not much to look at. It was a big, wooden barn with a rusty corrugated-iron roof. But inside it was truly impressive. The beaten-earth floor was immaculately clean and the machines were polished and lined up as if for exhibition at a fair. Citizen Bordonny knew the date of purchase, the oil and gasoline consumption and the horsepower of every one.

At the far end of the building there was a workshop with brick walls. It contained a strict minimum of tools but it was kept in such perfect order that Peppone was very nearly moved to tears. A tractor was currently under repair and the various parts of its motor were lined up on a work-bench. Peppone picked up one of the parts for closer examination.

"Who's been working on this?" he asked.

"I have," said Citizen Bordonny indifferently.

"With this lathe?" asked Peppone, pointing in surprise to an instrument that had something vaguely lathe-like about it.

"No, with a file," the guide answered.

Hanging from a big hook on the wall there was a connecting rod, tied together with heavy string. Bordonny took a screwdriver and struck the rod, causing it to ring like a bell.

"It's out of balance," he said. "I can tell from the sound. All it takes is a practised ear."

Peppone took off his hat and wiped the perspiration from his forehead.

"What do you know about that?" he exclaimed. "I thought there was only one man in the world who used that system. And here in the middle of Mother Russia I find another!"

"Who's that?" asked Don Camillo.

"The mechanic at Torricella," said Peppone. "A perfect wizard, who specialized in tuning racing-cars. A fellow that didn't look as if he had a penny to his name, but racers used to send him their cars from all over Europe. During the second year of the war his machine shop was hit by a bomb aimed at the bridge over the Stivone. He and his wife and two children were killed on the spot."

"Only one of his sons," said Bordonny. "The other was lucky enough to be in the army." There was a new tone in his voice as he added: "I'm happy to know someone who remembers my father."

They left the building in silence. Outside, the sky was black with an impending storm.

"I live in that house over there," said Bordonny. "We'd better take shelter there before it starts to pour. While we're waiting I can answer any further questions."

They reached the house just as the first drops of rain were beginning to fall. It was a simple dwelling, but cosy and warm, with smoke-blackened beams on the kitchen ceiling. Peppone had not yet recovered from his surprise when they sat down at the long table.

"The last time I went to your father's machine shop was in 1939," he said, as dreamily as if he were talking to himself. "Something was wrong with my little second-hand car and I couldn't get at the trouble."

"It was a connecting rod," said Bordonny. "And I was the one who fixed it. My father used me as a helper. Tell me, how did the car run?"

"It's still running . . . . So that slight boy with a lock of dark hair dangling over his forehead . . ."

"I was just nineteen," said Bordonny. "And at that time you didn't have a moustache, as I remember."

"No," said Don Camillo. "He grew that when he was thrown in jail for drunkenness and disorderly conduct. Of course his real crime was anti-Fascist agitation, and eventually it did him a good turn. After the war he won the status of political prisoner and martyr to the cause. That's how he became first mayor and then senator."

Peppone brought down his fist on the table.

"That's not the whole story!" he protested.

Bordonny was staring at Don Camillo.

"Your face isn't unfamiliar either," he said. "Do you come from the same place?"

"No, no," Peppone hastily interpolated. "He's been living around there, but he comes from another town. You couldn't possibly have known him. Tell me, how did you get here?"

Bordonny shrugged his shoulders.

"What's the use of going back over things which the Russians have generously forgotten?" he said in a voice which had once more turned cold. "If you want more explanations about the *kolkhos,* I'm ready to give them to you."

But Don Camillo did not leave it at that.

"My friend, don't let the fact that he's a Communist senator stand in your way. We don't have to consider politics. You can talk as man to man."

Bordonny looked in the eyes of first the one and then the other.

"I have nothing to hide," he asserted. "Everybody here at Grevinec knows my story. But since they don't talk about it, I'd rather not talk about it either."

Don Camillo held out his pack of Italian cigarettes.

Outside there was a raging storm, and rain beat against the windowpanes.

"For seventeen years I've been craving one of those cigarettes," said Bordonny, lighting one up. "I've never got used to *makorta* rolled in newsprint. It makes my stomach turn over."

Greedily he inhaled a few puffs and then let the smoke trickle slowly out of his mouth.

"It's a simple story," he said. "I was on the Russian front, at a truck repair centre, and one day the Russians walked in and took us over. It was at the end of 1942, and the wind and snow were murderously cold. They drove us ahead of them like a flock of sheep. Every now and then one of us fell to the ground and they left him with a bullet in his head on the muddy snow. I fell, too, but I knew enough Russian to make myself understood and when a Russian soldier gave me a kick and said 'Get up!' I was able to answer. '*Tovarisch,*' I said, 'I can't go on. Let me die in peace.' I was one of the last prisoners in the column and the others were already a hundred feet away, almost lost from sight in the snow. He aimed above my head and muttered: 'Hurry up and die, then, and don't get me into trouble.'"

Just then somebody bundled up in dripping burlap came into the kitchen. Unwinding this covering she revealed herself to be a handsome woman no more than thirty years old.

"My wife," said Stephan.

The woman smiled, murmured a few incomprehensible words and disappeared up a circular stair.

"God willed that I should live," Bordonny went on. "When I came to I found myself in a warm *isba*. The place where I had fallen was half a mile from here, between the woods and the village, and a seventeen-year-old girl who had gone to collect kindling had heard moans coming out of a pile of snow. She had strong arms and she tugged me along by my coat collar, like a sack of potatoes, without even setting down her bundle of wood."

"They're good people, these Russian peasants," said Peppone. "A fellow called Bagò, from Moinetto, was saved in the same way."

"Yes, a lot of fellows owe them their lives. But this girl wasn't Russian; she was a Pole whose family had been moved here because there was a shortage of agricultural workers. They shared what little food they had with me and kept me hidden for two days. I realized this couldn't go on for ever, and since the girl and I managed to communicate with each other in broken Russian, I told her to go and report that a lost Italian soldier had stumbled in on them only a few hours before. Reluctantly she consented to go. Soon she came back with a man armed with a pistol and two others with guns. I raised my hands and they beckoned to me to follow them. The Polish family's hut was the one farthest from the centre of the village, and I had to walk a good distance with the guns sticking into my back. Finally we came to the open space where you saw the silos. A truck loaded with bags of wheat was standing there and an unfortunate fellow was ruining the motor trying to get it started. I was so outraged that I turned to one of my captors and said: '*Tovarisch*, he's going to run down the battery and then he'll never get it going at all. The injection pump must be choked; tell him to pump out the gasoline.' My guard was amazed to hear me use a few Russian words. 'What do you know about it?' he asked suspiciously. 'That's my trade,' I told him. The battery was rapidly dying, and he pushed me over to the truck and ordered the driver to do what I had said. The face that looked out of the cab window was that of a very young boy in soldier's uniform. He didn't know what pump I was talking about, because he'd never driven a diesel before. I asked for a screwdriver, threw up the hood and cleaned out the fuel injector. 'Now it will start,' I said, and a few minutes later he drove it away.

"They shut me up in a small room of the local soviet but left me a cigarette for company. Ten minutes later they came back, and holding their guns against my back, pushed me over to a shed where there were primitive arrangements to repair tractors and agricultural machinery. They pointed out one of the tractors and told me to find out what was the matter with it. I asked for some boiling water to pour into the radiator and then tried to start it. Then I got down and said: 'It's a cylinder. The whole motor has to be taken apart and the cylinder made over. It will take quite some time.' With the miserable tools they gave me I worked like mad for forty-eight hours. Just as I was putting back the whole block an officer and two men armed with sub-machine-guns came along. They looked on while I put more boiling water in the radiator and tried the motor. God meant me to live, because it started right up and ran like a dream. I ran it around the shed and then brought it back to its original place. I wiped my hands on a rag, jumped down and stood in front of the officer with my arms above my head. They all started laughing. 'He's all yours, Comrade,' said the officer to the district Party leader. 'It's your responsibility; if he runs away, you'll pay for it.' I joined in the laughter. 'Captain,' I said, 'Russia's a big country, and I'm not likely to run any farther than that islolated *isba*, where there's a girl I've taken quite a fancy to, even if she did report me.' The officer looked me up and down. 'You're a good Italian worker,' he said. 'Why did you come to fight against the workers of the Soviet Union?' I told him that I came because I was sent. My only military activity was truck repairs and the only Russians I'd killed were two chickens I had accidentally run over. . . .''

The storm was raging more fiercely than ever. Bordonny got up and talked into an old army field telephone in one corner. Then he came back and said:

"They say you may as well stay here. The rest of your party is stuck over at Barn No. 3, which is at the other end of nowhere." And he sat down.

"Well, what happened next?" asked Don Camillo.

"I worked like a dog at repairing their machines and putting the workshop in order. By the time I was able to stop and think, the war was over. The Polish girl's father died, and we got married. As the years went by she and I were both given Soviet citizenship."

"And didn't you ever think of going home?" asked Don Camillo.

"What for? To see the mass of rubble where my father and brother were rotting away? Here they treat me as if I were one of their own, in fact better, because I'm good at my job. At home there's no one to remember me. I'm just one of the prisoners of war who disappeared in Russia. . . ."

Just then there was a loud noise and the door was thrown open. In came a stream of water and a strange wriggling monster that looked like a giant centipede. From somewhere Bordonny's wife appeared on the scene and rushed to close the door. The shiny oilskin covering of the monster fell to the floor and out popped half a dozen children, one handsomer than the next, ranging from six to twelve years of age.

"Your disappearance in Russia has been time well spent, I can see that!" exclaimed Don Camillo.

Bordonny stared at him again.

"I *do* have a feeling I've seen you before," he repeated.

"It's unlikely," said Don Camillo. "But even if you have, forget about it."

They were well-brought-up children and, although for the first few minutes they made quite a racket, a few words from their mother were enough to calm them down. They sat down on a bench near the stove and began talking in a low voice together.

"They're still small," the woman apologized in surprisingly good Italian. "They forgot that their grandmother is sick in bed upstairs."

"May we pay her a visit?" said Don Camillo.

"That would make her very happy. She seldom has a chance to see anybody."

They went up the circular stair to a low-ceilinged attic room. A shrivelled old woman was lying in a bed made up with neatly pressed white sheets. Bordonny's wife said something to her in Polish and she whispered a reply.

"She says may the Lord bless those who visit the sick," the wife explained. "She's very old and she can't help thinking in terms of the past."

At the head of the bed there was a holy picture and Don Camillo bent over to examine it.

"It's the Black Macdonna!" he exclaimed.

"Yes," murmured the wife, "the protectress of Poland. Old Poles are Catholics. On account of her age you must forgive her."

She spoke cautiously and there was a vague look of fear in her eyes.

Peppone put in a reassuring word.

"There's nothing to forgive. In Italy young people are Catholics, too. It's quite all right as long as they're on the level. Our enemies are the priests, because they mix politics with religion."

The old woman whispered something into her daughter's ear and the latter shot an enquiring glance at Bordonny.

"They're not here to do us any harm," he told her.

"Mother wants to hear how is . . . the Pope," his wife stammered.

"He's all too healthy!" answered Peppone.

Don Camillo extracted something from an inside pocket. The old woman stared at it with wide-open eyes and then reached out a bony hand. She whispered excitedly into her daughter's ear.

"She wants to know if that's really he."

"Himself and no other. Pope John XXIII."

Peppone turned pale and looked around him with a worried air.

"Comrade," said Don Camillo, taking him by the arm and impelling him towards the door, "go downstairs with Citizen Bordonny and see if it's still raining."

Peppone started to protest, but Don Camillo cut him short.

"Don't interfere with me, Comrade, if you value your skin."

And he stayed alone with the two women.

"Tell your mother she can talk freely, because I'm as much of a Catholic as she is."

The two women spoke at length together and then the younger one reported:

"She wants to thank you and give you her blessing. Now that she has that picture she feels that she can die in peace. It was very hard for her to see my father die without the last rites of the Church."

"But there are priests of a sort, who are free to visit you, aren't there?" asked Don Camillo.

She shook her head.

"They seem like priests," she explained, "but they are emissaries not of God but of the Party. What good are they to us Poles?"

The rain was still coming down in buckets. Don Camillo took off his jacket, pulled the hinged crucifix out of the false fountain pen, stuck it into the neck of a bottle and set it up on the bedside table. Then he took out the aluminium cup which served for a chalice.

A quarter of an hour later, Peppone and Bordonny, alarmed by the long silence, came upstairs and looked in the door. Before their startled eyes Don Camillo was celebrating Mass and the old woman, her hands folded and her eyes filled with tears, was following his every motion. After she had received communion it seemed as if new strength were flowing through her veins.

"*Ite, missa est* . . . ."

The old woman whispered breathlessly into her daughter's ear and the latter went to stand beside her husband.

"Father," she said excitedly, "will you marry us before God? Until now we've been married only in the sight of man."

Outside the rain was still coming down as hard as if clouds from all Russia had converged upon Grevinec. There was no wedding ring, but the old woman slipped a worn gold band off her fourth finger.

"Lord," said Don Camillo, "don't take it amiss if I skip a few words or even a few sentences. . . ."

Peppone stood there like a stone until Don Camillo pushed him down the stairs.

"Go and bring them up here, the whole lot of them!" he ordered.

The rain had begun to diminish, but Don Camillo was so wound up that he could not stop. In the twinkling of an eye he baptized all the children. And yet he did not, as he had threatened, skip a single word, much less a sentence. Only God could have given him the wind to get through it.

The whole thing lasted an hour, or perhaps it was a minute. Before he knew it Don Camillo was sitting once more at the kitchen table, with Peppone at his side and Bordonny across from him. The sun had come out and the children's eyes were shining in the dark corner. Don Camillo counted them: twelve for the children, four for their parents and two for the old woman. She was not with them downstairs, but her eyes were indelibly imprinted on his memory, for he had never seen a look such as theirs before.

Just then Comrade Nadia Petrovna appeared at the door.

"Is everything all right?" she inquired.

"Everything's perfect," said Don Camillo.

"We are most grateful to Comrade Oregov for assigning us a guide as competent as Citizen Stephan Bordonny," added Peppone, shaking their host's hand and starting towards the door. Don Camillo was the last to leave the house, and at the threshold he turned around to make the sign of the cross.

"*Pax vobiscum,*" he murmured.

And the old woman's eyes responded:

"*Amen.*"

THE RAINS CAME TO STAY

As IT WAS categorically stated on the visitors' programme, they were guests of the Grevinec *kolkhos* for lunch, and this spontaneous generosity aroused the expected enthusiasm among them. Peppone had prudently arranged for Don Camillo to sit beside him, and now Don Camillo whispered in his ear:

"Comrade, I have no use for people who find everything abroad superior to what they have at home, but I can't help saying that this bowl of healthy cabbage soup is infinitely preferable to our bourgeois spaghetti."

"Comrade," muttered Peppone, "after the trick you played this morning, you deserve a soup made of boiled nails and arsenic."

"This one is just about as good," retorted Don Camillo.

But, as usual, the vodka and roast mutton were highly satisfactory and Peppone was inspired to make a little speech, cast in a conventional mould, to which Comrade Oregov made an equally conventional reply. Luckily Don Camillo was in top form, buoyed up by two glasses of liquid fire and the heart-warming experience of the morning. From a ramp built of quotations from Marx, Lenin and Khrushchev he launched an oratorical sputnik which sent even Comrade Nadia Petrovna into a state of perceptible ecstasy as she translated it and caused the eyes of Comrade Yenka Oregov to shine with a reflected glow.

Don Camillo spoke of the *kolkhos* as if it were a living, breathing being, and his hearers got a new and agreeable feeling that they were happy and important people. After he had reached an operatic conclusion, Comrade Oregov leaped up and pumped his hand interminably, talking all the while in a rapid-fire patter.

"Comrade Oregov says that the Party needs men like you for its rural propaganda," Comrade Petrovna told him, "and he wishes that you would stay here. We have accelerated courses for learning Russian."

"Please thank Comrade Oregov on my behalf," answered Don Camillo. "After I have gone home and had time to make arrangements for my wife and children I may take him up on his offer."

"He says that you can have all the time you want," Comrade Petrovna assured him. "You can count on him to facilitate your return."

More vodka was brought to the table, and the visitors did not get away until the middle of the afternoon.

The torrential rain had transformed the road into a river of mud and the bus had some difficulty getting started. After five miles or so they came to the crossing of the road leading back towards the "Red Flag" *sovkos*. The irrigation canal running alongside had overflowed and the road was under a good fifteen inches of water. With Comrade Oregov's authorization the driver took a left turn in the direction of Tifiz and for a couple of hours the truck rolled over a narrow, winding track which was blessed with a solid bottom.

Unfortunately it began to rain again and the driver was faced with further trouble. The bus skidded from one side to the other, threatening to go off the road, and under continuous abuse the differential got out of order. The rain gave no indication of letting up and darkness was beginning to fall. Since the village of Tifiz was only two or three miles away the driver was sent ahead to bring back a tow truck or a tractor. But he came back with disappointing news. The only piece of working machinery in Tifiz was attached to the grain elevator. Since this offered no help out of the present situation and the *kolkhos* at Tifiz belonged to the distressing six per cent without telephones, the group had no choice but to walk the rest of the way. They set out, with a bitter wind blowing into their backs and mud up to their ankles.

By the time they came to the village it was completely dark and, since it was one of the unfortunate eight per cent without electric light, its aspect was anything but welcoming. The assembly room of the rural soviet was filled with sacks of fodder, but in a voice of unprecedented volume and severity Comrade Oregov gave orders that it should be cleared without delay. A group of men armed with brooms concluded the cleaning operation, leaving the visitors covered with dust at one end of the room, which had only kerosene lamps to light it. Don Camillo found himself standing next to Comrade Tavan, the tenant farmer, and he proceeded at once to undermine his morale.

"Comrade," he said audibly to Peppone, "do you remember what I said to you about the peasants this morning? At the *sovkos* which is run directly by the government, everything functioned efficiently. But here, where the *kolkhos* people manage their own affairs, there is nothing but disaster. Trucks and tractors are not running and the assembly room is used for a storehouse. Isn't it very much the same at home? At Le Pioppette, where many peasant houses have been rebuilt since the war, what do you find? Potatoes in the bathtub; kindling wood and chickens in the garage, while trucks and tractors rust outside. Believe me, Comrade, peasants haven't the stuff in them to live as free men under a socialist régime. All they know how to do is obey orders. How ridiculous to speak of 'giving the peasants land'! The land must belong to the State, every square inch of it. We must step up government-directed *sovkos* until such time as the peasants have acquired some sense of responsibility."

"That's not the half of it, Comrade," chimed in Scamoggia. "It will take centuries for sense of any kind to penetrate their noodles."

The surrounding light was dim, but Tavan's flapping ears had turned red enough to shine even in complete darkness. Don Camillo was getting ready to shoot off some more of his ammunition, but the heel of Peppone's right shoe came down on a corn on his left foot. If a gun barrel had been stuck into his belly, Don Camillo would have had no thought of surrender. But a corn irritated by a long walk in wet weather was strongly conducive to silence.

As the dust subsided, Comrade Oregov was seen standing with his legs wide apart in the middle of the room, issuing imperative orders. Trestles and boards were assembled to make a long table. Someone brought out a roll of burlap, and soon the table had a cloth upon it. Heat began to fan out of the stove, extra kerosene lamps provided more light and the table was set with plates, knives, forks, spoons and glasses. Comrade Oregov glanced at the corner where Peppone and his little band were awkwardly standing and guessed at the growing tension among them. In the twinkling of an eye he summoned three girls to pass around the vodka. After two good drinks the visitors' faith in the ultimate triumph of socialism was fully restored. That is, except in Don Camillo, whom the vodka cast into a deep depression.

Because they were prey to a genuinely Communist hunger they fell like wolves upon the bowls of steaming cabbage-and-potato soup. When he saw that their appetites were satisfied, Comrade Oregov called upon Comrade Petrovna to express his deep regret for the inconveniences of the afternoon. Don Camillo was once more in a diabolical mood and he stood up to respond to the apology.

"Actually we have enjoyed the adventure," he began, "because Comrade Oregov gave us a splendid example of how a Communist leader should behave. In my country there is a proverb which says that the master's pride lends nobility to his horse. In our era of mechanization and social progress, which has swallowed up both horse and master, it might be more apt to say that Comrade Oregov is ennobled by the rightful pride which the Communist Party takes in his achievement."

Comrade Oregov was delighted with this witticism and with the compliment which Don Camillo had paid him.

Peppone, as a senator, a Party official and leader of the mission, carried a brief case bulging with important secret papers. In the course of the dinner he imprudently put the brief case down on the floor, and Don Camillo, who was as usual sitting beside him, had an opportunity to open it and quickly examine the contents. Underneath the papers he found a bottle of brandy and a piece of excellent salami. Peppone became aware of his neighbour's discovery only when he quite unexpectedly heard Comrade Oregov thanking him for his generous gifts and insisting upon dividing them among all those present. The gifts, of course, were the bottle of brandy and the salami.

"Comrade," said Don Camillo, when he came back from making the presentation, "that was a splendid gesture. Just as splendid as the round of vodkas which you offered us with the change from your ten-thousand-lira bill."

Peppone shot him an angry look.

"He who laughs last laughs best," he retorted. "We have a long way to go before we get home."

Comrade Oregov was sitting at one end of the long table. At his right were the director and political secretary of the *kolkhos* and at his left Comrade Nadia Petrovna. Beside Comrade Petrovna was Comrade Salvatore Capece of Naples, who had wedged himself in between her and Comrade Nanni Scamoggia.

The brandy and salami showed typical bourgeois inertia and never got away from this end of the table.

"Comrade," said Capece, turning the full force of his melting eyes upon Comrade Petrovna, "if I had a guitar I could make a far prettier speech than that of Comrade Tarocci."

Comrade Petrovna said something to the director of the *kolkhos*, and he disappeared from the table. Nobody noticed, because the heat of the room, the vodka and the cigarette smoke had reduced the whole company to a state of somnolent euphoria. But when he came back, they were aroused by a loud shriek from the throat of Comrade Capece.

"It's a guitar!"

The *kolkhos* of Tifiz did not have a single working machine, but it did have a guitar, and also an accordion with a boy who knew fairly well how to play it. While Comrade Capece was tuning the guitar, the boy struck up a march on the accordion. At this moment the habitually taciturn tenant farmer, Tavan, had a sudden inspiration. He snatched the accordion from the boy's hands and sounded a chord which reduced the whole company to silence. Then he played 'The Horsefly' and 'The Mazurka of Migliavacca', and played them so well that the size of his ears became almost unnoticeable.

Comrade Salvatore Capece was ready to join in, and to the accompaniment of the accordion he burst into song. He sang '*O sole mio*', and all Naples was in his voice, from the Vomero to Possillipo, from Zi' Teresa to '*Funiculi, funicula*', from Moonlight on the Bay to the Problem of the South. If he hadn't given them an encore they would have torn him to pieces.

He sang half a dozen more songs, and Comrade Nanni Scamoggia began to foam at the mouth, because the singer never took his eyes off Comrade Nadia Petrovna and she was in a state of obvious enchantment.

Then Comrade Tavan broke into a polka. This had a magic effect. In a second, table and tableware were swept away and anyone who wanted to go on drinking had to take refuge in the adjacent *kolkhos* office, which was also the repository of the vodka. Everybody began to dance and the only one actually to take refuge from the horrendous sight was Don Camillo, who found the picture of Lenin on the office wall to keep him company.

Comrade Salvatore Capece finally tossed aside the guitar and began to dance with Comrade Nadia Petrovna. He held on to her so jealously that when Peppone had something urgent to get translated she had almost literally to tear out of his arms.

"Comrade," said Peppone when he had drawn her off into a corner, "after a day's hard work a man is entitled to some good, clean fun. And if a fellow is a spoil-sport, like Comrade Tarocci, and refuses to join in, then he deserves to be punished. Don't you agree?"

"I do," she answered promptly.

"Comrade Tarocci has many of the qualities of leadership, but in his own house his jealous, reactionary wife leads him by the nose. Even now, when he's thousands of miles away from home, he's afraid of letting himself go. He's simply got to join the dance!"

"Leave it to me!" said Comrade Petrovna.

Five minutes later a band of laughing girls burst into the office and pulled Don Camillo out into the main room and on to the dance floor. Peppone thoroughly enjoyed the scene, and while Don Camillo was being whirled about by the prettiest of the girls he signalled to Comrade Vittorio Peratto, the photographer from Turin, who whipped out his flash-camera and snapped a sensational picture. After that every one of the girls wanted to have her picture taken dancing with Don Camillo, and when the roll was finished Peppone said to Comrade Peratto:

"You're responsible to me for the negatives, and don't you forget it!"

There was a short pause while the windows were thrown open to clear the room of smoke, and fresh bottles of vodka were uncorked. But the gaiety did not subside. Comrade Li Friddi, the Sicilian, produced a mouth organ; Comrade Curullu, the Sardinian, gave an imitation of a drunk trying to fit a key in a keyhole in an attempt to sneak back into his house late at night; Comrade Gibetti, the Tuscan, sang an operatic air in a shrill falsetto voice, and Comrade Bacciga, from Genoa, held the whole company spellbound with a bag of magician's tricks.

"Organized recreational groups and television have raised the cultural level of the working class," Don Camillo said pantingly to Peppone.

"No doubt about it," Peppone replied. "And I have an idea that back home a display of picture postcards would be much better propaganda than any number of political manifestos."

"What sort of pictures?" inquired Don Camillo.

"Pictures of our beloved parish priest in false clothing, kicking up his heels at a dance."

"Don't count your chickens before they're hatched," retorted Don Camillo. "As you said yourself, we have a long way to go before we get back home!"

The dancing had resumed, and a little man about forty years old accosted Don Camillo.

"Comrade," he said in Italian, "are you the head of the group?"

"No, this stuffed clown beside me is the head. I'm only the cell leader."

"Well, I have something to tell you both. If your Neapolitan friend over there doesn't let go of that girl, the fellow from Rome is going to break his bones."

Without pausing to find out how the stranger happened to speak Italian, Peppone rushed away to forestall any possible trouble. Don Camillo made some wild gesture, and the stranger laughed and showed that he understood.

"Vodka, that's what you want, isn't it?" he inquired.

"*Da, da!*" responded Don Camillo, still unable to believe that the man spoke his language. And he pointed towards the office, which was also the vodka cellar.

Once they were in the office they were able to talk freely.

"I am a Rumanian," the stranger informed Don Camillo.

"Then how do you happen to speak Italian with a Neapolitan accent?"

"Because I come from Naples, that's why. In 1939 I was a sailor, and I met a Rumanian girl and followed her to Rumania."

"Did you catch up with her?" asked Don Camillo.

"I caught up with her, all right, but not in time."

"What do you mean? Was it too late? Had she already married another man?"

"No, it was too soon, and I had to marry her myself. Fortunately the war came along and the Russians moved into Rumania. They were recruiting agricultural workers and I volunteered to go. . . ."

While the stranger was telling his story, Peppone was waiting for a chance to get hold of Comrade Petrovna. At the end of a mazurka he took her away from Comrade Capece and whirled her into a waltz.

"Look here, Comrade," he said; "I have something to tell you. Comrade Scamoggia is an asset to the Party, but he isn't politically mature. He's subject to capitalistic errors. . . ."

"I've noticed them," said Comrade Petrovna. "But I think he'll outgrow them with time."

"I quite agree. But tonight they have taken the upper hand, and if you don't stop dancing with that guitar player, he may make trouble. I thought I'd tip you off, because I'm sure you wouldn't want the party to wind up in a fight."

They finished the waltz together and then parted company. Peppone went to the office, and Don Camillo brought him up to date on the Neapolitan's story.

"He's never been mixed up in politics," he explained. "He just wants us to help him get out of hot water."

Peppone shrugged his shoulders.

"He went looking for trouble, didn't he? Why didn't he stay in Rumania?"

"Because of my wife," the stranger explained. "I had to get away from her. And it's easier for a Neapolitan to be a Rumanian in Russia than it is in Rumania! I could be perfectly happy here, because I'm a barber and hairdresser, the only one for miles around. I go from one *kolkhos* to another, giving shaves and haircuts. But my real speciality is permanent waves. . . ."

"Permanent waves?"

"Women are women the world over, Chief, and if they have a chance to pretty themselves up they'll starve themselves to death to pay for it. As soon as one girl got a permanent, all the rest of them wanted one, too. My reputation spread like wildfire. . . ."

"I see," said Peppone. "But that doesn't explain why you're in hot water."

"Chief, can't you imagine what it is to be a young man in the middle of this enormous Russia? It's not true what they say about free love. When I came here from Rumania, I had that idea in mind. But if you start flirting with a Russian's wife or his girl, he'll beat you up just as promptly as the next one. At the first *kolkhos* I went to I was caught red-handed and kicked out in no time flat. At the second I had the same bad luck, and so on, right down the line."

"Well, why worry?" laughed Peppone. "Aren't there eighty thousand *kolkhos* to choose from?"

"Yes, but I'm only one man!" the barber retorted.

Peppone couldn't stop laughing, and Don Camillo decided to take advantage of his good humour.

"The poor fellow's joking," he put in. "The truth is he's crazy to get back to Naples. Can't we give him a hand?"

"What do you mean? We can't take him back in a suitcase, can we?"

"No. But Comrade Rondella was sent home, and you have travelling papers for a group of eleven."

"You're crazy! Under Comrade Oregov's eagle eye?"

"He can't keep tabs on us for ever."

"Don't be a fool," said Peppone. "The fellow can stay here and pursue his barber's trade and let the married women alone."

"I don't call that Communism!" said the barber.

"It's a funny story," admitted Peppone, "but I refuse to get mixed up in it." And he went out of the room.

"Don't desert me," the barber implored Don Camillo. "I'm not asking you to get yourself in trouble. Just tell me where you're going and when. I can get myself kicked from one place to another. Only God Almighty can stop a Neapolitan from going home, and Khrushchev isn't God."

Don Camillo copied out the tour schedule.

"That's all I can do for you," he said. "And forget that we ever met. I've forgotten it already."

The main room was more tumultuous than ever and Peppone was searching desperately for Comrade Petrovna. He was desperate because Comrade Capece and Comrade Scamoggia had disappeared also. Finally he caught sight of the girl and grabbed her by the arm.

"What's happened?" he asked her.

"I got there too late," she admitted. "They went out together and by the time I overtook them it was all over."

"Where is Capece?"

"In the haystack of Barn No. 7."

"And Scamoggia?"

"He's holding a cold compress to Capece's black eye."

"Nobody else knows about it?"

"Only Comrade Capece, who has the black eye for a souvenir, and Comrade Nadia Petrovna, who got slapped in the face!" She clenched her fists angrily. "He had the nerve to hit me!" she added.

This was no laughing matter. Comrade Petrovna was not an ordinary woman; she was high up in the Party and a Government employee.

"I quite understand," said Peppone gravely. "Shall I beat him up or shall I report him to Comrade Oregov?"

"There are times when personal feelings have to be sacrificed for the good of the Party," replied Comrade Petrovna. "Just let the whole thing go. Comrade

Scamoggia is still under the influence of vodka. When he comes to himself he'll see the stupidity of his behaviour."

Peppone shook his head.

"Comrade, Lenin has instructed us to tell the truth, no matter how disagreeable it may be. I happen to know that Scamoggia didn't have a single drop of either vodka or brandy. He wasn't drunk; he knew perfectly well what he was doing."

Comrade Petrovna looked more beautiful than ever and her eyes shone as if with tears. One cheek was slightly redder than the other and she covered it with her hand.

"Comrade," she said humbly, "it's not easy for me to admit, but I'm afraid I too am not politically mature."

Don Camillo suddenly appeared at Peppone's side.

"Anything wrong?" he queried.

"No, everything's in good order," said Peppone sternly.

THREE STALKS OF WHEAT

DURING THE NIGHT a furious wind out of nowhere swept over the plains and froze the soggy ground over. Don Camillo was the first to wake up, roused by the stentorian snoring of Peppone. Long icicles hung at the windows, but an agreeable warmth came out of the big stove. All around, on improvised cots, his eight companions, overcome by the vodka and uproarious gaiety of the night before, lay in a deep sleep. Don Camillo, like all the rest, had slept with his clothes on, and Peppone lay on the cot next to his own.

"If he didn't snore so shamelessly," Don Camillo thought to himself, "I'd be almost sorry to have given him so many headaches."

He looked around and silently called the roll. Yes, except for Comrade Yenka Oregov and Comrade Nadia Petrovna, they were all there, and Comrade Salvatore Capece still had a wet compress over his black eye.

"Lord," said Don Camillo, "have pity on these poor fellows and shed light upon their darkness."

He lowered his legs over the edge of the cot and started to put on his shoes. He got the left one on all right, but the right one seemed stuck to the floor. Apparently the lace was caught in a crack. He gave it a hard jerk, and Peppone suddenly stopped snoring. The reason for this coincidence was the simple fact that Peppone had tied Camillo's shoelace around his ankle.

"Comrade," Don Camillo said to him reproachfully, "I can't see why you mistrust me."

"After all the tricks you've played under my waking eyes, who knows what you might do while I'm asleep!"

They went to wash at a pump outside. The icy wind slashed their faces and the inhabitants of the thatch-roofed houses all seemed to have shut themselves up inside. But suddenly there were signs of life. A big truck arrived, and Comrade

Oregov, with a group of local men, suddenly appeared on the scene to greet it. Peppone and Don Camillo went to join them.

A boy jumped down from the truck and asked for help in unloading a motor-cycle. Then the driver got out and reported to Comrade Oregov. When he turned down his fur coat collar they saw that he was none other than Citizen Stephan Bordonny. The boy had ridden on the motor-cycle to get mechanical assistance from Grevinec, and now the visitors' bus driver, accompanied by Comrade Nadia Petrovna, came to see what was to be done next.

"Don't worry," Comrade Petrovna said to Peppone, after Comrade Oregov and Bordonny had held a brief consultation. "He has brought over the necessary parts and the bus will soon be repaired."

"Won't they have to tow the bus here?" asked Peppone.

"That's impossible," she told him. "The road is frozen over and the truck is too light for its tyres to get a good grip on the ice. They're going to carry out the repairs on the spot."

"I'm a mechanic myself," said Peppone. "If you'll give me a pair of overalls, I'll be glad to lend a hand."

Comrade Oregov was pleased with this offer, and Comrade Petrovna told Peppone that a pair of overalls would be provided.

"Make it two pairs," said Peppone. "Comrade Tarocci here is mechanically minded, and we can use his help."

Comrade Oregov approved of this plan and went off on the motor-cycle to the neighbouring village of Drevinka, whence he intended to notify his superiors by telephone of the forced delay.

"Comrade," Peppone said to Comrade Petrovna, "that leaves you in charge of the rest of the group. If any of them misbehaves, don't hesitate to discipline him. I call Comrade Scamoggia to your particular attention, because he's a troublemaker."

"I thought all night long about the way he insulted me," she replied. "He owes me an explanation."

There was a cold look in her eyes, but it was softened by the brand-new permanent wave which the Neapolitan barber had found time to give her hair.

By now the overalls had been found, and Peppone and Don Camillo drove away in the truck. Peppone confided to Don Camillo that he was alarmed by Comrade Petrovna's formidable air.

"That woman is in a dangerous frame of mind. She's quite capable of taking up lipstick and nail polish, if she can lay her hands on them."

"I don't doubt it," Don Camillo replied. "When it comes to politics, women are always extremists."

During the ride in the truck Citizen Bordonny did not open his mouth and behaved as if he could not understand what his two Italian passengers were saying. The bus driver had climbed in the back, lain down and fallen asleep, but Bordonny was not taking any chances.

Bordonny had brought all the necessary tools, and as soon as they reached the stranded bus he saw what was to be done. The rear end of the bus was easy to jack up, but in order that the jack shouldn't slip on the ice it was necessary to lay a board for it to stand on. The bus driver flatly refused to crawl underneath. His reluctance was natural enough and Peppone was surprised to hear Bordonny argue so violently with him. He tried to put in a word, but Bordonny went on shouting and finally the bus driver turned around and walked away in the direction of the *kolkhos*.

"To hell with him!" Bordonny muttered when the other had gone.

"I don't know that he's to be blamed," said Peppone, shaking his head. "He just didn't want to risk being pinned down under the bus."

"Bawling him out was the only thing I could do to get him out of the way," Bordonny explained.

Soon the truck was jacked up and work begun. While Bordonny was loosening screws and taking off nuts, he talked to his companions.

"This was the site of a fierce battle just before my capture, around Christmas of 1942. The Russians attacked in overwhelming numbers and when we retreated we left many of our dead behind. A group of some thirty artillerymen and *bersaglieri* were surrounded and taken prisoner, many of them wounded or sick. The Russians shut them up in a barn at a *kolkhos* near the one you've just visited at Tifiz, and when we retook the area a day later we found them dead. The Russians had machine-gunned them rather than let them get away. I was there when the bodies were discovered, and it was a terrible sight."

Don Camillo and Peppone went on working, although their fingers were numb with cold.

"We gathered up the dead bodies and buried them," Bordonny continued. "If you will walk for three-quarters of a mile towards the north you'll see a wagon track leading to the right. Just a hundred yards before you actually reach it, there's an irrigation ditch, with an overgrown hedge on one side. If you go a couple of hundred feet along the hedge you'll come to a big oak tree whose trunk is covered with ivy. The burial ground is right there, in the rectangle bounded by the road, the wagon track, the ditch and a line parallel to the road leading from the wagon track to the oak tree."

They worked on for another half hour without speaking.

"I can do the rest alone," said Bordonny. "In case anyone comes I'll sound the horn. If you look under the ivy you'll find something there."

Don Camillo walked resolutely away and Peppone had no choice but to follow him. The sky was dark and the wind continued to blow over the bare plain.

"If the wind lets up there'll be snow," said Don Camillo.

"I hope there's enough to snow you under," retorted Peppone.

They broke into a run and soon they came to the ditch. There was a thick coat of ice on the bottom and Don Camillo clambered down on to it to pursue the rest of the way. When they came to the great oak tree, which raised its bare branches towards the dark sky, they climbed up through an opening in the hedge. Before them lay a wide field, still covered with green stalks of wheat.

For a moment they stood still, gazing at the desolation of the scene. Then Don Camillo forced himself to take a few steps forward and with a trembling hand thrust aside the twining ivy. On the trunk of the tree there was carved a date: *Dec. 27, 1942*, and the single word *Italia*, with a cross above it.

Don Camillo let the ivy fall back, while Peppone slowly took off his cap and looked out over the field, thinking of the wooden crosses that were no longer there, of the scattered bones buried in the cold ground.

"*Requiem aeternam dona eis, Domine, et lux perpetuus luceat eis . . . .*"

Turning around he saw that at the foot of the oak tree, under the rude cross that Bordonny had carved upon it, Don Camillo was saying the Mass for the Dead.

"*Deus, cuius miseratione animae fidelium requiescunt: famulis et famulabus tuis, et omnibus hic et ubique in Christo quiescentibus, da propitius veniam peccatorum; ut a cunctis reatibus absoluti, tecum sine fine laetentur. Per eumdem Dominum . . . .*"

The tender stalks of wheat quivered under the impact of the wind.

"*My son, where are you?*"

Peppone remembered the despairing outcry of the headline over a newspaper story he had seen in the last years of the war.

"*Where are you, my son?*"

Bordonny was intent upon his work, but he kept one ear cocked for any approaching sound. When he heard someone coming from the direction of the *kolkhos*, he sounded his horn as a warning. It was not, as he had feared, the bus driver, but one of the Italians, the fellow with the big ears. He was walking very slowly and, as soon as he drew near, Bordonny halted him.

"Lend me a hand, Comrade, until the others return."

Tavan took off his coat and fell willingly to work, and meanwhile Peppone and Don Camillo hurriedly retraced their way. When they got to the bus, Peppone said to Tavan:

"Hand that tool over to me."

Comrade Tavan wiped his hands on a rag and put on his overcoat. He hung about Don Camillo, who had lit a cigar butt, and finally got up his courage to say:

"Comrade, if you're not busy, I'd like a word with you."

"The experts have taken over," Don Camillo replied. "There's no reason why we can't talk." And they started walking up the road together.

"Comrade," said Comrade Tavan with a slightly embarrassed air. "You have said a great many true things, with which I have to agree. But I can't go along with you when you condemn the whole peasant class. In the city, workers are thrown together; they are in contact with modern progress and in the centre of the political scene. Whereas peasants live in isolation and can't be expected to have any community feeling. It's hard to get new ideas into their heads; most often they don't understand them. But a few of them have caught on and are trying to improve their lot."

Comrade Tavan's dark-skinned, bony face and his flapping ears were somehow disarming.

"I know that you're a loyal and hard-working Party man," said Don Camillo. "Perhaps I spoke too hastily. In any case, I didn't mean to wound your class pride."

"You were right," the other replied. "The peasant class is just about the way you describe it, but it's in the process of change. It's the old people who are still holding it back, and in the country old people carry a lot of weight. They have all sorts of wrong ideas, but because they've worked like dogs all their life long, it's hard to contradict them. The Party has all the answers, but the old people still hold the reins. It appeals to their reason, but they listen to their hearts. Even when they are capable of thinking clearly their hearts still rule over their heads."

"Comrade, I'm from peasant stock myself and I know exactly what you mean. That's the peasant problem in a nutshell. And that's why we must step up our propaganda."

They walked on without speaking.

"Comrade," Tavan said abruptly, "my wife and children and I live with my father, who is seventy-five years old, and my mother, who is seventy-three. Our family has been settled on the same piece of land for over a century. My father and mother don't go into the village more than once a year and they've only once been to a big city. How am I to straighten out their ideas, especially after what happened to them? . . ."

Don Camillo looked questioningly at him.

"Comrade, if there's anything on your mind, come out with it. You're talking man to man, not to the Party."

Comrade Tavan shook his head.

"I had a brother five years younger than myself," he explained, "and he died in the war. My father managed to accept it, but my mother has never been reconciled. When she heard that I was making this trip she was beside herself, and I had to promise to do what she asked."

"Where was your brother killed?" asked Don Camillo.

"He went where they sent him," said Tavan, "and he was killed just here, in the battle that took place around Christmas of 1942." There was obvious relief in his voice. "My mother made me promise that I'd do everything I could to find the cross that marks his grave and put this in front of it . . . ."

And out of his pocket he pulled a wax votive candle.

"I understood, Comrade," said Don Camillo. "But how can you hope to find the place where he is buried?"

Tavan drew a faded photograph out of his wallet.

"Here it is," he replied. "The regimental chaplain gave this to my mother. There's the cross with my brother's name, and on the back are the name of the nearest village and a local map."

Don Camillo turned the photograph over and then gave it back to him.

"Don't you see, Comrade?" asked Tavan anxiously. "It's just about here, and somehow I must find it. But how can I ask these people to tell me?"

They had walked quite a way up the road and by now they were not far from the irrigation ditch and the oak tree, the very one that was marked on the map.

"Walk faster," said Don Camillo, at the same time quickening his own pace. When they came to the ditch he halted. "This is the road, here's the ditch with the hedge running along it, and there's the tree." And followed by Comrade Tavan he retraced his way along the bottom of the ditch and climbed out of it just below the oak. "There," he said, pointing at the wheat field, "this is the place where your brother lies."

He lifted up the ivy and showed him the cross and the date carved on the bark of the tree. Comrade Tavan looked out over the field, and the hand that was holding the candle trembled. Don Camillo took a few steps forward, bent down and dug a hole in the earth. Tavan understood and put the candle into the hole and lighted it. Then he stood up and stared straight ahead, holding his cap in his hand. Don Camillo took a knife from his pocket and cut out a clod of earth with three slender stalks of wheat growing in it. He put the clod in the aluminium cup which he always carried with him for use as a chalice. "I'll get hold of another cup somehow," he told himself. And he said to Tavan:

"Take this to your mother."

Then they walked back to the edge of the field.

"Make the sign of the cross, Comrade," said Don Camillo. "I'm going to do the same thing myself."

From where they stood they could see the flickering flame of the votive candle.

Then the sound of the horn caused them to hasten their steps back to the bus. Just before they got there Don Camillo stopped.

"Comrade," he said, "your mother will be happy, but the Party can't possibly approve."

"I don't give a damn about the Party," said Comrade Tavan emphatically.

And he fingered the cup containing the clod of earth and the stalks of wheat as tenderly as if they were alive.

THE CELL GOES TO CONFESSION

THERE WERE FEW passengers aboard the train for Moscow and very soon Don Camillo found himself alone in a compartment. When Peppone saw him pull out the famous book of excerpts from Lenin he went off in disgust to chat with Comrade Nadia Petrovna and Comrade Yenka Oregov, who had set up their headquarters at the front end of the car. Don Camillo put away the disguised breviary and took out his notebook.

"Thursday, 8 a.m. Tifiz *kolkhos*. Stephen Bordonny. War cemetery. Mass for the Dead. Comrade Tavan. 3 p.m. Departure by train."

Thursday? Was it only Thursday? He could hardly believe that he had been in the Soviet Union for no more than seventy-nine hours.

Once more darkness was falling, and not a single tree or house broke the monotony of the wind-swept plain. There were only endless wheat fields, which in mind's eye he could picture green and alive under the summer sun. But no amount of imagination was sufficient to warm his heart. He thought of the winter landscape of his native Bassa, with its heavy fog, drenched fields and muddy roads. There no wind was too icy to extinguish the natural warmth generated by the touch of man. A peasant trudging through that landscape did not feel cut off from the rest of the world. Invisible life-giving threads bound him to his fellows. Here there were no such bonds. A man was like a brick in a wall, a necessary but inter-changeable part of the national structure. At any moment he might be discarded and thrown on the scrap heap, and then he had no reason to go on living. Here, in short, man was desperately isolated and alone. Don Camillo shuddered. Then he was roused by the thought:

"Where the devil is that rascal Peppone?"

The door of the compartment creaked, and he saw the inquiring face of Comrade Tavan.

"Am I disturbing you?" Tavan asked.

"Come on in and sit down," replied Don Camillo.

Tavan sat down on the opposite seat. He took a roll of cardboard out of his pocket, and after a moment's hesitation showed it to his companion.

"Only a few more days and they won't have to suffer any longer," he explained, pointing to the cup containing the three stalks of wheat, which he had concealed inside. "They can get air from the open end of the tube. Do you think I ought to punch holes in the side as well?"

"No, I think they're quite all right the way they are. The important thing is not to let them get overheated."

Tavan stood the tube up against the back of the seat.

"But later on . . ." he began.

"Later on? When do you mean?"

"When I'm back home. . . ."

Don Camillo shrugged his shoulders.

"Comrade, I don't see anything difficult about transplanting three stalks of wheat."

"The difficulty's with my mother," said Tavan. "What am I going to say? 'This is some wheat that . . .'?" He paused and looked out of the window. "With eleven million square miles of land why did they have to sow wheat in that particular place?" he muttered.

Don Camillo shook his head.

"Comrade," he said, "if a country has twenty million war dead of its own, it can't make much ado over the fifty or a hundred thousand left on its soil by the enemy."

"That's not something I can tell my mother," objected Tavan.

"I'm not recommending it. Let your mother go on thinking about the wooden cross which the photograph showed over her son's grave. Tell her that you lit the candle in front of it. As for the three stalks of wheat, do whatever your heart prompts you. If you keep them alive and transplant them, then their seed will somehow keep alive the memory of your brother."

Tavan listened with a gloomy air and Don Camillo changed the subject.

"Comrade," he said, "what makes you raise such sentimental and bourgeois questions?"

"I like to discuss them," said Tavan, picking up the roll of cardboard and start-ing to go away. Before leaving he looked again out of the window.

"Eleven million square miles, and they had to pick on that one acre . . ." he repeated.

Don Camillo did not remain long alone. A few minutes later the door swung open again and Comrade Bacciga from Genoa came in. He sat down across from Don Camillo and because he was a hard-headed, direct sort of fellow he came straight to the point.

"Comrade," he said, "I've been thinking things over, and I see that you're in the right. This is no place to make deals in minds and nylons. And I'm sorry for the stupid things I said after you'd denounced me."

"I owe you an apology, too," said Don Camillo. "I should have talked to you man to man instead of bringing the matter up in front of the whole cell. But the fact is that Comrade Oregov had seen what you were at, and I wanted to clear it up before he did."

Comrade Bacciga mumbled something under his breath and then said:

"He got the stole, didn't he, even if the deal was illegal?"

"At least the story went no farther," said Don Camillo consolingly.

"Yes, but I got the short end of the deal," said Bacciga.

"You paid for your fun, that's all, Comrade," said Don Camillo.

"But what am I going to say to the person who gave me the stockings and told me to bring back the mink stole in return?" He went on grumbling under his breath and then added: "Comrade, let's be frank. Last night I saw the trick the Senator played on you and I heard him saying you have a bossy wife. Well, my wife is ten times as bad, I can tell you. She's the one that got me into it, and if I don't bring back the goods not even Comrade Togliatti himself can save me. I can't haul her up in front of the Party organization, because she's a stinking Fascist as well. Her daughters will take her side, and they're even worse than she is."

"Stinking Fascists, too?" inquired Don Camillo.

"Worse than that! They're Christian Democrats. Storm troopers, I call them!"

"I understand," said Don Camillo. "How can I help you?"

"Comrade, I work on the docks, and so I always manage to have a few American dollars in my pocket. America stinks, too, but dollars always come in handy. Do you get the point?"

"Not exactly, no."

"Comrade, for the sake of keeping peace at home I'm willing to part with my dollars. Is there anything wrong about that?"

"About your spending your dollars? Not a thing. The Soviet Union needs dollar exchange."

"I thought so," said Bacciga with relief. "And while we're about it, can you give me an idea of what they're worth?"

Don Camillo was thoroughly informed.

"The official exchange is four roubles for a dollar, but tourists are entitled to ten. Reactionary papers claim that there's a black market as well, and you can get twenty. But of course that's the usual anti-Communist propaganda."

"Of course," said Bacciga. "So once we get to Moscow I can do what I like with my money, is that it?"

"It's perfectly legitimate, Comrade."

Comrade Bacciga went away satisfied, but Don Camillo had no time to make a note of what had happened because Comrade Salvatore Capece was already at the door. The cold compress had been effective and his left eye was now circled with only a rim of pale blue.

"Comrade," he said, sitting down across from Don Camillo, "I don't know how you do it, but you gulp down that vodka as if it were brandy. But it's still vodka. There's no telling what it may do to you, and after the mischief is done, well, it's irrevocable."

Don Camillo nodded assent, and the other went on:

"The Senator told me that he'd settle with me later. Meanwhile I have a black eye and a lump as big as a nut on the back of my neck. What more of a settlement can he want? My wife's active in out local Party cell, and if there's any talk about all this foolishness she's sure to hear about it. She's hot-blooded and jealous. I needn't say any more, because it seems that you have to cope with very much the same thing."

"Don't worry, Comrade," said Don Camillo; "I'll take it up with the Senator myself."

Capece leaped to his feet with a look of obvious relief.

"Salvatore Capece, that's my name!" he exclaimed. "If you ever come to Naples, just ask for Salvatore Capece. Everyone there knows me!"

By now so much had happened that Don Camillo felt he really must jot it down. But fate would not have it that way. Before he could pull put his notebook Comrade Peratto blew in. As a Piedmontese from Turin he lost no time beating around the bush.

"Comrade," he said, "yesterday we had quite a bit of fun. That's always the way when there's drinking. But now the effects of the vodka are gone and I'm cold sober. The Senator can say what he likes, but I'm a professional photographer, not an amateur. And so here's the roll containing all the pictures I snapped last night. Do what you want with them."

Don Camillo accepted the roll.

"I'm grateful, Comrade. It's very decent of you."

"It's a matter of professional ethics," said Comrade Peratto, preparing to take his leave, "and also of masculine solidarity. My own wife is growing more jealous every day. I'll tell the Senator the film was exposed to the light."

After Peratto had gone Don Camillo lifted his eyes to heaven. "Lord," he said, "after all this I'm almost ashamed of not having a jealous wife." Then he took out his notebook and wrote down: "Wives are the opium of the people." Before he could add anything more Comrade Scamoggia appeared at the door. He threw himself down on the seat across from Don Camillo's, lit a cigarette and then let it hang from one corner of his down-turned mouth. He looked unusually serious and it was plain that there was something on his mind. Don Camillo looked at him inquiringly for a moment, and then as the other gave no signs of speaking he decided to complete his notes.

"Comrade!" Scamoggia interrupted, and Don Camillo hurriedly put the notebook away.

"Something wrong?" he asked innocently.

"Comrade, you know what happened last night," Scamoggia began.

"Have no fear about that," Don Camillo reassured him. "Capece was just here, and everything's in good order."

"Capece? What's he got to do with it?" said Scamoggia, very much surprised.

"He got the black eye, didn't he?" exclaimed Don Camillo.

"Oh, perhaps he did," said Scamoggia distractedly. "That's not what I came to talk about."

"Then I'm completely in the dark," said Don Camillo.

Scamoggia puffed the cigarette smoke slowly out of his mouth.

"Last night, in a moment of weakness, I hit somebody in the face."

"Yes, I know," said Don Camillo impatiently.

"Oh, I don't mean Comrade Capece. I mean the girl."

Don Camillo was thoroughly taken aback.

"You mean to say you hit Comrade Petrovna? How could you do a thing like that?"

Comrade Scamoggia threw out his arms as if to indicate that he himself could give no explanation.

"Comrade Petrovna is an intelligent woman," said Don Camillo. "She'll understand that it was all on account of the vodka."

"I hadn't been drinking, and she knows it," said Scamoggia. "That's the whole trouble." He threw his cigarette on the floor and stamped it out. Don Camillo had never seen him in such a state of depression.

"Don't be melodramatic, Comrade," he said. "She's a lovely girl."

"Exactly," said Scamoggia. "She's worth her weight in gold, and I can't treat her as if she were just a casual pick-up. I have no right to lead her on."

Don Camillo's country, La Bassa, was hundreds of miles from Rome and he couldn't fathom the workings of Scamoggia's city-slicker mind.

"Lead her on?" he said. "What do you mean?"

"It's no joke!" shouted the Roman heartbreaker. "When Nanni Scamoggia hits a girl in the face, it's not without some reason. Do I look to you like the kind of man that roughs up a woman just for the fun of it?"

Don Camillo shook his head.

"I see. You're afraid the girl has got the idea that you're seriously interested in her."

"Exactly."

"You don't want to get married, is that it, and you're afraid to tell her."

"That's it."

"Then it's perfectly simple. Just let things coast along, and in three days, when you go home, she'll realize that she has to get over it."

"But *I* won't get over it. That's the point."

Don Camillo saw that the situation was even more complex than he had imagined.

"In that case I can't give you any advice," he admitted.

"Yes, you can. You know how to think straight, and I'm counting on you. We had a long talk last night, after it was all over. I had to explain."

"Quite right."

"In a few months she'll be coming to Rome as interpreter to a guided tour. And then . . ." And after a moment of hesitation he added: "Comrade, can I trust you?"

"Just as if you were talking to your confessor."

"I wouldn't be caught dead in the confessional!"

"Quite right," said Don Camillo. "Nevertheless there are priests who have died rather than reveal the substance of a confession. If I were a priest that's the kind I'd be. So you can speak quite freely."

"When she comes to Rome she'd just as soon stay there, in order to be with me. Is it right for me to encourage her?"

"No," said Don Camillo peremptorily. "That would be dishonourable. A Comrade Scamoggia can't behave that way. There's a much more natural and honourable solution."

"What's that?"

"The girl's very good at her job and probably she enjoys the favour of the Party. When we get to Moscow she can doubtless obtain permission for you to stay here. The Soviet Union needs men with strong convictions and technical ability. Once you've settled yourself here the rest will be easy. You can satisfy both your heart and your conscience. Surely that's better than involving an innocent, lovesick girl in an affair in a foreign land."

Scamoggia's face lighted up.

"Comrade, my mind wasn't working and you've set it back on the right track. As you say, it's all quite simple. I'm glad I unburdened myself to you."

And after vigorously shaking Don Camillo's hand he went away.

"Lord," said Don Camillo, "the Comrade shepherd's job is to bring the lost sheep back to the Party fold."

"Not so," said the Lord; "that's the job of Comrade Devil!"

But perhaps this was not the Lord's voice; perhaps it was the voice of the wind howling over the steppes. Don Camillo had to leave the question unanswered because Peppone was standing before him.

"Why haven't you come to talk with us," said Peppone, "instead of sitting here and staring out of the window?"

"Comrade," said Don Camillo gravely. "A cell leader has a lot to do if he's to live up to his Party responsibilities."

Peppone stared at him suspiciously and then shrugged his shoulders. No matter how diabolical his enemy might be, what harm could he do shut up in a compartment of a train travelling through Mother Russia?

IN THE JAWS OF HELL

THIS WAS PEPPONE's great day! They had visited a tractor factory and a *kolkhos* and travelled by train for twenty consecutive hours through an endless expanse of fertile, cultivated land. These things had given them some idea of the Soviet

Union's agricultural resources and industrial efficiency, but they had not made an overwhelming impression. Indeed, a series of regrettable accidents had tipped the balance in favour of the West. But now, Peppone reflected, all doubts and misconceptions would be swept away; the Western point of view was doomed to annihilation. The luxurious, ultra-modern bus in which they were driving down the broad streets of Moscow was quite unlike the rickety vehicle in which they had been transported across the muddy roads of the Ukraine, and around them were not thatch-roofed hovels but towering skyscrapers. Don Camillo, the disguised representative of the Western point of view, was momentarily speechless.

"Don't let it get you down, Comrade," Peppone whispered into his ear. "Even what you can see with your own eyes is a mirage created by propaganda. Meanwhile, if you want some exercise, you can take a little walk around the Kremlin. The circumference only measures three miles."

He was repeating the data furnished by Comrade Nadia Petrovna, but there was as much pride in his voice as if he had built Moscow with his own two hands. As for Comrade Yenka Oregov, the visitors' admiring exclamations made him tremulous with joy. He was no cold and indifferent bureaucrat; in return for his salary of a thousand roubles a month he gave at least ten thousand roubles' worth of zeal and enthusiasm. He was happy in the conviction that he was a humble but essential part of the gigantic structure of the Communist State. "It takes a hundred kopeks to make a rouble and a thousand times a thousand roubles to make a million roubles. But without my kopek the million roubles would not be complete." This was the way he saw it, and his reasoning was not as absurd as it might have seemed, because the investment of a single kopek gave him the feeling that he was a millionaire. The visitors' gaping admiration filled him with pride, but when he saw that they had digested all they could of the wonders of Moscow he instructed Comrade Nadia Petrovna to inform them that the preliminary part of their tour of the city was over.

"Comrade Oregov says that you may want to stretch your legs," she announced, "and he advises you to return by foot to the hotel. It's only a few hundred yards away."

They got out of the bus in the middle of an imposing square. As if he had suddenly remembered an unimportant detail, Comrade Oregov wheeled around and led them into a small building which housed an escalator. The next thing they knew they were carried down into the bowels of the earth.

"Comrades," said Comrade Petrovna, when they got to the bottom, "this is the subway!"

The famous Moscow subway was grandiose in the Babylonian manner. Everywhere there was decoration: bronze and marble statuary, bas-reliefs, paintings and gleaming glass. It seemed almost as if the carpeting must be made of mink. Peppone and his companions were overpowered, and Comrade Oregov glowed with satisfaction. The first to speak was Comrade Scamoggia.

"Comrade," he said in a subdued voice to Comrade Petrovna, "next to you, this is the most gorgeous sight of the Soviet Union!"

She was taken by surprise but recovered herself sufficiently to answer:

"Comrade, this triumph of Soviet art and industry doesn't lend itself to jokes."

"But, Comrade, I'm not joking," Scamoggia insisted.

He spoke so earnestly that for a moment Comrade Petrovna forgot her Party dignity and gave him a capitalistic smile. Meanwhile Peppone nudged Don Camillo.

"Comrade," he said with a grin, "can you imagine what that priest with whom we have both had some dealings would say?"

The subway was beginning to be crowded with people: men and women in the usual ill-fitting clothes, with the usual gloomy expression on their faces.

"I know what he'd say," replied Don Camillo. "He'd say that it's better to eat steak out of an earthenware dish than an onion served on a golden platter."

"Materialism of the lowest degree!" said Peppone. But his imagination lingered over the steak.

These were the days of the famous thaw, and the Soviet government had chosen to lodge the visitors in the very best hotel. It was a structure as magnificent as the subway, with over a thousand rooms, elaborate reception halls and elevators in every corner. After lunch Don Camillo sat in an armchair in the lobby to watch the people go by. They were of every race and colour: black, brown, yellow and all shades of white, apparently coming from every corner of the globe and jabbering in a variety of languages. Soon the watchful Peppone came to sit down beside him.

"It's like the tower of Babel," remarked Don Camillo.

"So it seems," Peppone agreed. "But although they speak so many different tongues, they manage to understand one another. They all think the same way; that's the power of Communism. Did you notice the crowd we saw this morning standing in line to visit the tomb of Lenin? Because he brought light into darkness, men come from everywhere to pay him their respects."

Don Camillo gazed earnestly at Peppone.

"Comrade, when you were mayor you didn't know any of these things."

"Yes, I did. I knew them just as well as I do now, only I wasn't aware of it. Later I thought them over and crystallized my ideas. It's just what happened when Jesus Christ was in fashion. Only in the case of Christ it was superstition that bound men together, whereas now it's reason. The truth was always there, but it took Lenin to light a torch by which all men could see it. That's why every visitor to Moscow wants more than anything to visit his tomb."

"But isn't there somebody else in there with him?" asked Don Camillo.

"There is and there isn't," said Peppone. "Anyhow, Lenin is the one people come to see. You'll have a chance to look at him yourself."

"No, I won't," said Don Camillo, shaking his head.

"We're going there shortly, all of us," said Peppone. "I've just been talking over plans with Comrade Oregov."

"I have no debt of gratitude to discharge," said Don Camillo. "I don't follow the vagaries of fashion, and for me Christ is still the only true Light."

"But you have duties, as a cell leader."

"My duty as a priest comes first," said Don Camillo. Pulling a postcard out of his pocket, he set it down on a nearby table and began to write.

"I hope you're not up to some more of your tricks," grumbled Peppone.

"Isn't it legitimate for a fellow to have a friend whose address happens to be the Bishopric Square?"

"Except for the fact that nobody besides the Bishop has that address!"

Don Camillo held out the card for inspection.

"That's why I'm able to address it to plain Mr. So-and-so, which happens to be the bishop's name!"

Peppone glared at the card and gave it back to him.

"I'm not sticking my nose into your personal affairs."

"Nevertheless, if I were you, I'd add my signature," Don Camillo advised him.

"Are you crazy?"

"What if Christ were to come back into fashion?" insinuated Don Camillo.

Peppone took the card and scribbled his name at the bottom.

"Don't get me wrong," he said sternly. "It's only because your bishop happens to be a very lovable man."

Don Camillo got up and slipped the card into a mailbox attached to a column in the hall. When he came back he found the whole group gathered together.

"According to your wishes," said Comrade Nadia Petrovna, "we're going to visit the tomb of Lenin."

Don Camillo started to go along with the others, but at the door he stumbled and turned his ankle. If Peppone had not braced him with one arm he would have fallen flat on the floor.

"We'll send for the hotel doctor," said Comrade Petrovna. "I trust it's nothing serious, but you'd better stay here and rest."

Don Camillo seemed so very disappointed that Comrade Oregov felt the need to console him.

"You'll be able to visit the tomb another time," he said cheeringly.

And so Don Camillo hobbled back to his chair. He rubbed his ankle and of course it was immediately restored to normal. With a sigh of relief he pulled out of his pocket the famous book of excerpts from Lenin.

A half-hour went by, and Don Camillo was so completely absorbed in his thoughts that he forgot that he was Comrade Tarocci. Just at this point a voice said:

"Father!"

Don Camillo looked up and then kicked himself for his stupidity. But it was too late to cover it up. In the adjacent chair, which had been vacated by Peppone, sat a thin, dark-haired man about forty-five years old. Don Camillo recognized him at once and spontaneously called him by name.

"Comassi!" he exclaimed.

The newcomer held an open copy of *Pravda* before him and leaned over towards Don Camillo as if he were translating an article on the front page for his benefit.

"I knew you the minute I saw you," he explained, "even if you weren't wearing your cassock."

"I wanted to see Moscow," said Don Camillo, "but I had to wear suitable clothes."

"You mean you're still a priest?" the newcomer muttered.

"What else could I be?" said Don Camillo.

"So many people have switched their allegiance . . . ." said the other.

"My allegiance is of a kind that can't be switched. . . . But tell me, what are you doing here?"

"I came with a group of comrades from Prague. That's where I'm living. We go back tomorrow."

"And I suppose you'll report that I'm a Vatican spy."

"Don Camillo, you know me better than that!"

The Comassis were a good churchgoing family from Castelletto; only young Athos had fallen away. His story was the same as that of many of his contemporaries. On September 8, 1943, when Badoglio signed an armistice with the Allies, he cast off his soldier's uniform and made for home. Then when he was called up to the army of Mussolini's short-lived Fascist republic, he took to the hills. He was not seen again until April of 1945, when the Partisans came out of hiding and with them many last-minute recruits who had foresightedly grown long beards in order to appear veterans of the Partisan struggle. Young Comassi wore a red kerchief around his neck and held a position of command. He assumed charge of local operations, which consisted largely of obtaining forced contributions of money from the landowners, each one in proportion to the area of his land. Fists flew and many a landowner was lucky to escape with his life.

Seventy-five-year-old Count Mossoni, together with his seventy-year-old wife, a servant girl and a dog, lived quietly in an isolated manor house in the centre of the plain. One morning when their tenant farmer came to deliver a can of milk nobody answered the bell. He walked into the house and found it empty. Only the dog stood in one corner and could not be persuaded to leave it. The farmer called in some neighbours and they found that the dog was standing guard over the rim of an old, indoor well. At the bottom of the well lay the bodies of the count, the countess and the servant girl. Apparently thieves had broken in during the previous night, jimmied open a safe hidden behind a portrait hanging on the second-floor drawing room wall and killed all three human occupants of the house.

A dozen people had seen young Comassi leave the village by car that evening with a group of young toughs and a strange man who was apparently their leader. Other witnesses had noticed the car going up the Mossoni driveway. The three young toughs had kept watch outside while Comassi and the stranger went in. Twenty minutes later they all drove away together.

These were dangerous times and no one dared come forward and testify against them. For three years the affair was forgotten. But during the elections of 1948 posters were stuck up in the village telling the whole story of the murder and pointing out what kind of men the Reds were trying to put in power. The three young toughs were able to prove that they hadn't gone into the house and claimed they had never known the identity of the stranger. As for Comassi, he had once more disappeared. That is, until this moment, when Don Camillo discovered him at his side.   ★

"What are you doing in Prague?" he asked him.

"They say I have a good voice, and I make news broadcasts in Italian."

"That's a dirty job," said Don Camillo. "Does your family know?"

"No, they don't. But I'd like them to hear my voice and know that I'm alive."

"That wouldn't make them very happy. They're better off thinking that you're dead."

"But I want them to know," Comassi insisted. "That's my whole purpose in speaking to you. God must have meant to give me this chance."

"God! This is a fine time to remember Him! He wasn't in your thoughts when you murdered those poor old people!"

Comassi made an abrupt motion as if there were something he felt impelled to say. Then, apparently, he thought better of it.

"I understand," he murmured. "I can't expect you to believe me. But since you're a priest, you can't refuse to hear my confession."

The hotel lobby was thronged with people of every race and tongue. Black, brown and yellow faces mingled together and a discordant clamour filled the room. Don Camillo felt as if he were in the jaws of hell, and yet God was there, perhaps more vividly than anywhere else in the world. Christ's words rang in Don Camillo's ear: "Knock and it shall be opened unto you . . . ." He made the sign of the cross and Comassi followed his example, cautiously and deliberately, because there were hundreds of watchful eyes around him, beyond the paper curtain of the *Pravda*.

"O God of infinite mercy, here at Your feet is the sinner who has offended you . . . humbly seeking Your pardon . . . . Lord, do not turn me away . . . do not despise a humble and contrite heart. . . . *Cor contritum et humiliatum non despicies. . . .*"

In an almost inaudible voice Comassi repeated the prayer which Don Camillo recalled to him. Then he said what he had to say, and the words came from his heart, although he seemed to be reading them from the newspaper.

". . . we went in and threatened them with a gun. At first they wouldn't reveal the hiding place, but finally they did . . . . The leader told me to go up to the drawing-room on the second floor and take the money while he kept an eye on them. When I came back he was all alone. He took the money, saying that it would all go the Cause. . . . Then, just before the election, when the posters told the story, they helped me to get away . . . ."

"Why didn't you protest your innocence?"

"I couldn't. He was a higher-up of the Party. . . ."

"Then why don't you come forward now?"

"I can't. It would be even worse now than then. The Party would be involved in a scandal."

"You mean to say that you still respect the Party?"

"No, but I'm afraid. If I said anything they'd liquidate me."

"But what is the leader's name?"

The name was one so much in the news that Don Camillo could hardly believe it.

"Nobody must find out what I have told you, but I want my father and mother to know that I'm not a murderer. That much you can tell them. And I want them to listen to my radio broadcasts, not on account of what I say but simply in order to hear my voice. That way I can feel that I'm still alive, and not just a dead man crying in the wilderness. . . ."

He pulled a sealed envelope out of his pocket and surreptitiously transferred it to the pocket of Don Camillo.

"Here's the whole story, with my signature. You mustn't open the envelope, but you can tell that man that it is in your possession and that I want to go home. . . ."

Comassi was very pale and his voice trembled.

"*Ego te absolvo . . .*" said Don Camillo.

Comassi seemed to have recovered his peace of mind. He folded the newspaper and handed it to Don Camillo.

"You can keep it as a souvenir," he said. "You've never heard a confession in a stranger place than this . . . . Forget what I said to you about the letter; I should never have said it. There's nothing to be done, really . . . . I've passed the point of no return."

"Don't be so sure, Comrade," said Don Camillo. "God still has an outpost in Prague: He's better organized than you may think. Meanwhile I'll see to it that your father and mother listen to your broadcasts, not on account of what you say, but simply in order to hear your voice."

Comassi got up.

"God!" he said. "Who could have imagined that someone would speak to me of God in a place like this?"

"God has outposts everywhere, Comrade," said Don Camillo, "even in Moscow. God's organization is very old, but it's still working."

COMRADE NADIA'S COFFEE

"Comrade, I'm in trouble," said Scamoggia.

"Everyone has to stew in his own juice," replied Don Camillo.

"It's not my own trouble," Scamoggia explained; "it's somebody else's. Only it's been passed on to me and my duty is to pass it on to my immediate superior. Then you'll report it to the chief and he'll report it to the echelon above him. Isn't that the correct official procedure?"

Don Camillo, wearied by the Babylonian tumult of the lobby, had gone upstairs and thrown himself down on his bed.

"If it's an official matter, yes," he said, pulling himself into an upright position. "Sit down and tell me more about it."

Scamoggia shrugged his shoulders.

"I'll give you the story," he said, "and you can decide for yourself how official it is. Do you know Comrade Gibetti?"

"Of course," said Don Camillo.

Actually he knew only what he had read in Peppone's files. Gibetti was a Tuscan, forty years old, an electrical engineer, an active Partisan, well grounded in Party ideology. He had had no occasion to size the fellow up at first hand, because, like the Sicilian Li Friddi and the Sardinian Curullu, Gibetti was close-mouthed and never revealed what he was thinking.

"I like him,' said Scamoggia. "He's tough, like myself. And as a Partisan he risked his life without flinching."

"I know that," said Don Camillo.

"Did you know that during the war he fought here in Russia, somewhere near Stalino?"

"In view of his subsequent Partisan record, that's not to be counted against him."

"I agree, Comrade; it shouldn't matter, but in his case it does."

"Why so?"

"During the war he was only twenty-three years old. In spite of instructions he had an urge to fraternize with the enemy. And when the enemy happens to be a stunning seventeen-year-old girl, you can see that the fraternizing might go too far. It did, but then came the retreat, and it was all over."

Don Camillo threw out his arms.

"It's not a pretty story," he said, "but in war such things are bound to happen. In every country there are girls who got themselves into trouble with foreign soldiers."

"Yes," admitted Scamoggia, "but it's unusual to find a soldier who goes on thinking of an enemy girl for seventeen years after the war is over. And that's Gibetti's story." He puffed at his cigarette and then went on: "He told me all about it. Originally he wanted to take the girl home. He dressed her up in an army uniform and with the help of his comrades started to carry out this plan. Then his unit was encircled by the Russians and because he was afraid she might be shot he sent her away. He gave her all the tins of rations that he could get out of his friends and told her to hide out in an abandoned *isba*, where he promised to pick her up again if they escaped from the Russians' clutches. 'But if we're killed or captured,' he said, 'wait until it's all over and then go home. You can say that the Italians carried you away.'

"The battle lasted three days, and at the end the Russians had to beat a retreat for fear of being encircled in their turn. Gibetti returned to the *isba*, but she was no longer there. He went back to Italy with the thought of her still haunting his mind. After the armistice he took to the mountains as a Partisan, but he still hadn't forgotten her. At the end of the war he joined the Party, but even that was no help to him in retracing the girl. All he could do was send letters to her by any Party comrade who went to Russia. Either the letters never got mailed or else they didn't reach their destination; in any case he had no reply. Finally, seventeen years later, he found a chance to come to Russia himself, and at this particularly favourable time when the tension between the two countries is relaxed.

"On our original programme we were to visit Stalino, and the girl supposedly lives close by. But there has been a change of plans, and he doesn't know what to do. That's why he told me the story. 'You're on good terms with Comrade Nadia Petrovna,' he said. 'See if you can't do something for me. I'm willing to stay here, if necessary; I'd do anything to find that girl.'

"I told him to leave it to me and trust my discretion. Then I went to Comrade Nadia. She's a woman with a head on her shoulders and the first thing she said was that she must look into the girl's present situation. I gave her the name and address and she wrote to a friend of hers who holds down an important post in Stalino."

Scamoggia paused and took a typewritten sheet from his pocket.

"Here's the reply," he said.

Don Camillo turned the paper over in his hands.

"This doesn't mean anything to me," he said. "I don't know Russian."

"Here's Comrade Nadia's Italian translation," said Scamoggia, handing him another sheet of paper.

The letter was brief. It said that a Soviet mechanized unit had found the girl, clad in an Italian army coat, at an *isba* near the enemy lines. She claimed that the Italians had brought her there after they had withdrawn from the village of K., against her will, but that she had finally escaped them. She was taken back to K., handed over to the village authorities, accused of collaboration with the enemy and executed on the spot.

"But I can't tell this to Gibetti," Scamoggia concluded. "If you think he ought to be told, go ahead and tell him. If you don't, remember that he's dead set on staying here because he thinks he can find her. It's too much for me, and I'm washing my hands of it."

And he strode out of the room leaving Don Camillo alone. The Soviet Union has more than its share of devils and one of them began tugging at Don Camillo's cassock, the cassock which he still wore in spirit beneath his disguise. The devil whispered: "Go ahead, Don Camillo! Here's your chance to sink Gibetti!" But Don Camillo booted him away. A moment later Peppone came through the door and Don Camillo grabbed his arm.

"After all, you do outrank me," he said, shoving the papers into his hand. "I'm putting this little affair right in your lap."

Then since the papers alone were not sufficient to make his point he proceeded to furnish a full explanation. Peppone turned around to lock the door and then gave vent to his feelings.

"The élite!" he shouted. "Ten hand-picked men! And what do we see? Rondella made trouble from the start and had to be sent home. Scamoggia came with bottles of perfume in his pocket and the idea of playing Don Juan, and Capece went and set himself up as his rival. Bacciga's purpose was to deal on the black market, Tavan's to light a candle on his brother's grave. Peratto said he was going to take pictures for the Party paper and on the side he's selling others to the capitalist press—he thinks he's put it over on me but I know perfectly well what he's up to. And now Gibetti, who seemed to be beyond reproach, is contributing to the confusion! Is it possible that not a single man came to see the Soviet Union? Has every one of them got some personal motive up his sleeve?"

"You're too hard on them, Comrade," said Don Camillo consolingly. "Curullu and Li Friddi are as pure as driven snow."

"A pair of dummies, that's what they are! They don't say a word for fear of compromising themselves."

"And then you've forgotten Comrade Tarocci!"

"Tarocci?" mumbled Peppone. "Who's that?" Then he came to himself and stood with his legs wide apart, wagging his thumb in Don Camillo's face.

"You!" he shouted. "You'll send me home with a heart attack if you don't watch out!" And he threw himself on his bed in exhaustion. His usual aggressiveness had crumpled and he could hardly speak. "You're nothing but a blackmailer! You've got me into such a mess that if it became known I'd be a laughing-stock the world over. Ever since I ran into you in Rome my life has been hell. Every time you open your mouth my heart skips a beat and my stomach turns over. I have nightmares all night long and when I get up I feel as if all my bones were broken." He paused to wipe the perspiration from his brow. "If you wanted to get me down, you can be happy. I'm down and out."

Don Camillo had never seen Peppone in such a low state of mind or imagined that he could be at such a total loss as to what to do. He felt strangely sorry for him.

"God is witness that I never meant you any harm," he expostulated.

"Then why did you get me into this play-acting? There's no iron curtain any more. You've seen that there are people from every country in the world travelling around. You could have come here in plain clothes on your own. I'd have paid your fare. This way you may not have cost me money, but you've made me suffer the pains of the damned, and my pains aren't yet over. Perhaps it gives you some pleasure to travel at the expense of the Soviet Union. . . ."

Don Camillo shook his head.

"I didn't want to see the Soviet Union as a tourist. I wanted to see it through your eyes. It's one thing to see a show from the audience and another to be behind the scenes with the extras. Unless the Party has completely addled your brain you must know that I was on the level."

Peppone got up and went over to the stand where his suitcase was lying. He started to open it but stopped halfway.

"You've even taken my brandy!" he exclaimed. "What were you after when you insisted on giving it to Comrade Oregov, I'd like to know?"

"Nothing," said Don Camillo. "It was my loss as well as yours, because now I have to give you some of mine."

He produced his own bottle, and after swallowing a glassful Peppone was once more able to cope with the situation.

"Now then," said Don Camillo, once more showing him the two sheets of paper, "what do you propose to do?"

"Take care of it yourself," said Peppone. "I don't want to hear anything about it."

Don Camillo went straight to Gibetti's room. There he tackled the thorny matter without delay.

"Comrade Scamoggia has bad news, but he couldn't bear to tell it to you himself, so I'm here to tell you."

Gibetti leaped up from the bed where he was lying.

"You may as well forget about that girl," said Don Camillo. "She's married and has five children."

"It can't be true!" said Gibetti.

"Comrade, you know Russia, don't you?" said Don Camillo.

"No."

"Then how did you manage to fraternize with her so closely?"

"We understood each other without words."

"And how did you manage to write to her?"

"I knew how to write her name and the name of her village, and I got someone to teach me how to say: 'I'm still thinking of you. I'll be back. Write me a letter.' And she had my address."

Don Camillo pulled the typewritten Russian sheet out of his pocket.

"Here's the report from her native place. You can get someone to translate it for you and you'll find in it everything I've been saying."

Gibetti looked searchingly at the letter.

"Her name and the name of the village are there, all right," he admitted.

"And so is the rest of what I told you," said Don Camillo. "In case you don't believe me, you can easily enough check on it when you get home."

Gibetti folded the paper and tucked it into his pocket.

"I shan't do anything of the sort," he replied. "I trust you completely. Next time I lose my head over a woman I'll just look at this paper and find a quick cure." He smiled sadly and went on: "Comrade, you know my Party record, don't you? Well, I did what I did, and many things I shouldn't have done as well, chiefly for the purpose of getting myself to Russia and looking for the girl. How am I to behave from now on?"

"Go right on fighting for the Cause."

"But my cause was Sonia and now someone else has taken it over."

Don Camillo shrugged his shoulders.

"Think it through, Comrade, that's all I can say. I've talked to you not as a Party comrade but as a friend. In my Party capacity, I know nothing of the whole affair."

"I do, though, to my sorrow," mumbled Gibetti as he threw himself back on to the bed.

The group met over the dinner table, all except for Gibetti, who was feeling sick. Comrade Oregov was in good spirits, because the afternoon programme had gone off well. Comrade Bacciga was sitting beside Don Camillo, and managed to whisper in his ear:

"Comrade, I've made my deal. I exchanged my money and bought another mink stole."

"But how are you going to get it through the customs back home?" asked Don Camillo. "You can't very well pass off a mink stole as part of your personal linen."

"I'll sew it on to my overcoat collar. Plenty of men's overcoats are trimmed with fur. By the way, our reactionary press was, as usual, in error."

"I don't doubt it," said Don Camillo. "But what's the connection?"

"You told me that, according to the rate of exchange quoted by the reactionary papers, I'd get twenty roubles for every dollar. But I got twenty-six."

The vodka was going around and the conversation grew more and more gay.

"Comrade Tarocci," said Scamoggia, "it's a shame you couldn't come with us. A visit to the tomb of Lenin is something never to be forgotten."

"Quite right," said Comrade Curullu, who was sitting nearby. "To see the last resting-place of Stalin makes a tremendous impression."

The mention of Stalin was not exactly tactful, and Don Camillo hastened to fill in the awkward silence that followed.

"Of course," he said diplomatically. "I remember how impressed I was by the tomb of Napoleon in Paris. And Napoleon is a pigmy alongside Lenin."

But Comrade Curullu, fortified by vodka, would not stand for a change of subject.

"Stalin, that's the great man," he said gloomily.

"Well spoken, Comrade," chimed in Comrade Li Friddi. "Stalin is the outstanding hero of Soviet Russia. Stalin won the war."

Comrade Curullu downed another glass of vodka.

"Today, in the line of workers waiting to visit the tomb, there were some American tourists. The girls were dressed as if they were going to a preview of a Marilyn Monroe picture. Little idiots, I call them!"

"Quite right, Comrade," Li Friddi assented. "I was just as disgusted as you. Moscow isn't Capri or Monte Carlo."

"If Stalin were still alive, those little idiots wouldn't have been allowed to enter the country. Stalin had the capitalists scared to death."

Peppone, with the aid of Comrade Nadia Petrovna, was doing his best to distract Comrade Oregov's attention. But at a certain point Comrade Oregov pricked up his ears and demanded a translation of what was being said at the other end of the table. Peppone sent a mute S.O.S. signal to Don Camillo.

"Comrades," Don Camillo said gravely to the two recalcitrants, "nobody denies the merits of Stalin. But this is neither the time nor the place to speak of them."

"Truth knows neither time nor place!" Comrade Curullu insisted. "Even if today the Soviet Union has conquered the moon, the truth is that the Party has lost the revolutionary inspiration for which two hundred and fifty thousand men laid down their lives."

"Policies have to be adapted to the circumstances of the moment," Don Camillo timidly objected. "The end is what counts, not the means."

"The fact is that Stalin got everything he wanted without bothering to set foot outside the Soviet Union," insisted Curullu.

Don Camillo relapsed into silence and let the vodka take over. Little by little, all the comrades, except for Peppone, were overcome by nostalgia for Stalin. Peppone sat with clenched jaws, waiting for the inevitable explosion. Comrade Oregov confabulated excitedly with Comrade Nadia Petrovna and then leaped to his feet, pounding with his fist on the table. His eyes were feverishly bright and he was pale as a ghost. There was an icy silence until he shouted in strangely accented but comprehensible Italian:

"Long live Stalin!"

He raised his glass, and the others leaped to their feet and followed suit.

"Hurrah!" they all shouted together.

Comrade Oregov drained his glass and the rest of them did the same. Then he dashed it to the floor and they did likewise. Comrade Nadia Petrovna abruptly announced:

"Comrade Oregov wishes his Italian comrades a very good night."

The party broke up in silence. Don Camillo and Peppone were the last to leave the private dining-room, and Comrade Nadia Petrovna blocked their way.

"Comrades," she said, "may I offer you a cup of coffee?"

They stared at her, perplexed.

"It will be brewed in Italian style," she explained, smiling. "My house is only a short distance away."

Behind the ancient palaces and the American-style skyscrapers lay a proletarian section of the city. Comrade Petrovna lived on the fourth floor of a shabby house whose stairways reeked of cabbage and cooking oil. Her apartment consisted of a single room, furnished with two couches, a table, four chairs, a wardrobe and a stand for the radio. The curtains at the windows, some tasselled lampshades and the rug on the floor were obviously meant to be decorative, but did little to alleviate the bleakness of the surroundings.

"This is the comrade with whom I live," she said, introducing the girl who had opened the door. Although the girl was older, stockier and more rustic in appearance than Comrade Petrovna she was obviously cut from the same cloth. "She's an interpreter of French, but she speaks a fair amount of Italian as well," Comrade Petrovna added.

The coffee was already brewing over an alcohol burner in the middle of the table.

"We make it here," Comrade Petrovna explained, "because we share a kitchen with the next apartment, and it's across the hall." The flavour was unexpectedly delicious, and the two girls were gratified by their guests' appreciation. "I hope you're enjoying your trip to our great country," said Comrade Petrovna when the compliments were over.

Peppone, who was in a jovial mood, launched into an enthusiastic recapitulation of the wonders of the journey. But Comrade Petrovna's friend cut him short.

"We know all these things," she said. "Talk to us about Italy."

"Comrades," said Peppone, throwing out his arms in mock despair, "Italy is a small country, which might be a wonderful place to live in if it weren't infested with capitalists and clergy."

"But there's a good bit of freedom, isn't there?" put in Comrade Petrovna.

"On the surface the country is free," answered Peppone. "But the priests are secretly in control and they have spies everywhere. By the time we get home they will know every detail of our travels."

"Really?" said the other girl.

"You can tell her better than I," said Peppone, turning to Don Camillo.

"It's the truth," admitted Don Camillo. "I can swear to it."

"How terrible!" exclaimed Comrade Petrovna. "And how does the average worker get along? Comrade Scamoggia, for instance?"

"Scamoggia isn't an average unskilled worker," Peppone explained. "He's an expert mechanic with a busy workshop of his own."

"Approximately how much money does he make?" she asked with an apparently casual air.

"If you figure thirty liras to the rouble, then he makes about seven hundred roubles a month," said Peppone after a quick mental calculation.

The two girls exchanged a few words in Russian together and then Comrade Petrovna went on:

"It all depends on the purchasing power of the lira. How much does it cost, in roubles, to buy a man's suit or a pair of shoes?"

"That varies, according to the quality," put in Don Camillo. "A suit may cost anywhere between seven and fourteen hundred roubles; a pair of shoes anywhere from seventy to three hundred and fifty."

"What about the suit you are wearing?" asked Comrade Petrovna's room-mate of Peppone, fingering its luxurious senatorial fabric.

"Forty thousand liras," he replied.

"That's about one thousand three hundred and fifty roubles," interpolated Don Camillo.

"But to return to Scamoggia," said Peppone, "I repeat that he's a special case. Scamoggia . . ."

"Scamoggia, Scamoggia!" exclaimed the room-mate. "I'm always hearing that name. Is he the individual who behaved so dreadfully at the Tifiz *kolkhos*? I don't see how such a fellow can keep on belonging to the Party."

"He's not a bad fellow at all," said Peppone. "You mustn't judge him from appearances. He's a sharp-witted and loyal Party man."

"Perhaps his parents were unenlightened and didn't bring him up the right way."

"No, there's nothing wrong with his family. You have to know Rome to understand him. When Roman men are away from home, they put on a devil-may-care air. But within their own four walls they don't dare open their mouths for fear of their wives."

"Is Scamoggia afraid of his wife?" the room-mate inquired.

"Not yet. He hasn't got one," said Peppone, laughing. "But once he's married he'll be like all the rest."

Comrade Nadia Petrovna came back into the conversation with a question about Italian citrus-fruit production, which Peppone answered with a volley of statistics. She listened attentively and insisted on serving a second cup of coffee. Then she offered to guide the two men back to the hotel, but they insisted that they could find it alone. On the way, Peppone remarked that few Italian women had achieved such political maturity as that of Comrade Nadia Petrovna and her friend.

"Can you imagine one of our girls interested in heavy industry and fruit production in the Soviet Union?"

"No, I can't," said Don Camillo with a dead-pan expression. "An Italian girl is interested only in the young man who's courting her. She wants to make sure he isn't married, to find out about his family background, salary and reputation."

Peppone came to a sudden halt, as if some suspicion were crossing his mind.

"Are you insinuating that . . ."

"I'm insinuating nothing," retorted Don Camillo. "No Communist senator would come to Moscow as a marriage broker. He has more important things to do than to look out for pretty girls for his Party comrades."

"Quite right!" roared Peppone, oblivious of his companion's irony. "Pretty girls are far from my thoughts, and so are married women, in spite of the fact that my wife wants me to bring her back some furs just like her neighbour's."

This was obviously a sore point, and when he had got it off his chest he felt better. It was ten o'clock in the evening and an icy wind swept through the deserted streets. Moscow seemed like the capital of Soviet melancholy.

THE NEXT-TO-LAST WAVE

They left Moscow for the airport by bus early in the morning, when there was no one to be seen except street cleaners. Young girls and middle-aged women were spraying the streets with water, running mechanical sweepers and brushing up what these left behind with brooms. Don Camillo pointed out to Peppone how their every gesture seemed to indicate pride in the privilege of doing a man's work.

"It's a comforting sight," he concluded, "and one you can't see anywhere except in the Soviet Union."

"I shall be still more comforted on the day when in our own country we conscript priests for this job," mumbled Peppone.

An icy wind which seemed to come straight from the tundras of Siberia blew, unimpeded, through the empty streets. Only in the vast Red Square did it find human targets. What looked like bundles of rags, waiting for the street cleaners to come and carry them away, revealed themselves on second glance to be pilgrims lined up for the ritual visit to the mausoleum. Peasants from Uzbekistan, Georgia, Irkutsk and other remote parts of Russia had been ousted from their trains in the middle of the night and now sat, huddled together like sheep, on their suitcases, until such time as the approach to the tomb should be opened.

"Comrade," said Don Camillo, "how different this is from the days when poor mujiks travelled in wagons to St. Petersburg and camped out for days in the park until they had a chance to see the Tsar and his German bride."

"It's one thing to be a slave performing an act of submission to a tyrant and another to be a free citizen paying tribute to his liberator," Peppone retorted.

"Besides the fact that many of them come to make sure of the fact that Lenin and Stalin are really dead."

Peppone smiled blandly.

"When I think that by midnight tomorrow I shall be unloading the lot of you at the Milan railway station, I have to pinch myself to be sure it isn't a dream. Enjoy your fun while you can. The time is running out . . . ."

The adventure was nearly over. At nine o'clock the plane would disembark them at S., where they were to visit a shipyard, then they were to travel for three hours by boat to the city of O. and board another plane for Berlin. The boat trip was Comrade Oregov's idea. Planes, trains, buses, trolleys and subways had all contributed to a demonstration of Soviet efficiency in the field of transportation, but a voyage by sea was necessary to complete it. Comrade Oregov had submitted his final project to the higher-ups and was visibly proud that it had been accepted.

Punctually at nine o'clock the plane landed at S. The airfield was small, commensurate with the size of the town which had no importance except for its shipyard. In the broad, well-defended harbour, equipped for all possible repairs, there were ships of every description. Comrade Bacciga of Genoa felt immediately at home and was more loquacious than he had ever shown himself before. Among the various craft there was a gleaming new tanker and he described its tonnage and fittings with such familiarity and technical skill that Comrade Oregov felt his guidance was quite unnecessary. He left the little group of Italians in Comrade Nadia Petrovna's charge and went off to the shipyard to arrange the details of the visit.

Comrade Bacciga was in top form. He had a ready answer to every question and exclaimed at intervals:

"Shipbuilding is a Genoese speciality, but these fellows are experts and I take off my hat to them."

Don Camillo was on the alert, and after Bacciga had several times announced this opinion he said:

"They're experts, all right, and from away back. Just look at that old schooner! Isn't it a beauty?"

The others followed Don Camillo along the quay until they came to a place where the schooner was in full view. It seemed to be straight out of a nineteenth-century engraving, and yet a fresh coat of paint and varnish made it look at the same time brand-new.

"It's wonderful what respect the Russians have for everything that harks back to their glorious past!" Don Camillo exclaimed. "Comrades, this ship bears witness to a long and noble tradition." Then, after a few minutes of silent admiration, he turned to Bacciga. "Comrade longshoreman, for centuries we have been masters of the art of shipbuilding, but to see a schooner like this we had to come all the way to the Soviet Union."

Comrade Nadia Petrovna had gleaned further information from one of the workers.

"*Tovarisch* is the ship's name," she informed them. "It's used for cadet training."

"Three thousand tons," put in Comrade Bacciga, turning suddenly upon her. "It was originally called the *Cristoforo Colombo* and was a training ship of the Italian Navy."

Comrade Petrovna blushed.

"Forgive me, Comrade," she muttered. Then because she had caught sight of

Comrade Oregov, walking towards them in the company of a shipyard official, she went to receive instructions. Peppone tugged at Don Camillo's sleeve and drew him apart from the others.

"Can't you keep that big mouth of yours shut?" he whispered. "Now you've made a real blunder."

"It wasn't a blunder at all," said Don Camillo. "I knew all along that it was the *Cristoforo Colombo*. I'll never forget how badly I felt the day when they took it and the *Giulio Cesare* away."

Comrade Bacciga was standing nearby and Peppone turned to vent his ire on him.

"Couldn't *you* have shut up about it?"

"How could I, Chief?" said Bacciga. "I recognized it from the start."

"A loyal Party member wouldn't have allowed himself any such recognition."

"I may be a loyal Party member, but don't forget that I'm also a professional longshoreman," Bacciga retorted.

"What do you mean by that?"

"Water's water everywhere," said Bacciga, "but there's a big difference between the sea and the Po River. I can't look at the *Cristoforo Colombo* with as little emotion as if it were a river barge."

"The sailors of the famous cruiser *Potemkin* weren't of the same stamp as you," said Peppone sarcastically.

"But then they weren't Genoese," said Bacciga.

At eleven o'clock, with their heads crammed full of statistics, the Italians finished their tour of the shipyard. Their ship was not due to leave for another hour, and while Comrade Nadia Petrovna took the main body of the group to look at the town, Comrade Oregov, Peppone and Don Camillo went to have a drink in a workers' canteen. Comrade Oregov worked on a report of the day's activities, while the other two fortified their spirits for the coming sea voyage. A bitter wind and a mass of clouds in the sky seemed to foretell a storm.

The canteen was ill-lit and dirty, but it served excellent vodka. After the second round Peppone confided to Don Camillo:

"I'm afraid of being seasick. How about you?"

"Not in the least. Priests have been storm-tossed for nearly two thousand years, and they've always managed to come out alive."

"We'll see if you can still crack jokes when we're on the high seas," said Peppone.

Soon the cold wind drove the rest of the group indoors. They didn't look as if they had had much fun, and the dourest of them all was Comrade Curullu. After they had all sat down and a glass of vodka had loosened their tongues, Comrade Curullu proceeded to let off steam.

"Do you know where we have been, Comrade?" he asked Don Camillo.

Don Camillo put away his book of excerpts from Lenin.

"In a church!" Curullu continued. "And do you know what was going on?"

Don Camillo shrugged his shoulders.

"A wedding!" said Curullu excitedly. "Complete with priest and all the usual rubbish!" And he added, turning to Comrade Scamoggia: "And to think that you came here in the hope that there'd be no priests cluttering up the landscape! You should have seen this one! He was sleek and well fed and rigged out in even fancier vestments than ours. And the bride and groom! There they were, all dressed up, with their hands folded in prayer and a sickly, angelic smile on their faces! It was enough to make your stomach turn over."

"A disgusting sight to see in the Soviet Union!" chimed in Comrade Li Friddi. "You'd have thought we were in a backward village in Sicily."

They all looked expectantly at Don Camillo, and he had a ready reply.

"Comrades, the Soviet constitution allows every citizen to practise his own personal religion. And as long as the priests don't corrupt young people under eighteen years of age with their teachings, they are free to exercise their trade. This is nothing so very startling. The whole story of religious persecution is Vatican propaganda."

Comrade Oregov had pricked up his ears and with the aid of Comrade Nadia Petrovna was following the conversation. Don Camillo looked to him for a sign and he hastened to respond.

"He says that Comrade Tarocci is quite right," said Comrade Petrovna. "Paragraph 124 of the Constitution is observed to the letter. The Council for the Orthodox Church and the Council for Religious Bodies see to it that there is complete freedom of conscience; in fact they help the churches solve practical problems."

"That makes it perfectly clear," said Don Camillo. "The priests don't do whatever they please, as they do at home; they do only what the Constitution allows. It's quite a different situation."

"But it adds up to the same thing," protested Comrade Li Friddi. "Priests are priests, wherever you find them."

Don Camillo laughed.

"Comrade, in this enormous country there are only twenty-six thousand churches and thirty-five thousand clergy."

"That's too many of both," muttered Comrade Curullu.

"Remember that in 1917 there were forty-six thousand churches and fifty thousand priests, and in 1945 there were only four thousand churches and five thousand priests," said Don Camillo.

"Is that true?" Comrade Curullu asked incredulously, turning to Comrade Oregov.

After the usual translation Comrade Nadia Petrovna replied on his behalf:

"Those figures are substantially correct. Today priests and their churches receive no money except from their parishioners. During the war the Orthodox Church gave full patriotic support to the war effort. And the Party uses nonviolent, dissuasive means to combat superstition."

But vodka caused Comrade Curullu to give further vent to his disillusionment.

"Comrade," he said to Comrade Petrovna, "if in the last fourteen years the number of priests has grown from five thousand to thirty-five thousand, how can you say that there has been a combat against superstition?"

Comrade Petrovna hesitated a moment before relaying this question to Comrade Oregov, and he listened to her with a bowed head, as if he were personally responsible for this betrayal. Finally he looked up and threw out his arms in despair. There was no need for Comrade Nadia Petrovna to translate for him. This was the end of the discussion. Comrade Oregov returned to working over his report and the visitors spoke of other things. The canteen was filled with smoke, and Don Camillo felt a need of fresh air. He went out on to the street, and Peppone followed after. The wind had died down and they were able to stroll quietly up and down, side by side. Finally Peppone exclaimed:

"Thirty-five thousand priests. After a bloody revolution and thirty-two years of sacrifice on behalf of the people!"

"Don't get excited, Comrade," said Don Camillo soothingly. "Numbers shouldn't alarm you. These Russian priests are only government employees. They call the Pope an enemy of peace, and their old Patriarch Alexis once referred to Stalin as having been 'sent by God'. But although Communism has won over the priests it has lost the war against religion. And it has lost two other wars: the war against the peasants and the war against the *bourgeoisie*. After four decades of struggle the Soviet Union has gained atomic supremacy and conquered the moon; it has installed science in the place of superstition and subjugated both its own people and the peoples of the satellite nations; it has killed off ten million peasants in the process of agricultural reform and eliminated the old middle class. Yet today, in their search for God, the Russians are spending their hard-earned roubles to build churches. Agricultural production is below the pre-Revolutionary level and the Government has been forced to allow the peasants to have a portion of privately owned land and to sell its produce on the free market. At the same time there is a new and increasingly powerful *bourgeoisie*. Don't take offence, Comrade, but you yourself, with your well-tailored , double-breasted dark blue suit, the two salaries which you receive as a senator and a Party leader, your bank account and your intention of buying a high-powered car, are a budding bourgeois. Can you deny it?"

"What do you mean, a 'high-powered car'? I'm going to buy a second-hand standard model."

Don Camillo shook his head.

"It isn't the horsepower that counts; it's the principle of the thing."

Peppone took a leather case out of his pocket and extracted a big Tuscan-type cigar. Don Camillo, who for the past two days had been longing for the familiar aroma, heaved a formidable sigh and said bitterly:

"There you are! The *bourgeoisie* feast while the people are famished!"

Angrily Peppone broke the cigar in two and offered half of it to Don Camillo.

"Thirty-five thousand priests weren't enough," he muttered; "you had to come and join them!"

At this moment they heard the ship whistle.

The *Partisan* was a light but powerful and up-to-date craft, which ploughed steadily and speedily through the water. The first hour of the voyage left nothing to be desired. Unfortunately the devil intervened; the sky darkened again and the wind began to blow. In order that the giant waves should not throw the ship on to the rocky shore, the captain steered farther out to sea in search of calmer weather.

But the storm only increased in intensity and soon the ship was dangerously drifting. A sailor came down into the saloon and hurled a pile of canvas objects on the floor.

"The captain says to put on the life jackets and go up on deck," said Comrade Nadia Petrovna.

On deck all hell seemed to have broken loose. Rain poured down from the sky and waves beat mercilessly against the sides of the ship. The sky was pitch black and the wind was howling. The wheel rotated wildly and two lifeboats were swept away. All eyes were turned on the captain, who stood clinging to the rail of the bridge. He knew that all those present were looking to him for safety, but he avoided their gaze and stared helplessly out over the water. How long would the ship hold together? A giant wave lifted the stern and it seemed as if the bow would sink into the sea. After the wave had broken over the deck and the ship had regained its balance, the passengers looked around and counted their numbers. They were all there: Peppone and his group, Comrade Oregov and Comrade Petrovna, the captain and the six members of the crew. Huddled together, holding on to whatever object came to hand, they had miraculously survived the first inundation. But how would they manage to survive another? The ship slid along the side of the next wave and down into the hollow. Then it came to the surface again, but one of the portholes was shattered and the hold began to fill with water. Hopelessly Peppone turned to Don Camillo:

"For the love of God, do something!" he shouted.

Don Camillo summoned all his self-control.

"Lord," he said, "I am happy to die in Your service."

Forgetful of where he was and of the fact that none of his companions except Peppone knew him except under the name of Comrade Tarocci, he bared his head and reached into his pocket for the crucifix concealed in a fountain pen. He held it up over their heads and they fell on to their knees before him, even Comrade Petrovna, the captain and the crew. Only Comrade Oregov kept his cap pulled down over his eyes and clung to the stairway which led to the bridge, looking at the sight with amazement.

"Lord," Don Camillo prayed, "have mercy on Your unfortunate children."

As he spoke a wave dashed against the side of the ship and another threatened to break over the deck.

"*Ego vos absolvo a peccatis vestris, in nomine Patris et Filii et Spiritus Sancti. . . .*"

He traced a sign of the cross in the stormy air, and his hearers crossed themselves and crept forward to kiss the crucifix. A mountain of water broke over the deck, but God had other designs for them and did not allow it to sweep them away. They rose to their feet, suddenly confident that the worst was over. All of them had noticed that Comrade Oregov had neither taken off his cap nor fallen to his knees, but only now did they mentally question the consequences. He was standing stock-still, with clenched jaws and blazing eyes. Comrade Nadia Petrovna, the captain and the members of the crew were alarmed by his menacing stare, but the Italians were so happy to be alive they paid no attention.

✻

The ship was still shaken by the storm, but the sailors were able to man the pumps while the passengers went to wring out their drenched clothes. Comrade Oregov's attitude was quickly forgotten. As the storm gradually subsided shipboard life returned to normal. Two hours later men were talking among themselves just as they did every day. After all, nothing so very extraordinary had happened. A heavy sea, decks awash with water, a shattered porthole, two lifeboats swept away—the everyday occurrences of a sea voyage. No one thought of Comrade Oregov until the ship reached port and Comrade Nadia Petrovna mentioned his name. The gangplank was in place and Peppone and his group were about to walk down it when Comrade Nadia Petrovna planted herself in their way.

"We must wait for Comrade Oregov," she said with a tremor in her voice.

Just then the captain came along and led her away below deck. He brought her back a few minutes later and smilingly shook Don Camillo's hand.

"*Kak trevóga, tak do Bógo,*" he said.

"We can disembark," Comrade Petrovna explained. "Unfortunately one of the last waves carried Comrade Oregov away. The Party has lost an able and devoted servant. A valiant soldier is dead."

When they set foot on land, Don Camillo looked anxiously out to sea, half-expecting to see the ghost of Comrade Oregov between the lowering clouds and the storm-tossed water.

"May God forgive you your sins!" he said to himself, trying to convince himself of the truth of the captain's story. If the captain had written in his log that two lifeboats and Comrade Oregov had been lost at sea, what reason was there to doubt him?

The departure of the Berlin plane was delayed by the storm. In the bus which carried them to the airfield Don Camillo found himself sitting across from Comrade Scamoggia.

"Well, Comrade," he said, "the time has come to say good-bye. You'll be staying on after we have gone away."

"No, I'm going with you," Scamoggia replied.

"Wasn't Comrade Petrovna able to persuade you to stay?"

"I never even mentioned the possibility. I feel I'm still needed by the Italian Communist Party."

"Very good, Comrade! A Party stalwart must subordinate love to duty."

Comrade Scamoggia sighed and looked out of the window. The bus came to a stop at the airfield gate and they all got out. Comrade Nadia Petrovna and Peppone went into the office with the group's travelling papers. The police official glanced over them and passed on the list of names to his interpreter, who proceeded to call them out one by one.

"Pietro Bacciga . . . ."

Bacciga came in, and both Peppone and Comrade Petrovna confirmed his identity. When his name had been checked, Comrades Capece, Gibetti, Li Friddi and Peratto followed.

"Walter Rondella . . . ."

Peppone forgot that Comrade Rondella had been ignominiously shipped back home. He looked up and saw the Neapolitan barber whom they had met at the Tifiz *kolkhos* standing brazenly before him. Already he had approved the fellow's name as that of Rondella and Comrade Petrovna had assented. When Comrade Tarocci was called in Peppone was tempted to disavow him. But this vengeful impulse had no time to take root in his mind.

"Ten entries, ten exits," said the interpreter, as he handed the papers back to Peppone.

As they walked towards the plane Don Camillo asked Comrade Petrovna to tell him the exact meaning of the Russian words which the ship captain had pronounced at the moment of disembarcation.

"He was summing up what happened during the storm," she replied. " 'In dire extremity man remembers his God.' "

"An outdated Russian proverb," muttered Don Camillo.

As the travellers climbed into the plane Comrade Petrovna shook hands with them, one by one. When it came to the Neapolitan barber, who was also a refugee from Rumania, it was all she could do to contain her laughter. But the sight of Comrade Scamoggia froze the smile on her lips. Don Camillo was the last to climb aboard.

"Good-bye," he said.

"Pray for me, Comrade," Comrade Petrovna whispered, and there were tears rolling down her cheeks.

For a long time after the plane had left the ground Don Camillo could not stop thinking of the sorrowful expression in her eyes. Then he looked down at the endless expanse of mist-covered fields and remembered a Russian phrase which he had jotted down in his notebook: "*Spasitjel mira, spasi Rossiu!*—Saviour of the world, save Russia!"

A STORY THAT HAS NO END

"LORD," SAID DON CAMILLO to the crucified Christ above the altar, "for two whole weeks I've been back in my own familiar surroundings, and I still can't get over the feeling of distress from which I suffered during my travels. Mind You, Lord, it was distress, not fear; I had no reason to be afraid. I was deeply ashamed, like an old soldier used to fighting out in the open when he finds himself under false colours, charged with penetrating the enemy ranks in order to plot their destruction. The crucifix concealed in a fountain pen, the breviary masked as a volume of excerpts from Lenin, the clandestine Masses celebrated before a bedside table! . . ."

"Don't torment yourself, Don Camillo," Christ answered gently. "You weren't a coward, trying to knife his neighbour in the back; you were trying to help him. Would you refuse a dying man a drink of water if it were necessary to lower yourself to practise deceit in order to bring it to him? The heroism of a soldier of

Christ is humility; his only enemy is pride. Blessed are the meek . . ."

"Lord, you are speaking from a Cross that has all the glory of a throne, a throne which you won in open battle, without the humiliation of disguise. You never appeared to men in the likeness of the Devil. . . ."

"Don Camillo, didn't the Son of God humble himself when he consented to live like a man and die like a common criminal? Just look at your God, at His wounded sides and the ignominious crown of thorns on His head!"

"Lord, I am looking at You," insisted Don Camillo, "but I see only the divine light of Your supreme sacrifice. No light at all, not even the wavering flare of a match, illuminates the wretched figure of 'Comrade Don Camillo'. "

Christ smiled.

"What about the light you kindled in the eyes of the old peasant woman of Grevinec? And the candle you lit on the unmarked grave of a soldier whose family did not even have the satisfaction of knowing where he lay? Then think back to the storm at sea and the terror of your miserable companions at the thought that their last hour had come. When you held up your crucifix and asked God to forgive them their sins, did they ridicule the transformation of Comrade Tarocci into a priest of the Church? No, they fell down on their knees and tried to kiss that tiny figure with the collapsible arms. Haven't you ever wondered what got into them?"

"But, Lord, any other priest would have behaved the same way," murmured Don Camillo.

"Remember that only Peppone knew who you were. For all the others you were simply Comrade Tarocci. How do you explain their change of heart?"

Don Camillo threw out of his arms. Only now did he realize what an incredible episode it had been.

"You see," said Christ, "that some light must have been shed by 'Comrade Don Camillo'."

For most of the two weeks since his return Don Camillo had been trying to put his travel notes in order for the Bishop's perusal. It was no easy job for, although the Bishop was old and forgetful, he had very exacting notions of grammar.

Ever since they had said good-bye at the Milan railway station, Don Camillo had had no news of Peppone. The Neapolitan barber had dropped out of the group in West Berlin; Comrade Tavan, with his three stalks of wheat, had left the train at Verona, and Don Camillo had got off, along with Comrade Bacciga and Comrade Peratto, at Milan.

"Shouldn't you travel with us as far as Parma or Reggio Emilia?" Scamoggia had asked him. But Don Camillo claimed to have urgent business in Milan. This was quite true because there he had left his cassock and he was in a hurry to recover it. Peppone had counted his little troop and just as Don Camillo was leaving the train he heard him shout gaily at Scamoggia:

"There are only six of us from now on. Take this money and buy six bottles of wine. I want to treat you."

Peppone's laughter continued to ring in his ears and he racked his brain to know what had caused it. On the evening of the fourteenth day after his homecoming Peppone himself turned up to give him an explanation. For a moment Don

Camillo failed to recognize his old friend. He had left him wearing a double-breasted dark-blue suit, a white shirt and a grey silk tie, and now here he was in his outfit of times long gone by: a corduroy jacket, wrinkled trousers, a cap pulled down over the back of his head, a handkerchief knotted around his neck and a peasant's black wool cape over his shoulders. Don Camillo stared at him for some minutes and then shook his head.

"How silly of me to forget," he exclaimed, "that the representative of the working class has to carry his load in a senatorial suit in Rome and in the rig of a mayor in his native village. It must be hard lines for you to travel only at night. Won't you sit down?"

"I can say what I have to say standing up," grumbled Peppone. "I've come to pay my debt." He pulled a candle out of his pocket and put it down on Don Camillo's desk. "This is to thank the Lord for having saved me from shipwreck."

" 'In dire extremity man remembers his God,' as the Russian sea captain said," answered Don Camillo. "Usually when the extremity is past he proceeds to forget Him. I congratulate you on your good memory."

"And this is to thank the Lord for saving me from a certain priest whom the Devil sent to torment me," added Peppone lugubriously, drawing forth another candle, a giant one, four feet long and eight inches in diameter.

Don Camillo's jaw dropped.

"I had it made to order," Peppone explained. "It's big, if you like, but if it were really to represent the danger of that priest it would have to be four times bigger."

"You flatter me," said Don Camillo. "A country priest doesn't really deserve such consideration."

"There are country priests more dangerous than the Pope in person," said Peppone. He threw a parcel and three letters on to the desk and added: "These were sent to me with the request that I should turn them over to Comrade Tarocci. I don't like it, not a bit. I warn you that if I receive any more I shall burn them."

Don Camillo opened the parcel, which was full of photographs, and looked hastily at one of the letters, which was addressed in the same writing.

"They are . . ." he began.

"I'm not sticking my nose into your business, Father," said Peppone.

"But they pertain to Comrade Tarocci, who as cell-leader is obliged to inform his superior. They are pictures sent by Comrade Peratto, and he says I am to do what I please with them. Look at this group, where we are in the front row together. Doesn't it interest you?"

Peppone snatched the picture, examined it, and said between clenched teeth:

"I hope you're not going to get me into any more trouble!"

"Don't worry, Senator. Comrade Peratto has sent another set, of a strictly unofficial nature, which he asks me to place without mentioning his name. The Party doesn't pay him very well and he wants to make a bit of money."

"Would you play a dirty trick like that?"

"It's up to you. What if we fail to give him satisfaction and he sends a picture that has me in it to a Party paper?"

Peppone lowered himself into a chair and wiped the perspiration from his forehead. While he looked through the pictures Don Camillo read the second letter and informed him of its contents.

"This one is from Comrade Tavan. He thanks me for my good advice and says it has done wonders for his mother. He has planted the three stalks of wheat and goes to look at them every day. 'If they were to wither,' he says, 'I'd feel that my brother was even more dead than before.' And he sends his best wishes to the Comrade Senator."

Peppone only grunted in reply.

The third letter was a very short one, enclosing some money.

"It's from Comrade Gibetti," said Don Camillo. "When he got home he began to wonder about the contents of the Russian letter which told the story of the girl with whom he was in love. Finally he got it translated and found that she was dead. He has sent me a thousand liras to say a Mass for her soul. I'm going to send back the money and tell him I'll say a Mass for her every month."

Peppone brought his fist down on the desk.

"Who the devil told these fellows that you were a priest?" he thundered. "That's what I'd like to know!"

"Nobody told them. They simply got the idea."

"But how did they get it?"

"It was a question of seeing the light," said Don Camillo. "Since I'm no electrician, I can't explain."

Peppone shook his head.

"Perhaps the fault is mine. Perhaps there on the ship my tongue slipped and I called you 'Father'."

"I don't remember your doing any such thing."

Peppone showed him a picture in which Comrade Oregov occupied a prominent place.

"When I saw him for the last time," he said with bowed head, "the fury of the storm was over. How did it happen that a wave washed him into the sea? What happened up on the deck after we had gone below?"

"Only God can say," said Don Camillo. "And He alone knows how often the poor fellow is in my thoughts."

Peppone gave a deep sigh and got up.

"Here are the pictures I'd choose," he said.

"Agreed," said Don Camillo. "And what am I to do with the candles?"

Peppone shrugged his shoulders.

"The big one can be for the escape from shipwreck," he muttered.

"That's what you said for the smaller," Don Camillo reminded him.

"The smaller can be for the escape from the priest," shouted Peppone, and he went away without saying good-bye.

Don Camillo went over to the church. There was no candlestick large enough to contain the giant candle, but he managed to fit it into a big bronze vase. When he had put both candles on the altar and lit them Don Camillo said:

"Lord, Peppone is mindful of you."

"And of you, too, if I'm not mistaken," Christ replied.

When the Bishop had read Don Camillo's report, he sent for him. "Now give me the whole story," he said.

Don Camillo talked for several hours uninterruptedly and when he had finished the Bishop exclaimed:

"It's incredible! Conversion of Comrade Tavan and Comrade Gibetti, liberation of a Neapolitan barber, communion given to the old Polish woman, the marriage of her daughter to an Italian veteran and the baptism of their six children, the veteran's confession and rehabilitation, a Mass for the Dead celebrated in a forgotten cemetery and the absolution given to eighteen persons in imminent danger of death! And besides this you became a cell leader. All in the space of six days in the territory of the anti-Christ! I can hardly believe it!"

"Your Grace, besides my word there are the photographs and the letters. And I have a senator for a witness."

"A senator!" groaned the old man. "Then the damage is irreparable."

Don Camillo looked bewildered.

"My son, can't you see that under these conditions I'll simply have to raise you to the rank of *monsignore.*"

"*Domine, non sum dignus,*" he murmured, raising his eyes to heaven.

The Bishop shook his head.

"Just what I said myself, many years ago, but no one paid any attention. God be with you!"

In the month that followed, the Russian adventure ceased to occupy Don Camillo's mind. But one morning as he was coming out of the church he caught Smilzo pasting a poster on the rectory wall. He did not make his presence known but when Smilzo came down from the ladder and almost knocked him over, he asked:

"Comrade, what if someone were to tear down your poster while the paste is still fresh and ram it down your throat?"

"Father, no man alive would do a thing like that!" Smilzo replied.

"Just suppose such a man *is* alive and standing here before you!"

He had taken hold of the lapels of Smilzo's ragged jacket and seemed to have no intention of letting them go.

"All right . . . . That would be a very different situation."

Don Camillo went on in a different tone:

"Look here; do I ever stick up posters on your 'People's Palace'? Why do you have to inflict your political idiocies on me?"

"This isn't politics," said Smilzo. "It's the announcement of a cultural event."

Without releasing his grip on Smilzo's jacket Don Camillo looked up and read a notice to the effect that Senator Giuseppe Bottazzi was to talk the following evening about his recent trip to the Soviet Union. A period of questions and answers would follow.

"You're right," he said, letting go of Smilzo's jacket. "It's a strictly cultural proposition. Where can I get a ticket?"

"Everybody's welcome and entrance is free," said Smilzo, straightening out his lapels. "And there are no holds barred on the questions."

"Even questions from me?"

"Even from the Bishop," said Smilzo, beating a cautious retreat. "We particularly want to educate the clergy."

He had retreated too far for Don Camillo to lay hands on him again, and besides the priest had other matters on his mind. He went into the rectory and picked up his pen. Half an hour later a boy delivered a letter to Peppone, which read as follows:

"Dear Comrade Senator: I can hardly wait to come to tomorrow night's meeting. Just let me submit one advance question: Why are you looking for trouble? Best regards from—Comrade Tarocci."

In the late afternoon Peppone was unexpectedly called to Rome and the next morning Smilzo had to add a postscript to the poster: *Because of the unavoidable absence of the speaker the meeting is postponed to an indefinite date.*

Once more, when he climbed down from the ladder, Smilzo found himself face to face with Don Camillo.

"Too bad!" said the priest. "Who knows how long the clergy will have to remain wrapped in the ignorance of the Dark Ages?"

Smilzo quickly picked up his ladder and retreated to a position of safety.

"Don't you worry, Father. We'll open their eyes!"

No later date was ever announced, and after rain had washed the poster away it received no further mention. Six months went by, and because Don Camillo had no opportunity of talking about his Russian trip he began to wonder whether it was all a dream. But one morning, when he was putting his papers in order, the sexton came to tell him that a stranger was at the door. To his utter amazement Don Camillo saw, over the sexton's shoulder, the face of Comrade Nanni Scamoggia.

"How did you get here?" he asked.

"There are such things as trains," said Scamoggia. "And I persuaded Comrade Bottazzi to give me your address."

"I see," said Don Camillo, although he didn't see at all. "What's the reason for your visit?"

Scamoggia was still the same devil-may-care fellow as before. This was quite plain from the way he lit his cigarette and threw himself into a chair. But his nonchalance did not deceive Don Camillo, who remembered the tears in Comrade Nadia Petrovna's eyes.

"I have a problem, Comrade . . . I mean Father. It's that girl. . . ."

"Yes. What happened to her?"

"She came to Rome two months ago with a Russian women's delegation. When they left she cut loose and stayed behind."

"So what did you do?"

"In my Party position I couldn't have dealings with a traitor to the Soviet Union. . . ."

"So what next?"

"In order to marry her I had to leave the Party," said Scamoggia, tossing his cigarette butt into the fire.

"Is that the problem?"

"No, it's this. We've been married for a month now, and every day she says the civil ceremony isn't enough. She wants a church wedding."

"I don't see much to worry about," Don Camillo observed calmly.

"You wouldn't," said Scamoggia. "But don't forget that the very sight of a priest turns my stomach."

"I understand, Comrade. You have a right to your own opinions. But if that's the case, why have you come to me?"

"Because if a priest does have to be dragged into it, I'd rather he were a regular fellow. And you're a sort of ex-comrade, like myself. In fact, you're my former cell leader."

"Not a bad idea," said Don Camillo.

Scamoggia went to open the door and shouted:

"Nadia!"

A second later Comrade Petrovna entered the room. As soon as she saw Don Camillo, she rushed to kiss his hand.

"How revolting!" muttered Scamoggia. "So short a time in this country and she knows all the rules!"

All their papers were in good order and the marriage ceremony was a rapid affair. Peppone had to accept the job of giving the bride away. But he did it with a smile. Before the couple went away Don Camillo took the girl aside and asked her to tell him the true story of Comrade Oregov.

"It was an ugly affair," she explained. "When the rest of us went below deck, Comrade Oregov ordered the captain to lock us all up and put handcuffs on you and Comrade Bottazzi. He raved about betrayal, and Vatican spies and commissions of inquiry. Finally he appeared to be quite mad. He and the captain came to blows and the captain knocked him against the rail. Just then a wave swept him away. This is the whole truth, but only the captain, you and I know it. It's all very sad. . . ."

After the bride and groom had left, Don Camillo and Peppone sat warming their hands at the fire in the study. For some time they were silent, and then Don Camillo exclaimed:

"I must jot that down before I forget it."

He pulled the famous notebook out of his pocket and said aloud as he was writing:

"Two more conversions and another marriage . . ."

"Put down whatever you like," roared Peppone. "It will all go on your bill on the day of the Great Uprising!"

"Won't you give me a small discount?" asked Don Camillo. "I'm an ex-comrade, after all."

"We'll let you choose the place where you are to be hanged," jeered Peppone.

"I can tell you that right now," retorted Don Camillo. "Right beside you!"

It was a cold winter day and the mist rising from the river clouded over the end of this newly finished story, which already was older than time.